The Adventures
of
Langdon St. Ives

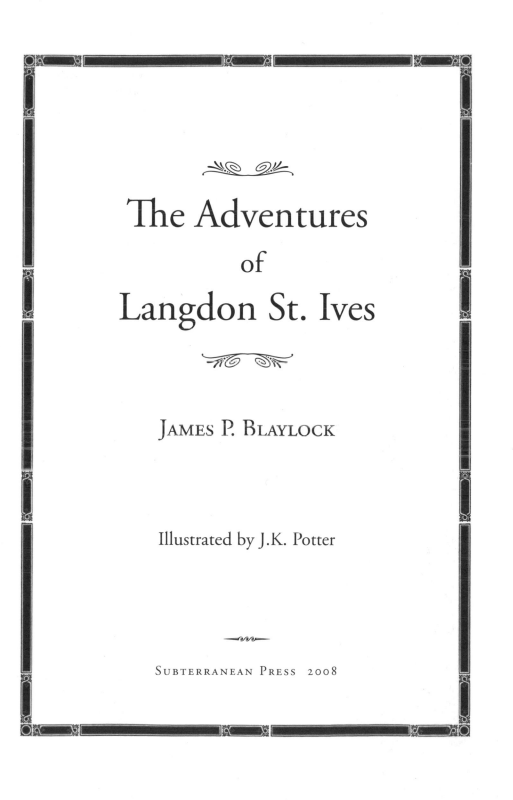

The Adventures

of

Langdon St. Ives

James P. Blaylock

Illustrated by J.K. Potter

Subterranean Press 2008

First Edition

ISBN
978-1-59606-170-5

Subterranean Press
PO Box 190106
Burton, MI 48519

www.subterraneanpress.com

Table of Contents

Introduction

by Tim Powers

NOBODY WHO KNEW him in 1972 would have guessed that James Blaylock would one day be the most original science fiction writer alive, which he now is, Cordwainer Smith and Philip K. Dick no longer being with us. Blaylock also writes fantasy, and some people would say that's all he writes—but those people would be noting the consistent tone and assuming a consistent substance. Lovecraft's several science fiction stories often get categorized as supernatural horror for the same reason.

In 1972, though, when he and I were in college, I don't think many people would have guessed he'd be a writer at all. He was a dedicated surfer in his spare time, and his part-time job was doing construction clean-up—knocking down garages and sawing the roofs off of houses, sometimes at the wrong addresses by mistake. And for a while, before changing his major to English, he was a Psychology major. That didn't work out, luckily—I can't think of anybody less suited to that narrow discipline than Blaylock—though the world may have thereby lost a spectacular psychiatrist. I picture a sort of mix of Carl Jung and Federico Fellini.

He was already a writer, though. So was I. Neither of us had had anything published, but we were busily writing stories, and soon began long, never-to-be-finished novels. Of course we both read incessantly, the assigned books for our English literature classes blending in with the stuff we were reading on our own incentive, and it quickly became clear that, although in many ways we were writing the same sorts of adventure-and-grotesquerie stories, we were approaching them from very different points of the literary compass. I had grown up on writers like Fritz Leiber and Theodore Sturgeon, Henry Kuttner and Leigh Brackett, while Blaylock was operating from a foundation of Robert Louis Stevenson, Mark Twain, and P. G. Wodehouse.

And Lawrence Sterne. A lot of people love *Tristram Shandy*, but I don't think anybody since Sterne himself has been as compatible to that book as Blaylock is. Corporal Trim's *apologia* in it, which the character Doctor Slop admires for the depth of its philosophy as much as for its insight into physiology, could be a summary of Blaylock's *oeuvre*: "I infer, an' please your worship, replied Trim, that the radical moisture is nothing in the world but ditch-water—and that the radical heat, of those who can go to the expence of it, is burnt brandy,—the radical heat and moisture of a private man, an' please your honour, is nothing but ditch-water—and a dram of geneva—and give us but enough of it, with a pipe of tobacco, to give us spirits, and drive away the vapours—we know not what it is to fear death."

Trim's philosophy is echoed by many Blaylock characters, as when St. Ives says, in *Lord Kelvin's Machine*, "We *must* have our hand in. It's nothing more nor less than the salvation of the Earth, secularly speaking, that we're involved in," and Hasbro asks, "Shall we want lunch first, sir?" and St. Ives replies, "Kippers and gherkins, thank you."

And the business about radical heat and radical moisture particularly anticipates Blaylock, who likewise doesn't hesitate to deal with principles of science in his fiction, especially in the St. Ives stories.

He is, as I said, a science fiction writer.

As in the Sterne passage, it's generally antique science, to be sure. "It's a little-known fact," says Bill Kraken in *Homunculus*, "that the equator, you see, is a belt—not cowhide, mind you, but what the doctor called elemental twines. Them, with the latitudes, is what binds this earth of ours. It isn't as tight as it might be, though, which is good because of averting suffocation."

Maybe a better term would be crazy science. But it's presented solemnly.

And it's perfectly appropriate to the Victorian world Blaylock writes about—which isn't precisely the Victorian world that actually existed. Fellow-writer K. W. Jeter got Blaylock and I interested in 19th century London with his 1979 novel *Morlock Night*, and he introduced us to the cornerstone research work for the period, Henry Mayhew's *London Labor and London Poor*—but somehow Blaylock's London, accurate as it is in its geography and demographics, is a more magical city than the real one could ever have been. Blaylock can't help but impose his own weird and amiable and Byzantine perspective on it.

And while it might not be a perspective that exactly reflects the actual 19th century's, neither does it reflect that of the 20th or 21st centuries. Blaylock isn't really a citizen of those, literarily.

Raymond Chandler said once of his fictional private detective Philip Marlowe that he was a realistic character except in that such a person would never in real life become a private detective. The science fiction and fantasy fields have, more often than we could have hoped for, been the venue of writers who seem to have landed there by some mistake, who seem as if they should "in real life" have been writing a more obviously elevated sort of fiction. I think of Dick, and Ballard, and Tiptree, and Wolfe. And Blaylock, with his uniquely eccentric characters and locales and melodrama and humor, is certainly one of them too. —◦

The Ape-Box Affair

A GOOD DEAL OF controversy arose late in the last century over what has been referred to by the more livid newspapers as "The Horror in St. James Park" or "The Ape-Box Affair." Even these thirty years later, a few people remember that little intrigue, though most would change the subject rather abruptly if you broached it, and many are still unaware of the relation, or rather the lack of relation, between the actual ape-box and the spacecraft that plunked down in the Park's duck pond.

The memoirs of Professor Langdon St. Ives, however, which passed into my hands after the poor man's odd disappearance, pretty clearly implicate him in the affair. His own orang-outang, I'll swear it, and the so-called Hooded Alien are one and the same creature. There is little logical connection, however, between that creature and "the thing in the box" which has since also fallen my way, and is nothing more than a clockwork child's toy. The ape puppet in that box, I find after a handy bit of detective work, was modeled after the heralded "Moko the Educated Ape" which toured with a Bulgarian Gypsy fair and which later became the central motif of the mysterious Robert Service sonnet, "The Headliner and the Breadliner." That the ape in the box became linked to St. Ives's shaven orang-outang is a matter of the wildest coincidence—a coincidence that generated a chain of activities no less strange or incredible. This then is the tale, and though the story is embellished here and there for the sake of dramatic realism, it is entirely factual in the main.

—*∽∽*—

PROFESSOR ST. IVES was a brilliant scientist, and the history books might some day acknowledge his full worth. But for the Chingford Tower fracas and one or two other rather trivial affairs, he would be heralded by the Academy, instead of considered a sort of interesting lunatic.

His first delvings into the art of space travel were those which generated the St. James Park matter, and they occurred on, or better yet, were culminated in 1892 early in the morning of July 2. St. Ives' spacecraft was ball-shaped and large enough for one occupant; and because it was the first of a series of such crafts, that occupant was to be one Newton, a trained orang-outang who had only to push the right series of buttons when spacebound to motivate a magnetic homing device designed to reverse the craft's direction and set it about a homeward course. The ape's head was shaven to allow for the snug fitting of a sort of golden conical cap which emitted a meager electrical charge, sufficient only to induce a very mild sleep. It was of great importance that the ape remain docile while in flight, a condition which, as we shall see, was not maintained. The ape was also fitted with a pair of silver, magnetic-soled boots to affix him firmly to the deck of the ship; they would impede his movements in case he became restive, or, as is the problem with space travel, in case the forces of gravity should diminish.

Finally, St. Ives connected a spring-driven mechanism in a silver-colored box which puffed forth successive jets of oxygenated gas produced by the interaction of a concentrated chlorophyll solution with compressed helium—this combination producing the necessary atmosphere in the closed quarters of the ship.

The great scientist, after securing the ape to his chair and winding the chlorophyll box, launched the ship from the rear yard of his residence and laboratory in Harrogate. He watched the thing careen south through the starry early-morning sky. It was at that point, his craft a pinpoint of light on the horizon, that St. Ives was stricken with the awful realization that he had neglected to fill the ape's food dispenser, a fact which would not have been of consequence except that the ape was to receive half a score of greengage plums as a reward for pushing the several buttons which would affect the gyro and reverse the course of the ship. The creature's behavior once he ascertained that he had, in effect, been cheated of his greengages was unpredictable. There was nothing to be done, however, but for St. Ives to crawl wearily into bed and hope for the best.

—◦◦◦—

SEVERAL WEEKS PREVIOUS to the launching of the craft (pardon the digression here; its pertinence will soon become apparent) a Bulgarian Gypsy caravan had set up a bit of a carnival in Chelsea, where they sold the usual salves and potions and such rot, as well as providing entertainments. Now, Wilfred Keeble was a toymaker who lived on Whitehall above the Old Shades and who, though not entirely daft, was eccentric. He was also the unloved brother of Winnifred Keeble, newly monied wife of Lord Placer. To be a bit more precise, he was loved well enough by his sister, but his brother-in-law couldn't abide him. Lord Placer had little time for the antics of his wife's lowlife relative, and even less for carnivals or circuses of gypsies. His daughter Olivia, therefore, sneaked away and cajoled her Uncle Wilfred into taking her to the gypsy carnival. Keeble assented, having little use himself for Lord Placer's august stuffiness, and off they went to the carnival, which proved to be a rather pale affair, aside from the antics of Moko the Educated Ape. Actually, a far as Keeble was concerned, the ape itself was nothing much, being trained merely to sit in a great chair and puff on a cigar while seeming to pore over a copy of the Times which, more often than not, it held upside down or sideways or chewed at or tore up or gibbered over.

Olivia was fascinated by the creature and flew home begging her father for a pet ape, an idea which not only sent a thrill of horror and disgust up Lord Placer's spine, but which caused him to confound his brother-in-law and everything connected with him for having had such a damnable effect on his daughter. Olivia, her hopes dashed by her father's ape loathing, confided her grief to Uncle Wilfred who, although he knew that the gift of a real ape would generate conflicts best not thought about, could see no harm in fashioning a toy ape.

He set about in earnest to create such a thing and, in a matter of weeks, came up with one of those clockwork, key-crank jack-in-the-boxes. It was a silver cube painted with vivid circus depictions; when wound tightly, a comical ape got up as a mandarin and with whirling eyes would spring out and shout a snatch of verse. Wilfred Keeble was pretty thoroughly pleased with the thing, but he knew that it would be folly to go visiting his brother-in-law's house with such a wild and unlikely gift, in the light of Lord Placer's hatred of such things. There was a boy downstairs, a Jack Owlesby, who liked to earn a shilling here and there, and so Keeble called him up and, wrapping the box in paper and dashing off a quick note, sent Jack out into the early morning air two and six richer for having agreed to deliver the gift. Having sat up all night to finish the thing, Keeble crawled wearily into bed at, it seems, nearly the same hour that Langdon St. Ives did the same after launching his spacecraft.

—∿∿∿—

THREE PEOPLE—TWO INDIGENT gentlemen who seemed sea-captainish in a devastated sort of way, and a shrunken fellow with a yellow cloth cap who was somehow responsible for the chairs scattered about the green—were active in St. James Park that morning; at least those are the only three whose testimony was later officially transcribed. According to the Times report, these chaps, at about 7:00 AM, saw, as one of them stated, "a great fiery thing come sailing along like a bloody flying head,"—an adequate enough description of St. Ives' ship which, gone amok, came plunging into the south end of the Park's duck pond.

This visitation of a silver orb from space would, in itself, have been sufficient to send an entire park full of people shouting into the city, but, to the three in the park, it seemed weak tea indeed when an alien-seeming beast sailed out on impact through the sprung hatch, a bald-headed but otherwise hairy creature with a sort of golden dunce cap, woefully small, perched atop his head. Later, one of the panhandlers, a gentleman named Hornby, babbled some rubbish about a pair of flaming stilts, but the other two agreed that the thing wore high-topped silver boots, and, to a man, they remarked of an "infernal machine" which the thing carried daintily between his outstretched hands like a delicate balloon as it fled into Westminster.

There was, of course, an immediate hue and cry, responded to by two constables and a handful of sleepy and disheveled horse guards who raced about skeptically between the witnesses while poor Newton, St. Ives's orang-outang, fuddled and hungry, disappeared into the city. At least three journalists appeared within half an hour's time and were soon hotfooting it away quick as you please with the tale of the alien ship, the star beast, and the peculiar and infernal machine.

Newton had begun to grow restless somewhere over Yorkshire, just as the professor had supposed he would. Now all of this is a matter of conjecture, but logic would point with a stiffish finger toward the probability that the electronic cap atop the ape's head either refused to function or functioned incorrectly, for Newton had commenced his antics within minutes of takeoff. There were reports, in fact, of an erratic glowing sphere zigging through the sky above Long Bennington that same morning, an indication that Newton, irate, was pretty thoroughly giving the controls the once-over. One can only suppose that the beast, anticipating a handful of plums, began stabbing away at the crucial buttons unaffected, as he must have been, by the cap. That it took a bit longer for him to run thoroughly amok indicates the extent of his trust in St. Ives. The professor, in his papers, reports that the control panel itself was finally dashed to bits and the chlorophyll-atmosphere box torn cleanly from the side of the cabin. Such devastation couldn't have been undertaken before the craft was approaching Greater London; probably it occurred above South Mimms, where the ship was observed by the populace to be losing altitude. This marked the beginning of the plunge into London.

Although the creature had sorted through the controls rather handily, those first plum buttons, luckily for him, activated at least partially St. Ives's gyro homing device. Had the beast been satisfied and held off on further mayhem, he would quite possibly have found himself settling back down in Harrogate at St. Ives's laboratory. As it was, the reversing power of the craft was enough finally to promote, if not a gentle landing, at least one which, taking into account the cushion of water involved, was not fatal to poor Newton.

———⟨≈⟩———

JACK OWLESBY, MEANWHILE, ambled along down Whitehall, grasping the box containing Keeble's ape contraption and anticipating a meeting with Keeble's niece whom he had admired more than once. He was, apparently, a good enough lad, as we'll see, and had been, coincidentally enough, mixed in with Langdon St. Ives himself some little time ago in another of St. Ives's scientific shenanigans. Anyway, because of his sense of duty and the anticipation of actually speaking to Olivia, he popped right along for the space of five minutes before realizing that he could hardly go pounding away on Lord Placer's door at such an inhuman hour of the morning. He'd best, thought he, sort of angle up around the square and down The Mall to the park to kill a bit of time. A commotion of some nature and a shooting lot of people drew him naturally along and, as would have happened to anyone in a like case, he went craning away across the road, unconscious of a wagon of considerable size which was gathering speed some few feet off his starboard side. A horn blasted, Jack leapt forward with a shout, clutching his parcel, and a brougham, unseen behind the wagon, plowed over him like an express, the driver cursing and flailing his arms.

The long and the short of it is that Jack's box, or rather Keeble's box, set immediate sail and bounced along unhurt into a park thicket ignored by onlookers who, quite rightly, rushed to poor Jack's aid.

The boy was stunned, but soon regained his senses and, although knocked about a good bit, suffered no real damages. The mishaps of a boy, however, weren't consequential enough to hold the attention of the crowd, not even of the Lord Mayor, who was in the fateful brougham. He had been rousted out of an early morning bed by the reports of dangerous aliens and inexplicable mechanical contrivances. He rather fancied the idea of a smoke and a chat and perhaps a pint of bitter later in the day with these alien chaps and so organized a "delegation," as he called it, to ride out and welcome them.

He was far more concerned with the saddening report that the thing had taken flight to the south than with the silver sphere that bobbed in the pond. The ship had been towed to shore, but as yet no one had ventured to climb inside for fear of the unknown—an unfortunate and decisive hesitation, since a thorough examination would certainly have enabled an astute observer to determine its origin.

It was to young Jack's credit that, after he had recovered from the collision, he spent only a moment or so at the edge of the pond with the other spectators before becoming thoroughly concerned over the loss of the box. The letter from Keeble to Olivia lay yet within his coat, but the box seemed to have vanished like a magician's coin. He went so far as to stroll nonchalantly across the road again, reenacting, as they say, the scene of the crime or, in this case, the accident. He pitched imaginary boxes skyward and then clumped about through bushes and across lawns, thoroughly confounded by the disappearance. Had he known the truth, he'd have given up the search and gone about his business, or what was left of it, but he had been lying senseless when old grizzled Hornby, questioned and released by the constables, saw Jack's parcel crash down some few feet from him as he sat brooding in the bushes. In Hornby's circles one didn't look a gift horse in the fabled mouth, not for long anyway, and he had the string yanked off and the wrapper torn free in a nonce.

Now you or I would have been puzzled by the box, silvery and golden as it was and with bright pictures daubed on in paint and a mysterious crank beneath, but Hornby was positively aghast. He'd seen such a thing that morning in the hands of a creature who, he still insisted, raged along in his wizard's cap on burning stilts. He dared not fiddle with it in light of all that, and yet he couldn't just pop out of the bushes waving it about either. This was a fair catch and, no doubt, a very valuable one. Why such a box should sail out of the skies was a poser, but this was clearly a day tailor-made for such occurrences. He scuttled away under cover of the thick greenery until clear of the mobbed pond area, then took to his heels and headed down toward Westminster with the vague idea of finding a pawn broker who had heard of the alien threat and would be willing to purchase such an unlikely item.

Jack, then, searched in vain, for the box he'd been entrusted with had been spirited away. His odd behavior, however, soon drew the attention of the constabulary who, suspicious of the very trees, asked him what he was about. He explained that he'd been given a metallic looking box, and a very wonderful box at that, and had been instructed to deliver it across town. The nature of the box, he admitted, was unknown to him for he'd glimpsed it only briefly. He suspected, though, that it was a toy of some nature.

"A toy is it, that we have here!" shouted Inspector Marleybone of Scotland Yard. "And who, me lad, was it gave you this toy?"

"Mister Keeble, sir, of Whitehall," said Jack very innocently and knowing nothing of a similar box which, taken to be some hideous device, was a subject of hot controversy. Here were boxes springing up like the children of Noah, and it took no longer than a moment or two before two police wagons were rattling away, one to ferret out this mysterious Keeble, in league, like as not, with aliens, and one to inquire after Lord Placer down near the Tate Gallery. Jack, as well as a dozen policemen, were left to continue futilely scouring the grounds.

—⁓—

SOMEHOW NEWTON HAD managed, by luck or stealth, to slip across Victoria Street and fall in among the greengrocers and clothing sellers along Old Pye. Either they were fairly used to peculiar chaps in that section of town so took no special notice of him, or else Newton, wittily, clung to the and shadows and generally laid low, as they say. This latter possibility is most likely the case, for Newton would have been as puzzled and frightened of London as had he actually been an alien; orang-outangs, being naturally shy and contemplative beasts, would, if given the choice, spurn the company of men. The incident, however, that set the whole brouhaha going afresh was sparked by a wooden fruit cart loaded, unfortunately, with nothing other than greengage plums.

Here was a poor woman, tired, I suppose, and at only eight o'clock or so in the morning, with her cart of fresh plums and two odious children. She set up along the curb, outside a bakery. As fortune would have it, she was an altogether kindly sort, and she towed her children in to buy a two-penny loaf, leaving her cart for the briefest of moments.

She returned, munching a slab of warm bread, in time to see the famished Newton, his greengages come round at last, hoeing into handfuls of the yellowy fruit. As the Times has the story, the ape was hideously covered with slime and juice, and, although the information is suspect, he took to hallooing in a resonant voice and to waving the box like a cudgel above his head. The good woman responded with shouts and "a call to Him above in this hour of dreadful things."

As I see it, Newton reacted altogether logically. Cheated of his greengages once, he had no stomach to be dealt with in such a manner again. He grasped the tongue of the cart, anchored his machine firmly in among the plums, and loped off down Old Pye Street toward St. Ann's.

Jack Owlesby searched as thoroughly as was sensible—more thoroughly perhaps, for, as I said, he was prompted and accompanied by the authorities, and as soon as the crowd in the park got wind of the possible presence of "a machine," they too savaged the bushes, surged up and down the road behind the Horse Guards, and tramped about Duck Island until the constables were forced to shout threats and finally give up their own search. The crowd thinned shortly thereafter, when a white-coated, bespectacled fellow hailing from the Museum came down and threw a tarpaulin over the floating ship.

Jack was at odds, blaming himself for the loss, but mystified and frustrated over its disappearance. There seemed to be only one option—to deliver the letter to young Olivia and then return the two and six to Mr. Keeble upon returning to the Old Shades. He set out, then, to do just that.

⸺ꙮꙮꙮ⸺

INSPECTOR MARLEYBONE WAS in an itch to get to the bottom of this invasion, as it were, which had so far been nothing more than the lunatic arrival of a single alien who had since fled. Wild reports of flaming engines and howling, menacing giants were becoming tiresome. But, though rumors have always been the bane of the authorities, they seem to be meat and drink to the populace, and here was no exception. Bold headlines of "Martian Invasion" and "St. James Horror" had the common man in a state, and it may as well have been a bank holiday in London by 9:00 that morning. A fresh but grossly overblown account of the plum-cart incident reached poor Marleybone at about the time he arrived back at the Yard, just as he had begun toying with the idea that there had been no starship, nor hairy alien nor dread engine, and that all had been a nightmarish product of the oysters and Spanish wine he'd enjoyed the night before. But here were fresh accounts, and the populace honing kitchen knives, and a thoroughly befuddled Wilfred Keeble without his cap, being ushered in by two very serious constables.

Keeble, who normally liked the idea of romance and grand adventure, didn't at all like the real thing, and was a bit groggy from lack of sleep in the bargain. He listened, puzzled, to Marleybone's questions, which seemed, of course, madness. There was no reference, at first, to strange metallic boxes, but only to suspected dealings with alien space invaders and to Marleybone's certainty that Keeble was responsible, almost singlehandedly, for the mobs which, shouting and clanking in their curiosity, came surging up and down the road at intervals on their way to gaze at the covered ball in the pond, and to search for whatever wonderful prizes had rained on London from the heavens.

Keeble pleaded his own ignorance and innocence and insisted that he was a toy-maker who knew little of invasions, and would have nothing to do with such things had he the opportunity. Marleybone was wary but tired, and his spirits fell another notch when Lord Placer, his own eyes glazed from a night of brandy and cards at the club, stormed in in a rage.

Although it was all very well to ballyrag Keeble, it was another thing entirely with Lord Placer, and so the inspector, with an affected smile, began to explain that Keeble seemed to be mixed into the alien affair, and that a certain metallic box, thought to be a threatening device of some nature or another, had been intercepted, then lost, en route from Keeble to Lord Placer. It wasn't strictly the truth, and Marleybone kicked himself for not having taken Jack Owlesby in tow so that he'd at least have someone to point the accusatory finger at. Lord Placer, although knowing even less at this point than did his brother-in-law (who, at the mention of a silver box saw a glimmer of light at the end of the tunnel) was fairly sure he could explain the fracas away even so. Wilfred Keeble, he stated, was clearly a madman, a raving lunatic who, with his devices and fables, was attempting to drive the city mad for the sake of company. It was a clear go as far as Lord P. could determine, and although it did not lessen the horror of being dragged from a warm bed and charged as an alien invader, it was at least good to have such a simple explanation. Lunacy, Lord Placer held, was the impetus behind almost everything, especially his brother-in-law's actions, whether real or supposed.

Finally Marleybone did the sensible thing, and let the two go, wondering why in the devil he'd called them in in the first place. Although he believed for the most part Keeble's references to a jack-in-the-box, he was even more convinced of Lord Placer's hypothesis of general lunacy. He accompanied Lord Placer to his coach, apologizing profusely for the entire business. Lord P. grunted and agreed, as the horses clopped away, to contact Scotland Yard in the event that the mysterious machine should, by some twist of insane fate, show up at his door.

Lady Placer, the former Miss Keeble, met her husband as he dragged in from the coach, mumbling curses about her brother. If anyone in the family had, as the poet said, "gone round the bend," it was Winnifred, who was slow-witted as a toothpick. She was, however, tolerant of her brother, and couldn't altogether fathom her husband's dis-like of him, although she set great store in old Placer's opinions, and thus often found herself in a muddle over the contrary promptings of her heart and mind. She listened, then, with great curiosity to Lord Placer's confused story of the rumoured invasion, the monster in the park, and his own suspected connection with the affair, which was entirely on account of her damned brother's rumminess.

Winnifred, having heard the shouting newsboys, knew something was in the air, and was mystified to find that her own husband and brother were mixed up in it. She was thoroughly awash when her husband stumbled away to bed, but was not overly worried, for confusion was one of the humours she felt near to and was comfortable with. She did wonder, however, at the fact that Lord Placer was involved in such weird doings, and she debated whether her daughter should be sent away, perhaps to her aunt's home near Dover, until the threat was past. Then it struck her that she wasn't at all sure what the threat was, and that spaceships might land in Dover as well as London, and also that, at any rate, her husband probably wasn't in league with these aliens after all. She wandered out to her veranda to look at a magazine. It was about then, I'd calculate, that the weary Marleybone got wind of the plum business and headed streetward again, this time in the company of the Lord Mayor's delegation.

It's not to be thought that, while Scotland Yard was grilling its suspects, Newton and Jack Owlseby and, of course, old Hornby who was about town with one of the two devices, stood idle. Newton, in fact, set out in earnest to enhance his already ballooning reputation. After making off with the plum cart, he found himself unpursued, and deep into Westminster, heading, little did he know, toward Horseferry Road. It's folly for an historian in such a case to do other than conjecture, but it seems to me that, sated with plums but still ravenous, as you or I might be sated with sweets while desiring something more substantial, he sighted a melon cart wending its way toward the greengrocers along Old Pye. Newton moored his craft in an alley, his box rooted in the midst of the plums, and hastened after the melon man, who was anything but pleased with the ape's appearance. He'd as yet heard nothing of the alien threat, and so took Newton to be an uncommonly ugly and bizarrely dressed thief. Hauling a riding crop from a peg on the side of the cart, the melon man laid about him with a will, cracking away at the perplexed orang-outang with wonderful determination, and shouting the while for a constable.

Newton, aghast, and taking advantage of his natural jungle agility, attempted to clamber up a wrought-iron pole which supported a striped canvas awning. His weight, of course, required a stout tree rather than a precariously moored pole, and the entire business gave way, entangling the ape in the freed canvas. The grocer pursued his attack, the ruckus having drawn quite a crowd, many of whom recognized the ape as a space invader, and several of whom took the trailing canvas, which had become impaled on the end of Newton's conical cap, to be some sort of Arab headgear. That, to be sure, explains the several accounts of alien-Mohammedan conspiracies which found their way into the papers. References to an assault by the invader against the melon man are unproven and, I think, utterly false.

When Newton fled, followed by the mob, he found his plum cart as he had left it—except for the box, which had disappeared.

—~~~—

JACK OWLESBY HADN'T walked more than a half mile, still glum as a herring over Keeble's misplaced trust, when, strictly by chance, he glanced up an alley off St. Ann's and saw a plum cart lying unattended therein. The startling thing was that, as you can guess, an odd metallic box was nestled in among the plums. Jack drew near and determined, on the strength of the improbability of any other explanation, that the box was his own, or, rather, Olivia's. He had seen the thing only briefly before it had been wrapped, so his putting the gypsy touch to it can be rationalized, and even applauded. Because he had no desire to encounter whoever stole the thing, he set out immediately, supposing himself to have patched up a ruinous morning.

Old Hornby had not been as fortunate as had Jack. His conviction that the box was extra-terrestrial was scoffed at by several pawnbrokers who, seeming vaguely interested in the prize, attempted to coerce Hornby to hand it over to them for inspection. Sly Hornby realized that these usurious merchants were in league to swindle him, and he grew ever more protective of the thing as he, too, worked his way south. His natural curiosity drew him toward a clamoring mob which pursued some unseen thing.

It seemed to Hornby as if he "sniffed aliens" in the air and, as far as it goes, he was correct. He also assumed, this time incorrectly, that some profit was still to be had from these aliens, and so, swiftly and cunningly, he left the mob on Monck Street, set off through the alleys, and popped out at about the point that Horseferry winds around the mouth of Regency Street, head-on into the racing Newton who, canvas headgear and all, was outdistancing the crowd. Hornby was heard to shout, "Hey there," or "You there," or some such, before being bowled over, the ape snatching Hornby's treasured box away as it swept past, thinking it, undoubtedly, the box that had been purloined in the alley.

Jack Owlesby, meanwhile, arrived at Lord Placer's door and was admitted through the rear entrance by the butler, an affable sort who wandered off to drum up Miss Olivia at Jack's insistence. Lord Placer, hearing from the butler that a boy stood in the hall with a box for Olivia, charged into Jack's presence in a fit of determination. He'd played the fool for too long, or so he thought, and he intended to dig to the root of the business. He was well into the hall when he realized that he was dressed in his nightshirt and cap, a pointed cloth affair, and wore his pointy-toed silk house slippers which were, he knew, ridiculous. His rage overcame his propriety, and, of course, this was only an errand boy, not a friend from the club, so he burst along and jerked the box away from an amazed Jack Owlesby.

"Here we have it!" he shouted, examining the thing.

"Yes, sir," said Jack. "If you please, sir, this is meant for your daughter and was sent by Mr. Keeble."

"Keeble has a hand in everything, it seems," cried Lord Placer, still brandishing the box as if it were a great diamond in which he was searching for flaws. "What's this bloody crank, boy? Some hideous apparatus, I'd warrant."

"I'm sure I don't know, sir," replied Jack diplomatically, hoping that Olivia would appear and smooth things out. He was sure that Lord Placer, who seemed more or less mad, would ruin the thing.

Casting caution to the winds, Lord Placer whirled away at the crank while peering into a funnel-like tube that protruded from the end. His teeth were set and he feared nothing, not even that this was, as he had been led to believe, one of the infernal machines rampant in the city. Amid puffings and whirrings and a tiny momentary tinkling sound, a jet of bright chlorophyll-green helium gas shot from the tube, covering Lord Placer's face and hair with a fine, lime-colored mist.

A howl of outrage issued from Lord Placer's mouth, now hanging open in disbelief. It was an uncanny howl, like that of moaning elf, for the gaseous mixture, for a reason known only to those who delve into the scientific mysteries, had a dismal effect on his vocal cords, an effect not unnoticed by Lord P., who thought himself poisoned and leapt toward the rear door. Winnifred, having heard an indecipherable shriek while lounging on the veranda, was met by Olivia, fresh from a stroll in the rose garden, and the two of them were astounded to see a capering figure of lunacy, eyes awhirl in a green face, come bellowing with an elvish voice into the yard, carrying a spouting device.

Winnifred's worst fears had come to pass. Here was her husband, or so it seemed, gone amok and in a weird disguise. Lady Placer, in a gesture of utter bewilderment, clapped a hand to her mouth and slumped backward onto the lawn. Olivia was no less perplexed, to be sure, but her concern over her mother took precedence over the mystery that confronted her, and she stooped to her aid. Lady Placer was a stout-hearted soul, however, and she was up in a moment. "It's your father," she gasped in a voice that sounded as if it knew strange truths, "go to him, but beware."

Olivia was dumbfounded, but she left her mother in the care of the butler, and launched out in the company of Jack Owlesby (who was, by then, at least as confused as the rest of the company) in pursuit of her father, who was loping some two blocks ahead and still carrying the box.

It was at this point that the odd thing occurred. Newton, having lost the crowd, still swung along down Regency past stupefied onlookers. He rounded onto Bessbourough and crossed John Islip Road, when he saw coming toward him a kindred soul. Here then came Lord Placer in his own pointed cap and with his own machine, rollicking along at an impressive clip. Now apes, as you know, are more intelligent in their way than are dogs, and it's not surprising that Newton, harried through London, saw at once that Lord Placer was an ally. So, with an ape's curiosity, he sped alongside for the space of a half block down toward Vauxhal Bridge, from which Lord Placer intended to throw himself into the river in hopes of diluting the odious solution he'd been doused with. Why he felt it necessary to bathe in the Thames is a mystery until we consider what the psychologists say—that a man in such an addled state might well follow his initial whims, even though careful contemplation would instruct him otherwise.

Inspector Marleybone, the Lord Mayor, and the delegation whipped along in their brougham in the wake of the mob. As is usual in such confusion, many of those out on the chase knew little or nothing of that which they pursued. Rumors of the alien invasion were rampant but often scoffed at, and secondary rumors concerning the march of Islam, and even that the walls of Colney Hatch had somehow burst and released a horde of loonies, were at least as prevalent. Marleybone blanched at the sight of clubs and hay forks, and the Lord Mayor, aghast that London would visit such a riot on the heads of emissaries from another planet, demanded that Marleybone put a stop to the rout; but such a thing was, of course, impossible and they gave off any effort at quelling the mob, and concentrated simply on winning through to the fore and restraining things as best they could. This necessitated, unfortunately, taking a bit of a roundabout route which promoted several dead-ends and a near collision with a milk wagon, but finally they came through, careening around the corner of Bessborough and Grosvenor and sighting the two odd companions hotly pursued by a throng that stretched from the Palace to Millbank. Here they reined in.

The Lord Mayor was unsure as to exactly what course of action to take, considering the size and activity of the crowd and the ghastly duo of cavorting box-carriers that approached. If anyone remembers Jeremy Pike, otherwise Lord Bastable, who served as Lord Mayor from '89 almost until the war, you'll recall that, as the poet said, he had a heart stout and brave, and a rather remarkable speech prepared for the most monstrous audience he was likely to encounter.

So the Lord Mayor, with Marleybone at his heels, strode into the road and held up his hands, palms forward, in that symbolic gesture which is universally taken to mean "halt." It is absurd to think that there is any significance to the fact that Newton responded correctly to the signal, despite the suggestion of two noted astronomers, because their theory—the literal universality of hand gestures—lies in Newton's other-worldliness, which, as we know, is a case of mistaken identity. Anyway, the pair of fugitives halted in flight, I believe, because it was at that point, when presented with the delegation, that Lord Placer's eyes ceased to revolve like tops and it looked as if he were "coming around." He was still very much in some nature of psychological shock, as would anyone be if thrown into a like circumstance, but he was keen-witted enough to see that here was the end of the proverbial line. As Lord Placer slowed to a stop, so did Newton, himself happy, I've little doubt, to give up the chase.

The mob caught up with the ambassadorial party in a matter of moments, and there was a great deal of tree climbing and shoulder hoisting and neck craning as the people of London pressed in along the Thames. Marleybone gazed suspiciously at Lord Placer for the space of a minute before being struck with the pop-eyed realization of the gentleman's identity.

"Ha!" shouted the Inspector, reaching into his coat for a pair of manacles. Lord Placer, sputtering, proffered his box to the delegation, but a spurt of green fume and the tick of a timing device prompted a cry of, "The devil!" from Marleybone and, "The Infernal Machine!" from a score of people on the inner perimeter of the crowd, and everyone pressed back, fearing a detonation, and threatening a panic. Another burst of green, however, seemed to indicate that the device had miscarried somehow, and a smattering of catcalls and hoots erupted from the mob.

Lord Placer, at this point, recovered fully. He tugged his cloth cap low over his eyes and winked hugely several times at Olivia as she pushed through to be by his side. Olivia took the winks to be some sort of spasm and cried out, but Jack Owlesby, good lad he, slipped Lord P. a wink of his own, and very decorously tugged Olivia aside and whispered at her. Her father made no effort to rub away the chlorophyllic mask.

The Lord Mayor stepped up, and with a ceremonious bow took the glittering aerator from Lord Placer's outstretched hands. He held the thing aloft, convinced that it was some rare gift, no doubt incomprehensible to an earthling. He trifled with the crank. As another poof of green shot forth, the crowd broke into applause and began stamping about in glee.

"Londoners!" the Lord Mayor bawled, removing his hat. "This is indeed a momentous occasion." The crowd applauded heartily at this and, like as not, prompted Newton, who stood bewildered, to offer the Lord Mayor his own curiously wrought box.

A bit perturbed at the interruption but eager, on the other hand, to parley with this hairy beast who, it was apparent, hailed from the stars, old Bastable graciously accepted the gift. It was unlike the first box, and the designs drawn upon the outside, although weird, seemed to be of curiously garbed animals: hippoes with toupees and carrying Gladstone Bags, elephants riding in ridiculously small dog-carts, great toads in clam-shell trousers and Leibnitz caps, and all manner of like things. Seeing no other explanation, the Lord Mayor naturally assumed that such finery might be common on an alien star, and with a flourish of his right arm, as if he were daubing the final colours onto a canvas, he set in to give this second box a crank-up.

The crowd waited, breathless. Even those too far removed from the scene to have a view of it seemed to know from the very condition of the atmosphere that what is generally referred to as "a moment in history" was about to occur. Poor Hornby, his feet aching from a morning of activity, gaped on the inner fringe of the circle of onlookers, as Lord Placer, perhaps the only one among the multitude who dared move, edged away toward the embankment.

There was the ratchet click of a gear and spring being turned tighter and tighter until, with a snap that jarred the silence, the top of the box flew open and a tiny ape, singularly clad in a golden robe and, of all things, a night cap not at all unlike Lord Placer's, shot skyward, hung bobbing in mid-air, and, in a piping voice called out Herodotus's cryptic and immortal line: "Fear not, Athenian stranger, because of this marvel!" After uttering the final syllable the ape, as if by magic, popped down into the box, pulling the lid shut after him.

The Lord Mayor stared at Marleybone in frank disbelief, both men awestruck, when Lord Placer, his brass having given out and each new incident compounding his woe, broke for the stairs that led to the causeway below the embankment and sailed like billy-o in the direction of home. About half the mob, eager again for the chase, sallied out in pursuit. When their prey was lost momentarily from view, Jack Owlesby, in a stroke of genius, shouted, "There goes the blighter!" and led the mob around the medical college, thus allowing for Lord Placer's eventual escape. Marleybone and the Lord Mayor collared Newton, who looked likely to bolt, and were confronted by two out-of-breath constables who reported nothing less than the theft of the spacecraft by a white-coated and bearded fellow in spectacles, ostensibly from the museum, who carried official looking papers. After towing Newton into the brougham, the delegation swept away up Millbank to Horseferry, lapped round behind Westminster Hospital and flew north back across Victoria without realizing that they were chasing phantoms, that they hadn't an earthly idea as to the identity or the whereabouts of the mysterious thief.

The Lord Mayor pulled his folded speech from his coat pocket and squinted at it through his pince-nez a couple of times, pretty clearly worked up over not having been able to utilize it. Marleybone was in a foul humour, having had his fill of everything that didn't gurgle when tipped upside down. Newton somehow had gotten hold of the jack-in-the-box and, to the annoyance of his companions, was popping the thing off regularly. It had to have been at the crossing of Great George and Abingdon that a dog-cart containing a tall, gaunt gentleman wearing a Tamerlane beret and with an evident false nose plunged alongside and kept pace with the brougham. To the astonishment of the delegation, Newton (a powerful beast) burst the door from its hinges, leapt out running onto the roadway, and clambered in beside Falsenose, whereupon the dog-cart howled away east toward Lambeth Bridge.

The thing was done in an instant. The alien was gone, the infernal machine was gone, the ship, likewise, had vanished, and by the time the driver of the brougham could fathom the cacophony of alarms from within his coach, turn, and pursue a course toward the river, the dog-cart was nowhere to be seen.

A thorough search of the Victoria Embankment yielded an abandoned, rented dog-cart and a putty nose, but nothing else save, perhaps, for a modicum of relief for all involved. As we all know, the papers milked the crisis for days, but the absence of any tangible evidence took the wind from their sails, and the incident of "The Ape-Box Affair" took its place alongside the other great unexplained mysteries, and was, in the course of time, forgotten.

How Langdon St. Ives (for it was he with the putty nose), his man Hasbro (who masterminded the retrieval of the floating ship), and Newton the orang-outang wended their way homeward is another, by no means slack, story. Suffice it to say that all three and their craft passed out of Lambeth Reach and down the Thames to the sea aboard a hired coal barge, from whence they made a rather amazing journey to the bay of Humber and then overland to Harrogate.

This little account, then, incomplete as it is, clears up some mysteries—mysteries that the principals of the case took some pains, finally, to ignore. But Lord Placer, poor fellow, is dead these three years, Marleybone has retired to the sea-side, and Lord Bastable…well, we are all aware of his amazing disappearance after the so-called "cataleptic transferrence" which followed his post-war sojourn in Lourdes. What became of Jack Owlesby's pursuit of Olivia I can't say, nor can I determine whether Keeble hazarded the making of yet another amazing device for his plucky niece, who was the very Gibraltar of her family in the months that followed the tumult.

So this history, I hope, will cause no one embarrassment, and may satisfy the curiosities of those who recall "The Horror in St. James Park." I apologize if, by the revelation of causes and effects, what was once marvelous and inexplicable slides down a rung or two into the realm of the commonplace; but such explication is the charge of the historian—a charge I hope to have executed with candor. —

The Hole in Space

BY NOW YOU'VE heard of the doings at Chingford-by-the-Tower and of the great orange cataract of flame that the Watford-Enfield scouts saw over Chingford Common on the evening of October 24. You also know that the whole affair blew over in a fortnight, was laughed down as a prank played on the scouts by a gang of local toughs, those same toughs who, during the Baden Powell Jamboree in St. James Park, pitched the four scoutmasters into the duck pond. The burnt tents and rampaging scouts of the Chingford Common incident, however, had a run-in with something other than local bullies: vastly other, I believe I can say with complete truth. Virtually no one knows what actually occurred on that wild night—no one but me, Jack Owlesby, and, I pray, Professor Langdon St. Ives and his man Hasbro. Had I not returned miraculously Sunday last, worn but serviceable, the Watford-Enfield boys would remain known as the Chingford Cuckoos and the Scout's Rest on Jermyn Street would fold its tent shamefacedly and slink away.

But I haven't crossed and recrossed a million miles of deep space simply to explain away the Chingford fracas, nor to stand witness for the Enfield toughs, nor to help eradicate the blot that this pall of suspected lunacy has dropped over the Scout's Rest, although this last task I would undertake cheerfully, for the old Rest has been my succor and my hearth rug, as I believe they say, since the good years of my youth.

My rooms, in fact, are above the Rest there on Jermyn Street, about halfway between Charing Cross Road and the Dunhill shop—the corner of Regent and Jermyn to be precise. It was but eight short weeks ago, if I remember aright, that an oddly uniformed boy nipped round with a telegram of what appeared to be the urgent sort. I had returned to the digs about thirty minutes past from lunch at the Old Shades on Whitehall; you know, off Trafalgar Square: Cornish pasty and mash and a pint of the best a shilling. Can't be beat, I say. Anyway, here came a fearful pounding on the door and I opened it to find a small stout chap got up in joke clothes, in a Fauntleroy suit and with a sort of greenish wiggy thing atop his head. There was something of the jolly porcine about him, like a pig on holiday. He handed me a note, uttering something made senseless by a foreign accent, and I tipped him twopence for the effort. He tripped off down the stairs looking altogether pleased. The telegram ran as follows:

> Jack Owlesby
> Jermyn House
> #24 Jermyn St.
> London
>
> Jack: Project finished. Make haste. 24th of O. absolute necessity. Full moon. Bring woolies and secure copy of Birdlip's Last Word on Rare Succulents and Tropical Begonias from Dr. Lester, special collections, Brit. Mus.
>
> Professor Langdon St. Ives
> The High Road
> Chingford-by-the-Tower
> Chingford

Another person might have been stupefied by such a telegram, but I wasn't. I was out and hoofing it up Charing Cross in a nonce to secure, as St. Ives had requested, the Birdlip volume from Dr. Lester. I'll admit that this part of the instructions was a puzzler. The rest was clear as a lark among peahens, but this plant book threw me. One doesn't diddle about, however, when Langdon St. Ives calls; one hops to in the manner of the famous rickshaw boy in the fable, and sets about his mission. So, as I say, I set out at a brisk pace and returned with the book in hand—something more of a manuscript than a book—in a matter of an hour. By five o'clock I was packed and rattling away out of King's Cross Station toward Chingford, the book propped open on my knee and the compartment cheerful with the reek of a merry pipe and the steam from a thermos of coffee and a pair of hotcross buns bought smoking from a car at the station. The illustrated volume was otherworldly, the Latin incomprehensible, and I could only marvel at the foreign climes that produced the strange fauna that peopled the pages of the book.

It was storming outside and the dusk was lit with flashes of lightning that illuminated raindrops the size of goose eggs. The wind was blowing in fits and gusts out of the east, a chill wind off the North Sea, and I was ruminating on the jolly atmosphere of the warm compartment and was congratulating myself for having the upper hand over what have been referred to as the inclemencies of climate, and that in spades, when into the compartment burst a red faced sweating chap with a heavy, fat face and, oddly, with what might be called a family relationship to the man who had delivered the Professor's telegram—the same swinish features, the small eyes, the stout build.

I was on the brink of suggesting that he had stumbled by accident into the first class car, when what he wanted was either the third class down back, or, more likely, the coal car, when he lunged across and whisked the window down with a twirl of his coarse wrist.

"Quite a night, what?" I said, leading into the whole thing delicately. The wind, however, came howling through at about that time carrying this goose-egg rain upon it like a flood tide, and my words were lost in the deluge. I felt like old Lear, the king in the play who made the crazy speech out on the blasted heath to his knave, poor Tom Foolery, who was wrapped in a winding sheet.

"Quite a filthy night!" I repeated, cupping my hands over my mouth.

He turned and gave me a look, as if I had shouted a madness. Then he squinted along over his nose and said something like, "aaargh," and pointed out the window toward the east and the lights of Stoke Newington. Anxious not to offend, and supposing that some visual treat was looming out there somewhere, I bent down and thrust my head out into the storm.

In a trice shrivel-face had me by the seat of the trousers and the collar of my mack and I found myself hurtling like the Hesperus toward a blur of rock and gravel along the tracks. The fates, however, have always kept a judicious eye on Jack Owlesby, and apparently they cast a quick vote and decided to play out a bit of slack. I landed tumbling and whooping in a stand of gorse.

I lay still for a moment, taking stock, as they say, and letting the rain, which by now was falling in sheets instead of drops, wash the wildness from my eyes and clear away the muddle. Leave it to being pitched out the window of a moving train to create a muddle. Two things appeared certain as I lay there plucking at gorse spines. The first was that bugs of one sort or another inhabited the bush. The second was that foul play had stuck its beak into the affair and had begun to prod about and stir things up filthily.

This was just the sort of thing, however, that spurs we Owlesbies into action. *Dies Infustus,* I think they call it—the day of unfavorable omen. Such a day might send the average man scurrying, but it simply propels Jack Owlesby deeper into the grim fray. The bugs, once I clamped my eye on them, also played a part in spurring me on, and I, sans book, pipe, tea, and hot-cross buns, wandered away up Forest Road toward Woodford. In Woodford I managed to dry out a bit and to secure a noggin or two of hot punch before hitching a ride with a lorry driver returning that night to Buckhurst Hill. He dropped me at Epping Gate and I trudged the last half mile to Chingford-by-the-Tower on foot. The storm had broken by this time but enough clouds were scudding about to obscure the moon and make the night fearfully black and stark. The wind, although it had lessened considerably down below, was lashing things about with a vengeance upstairs, and the clouds and stars were bobbing and shooting through the night sky in a sort of mad cosmic dance.

It was the sort of night that prompts one to muse on the infinite and to consider what might be out there, beyond the scattering of stars that we egotistically consider our own. I used to think, when I was a lad, that there was likely a big stone wall that one would encounter should one run one's space galleon far enough out into the void. I chose a wall, I believe, simply to provide a boundary. The idea of the endlessness of anything was something I was unprepared to grapple with. I even dreamed about it—of just such a night—blasting away beyond the planets through a heaven alive with stars whirling like pinwheels, only to run headlong, finally, into a wall painted up with strange and leering lunatic faces. I remember that old Sidcup Catford, the Dean of Lewisham Boys Academy, was along in the ship, and that he blamed me for having drawn comic faces on the walls of heaven. It ruined the dream, old Catford showing up like that. Funny to discover these long years later that the walls exist after all, even if they're not made of stone.

Anyway, here I was feeling fearfully bucked by the rum and the pint of stout I chased it with, and musing, as I've already said, on the infinite, when I sighted Chingford Tower, strangely aglow in the distance. The vision was heartening, because St. Ives Manor would soon pop up from behind the rows of yew trees on the left. And up it popped like a shot, smoke from the chimney and St. Ives' man Hasbro visible within the bright interior, brewing up the late afternoon tea.

I drained a cup or two before the fire, and had warmed up considerably, when through the door strode Professor Langdon St. Ives with a strength of purpose that was admirable. He always displayed that same strength of purpose whether tying into a bowl of soup or preparing to save the world from an alien threat. It's the sort of thing that I might muster for an hour or so on a good day, but which would drain me entirely before midafternoon. Those sorts of purposeful, hie-on-into-the-fray chaps seem always to stride about for some reason, mere walking or strolling being foreign to their very being. Carlyle, I think it was, pointed that out in his treatise on heroes and great men, although it might have been Newman. Either one of them were up to it.

So there I was, firmly ensconced at Chingford-by-the-Tower, slurping away at a cup of what appeared to be some oriental notion of tea, Malay Oolong, if I'm any judge, and here was the greatest physicist since what-was-his-name, gazing at me through slit lids, as they say, with as businesslike an eye as has ever seen daylight.

"Did you bring it, Jack?" he asked.

"Bring it?"

"The book. Birdlip's succulents. Telegram."

"Oh, ah," I replied weakly. "Yes, and then again, no."

"Hah!" cried the Professor, rising up out of his seat. "Did they pinch it?"

"Yes, indeed," I said, mystified by his enthusiasm. "They pinched it. Or rather, *he* did, whoever he was. I hadn't time to inquire, and he wasn't inclined to chat. He took the book and flung me out the window."

"Capital!" shouted the Professor, accepting these odd goings-on in the jolliest of spirits. I wasn't half so sanguine, in fact I was more or less hipped, but this fell into the line-of-duty category, and like a good soldier I awaited further orders.

Hasbro cleared away the tea apparatus and, in a wink, slid round with a tray of essentials: small cakes and glasses and a bottle of Spanish sherry—none of your French vinegar fattened up with cheap brandy. Tea, I've always said, is your man for the pick-me-up, the restorative. But it doesn't stick with you, if you follow me; it's gone as soon as it clears your gums. It takes the real fuel oil to keep the fire lit, and I can tell you that it slipped down the throat like a healing zephyr, giving me what the ancients referred to as the will to live.

St. Ives sat nodding, his mind running on before him, his lips pursed in a knowing and thoughtful way. "Say on, Jack," he said suddenly. "Was it an obese man in a Chinese mandarin jacket and a Leibnitz hat? A beady-eyed man with a face screwed up like a prune? A face like a peccary?"

"That's the bird," I said. "Only without the Chinese clothes. And now that you mention it, no hat either. But he had the warthog face and a flat nose like a whacking great beacon."

St. Ives nodded with apparent satisfaction. "You see, Jacky," he said, "there are those roundabout us who would rather we didn't make this little...voyage. You've met one of their chiefs, I'm afraid."

"Saboteurs is it?"

"Just so. But I've been onto them now for a month. I suspected them after the first voyage, after we'd successfully charted the hole. It's the crowd that Birdlip hinted at in his last letters."

I was thunderstruck. "The same crowd that planted the bomb under Birdlip's laboratory?"

"Just so. And they wouldn't hesitate for a moment to blow us all to Kingdom Come, Jack." He slumped now, and tugged at his chin in the fashion of a man treading the mental pathways, a man who didn't entirely like the look of the landscape. "And now they've gotten off with the book! Or at least its facsimile. They've played their hand. I know them now."

"So it was a ruse, the succulent book?"

"Clever, eh?"

"Indeed," I said, although I wasn't feeling it. I was hipped again. "Quite a gag. I laughed myself into a ditch full of gorse, lost my pipe, my thermos bottle, and my dinner into the bargain, and then I walked from Stoke Newington to Woodford."

"Your thermos bottle do you say?"

"Absolutely."

"Keeble's device for the maintenance of temperature within an enclosed space?"

"That's it exactly. Very nearly irreplaceable, too."

"Do you know that it was the invention of the thermos bottle that excluded Keeble from the Royal Academy?"

"I didn't know that," I said. (William Keeble, I'll reveal here, is my protector and benefactor, a toy maker and inventor extraordinaire.) "Why on earth would they *exclude* him?"

"He explained his device to the members, do you see?—telling them that it kept hot things hot and cold things cold."

"Ah." I nodded.

"But they were skeptical. It sounded like gibberish to them, hot things hot and cold things cold. It was a conundrum, a contradiction in terms. They held the device in their hands, peered inside, sniffed it, handed it round. It was Lord Kelvin himself who asked the decisive, ruinous question. The question for which there was no answer."

"Ah," I said, waiting.

"Kelvin looked at him over the top of his spectacles in that way he has, and asked, quite simply, and with great finality, 'how does it *know?*'"

I stared at St. Ives, blinking once or twice, waiting for his words to convey some meaning to my mind. It had been a long and trying day.

"The question baffled poor Keeble. He didn't expect it. But they were adamant. It's the scientific method or nothing with them, you know, and too often nothing comes of it. Far too often. Do you follow me?"

I poured myself another glass of sherry and nodded. "The succulents and begonias book—I take it you don't rue the loss. And yet your telegram seemed to hint that the volume was of a vital nature."

"And perhaps it was, in its roundabout way. Tell me, do you read the work of Mr. Poe?"

"Too morbid for my taste."

"He's a master of the crime story. Pioneered the device of the false clue, the red herring, the specious oddity that throws your man off the track."

"Or onto the track, in my case," I said, cramming a cake into my mouth, a very delicate seeded cake tasting of anise, and I nodded my appreciation at Hasbro as he reentered the room bearing what appeared to be manuscript pages.

"Quite so. But you see, I knew that these—these pig men, I suppose we can call them, would purloin that telegram and then deliver it themselves. They're keen on the manuscript, you see. As a *ruse de guerre,* I deposited the false volume, the mockup, with Dr. Lester, then gave the missive to Bill Kraken and had him dash down to London to deliver it."

"Bill Kraken!" I was aghast. Of all the unreliable drunkards! "You can't mean old Cuttle Kraken's mad brother?"

"The same." The Professor uttered a sort of sigh and drained his glass, helping himself to one of the cakes. He took the manuscript from Hasbro. "Pour yourself a glass of this sherry," he said, smiling at the man. "We're a company now."

"Yes, sir," Hasbro said, pouring himself an unconvincing dribble.

"Unfortunately poor Bill was knocked on the head in a tavern in Limehouse. He'll recover, thank God, but they weren't kind to him. They took the message around to your digs themselves, delivered it to you, and then accosted you on the train in order to steal the book after old Lester had entrusted it to you."

I was dumbstruck. "And so the book is gone! I still don't fathom…"

"*This* is the Kraken-Birdlip manuscript," St. Ives said, winking at me and handing me the loose pages that he'd taken from Hasbro. Imagine my surprise when I discovered that I was indeed reading Birdlip's treatise on succulents and begonias. I gave St. Ives the searching stare and awaited a further explanation. I had been practiced upon, and I wasn't smiling and winking, although he was, apparently tremendously pleased with himself.

"Another ruse?" I asked him.

"Indeed. Ruse upon ruse. This, of course, is the treatise on alien botanicals prepared by Cuttle Kraken and Dr. Birdlip after their first venture through the hole. After Cuttle's death in the explosion, Birdlip spirited it away, consigning it to me before he went into hiding. It constitutes evidence, of course, which ought to have been destroyed in the conflagration in Birdlip's laboratory. But as you can see, it wasn't destroyed. How the pig men divined the truth is hard to say, but I became certain that they had." He laughed now, out of high spirits. "I had almost said 'deveined' as if the truth were a shrimp."

"And so you fabricated this, this *red herring de guerre*, this *shrimp de mer*, just in order to confound them?"

"Just so."

St. Ives was triumphant, proof positive that my little contribution to his scheme was well worth a few gorse spines, but before I could utter a word there was a tremendous explosion that brought me catapulting out of my chair, dumping a half glass of sherry down the front of my trousers. I saw that Hasbro stood at the open French window, his hair whisking about on the wind and a regular torrent of rain from a renewed storm sluicing into the room. In his hands was a long smoking rifle of monstrous proportions—a death-dealer from the look of it.

"What-ho Hasbro?" St. Ives stood up unflustered, peering out into the night.

"Prowlers, sir."

"Did you bring any down?"

"Yes, sir. I seem to have dropped one, as the white hunter would say. He's lying on the lawn, apparently immobilized."

The Professor had a lantern in hand in a nonce, and we were out the door and into the rain, warily approaching the creature, Hasbro brandishing his weapon, ready to blow the interloper to Kingdom Come. The fallen man, if a man he was, apparently now trod on more hallowed ground than had been available in the environs of Chingford-by-the-Tower.

I'll admit that I'd had a sip or two that evening, but I was sober enough to see with relative clarity, and, I might add, I'm a man who prides himself in his straightforward veracity. Ask any of the lads at the old Scout's Rest, and they'll back me to a man. Jack Owlesby, they'll say, is solid as the Rock. And it took that sort of solidity, I can assure you: when St. Ives held the lantern over the wound, it ran with green blood—a murky and fibrous green, as if spun into tangled clumps of dirty Irish cobweb. St. Ives was grim, but was not particularly taken aback. He reached down and popped the corpse's shoe off, and, with a wide gesture, as if introducing a fairly so-so pianist, waved at the thing's cloven hoof, the ghastliest bit of anatomical peculiarity I'd hitherto had the pleasure to encounter. The beast had the foreleg of a pig, and, indeed, appeared to be the very gentleman, if gentleman I can call him, who had propelled me through the open train window that very afternoon. He was dead as a Yorkshire ham, and already he had begun to stink.

Another thing Jack Owlesby isn't is a coward. I mean to say, I was pitched from the window of a moving train, an incident that would discourage the stoutest heart, and yet I trudged like a trooper through the night to a rendezvous with a scientist— not mad, strictly speaking, but eccentric, given to flights of fancy—whose intention it was to shoot me into outer space in an utterly unlikely machine. Mere pluck isn't in it, from my point of view. But when I caught sight of that hoof, attached to the end of a pinkish but rather human-looking leg, I let fly a "Yoicks!" that might have been heard as far away as Stoke Newington, and took off, as my old mother would say, like a dirty shirt toward St. Ives Manor, where I finished off the sherry bottle and opened a second without invitation.

Later, St. Ives and Hasbro slid back in, having deposited the corpus delecti with the local vivisectionist. I was storming the gates of fear with another scupper of Spanish sherry, but I was sober as a judge, much to my dismay. The whole rum puncheon ran contrary to what one might call my better judgment—a dead man, after all, or some facsimile of one—but the Professor had a different way of seeing things. Langdon St. Ives has always seen things in his own light, although the wavelength is off the visible spectrum, a sublunar light, if you follow me, but, admittedly, the light of rare genius. He assured me that if we all kept a judicious eye peeled for scalawags, we'd last out the night in good health. Consider for a moment how cheered I was by this observation.

And it was a vigil that we kept: Hasbro with his elephant rifle scouring the grounds; Professor St. Ives at the lookout, first at one window, then at the next; and I holding sway before the fireplace, guarding the chimney flue and the sherry bottle lest the hoofed men try to slip in from above. A roaring fire, I've heard, fends off even the most fearsome night denizens, and by God I kept the fire hot. And in the long night I learned several bits of information that served merely to increase the general rumminess. First, I caught on that these cloven-hoofed pig men were not at all human, a fact I had rather suspected, and that they were intent upon putting the damper on our mission into space. It seems that these aliens, these Citronites (Birdlip and the elder Kraken had, apparently, dubbed their planet Citrona after finding vast tangerine orchards in evidence) had been slipping in through what Birdlip and St. Ives have dubbed "black holes"—a single black hole, actually.

In fact I don't have an earthly idea, but I picture the mouth of a train tunnel, seen from a distance and cut through solid rock. But these holes, these tunnels if you will, are apparently cut through *solid* space—something that meant worlds to a man like St. Ives, but meant nothing to a man like me. They were garden gates, if you will, from... elsewhere, and they led, as it was explained to me, from one place to another. A chap might be capering along through the void when a bloody great hole opens up next door, and, if the chap isn't ready for it, sucks him in like water through a pump hose. The puzzler, at least to me, is that a hole can appear in the void. The Professor cleared that up effortlessly. It seems as if this hole isn't a hole, not really, not in the sense of its having dimension, or at least measurable dimension. It's like the thingummy that is all things to all men, apparently, the hole that is both the alpha and the omega, the window that is at once a hiatus and a hindrance. Kraken and Birdlip, suffice it to say, navigated the avenues of this aperture, popping down into the jungle groves of Citrona where they meddled with their botanicals for a week or so before whizzing back through. The real rat's nest, however, is this: they were pursued on their return by these pig-faced men, an indeterminate number of them, who blew Birdlip's laboratory to dust, murdering Cuttle Kraken. Their misuse of Cuttle's brother drove the poor man to drink and madness.

I awoke on the chair by the fireplace, stiff as a post, and was greeted immediately by the steadfast Hasbro who bore in a pot of mocha java. I sugared it twice, once for taste and once to recapitulate with the depleted blood sugars, and after the coffee and an ablution was ready for all the pig men in Essex. The pig men, however, didn't show, and neither did Langdon St. Ives who, I found, was off on some mysterious errand.

When I went out at last onto the veranda, the sun was halfway up the morning sky chivvying for position with a single cloud that hightailed it toward the horizon in the wake of its passel of erstwhile companions. It was one of those clean autumn mornings that makes a chap throw back both arms and suck in a lung full of air, then let it out in a hearty wheeze, and that was entirely my ambition when I was interrupted by Hasbro, who stepped out into the open air and said, "The Professor desires our company in the tower, sir."

We crossed the meadow, finding St. Ives within the confines of the stone tower, a circular vaulted room with a polished stone floor and high windows radiating sunlight. A veritable scourge of sucking noises proceeded from a great conical device raised on an iron platform in the center of the floor, and it didn't take more than a moment to deduce the fact that this device, a gothic assemblage of metal and glass, was the Professor's spacecraft. I had been expecting a saucer, perhaps ringed with porthole windows and with a whirring combine beneath. This ship, however, had the appearance of a ruddy great bullet that had been decorated in the style of Chartes Cathedral.

St. Ives puttered about, tugging on one thing and another and grappling with levers and switches. Hasbro took up a position outside the tower door, armed with his weapon. Unbeknownst to me, the hour of our departure was approaching, and the Professor and Hasbro knew that the pig men had to act if they were going to squelch things for good and all. St. Ives fully expected a cutting out expedition, and we were all of us on our guard. I was put to work, I can tell you, and I sweated like a banshee all afternoon over a complexity of whatnots and doodads. There were gyros to ameliorate and fluxion sponges to douse, and all of it accomplished within the space of thirty-eight seconds, with no margin of error, lest, as Shakespeare himself was wont to say, we tread untimely the fields of Elysium, pig men be damned. It was an unforgiving machine that could dash out our brains on the instant, and so my earthbound familiarity with the controls was vital if I were to be midshipman among the stars.

Late in the afternoon I was tolerably familiar with endless buttons and dials and switches, and I moved about the cork floor in my stocking feet with something like confidence. The cork that made up the immense undercarriage of the ship, and which must have cost Spain half her annual production, was apparently the key to mass and buoyancy, the two great levelers of an air-going craft just as they were at sea. Stone ships, as the Professor put it, sink like the popular phrase. Long past noon, and with a growing peckishness, I found myself quite alone, left to batten down the hatches before popping over to the manor for a meat pie and a pint. The Professor and Hasbro had gone thither a half hour past. I stood now on the small iron quarterdeck, I guess you would call it, and spied through the tower window a man on the meadow, a stout man, with a suspicious creeping gait, who must have been hidden from view of the manor by the tower itself.

I had the uncanny notion that I had seen the man before, and of course I had, for he could have been a twin of the man who had stopped on the lawn last night to parlay with Hasbro's bullet. But that man by now had almost certainly been reduced to the sum of his parts. This one, like his fellows, possessed an uncannily rolled up face and tiny eyes, and he walked along on the tips of his toes like a chap might walk over hot sand. He was dressed in lederhosen in the manner of a comical German, and he carried a bamboo whangee, as if this unlikely stick would lend him the innocent air of a man on a walking tour. On his head was an oversized hat of the variety commonly called a poma, with a rounded point at its crown and with a turned up brim. Smoke seemed to rise from his ears.

I shouted at him through the tower window: "What ho the masquerade!" I called out wittily, at which the man leapt into the air, looking around with a caught-in-the-act countenance. In a nonce he had pulled off his cap, removing from the smoking interior a black fizz bomb the size of a twelve pounder cannonball. Even in the afternoon sunlight the fuse was visibly sparking. He turned and ran even as he pitched the bomb at the tower, fleeing away in mincing steps toward Epping Forest. He had a tolerably good aim, I'll give him that, for the black orb shattered the glass of one of the lower windows and clunked down onto the floor.

"Here's a jolly filthy mess," I said to myself, clambering downwards. I'll admit that my mind contemplated the open door, through which I was tempted to flee, but there's something in a man that doesn't love a bomb, and it was that which inclined me to risk everything on the chance of pinching out the fuse. I went for it like billy-o, scooping the thing up and, casting danger to Aeolus and his kin, attempted to smother the sputtering flame. It was no go. The fuse would stay lit despite my antics. And a fine fool I must have looked, juggling the bomb like a hot potato, dancing about on my toes, when I heard a voice shout, "Throw it away, sir! Out the door with it!" And without a second thought I did just that—pitched it through the open door, out onto the meadow, where it rolled like a game of nine-pins down the hill toward the forest, gathering speed, bouncing and hopping toward the very place where the pig man had taken shelter.

Hasbro entered the tower. "I trust you're unharmed, sir?" he asked.

"Quite," I told him, although in truth my fingertips were singed from my unsuccessful efforts with the flaming wick.

"Then I suggest that we ascend to the upper reaches, sir, so that we might have the advantage of elevation."

Bounding up the stairs again was the work of a moment, and we had no sooner poked our heads through the porthole on the second balcony when a whopping great bang, a puff of black soot, and a regular bingo of fine orange spark and flame whooshed up from the forest. A cascade of tree limbs, leaves, and dirt rained roundabout for a time until the air over the wood was empty but for suspended dust, a bit of curling smoke, and the pig man's hat turning end over end, buoyed for a moment on the recently charged atmosphere before falling groundward.

We watched for movement in the fringe of the trees, but there was nothing, only the still-settling dust. The Professor appeared on the veranda and waved to us. We made our way down the stairs again and out onto the meadow, joining him. "Jolly stupid chaps, aliens," I muttered as the three of us approached the woods.

"Their powers of observation are singularly weak," said the Professor. "If only their explosive devices were equally inadequate, we might almost find the creatures amusing."

"That chap with the bomb might have been the dead man on the lawn. Absolute likeness. Why do they all look so frightfully piggish?"

"It has been observed," said Hasbro, "that to the Asian gentleman all white Europeans look quite moderately alike. This is a similar phenomenon, I believe."

"Perhaps even more so," I said, "these being space aliens."

"Entirely within the sphere of the possible, sir."

"We're dealing with an entire race of pig men."

"So it would seem," the Professor said. "Pig men down to the ground."

Just inside the line of trees we found a fine crater blown into the earth, but there was no sign of the alien, no hooves or sow's ears or soused pig's face. The singed hat lay in the crater, as if perhaps he had lost it as he fled.

"I have a hunch," St. Ives said, "that these aliens have a base right here in Epping Forest, perhaps even a spacecraft, hidden in the woods."

"Let's flush the buggers out," I said. "Ferret them out like stoats. Stoat them out like ferrets. They seem a stupid enough bunch."

"Perhaps too stupid." The Professor looked thoughtful. "Rather like dealing with a dozen escaped loonies from Chigwell Hatch. Impossible to read them."

"You've got a point there," I said. In the heat of the recent victory, however, I was fired up, and determined to be on the offensive for once. "But we can't simply allow them to storm in waving fizz bombs whenever they feel up to it. After all, there might be dozens of them."

"I doubt it, sir, if you'll pardon a word or two," Hasbro put in. "If there were a quantity of them, they could have overpowered us easily. They are wary, I believe, because there are so few of them."

"Quite so," responded St. Ives. "And, more to the point, we've really little to fear from the handful we suppose are in the woods, as long, that is, as we stay alert. I believe it was Addison who said something about leaping over single foes to attack entire armies, and that, in fact, is just the point. When one's roof leaks, one doesn't merely place a bucket beneath the drip. One climbs atop the roof and jolly well plugs the hole. Do you follow me?"

I said that I did, and we left Hasbro standing guard with his elephant gun and a brass bell to ring if he needed reinforcements. The Professor and I returned to the manor. We were to sail at dusk—blast off, I should say—and we spent the remainder of the afternoon loading supplies and closing up shop. Birdlip's manuscript caught my eye as I was hauling beakers of water, and I realized that the succulents and begonias were still a mystery to me. I picked the thing up and waved it at St. Ives. "About the manuscript," I began, but the Professor interrupted me with his inscrutable smile.

"Ah, yes," said he. "The false clue."

"Quite," said I, "but why? Why slip the pig men a worthless book?"

"Birdlip's manuscript, my dear Owlesby, refers to certain plants—begonias, if you will, of outstanding girth, large as a man's head, veritable trees. They shimmered, according to Birdlip and Kraken, and were surrounded by a halo, an aura of roseate darkness that suggested the black hole through which the two scientists had made an entrance into the universe where they had very much found themselves. These begonias appeared to be parasitical, attached as they were to the immense tangerine trees of which I have already spoken."

"Immense?"

"Quite. Fully as large as the greater Norwegian alder, which, I needn't add, is quite the largest tree on the globe, although it's worthless for anything but firewood and the carving of figureheads. But do you know what the corker was?"

"I'm ashamed to say I do not."

"Tangerines were sprouting and growing on the trees like…"

The Professor groped for a word.

"Like banshees," I said helpfully.

"I don't follow you," said he. "The simile conveys no meaning to my mind."

"It's a general purpose word that I use for comparison. Works virtually anywhere."

"Yes," said he. "Well. Kraken advanced the hypothesis that these begonias were somehow connected to the black hole, and that energy, or something quite like it, was jolly well sailing through the hole from our universe into theirs."

"A bleed-off, would you call it?"

"Exactly."

"And that's why the trees are big as legends and growing fruit like popping corn." It only has to snow once before Jack Owlesby gets the drift, as my old mother used to say, and I could see in an instant what these filthy alien interlopers were up to and why they'd handed me a fizz bomb for my troubles.

"There you have it," said St. Ives, shaking snuff onto the edge of his thumb.

"These aliens are drawing off the essential humors," said I, by way of clarification.

"Filching our essences," agreed the Professor. "And to bring up their plans with a round turn, I slipped an expurgated edition into the Museum and told old Dr. Lester that he was to release it only to you. The aliens, I found, tried to obtain the thing no less than eight times. Lester supposed it was the same whey-faced man dressed like lunacy each time. In his final attempt he was dressed as a red Indian, feathers protruding from his hat at a dozen angles and painted up like a grandee and wearing a pair of golden Arab slippers with the toes curled back in a point. Lester threatened to set the constable on him, and he fled through a rear exit and never made another attempt."

"Who first put them on to Birdlip?"

"Kraken's son, mad Bill."

"Their agent?"

"I'm afraid so, poor devil. No fault of his own, though. They worked on his mind, what there was of it."

"Ah," I said sadly. "That explains the Fauntleroy suit and the wig. It was their idea."

"Apparently so, though Lord knows why. The note was my own. I knew that you'd fetch the book from Lester, that the aliens would steal it and discover the false clue: that we blast off tomorrow, on the 24th."

"The night of the full moon."

"Just so. Actually," he said, grinning like a grampus, "we blast off tonight." He checked his pocket watch. "In an hour and a half exactly."

With that the Professor tucked the unexpurgated copy of Birdlip's manuscript into his coat and busied himself with a crate of tinned foods and a cask of ship's biscuit. When we returned to the tower we found Hasbro watering yew sproutlets in the greenhouse on the second level. I was sharp enough from the outset to realize that these shrubs and ferns and such would provide us with the necessary oxygen. St. Ives's craft was turned out like a ship of the line.

This is the part of the adventure where the minutes drag past like starfish, which, if you follow me, have enough legs to hie along like anything, but instead can do nothing but creep. Night had fallen an hour before, and the weather was exceptional—nothing between us and the hovering stars but vacant space, not even a cloud.

We popped right to it, sealing hatches, zipping up atmosphere bulwarks, setting gyros and elasto-turbans, battening hatches, and all that sort of thing. I was smitten by a sense of adventure, and had there been a bowline or a capstan bar I would have hauled upon it with the heartiest sort of heave-ho, the consummate deckhand. By half past eight we were strapped into cushioned loungettes in the prow. Hasbro unshipped the deadlights and found his way back to his own loungette, all of us silent as we gazed out through the thick glass of the portholes through the top of Chingford Tower, which was unlidded, roofless, open to the elements so as to reveal a circle of sky as through the lens of a telescope.

The Professor jabbed buttons, nodded meaningfully to Hasbro and I, and then reached across and heaved on a bloody great anti-something-or-other crank with silver wires sprouting from it like tentacles. There was a wild crash and clatter and a cacophonous whir reminiscent of a scourge of locusts setting up for a concert. In that moment there was a muffled explosion that brought the Professor up short. "What...?" he began to ask, but the entire tower quivered like a column of aspic, and we jolly well ripped out through the roofless roof like a comet trailing a universe of sparks.

I'll admit that I myself was smug in my ignorance, and not only about our having given the pig men the slip. I had a hand, you see, in making earth safe from their depredations: we were more than a match for a gaggle of ill-dressed loonies. I could visualize them leaping to their feet about now, from where they were hunkered down in Chingford Forest, punching each other on the shoulder, leaping up and running hatless onto the meadow. Imagine my surprise when that's precisely what I *did* see, not forty feet below us.

Odd thing, spaceships, they have these gyro gizmos that make a chap feel right side up in spite of the fact that he's not—saves him a good deal of uneasiness, I suppose. It took a moment, then, for me to understand what had happened. The aliens, apparently, had chucked in one of their fizz bombs just as we launched our craft, and the concussion in the base of the tower had cannoned us upward, setting the bloody ship mad. Dials were spinning like whirligigs, and St. Ives was a veritable octopus, arms flailing hither and yon in an effort to stabilize our madcap flight.

The ship capered along haywire above the green, and the pig men, dressed for a masquerade, ran in a wild rout in our wake, carrying lighted torches. St. Ives and Hasbro enlivened the necessary retros and stabilizers, and we banked into one last side-crushing loop before bowling off westward toward the common. Pig men gave way to costumed Boy Scouts about then, several hundred of the blighters on the evening march, who broke and ran like mice as we flew overhead, all shot up with flame and whizzing a universe of parti-colored sparks. We were out of sight quickly enough after setting aflame several score of tents, and (here I only speculate from newspaper accounts) the Scouts were regrouping when from over the rise, led by a gigantic alien dressed as a cartoon devil, came the pig men, shouting unfathomable drivel and brandishing torches.

The rest of the Chingford Common fracas is history, and a dozen wild and equally unlikely stories have been offered by unfortunate witnesses, so I won't say more about it except that none of those stories holds a candle to the truth, which, the philosopher tells us, is often the case. As for the ship, we managed to yank it up into the proper trajectory and, through the skills of science and the will of God, raced outward through the void toward the black hole that yawned like a tunnel of infamy off the port side of Mars.

—⁓—

IN TRUTH, THERE'S not much more to say—not yet anyway. We whizzed along for six days before it occurred to me to ask the Professor just how long we'd be engaged in our modest heroics. He was evasive. That is to say, he hinted that the mission might be a protracted one indeed, and that the business of shutting a door sometimes requires stepping through that door and slamming it firmly shut behind one—a notion that in my weakness I understood to have been revealed to me in what might be called an untimely fashion, if you follow me.

On the thirteenth day, late in the long and lightless afternoon, with Earth in our wake reduced to a speck of flame in the vast heavens, we saw the orbicular shadow of what a futuristic poet might, in his paroxysms of language, call something slightly more grand than a simple black hole: an ebony hiatus, perhaps, the looming mouth of a dark destiny encircled by a whirling vaporous darkness and shot through with rainbow lights as if a thousand twirling prisms danced above the abyss.

"There she blows," Hasbro muttered helpfully, mixing grog in a chemical beaker.

"Still a good way off," I responded, awestruck by the sight and helping myself to the contents of the beaker.

"Its appearance is deceptive," said the Professor, winking at me. "It looks as if it's a thousand miles across from this distant perspective, when actually it's a tiny thing, not much broader, shall we say, than the base of this ship, although all talk of breadth is purely conceptual. You see, Jack, there are walls."

"I was sure there were!" I shouted, slightly illuminated by the grog. And I told him about the dream and old Sidcup Catford and the rock wall. The Professor saw more merit in my metaphoric dreaming than I had anticipated. Space, it turns out, is just that: a void peopled by an occasional star or a family or two of meteorites or a misanthropic comet. Our mistake is to suppose that life exists out among the stars that we discern in the night sky. It's out there, all right, but behind a wall, through a door, as it were, a door through which Birdlip and Kraken had plunged in their own star vehicle, unwittingly leaving it open behind them not unlike the door of the proverbial barn.

"A glass of grog with you, sir," Hasbro said, handing across the beaker for what might have been the sixth time. I filled my glass and drank it off, realizing as it settled its fiery weight in the pit of my stomach that I was drunk as a lord and with none of the wealth to go with it.

"If we fail, Jacky, don't expect to see either of us this side of Paradise," the Professor said. "We'll be strangers in a filthy strange land."

"I say," I said, trying to rise. "What's this we and you? We're a company!" My legs, apparently, had turned to jelly, for I remained helplessly in my seat. Hasbro and the Professor donned lead shoes and strode to the hatch, which led below to the 'tween deck, as it were. I tried to throw myself from the loungette, for I saw their intention as clear as rainwater, and I would have damn well followed them but for the physics of leaden rum and leadless shoes.

"Take heart, Jacky boy," the Professor said. "Let the craft bear you home. Watch for us when the moon is one day past full and Mars rises above the horizon in the early evening." With that utterance they disappeared through the hatch, and that's the last I've seen of Professor St. Ives and his man Hasbro. I sat like a pudding, stupefied in my chair, listening for a time to a banging and clattering from below. Abruptly there came a lurch and crash and the whirl and swoosh of a great flaming exhalation through the scuttle that bespoke the jettisoning of the forward section. I and my capsule arced away in a trajectory that would ultimately point my prow toward home and the long plunging fall.

Through the glass, as my ship came around on a broad tack, I could see the double aft section hurtling toward the lee shore of Mars, carrying in it two of England's—aye, of the world's—greatest men: heroes to the core. I could do nothing but watch in mute wonder as they plunged toward the dark and whirling vortex of the hole. Their ship, now a cone with the top shorn off, broke again in two, the massive lower section towing, if that's the word, on the end of what appeared to be a long chain of highly polished droplets of metal. The sides of that aft section fell away and tumbled slowly off into the emptiness, baring the massive cork that I had occasion to comment upon previously.

And so, the heavens revolving around her, her conical bowsprit pointed into that gullet of dark mystery, she sailed into temporary oblivion, hauling behind her an incredible cork etched with an equally incredible and, I must say, vastly inspiring legend: "Fitzall Sizes"—a legend that might as easily define the vast capacities of those two forthright and intrepid adventurers. —⌒

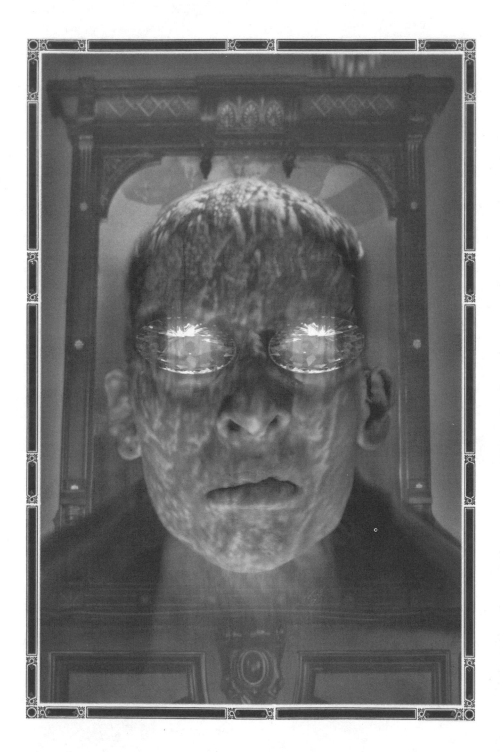

The Idol's Eye

I WON'T SAY THAT this was the final adventure of Professor Langdon St. Ives and his man Hasbro—Colonel Hasbro since the war—but it was certainly the strangest and the least likely of the lot. Consider this: I know the Professor to be a man of complete and utter veracity. If he told me that he had determined, on the strength of scientific discovery, that gravity would reverse itself at four o'clock this afternoon, and that we'd find ourselves, as Stevenson put it, scaling the stars, I'd pack my bag and phone my solicitor and, at 3:59, I'd stroll out into the center of Jermyn Street so as not to crack my head on the ceiling when I floated away. And yet even *I* would have hesitated, looked askance, perhaps covertly checked the level of the bottles in the Professor's cabinet if he had simply recounted to me the details of the strange occurrence at the Explorers Club on that third Thursday in April. I admit it the story is impossible on the face of it.

But I was there. And, as I say, what transpired was far and away more peculiar and exotic than the activities that, some twenty years earlier, had set the machinery of fate and mystery into creaking and irreversible motion.

It was a wild and rainy Thursday, then, that day at the club. March hadn't gone out like any lamb; it had roared right along, storming and blowing into April. We—that is to say, the Professor, Colonel Hasbro, Tubby Frobisher, John Priestly (the African explorer and adventurer, not the novelist), and myself, Jack Owlesby—were sitting about after a long dinner at the Explorers Club, opposite the Planetarium. Wind howled outside the casements, and rain angled past in a driving rush, now letting off, now redoubling, *whooshing* in great sheets of grey mist. It wasn't the sort of weather to be out in, you can count on that, and none of us, of course, had any business to see to anyway. I was looking forward to pipes and cigars and a glass of this or that, maybe a bit of a snooze in the lounge and then a really first-rate supper—a veal cutlet, perhaps, or a steak and mushroom pie and a bottle of Burgundy. The afternoon and evening, in other words, held astonishing promise.

So we sipped port, poked at the bowls of our pipes, watched the fragrant smoke rise in little lazy wisps and drift off, and muttered in a satisfied way about the weather.

Under those conditions, you'll agree, it couldn't rain hard enough. I recall even that Frobisher, who, to be fair, had been coarsened by years in the bush, called the lot of us over to the window in order to have a laugh at the expense of some poor shambling madman who hunched in the rain below, holding over his head the ruins of an umbrella that might have been serviceable twenty or thirty years earlier but had seen hard use since, and which, in its fallen state, had come to resemble a ribby-looking inverted bird with about half a dozen pipe-stem legs. As far as I could see, there was no cloth on the thing at all. He had the mannerisms correct, that much I'll give him. *He* seemed convinced that the fossil umbrella was doing the work. Frobisher roared and shook and said that the man should be on the stage. Then he said he had half a mind to go down and give the fellow a half crown, except that it was raining and he would get soaked. "That's well and good in the bush," he said, "but in the city, in civilization, well…" He shook his head. "When in Rome," he said. And he forgot about the poor bogger in the road. All of us did, for a bit.

"I've seen rain that makes this look like small beer," Frobisher boasted, shaking his head. "That's nothing but fizz-water to me. Drizzle. Heavy fog."

"It reminds me of the time we faced down that mob in Banju Wangi," said Priestly, nodding at St. Ives, "after you two"—referring to the Professor and Hasbro—"routed the pig men. What an adventure."

It's moderately likely that Priestly, who kept pretty much to himself, had little desire to tell the story of our adventures in Java, incredible though they were, which had transpired some twenty years earlier. You may have read about them, actually, for my own account was published in *The Strand* some six months after the story of the Chingford Tower fracas and the alien threat. But as I say, Priestly himself didn't want to, as the Yanks say, spin any stretchers; he just wanted to shut Frobisher up. We'd heard nothing but "the bush" all afternoon. Frobisher had clearly been "out" in it—Australia, Brazil, India, Canton Province. There was bush enough in the world; that much was certain. We'd had enough of Frobisher's bush, but of course none of us could say so. This was the club, after all, and Tubby, although coarsened a bit, as I say, was one of the lads.

So I leapt in on top of Priestly when I saw Frobisher point his pipe stem at St. Ives. Frobisher's pipe stem, somehow, always gave rise to fresh accounts of the ubiquitous bush. "Banju Wangi!" I half shouted. "By golly" I admit it was weak, but I needed a moment to think. And I said it loud enough to put Frobisher right off the scent.

"Banju Wangi," I said to Priestly. "Remember that pack of cannibals? Inky lot of blokes, what?" Priestly nodded, but didn't offer to carry on. He was satisfied with simply recalling the rain. And there *had* been a spectacular rain in those Javanese days, if you can call it a rain. Which you can't, really, no more than you would call a waterfall a faucet or the sun a gaslamp. A monsoon was what it was.

Roundabout twenty years back, then, it fell out that Priestly and I and poor Bill Kraken had, on the strength of Dr. Birdlip's manuscript, taken ship to Java where we met, not unexpectedly, Professor St. Ives and Hasbro, themselves returning from a spate of very dangerous and mysterious space travel. The alien threat, as I said before, had been crushed, and the five of us had found ourselves deep in cannibal-infested jungles, beating our way through toward the Bali Straits in order to cross over to Penginuman where there lay, we fervently prayed, a Dutch freighter bound for home. The rain was sluicing down. It was mid-January, smack in the middle of the northwest monsoons, and we were slogging through jungles, trailed by orangutans and asps, hacking at creepers, and slowly metamorphosing into biped sponges.

On the banks of the Wangi River we stumbled upon a tribe of tiny Peewatin natives and traded them boxes of kitchen matches for a pair of long piroques. Bill Kraken gave his pocket watch to the local shaman in return for an odd bamboo umbrella with a shrunken head dangling from the handle by a brass chain. Kraken was, of course, round the bend in those days, but his purchase of the curious umbrella wasn't an act of madness. He stayed far drier than the rest of us in the days that followed.

We set off, finally, down the Wangi beneath grey skies and a canopy of unbelievable green. The river was swollen with rain and littered with tangles of fallen tree trunks and vegetation that crumbled continually from either shore. Canoeing in a monsoon struck me as a trifle *outré* as the Frenchman would say, but St. Ives and Priestly agreed that the very wildness of the river would serve to discourage the vast and lumbering crocodiles which, during a more placid season, splashed through the shallows in frightful abundance. And the rain itself, pouring from the sky without pause, had a month before driven most of the cannibal tribes into higher elevations.

So we paddled and bailed and bailed and paddled, St. Ives managing, through a singular and mysterious invention of his own, to keep his pipe alight in the downpour, and I anticipating, monsoon or no, the prick of a dart on the back of my neck or the sight of a toothy, arch-eyed crocodile, intent upon dinner.

Our third night on the river, very near the coast, we found what amounted to a little sandy inlet scooped into the riverside. The bank above it had been worn away, and a cavern, overhung with vines and shaded by towering acacias and a pair of incredible teaks, opened up for some few yards. By the end of the week it would be underwater, but at present it was high and dry, and we required shelter only for the night. We pushed the piroques up onto the sand, tied them to tree trunks, and hunched into the little cavern, lighting a welcome and jolly fire.

That night was full of the cries of wild beasts, the screams of panthers and the shrill peep of winging bats. More than once great clacking-jawed crocodiles crept up out of the river and gave us the glad eye before slipping away again. Pygmy hippopotami stumbled up, to the vast surprise of the Professor, and watched us for a bit, blinking and yawning and making off again up the bank and into the undergrowth. St. Ives insisted that such beasts were indigenous only to the continent of Africa, and his observation encouraged Priestly to tell a very strange and sad tale—the story of Doctor Ignacio

Narbondo. This Doctor Narbondo, it seems, practiced in London in the eighteenth century. He claimed to have developed any number of strange serums, including one which, ostensibly, would allow the breeding of unlike beasts: pigs with fishes and birds with hedgehogs. He was harried out of England as a vivisectionist, although he swore to his own innocence and to the efficacy of his serum. Three years later, after suffering the same fate in Venice, he set sail from Mombasa with a herd of pygmy hippos, determined to haul them across the Indian Ocean to the Malay Archipelago and breed them with the great hairy orangutans that flourished in the Borneo rain forests.

He was possessed, said Priestly, with the idea of one day docking at Marseilles or London and striding ashore flanked by an army of the unlikely offspring of two of the most ludicrous beasts imaginable, throwing the same fear into the civilized world that Hannibal must have produced when, with ten score of elephants, he popped in from beyond the Alps. Narbondo, however, was never seen again. He docked in Surabaja, disappeared into the jungles with his beasts, and, as they say of Captain England in Mauritius, went native. Whether Narbondo became, in the years that followed, the fabled Wildman of Borneo is speculation. Some say he did, some say he died of typhus in Bombay. His hippopotami, however, riddled with Narbondo's serum, multiplied within a small area of Eastern Java.

The explanation of the existence of the hippos seemed to whet St. Ives's curiosity. He questioned Priestly for an hour, in fact, about this mysterious Doctor Narbondo, but Priestly had merely read about the mad doctor in Ashbless's *Account of London Madmen* (a grossly unfair appellation, at least in regard to Doctor Narbondo) and he could remember little else.

St. Ives, Hasbro, and I, of course, already knew of the existence of this Narbondo, and of his secret identity, for he was not, as Frosbinder alleged, Ignacio Narbondo, who lies frozen in a Scandanacian Tarn. He was (and still is) Ignacio Narbondo's long lost twin brother Ivan, who had stolen his brother's name and traded on his reputation before the name and reputation fell into disrepute. His flight from England had less to do with vivisection than with the sworn enmity of the enraged Ignacio, an enmity that is now long cooled, if you'll allow me a moment of levity.

Half a dozen times that night I awakened to the sounds of something crashing in the forest above, and twice, blinking awake, I saw wide, hairy faces, upside down, eyes aglow, peering at us from overhead—jungle beasts, hanging from the vine-covered ledge above to watch us as we slept. Visions of the supposed Narbondo's hippo-apes flitted through my dreams, and when daylight wandered through the following morning, I was convinced that many of the past night's visitations had not been made merely by the creatures of dreams, but had actually been the offspring, so to speak, of the misanthropic Doctor Narbondo.

We had a brief respite from the rain that morning, and, determined to make the most of it, we loaded our gear aboard the piroques and prepared to clamber in. The sun broke through the clouds about then, and golden rays slanted through the forest ceiling, stippling the jungle floor and setting off an opera of bird cries and monkey whistling. We stood and stared at the steamy radiance of the forest, beautiful beyond accounting, then turned toward the canoes. A shout from Hasbro, however, brought us up short. He'd seen something, that much was certain, in the jungle beyond the riverside cavern.

"What ho, man?" said St. Ives, anxious to be off yet overwhelmed with scientific curiosity.

"A temple of sorts, sir," said Hasbro, pointing away into the forest. "I believe I see some sort of stone monolith or altar, sir. Perhaps a shrine to some heathen god."

And sure enough, bathed now in sunlight was a little clearing in the trees. In it, scattered in a circle, were half a dozen stone rectangles, one almost as large as an automobile, all crumbling and half-covered with creepers and moss.

Bill Kraken, still suffering from the poulp madness that had so befuddled him in the past months, gave out a little cry and dashed past Hasbro up the bank and into the forest. The rest of us followed at a run, fearing that Bill would come to harm. If we had known what lay ahead, we would have been a bit quicker about it even yet.

What we found in the clearing was that circle of stone monoliths, crumbling, as I've said, with age. Dozens of bright green asps rested in the sunshine atop the stones, watching us through lazy eyes. Four wild pigs, rooting for insects, crashed off into the vegetation, setting off the flight of a score of apes which had, hitherto, been hidden away overhead in the treetops. In the midst of the circle of stones sat a peculiar and indescribably eerie statue, carved, it seemed, entirely of ivory. It was old, though clearly not so old as the monoliths surrounding it, and it was minutely carven; its mouth looked as if it were ready to speak, and its jaw was square and determined and revealed just a hint of sadness. On closer inspection it clearly wasn't ivory that it had been carved from, for the stone, whatever it was, was veined with thin blue lines.

It was uncanny. Professor St. Ives speculated at first that it was some sort of rare Malaysian marble. And very fine marble at that—marble that Michelangelo would have blathered over. More astonishing than the marble, though, were its eyes—two great rubies, faceted so minutely that they threw the rays of the tropical sun in a thousand directions. And it was those ruby eyes that not only cut short our examination of the ruined ring of altars and the peculiar idol, but which were the end of poor old Bill Kraken, a fine scientist in his own right before falling into the hands of the aliens after Birdlip's demise.

It was the flash of sunlight from those rubies that had instigated Kraken's charge up the slope and into the clearing. While the rest of us had gathered about commenting on the strange veined stone, Bill had stood gaping, clutching his umbrella, hypnotized by the ruby lights which, as the forest foliage swayed in the breezes overhead, now shading the jungle floor, now opening and allowing sunlight to flood in upon us, played over his face like the glints of light thrown from one of those spinning mirrored globes that dangle from the ceiling of a ballroom.

Suddenly and in an instant, as if propelled from a catapult, he sprang past St. Ives, hurled Priestly aside, and jabbed the tip of his umbrella in under one of the ruby eyes—the left eye, it was; I remember it vividly. He pried furiously on the thing as St. Ives and Hasbro attempted to haul him away. But he had the strength of a madman. The eye popped loose, rolling into the grasses, and Mad Bill shook off his two friends, wild in his ruby lust. He cast down his umbrella and dived for the gem, convinced, I suppose, that St. Ives and Hasbro and, no doubt, Priestly and myself were going to wrestle him for it. What brought him up short and froze the rest of us to the marrow there in that steamy jungle sun was a long, weary, ululating howl—a cry of awful pain, of indefinable grief—that soared out of the jungle around us, carried on the wind, part of the very atmosphere.

Our first thought after that long frozen instant was, of course, of cannibals. Bill snatched up the stone and leapt down the path toward the piroques with the rest of us, once again, at his heels.

Before night fell we had paddled out into the Bali Straits, never having caught a glimpse of those supposed cannibals nor seen the hint of a flying spear. There lay the Dutch freighter the *Peter Van Teeslink*. A week later Bill Kraken died of a fever in Singapore, shouting before he went of wild jungle beasts and of creatures that lay waiting for him in the depths of the sea and of a grinning sun that blinded him and set him mad.

We buried him there in Singapore on a sad day. St. Ives was determined to bury the ruby with him—to let him keep the plunder which had, it seemed certain, brought about his ruination. But Priestly wouldn't consider it. The ruby alone, he said, would pay for the entire journey with some to spare. To bury it with Kraken would be to submit, as it were, to the lusts of a madman. And Kraken, only six months previously, had been as sane as any of us. Keep the ruby, said Priestly. If nothing else it would provide for Kraken's son, himself almost as mad as his father. Hasbro agreed with Priestly as did, after consideration, St. Ives. The Professor, I believe, had an uncommon and inexplicable (in the light of his scientific training) fear of the jewel. But that's just conjecture. In the forty-five years I've known him he's demonstrated no fears whatsoever. He's too full of curiosity. And the ruby, finally, was a curiosity. It was certainly that.

Such were the details of our journey down the Wangi River as I related them that day at the Explorers Club. Everyone present at the table except Tubby Frobisher had, of course, been along on that little adventure, and I rather suspected that Tubby would just as soon I'd kept the story to myself, he being full of his own wanderings in the bush and having no acquaintance whatsoever with eastern Java or Bill Kraken. It was the ruby, in the end, that fetched his attention.

For some moments he'd been hunched forward in his chair, squinting at me, puffing so on his cigar that it burned like a torch. He slumped back as I ended the tale and plucked the cigar from his mouth. He paused for a moment before standing up and stepping slowly across to the window to look for his stranger on the street. But the man had apparently moved along.

There was a crashing downstairs about then—a slamming of doors, high voices, the clattering of failing cutlery. "Close that off!" shouted Frobisher down the stairwell. There was an answering shout, indecipherable, from below. "Shut yer gob!" Frobisher shouted, tapping ashes onto the rug.

One of the club members, Isaacs, I believe, from the Himalayan business, advised Frobisher to shut his. Under other circumstances, I'm sure, Tubby would have flown at the man, but he was too full of our Javanese ruby, and he barely heard the man's retort. It was quiet again downstairs. "By God," said Frobisher, "I'd give my pension to have a look at that damned ruby!"

"Impossible," I said, relighting my pipe which I'd let grow cold during my narrative. "The ruby hasn't been seen in five years. Not since Giles Connover stole it from the museum. It was the ruby that brought about his end; that's what I believe—just as surely as it brought about the death of Bill Kraken."

I expected St. Ives to disagree with me, point out that I was possessed by superstition, that logic didn't and couldn't support me. But he kept silent, having once been possessed, I suppose, by the same unfounded fears—fears that had been a product of the weird, moaning cry that had assailed us there in the jungle some twenty years before.

"It certainly has had a curious history," said St. Ives with just the trace of a smile on his face. "A very curious history."

"Has it?" said Frobisher, stabbing his cigar out into the ashtray. "You didn't manage to sell it, then?"

"Oh, we sold it," St. Ives said. "Almost at once. Within the week of our return, if I'm not mistaken."

"Four days, sir, to be precise," put in Hasbro, who had an irritating habit of exactitude, one that had been polished and tightened over his eighty- odd years. "We docked on a Tuesday, sir, and sold the ruby to a jeweler in Knightsbridge on the following Saturday afternoon."

"Quite," said St. Ives, nodding toward him.

A waiter wandered past about then with a tea towel over his arm. Simultaneously there was another crash downstairs, a chair being upset it sounded like, and an accompanying shout. "What the devil is that row?" demanded Frobisher of the waiter. "This is a club, man, not a bowling green"

"Quite right, sir," the waiter said. "We've had a bit of a time with an unwanted guest. Insists on coming in to have a look around. He's very persistent."

"Throw the blighter into the rubbish can," said Frobisher. "And bring us a decanter of whisky, if you will. Laphroaig. And some fresh glasses."

"Ice?" the waiter asked.

Frobisher gave him a wilting look and chewed on his cigar. "Just the filthy whisky. And tell that navvy downstairs that Tubby Frobisher will horsewhip him on the club steps at three o'clock if he's still about." Frobisher checked his watch. "That's about six and a half minutes from now."

"I'll tell him, sir, just as you say. But the man is deaf as a stone, as far as I can make out, and he wears smoked glasses, so he's quite possibly blind too. Threats haven't done much to dissuade him."

"Haven't they, by God!" shouted Frobisher. "Dissuade him, is it! I'll dissuade the man. I'll dissuade him from here to Chelsea. But let's have that whisky first. Did I say we needed glasses too?"

"Yes, sir," said the waiter. And off he went toward the bar.

"So this ruby," Frobisher said, settling back in his seat and plucking another cigar from inside his coat. "How much did it fetch?"

"A little above twenty-five thousand pounds," said St. Ives, nodding to Hasbro for affirmation.

"Twenty-five thousand six hundred fifty, sir," the colonel said.

Frobisher let out a low whistle.

"And it brought almost twice that at an auction at Sotheby's two weeks after," I put in. "Since then it's been bought and sold a dozen times, I imagine. The truth is, no one wants to keep it. It was owned, in time, by Isador Persano, and we all know what came of that, and later by Lady Braithewaite-Long, whose husband, of course, was involved in that series of ghastly murders near Waterloo Station."

"Don't overlook Preston Waters, the jeweler," said Priestly with an apparent shudder—a recollection, no doubt, of the grisly horror that had befallen the very Knightsbridge jeweler who had given us the twenty-five thousand pounds.

"The thing's cursed, if you ask me," I said, clearing debris from the table to make room for our newly arrived decanter of Scots whisky. Frobisher, sighing heartily, poured a neat bit into four glasses.

"None for me, thanks," Priestly said when Frobisher approached the fifth glass with the upturned decanter. "I'll just nip at this port for a bit. Whisky eats me up. Tears my throat bones to shreds. I'd be on milk and bread for a week."

Frobisher nodded, pleased, no doubt, to consume Priestly's share himself. He tilted his glass back and sucked a bit in, rolling it about in his mouth, relishing it. "That's the stuff what?" he said, relaxing. "If there were one thing that would drag me back in out of the bush, it wouldn't be gold or women, I can tell you. No, sir. Not gold or women."

I assumed that it was whisky, finally, that would drag Tubby Frobisher out of the bush, though he never got around to saying so. I got in ahead of him. "Where do you suppose that ruby lies today, Professor?" I asked, having a taste of the Scotch myself. "Did the museum ever get it back?"

"They didn't want it, actually," said St. Ives. "They were offered the thing free, and they turned it down."

"The fools," Frobisher said. "They didn't go for all that hocus-pocus about a curse, I don't suppose. Not the bloody museum."

St. Ives shrugged. "There's no denying that it cost them a tremendous amount of trouble—robbery and murder and the like. And it's possible that they thought the man who offered it to them was a prankster. No one, of course, with any sense would give the thing away. I rather believe that they never considered the offer serious."

"I'd bet they were afraid of it," said Priestly, who had come to fear the jewel himself in the years since our return. "I wish now that we'd buried the bloody thing with Kraken. Do you remember that ghastly cry in the jungle? That wasn't made by any cannibals."

Hasbro raised an eyebrow. "Who do you suggest cried out, sir?" he asked in his cultivated butler's tone—a tone that alerted you to the sad fact that you were about to say something worthless and foolish.

Priestly gazed into his port and shrugged.

"I like to believe," said St. Ives, always the philosopher, "that the jungle itself cried out. That we had stolen a bit of her very heart, broken off a piece of her soul. I was possessed with the same certainty that we'd committed a terrible crime that possesses me when I see a fine old building razed or a great tree cut down—a tree, perhaps, that had seen the passing of two score generations of kings and, being a part of those ages, has been imbued with their history, with their glory. Do you follow me?"

Hasbro nodded. I could see he took the long view, Priestly appeared to be lost in the depths of his port, but I knew that he felt pretty much the same way; he just couldn't have stated it so prettily. Leave it to the Professor to get to the nub.

"Trash!" said Frobisher. "Gouge 'em both out, that's what I would have done. Imagine a pair of such rubies. A matched pair!" He shook his head. "Yes, sir," he finished, "I'd give my pension just to get a glimpse of one. Just a glimpse."

St. Ives, smiling just a bit, wistfully perhaps, reached into the inside pocket of his coat, pulled out his tobacco pouch and unfolded it, plucking out a ball of tissue twice the size of a walnut. Inside it was the idol's eye—the very one.

Frobisher leapt with a shout to his feet, his chair slamming over backward on the carpet. Isaacs, dozing in a chair by the fire, awoke with a start and shouted at Frobisher to leave off. But Tubby, taken so by surprise at St. Ives's coolness and by the size of the faceted gem that lay before him, red as thin blood and glowing in the firelight, failed to hear Isaacs's complaint. He stood and gaped at the ruby, his pension secure.

"How..." I began, at least as surprised as Frobisher. Priestly acted as if the thing were a snake; his pipe clacked in his teeth.

There was a wild shout from downstairs. Running footsteps echoed up toward us. A *whump* and crash followed as if something had been hurled into the wall. Then, weirdly, a blast of air sailed up the stairwell and blew past us, as if a door had been left open and the winds were finding their way in.

But the peculiar thing, the thing that made all of us, in that one instant, abandon the jewel and turn, waiting, watching the shadow that rose slowly along the wall of the stairwell, was the nature of that wind, the smell of that wind.

It wasn't the wet, cold breeze blowing down Baker Street. It wasn't a London breeze at all. It was a wind that blew down a jungle river—a warm and humid wind saturated with the smell of orchid blooms and rotting vegetation, that seemed to suggest the slow splash of crocodiles sliding off a muddy bank and the rippling silent passage of a tiger glimpsed through distant trees. The shadow rose on the stairs, frightfully slowly, as if whatever cast it had legs of stone and was creeping inexorably along—clump, clump, clump—toward some fated destination. And within the footsteps, surrounding them, part of them, were the far-off cries of wild birds and the chattering of treetop monkeys and the shrill cry of a panther, all of it borne on that wind and on that ascending shadow for one long, teeming, silent moment

And what we saw first when the walker on the stairs clumped into view was the bent tip of an umbrella—the sprung umbrella hoisted by Frobisher's stroller. Ruined as the umbrella was, I could see that the shaft was a length of deteriorated bamboo, crushed and black with age and travel. And there, at the base, dangling by a green brass chain below the grip that was clutched in a wide, pale hand, was what had once been a tiny, preserved head, nothing but a skull now, yellow and broken and with one leathery strip of dried flesh still clinging in the depression below the eye socket.

We all shouted. Priestly smashed back into his chair. St. Ives bent forward in eager anticipation. We knew, wild and impossible as it seemed, what it was that approached us up the stairs on that rainy April day. It wore, as the waiter had promised, a pair of glasses with smoked lenses, and was otherwise clad in cast-off misshapen clothing that had once been worn, quite clearly, by people in widely different parts of the world: Arab bloused trousers, a Mandalay pontoon shirt, wooden shoes, a Leibnitz cap. His marbled jaw was set with fierce determination and his mouth opened and shut rhythmically like the mouth of a conger eel, his breath *whooshing* in and out. He reached up with his free hand and tore the smoked glasses away, pitching them in one sweeping motion against the wall where they shattered, spraying poor, dumbfounded Isaacs with glass shards.

In his right eye shone a tremendous faceted ruby, identical to the one that lay before St. Ives. Light blazed from it as if it were alive. His left eye was a hollow, dark socket, smooth and black and empty as night. He stood at the top of the stairs, chest heaving, creaking with exertion. He looked, so to speak, from one to the other of us, fixing his stare on the ruby glowing atop the table. His arm twitched. He let go of Bill

Kraken's umbrella, and the thing dropped like a shot to the floor, the jawbone and half a dozen yellow teeth breaking loose and spinning off across the oak planks. His entire demeanor seemed to lighten, as if he were drinking in the sight of the ruby like an elixir, and he took two shuffling steps toward it, swinging his arm ponderously out in front of him, pointing with a trembling finger toward the prize on the table. There could be no doubt what he was after, no doubt at all.

And for me, I was all for letting him have it. Under the circumstances it seemed odd to deny him. St. Ives was of a like mind. He went so far as to nod at the gem, as if inviting the idol (we can't mince words here, that's what he was) to scoop it up. Frobisher, however, was inclined to disagree. And I can't blame him, really. He hadn't been in Java with us twenty years past, hadn't seen the idol in the ring of stones, couldn't know that the sad umbrella lying on the floor had belonged to Bill Kraken and had been abandoned, as if in trade, for the priceless, ruinous gem among the asps and orchids of that jungle glade.

He stepped forward then, foolishly, and said something equally foolish about horsewhipping on the steps of the club and about his having been in the bush. A great, marbled arm swept out, *whumping* the air out of foolish old Frobisher and knocking him spinning over a library table as if he had been made of *papier-mâché*. Frobisher lay there senseless.

St. Ives at that point played his trump card: "Doctor Narbondo!" he said, and then waited, anticipating, watching the idol as it paused, contemplating, stricken by a rush of ancient, thin memory. Priestly hunched forward, mouth agape, tugging at his great white beard. I heard him whisper, "Narbondo!" as if in echo to St. Ives's revelation.

The idol stared at the Professor, its mouth working, moaning, trying to speak, to cry out. "Nnnn..." it groaned. "Nnnar, Nnarbondo!" it finally shouted, screwing up its face awfully, positively creaking under the strain.

Doctor Narbondo! It seemed impossible, lunatic. But there it was. He lurched forward, pawing the air, stumbling toward the ruby, the idol's eye. One pale hand fell on the edge of the table. The glasses danced briefly. Priestly's port tumbled over, pouring out over the polished wood in a red pool. The rain and the wind howled outside, making the fire in the great hearth dance up the chimney. Firelight shone through the ruby, casting red embers of reflected light onto Narbondo's face, bathing the cut-crystal decanter, three-quarters full of amber liquid, in a rosy, beckoning glow.

Narbondo's hand crept toward the jewel, but his eye was on that decanter. He paused, fumbled at the jewel, dropped it, his fingers clutching, a sad, mewing sound coming from his throat. Then, with the relieved look of a man who'd finally crested some steep and difficult hill, as if he'd scaled a monumental precipice and been rewarded with a vision of El Dorado, of Shangri-la, of paradise itself, he grasped the decanter of Laphroaig and, shaking, a wide smile struggling into existence on his face, lifted it toward his mouth, thumbing the stopper off onto the tabletop.

Hasbro responded with instinctive horror to Narbondo's obvious intent. He plucked up Priestly's unused glass, said, "Allow me, sir," and rescued the decanter, pouring out a good inch and proffering the glass to the gaping Narbondo. I fully expected that Hasbro would sail across and join Frobisher's heaped form unconscious on the floor. But that wasn't the case. Narbondo hesitated, recollecting, bits and pieces of European culture and civilized instinct filtering up from unfathomable depths. He nodded to Hasbro, took the proffered glass, and, swirling the whisky around in a tight, quick circle, passed it once under his nose and tossed it off.

A long and heartfelt sigh escaped him. He stood there just so, his head back, his mouth working slowly, savoring the peaty, smoky essence that lingered along his tongue. And Hasbro, himself imbued with the instincts of the archetypal gentleman's gentleman, poured another generous dollop into the glass, replaced the stopper, and set the decanter in the center of the table. Then he uprighted Frobisher's fallen chair and motioned toward it. Narbondo nodded again heavily, and, looking from one to the other of us, slumped into the chair with the air of a man who'd come a long, long way home.

—◊◊◊—

THUS ENDS THE story of, as I threatened in the early pages, perhaps the strangest of all the adventures that befell Langdon St. Ives, his man Hasbro, and myself. We ate that cutlet for supper, just as I'd planned, and we drained that decanter of whisky before the evening was through. St. Ives, his scientific fires blazing, told of his study over the years of the history of the mysterious Doctor Narbondo, of his slow realization that the curiously veined marble of the idol in the forest hadn't been marble at all, had, indeed, been the petrified body of Narbondo himself, preserved by jungle shaman and witch doctors using Narbondo's own serums. His eyes, being mere jellies, were removed and replaced with jewels, the optical qualities of the oddly wrought gems allowing him some vague semblance of strange vision. And there he had stood for close upon two hundred years, tended by priests from the tribes of Peewatin natives until that fateful day when Bill Kraken had gouged out his eye. Narbondo's weird reanimation and slow journey west over the long years would, in itself, be a tale long in the telling, as would that of St. Ives's quest for the lost ruby, a search that led him, finally, to a curiosity shop near the Tate Gallery where he purchased the gem for two pound six, the owner sure that it was simply a piece of cleverly cut glass.

At first I thought it was wild coincidence that Narbondo should arrive at the Explorers Club on the very day that St. Ives appeared with the ruby. But now I'm sure that there was no coincidence involved. Narbondo was bound to find his eye, and if St. Ives hadn't retrieved it from the curiosity shop, then Narbondo would have.

The doctor, I can tell you, is safe and sound and has done us all a service by renewing Langdon St. Ives's interests in the medical arts. Together, take my word for it, they work at perfecting the curious serums. Where they work will, I'm afraid, have to remain utterly secret. You can understand that. Curiosity seekers, doubting Thomases, and modern-day Ponce de Leons would flock forth gaping and demanding if his whereabouts were generally known.

And so it was that Doctor Narbondo returned. He had no army of supporters, no mutant beasts from the Borneo jungles, no hippos and apes with which to send a thrill of terror across the continent, no last laugh. Cold reality, I fear, can't measure up to the curious turnings of a madman's dreams. But if it was a grand and startling homecoming he wanted when he set sail for distant jungle shores two hundred years ago, he did quite moderately well for himself, I think you'll agree. —⟡

Homunculus

OWLESBY'S MEMOIRS

"I'm possessed by the most evil aching of the head—such that my eyes seem to press down to the size of screwholes, so that I see as if through a telescope turned wrong end to. Laudanum alone relieves it, but fills me with dreams even more evil than the pain in my forebrain. I'm certain that the pain is my due—that it is a taste of hell, and nothing less. And I can feel myself decay, feel my tissues drying and rotting like a beetle-eaten fungus on a stump, and my blood pounds across the top of my skull. I can see my own eyes, wide as half crowns and black with death and decay, and Narbondo ahead with that ghastly shears. I pushed him along! That's the truth of it. I railed at him. I hissed. I'd have that gland, is what I'd have, and before the night was gone. I'd hold in my hand my salvation..."

What a delicate speculation it is, after drinking whole goblets of tea, and letting the fumes ascend into the brain, to sit considering what we shall have for supper—eggs and a rasher, a rabbit smothered in onions, or an excellent veal cutlet! Sancho in such a situation once fixed upon cow-heel; and his choice, though he could not help it, is not to be disparaged.

William Hazlitt
"On Going a Journey"

I should wish to quote more, for though we are mighty fine fellows nowadays, we cannot write like Hazlitt. And, talking of that, Hazlitt's essays would be a capital pocketbook on such a journey; so would a volume of Ashbless poems; and for Tristrarn Shandy *I can pledge a fair experience.*

Robert Louis Stevenson
"Walking Tours"

Prologue

London 1870

ABOVE THE ST. Georges Channel clouds thick as shorn wool arched like a bent bow from Cardigan Bay round Strumble head and Milford Haven, and hid the stars from Swansea and Cardiff. Beyond Bristol they grew scanty and scattered and were blown along a heavenly avenue that dropped down the sky toward the shadows of the Cotswold Hills and the rise of the River Thames, then away east toward Oxford and Maidenhead and London. Stars winked and vanished and the new moon slanted thin and silver below them, the billowed crescent sail of a dark ship, swept to windward of stellar islands on deep, sidereal tides.

And in the wake of the moon floated an oval shadow, tossed by the whims of wind, and canting southeast from Iceland across the North Atlantic, falling gradually toward Greater London.

Two hours yet before dawn, the wind blew in fits above Chelsea and the sky was clear as bottled water, the clouds well to the west and east over the invisible horizon. Leaves and dust and bits of paper whirled through the darkness, across Battersea Park and the pleasure boats serried along the Chelsea shore, round the tower of St. Luke's and into darkness. The wind, ignored by most of the sleeping city, was cursed at by a hunchbacked figure who drove a dogcart down the Chelsea Embankment toward Pimlico, a shabby vehicle with a tarpaulin tied across a humped and unnatural load.

He looked back over his shoulder. The end of the canvas flapped in the wind. It wouldn't do to have it fly loose, but time was precious. The city was stirring. The carts of ambitious costermongers and greengrocers already clattered along to market, and silent oyster boats sailed out of Chelsea Reach toward Billingsgate.

The man reined in his horse, clambered down onto the stones, and lashed the canvas tight. A putrid stench blew out from under it. The wind was from the northeast, at his back. Such was the price of science. He put a foot on the running board and then stopped in sudden dread, staring at an open-mouthed and wide-eyed man standing on the embankment ahead with a pushcart full of rags. The hunchback gave him a dark look, most of it lost in the night. But the ragpicker wasn't peering at him, he was staring skyward where, shadowing the tip of the moon overhead, hovered the dim silhouette of a great dirigible, a ribby gondola swinging beneath. Rhythmic humming filled the air, barely audible but utterly pervasive, as if it echoed off the dome of the night sky.

The hunchback leaped atop the seat, whipped his startled horse, and burst at a run past the stupefied ragpicker, knocking his barrow to bits against a stone abutment. With the wind and the hum of the blimp's propellers driving him along, the hunchback scoured round the swerve of Nine Elms Reach and disappeared into Westminster, the blimp drifting lower overhead, swinging in toward the West End.

——⁓——

ALONG JERMYN STREET the houses were dark and the alleys empty. The wind banged at loose shutters and unlatched doors and battered the new wooden sign that hung before Captain Powers' Pipe Shop, yanking it loose finally in the early morning gray and throwing it end over end down Spode Street. The only light other than the dim glow of a pair of gaslamps shone from an attic window opposite, a window which, if seen from the interior of Captain Powers' shop, would have betrayed the existence of what appeared to be a prehistoric bird sporting the ridiculous rubber beak of a leering pterodactyl. Beyond it a spectacled face, half frowning, examined a rubber ape with apparent dissatisfaction. It wasn't the ape, however, that disturbed him; it was the wind. Something about the wind made him edgy, restless. There was too much noise on it, and the noises seemed to him to be portentous. Just when the cries of the windy night receded into regularity and faded from notice, some rustling thing—a leafy branch broken from a camphor tree in St. James Square or a careering crumple of greasy newspaper—brushed at the windowpane, causing him to leap in sudden dread in spite of himself. It was too early to go to bed; the sun would chase him there soon enough. He stepped across to the window, threw open the casement, and shoved his head out into the night. There was something on the wind—the dry rustle of insect wirrings, the hum of bees...He couldn't quite name it. He glanced up at the starry sky, marveling at the absence of fog and at the ivory moon that hung in the heavens like a coathook, bright enough, despite its size, so that the ghosts of chimney pots and gables floated over the street. Closing the casement, he turned to his bench and the disassembled shell of a tiny engine, unaware of the fading of the insect hum and of the oval shadow that passed along on the pavement below, creeping toward Covent Garden.

It wasn't yet four, but costermongers of all persuasions clustered at the market, pushing and shoving among greengrocers, ragpickers, beggars, missionaries, and cats. Carts and wagons full of vegetables were crammed in together along three sides of the square, heaped with onions and cabbages, peas and celery. On the west side of the square sat boxes and baskets of potted plants and flowers—roses, verbena, heliotrope and fuschia—all of it emitting a fragrance which momentarily called up memories, suspicions of places at odds with the clatter and throng that stretched away down Bow Street and Maiden Lane, lost almost at once among a hundred conflicting odors. Donkey carts and barrows choked the five streets leading away, and flower girls with bundles of sweet briar competed with apple women, shouting among the carts, the entire market flickering in the light of gaslamps and of a thousand candles thrust into potatoes and bottles and melted heaps of wax atop brake-locked cartwheels and low window sills, yellow light dancing and dying and flaring again in the wind.

A tall and age-ravaged missionary advertising himself as Shiloh, the Son of God, stood shivering in sackcloth and ashes, shouting admonitory phrases every few seconds as if it helped him keep warm. He thrust tracts into random faces, as oblivious to the curses and cuffs he was met with as he throng around him was oblivious to his jabber about apocalypse.

The moon, yellow and small, was sinking over Waterloo, and the stars were one by one winking out when the dirigible sailed above the market, then swept briefly out over the Victoria Embankment on its way toward Billingsgate and Petticoat Lane. For a few brief seconds, as the cry went round and thousands of faces peered skyward, the slat-sided gondola that swayed beneath the blimp was illuminated against the dying moon and the glow it cast on the clouds. A creaking and shuddering reached them on the wind, mingled with the hum of spinning propellers. Within the gondola, looking for all the world as if he were piloting the moon itself, was a rigid figure in a cocked hat, gripping the wheel, his legs planted widely as if set to counter an ocean swell. The wind tore at his tattered coat, whipping it out behind him and revealing the dark curve of a ribcage, empty of flesh, ivory moonlight glowing in the crescents of air between the bones. His wrists were manacled to the heel, which itself was lashed to a strut between two glassless windows.

The gondola righted itself, the moon vanished beyond rooftops, and the dirigible had passed, humming inexorably along toward east London. For the missionary, the issuance of the blimp was an omen, the handwriting on the wall, an even surer sign of coming doom than would have been the appearance of a comet. Business picked up considerably, a round dozen converts having been reaped by the time the sun hoisted itself into the eastern sky.

It was with the dawn that the blimp was sighted over Billingsgate. The weathered gondola creaked in the wind like the hull of a ship tossing on slow swells, and its weird occupant, secured to the wooden shell of his strange swaying aerie like a barnacle to a wave-washed rock, stared sightlessly down on fishmongers' carts and bummarees and creeping handbarrows filled with baskets of shellfish and eels, the wind whirling the smell of it all east down Lower Thames Street, bathing the Custom House and the

Tower in the odor of seaweed and salt spray and tidal flats. A squid seller, plucking off his cap and squinting into the dawn, shook his head sadly at the blimp's passing, touched two fingers to his forehead as if to salute the strange pilot, and turned back to hawking and rubbery, doleful-eyed occupants of his basket, three to the penny.

Petticoat Lane was far too active to much acknowledge the strange craft, which, illuminated by the sun now rather than the reflected light of the new moon, had lost something of its mystery and portent. Heads turned, people pointed, but the only man to take to his heels and run was a tweed-coated man of science. He had been haggling with a seller of gyroscopes and abandoned shoes about the coster's supposed knowledge of a crystal egg, spirited away from a curiosity shop near Seven Dials and rumored to be a window through which, if the egg were held just so in the sunlight, an observer with the right sort of eyesight could behold a butterfly-haunted landscape on the edges of a Martian city of pink stone, rising above a broad grassy lawn and winding placid canals. The gyroscope seller had shrugged. He could do little to help. To be sure, he'd heard rumors of its appearance somewhere in the West End, sold and resold for fabulous sums. Had the guv'nor that sort of sum? And a man of science needed a good gyroscope, after all, to demonstrate and study the laws of gravity, stability, balance, and spin. But Langdon St. Ives had shaken his head. He required no gyroscope; and yes, he did have certain sums, some little bit of which he'd gladly part with for real knowledge.

But the hum of the blimp and the shouts of the crowd brought him up short then, and in a trice he was pounding down Middlesex Street shouting for a hansom cab, and then craning his neck to peer up out of the cab window as it rattled away east, following the slow wake of the blimp out East India Dock Road, losing it finally as it rose on an updraft and was swallowed by a white bank of clouds that fell away toward Gravesend. ❧

ONE

The West End

ON APRIL 4 of the year 1875—thirty-four centuries to the day since Elijah's flight away to the stars in the supposed flaming chariot, and well over eighty years after the questionable pronouncement that Joanna Southcote suffered from dropsy rather than from the immaculate conception of the new messiah— Langdon St. Ives stood in the rainy night in Leicester Square and tried without success to light a damp cigar. He looked away up Charing Cross Road, squinting under the brim of a soggy felt hat and watching for the approach of—someone. He wasn't sure who. He felt foolish in the top shoes and striped trousers he'd been obliged to wear to a dinner with the secretary of the Royal Academy of Sciences. In his own laboratory in Harrogate he wasn't required to posture about in stylish clothes. The cigar was beginning to become irritating, but it was the only one he had, and he was damned if he'd let it get the best of him. He alternately cursed the cigar and the drizzle. This last had been falling—hovering, rather—for hours, and it confounded St. Ives' wish that it either rain outright or give up the pretense and go home.

There was no room in the world of science for mediocrity, for half measures, for wet cigars. He finally pitched it over his shoulder into an alley, patted his overcoat to see if the packet beneath was still there, and had a look at his pocket watch. It was just shy of nine o'clock. The crumpled message in his hand, neatly blocked out in handwriting that smacked of the draftsman, promised a rendezvous at eight-thirty.

"Thank you, sir," come a startling voice from behind him. "But I don't smoke. Haven't in years." St. Ives spun round, nearly knocking into a gentleman under a newspaper who hurried along the cobbles. But it wasn't he who had spoken. Beyond, slouching out of the mouth of an alley was a bent man with a frazzle of damp hair protruding from the perimeter of a wrecked Leibnitz cap. His extended hand held St. Ives' discarded cigar as if it were a fountain pen. "Makes me bilious," he was saying. "Vapors, it is. They say it's a thing a man gets used to, like shellfish or tripe. But they're wrong about it. Leastways they're wrong when it comes to old Bill Kraken. But you've got a dead good aim, sir, if I do say so myself. Struck me square in the chest. Had it been a snake or a newt, I'd have been a sorry Kraken. But it weren't. It were a cigar."

"Kraken!" cried St. Ives, genuinely astonished and taking the proffered cigar. "Owlesby's Kraken is it?"

"The very one, sir. It's been a while." And with that, Kraken peered behind him down the alley, the mysteries of which were hidden in impenetrable darkness and mist.

In Kraken's left hand was an oval pot with a swing handle, the pot swaddled in a length of cloth, as if Kraken carried the head of a Hindu. Around his neck was a small closed basket, which, St. Ives guessed, held salt, pepper, and vinegar. "A pea man, are you now?" asked St. Ives, eyeing the pot. Standing in the night air had made him ravenous.

"Aye, sir," replied Kraken. shaking his head. "By night I am, usually up around Cheapside and Leadenhall. I'd offer you a pod, sir, but they've gone stone cold in the walk."

A door banged shut somewhere up the alley behind them, and Kraken cupped a hand to his ear to listen. There was another bang followed close on by a clap of thunder. People hurried past, huddled and scampering for cover as a wash of rain, granting St. Ives' wish, swept across the square. It was a despicable night, St. Ives decided. Some hot peas would have been nice. He nodded at Kraken and the two men hunched away, sloshing through puddles and rills and into the door of the Old Shades, just as the sky seemed to crack in half like a China plate and drop an ocean of rain in one enormous sheet. They stood in the doorway and watched.

"They say it rains like that every day down on the equator," said Kraken, pulling off his cap.

"Do they?" St. Ives hung his coat on a hook and unwound his muffler. "Any place special on the equator?"

"Along the whole bit of it," said Kraken. "It's a sort of belt, you see, that girds us round. Holds the whole heap together, if you follow me. It's complicated. We're spinning like a top, you know."

"That's right," said St. Ives, peering through the tobacco cloud toward the bar, where a fat man poked bangers with a fork. Lazy smoke curled up from the sausages and mingled with that of dozens of pipes and cigars. St. Ives was faint. Nothing sounded as good to him as bangers. Damn pea pods. He'd sell his soul for a banger, sell his spacecraft even, sitting four-fifths built in Harrogate.

"Now the earth ain't nothing but bits and pieces, you know, shoved in together." Kraken followed St. Ives along a trail of sausage smoke toward the bar, crossing his arms in front of his pot. "And think of what would come of it if you just set the whole mess aspin. Like a top, you know, as I said."

"Confusion," said St. Ives. "Utter confusion."

"That's the very thing. It would all go to smash. Fly to bits. Straightaway. Mountains would sail off. Oceans would disappear. Fish and such would shoot away into the sky like Chinese rockets. And what of you and me? What of us?"

"Bangers and mash for my friend and me," said St. Ives to the publican, who looked at Kraken's peapot with disfavor. "And two pints of Newcastle." The man's face was enormous, like the moon.

"What of us, is what I want to know. It's a little-known fact."

"What is?" asked St. Ives, watching the moon-faced man spearing up bangers, slowly and methodically with pudgy little fingers, almost sausages themselves.

"It's a little-known fact that the equator, you see, is a belt—not cowhide, mind you, but what the doctor called elemental twines. Them, with the latitudes, is what binds this earth of ours. It isn't as tight as it might be, though, which is good because of averting suffocation. The tides show this—thank you, sir; God bless you—when they go heaving off east and west, running up against these belts, so to speak. And lucky it is for us, sir, as I said, or the ocean would just slide off into the heavens. By God, sir, this is first-rate bangers, isn't it?"

St. Ives nodded, licking grease from his fingertips. He washed a mouthful of the dark sausage down with a draught of ale. "Got all this from Owlesby, did you?"

"Only bits, sir. I do some reading on my own. The lesser known works, mostly."

"Whose?"

"Oh, I ain't particular, sir. Not Bill Kraken. All books is good books. And ideas, if you follow me, facts that is, are like beans in a bottle. There's only so many of them. The earth ain't but so many miles across. I aim to have a taste of them all, and science is where I launched out, so to speak."

"That's where I launched out too," said St. Ives. "I'll just have another pint. Join me?"

Kraken yanked a faceless pocket watch out of his coat and squinted at it before nodding. St. Ives winked and pushed away once more toward the bar. It was an hour yet before closing. A tramp in rags sidled from table to table, uncovering at each the stump of a recently severed thumb. A man in evening clothes lay on the floor, straight out on his side, his nose pressed against a wall, and three stools, occupied by his sodden young friends, propped him up there as if he were a corpse long gone in rigor mortis. There was an even cacophony of sounds, of laughter and clanking dishes and innumerable conversations punctuated at intervals by a loud, tubercular cough. More floor was covered by shoe soles and table legs than was bare, and that which was left over was scattered with sawdust and newspaper and scraps of food. St. Ives mashed the end of a banger beneath his heel as he edged past two tables full of singing men—seafaring men from the look of them.

Kraken appeared to be half asleep when minutes later St. Ives set the two pint glasses on the tabletop. The pleasant and solid clank of the full glasses seemed to revive him. Kraken set his pea pot between his feet. "It's been a while, sir, hasn't it?"

"Fourteen years, is it?"

"Fifteen, sir. A month before the tragedy, it was. You wasn't much older'n a bug, if I ain't out of line to say so," He paused to drink off half the pint. "Them was troublesome times, sir. Troublesome times. I ain't told a soul about most of it. Can't. I've cheated myself of the hereafter; I can't afford Newgate."

"Surely nothing as bad as that…" began St. Ives, but he was cut short by Kraken, who waved broadly and shook his head, falling momentarily silent.

"There was the business of the carp," he said, looking over his shoulder as if he feared that a constable might at that moment be slipping up behind. "You don't remember it. But it was in the *Times,* and Scotland Yard even had a go at it. And come close, too, by God! There's a little what-do-you-call-it, a gland or something, full of elixir. I drove the wagon. Dead of night in midsummer, and hot as a pistol barrel. We got out of the aquarium with around half dozen, long as your arm, and Sebastian cut the beggars up not fifty feet down Baker Street, on the run but neat as a pin. We gave the carps to a beggar woman on Old Pye, and she sold the lot at Billingsgate. So good come of it in the end.

"But the carp affair was the least of it. I'm ashamed to say more. And it wouldn't be right to let on that Sebastian was behind the worst. Not by a sea mile. It was the other one. I've seen him more than once over the fence at Westminster Cemetery, and late at night too, him in a dogcart on the road and me and Tooey Short with spades in our hand. Tooey died in Horsemonger Lane Gaol, screaming mad, half his face scaled like a fish."

Kraken shuddered and drained his glass, falling silent and staring into the dregs as if he'd said enough—too much, perhaps.

"It was a loss when Sebastian died," said St. Ives. "I'd give something to know what became of his notebooks, let alone the rest of it."

Kraken blew his nose into his hand. Then he picked up his glass and held it up toward a gaslamp as if contemplating its empty state. St. Ives rose and set out after another round. The moon-faced publican poured two new pints, stopping in between to scoop up mashed potatoes with a blackened banger and shove it home, screwing up his face and smacking his lips. St. Ives winced. An hour earlier a hot banger had seemed paradisial, but four bangers later there was nothing more ghastly to contemplate. He carried the two glasses back to the table, musing on the mutability of appetite and noting through the open door that the rain had let off.

Kraken met him with a look of anticipation, and almost at once did way with half the ale, wiping the foam from his mouth with the sleeve of his shirt. St. Ives waited.

"No, sir," said Kraken finally. "It wasn't the notebooks I'm sorry for, I can tell you." Then he stopped.

"It wasn't?" asked St. Ives, curious.

"No, sir. Not the bleeding papers. Damn the papers. They're writ in blood. Every one. Good riddance, says I."

St. Ives nodded expansively, humoring him.

Kraken hunched over the table, waggling a finger at St. Ives, the little basket of condiments on his neck swaying beneath his face like the gondola of a half-deflated balloon. "It was that damn *thing*," whispered Kraken, "what I'd have killed."

"Thing?" St. Ives hunched forward himself.

"The thing in the box. I seen it lift the corpse of a dog off the floor and dance it on the ceiling. And there were more to it than that." Kraken spoke so low that St. Ives could barely hear him above the din. "Them bodies me and Tooey Short brought in. There was more than one of them as walked out on his own legs." Kraken paused for effect and sucked down the last half inch of ale, clunking the glass back down onto the oaken tabletop. "No, sir. I don't rue no papers. And if they'd asked me, I'd 'a' told them Nell was innocent as a China doll. I loved the young master, and I cry to think he left a baby son behind him, but by God the whole business wasn't natural, was it? And the filthy shame of it is that Nell didn't plug that damned doctor after she put one through her brother. That's what I regret, in a nut."

Kraken made as if to stand up, his speechifying over. But St. Ives, although shaken by bits of Kraken's tale, held his hand up to stop his leaving. "I have a note from Captain Powers," said St. Ives, proffering the crumpled missive to Kraken, "asking me to meet a man in Leicester Square at eight-thirty."

Kraken blinked at him a moment, then peered over his shoulder toward the door and squinted round the pub, cocking an ear. "Right ho," he said, sitting back down. He bent toward St. Ives once again. "I ran into the Captain's man, up in Covent Garden, at the market it was, three days back. And he mentioned the..." Kraken paused and winked voluminously at St. Ives.

"The machine?"

"Aye. That's the ticket. The machine. Now I don't claim to know where it is, you see, but I've heard tell of it. So the Captain put me onto you, as it were, and said that the two of us might be in a way to do business."

St. Ives nodded, pulse quickening. He patted his pockets absentmindedly and found a cigar. "Heard tell of it?" He struck a match and held it to the cigar end, puffing sharply. "From whom?"

"Kelso Drake," whispered Kraken. "Almost a month ago, it was. Maybe six weeks."

St. Ives sat back in surprise. "The millionaire?"

"That's a fact. From his very lips. I worked for him, you see, and overheard more than he intended—more than I wanted. A foul lot, them millionaires. Nothing but corruption. But they'll reap the bread of sorrow. Amen."

"That they will," said St. Ives. "But what about the machine—the ship?"

"In a brothel, maybe in the West End. That's all I know. He owns a dozen. A score. Brothels, I mean to say. There's nothing foul he don't have a hand in. He owns a soap factory out in Chingford. I can't tell you what it is they make soap out of. You'd go mad."

"A brothel that might be in the West End. That's all?"

"Every bit of it."

St. Ives studied the revelation. It wasn't worth much. Maybe nothing at all. "Still working for Drake?" he asked hopefully.

Kraken shook his head. "Got the sack. He was afraid of me. I wasn't like the rest." He sat up straight, giving St. Ives a stout look. "But I'm not above doing a bit of business among friends, am I? No, sir. I'm not. Not a bit of it." He watched St. Ives, who was lost in thought. "Not Bill Kraken. No, sir. When I set out to do a man a favor, across town, through the rain, mind you, why it's, 'keep your nose in front of your face. Let it rain!' That's my motto when I'm setting out on a job like this one."

St. Ives came to himself and translated Kraken's carrying on. He handed across two pound notes and shook his hand. "You've done me a service, my man. If this pans out there'll be more in it for you. Come along to the Captain's shop on Jermyn Street Thursday evening. There'll be a few of us meeting. If you can round up more information, you won't find me miserly."

"Aye, sir," said Kraken, rising and fetching up his pea pot. He secured the cloths and tied them neatly about the lip of the pot. "I'll be there." He folded the two notes and slipped them into his shoe, then turned without another word and hurried out.

St. Ives' cigar wouldn't stay lit. He looked hard at it for a moment before recognizing it as the damp thing he'd pitched at Kraken an hour and a half earlier. It seemed to be following him around. The man without the thumb loomed in toward him. St. Ives handed him a shilling and the cigar, found his coat on the rack, checked the inside pocket for his parcel—actually a sheaf of rolled paper—and set out into the night.

—◆◆◆—

POWERS' PIPE AND Tobacco Shop lay at the corner of Jermyn and Spode, with long, mullioned windows along both the south and east walls so that a man—Captain Powers, for instance—might sit in the Morris chair behind the counter and, by rotating his head a few degrees, have a view of those coming and going along either street. On the night of the fourth of April, though, seeing much of anything through the utter darkness of the clouded and rainy night was unlikely. The thin glow cast by the two visible gaslamps, both on Jermyn Street, was negligible. And the light that shone from lit windows here and there along the street seemed to have an antipathy to flight, and hovered round its sources wary of the damp night.

Captain Powers would hear the sound of approaching feet on the pavement long before the traveler would appear in one of the two yellow circles of illuminated sidewalk, then disappear abruptly into the night, the footsteps clop-clopping away into silence.

The houses across the street were inhabited by the genteel, many of whom wandered into the pipe shop for a pouch of tobacco or a cigar. It would have been lean times for the Captain, however, if it hadn't been for his pension. He'd been at sea since he was twelve and had lost his right leg in a skirmish fifty miles below Alexandria, when his sloop sank in the Nile, blown to bits by desert thieves. He had saved a single tusk of a fortune in ivory, and twenty years later William Keeble the toymaker had made him a leg of it, the best by far of any he'd worn. Not only did it fit without taking the skin off that little bit of leg he had left, but it was hollow and held a pint of liquor and two ounces of tobacco. In a pinch he could smoke the entire leg, could press a button at the tip and manipulate a hidden plate, the size of a half crown, which would slide back to reveal the bowl of a pipe. A tube ran up the inside of his pantleg and coat, and he could walk and smoke simultaneously. The Captain had only done so once, largely because of a sort of odd fascination with the idea of Keeble's having built it. The bewildered stares of passersby, however, had seemed to argue against the wisdom of revealing in public the wonderful nature of the thing. Captain Powers, grizzled from sea weather and stoic from thirty years of discipline before the mast, was a conservative at heart. Dignity was his byword. But friendship precluded him from letting on to Keeble that he had no real desire to be seen smoking a peg leg.

Keeble's house, in fact, sat opposite Powers' store. The Captain looked across the top of his companion's head at the lamp burning in the attic shop. Below was another room alight—the bedroom of Jack Owlesby; and on the left yet another, the bedroom, quite likely, either of Winnifred—Keeble's wife—or of Dorothy, the Keeble daughter, home for a fortnight now from finishing school.

His companion cleared his throat as if about to speak, so Captain Powers let his gaze fall from the window to his friend's face. It had the unmistakable look of nobility to it, of royalty, but it was the face of Theophilus Godall of the Bohemian Cigar Divan in Rupert Street, Soho, a face that at that moment was drawing on an old meerschaum pipe. Carved on either side of the bowl was the coat of arms of the royal family of Bohemia, a house long since scattered and flown from a fallen country. The pipe had had, no doubt, a vast and peculiar history before passing into the hands of Godall, and who knew what sort of adventures had befallen it since?

"I was with Colonel Geraldine," Godall was saying, "in Holborn. Incognito. It was late and the evening had proven fallow. All we'd accomplished was to have spent too much good money on bad champagne. We'd had a pointless discussion with a fellow who had a promising story about a suicidal herb merchant on Vauxhall Bridge Road. But the fellow—the second fellow, that is, the herb merchant—turned out to be already dead. Hanged himself these six months past with his own gaiters, and the first fellow turned out to be uninteresting. I wish I could say he meant well, but what he meant was to drink our champagne.

"Before he left, though, in came two of the most extraordinary men. Obviously bound for the workhouse but neither had any color to him. They had the skin of frog bellies. And they had no notion of where they were. Not the foggiest. They had a sort of dazed look about them, as if they'd been drugged, you might say. In fact that's what I thought straightaway. Geraldine spoke to the larger of the two, but the man didn't respond. Looked at him in perfect silence. Not insubordinately, mind you. There was none of that. There was simply no hint of real consciousness."

The Captain shook his head and tapped the ashes of his pipe into a brass bowl. He looked at the clock under the counter—nearly ten-thirty. The rain had slackened. He could see none at all falling across the illuminated glass of the streetlamp. Footsteps approached slowly, drawing up along Jermyn Street. They stopped altogether. Captain Powers winked at Theophilus Godall, who nodded slightly. The footsteps resumed, angling away across the road toward Keeble's house. It was just possible that it was Langdon St. Ives, come round to Keeble's to discuss his oxygenator box. But no, St. Ives would have stopped in if he'd seen a light. He'd have spoken to Kraken by now and be full of alien starships. This was someone else.

A hunched shadow appeared on the sidewalk opposite—the shadow of a hunchback, to be more exact—and hurried past the gaslamp into darkness, but the Captain was certain that he'd stopped beyond it. He had for five nights running. "There's your man across the road," said the Captain to Godall.

"Are you certain of it?"

"Aye. The hunchback. It's him all right. He'll hang round till I switch out the lights."

Godall nodded and resumed his story. "So Geraldine and I followed the two, halfway across town into Limehouse where they went into a pub called the Blood Pudding. We stayed long enough to see that it was full of such men. The two of us stood out like hippopotami. But I can't say we were noticed by any but him." And Godall shrugged back over his shoulder at the street. "He was a hunchback, anyway. And although I'm not familiar with this fellow Narbondo, it could conceivably have been he. He was eating live birds, unless I'm very much mistaken. The sight of it on top of champagne and kippers rather put us off the scent, if you follow me, and I'd have happily forgotten him completely if it weren't for your having got me onto this business of yours. Is he still there?"

The Captain nodded. He could just see the hunchback's shadow, still as a bush, cast across a bit of wall.

A new set of steps approached, accompanied by a merry bit of offkey whistling.

"Get your hat!" cried Captain Powers, standing up. He stepped across and turned down the lamp, plunging the room into darkness. There, striding purposefully up toward Keeble's door carrying his packet of papers was Langdon St. Ives, explorer and inventor.

In an instant the hunchback—Dr. Ignacio Narbondo—had vanished. Theophilus Godall leaped for the door, waved hastily at Captain Powers, and made away into the night, east on Jermyn toward Haymarket. Across the street, William Keeble threw back the door and admitted St. Ives, who squinted wonderingly at the dark, receding figure that had hurried from the suddenly darkened tobacco shop. He shrugged at Keeble. The Captain's doings were always a mystery. The two of them were swallowed up into the interior of Keeble's house.

The street was silent and wet, and the smell of rain on pavement hung in the air of the tobacco shop, reminding the Captain briefly of spindrift and fog. But in an instant it was gone, and the thin and tenuous shadow of the sea vanished with it. Captain Powers stood just so, contemplating, a lazy shaving of smoke rising in the darkness above his head. Godall had left his pipe in his haste. He'd be back for it in the morning; there was little doubt of that.

A sudden light knock sounded at the door, and the Captain jumped. He'd expected it, but the night was full of dread and the slow unraveling of plots. He stepped across and pulled open the heavy door, and there in the dim lamplight on the street stood a woman in a hooded cloak. She hurried past him into the room. Captain Powers closed the door.

—*◊◊◊*—

St. Ives followed William Keeble up three flights of stairs and into the cluttered toyshop. Logs burned in an iron box, vented out into the night through a terra cotta chimney, and the fire was such that the room, although large, was warm and close, almost hot. But it was cheerful, given the night, and the heat served to evaporate some of the rainwater that dripped in past the slates of the roof. A tremendous and alien staghorn fern hung very near the fire, below the leaded window of the gable that led out onto the roof, and a stream of water, nothing more than a dribble, ran in along the edge of the ill-scaled casement and dripped from the sill into the mossy, decayed box that held the fern. Every minute or so, as if the rainwater pooled up until high enough to run out, a little waterfall would burst from the bottom of the planter and fall with the hiss of steam into the firebox.

Darkened roof rafters angled sharply away overhead, stabilized by several great joists that spanned the twenty-foot width of the shop and provided avenues along which tramped any number of mice, hauling bits of debris and working among the timbers like elves. Hanging from the joists were no end of marvels: winged beasts, carved dinosaurs, papier-mâché masks, odd paper kites and wooden rockets, the amazed and lopsided head of a rubber ape, an enormous glass orb filled with countless tiny carven people. The kites, painted with the visages of birds and deepwater fish, had hung among the rafters for years, and were half obscured by cobweb and dust amid the brown stains of dirty rainwater. Great shreds had been chewed away by mice and bugs to build homes among the hanging debris.

The red pine floor, however, was swept clean, and innumerable tools hung over two work benches, unordered but neat, brass and iron glinting dully in the light of a half-dozen wood and glass sconces. Coughing into his sleeve, Keeble cleared a score of mauve seashells and a kaleidoscope from the benchtop, then swept it clean with a horsehair brush, the handle of which was elegantly carved into the form of an elongated frog.

St. Ives admired it aloud.

"Like that do you?" asked Keeble.

"Quite," admitted St. Ives, an admirer of William Morris's philosophy concerning beauty and utility.

"Press its nose."

"Pardon me?"

"Its nose," said Keeble. "Press it. Give it a shove with your fingertip."

St. Ives dubiously obeyed, and the top of the frog's head, from nose to mid-spine, slid back into its body, revealing a long, silver tube. Keehie pulled it out, unscrewed a cap at the end, found two glasses wedged in behind a heap of wooden planes, and from the tube poured an equal share of liquor into each. St. Ives was astonished.

"So what have you got?" asked Keeble, draining his glass and hiding it away once again.

"The oxygenator. Finished, I believe. I'm counting on you for the rest. It's the last of the lot. The rest of the ship is ready. We'll launch it in May if the weather clears up." St. Ives unrolled his drawing onto the benchtop, and Keeble leaned over it, peering intently at the lines and figures through startlingly thick glasses.

"Helium, is it?"

"And chlorophyll. Powdered. There's an intake here and a spray mechanism and filter there. The clockworks sit in the base—a seven-day works should do it, at least for the first flight." St. Ives sipped at his lass and looked up at Keeble. "Birdlip's engine; could it be duplicated on this scale?"

Keeble pulled off his glasses and wiped them on a handkerchief. He shrugged. "Perpetual motion is a tricky business, you know—rather like separating an egg from its shell without altering the shape of either, and then suspending the two there, one a quivering, translucent ovoid, the other a seeming solid, side by side. It's not done in a day. And the whole thing is relative, isn't it? True perpetual motion is a dream, although a sage named Gustatorius claimed to have produced it alchemically in 1410 in the Balkans, for the purpose of continually turning the back lens of a kaleidoscope. A wonderful idea, but alchemists tend to be frivolous, taken on the whole. Birdlip's engine, though, is running down. I'm afraid his appearance this spring may be his last."

St. Ives glanced up sharply. "Are you?"

"Yes indeed. When it passed five years ago it was low, fearfully so, and far to the north of its passing in '65. So I've a suspicion that the engine is declining. The blimp may well drop into the sea, but I rather think it's tending toward Hampstead where it was launched. There's a homing element in the engine; that's what I think. A chance product of its design, not anything I intended."

St. Ives rubbed his chin, unwilling to let Keeble's revelation push him off his original course. "But can it be miniaturized? Birdlip has been up for fifteen years. In that time I can easily reach Mars, Saturn even, and return."

"Yes, in a word. Look at this." Keeble slid open a drawer and pulled out a wooden box. The joints were clearly visible, and the box was painted with symbols that appeared to be Egyptian hieroglyphs—walking birds and amphibians, eyeballs peering out of pyramids—but there was no sign of a hinge or a latch.

It immediately occurred to St. Ives that the box was a tamper-proof bottle of some sort, perhaps a tiny, self-contained still, and that he would be asked to poke the nose of a painted beast in order to reveal an amber pool of Scotch whisky. But Keeble set the box squarely atop the bench, spun it round forty-five degrees or so, and the lid of the box opened on its own.

St. Ives watched as the lid rose and then fell back. From out of the depths of the box rose a strangely authentic-looking miniature cayman alligator, its long, toothed snout opening and shutting rhythmically. Four little birds followed, one at each corner, and the cayman snapped up and devoured the birds one by one, then grinned, rolled its eyes, made a sound like a rusty hinge, and sank into its den. After a ten second pause, up it rose again, followed by miraculously restored birds, fated to be devoured over and over again into infinity. Keeble shut the lid, rotated the box a few degrees farther along, and smiled at St. Ives. "It's taken me twelve years to perfect that, but it's quite as workable now as is Birdlip's engine. It's for Jack's birthday. He'll be eighteen soon—fifteen years he's been with us—and he's the only one, I fear, who sees these things with the right sort of eye."

"Twelve years it took?" St. Ives was disappointed.

"It could be done more quickly now," said Keeble, "but it's fearsomely expensive." He was silent for a moment while he put the box away in its drawer. "I've been approached, in fact, about the device—about the patent, actually."

"Approached?"

"By Kelso Drake. He seems to have dreams of propelling entire factories with perpetual motion devices. I haven't any idea how he got onto them in the first place."

"Kelso Drake!" cried St. Ives. He almost shouted, "Again!" but hesitated at the melodramatic sound of it and the moment passed. It was an odd coincidence, though, to be sure. First Kraken's suspicion of Drake's possessing the alien craft, and now this. But there could hardly be a connection. St. Ives pointed at the plans lying on the bench. "How long then, a month?"

"I should think so," said Keeble. "That should do nicely. How long are you in London?"

"Until this is accomplished. Hasbro stayed on in Harrogate. I've got rooms at the Bertasso in Pimlico."

Keeble, winking at St. Ives, began unscrewing the handle of a heavy chisel with an iron two inches wide. There was a bang at the casement overhead, as if it had been suddenly blown closed in the wind. Keeble dropped the chisel in surprise, the inevitable liquor within the handle flowing out over the drawing of the oxygenator device.

"Wind," said St. Ives, himself shaking from the sudden start. But just as he mouthed the word, a bolt of lightning lit the night sky, illuminating a shadowy face that peered in over the sill, and precipitating a wash of sudden, heavy rain.

Keeble cried out in horror and surprise. St. Ives jumped across to the tilted stepladder that led to the boxy little gable. There was a shout from above—a cry actually—and the sound of something scraping across he slates. St. Ives flung open the window in the face of the rain, and climbed out into the night, just as a head and shoulders disappeared over the edge of the roof.

"I've got him!" came a shout from below, the voice of Jack Owlesby, and St. Ives started toward it, thinking to follow the man down. But the slick roof would almost certainly land him in the road, and he could just as easily use the stairs as Keeble had done. As he clambered back in at the casement there was another shout and a creaking and snapping, followed by curses and the swish of tearing vegetation.

St. Ives bolted for the stairs, taking them two at a time, passing a bewildered Winnifred Keeble on the second floor landing. Further cries drew him on toward the gaping front door and into the street where Keeble wrestled with the marauder, the two of them slogging through an ankle-deep puddle.

Lights flared on in Powers' shop, then abruptly winked out again, then back on. Windows slammed open along the street, and cries of "Pipe down!" and "Shut yer gob!" rang out, but none of them louder than Keeble's shouts of pain. He held his assailant round the chest, having grappled the man from behind as he attempted to flee, and the man stamped the toymaker's toe with the heel of his boot, unable to shake Keeble off.

St. Ives rushed at the pair through the rain, hollering for his friend to hold on, as the criminal—a garret thief, likely—pulled the both of them down the road. Captain Powers, just then, erupted from the mouth of the tobacco shop, stumping along on his peg leg and waving a pistol.

Just as St. Ives drew near, thinking to throw his coat over the thief's head, Keeble set him free and reeled away, hopping on one foot toward the curb. St. Ives' coat, flung like a gill net, fluttered into the mud of the roadway, and the man was gone, loping up Spode Street into the night. Captain Powers aimed his pistol at the man, but the range was too great for any but a chance hit, and the Captain wasn't one to be cavalier with his shooting. St. Ives dashed after the retreating figure, leaping onto the sidewalk in front of the pipe shop, then nearly colliding with a cloaked woman who appeared out of an adjacent alley, as if, perhaps, she'd come along the short cut from Piccadilly. St. Ives dodged into a wall, and his chase was at an end, the criminal disappearing utterly, his footfalls dying away. St. Ives turned to apologize to the woman, but there was nothing to see but the dark tweed of her cloak and hood, receding into the gloom along Jermyn. A gust of wind whistled along after her, rippling the surface of puddles beneath gaslamps. And on it, unseasonably cold, came the last quick scatter of pre-dawn raindrops. —⌀

TWO

The Trismegistus Club

S T. IVES HAD always felt at home in Captain Power's shop, although he
would have been in a hard way to say just how. His own home—the home of his
childhood—hadn't resembled it in the slightest. His parents had prided themselves in
being modern, and would brook no tobacco or liquor. His father had written a treatise
on palsy, linking the disease to the consumption of meat, and for three years no meat
crossed the threshold. It was a poison, an abomination, carrion like eating broiled dirt,
said his father. And tobacco: his father would shudder at the mention of the word. St.
Ives could remember him standing atop a crate beneath a leafless oak, he couldn't say
just where—St. James Park, perhaps—shouting at an indifferent crowd about the evils
of general intemperance.

His theories had declined from the scientific to the mystical and then into gibberish, and now he wrote papers still, sometimes in verse, from the confines of a comfortable, barred cellar in north Kent. St. Ives had decided by the time he was twelve that
intemperance in the pleasures of the senses was, in the main, less ruinous than was
intemperance along more abstract lines. Nothing, it seemed to him, was worth losing
your sense of proportion and humor over, least of all a steak pie, a pint of ale, and a
pipe of latakia.

All of which explained, perhaps, why the Captain's shop struck him so absolutely
agreeably. From one angle it was admittedly close and dim, and there was no profit examining the upholstery on the several stuffed chairs and settee that were wedged together toward the rear of the shop. The springs which here and there protruded from rents in
the upholstery and which carried on them tufts of horsehair and cotton wadding had, in
their day, quite possibly been crowning examples of their type. And the Oriental carpets
scattered about might have been worthy of a temple floor fifty or sixty years earlier.

Great pots of tobacco stood atop groaning shelves, now and then separated by a
row of books, all tilted and stacked and quite apparently having nothing at all to do

79

with tobacco, but being, it seemed to St. Ives, their own excuse—a very satisfactory thing. Everything worth anything, he told himself, was its own excuse. Three or four lids were askew on the tobacco canisters, which leaked an almost steamy perfume into the still air of the room.

William Keeble hunched over one, dangling his long fingers in at the mouth of the jar and pulling out a tangle of tobacco that glowed golden and black in the gaslight. He wiggled it into the bowl of his pipe, then peered in at it as if in wonder, working it over from as many angles as possible before setting it aflame. There was much in the gesturing to attract a man of science, and for a moment the poet within St. Ives grappled with the physicist, both of them clamoring for the floor.

St. Ives' study at Heidelberg under Helmholtz had brought him into contact for the first time with an opthalmoscope, and he could remember having peered through the wonderful instrument into the eye of an artistic fellow student, a man given to long walks in the forest and to gazing at idyllic landscapes. Just as the operation began, the man had seen through an unshuttered window the drooping branches of a flowering pear, and a little tidepool of gadgetry that ornamented the interior of his eye, suddenly enlivened at the sight, danced like leaves in a brief wind. For a frozen moment after St. Ives removed the instrument and before a blink sliced the picture neatly off, the pear blossoms and a sketch of cloud drift beyond were reflected in the lens of the man's eye. The conclusions St. Ives had drawn tended, he had to admit, toward the poetic, and were faintly at odds with the methods of scientific empiricism. But it was that suggestion of beauty and mystery which attracted him so overwhelmingly to the study of pure science and which—who could say?—compelled him to wander down the crooked avenues that might at last lead him to the stars.

The Captain's tobacco canisters—no two of them alike, and gathered from distant parts of the globe—reminded him, open as they were, of a candy shop. The feeling was altogether appropriate and accurate. His own pipe had gone dead. Here was the opportunity of having a go at some new mixture. He rose and peeked into a Delft jar containing "Old Bohemia."

"You won't be disappointed in that," came a voice from the door, and St. Ives looked up to see Theophilus Godall pulling off a greatcoat on the threshold. The street door slammed behind him, jerked shut by the wind. St. Ives nodded and tilted his head at the tobacco canister as if inviting Godall's commentary. There was something about the man, St. Ives decided, that gave him an air of worldliness and undefined expertise—something in the shape of his aquiline nose or in the forthrightness of his carriage.

"That was originally mixed by a queen of the royal house of Bohemia, who smoked a pipe at precisely midnight each evening, then drank off a draught of brandy and hot water in a swallow and retired. It has medicinal qualities that can't be disputed." St. Ives could see no way out of smoking a bowl. He began to regret his inability to do justice to the rest of the queen's example, then saw, out of the corner of his eye, Captain Powers emerge from the rear of his shop carrying a tray and bottles. Godall smiled cheerfully and shrugged.

Behind the Captain, cap in hand, plodded Bill Kraken, his hair a wonder of wind-whipped happenstance. Jack Owlesby bent in through the door behind Godall, bringing the number of people in the room to seven, including St. Ives' man Hasbro, who sat reading a copy of the *Peloponnesian Wars* and sipped meditatively at a glass of port.

The Captain stumped across to his Morris chair and sat down, waving haphazardly at the collection of bottles and glasses on the tray.

"Thank you, sir," said Kraken, bending over a bottle of Laphroaig. "I'll have a nip, sir, since you ask." He poured an inch of it into a glass, tossing it off with a grimace. He seemed to St. Ives to be in a bad way—pale, disheveled. Hunted was the word for it. St. Ives regarded him narrowly. Kraken's hand shook until, with a visible lurch, he shuddered from top to bottom, the liquor taking hold and supplying a steadying influence. Perhaps his pallid and quaking demeanor was a product of the absence of alcohol rather than of the presence of guilt or fear.

The Captain tapped on the countertop with his pipe bowl and the room fell silent "I was inclined to believe, just like yourselves, that last Saturday night's intruder was a garret thief, but that's not the case."

"No?" asked St. Ives, startled by the abrupt revelation. He'd had such a suspicion himself. There was too much deviltry afoot for it all to be random—too many faces in windows, too many repeated names, too many common threads of mystery for him to suppose that they weren't part of some vast, complicated weft.

"That's right," said the Captain, putting a match to his pipe. He paused theatrically, squinting roundabout. "He was back this afternoon."

Keeble nodded. It had been the same man. Keeble couldn't have forgotten the back of the man's head, which is all of him he'd seen this time again. Winnifred had been at the museum, cataloguing books on lepidoptery. Jack and Dorothy, thank God, had been away at the flower market buying hothouse begonias. Keeble had been asleep an hour. He'd been dabbling at the engine, and had put the whole works—the plans, the little cayman device, notes—in a hole in the floor that no one, not another living soul, could sniff out. Then he'd given up the ghost at noon and welcomed the arrival of blinking Morpheus. A crash had brought him out of it. The casement window again. He was sure of it. Footfalls sounded. The cook, who was coming in through the back door with a chicken, was confronted by the thief, and slammed him in the face with the plucked bird before snatching at a carving knife. Keeble had rushed out in his nightshirt and, once again, pursued the man into the street. But dignity demanded he give up the chase. A man in a nightshirt, after all. It wasn't to be thought of. And his foot—it was barely healed from the last encounter.

"What was he after?" asked Godall, breaking into Keeble's narration. "You're certain it wasn't valuables?"

"He ran past any number of them," said Keeble, pouring himself a third glass of port. "He could have filled his pockets between the attic and the front door."

"So nothing was taken?" St. Ives put in.

"On the contrary. He stole the plans for a roof-mounted sausage cooker. I'd intended to try it out in the next electrical storm. There's something about a lightning storm that puts me immediately in mind of sausages. I can't explain it."

Godall, incredulous, plucked his pipe out of his mouth and squinted. "You're telling us he broke into the house to steal the plans for this fabulous sausage machine?"

"Not a bit of it. I rather believe he was after something else. He'd been at the floor with a prybar. He'd seen me slip the plans into the cache. I'm certain of it. But he couldn't get at them. I've a theory that he balanced the casement open with a stick so as to be able to shove out in a nonce. But the stick slipped, the casement banged home and latched, and in a panic he snatched up the nearest set of plans and ran for it, thinking to be out the back before I awoke. The cook surprised him."

"What can he do with these plans?" asked the Captain, tapping his pipe out against his ivory leg.

"Not a living thing," said Keeble.

Godall stood and peered out to where wind-whirled debris danced and flew along Jermyn Street in the night. "For my money Kelso Drake will market such a device within the month. Not for profit, mind you—there wouldn't be much profit in it—but as a lark, to thumb his nose at us. He was after the perpetual motion engine then?"

Keeble began to assent when a banging at the door cut him off. The Captain was out of his chair at once, his finger to his lips. There was no one beyond the seven of them whom they could trust, and no one, certainly, who had any business at a meeting of the Trismegistus Club. Kraken slipped away into a rear chamber. Godall shoved a hand beneath his coat, an act which startled St. Ives.

At the newly opened door stood a young man who was, largely because of a disastrous complexion, of indeterminate age. He might have been thirty, but was more likely twenty-five: of medium height, paunchy, brooding, and slightly stooped. The smile that played across the corners of his mouth was evidently false and served in no way to animate his cold eyes—eyes ringed and dark from an excess of study under inadequate light. He seemed to St. Ives to be a student. Not a student of anything identifiable or practical, but a student of dark arts, or of the sort who wags his head morosely and knowingly over cynical and woeful poetry and who has ingested opiates and stalked through midnight streets, without destination, but out of an excess of morbidity and bile. His cheeks seemed almost to be sucked inward, as if he were consuming himself or were metamorphosing into a particularly picturesque fish. He needed a pint of good ale, a kidney pie, and a half-dozen jolly companions.

"I am addressing a meeting of the Trismegistus Club," said he, bowing almost imperceptibly. No one answered, perhaps because he had addressed no one or perhaps because it seemed as if he expected no response. The wind whistled behind him, trifling with the tattered hem of his coat.

"Come in, mate," said the Captain after a long pause. "Pour yourself a glass of brandy and state your business. This is a private club, you see, and no one with a full deck would want to join, if you follow me. We're all idle and we have little regard for hands, you might say, looking for a sail to mend."

The Captain's speech didn't wrinkle the man in the least. He introduced himself as Willis Pule, an acquaintance of Dorothy Keeble. Jack's eyes narrowed. He was certain the claim was a lie. He was familiar with Dorothy's friends, and even more, he was familiar with the sorts of people who could likely be Dorothy's friends. Pole wasn't one of them. He hesitated to say so only out of a spirit of hospitality—it was the Captain's shop, after all—but the man's very presence became an immediate affront.

Godall, his hand yet in his coat, addressed Pule, who hadn't touched a glass despite the Captain's offer. "What do *you* suppose we are?" he asked.

The question seemed to take Pule aback. "A club," he stammered, looking at Godall, then glancing quickly away. "A scientific organization. I'm a student of alchemy and phrenology. I've read of Sebastian Owlesby. Very interesting matter."

Pule chattered on nervously in an unfortunately high voice. Jack was doubly insulted—first at the mention of Dorothy, now at the mention of his father. He'd have to pitch this Pule into the road. But Godall got in before him, waving his free hand and thanking Pole for his interest. The Trismegistus Club, he said, was an organization devoted to biology, to lepidoptery, in fact. They were compiling a field guide to the moths of Wales. Their discussions could be of no use to a student of alchemy. Or of phrenology, for that matter, which, insisted Godall, was a fascinating study. They were awfully sorry. The Captain echoed Godall's general sorrow, and Hasbro instinctively arose and showed Pole the door, bowing graciously as he did so. A silent moment passed after Pule's ejection. Then Godall stood, pulled his coat from its hook, and hurried out.

St. Ives was astonished at Godall's so quickly and handily ejecting Pule, who was, to be sure, not at all the right sort, but who might have been well intentioned. There could be little harm, after all, in his praising Owlesby, though Owlesby's experimentation was not entirely praiseworthy. In fact, when he considered it, St. Ives wasn't sure what part of Owlesby's work Pule had such admiration for. None of the rest of them could enlighten him. No one, apparently, knew this Pule.

Kraken peeked out of the rear chamber, and Captain Powers waved him into the room. Godall and Pule were forgotten for the moment as Kraken, at the Captain's bidding, spouted the story of his months as a hireling of Kelso Drake, the millionaire, punctuating it with accounts of his readings into scientific and metaphysical matters, the deep waters of which he sailed on a daily basis. And what he found there, he could assure them, would astonish the lot of them. But Kelso Drake—nothing about Kelso

Drake would astonish Bill Kraken. Kraken wouldn't put up with the likes of Drake, not for all the money the man possessed. He gulped at his scotch. His face grew red. He'd been fired by Drake, threatened with a thrashing. He'd see who was thrashed. Drake was a coward, a pimp, a cheat. Let Drake get in his way. Drake would reel from it. Kraken would show him.

Had Kraken news of the machine, asked St. Ives delicately. Not exactly, came the answer, it was in the West End, in one of Drake's several brothels. Was St. Ives aware of that? St. Ives was. Did Kraken know which of the brothels it might be in? Kraken did not. Kraken wouldn't go into Drake's brothels. They wouldn't hold Drake and him at once. They'd explode. Bits of Drake would fall on London like a blighted rain.

St. Ives nodded. The evening would reveal nothing about the alien craft. He might have guessed it. Kraken was proud of himself, of the stuff he was made of. He launched suddenly into a vague dissertation on the backward spinning of a spoked wheel, then broke off abruptly to address Keeble. "Billy Deener," he seemed to say.

"What?" asked Keeble, taken by surprise.

"I say, Billy Deener. The chap who broke in at the window."

"Do you know him?" asked Keeble, startled. The Captain sat up and ceased drumming his fingers on the countertop.

"Know him!" cried the slumping Kraken. "Know him!" But he didn't bother to elaborate. "Billy Deener is who it was, I tell you. And if you're sharp, you won't get within a mile of him. Works for Drake. So did I, once. But no more. Not for the likes of him." And with that Kraken reached once again for the scotch. "A man needs a drink," he said, meaning, St. Ives supposed, men in general and intending to do right by all men who weren't there to satisfy that particular need. Moments later he slid into a chair and began to snore so loudly that Jack Owlesby and Hasbro hauled him into the back room on the Captain's orders and arrayed him on a bed, shutting the door behind them on their return.

"Billy Deener," said St. Ives to Keeble. "Does it mean anything to you?"

"Not a blessed thing. But it's Drake. That much is clear. Godall was right."

Keeble seemed to pale at the idea, as if he'd rather it weren't Drake. A common garret thief was far preferable. Keeble poured out a draught of the scotch left in the bottle, then clacked the bottle down onto the tray just as Theophilus Godall slipped back in out of the night, easing the door shut behind him.

"I'll apologize," he said straightaway, "for my behavior—hardly the sort one would expect from a gentleman, which, I profess, is what I heartily wish myself to be considered." The Captain waved his hand. Hasbro tut-tutted. Godall continued, "I hurried Mr. Pule on his way only because I knew him. He is, I'm sure, ignorant of that. He meant us no good, I can assure you. He was in the company, day before yesterday, of your man Narbondo." He nodded at the surprised Captain. "The two struck me as being passing familiar with each other, and although we might have led this Pule along a bit to see what stuff he was made of, I thought the idea rather a dangerous one, in the light of what I perceive as a situation of growing seriousness. Forgive me if I acted in haste. My rushing away was merely a matter of desiring to confirm my suspicions. I followed him to Haymarket where he met our hunchback. The two of them climbed into a hansom cab and I returned with as much haste as propriety allowed."

St. Ives was stunned. Here was a fresh mystery. "Hunchback?" he asked, swiveling his head from Godall to the Captain, who squinted grimly at him and nodded. "Ignacio Narbondo?" Again the Captain nodded. St. Ives fell silent. The woods, apparently, had thickened. And as mysterious as the rest of it was the mere fact that Captain Powers was so well acquainted with Narbondo, quite apparently had an eye on the machinations of the evil doctor. But why? How? It wasn't a question that could be asked outright.

And Langdon St. Ives wasn't the only one mystified. Jack Owlesby, perhaps, was the one among them most seething with angry curiosity. He hardly knew the Captain, who, it seemed to Jack, carried on a strange sort of business for a tobacconist. He knew Godall not a bit. He was certain of only one thing—that he would marry Dorothy Keeble or blow his brains out. The slightest hint that she was being swept unwittingly into a maelstrom of intrigue made him fairly burst with anger. The idea of Willis Pule flattened him with irrational jealousy. His window, he reminded himself, overlooked the Captain's shop. He'd be a bit more attentive in the future; that was certain.

It was almost one in the morning, and nothing had been accomplished. Like a good poem, the night's doings had aroused more questions, had unveiled more mysteries, than they had solved.

The seven of them agreed to meet in a week—sooner if something telling occurred—and they departed, Keeble and Jack across the road, Hasbro and St. Ives toward Pimlico, Theophilus Godall toward Soho. Kraken stayed on with the Captain, unlikely to awaken before morning, despite the shrieks of the wind rattling at the shutters and whistling under the eaves. —◌

THREE

A Room with a View

THE OPEN DOORS of the public and lodging houses along Buckeridge Street were wreathed with smoke, which wandered out to be consumed by the London fog, yellow and acrid in the still air. A gaunt man could be seen through one such door, sitting at a table in a dim corner, half a glass of claret before him, boldly clipping the gats off counterfeit half crowns and filing the edges smooth with a tiny, triangular iron. He'd been at the work all evening, tirelessly tossing cleaned blue coin into a basket and covering the heap with a scattering of religious tracts that prophesied the coming doom.

He employed no agents to sell the coin, preferring to distribute it at greater profit and peril through the faithful—his lambs, who understood that they did the work of Shiloh, the New Messiah. They'd be very pretty coins, once they'd been plated, and would further the work of God. The time approached when such work would be at an end. The Reverend Shiloh had honed the coming of the apocalyptic dirigible to the day. Twice it had passed in the early morning, and the last time, more than four long years ago, it had appeared to him out of the west, emblazoned by a dying moon, its impossibly animate pilot peering down out of the heavens.

Historically speaking, the current years should have been fraught with disaster and portent, but recent months had little to recommend themselves beyond the crowning of the Queen as Empress of India and a spate of lackluster scuffling in Turkestan. The next month would see changes, though—that was certain—changes that would knock the Earth askew of its axis and which, Shiloh knew, would reveal the truth of his monumental birth and the identity of his natural, or unnatural, father. It had been twelve years since he'd confronted Nelvina Owlesby on a balcony in Kingston, a blooming trumpet flower vine behind her, shading the two of them from a noon sun. She, in a passion of momentary spiritual remorse, had confessed to him the existence and the fate of the tiny creature in the box. But she was unfaithful. She had recanted, and disappeared into the Leeward Islands that night, and for a dozen years he had waited to see if she had cheated him. The day was nigh. And in the long night to come no end of people would pay. In fact, it was easier to count the few who wouldn't, scattered here and there about London, passing out tracts, doing his work. Bless the lot of them, thought Shiloh, tossing another coin into the heap. "As ye sow," he said, half aloud.

More than anything he would have liked to see the ruination of those who had condemned his mother, who had diagnosed her dropsical when she knew that she carried within her the messiah; those who had denied his very existence, who scoffed at the notion of the union of woman and god. But they were dead, the filth, long years since—beyond his grasp. And so he carried out his father's work. He was certain that the tiny man in the box, the homunculus possessed by Sebastian Owlesby, had been his father. Let the doubting Thomases doubt. There was no end of gibbets in hell.

Idly he snipped a gat with a scissors, rubbing the slick coin with his fingers and gazing out toward the street at the hovering fog. If there was the slightest chance, the remotest chance, that the hunchback could resurrect his mother, Joanna South-cote, whose body lay beneath the loam of Hammersmith Cemetery—if the vanished flesh could be regained, revitalized…Shiloh clutched at his basket, overwhelmed at the thought. The act would be worth a thousand of Narbondo's animated corpses, a million of them. They weren't, after all, ideal converts, but they worked without protest, demanded nothing, and thought not at all. Perhaps they were ideal converts. Shiloh sighed. The last of his coins was clean.

He arose, wrapped himself in a dark and tattered cloak, drained the lees of his claret, and strode toward the tilting stairs, glaring into the eyes of anyone who dared to look at him. The floor above was dark save for the light of a single tallow candle that burned in a greasy wall niche. The smoke-blackened triangle that fanned away on the wall above it was the least of the filth that stained the plaster.

Shiloh kicked loose the stuck door, lifted the edge by the latch, and pushed it in a foot where it stuck fast, wedged against the floor. The room beyond was bare but for a heap of bedclothes in one corner, a tilted wooden chair, and a little gate-leg table leaning against the wall.

He stepped across to the street end of the room and pulled aside a bit of curtain. Beyond were the artifacts of a little shrine: a silver crucifix, a miniature portrait of his mother's noble face, and a sketch of the man Shiloh knew to he his father, a man who might have danced in the palm of the evangelist's hand, had Shiloh less an aversion to dancing and had the homunculus not been spirited away and set adrift these last fourteen years. The sketch had been done by James Clerk Maxwell, who, in the months he'd possessed the so-called demon, hadn't the vaguest notion what it was, no more than did the Abyssinian, dying of some inexplicable wasting disease, who had sold it to Joanna Southcote eighty-two years ago and had set into motion the creaking, leaden machinery of apocalypse.

Shiloh lifted the odds and ends in the shrine, raised a cleverly disguised false bottom, and dumped in the coin. Then he retrieved from the space a bag of finished, plated coin, replaced the floor and the relics, wrapped himself once again in his cloak, and left. He spoke to no one as he made his way toward the street, where a biting wind whistled across the cobbles and persuaded almost everyone to stay indoors. A single stroller, a portly man with a stick and eyepatch, limped along in his wake, his free hand pressed against his cap to stop the wind's stealing it. Shiloh paid him little heed as he hurried on into Soho.

———

THE HOUSES FRONTING the narrow stretch of Pratlow Street cramped between Old Compton and Shaftesbury were miserable with neglect. Whereas years and weather sometimes soften the faces of buildings, betraying some few elements of passing history, some reflection of the subtle artistry of nature, on Pratlow Street no such effects had been accomplished. Here and there shutters hung canted across windows perpetually dark, their slats held together by nails and screws that were little more than rusty powder. Some feeble attempt had been made once at enlivening a storefront with a gay color of paint, but the painter had had a singularly dull sense of harmony and had, moreover, been dead these past twenty years. His efforts lent the street an even more ghastly and barren personality, if only by contrast, and the glaucous paint, peeling and alligatored over seasons by what little sunlight penetrated the general gloom of the street, popped loose in brittle showers of chips after each rain.

It was perhaps more difficult to find a window pane that remained entire than it was to find one broken, and the only evidence of industry was in the removal of dirty glass shards from some few of the bottom floor windows and the subsequent dumping of the broken glass onto the cobbles of the street. The effort, perhaps, was made to facilitate the sort of person who would crawl in at the window rather than step in at the door, a purely practical matter, since few of the doors hung square on their rusted hinges, and were in such appalling disrepair as to dissuade any honest man from attempting to breach them.

The effect of the place beneath the pall of smoky fog was so unutterably dismal that the man turning onto it from Shaftesbury started in spite of himself. He pulled his eyepatch down toward his nose, as if it were merely a prop and he desired to hide a fraction more of the street from view. He looked straight ahead at the broken stones of the roadway, ignoring the jabber of a ragged child and the appeals of dark shapes hunched in the shadows of ruined stoops. Halfway down the street he unlocked a bolted door and hurried through, climbing the stairs of a dark, almost vertical well. He entered a room that looked out across an empty courtyard at another house, the windows of which were lit with the glow of gaslamps. Fog drifted in the air of the courtyard, now clearing, now thickening, swirling and congealing and allowing him only occasionally a view of the room opposite—a room in which stood a particularly stooped hunchback, peering at a wall chart and holding in his hand a scalpel, the blade glowing in the lamplight.

—◈—

IGNACIO NARBONDO PONDERED the corpse before him on the table. It was a sorry thing—two weeks dead, of a blow to the face that had removed its nose and eye and so mangled its jaw that yellowed teeth gaped through a wide rent, their gums shrunk back alarmingly. Animating it would accomplish little. What in the devil would it do if it could walk again, beyond horrifying the populace? It could beg, Narbondo supposed. There was that. It could be passed off by the charlatan Shiloh as a reformed sinner, far gone in the ravages of pox but walking upright by a miracle of God. Narbondo grunted with laughter. His limp, oily hair hung in wormy curls to his twisted shoulders, which were covered by a smock stained ochre with old blood and dirt.

Along one wall were heaps of chemical apparatus: glass coils, beakers, bell jars, and heavy glass cubes, some empty, some half-filled with amber liquid, one encasing the floating head of an enormous carp. The eyes of the fish were clear, unglazed by death, and seemed to swivel on their axes, although this last might have been an optical trick of the bubbling fluid in the jar. A human skeleton dangled by a brass chain in a corner, and above it, perched along a wide shelf, were oversize specimen bottles containing fetuses in various stages of growth.

Vast aquaria bubbled against the wall opposite, thick with elodea and foxtail and a half-dozen multi-colored koi the length of a man's arm. Narbondo gave up looking at the corpse and limped across to the aquaria, regarding the fish carefully. He reached into a tin bucket and pulled out a clot of brown, threadlike worms, knotted and wriggling, and dumped them onto the surface of the water. Five of the koi lashed about, mouths working, sucking down little clumps of worms. Narbondo watched for a moment the sixth carp, which paid no attention to the meal, but swam along the surface, gulping air, listing to one side, resting now and then until beginning to sink into the weeds, then lurching once more with a great effort toward the surface.

The hunchback snatched up a broad net from a box beneath the aquaria. He pushed back a glass top, stood atop a stool, and with a single, quick sweep, scooped up the struggling fish, tucked the middle finger of his free hand under its gill, and plucked the great fish from the water, slamming it down at once onto a cork board a foot from the head of the supine corpse and nailing its tail and head to the board with pushpins. The fish writhed helplessly for the few seconds it took Narbondo to slice it open. He paused briefly to spray it with fluid from a glass bottle, then scooped out its intestines and organs, clipping them loose and sweeping them into a box at his feet.

There was a sudden pounding at the door. Narbondo cursed aloud. The door swung open to reveal Shiloh the evangelist, cloaked and holding his leather bag. Narbondo ignored him utterly, prodding a little pulsing, bean-shaped gland out of the organ cavity of the carp. He nipped through the threads that held it, slid a thin spatula under it, and lifted it into a vial of amber liquid, corking it and setting it alongside the fetuses. He yanked the gutted carp from the cork board and dropped it into the box below, kicking it under the table. He leered up at the old man, who watched the affair with a mixture of wonder and loathing. "Cat food," said Narbondo, nodding at the dead fish.

"A tragic waste," said Shiloh. "God's children starve for want of bread."

"Feed the multitude with it, then," cried Narbondo, suddenly enraged at the old man's hypocrisy. He yanked the fish out by the tail and waved it in the air, droplets of blood spattering the floor. "A half-dozen more of these and you can feed Greater London."

Shiloh stood silent, grimacing at the blasphemy. "People hunger on this very street—hunger and die."

"And I," croaked Narbondo, "make them walk again. But you're right. It's a filthy shame. There but for fortune, and all."

He stepped across and unlatched the casement that faced the street, swung the window open, and tossed the carp onto the pavement below, the fish bursting in a shower of silver scales. Narbondo emptied the box of entrails after it, nearly onto the head of two men and an ancient old woman who had already begun to fight over the fish. Cries and curses rose from the street. Narbondo cut them short by slamming closed the window. He turned contemptuously and without warning snatched the leather bag from the old man's hand.

The evangelist cried out in surprise, caught himself, and shrugged. "Who is this poor brother?" he asked, nodding at the corpse.

"One Stephanus Biddle. Run over two weeks back by a hansom cab. Stomped to bits by the horses, poor bastard. But dead is dead, I always say. We'll enliven the slacker. He'll be passing round tracts with the best of them by midday tomorrow, if you'll kindly trot along and leave me alone." Narbondo emptied the bag onto the table, then inspected one of the coins. "You'd make money by selling these to the utterer yourself instead of making me do it. You pay dearly for my time, you know."

"I pay for the speedy recovery of God's kingdom," came the reply, "and as for selling the coin myself, I have neither the desire for risk nor the inclination to hobnob with criminals of that sort. I..."

But Narbondo cut him short with a hollow laugh. He shook his head. "Come round tomorrow noon," he said, nodding toward the door. And just as he did so, it swung to and in walked Willis Pule with an armload of books, nodding ingratiatingly at Shiloh and holding out a moist hand that had, a moment earlier, been fingering a promising boil on Pule's cheek. The evangelist strode through the open door, disregarding the proffered hand, a look of superiority and disgust on his face.

The window curtains in the second floor of the building across the courtyard slid shut, unseen by Pule and Narbondo, who bent over the still form on the table. A moment later the street door of that same building opened, and the man in the eyepatch tapped down the half-dozen stairs of the stoop and into the street, hurrying away in the wake of the receding evangelist, who pursued a course toward Wardour Street, bound for the West End.

—⁓—

LANGDON ST. IVES trudged along through the evening gloom. The enlivening effects of the oysters and champagne he'd foolishly consumed for lunch had diminished and been replaced by a general despair, magnified by his fruitless search for a brothel, of all things, that he wouldn't be able to recognize if he stumbled upon it. And he had undertaken the embarrassing errand on the advice of a man addled by years of drink, who understood the earth to wear a belt for the purpose of supporting a pair of equatorial trousers.

It was the song and dance of getting round to the nub that was most bothersome— of making the proprietor understand that it wasn't just casual satiation that he desired, that the act must somehow involve machinery—a particular machine, in fact. Lord knows what conclusions were drawn, what criminal excesses were even at that moment being heaped onto the doorstep of technology. More champagne would, perhaps, have been desirable. Halfway measures weren't doing the trick. If he were drunk, staggering, then his ears wouldn't burn quite so savagely at each theatrical and idiotic encounter. And if, in the future, he were to run across one of his would-be hosts in public, he could blame the entire sordid affair on drink. But here he was sober.

On the advice of a cabbie he approached a door with a little sliding window, knocking thrice and stepping back a foot or two so as not to seem unnaturally anxious. The door swung open ponderously and a jacketed butler peered out, slightly offended, apparently. The man looked overmuch like Hasbro, who St. Ives heartily wished were along on this adventure. The look on the man's face seemed to suggest that St. Ives, with his pipe and tweed coat, should be knocking on the rear door off the alley. "Yes?" he said, drawing the word out into a sort of monologue.

St. Ives inadvertently pushed at the false beard glued to his chin, a beard which perpetually threatened to succumb to the pull of gravity and drop ignominiously to the ground. It seemed firm enough. He smashed his eye socket around his monocle, squinting up his free eye and staring through the clear lens of the glass. He affected a look of removed and distinguished condescension.

"The cab driver," he said, "advised me that I might find some satisfaction here." He harrumphed into his fist, regretting almost at once his choice of words. What in the world would the man make of his desire for satisfaction? A challenge, perhaps, to a duel? A coarse reference to satisfied lusts?

"Satisfaction, sir?"

"That's correct," said St. Ives, brassing it out. "Not to put too fine a point on it, it was suggested to me that you could put me in the way of, shall we say, a particular machine."

"Machine, sir?" The man was maddening. With a suspicion that at once became certainty, St. Ives understood that he was being had on, either by the cabbie or by this leering, mule-faced man, whose chin appeared to have been yanked double with a tongs. The man stood silent, peering at St. Ives through the half-shut door.

"Perhaps you're unaware, my good fellow, to whom you speak." Silence followed this. "I have certain…desires, shall we say, involving mechanical apparatus. Do you grasp my meaning?" St. Ives squinted at aim, losing his monocle in the process. It clanked against a coat button on his chest. He shoved at his beard.

"Ah," said the suddenly voluble man in the doorway. "If you'll use the alley door next time. Wait a moment." The door eased shut. Footsteps receded. The door once again swung open and the butler handed out a parcel. St. Ives took it, and opened it unable to think of anything else to do, and found himself possessed of an eight-hour clock sporting a pair of iron gargoyles on either side of a cracked oval glass.

"I'm not," began St. Ives, when he was struck from behind and shouldered into the street. An old man in a cloak ascended the stairs, brushed past the butler and disappeared growling into the recesses of the house. The door slammed shut.

Damn me, thought St. Ives, staring first at the clock, then at the house. He began once again to ascend the stairs, but was struck halfway up with a sudden fit of inspiration. He turned, tucked the broken clock under his arm, fixed his monocle in his eye, and set out down the road, determined to give up his quest for the moment and to seek out a clock-maker instead. In his haste he nearly collided with a round, eyepatched man tapping along with a stick in the opposite direction.

"Sorry," St. Ives mumbled.

"S'nothing," came the reply, and in moments both had turned their respective corners, two ships passing, as it were, in the afternoon.

—◦◦◦—

The portly man tapped along, highly satisfied with the day's adventure. He entered Rupert Street, Soho, and disappeared into the open doorway of the Bohemian Cigar Divan, patting his pockets absentmindedly as if searching for a cigar. —◦

FOUR

Villainies

W ILLIS PULE ADMIRED himself in the window of a bun shop on King Street. His was an intelligent face, uncoarsened by sunlight or wind and with a broad forehead that bespoke a substantial cranium. His complexion, it was true, was marred by an insidious acne, one that beggared all efforts to eradicate it. Pumice, lye, alcohol baths, nothing had diminished it. He'd abstained from eating aggravating foodstuffs, to no effect at all. The red lump on his cheek shone as if it were polished. He should have powdered it, but he sweated so fearfully that the powder might simply have dribbled away.

He pried his eyes away from his skin and regarded for a moment his profile. He'd seen the dusty storage rooms of European libraries thought to be fables by the common breed of historian, and he'd knowledge of alchemy that the likes of Ignacio Narbondo hadn't dreamed of.

It was during his studies that he first learned of the existence of the homunculus. References to it and to its craft dated into antiquity, but were tiresomely sporadic and vague, linked by the most tenuous threads of pale suggestion until its sudden appearance in London some hundred years ago. The bottle imp, maligned by the dying sea captain whose log narrated the grim story of his own decline into madness and death, was without doubt the same creature sold some few years later to Joanna Southcote by an Abyssinian merchant, who followed the sea captain into an early and unnatural grave. There had been references to the thing's having power over life and death, over motion and energy, over the transmutation of metals. It had been the source of the inspiration of Newton, of James Maxwell, the ruination of Sebastian Owlesby.

A trail of horror seemed to follow the thing. All a matter of ignorance, Pule was certain. Ignorance and bungling had squandered the thing's powers, and Narbondo's losing it was the greatest blunder of all. But the hunchback was useful. They would all be useful to Willis Pule before he was through.

And the stakes seemed to be growing. His discovery that the thing in the box had disappeared after Sebastian Owlesby's murder had led him along a clear trail to William Keeble, and, he smiled to think of it, to his fetching daughter. And then there was the matter of a second box and the very interesting transaction between Owlesby and the West African Gem Company a month before Owlesby's death. If there wasn't profit to be made here, Pule was blind. Damn Keeble and the moronic Trismegistus Club. He'd deal with the lot of them.

Around the distant corner, right on time, came Dorothy Keeble, alone. Pule's chest heaved. His days of patient observation hadn't been for nought. His hand shook in his coat pocket, and he realized that he was breathing through his mouth. Fearing vertigo, he clutched at the iron railing across the window of the bun shop and attempted to whistle a nonchalant air.

"Dorothy Keeble?" he asked when the girl was some few feet off. Her jersey dress, dark red with ivory lace, narrowed in around her waist in such a way as to make Pule light-headed. She regarded him curiously. Her skin was almost transparent it was so light, and her hair, impossibly black, fell around her shoulders in loose curls. Pule was gripped by an urge to touch it, to fondle the skin of her face, which was, compared to his own, like ivory next to wormwood. He struggled to control himself. "We have, I believe, a mutual friend."

"Have we?" she asked.

"Jack Owlesby," said Pule, reciting his prepared lie. "We were in school together. Great friends."

"I'm pleased to meet you, Mr...."

"Pule," came the reply. "Willis Pule."

"Shopping for buns, were you, Mr. Pule? I won't keep you then. I'll tell Jack I've met you." She started on her way, and Pule turned to follow, suddenly angry at her obvious indifference.

"I'm a student of arcane history," he said. "I studied at Leipzig and Munich."

"I'm sure that's very nice," said Dorothy, hurrying along. "I'll tell Jack. He'll be happy to know what you've gotten up to. Don't let me interfere with your errand." She nodded at him and then ignored him. Pule fumed.

"Perhaps you'd take a cup of tea with me?"

"I'm terribly sorry."

"Tomorrow, then."

"I'm afraid not. Thank you awfully."

"Why not?"

Dorothy gave him a look of surprise. "What a question! Won't my simple refusal suffice?"

"No, it won't," said Pule, clutching at her arm. Dorothy jerked away, prepared to slam him with her bag. His skin seemed to be writhing as he stood gaping at her on the sidewalk. He sputtered, unable to speak.

"Good day to you," said Dorothy.

"You'll see me again," cried Pule at her back. "And so will your father." She walked on more quickly, not taking the bait.

"Wait until I've played my hand!" Pule yelled. And then he caught himself. He gasped for air and leaned against the brick of a row house. It would do no good to lose his temper now. He would wait. In time—soon—she would see reason. He glanced at a dark window. The sight of his face reflected in it didn't compose him. His hair was awry, and his mouth, normally sensitive and aloof, was contorted in a rictus of loathing. He made a conscious effort to relax, but his face seemed to have frozen in the grip of a maniacal passion.

A scrawny, half-hairless cat wandered out just then from under a fence. Pule stared at it, hating it. He snatched the cat up by the neck and held it kicking at arm's length. He sloughed off his jacket, letting it fall down his right arm to envelop the struggling beast, then shoved the burden under his arm and strode away in the direction of Narbondo's cabinet, visions of the cat dismembered flickering across his mind like etchings on a copper plate.

———

St. Ives let himself in through the front door of the Bertasso Hotel on Belgrave and tramped up two flights of carpeted steps to his room. The red wallpaper, rampant with stylized fleurs de-lis, almost made his hair stand on end. He despised the current fashion in gaudy furnishings. It was little wonder society was going to bits, surrounding itself as it did with fakery and ugliness. He was beginning to sound like his father. But it was entirely rational—empirical study would bear him out. Men were products of that with which they surrounded themselves. And men of substance could hardly spring from the cracker-box, factory-made trash they cluttered their homes and inns with. He was in a foul mood, he realized, having played the fool all afternoon. The clock gag probably wouldn't work. He'd be beaten by hired toughs. He'd have been wise to solicit the help of the Captain, who was, admittedly, far more worldly wise than he.

St. Ives himself had strayed within the confines of a house of prostitution only once, when, as a student in Heidelberg, he and a friend wandered into a questionable district after a night of revelry. He hadn't said a thing at the time. Drink had that effect on him—it thickened his tongue, made him mute. He'd merely grinned foolishly, and the grin had been correctly interpreted by an emaciated old woman in a robe who led him to a room full of painted women. "They were big girls," his artist friend had said, accurately and with an air of satisfaction as the two of them had returned to their flat near the university. "Yes," St. Ives had responded, able to add nothing to the pronouncement. Perhaps that was the key here. If he'd arrived drunk and leering on the doorstep of the house on Wardour Street he'd have been admitted. But now he'd have to depend upon masquerading as a clock repair man. The next morning would tell the tale.

He pushed his door open and discovered on a little circular table by his bed a wrapped packet, which had, apparently, just arrived by post. He tore it open and yanked out a sheaf of paper, a hundred fifty pages or so of foolscap, covered in tight handwriting—recognizable handwriting. He sat down hard on his bed. He held in his hands loose papers from the notebooks of Sebastian Owlesby, lost these fifteen years past. He looked at the envelope. It had been posted in London. But by whom? He leafed through it, page by page.

Kraken hadn't exaggerated. Not a bit. There were discussions of vivisection, of the animation of corpses. It was Owlesby's self-documented decline into madness—a day by day account, describing how, some few weeks before his death, he implored his sister to kill him. His experimentation had taken a nasty turn, urged on by the self-seeking Ignacio Narbondo until, in late May of 1861, his ghastly experimentation had required the brain of a living man, and Owlesby and an unnamed accomplice had clipped with a great pair of bone cutters the head from a sleeping indigent in St. James Park and borne the bloody prize home in a sack.

Owlesby had been certain that the homunculus had the power to arrest entropy, to reverse, at least superficially, the process of decay, and had managed to make use of it at the expense of his own sanity. The reasons for his decline were vague. He himself only half understood them. St. Ives became convinced that it was the decay of Owlesby's soul, the slide into deviltry, that hammered away at the shell of sanity until it began to crumble.

Moments of rationality had staggered Owlesby. Nell must kill him if he lapsed again into madness. He had withdrawn his interests in the West African Gem Company in the form of a great emerald, his son Jack's inheritance, and had prevailed upon Keeble to build a box to house it—a box almost identical to the lead-lined cube that held the homunculus.

The notebooks rambled. Owlesby fell into irrationality. There was mention of a second murder, of a brush with Scotland Yard, of the departing of the faithful Kraken, and in the end, of the necessity of obtaining certain glands—youthful glands, and of a nightmarish journey one foggy night into Limehouse. Narbondo had been pitched into the Thames and had swum to the opposite shore. Owlesby had prayed for the hunchback's death, but fate wasn't so kind. They'd have to try again, perhaps feed a stray child opiates. The entries stopped, a day before Owlesby's death. St. Ives was aghast. He dropped the papers onto the tabletop as if they had become suddenly the dried, scaly carcass of a rat. At the end of the journal, in a different hand—a woman's hand—were the words, "I gave the box to Birdlip," and nothing more.

St. Ives was astonished. The box to Birdlip! But which box? The emerald box? Which of the two, the emerald or the homunculus, was aloft in Birdlip's blimp? And who, besides himself, was aware of the whereabouts of the box? Narbondo, certainly, would be interested. St. Ives thought about it. The hunchback would kill to know where the box lay. What had all of this to do with Narbondo's lurking in the shadows of Jermyn Street opposite the Captain's shop? Nothing? Impossible. St. Ives knuckled his brow. Strange things were afoot—that was sure. But as compelling as the mystery of Birdlip's descent and of the blimp's alien passenger might be, St. Ives was doubly determined to find the thing's spacecraft. Failing that, he'd return to Harrogate straightaway to outfit his own craft with the oxygenator box that Keeble was even then working away on. First things first, after all. For fifteen years Birdlip had taken care of himself, and apparently, one of the boxes. He could be trusted to carry on. But it was a damnable and enticing mystery nonetheless. St. Ives packed tobacco into his pipe, held a match to it, and puffed away, the rising clouds of smoke bumping against the low ceiling and flattening in a general haze.

—∿∿—

"PEAS HERE!" SHOUTED Bill Kraken, thumping along down Haymarket toward Orange Street. It was nearing midnight, and Haymarket and Regent Street were mobbed with an assortment of revelers, made up in a large part by prostitutes on the arms of newly met gentlemen, strolling out of the Argyle Rooms and the Alhambra Music Hall. The weather was startlingly warm. A sort of trade wind had blown for three days and the air was tropical and clean. A wash of stars shone overhead, and the effect of the weather and the night sky and the coming of summer seemed to lend the city a breezy spirit.

Kraken could feel it himself. He was almost jaunty with it, and had sat into the morning reading metaphysics in a tuppenny copy of Ashbless' *Account of London Philosophers* that he'd bought at Seven Dials. The bugs that infested its spine had reduced a good portion of the Morocco cover to dust, but had, apparently, failed to reduce the philosophers themselves. Kraken had the volume in his coat pocket. There was no telling how many idle hours he would spend before he discovered what he sought.

An enormous full moon, harvest orange in the warm sky, hung directly overhead, grinning down on the throng and illuminating the white satin bonnets and silk coats of courtesans and the grimed faces of shoe blacks and crossing sweepers. Music tumbled out of cafes as if it were blood coursing through the arteries and veins of the West End, and even Kraken, tired from a day that had added miles to his wanderings about London, felt as if his own blood pulsed to the heat and noise of the moonlit street. The scent of coffee whirled past him in a rush, and four French girls, wide-eyed and chattering among themselves, stepped gaily from the door of a Turkish divan, nearly treading on his toes. For a moment he considered addressing them. But the moment passed, and just as well. What would they say to a pea pod man? Nothing he'd want to hear; that was certain. But the night was warm and almost magic with suggestion, and his mission on behalf of Langdon St. Ives and Captain Powers had been faithfully if unsuccessfully executed since eight that same morning.

He leered momentarily at his reflection in the unlit window of a hatter's shop and pulled the bill of his cap down over his left eye, considered it, then cocked it back onto his head with the air of a man satisfied with himself and faintly contemptuous of the rest of the populace.

Beside him materialized the face of a grinning woman. She'd been there for a bit, he was certain, but he'd just that moment focused on her. He winked. In his coat pocket, such as it was, lay a tin flask of gin he'd bought from a river vendor under Blackfriar's Bridge. It was two thirds empty—or one third full, from the long view. It was a good night for optimism. Kraken winked at the reflection again and held the bottle aloft, raising his eyebrows in a silent query.

The woman nodded and smiled. She hadn't, Kraken noticed, any front teeth. He poured a warm, juniper-tinged trickle down his throat, smacked his lips, and turned, handing across the flask. What were a few teeth? Several of his own were gone. She wasn't, taken altogether, utterly unappealing. That is to say, there was something about her, in the pleasant pudding of her cheeks, perhaps, or in the way she fleshed out the tattered merino gown she wore so thoroughly—almost as if she'd been poured into it from a bucket. A large bucket, to be sure. She'd seen better days in some distant time. But haven't we all, thought Kraken, buoyed by the Socratic wisdom of the London Philosophers.

The woman handed the tin back empty. She had a nose like a peach. She caught Kraken's forearm in the crook of her meaty elbow, pinioned it, and hauled him away down Regent toward Leicester Square in a fit of romantic cackling, lifting the lid from the pea pot and plunging her free right hand in among the peas. Let her eat, thought Kraken generously. He patted her arm.

"Do you know anything about the stars?" he asked, settling on an appropriate subject.

"Heaps," she replied, dipping once again into the peas.

"There aren't but a few," said Kraken, gazing heavenward. "Sixty or eighty. The heavens are a great mirror, you see. It's a matter of atmosphere, is what it is, of the reflected light of the sun, which…"

"A looking glass, is it? Heaven?"

"In a manner of speaking, miss. The sun, you see, and the moon…"

"A bleedin' looking glass? The moon? You've been suffern', love, haven't you?" She steered him down Coventry past a line of cafes. Kraken searched for the right words. The concept was a broad one for someone less schooled in the scientific and metaphysical arts than he. "It's astronomy is what it is."

"The moon's nothing but astronomy," agreed the woman, prying among her remaining teeth for a peapod string. "Drives them all mad." And she indicated with a sweep of her hand the entire street.

"The '*spiritus vitae cerebri*,'" intoned Kraken agreeably, "is attracted to the moon in the same manner as the needle of the compass is attracted toward the Pole." He was proud of his storehouse of quotations from Paracelsus, although they were quite likely wasted here. The woman gave his arm a squeeze, screwed her face up awfully so that her eyes seemed to disappear behind the flesh of her nose. She gouged Kraken playfully with a bent finger.

Before them was a lit house, on the door of which hung a sign reading, "Beds to be had within." Kraken found himself in a state of mingled desire and regret, being dragged up the stoop and finally into a darkened room little bigger than a pair of end to end closets. He stumbled against a disheveled bed and collapsed onto his face, hunched over his peapot, the lid of which sailed off and clattered into the opposite wall.

The bedclothes wanted perfume—a tubful. He pushed himself up. "Miss," he said, peering around him in the dark. A hand shoved him roughly down again. She was frolicsome, Kraken had to admit. "If you've a drop of something," he began, wondering if he were reading aright the heavy breathing and shuffling behind him. A warm hand grasped the thong round his neck, and, as he once again began to clamber onto his elbows, yanked the peapot from under him—rather roughly, he thought. He collapsed sideways when his right hand flopped up to allow the pot to travel beneath it. He'd have to be a bit more forward. That was the ticket.

He rolled over to have a look at his companion in the moonlight that illuminated the room. A woman of that stature…He anticipated a monumental revelation. But standing over him was a man, slowly chewing at his own tongue. He wore a black chimney pipe hat, smashed in and perched atop his head like a carton. Raised above it was the peapot. "Deener!" shouted Kraken. The peapot smashed down at him. There was a grunt of effort from the man in the hat. Kraken lurched aside, his left hand shielding his face. His wrist snapped down as the peapot glanced off it, smashing against his cheek. Kraken rolled into a wall. There seemed to be nothing in the tiny room but the villainous bed—nowhere to retreat.

The man swung the pot by its thong, bouncing it off Kraken's forehead and hauling it back for another blow. He seemed to be growling through his gaping mouth, and Kraken noticed in a moment of frozen clarity the droplets of spittle that flew in a little arc as the man's head was tossed backward with the momentum of his next swing.

Kraken regretted in a mist that his own head seemed to have stopped the peapot very handily, and through eyes suddenly blurred behind a wash of gore from his forehead, he watched with removed wonder as Billy Deener very slowly hauled a pistol from his coat, cocked it, and aimed it.

—◊—

THE BEING CONFRONTING a sleepy William Keeble chewed at the end of an ostentatious cigar. Keeble didn't half like his looks. He liked them less, in fact, than he had when

the man had visited him once before. It was his moneyed air that was so annoying—an air that betrayed a sort of Benthamite smugness and superiority, that exclaimed its own satisfaction with itself and its faint dissatisfaction with, in this case, William Keeble, who had been surprised in his nightshirt and cloth cap and so was automatically one down.

Kelso Drake hauled his cigar from his mouth and pried his lips apart into an oily, condescending smile. He wore a MacFarlane coat and a silk hat, both of which had left Bond Street, it was reasonably certain, not more than a week or so earlier. Keeble felt a fool in his cloth pointy-hat—doubly so, for he was wearing the one onto which Dorothy had embroidered a comical face, one eye of which was closer to the sideways nose than was the other, an eccentricity which gave the stitched countenance a look of cockeyed lunacy. Drake wouldn't understand such a thing. Keeble could see that in a glance.

The industrialist's desires hadn't changed. He was prepared to offer Keeble a sum of money—a substantial sum for the plans to the engine, for the patent. Keeble wasn't at all interested. Drake's eyes narrowed. He doubled the sum. Keeble didn't care for sums. Damn all sums. He was suddenly powerfully thirsty. On the hall table sat a walrus tusk, carved into the semblance of the beast that had sprouted it. Keeble imagined twisting its foolish head off and draining the peaty contents. But he'd have to offer Drake a glass, and he wasn't about to. Damn Drake and all of his affairs. He and his notion of textile mills run by perpetual motion engines made Keeble sick. The idea of a textile mill alone—a mill of any sort—made Keeble sick. Practicality in general made him sick, and the contrived practicality of Drake's utilitarian vision instilled in him an inexplicable mixture of indifference and loathing that made him long for his bed and a glass with which to chase Drake into nonexistence.

Drake champed at his cigar, rolling it in his mouth, his eyes squinting up into tight little slits. This wasn't, insisted Drake, merely a casual offer. He had certain methods. He had vast resources. He could exert pressure. He could buy and sell Keeble a dozen times. He could ruin him. He could this; he could that; he could the other. Keeble shrugged in his ridiculous cap. The clock on the wall opposite the hall table suddenly went off, pealing in a sort of doleful, leaden tone, utterly out of keeping with the little clockwork apes who charged grinning out of their lair in the interior and banged away with mallets at a bell-shaped iron octopus.

Drake frowned at it, recoiling slightly. The door opened behind him, and Dorothy, a troubled look on her face, stepped through, stopping in sudden surprise at the sight of the stranger's back. Keeble motioned with his eyes toward the stairway, but Dorothy hadn't taken a half step toward them when Drake turned, a broad smile betraying splayed yellow teeth. He clamped his mouth shut at the sight of Dorothy's involuntary grimace, and bowed slightly, flourishing his hat. "Kelso Drake, ma'am," he said rolling his chewed cigar from one side of his mouth to the other. "Very happy to make your acquaintance."

Dorothy nodded and proceeded toward the stairs, saying, "Pleased, I'm sure," over her shoulder, impolite as it seemed. Her father nodded his head toward the stairs in quick little jerks, stopping abruptly when Drake turned and looked at him quizzically. The questioning look turned once again into a leer, as if Drake's face naturally molded itself that way out of long practice. "What was I saying?" he asked the toymaker. "I was momentarily," he paused and pretended to search for a word, then said theatrically, "distracted."

"You were just saying good day," Keeble stated flatly. "You've got my answer. There isn't any room for discussion."

"No, I suppose there isn't. I'm averse to discussion anyway. A waste of time. Very pretty daughter, that one. Fetching, you might say. You have three days."

"I don't need three days."

"Thursday, let's say. And do stay sober. This business will require all of your efforts, regardless of the outcome." And with that, Drake raised his stick and neatly flipped Keeble's nightcap from his head, turned, and strode through the yawning door. He climbed into the interior of a waiting brougham and was gone.

Keeble stood still for a moment, as if his blood had solidified. His neck and face were hot. Without turning his head he plucked up the cap from where it had fallen on the hall table. A door shut with a bang upstairs. Had Dorothy listened? Had she witnessed Drake's departure? Keeble peered up the stairwell, a forced grin stretching his mouth. The stairs were empty. He pulled on the cloth cap and reached for the walrus tusk. There was really nothing to think about. Drake was all bluff. He wouldn't dare come meddling round again. He'd be sorry for it if he did. Keeble's hand shook as he drained the tusk, and he set it back onto the table uncapped. What did he care for threats? He stood thinking for a moment then tottered away up the stairs to bed. —⌒

FIVE

Shadows on the Wall

T HE DARKNESS OF Hammersmith Cemetery was complete. Not a star shone in the clouded heavens, and the occasional gaslamps that burned in oval niches in the block wall of scattered crypts illuminated nothing but a few befuddled moths that stumbled out of the night, fluttered woodenly around the flame, then disappeared once again into darkness. A heavy river fog lay along the ground, and the old yew trees and alders whose bent branches shaded the grounds dripped moisture onto the neck and shoulders of Willis Pule, who clumsily stamped on the backside of a spade. He pulled the collar of his coat around his neck and cursed. His doeskin gloves were a ruin, and on the palm of his hand below his thumb a blister the size of a penny threatened to tear open.

He looked at his companion's face. He loathed the man—doubly so for his poverty and stupidity. His face was expressionless. No, not entirely. There was a trace of fear on it, perhaps, a shimmer of dread at the sound of the sudden creaking of a limb overhead, at the sigh of rustling leaves. Pule smiled. He raised his left foot again and brought it down sharply on the spade. It slid off, and the shovel dug in a mere inch or two and canted to the side.

There was something utterly distasteful about this sort of work, but the evening's prize couldn't be trusted to the navvy alone. Why it was Pule who wielded the second spade and not Narbondo, Pule was at a loss to say. And if they were found out, there wasn't a bit of doubt that the doctor and his dogcart would be long gone and that Pule would be left to explain himself to the constable. One day that would change. Pule stared through the gloom toward Palliser Road, but the tree trunks just ten yards hence were dark and ghostly in the fog, and the feeble light of his half-shrouded lantern seemed to make the surrounding headstones and crypts even dimmer and more obscure than they were.

The sudden chiming of a distant clock, low and sullen through the fog, startled him. He dropped his spade. A smile danced momentarily on his companion's lips and eyes, and then was gone, replaced by the heavy dull slump of stolid indifference. Pule, seething, picked up his spade, grasped it near the base of its ash handle, and thrust it into the dirt. It penetrated several inches and then jammed to a sudden arm-chattering stop against a coffin lid. Pule grunted inadvertently with a thrill of pain and dropped the shovel.

His companion, never missing a stroke, skived the dirt from atop the box, his shovel glancing against the wood and scudding across it. The noises grated unnaturally loud in the heavy silence. Pule let his shovel lie. He'd had enough.

He bent once again over the headstone, cracked to bits years earlier and half covered with moss and mud. Fragments of it were gone altogether. The largest chunk, about a foot square, was cut with deep, angular letters that spelled out half a name—COTE—and below that the number 8 and the vine-draped shoulder of a carven skeleton. The remains of Joanna Southcote lay in the coffin. Her posturing son, himself almost a corpse, would be wild with joy over the worm-gnawed bones within. To Pule, one ruined skeleton pretty much resembled another.

The coffin seemed surprisingly solid for having sat so long in the ground; only one corner, from the look of it, had succumbed to the perpetual dampness and begun to rot, the wood separating into long, mushy fragments along grain lines. Pule's companion clambered in beside the head end, dug around until he could get a purchase on the edges, and heaved it upward.

Pule grappled with it in an attempt to lever it further up out of the hole. The bottom of the coffin was wet in his hands, and his fingers smashed into clinging bits of mud and bugs. The coffin began to slide from his grasp, then gave suddenly with a sharp crack, the bottom boards splitting down the center and collapsing outward in a spray of debris, covering the face of the man in the hole. From the bottom of the coffin slid the gauze-wrapped corpse, rolling stiffly onto its side. Folds of rotten winding sheet ripped away to reveal long strands of webby hair standing away from a mouldering face. Little pouchlets of flesh hung from cheekbones like fungus on a decayed tree. Ivory bone beneath shone faintly in the lamplight.

Pule stood transfixed, holding in either hand shreds of the rotted boards. The man in the open grave appeared to be strangling. His face, twisted away from the gaping countenance of the corpse, seemed about to burst. With monumental resolve, he twisted from beneath the ghastly remains, edged sideways a few precious inches, and very slowly and deliberately hoisted himself out of the hole. Then he walked calmly and stiffly away toward the lighted crypts, disappearing finally in the fog.

Pule stifled an urge to shout at him and another to shout for Narbondo. He unrolled a tarpaulin onto the ground, set his teeth, climbed into the hole and grasped the shrouded skeleton round its arms. He hauled it out and onto the canvas, folding the cloth around it, then set out toward the road, abandoning the light and dragging the tarpaulin across the wet grass, bumping over graves. The yawning black rectangle behind him vanished in mists through which glowed for a time the diffused yellow light of the veiled lantern.

—◦◦◦—

BILL KRAKEN AWOKE to find himself in a strange bed. There was no confusion about it. He didn't for a moment believe himself to be in his own shabby room. He felt pleasantly elevated, as if he were floating inches above the bed, and he heard a rushing sound in his ears that reminded him of a cold night he'd spent one early spring in a riverside cannery in Limehouse. But he wasn't in Limehouse. And he was quite pleasantly warm beneath a feather comforter the likes of which he hadn't seen for upwards of fifteen years.

His head felt enormous. He touched his forehead and discovered that it was wrapped like the head of an Egyptian mummy. And there was a dull ache in his chest, as if he'd been kicked by a horse. On a little table beside the bed lay a familiar book. He recognized the tattered ochre binding, a long fragment of which was curled back onto itself, as if someone had the nervous habit of rolling it between thumb and forefinger while reading. It was the *Account of London Philosophers* by William Ashbless. He picked it up happily and squinted at the cover. Dead in the center, as if it had been measured out, gaped a hole as round as the end of a finger. He opened the book, and page by page followed the little cavity down to a conical lead slug, its nose just touching the one hundred and eightieth page, stopping short of aerating a treatise on poetics. Kraken read half a page. It separated mankind into two opposing camps, like armies set to do battle—the poets, or wits, on the one side, and the men of action, or half wits, on the other. Kraken wasn't certain that the philosophy was sound, but the refusal of the bullet to damage the page seemed to signify he would have to study it further.

He knew, in a sudden rush, what bullet it was imbedded in the book. It was a miracle, the unmistakable finger of God. His peapot was gone along with his livelihood. He was sick of peapots anyway. He'd rather go back to hawking squids. If you were beaten in the head with a squid it didn't amount to so very much.

He was startled by a noise from somewhere else in the house. Through a half-open door he could see a second room, aglow with gaslight. A shadow appeared and disappeared on the wall, as if someone had stood up, perhaps from a chair, had gestured widely, and had sat back down or moved away from the lamp. The shadow belonged to a woman. There was her voice. Kraken had little interest in the woman's concerns, beyond a curiosity about the identity of his benefactors. A man spoke. Another shadow appeared, shrinking against the whitewashed wall, sharpening. A shoulder thrust into view, followed by a head—the head of Captain Powers. That explained the clay pipes, tobacco pouch, and matches next to the volume of Ashbless. The darkness beyond his window was Jermyn Street. He'd been saved by Captain Powers. And, of course, by the collected London Philosophers.

There was a sobbing in the room beyond. "I cannot!" the woman cried. The sobbing resumed. Captain Powers said nothing for moments. Then the weeping fell off, and his voice interrupted the silence. "The Indies." Kraken heard only a fragment. "St. Ives is all right." Mumbling ensued. Then, in a sudden, impassioned tone, almost shouted, came the words, "Let them try!" The woman's shadow reappeared and embraced the shadow of the Captain. Kraken picked up Ashbless and leafed through it idly, peeking up over the top of the spine.

Again the Captain hove into view, following his shadow, stumping along on his wooden leg. He fiddled with the latch of a sea chest that lay against the wall, then swung the chest open and began to haul out odds and ends: a brass spyglass, a sextant, a pair of sabers bound together with leather thongs, a carved rosewood idol, the ivory head of a pig. Then out came a false bottom built of oak plank, as if it were a piece of the floor that lay below the chest. Kraken started. Perhaps it *was* a piece of the floor. The Captain bent at the waist, and the top half of him disappeared into the box, his left hand steadying himself on the edge, his right hand groping downwards. He straightened again. In his hand was a wooden box, very smooth and painted over with pictures of some sort. It was too distant and too much in shadow for Kraken to make it out.

"Is it safe here?" asked the woman.

"I've kept it these long years, haven't I?" said the Captain staunchly. "No one knows of its existence but you, now, do they? A few days, a week—and Jack will have it." The Captain bent over the chest once again, hiding the box and replacing the oak plank. He very methodically slipped the odds and ends in atop it.

Kraken goggled in wonder. He felt like crying out, but doing so would be a dangerous business. There were vast secrets afloat. He was a small fish in very deep waters—almost a dead small fish. He lay Ashbless back onto the table, pulled the bedclothes up around his chin, and closed his eyes. He was tired, and his head ached awfully. When he awoke, sun played in through the sheer curtains beside his head, and the Captain sat beside him, quietly smoking a pipe.

———

WIND WHISTLED BEYOND the casement while St. Ives squinted into the little cheval glass atop his nightstand. The previous day's sun had, apparently, been blown out of sight, and the wind whipped the branch of a Chinese elm against the window as if the branch were rushing at him, enraged that it couldn't get into the room and warm itself at the fire. It was a disgraceful way to treat the scattering of green leaves that had just that week poked out in search of spring, only to find themselves flayed to bits by unfriendly weather.

St. Ives dabbed more glue onto the back of the mustache. It wouldn't do to have it blow off in a sudden gust. He worked his hair into a sort of willowy peak, and brushed his eyebrows upward to give himself the look of a disheveled simian, the same he'd worn the day before. Lord knew what the wind would do to it—heighten the effect, perhaps. He arose, pulled on a greatcoat, slipped Owlesby's manuscript under the carpet, picked up the newly repaired clock, and stepped out into the hall. He paused, thinking, and went back into the room. There was no use calling attention to the manuscript—better to make it seem trivial. He yanked it out from under the rug and set it atop the nightstand, shuffling the papers and laying his book and pipe atop them for good measure.

He trudged along in a foul humor with the repaired clock under his arm. It seemed as if precious little were being accomplished. He'd been almost a month in London, and still he hadn't glimpsed the fabled ship of the alien visitor. And he wasn't at all certain what he'd do if his mission to Wardour Street were successful. The ship, by all accounts, might be prodigiously old. It might be nothing but the rusted shell of the thing's craft—nothing but the decayed shadow of a starship, good for little beyond its value as a curiosity, turned, quite likely, into some loathsome article of bodily gratification. His own ship, after all, was almost spaceworthy. The oxygenator would be done any day. Perhaps that very night Keeble would bring it to the Trismegistus meeting. If so, St. Ives would be gone in the morning. He wouldn't suffer another fog. His efforts with the clock would either be satisfactory or they wouldn't be. He was bound for home either way.

It was true that odd things were in the wind—the business with Narbondo and Kelso Drake and poor Keeble. But St. Ives was a man of science first, an amateur detective second. The Trismegistus Club would get along without him. They could always summon him from Harrogate, after all, if his assistance were required to eradicate a menace.

He walked around to the rear of the house on Wardour Street and rang the bell. The half-timbered structure gave onto a small court in which languished a granite fountain, little more than a scummed pool with a rustling, water-spitting fish in the center. From the edge of the fountain a cobbled walk led out to a muddy alley. Some few windows stared blindly out onto the court curtained with blood-red fabric. The house must be dark as a tomb inside, thought St. Ives, an odd thing on such a day, blustery and clear as it was. He rang the bell again.

The alley seemed from St. Ives' vantage point to run along for a hundred feet or so before emptying onto a thoroughfare—Broadwick, perhaps. In the other direction it dead-ended into a stone wall, the top of which was studded with broken bottles. He heard a scuffling of feet. The door opened a crack and a meaty-looking woman peered out, white as a bled corpse. St. Ives jumped involuntarily, shaded his eyes, and realized that her face was covered in baking flour. Her nose was monumental and was somehow clean of flour, perched there like a mountaintop above a layer of cloud. She stared at him through fleshy slits, silent.

"Clock repair," said St. Ives, grinning widely at her. If there was one thing that gave him the absolute pip, it was perpetually frowning people who had no business being such. Stupidity explained it—the sort of stupidity that almost demanded a poke in the eye. The woman grunted. "I've repaired your clock," St. Ives assured her, displaying the item in question. She ran the back of her hand across her cheek, smearing the flour, then emitted a wet sniff. She reached for the clock, but St. Ives dragged it to safety. "There's the matter of the bill," he said, grinning even more widely.

She disappeared into the dark house, leaving the door ajar. It wasn't an invitation, certainly, but it was too good an opportunity to pass up. He stepped in, prepared to have a look about, but stopped abruptly, shutting the door behind him. There at a table, messing with a score of dominoes, sat a fierce-looking man, his beetling forehead spanned by a single unbroken stretch of eyebrow. There was something malevolent about him, something unwholesome, almost idiotic. A chimney pipe hat, dented and stained, sat on the table beside the dominoes. The man looked up at him slowly. St. Ives smiled woodenly, and the smile seemed to infuriate the domino player, who half rose to his feet. He was interrupted by the issuance of the mule-faced butler from whom St. Ives had received the clock. Roundabout him, filling the kitchen, hovered an atmosphere heavy with indefinable threat—a sort of pall of it that floated like a flammable gas, waiting to he set off.

"How much?" asked the butler, counting a handful of change.

St. Ives gave him a cheerful look. "Two pounds six," he said, holding onto the clock.

The man widened his eyes. "I'm sorry?"

"Two pounds six."

"A new clock wouldn't have been as much."

"The lens," said St. Ives, lying, "had to be pressed in a kiln. They aren't generally available. It's a complex process. Very complex. Involves tremendous heat and pressure. The damned things explode, often as not, and blow any number of men to bits."

"You picked up the clock yesterday," said the squinting butler, "and you're telling me this about heat and pressure and blowing up? There isn't an hour's labor here. Not half that."

"In fact," said St. Ives, brassing it out again, "that's what you're paying for. There's not another clocksmith in London who could have gotten it done so quick. I believe I mentioned it's a complex process. Great deal of heat. Exorbitant, really."

The butler turned in the middle of St. Ives' mumbling and stepped out of the kitchen toward the interior of the house. St. Ives followed him, hoping that the domino player would go back to his game and that the bulbous cook would abandon her diddling with meat cleavers and attend to her baking. The butler passed on into a long hallway, apparently oblivious to St. Ives having followed him. Voices drifted out from unseen rooms. A carpeted stairway angled away at his left.

St. Ives' heart thundered like a train in open country. He decided upon the stairs. He'd have a quick look and then pretend to have gotten lost. What would they do, shoot him? It was hardly likely. Why should they? He took the steps two at a time, still clutching the clock, and arrived at a landing illuminated by leaded windows beneath which sat a heavy, oaken Jacobean settle. A deserted hallway ran off in either direction revealing on the right a half-dozen closed doors, and on the left a stretch of plaster wall hung with brass sconces that lit, finally, a wooden balustrade that overlooked what appeared to be a broad, high-ceilinged room.

St. Ives hesitated. Would he ascend another flight, or have a look over the balustrade? A door slammed. He turned toward the stairs once again, putting a foot down silently on an immense copper-colored rose in the stair runner. Three steps farther up he paused, crouched, and, hidden by the angle of the ascending wall of the stairwell, peered between two turned posts. Along the hallway toward the landing below staggered the old man who'd elbowed him into the gutter the previous day. He seemed mesmerized, vacant, and he walked with a hesitating step. He wore a haggard, drawn expression in his eyes and in the downward curve of his mouth, as if consumed with remorse or disease— possibly both. His cloak was rumpled and stained, and his hand shook with palsy or fatigue. St. Ives at first was prompted to ask him if he needed support; he'd surely pitch down the stairs head first if he attempted to navigate them. But the atmosphere of evil and dread in the house pushed him deeper into shadow instead. This was no time for chivalry. The old man slumped against the wall, brightened a bit, and licked his lips. He wiped a hand across his face, leaving on it a feral, satisfied look.

St. Ives rose slowly to his feet, determined to see the top of the stairs. He'd left the kitchen a minute or so earlier; surely they'd be after him at any moment. Facing downward, he trod backward onto the step above, planting his heel firmly onto the top of someone's boot.

"There you are!" he half shouted, making a bluff, if idiotic, show of poise and half expecting to be precipitated down the stairs himself. He turned to look into the face of an incredibly fat man in a turban. Another man with a mangled arm stood on the stairs above. Both stared at him, or past him, St. Ives couldn't say which. He stared back, then looked over his shoulder to see if there was something ascending the staircase who was worth staring at with such fixed attention. There wasn't.

Their faces were ghostly, a lifeless white, faintly marbled with fine blue veins, and their eyes were fixed, as if made of glass. St. Ives could see a throbbing pulse beating along the neck of the turbaned man, slowly and rhythmically as if he'd been gilled in some earlier larval stage. A hand clamped onto St. Ives' arm, and the man took a step downward. Had St. Ives not stepped back himself, he would have been trodden on, and the two of them would have tumbled together down the stairs. His two companions said nothing, simply propelled him along. The old man, somewhat recovered, met them on the landing. He looked suddenly fierce, scowling at St. Ives.

"This is a nest of unspeakable sin," he croaked.

St. Ives smiled at him. "I've fixed this clock," he began, but the old man paid him little heed. He was obviously less inclined to listen than to speak.

"My children," he said to the pale men. Both of them gave him a little trilling bow, but neither spoke.

"I'm owed two pound six for my attention to the clock here," said St. Ives, suddenly wondering if the old man weren't some sort of proprietor. He seemed far too familiar with the place to be a mere customer.

"I know nothing of that," came the reply. "What do I care for clocks? For time? It's the infinite I pursue. The spiritual. Help me down the stairs, my child." The man with the twisted arm stepped at once out over the stairs—entirely past the first tread—and toppled forward, rolling end over end like a sack of onions, somersaulting off the bottom landing into the room below. He lay still. His companion in the turban seemed hardly to notice. The old man, however, grappled the banister with both hands and creaked down the stairs as hastily as he could, oh-oh-ohing. St. Ives and his captor followed mechanically.

The absent butler stormed into the room just then, followed by the domino player, who wore his tilted hat and carried a pistol in his right hand. The old man waved them off and bent over the still body. The injured man shook himself, rose unsteadily to his knees, then to his feet, and walked squarely into a long, drop-front desk against the wall, kicking one of the legs out from under it and going down once again, pulling the desk with him in a rattle of ink and blotters and books.

The front of the desk fell forward on its hinge and cracked him in the head. Loosed from the interior was an assortment of unidentifiable artifacts: an India rubber face with immense, yawning lips; a stupendous corset hung with whalebone stays and brass hooks; a leather halter of some inconceivable sort, attached to a block and tackle affair as if the halter and its wearer could be suspended, perhaps, from the ceiling; and finally, a brass orb the size of a grapefruit from which issued a quick spray of sparks. The butler and the old man went for the orb simultaneously, but the butler snatched it up first and pushed the other away, shoving the orb back into the fallen desk and slamming the front. What on earth, wondered St. Ives, bewildered as much by the unfathomable litter as by the flopping man it now entangled.

The butler, enraged, latched onto the back of the old man's cloak, preventing him from wading in to the injured man's assistance. "My child," the old man sobbed. "My boy! My sweet," But the sentence was left unfinished. Chimney pipe, his face frosted with a vacant grin, shoved his pistol into his coat, bent over, and hauled the man free, dragging him out of the tangle of paraphernalia by his ears, one of which tore off in his hand. He pitched it down in disgust and kicked his victim in the side of the head. No blood flowed from the rent where the ear had been severed. Mystery upon mystery. St. Ives began to think of the alley behind the house. He'd have to remember not to run toward the walled end. No one was going to give him two pound six for the clock. No one was going to give him anything at all for the clock. His hope was that the old man—whoever he was—and his two strange charges were of more immediate concern to the butler and his vicious accomplice, who, at that moment, was methodically beating the daylights out of the collapsed, half-earless man on the floor.

St. Ives disengaged his arm, surprisingly easily as it turned out, and edged around a chair, holding the heavy clock in both hands.

"Get these scum out of here," hissed the butler at the old man, who mewled helplessly, clinging to his turbaned friend for support. "Don't bring them here again. Your privilege doesn't extend that far."

The old man pulled himself straight, threw his cloak back theatrically, and began to rage in a hoarse voice about damnation. St. Ives disappeared into the kitchen to the sound of the butler's cursing and to shouts about who would teach whom about damnation. He sprinted for the back door, but met, halfway there, the leering figure of the toothless, befloured cook, slapping the flat edge of her cleaver onto her meaty palm.

St. Ives wasn't inclined to chat. He bowled straightaway into her, and the hastily swung cleaver rang off the iron case of the clock, dead between St. Ives' curled fingers. He shouted inadvertently, dashing the clock to the floor, and burst out into the yard, gathering the hem of his greatcoat with his right hand and leaping over the stile into the alley, loping toward its exit a hundred feet down, lost now in a swirl of fog. And as he ran, not daring to look back, thinking of the pistol in chimneypipe's coat, he understood suddenly who the bully was—could see that same malevolent face outlined in Keeble's garret window, a crack of lightning illuminating the rainy night sky around it. —◦

SIX

Betrayal

C APTAIN POWERS' SHOP was dense with tobacco smoke—indicative, thought St. Ives, of the serious nature of the night's business. Quantity of pipe smoke, he mused, was proportionate to the nature and intensity of the thoughts of the smoker. The Captain, especially lost in deep musings, puffed so regularly at his pipe that smoke encircled his head like clouds around the moon. They were waiting for Godall, who arrived, finally, laden with beer. St. Ives had told no one of Birdlip's newly discovered manuscript. There was too much to say to have to repeat the story singly to the members. At eight o'clock, by mutual, nodded consent, the Trismegistus Club came to order.

"I've gotten something interesting in the post," said St. Ives, sipping from a pint glass and waving the sheaf of foolscap at his companions. "Owlesby's notebooks, or part of them."

Keeble, who until that moment had seemed peculiarly withdrawn, bent forward in anticipation. And Jack, sitting beside him, seemed to slump in his chair, fearful, perhaps, that some unwholesome revelation about his unfortunate father was in the offing. Kraken shook his bandaged head sadly. Only the Captain seemed unmoved, and St. Ives supposed that his being unacquainted with Owlesby explained his apparent indifference.

"It would be easiest," St. Ives insisted, "if I merely read a bit of it aloud. I'm not the chemist or biologist that Owlesby was, and I was unacquainted with the peculiar hold that Narbondo apparently had on him. And that, I fear, was part and parcel of Owlesby's death."

Godall closed his left eye and squinted at him at the mention of Narbondo, and St. Ives was struck of a sudden with the peculiar notion that Godall's look reminded him of something—of being elbowed into the gutter by the nameless old man in the cloak. St. Ives ignored it and went on, warming to his task. "So here it is, in Owlesby's own hand. There's too much of it altogether, but the last pages are the telling part. He cleared his throat and began:

> "We've had the worst sort of luck all week: Short and Kraken brought in a fresh cadaver—took him off the gibbet themselves—and there he lies, full of fluids but stony dead despite it. If we can't find a carp and a fresh gland, he'll decompose before we have a chance at him. A terrible waste. My great fear is that all of this will come to nothing but murder and horror. But I've taken the first steps. That's a lie. First steps be damned. I'm halfway along the road by now, and it's twisted and turned so that there's no chance of finding my way back.
>
> "We ate in Limehouse last night. I wore a disguise—a putty nose and a wig—but Narbondo laughed it to ruin. There's no hope of disguising that damned hump of his. I'm not much given to metaphor, but it seems harder by the day to disguise my own loathsome deformities. It's the thing in the box, the bottle imp, that's caused it. If a man weren't tempted, he wouldn't fall.
>
> "But such talk is defeatist. That's what it is. Eternal life is within my grasp. If only we hadn't bungled so badly in Limehouse. The costerlad was a jewel—wicked as they come. It was a service to dispose of him. I swear it. Damn Narbondo's bungling. We've had a tremendous pair of shears forged at Gleason's (they think me a tree surgeon) and can snip the head off…"

"And there the narrative breaks," said St. Ives.

"He was interrupted, perhaps," said the Captain.

Godall shook his head. "He couldn't bear it, gentlemen. He couldn't write the word."

St. Ives glanced up at Jack, who would have been a child himself at the time that his father had written the confessions. He might be better off not hearing this. God bless Sebastian Owlesby's doubts, thought St. Ives. They're at once the horror of this and the man's only redemption.

"Read the rest," said Jack stoutly.

St. Ives nodded and resumed the narrative:

> "The lad couldn't have been above seven or eight. There was a fog, and not enough light from the streetlamps to amount to a thing. He was bound for the corner of Lead Street and Drake, I think, to buy a bucket of beer—for someone. For his father, I suppose. He had a pumpkin jack o'lantern, of all things, in his left hand, and the bucket in his right.

And we walked in shadow twenty paces behind. The street was silent as it was dark. Narbondo carried the shears from Gleasons. He'd have me along, he said, to share the glory, and would have none of my waiting in the alley off Lead Street in the dogcart, which was, I still insist, the only sensible course.

"So there we were, a musty wind cold as a fish blowing up off the Thames, and the mists swirling deeper by the moment, and the grinning face of that lit jack o'lantern swinging back and forth and back and forth, its face appearing with a dull orange glow at the top of the arc of each swing. There was a sudden gust out of an unsheltered alley, and the lad's lantern blew out. He disappeared in the night, and we could hear his bucket clank against the cobbles. Narbondo hopped forward. I grasped at his cloak to stop him—I could see the black truth in it, as that yellow, toothy light had blinked out in the pumpkin and on in my head—in my soul.

"I flew after him, and the two of us surprised the lad in the act of relighting his unlikely lantern. He stood up, a scream clipped off by those ghastly shears.

"The rest of it is a nightmare. That I fled out of Limehouse and returned in safety to my cabinet is testimony to the existence of dumb luck (if surviving that night of horror can be considered in any way lucky) and to the all-obscuring darkness and fog. It was as if evil had precipitated out of the solution of night and hid me like a veil. Narbondo wasn't so lucky, but the beating he took couldn't have been a result of his crime. If they'd known it, he wouldn't have been thrown into the river alive. Perhaps he was beaten because of what he is, like a man kills a rat or a roach or a spider.

"So the murder was for nought. And the corpse from the gibbet lies mouldering on the slab. Narbondo will go out again tonight—we must have the serum."

St. Ives paused in his reading to drain half a bottle of ale. The Captain sat paralyzed in his chair, stone-faced. "Owlesby," said St. Ives hurriedly, glancing first at the Captain, then at Jack, "was out of his wits. What he accomplished—what he committed—can't be justified, but it can be explained. And in the most roundabout way can be excused—forgiven at least if you keep in mind the poison that had trickled into his soul. His discussion of the night in Limehouse is accurate—to a degree. But he dissembled throughout. That much is clear. He admits it in the pages that follow. And as I say, what he admits is all the more horrifying, but it explains a great deal. Poor Nell!"

The Captain seemed to stiffen even more at the sound of the name, and he clanked his heavy glass onto the wooden arm of his Morris chair, brown ale sloshing out onto the oak. St. Ives noted that Kraken had disappeared during the course of the narrative. Poor man, thought St. Ives, searching for his place in the journals. Even after fifteen years, the story of his master's decline is too fresh for him. But the story had to be told. There was nothing for it but to go on, now that he'd launched out:

> *"I'm possessed by the most evil aching of the head—such that my eyes seem to press down to the size of screwholes, so that I see as through a telescope turned wrong end to. Laudanum alone relieves it, but fills me with dreams even more evil than the pain in my forebrain. I'm certain that the pain is my due—that it is a taste of hell, and nothing less. The dreams are full of that Limehouse night, of the toothy grin of that damned pumpkin, swinging swinging swinging in the fog. And I can feel myself decay, feel my tissues drying and rotting like a beetle-eaten fungus on a stump, and my blood pounds across the top of my skull. I can see my own eyes, wide as half crowns and black with death and decay, and Narbondo ahead with that ghastly shears. I pushed him along! That's the truth of it. I railed at him, I hissed. I'd have that gland, is what I'd have, and before the night was gone. I'd hold in my hand my salvation.*
>
> *"And when he failed, when he ran down East India Dock Road in that stooped half hop, terrified, it was I who set them on him. It was I who cried out to stop him. He little knows it. He'd outdistanced me. He was certain it was the police who shouted. And when they were beating him, by God I wasn't slack. I was a ruin of failure and loathing and rot as I stamped on his hands and helped those drunken toughs drag him into the river where it splashed and roiled and slammed itself to fury below the Old Stairs, and I hoped by God to see him dead and picked by fishes.*
>
> *"But there I was unlucky. Like the ghost at the feast, he came unlooked for in the night as I sat in a waking horror in the cabinet, listening to the thing in the box, staring, half expecting the tread of feet on the stair that would announce the end, the gibbet, the headsman's axe. There it came. Three in the morning it was. Deadly silent. A tramp, tramp, tramp on the wooden stairs—very heavy—and a shadow across the curtain. A hunched shadow. The door fell open on its hinge, and the hunchback stood against a scattering of lights and a clearing sky with such a look of abomination about him that his collapse onto the tiles failed to eradicate it—just as it failed to eradicate my horror of him.*

"I should have killed him. I should have slit his throat. I should have cut out the toad under his fifth rib and put it in a cage. But I didn't. Fear kept me from it. Fear, perhaps, of my own evil. It seemed to me that his face was my own, that he and I were one, that Ignacio Narbondo had somehow drawn part of me in with him, consumed the only part of me that had ever been worth a farthing, and had left a strengthless, malignant pudding, poured into the chair where I sat until half past ten the next morning.

"And it was thus that Nell found me. I begged her to kill me. I hadn't the courage to perform the deed. I pleaded. I told her of the costerlad. I swore at the same time that I was done with the pursuit—that the creation of life itself wasn't worth hell. But I lied. The thing in the box can arrest entropy. He can separate tepid water into ice and steam if he likes. He can animate the carcass of a rat dead in a wall for months and dance it about the room like a marionette. He's prodigiously old, and the only consequence of his thwarting time is his shrunken state. But he must be kept in a box.

"My fitting Keeble's clever structure with a screen through which I can communicate with him has led, I fear, to my own decay. I can't say just how I'm bartering with him—knowledge for freedom. If he could but find his craft and a pilot of sufficient stature to navigate it, he'd be lost among the stars in a moment. But that won't come to pass. Not until I have what I possess—we, I should say, for the hunchback has recovered, and swears he'll return to Limehouse tonight if the streets are hidden by a sufficiently thick blanket of murk.

"Shall I go with him? Will he draw me along at his heels like a shadow, a daily more fitting shadow? Or will nightfall bring an end to an unhappy and unnatural existence? I can't for the life of me imagine waking on the morrow. For the first time in my life the morning is cloaked in black."

"There's not much more," said St. Ives, putting a match to his cold pipe with a shaking hand. He'd read the manuscript earlier, but he couldn't quite get this last part straight in his mind. Nell, it was certain, was without guilt. Even more than that. She was heroic. That the act of shooting her brother, of spiriting away the damned homunculus and giving it to Birdlip to take perpetually aloft, had led to her exile and remorse was the greatest tragedy. Kraken had been correct. St. Ives dropped the manuscript to the floor. Somehow the act of reading it aloud had emptied him of any desire to look at it again.

The Captain heaved himself to his feet and stumped across to a tobacco jar, yanking off the lid and pulling out two fingersful of curly black tobacco, wadding it into the end of his enormous pipe. "I shipped with a Portagee once," he said, "who knew of that thing—that bottle imp. He'd owned it straight out for a month and went stark staring mad in a typhoon off Zanzibar. Traded it away to a Lascar on a sloop in the Mozambique Channel." He shook his head at the enormity of the whole thing and sat back down.

"And the rest of it," asked Godall keenly. "The other hundred-odd pages—are they as wild as this part?"

"Increasingly so," said St. Ives. "The decline was swift—almost from the day he bought the thing in the box."

"In the bottle," put in Keeble, staring out the window at the street. "There wasn't any box until I built it."

St. Ives nodded. "He seemed possessed by the thing—by the idea that he could not only animate the dead, an effect, I gather, that he'd discovered without the aid of the homunculus, but that *with* it, somehow, he could perpetuate life. Indefinitely. Perhaps that he could create life. And perhaps he *could.* There's a reference to a successful experiment in which he spawned mice from a heap of old rags, and another in which he revivified an old man from Chingford, who was dying of general paresis. Sheared forty years from him, according to Owlesby. All of it fearfully alchemical, although, as I say, it's out of my province.

"He was certain that the spacecraft belonging to the homunculus was in London, and he hoped to find it in order to sell it, as it were, to the damned creature in exchange for power over death and time. Whether his decline into madness and debasement was a result of scientific greed or of slow poisoning due to contact with the homunculus is impossible to say. Even Owlesby, obviously, didn't know.

"Apparently Owlesby was jealous of owning the thing to the point of refusing to let Narbondo at it. Nell's absconding with it must have infuriated the hunchback. She snatched the secret of life out of his hands, as it were, and gave it to Birdlip..."

"Who in a matter of weeks might well drop out of the skies on us," said Godall.

The Captain frowned. St. Ives nodded.

"Well," said Keeble, topping off his glass from an open bottle of ale, "this is all a very sad business, very sad. If I were asked, I'd say meet the dirigible when it lands— and I'll bet my ape clock it touches down on Hampstead Heath where it launched— and snatch the box. Between the lot of us such a thing would be nothing. Then we tie it into a bag full of stones and drop it off the center of Westminster Bridge when the river's in flood. The box isn't tight, I can attest to that. Regardless of the thing's powers, it's got to breathe, hasn't it? It's not a fish; it's a little man. I've seen it. We'll drown it like a cat, if only to keep it out of the clutches of this humpback doctor." Keeble paused, his chin in his hand. "*And* for what it did to Sebastian. I'll kill it for that. But there's no use, really, hashing over this Limehouse business. It's water under the bridge is what it is. Nothing more than that. And murky water too. So I'll just change the subject for a moment here, gentlemen, and call your attention to the date. It's Jack's birthday is what it is, and I've got a bit of something to give him."

Jack blushed, disliking, even among friends, being the center of attention. St. Ives grimaced in spite of himself. Perhaps he shouldn't have been waving Sebastian's memoirs about so freely. On his son's birthday, for God's sake. Well, this was the Trismegistus Club, and the ends they pursued would lead them along grim paths—there was no doubt of that. There was nothing to be accomplished by pretense and timidity. Better to clear the air with the truth straightaway. Far better to do that than to hide things and make them seem even more despicable and terrifying by doing so.

St. Ives wished, though, that he had known it was Jack's birthday so as to have some trifle wrapped up. But he could remember no one's birthday—not even his own most of the time. Keeble produced a square parcel about the size and shape of a jack-in-the-box. St. Ives was fairly certain he knew what it was, that he'd witnessed the rising of its clockwork cayman not too many days past.

"A toast to young Mr. Owlesby," said Godall heartily, raising his glass. The rest of the company followed suit, giving Jack three cheers.

From the shadows of the back room, Kraken raised his own glass—or flask, rather, which was two-thirds empty of gin. It seemed to Kraken to be perpetually in that state. How it could be more often empty than full was an utter mystery. Kraken hadn't delved particularly widely into the mathematics, and so he was willing to admit that there were forces at work on his gin that he couldn't yet fathom. He'd be after them though. He'd seek them out. Like beans in a bottle, he said to himself. Facts were nothing more. And mathematics were facts, weren't they? Numbers on a page were like bugs on a paving stone. They looked a mess, scurrying around. But they were a matter of nature. And nature had her own logic. Some of the bugs were setting about gathering supper—bits and pieces of this and that. Lord knew what they ate, elemental matter, most likely. Others were laying out trails, hauling bits of gravel to build a mound, measuring off distances, scouting out the land, all of them here and there on the pavement—a mess to the man ignorant of science, but an orchestrated bit of music to...to a man like Kraken.

He wondered if someday he couldn't write a paper on it. It was...what was it? An analogy. That's what it was. And it must, thought Kraken, explain the business of disappeared gin in a flask. The beauty of science was that it made things so clear, so logical. The cosmos, that was what science was after—the whole filthy cosmos. He smiled to think that he understood it. He'd only just run across the word in Ashbless. He'd seen it a hundred times, of course. Such were words. You were blind to them for years. Then one reached out and slammed you, and bingo, like lit candles in a dark room, it turned out they were everywhere—cosmos, cosmos, cosmos. The order of things. The secret order, hidden to most. A man had to get down on his knees and peer at the paving stones to see the bugs that hurried there, navigating about their little corner of the Earth with the certainty of a mariner setting a course by the immutable patterns of the stars.

A thrill shot up his spine. He'd rarely seen things so clearly, so...so...cosmically. That was the word. He shook his flask. There was a dram or so sloshing in the bottom. Why the devil *was* it more often empty than full? If a quantity could be poured in, the same quantity could be poured out. He'd filled it that very morning down at Whitechapel—brim full. But it hadn't stayed full for a half hour. It had been mostly empty all day. Hours of emptiness. And if it weren't for the bottle of whisky under the bed, he'd be powerfully dry by now.

Kraken grappled with the problem. It didn't seem fair to him. Like bugs, he reminded himself, screwing his eyes shut and imagining a scurrying lot of number-shaped bugs on a piece of gray slate. It didn't seem to do any good. He couldn't quite apply the bugs to the problem of the flask. He squinted through the open door into the room beyond.

He'd spent the last half hour with his hands over his ears, pressing out the sad business of Sebastian Owlesby's memoirs. He knew it all well enough—too well. He drained the flask, reached under the bed, and drew out the whisky. He was a gin man, truth to tell, but in a pinch...

Young Jack was waving some sort of box. Kraken squinted at it. He was certain he'd seen it before. But no, he hadn't. Here came some sort of business from inside—a beast of some sort, and tiny birds. The beast—a crocodile apparently tore at one of the birds, gobbled it up, then sank out of sight. Kraken puzzled over it, unsure, exactly, of the purpose of it. He sat for a moment, knuckling his brow, then got up off his bed and edged across to the open door.

Off to his left was another, dark room—the room where lay the sea chest. His heart raced. There was a tumult of talk and laughter as everyone gathered round Jack's birthday present, Keeble's engine. Kraken sidled into the dark room, drawn by bleary curiosity. He stubbed his toe into the chest before he saw it, grunting in such a way that he was certain would turn heads in the outer room. But no heads turned. Everyone, apparently, was far too keen on the marvelous toy.

Kraken bent over the chest, running his hands over the front until he found the flat, circular iron hasp. He fiddled with it, not knowing entirely how the mechanism worked and uncertain, even, what in the world he was after—certainly not the emerald. He'd have to be silent as a beetle. It wouldn't do to be heard. Lord knows what the Captain would think to see him rummaging in the chest. The hasp snapped up suddenly, rapping across Kraken's knuckles. He shoved three fingers into his mouth. They'd suppose him a common thief, of course. Or worse—they'd suppose he was in league with whomever it was they were at odds with.

Light from the rooms without lay feebly across the contents of the trunk. Kraken rummaged through them, shushing them to silence each time they rattled and swished, and shushing himself for good measure. He shoved his head amid the objects, which he'd managed to push to either side of the trunk. The cold brass of the spyglass pressed his cheek, and the smell of oak and leather and dust rose about his ears—very pleasant smells, in fact. It would be nice to remain so, his head buried like the head of an ostrich among fabulous things. He could easily have gone to sleep if he weren't standing up. He could hear blood rushing through his head—ebbing and flowing like the tides, as Aristotle would have it—and in among the general roaring of it he could just hear something else, a voice, it seemed, coming from somewhere very far away.

He puzzled over it, aware that the gash on his forehead had begun to throb. He couldn't for the life of him determine what to do next. Why am I standing here with my head in the chest, he asked himself. But only one answer was forthcoming: strong drink. Kraken smiled. "Whisky is risky," he said half aloud, listening to his voice echo up out of the chest. He was mad to drink whisky. Gin didn't do this to a man—make a fool of him. He was suddenly desperately afraid. How long had he been here, stooped over the chest? Was the room behind him filled with the faces of his friends, all of them stretched with loathing?

He extricated his head slowly, careful not to start an avalanche of nautical debris. In his hands he held the hidden box. A thrill of fear and excitement rushed along in his veins, washing away all rational thought. There it was again—the voice, tiny and distant, as if someone were trapped, perhaps, in the wall. He could understand none of it. He wasn't sure, suddenly, that he wanted to understand it, and was smitten with the wild certainty that the voice spoke from within his own head—a devil.

He was possessed. He'd read Paracelsus. It struck him at once that this was almost certainly a matter of Mumia, that the woman who'd lured him to the den where he'd been beaten was a witch. She'd used him, sensing that he was burdened with Mumia from the bodies he'd carted about London in the night. The sins of his past were rising like spectres, pointing at him. He shook with fear. It was *more* whisky he required, not less. He silenced the tiny voice, clacking his teeth to shut out the noise, then leaped in sudden horror as the noise turned into a fearful shouting.

He banged down the lid of the chest and jumped clear. The outer room was a tumult. That's where the noise had come from! Kraken peered around the doorjamb, only to lurch back into the comparative safety of the dark room. Kelso Drake stood without, in the open doorway of the shop. He'd come at last. Having Kraken beaten and shot hadn't satisfied him. He'd come to finish the job. Kraken pressed back into the room, bumping against a closed window. He unhooked the latch, swung it open, and crawled out across the sill and slid into the mud of the alley, where he lay breathing heavily. He stood up, casting a glance over his shoulder at Spode Street, then loped away toward Billingsgate. In a few hours the thronging crowd at the fishmarket would hide him and his prize from his enemies. —⁂

SEVEN

The Blood Pudding

T HE POUNDING STARTLED the lot of them, except, perhaps, Godall, who wore on his face a look of shrewd curiosity. The Captain took a step forward as if to open the door, but it was thrown open almost at once by Kelso Drake, who smiled benignly and bowed just a bit before striding into the room. Keeble leaped up and threw his coat over Jack's lap to hide the toy.

Drake stood just inside the door, bemused in his top hat, looking about him at the shop with the air of a man half baffled that such a place could exist, and coming to the conclusion that perhaps it could, given the quality of the men whom he confronted. He swept an invisible fleck from his sleeve and rolled his cigar to the other side of his mouth.

"Light?" asked the Captain, holding a long match aloft.

Drake shook his head and squinted.

"Rather eat them, would you?" said the Captain, tossing the match into a bowl. Keeble had gone white, a peculiarity Drake seemed to relish.

He smiled at the toymaker. "You've brought it along, then," he said, nodding at the half-concealed box in Jack's lap. "It's good when a man sees reason. The world is too full of unpleasantries as it is."

"The only unpleasantry I can see," cried the Captain, reaching beneath the counter, "is you! Get out of my shop while you can still stand on yer pegs!" And with that he hauled out a braided leather cosh the length of his forearm and slapped it against his ivory leg.

Drake ignored him. "Come, come, my man," he said to Keeble "Hand it across. The machine will do as well as the plans. My workmen can puzzle it out."

Jack was bewildered. Only Keeble and St. Ives entirely understood. St. Ives groped beside his chair for the neck of an empty ale bottle. Here was a dangerous man. It quite likely wouldn't come to blows—that wasn't Drake's way. But the man who'd tried to purloin Keeble's plans was quite clearly the domino player on Wardour Street. They'd best all be cautious. Who could say what sorts of ruffians waited in the shadows outside?

125

"You've had my answer," gasped Keeble, shaking visibly. "It hasn't changed."

"Then," said Drake, removing a chewed cigar from his mouth, "we'll attempt coercion." He stood silently for a moment as if lost in thought. The rest of the company was frozen, waiting for Drake's pronouncement. But instead of threatening and bribing, he merely tipped his hat and turned toward the door, saying, "*Very* pretty daughter, that Dorothy of yours. Reminds me of a girl I had once…Where was it?" He turned once again toward Keeble with a mock questioning look on his face, only to find Jack catapulting out of his chair in a fury. The box flew, Keeble caught it, and Jack punched wildly at Drake, missing the leering face by a foot and sprawling into Godall, who reached across and grasped the Captain's wrist as he brought the sap back for a swing that would have left Drake senseless.

The millionaire had feinted toward the door to avoid Jack's blow, and saw the Captain's attempt out of the edge of his eye. The look on his face changed from leering indifference and amusement to black hatred in an instant, and his hat flew off onto the floor as he checked his feint and jerked around in anticipation of the blow. But Godall still held the wrist of the furious Captain Powers, and Drake recovered, edging just a bit toward the door.

He stooped to retrieve his hat, but the Captain, stepping forward, pinned it to the floor with his peg leg, smashing the crown sideways, then, transferring the cosh to his free hand, flattened the hat utterly with three quick blows.

"That'll be your head, swabby, if I catch you around here again. You or any of your bully boys. You're filth—bilgewater, the lot o' ye, and I'd just as soon stamp you to jelly as look at ye!"

Drake's grin was palsied. He neglected the hat, turned as if to say one last thing to Keeble, but never got it out. The Captain, jerking free from Godall, struck Drake on the shoulder, sending him sprawling through the open door, then crouched, grabbed at the ruined hat and sailed it out into the night like a flying plate, banging the door shut in its wake. He opened a fresh bottle of ale and poured it into his glass with a shaking hand. Godall sat down. The Captain drained half the glass, turned to his aristocratic friend, and said, "Thanks, mate," then sat down himself.

Jack was once again possessed of the box. He stared at a spot on the floor, thoughtful or embarrassed. Keeble seemed to be staring at the same spot. St. Ives cleared his throat. "This business is growing curious," he said. "I don't half understand why we have to be embroiled in such complications—as if Narbondo's machinations aren't enough. Now we have two villains to deal with. We keep the weather eye on one of them, and all along the other one's watching us. And, I'm afraid, gentlemen, that I'll have to leave you to it—my train departs King's Cross Station tomorrow morning at ten sharp, now that the oxygenator is finished. I can't afford to put if off. Conditions are almost right."

Keeble waved his hand haphazardly. "Drake is my affair," he said, sighing, as if he were tired of the whole issue. "I'm not sure I won't sell him the plans. What difference would it make?"

"You can't!" cried Jack, half rising from his chair. And just as he shouted, lightning lit the road as if it were midday and thunder rattled the windows, rolling away for almost a minute before silence fell. Rain thudded against the panes and fell off, then thudded again in a wash of great drops that whirled and flew in the wind. The abrupt arrival of the weather seemed to furl Jack's sails, for he slumped into his chair and was silent.

"The lad is right," said Godall, knocking his pipe against the edge of a glass ashtray. "Drake mustn't have the engine. He'll have what's coming to him and no more—no less, I should say. I've come up with a bit of information myself that will, if I'm not mistaken, satisfy all of you on several points. Drake and Narbondo are in league, I mean to say. Or at least the one does business with the other. I've taken a room across from the doctor's cabinet—Drake has visited Narbondo more than once.

"I followed the two of them yesterday afternoon—not together, mind you; Drake wouldn't be seen abroad with Narbondo. They met at a public house in the Borough, a low sort of place that appears to have sprung up fairly recently. It's at the back of one of those old sprawling innyards, long ago fallen into disuse, and even the local people avoid it. There's rooms, as I say, that back up onto an alley; if there's a front entrance, I couldn't find it. Likely enough it lets out into the old inn, which is a regular warren of gables and attic rooms and hallways that seem to lead nowhere. If a man was scouting out an appropriate location for an opium den, he'd have to look no farther. There's not much else could be done with it, though.

"Anyway, these rooms—three of them with the walls broken out to connect them—let out onto the alley. There's not a window in the alley wall, and it's dark as pitch inside the pub and cold as a winding sheet. Luck for me, in fact, for I'm certain that if they'd gotten a glimpse of the cut of my clothes, they'd have seen me out."

Godall paused over his pipe and studied the street, where sluicing rain was illuminated every minute or two by ragged lightning.

"Damn, but there's a draft in here," said the Captain. He pulled a plaid muffler from under the counter and wrapped it round his shoulders, then waved his pipe at Godall as if to suggest he resume his story.

"There's nothing to identify the place but a curious sign over one of the alley doors, and not a hanging sign either, but painted on and ill done: The Blood Pudding, it reads. Inside were a dozen or more men, sitting idle, not speaking, mind you, and there weren't more than two of them had anything to drink. Even those weren't interested in their glass, although one kept peering at it as if there was something in among the bubbles to see, as if he *remembered* that there was something there he liked mightily once, but couldn't quite fathom it now. The odd thing about him was that he looked as if he'd been dead for a month.

"It wasn't just lack of sun, either. There was something unwholesome about him—about all of them, for that matter, that all the fresh air wouldn't undo. One stood up after consuming a quantity of the most loathsome-looking black pudding and walked face first into the wall before he got his bearings and set a course for the door.

"Kelso Drake appeared a quarter of an hour after the doctor, who was involved, at the time, in a meal consisting entirely of live birds—sparrows if my knowledge of the science of ornithology is not amiss. He caught and consumed them beneath a drape that hung to the floor. The nature of the meal was evident, for the peeping and chirping of the poor things filled the darkened room, and the rustle of their wings against the drape played against the crush and snap of tiny bones.

"Drake was taken aback, I can tell you, when the hunchback appeared from beneath the drape, chin bloodied, and a scattering of broken meats littering the table before him."

"By God," interrupted the Captain, standing up and peering toward the rear of the shop, "there's a window open that shouldn't be, or I'm a lubber." He stumped round the counter, lit a candle, and disappeared into the room that contained, since Kraken's visit, a half-emptied sea chest. His shout brought the rest of the club to their feet.

Gaslamps were lit and the window was pulled shut and bolted. On the floor lay the spyglass, the sextant, and two bits of oak plank. The Captain leaned into the chest, hauled out the pig and the sabers, and realized almost at once that the emerald box was gone. He slammed down the lid, threw the window open once again, and leaned out into the alley in a wash of rain. There was nothing to see in either direction when lightning obliged him by brightening the otherwise dark night. He turned to his companions, dripping rain from his beard, and gestured helplessly.

"Something stolen?" asked St. Ives, a rhetorical question, given the debris on the floor and the open window.

"Aye," gasped the Captain, reeling toward a chair. But he hadn't sat for more than a few seconds before he was up and through the door, bursting into Kraken's empty room with a shout. Silence met him.

"Kraken gone!" cried St. Ives.

"The scoundrel!" shouted the Captain.

"Perhaps," said Godall passionlessly, "Kraken himself has been the *victim* of this thief. Let's not leap to conclusions."

"Of course," said St. Ives. "I'd bet on the man with the chimney pipe hat here—the one who was after the plans to the engine. I ran afoul of him myself recently. I'd bet he's sneaked in through the casement, robbed the Captain's sea chest, and done Kraken a mischief while Drake waylaid us in the shop; that's the ticket." St. Ives stroked his chin, squinting at nothing. "But why should this man *necessarily* be in league with Drake?" He addressed the question to no one, but Godall answered.

"Drake owns the house in Wardour Street—one among many. Your disguise, by the way, was a bit on the transparent side. It was me that you bumped into after you'd gotten hold of the clock."

The captain interrupted the exchange by raging back into the room waving the almost empty whisky bottle that he'd found under Kraken's bed. "This is all stuff!" he cried. "The man's made off with...with my property, and no mistake. There was no man in a hat—not here anyway, kidnapping and robbing and clattering about under our noses. No, sir. Kraken's made away with the goods, and there's no use making up tales."

"What goods?" asked St. Ives innocently. "Perhaps we can recover them."

The Captain fell silent and collapsed into an armchair, precipitating a little cloud of dust. He buried his face in his hands, his anger apparently having fled in the face of St. Ives' question. The Captain looked up at his congregated friends, started to speak, glanced at Jack, and shook his head. "Leave me to think," he said simply, and slouched deeper into his chair, suddenly tired and old, his face lined with a hundred thousand sea miles and the weather of countless storms and suns.

Thunder rattled the casement, and the party gathered coats and hats and silently made ready to bend out into the road, awash now with the downpour. Jack and Keeble had only to cross Jermyn Street to shelter, but St. Ives and Godall had a longer journey. The muffled chiming of a clock could be heard through the pelting rain—two doleful peals that announced, more than anything else, the certainty that hansom cabs would long since have ceased to run, and that the walk, for St. Ives at least, would be a long and sodden one. The Bohemian Cigar Divan lay some half mile to the northeast, and the Bertasso in Pimlico some three miles to the southeast, but for six blocks or so, Godall and St. Ives walked together down Jermyn toward Haymarket. Neither was satisfied with the half-finished meeting. Things were hotting up at such a rate that action of some sort seemed to be called for. Biweekly meetings over cigars and ale would avail them little.

St. Ives knew almost nothing of Godall, who was a friend, after all, of Captain Powers, and a fairly recent friend at that. But he was very apparently enmeshed in the Narbondo-Drake business, for reasons St. Ives couldn't entirely fathom. Why, in fact, was Captain Powers so thoroughly caught up? Why *had* Narbondo been seen lurking outside the smoke shop, if indeed he had? Mightn't he as easily have been watching Keeble's house, on the advice, possibly, of Kelso Drake? It was a muddle. St. Ives longed to be back in Harrogate, in among his scientific apparatus, consulting the staid and learned Hasbro, losing himself in matters of physics and astronomy. He could almost smell the steel chips and hot oil of the workshop of Peter Hall, the little Dorchester blacksmith who constructed the shell of the riveted spacecraft. There were too damned many distractions in London, all of them chattering for attention.

Just that afternoon had come a note from the Royal Academy. On the strength of his knowledge of Birdlip and his friendship with the uncommunicative William Keeble, St. Ives was invited to participate in certain programs involving the study of Birdlip's amazing craft, which had been sighted over the Denmark Strait far up into the thin air of the stratosphere, swinging toward Iceland on a course that would sweep it once again over Greater London. Balloon expeditions were being readied in Reykjavik. There was some reason to suppose that the blimp would ultimately descend, perhaps land, in the following weeks. It might—who could say?—simply fall onto London rooftops like a spent balloon. The professor's particular knowledge might be useful. And didn't he know the toymaker William Keeble? Couldn't he, perhaps, use his influence…Coersion is what it was. Here was an offer. St. Ives was to drop his work, lock the doors of his laboratory, send Hasbro to Scarborough on holiday. And in exchange, the Royal Academy would blink the ignorance and scientific prejudice out of their eyes, clean their spectacles, and agree to consider him something more than a lunatic eccentric. Why couldn't a man just go about his work? Why must he always be meddled with? Who were all these people and what legitimate claim had they on his time? None whatsoever. The answer was clear as Whitefriar's crystal, and yet hardly a day went by but what some new mystery, some complaint, some request arrived by post, some odd man in a chimney pipe hat peered in the window at you, or some long lost Kraken appeared from an alley and stole an unidentifiable trifle from a friend on the most rainy, miserable night imaginable—a night that had no business showing its face in the spring, for God's sake.

Water ran from the brim of his felt hat like a beaded curtain and soaked his overcoat until it hung heavy as chain mail. And just when it seemed that the rain was letting up and the shadows of recessed doorways in the houses across the street began to solidify out of the mists, there was a bang and a crash as lightning lit the rooftops and ripped to bits whatever forces had attempted to subdue the weather. Wind tore along the street, whipping the tails of St. Ives' coat and sending a chill through him that anticipated a lancing deluge from the starless heavens. The two men bounded as one into the doorway of a dark house where the wind and wet, at least, were powerless to follow.

"Deadly night," said St. Ives blackly.

"Mmm," responded his companion.

"What do you suppose Kraken stole?" asked St. Ives. "Not that it's my business entirely—although I have a sneaking suspicion it will become so. It's just that the Captain seemed so peculiarly…devastated by it. It's a side of him I hadn't seen."

Godall lit his pipe in silence, his tobacco, pipe, and equipment miraculously dry. St. Ives didn't bother to look at his own. Some day soon—after the successful launching of the starship—he'd set about developing a method to maintain the suitability of his smoking apparatus in even the most hellish weather. There would then be one thing in his life that was a certainty, a constant, that the forces of weather and chaos couldn't make a hash of.

"I'm not at all sure how you've managed to keep your tobacco and matches dry," said St. Ives, "but my own are muck."

"Here, my good fellow," responded Godall graciously, offering his open pouch. "Thank the Captain. It's his blend. Superior to any of my own, too." The two men passed matches and tampers back and forth, speaking in low tones and watching the rain roar down in an undulating, opaque curtain, looking for all the world as if the gods were shaking out a cosmic sheet in the roadway.

"I'm not certain about the theft," said Godall, when St. Ives' pipe was alight. "But you've struck it, I believe, when you said it would become our business soon enough. The next few days should clarify things a bit, though I suppose the clarification will only serve to deepen the mystery." Godall paused for a moment, contemplating, then said: "Those men at The Blood Pudding. They were dead men; I'm certain of it. And your reading Owlesby's narrative tonight is what makes me so certain. What do you think, as a man of science? *Could* Owlesby animate corpses?"

"If Sebastian said he could, he could' said St. Ives simply. "How he did it I'm not certain, but it involved enormous carp, somehow. And the homunculus, the thing in the box, wasn't required. It's apparent from the manuscript that Owlesby thought the creature would reveal the secret of perpetual life to him. Keeble thought so too. What Keeble did, or attempted to do with engines—that's what Owlesby would accomplish with human beings. That's partly the explanation of poor Keeble's decline—forgive me for speaking in such terms of a friend. But damn me, this business has been ruinous. Keeble blames himself, I think, for having put Owlesby onto the creature in the first place, for having filled Owlesby with notions of overcoming inertia."

"And so his caring for Jack these past fifteen years," said Godall.

St. Ives shrugged. "Yes and no. He'd have done so anyway. The two of them—Keeble and Owlesby—were close as brothers, and Winnifred Keeble and Nell were inseparable since childhood."

"Ah, Nell," said Godall, nodding almost imperceptibly. "Well, there it is. The men at The Blood Pudding were dead men, as I say, and I watched Narbondo through the curtain two days ago revive what was almost certainly a corpse. How Drake ties in I'm not yet sure, although it seemed to me that the two were striking some sort of bargain there—that Narbondo, perhaps, supply Drake with an army of willing workers—workers the union bosses would find unmalleable. Or, now that I listen to your story of the creature in the box, it's entirely possible that Drake hopes to purchase that which Owlesby desired, and that he believes Narbondo can deliver it. In which case the landing of this blimp might prove interesting, if, as you say, the hunchback understands the homunculus to be aboard."

"He might," said St. Ives. "But there's no certainty of it."

"And there's another party," said Godall, "a self-styled messiah with the unlikely name of Shiloh, who has a hand in the mystery. He's the one, by the by, who brushed you into the roadway moments before I appeared in front of Drake's brothel."

"The old man!" cried St. Ives, the nature of the two empty-eyed men on the stairs and of the bloodless ear suddenly revealed. St. Ives shook his head. It was a loathsome business, but none of it precluded his being on the express next morning, bound for Harrogate. He'd be only hours out of London, in terms of clock time, and could sail back in, pistol in hand, as it were, when the call came. In figurative terms, thank heaven, Harrogate was light years distance from London, and such was the nature of reality that he'd traverse the miles in little over four hours, and eat cakes and tea in a room hung with star charts and bookshelves.

"When do you return?" asked Godall suddenly, breaking in upon St. Ives' reverie.

"I hadn't thought much along those lines," the physicist admitted.

"I rather fear for this man Kraken," said Godall. "He struck me as being a bit mad, in truth, but harmless. He'd best be found. And I'm fairly certain that none of us are man enough to see this thing through alone. It's collective spirit that will defeat them in the end."

"Of course, of course." St. Ives' pipe went dead. There was truth in Godall's statement. He could, he supposed, return to London in a few days. A week, say. Five days at most. Three. But fixing a date rather kicked the daylights out of his cakes and tea. "If anything develops," St. Ives heard himself saying, "send for me straightaway and I'll be on the next train. If I don't hear from you before, I'll see you next Thursday evening at the shop. These meetings should become a bit more regular, at least until after the appearance of Birdlip."

"Agreed," said Godall, who thrust out his hand, then hunched out into the slackening rain, striding away toward Soho, the words "Good luck" sailing back over his shoulder on the breeze. St. Ives set out down Regent, hunkering into his coat, wondering how it was that Godall seemed so damned efficient, how he wore so well his mantle of intrigue and mystery.

—⁓—

THE LIGHTS OF the Captain's shop glowed far behind them now through the rain, and just visible in the dimly lit room was the Captain himself, unmoving. The Captain's mind was empty, the dust beaten out of it by this sudden enormity. What would he say to her? To Jack? If he found Kraken…he didn't know what he would do. It was his own damned fault, waving the box around with Kraken supposedly unconscious in an adjacent room. Suddenly he stiffened. It wasn't just the box, after all, that had been waved around. He checked his pocket watch. Quarter past two. Three o'clock would tell the tale.

The hands crept round, the Captain regarding, then casting away, plan after plan. At five until three, he listened for the knock at the door. He paced from room to room, dimming lights, watching through windows. No one came. The streets were silent but for the patter of rain. Perhaps she'd forgotten, was asleep. Four o'clock passed, five. At ten next morning, when a customer rapped at the mysteriously locked door of the shop, he awakened Captain Powers, who leaped up with a shout from a dream involving dark London alleys and stooped criminals. He couldn't face the day alone; it was time to take Godall completely into his confidence. —⁓

EIGHT

At the Oceanarium

A T THE SAME time that St. Ives was reading Owlesby's manuscript to the horrified members of the Trismegistus Club at Captain Powers' shop, Dr. Ignacio Narbondo and Willis Pule were driving along Bayswater Road toward Craven Hill. The sky was a confusion of whirling clouds, and there was no moon to brighten the road, which was still dry despite little flurries of raindrops that swept along now and then, causing the two men to yank the collars of their coats tighter around their necks. The dome of the oceanarium lay like the shadow of a humped beast through the oaks, the broad branches of which shaded the road and adjacent park into utter obscurity.

The hunchback reined the horse in some twenty yards from the darkened building, keeping well back into black forest shadows. Nothing stirred but the sighing wind and the occasional patter of drops. The stone block of the oceanarium was gray with age and stained brown in long vertical streaks from the rusting iron sashes of banks of windows. Vines crept up along the wall, trimmed around windows and just beginning to leaf out in the late April spring. No lights shone from within, but the two men knew that somewhere a groundskeeper kept watch, poking around, perhaps, with a lit candle. Pule hoped the man was asleep, and his dog with him. He crept along the edge of the building, below the windows, listening and watching and trying each window in turn, ready to cut and run at the least sound.

He grasped the stile of a broad double casement and pulled, the window creaking suddenly open in a little spray of rust chips. Pule hauled himself up, scrabbling for a toe-hold against the stones and scraping the skin from his palms against the rough sill. He fell back onto the ground, cursing under his breath the night, the windows, the invisible watchman and his dog, and especially Doctor Narbondo, comfortably seated on the dogcart, ready to flee at the sound of trouble. Pule knew, though, that he'd be loathe to leave without the carp, that Joanna Southcote would become nothing but a decomposed heap of dust and bone without the fish—that her doddering son wouldn't be half so anxious to part with his bag of half crowns if their attempt were a failure.

Pule struggled once again at the window—physical strength had never been his forte. He loathed it, in fact. It was beneath him. All of this intrigue was beneath him. Soon, though, when certain things were in his possession…He found himself teetering across the sill, flailing his legs to keep from tumbling back into the night. He tipped head foremost, finally, into the building. His coat caught on the hinge of the casement, yanking him sideways. Debris clattered from his pocket onto the stone floor, and he cursed as he saw dimly his half candle roll under the iron legs of an aquarium. Moments later he was on his hands and knees on the damp floor groping for it.

The air was heavy with the musty smell of aquaria and water weeds and the salt that crusted glass lids from the fine spray of aerating bubbles. Pule could hear the echoing drip of leaking tanks and the swish of bubbles on the otherwise still surface water. Thank God his matches hadn't fallen into any puddles. He crouched behind a vast, rectangular stone monolith that supported a bank of dark aquaria, and he struck a match against the rough granite in a hiss of igniting sulphur. He lit the piece of candle, shoving it securely into a brass candlestick.

He peered out into the dark room, satisfied that he was alone, then rose and stepped across toward the opposite wall.

He'd strolled about that same room a half-dozen times in the last month, familiarizing himself with the islands of aquaria, with the position and nature of closets of nets and siphons and buckets and the great rubber bladders that fed air into the tanks. He found a broad, square net and a step stool, and hauled them both back to the center of the room. He waved his candle at a long, low tank, squinting through the glare off the glass, and watching the silver bulk of the great carp that lay barely moving among the rocks and weed.

Pule stepped to the top of the stool. He pulled the glass top from the tank, then climbed down and laid it carefully onto the floor. In a moment he was up again, dipping his net into the aquarium. He'd have to be quick. If the carp were given half a chance, they'd sail to the far end of the tank and hover there, and he'd have to move the stool to get at them. That wouldn't do. He carefully yanked out clumps of weed, dropping them with a wet splat to the floor. There was no use tangling his net in them. It was a carp he wanted, not a mess of greenery. Through the dim water he could see one resting on the gravel, a mottled koi some foot and a half in length. That would suffice. Pule eased the net into the water, wiggled it to unfurl the corners, and with a sudden lunge, swept it down and over the tail of the sleeping fish, yanking it out of the water before it had a chance to awaken. He groped for its head, trying to hook a finger under a gill. Water splashed out of the aquarium, drowning the front of his coat.

The carp thrashed suddenly sideways, jerking away from Pule's hand. He lunged at it and cradled the fish in his arms, feeling the step stool canting over as he did so, aware, suddenly, of a light being trimmed behind him and of the barking of a dog.

"Here now!" came a startled voice as Pule and the fish toppled over sideways into a mess of sodden waterweeds. Trailing anacharis and ambulia, Pule wrenched at his fish, slamming it against the stone monolith as he rolled against it. The dog growled and snatched at his pantleg. Pule yelled obscenities, ululating madly at the dog and his master, hoping that the watchman—an old man with a game leg—wouldn't be quick to engage an obviously lunatic fish thief. More than that, he hoped that Narbondo would hear the ruckus and get his filthy cart under the window.

He kicked at the dog, clamped now to his pantleg, and managed only to drag it along behind him. Its master limped in, crouched and waving his arms, grappling after the dog as if worried only that Pule might make away with it as well as with the carp. Pule turned, thrusting the fish through the window—there was no way he'd clamber out holding it—and felt it snatched from his grasp. A spray and wind-driven rain stung his eyes as he boosted himself through, easily now, with the dog yammering behind him and the window sill some two feet lower now that he was inside the building rather than outside.

The distance to the ground, however, was greater than he'd calculated, and he found himself, after a wild, thrashing tumble, twisted in the mud between the stones of the building and the wheel of the dogcart. Narbondo cursed wildly, Pule cursed him back, and the watchman clutched his little dog, staring inertly at the two from beyond the open window. The hunchback whipped up the horses as Pule grabbed the sideboard and attempted to hoist himself in, kicking furiously to keep up with the horse and falling in a heap into the bed, face first into the carcass of the great fish.

He was tempted, as he lay gasping and panting, smearing scaly ooze from his cheek with a coat sleeve, to pummel Narbondo senseless with the carp, to pitch the hunchback off the front of the dogcart into the way of the galloping horse, to run across his twisted face with the ironclad cartwheels and leave him to die in the muck of the roadway. But his time would come.

Pule picked up the heavy fish and thrust it into a half keg splashing with water barely deep enough to submerge it. He swam it back and forth to revive it, but the thing was half crushed. The water, in seconds, was a mess of blood and scales.

"He's done!" shouted Pule at the back of Narbondo's bouncing head.

The hunchback shouted something, but his words were lost in the wind. The cart bumped and clattered and raced between the shadowy oaks, careering this way and that into potholes, nearly going over into a ditch, the mud flung up from the horse's hooves spattering around Pule, who hung on with both hands now, satisfied to leave the fish to its own devices. With a suddenness that catapulted Pule into Narbondo's back, the horse reared to a stop, and in an obscuring deluge of rain, the hunchback clambered over into the back of the cart, jerking his head at Pule.

"Take the bloody reins!" he gasped, throwing open his bag and reaching into it for a scalpel. He paused long enough to fetch Pule a shove that nearly pitched him out of the wagon, and in moments they were away again, Pule driving, the doctor laying the fish open with his blade, muttering under his breath some foul business that was swept behind them on the wind and rain and so lost entirely on Pule, who was filled with his own black thoughts of death and revenge.

—*ovo*—

THERE WAS NO real reason to be fearful, quite likely. No one suspected her, yet she felt inclined toward darkness, toward venturing out at night. She prayed that the day would soon come that it would be otherwise. Captain Powers would see to it. She hurried along down Shaftsbury, hidden in her cloak through nearly empty streets, her umbrella slanted back to stop the wind and rain that drove in from the west. The weather was far too evil for anyone to be out and about, and the hour was late—long after midnight.

Her life of homeless wandering in the Indies, later for three years in South Carolina, and now, finally, in London—the home of her youth, but now the place in the world most laden with suspicion and fear—had been relieved by her having found a single, safe port, as it were, an island in a sea of tumult and remorse. Captain Powers was that island—a man whom nothing could unsettle, who with his peg leg could stride purposefully across heaving decks awash with seawater, could steer a course by the shadows of stars.

But what particularly suited her was the Captain's obvious regard for curious, frivolous things. In the midst of his stony practicality was a litter of oddities— his ridiculous smoking leg, a monkey-tooth necklace he'd been given by a jungle explorer in exchange for two bottles of scotch, a pipe that burned tobacco and emitted soap bubbles simultaneously, a collection of trifles purported to yield good luck and which he carried in his pocket. "I've got my luck in my pocket," he'd say, displaying the collection to a stranger, holding in the palm of his hand a red and black bean from Peru, a red agate marble, a tiny ivory ape, and an Oriental coin with a hole drilled through it. He could tell a good deal about a man, he would say, by the nature of the man's reaction. William Keeble and Langdon St. Ives had seen the value of it all straight off.

Nell surprised herself to discover that she was only a block from the smoke shop. It was early yet, for her particular purposes; the club meeting would no doubt still be underway. If she could find some sort of shelter she would wait. It wasn't at all unpleasant watching the rain if one were safely out of it. She turned down Regent Street toward St. James Park. She'd sit under the shelter and imagine a concert, or imagine nothing at all, but simply hide behind the darkness and the weather.

The rain diminished briefly, and the night fell silent but for her footfalls on the pavement. Behind her, clattering slowly down Regent, came a brougham, its lamp burning yellow in the misty night. It drew up apace and slowed, as if shadowing her. The driver, however, paid her no heed, but slouched on his seat looking ahead of him, the ribands slack in his hands, as if the vehicle were simply slowing down out of inertia. Nell forced herself to ignore it. She pulled her cloak around her and strode on. She debated whether to turn off down the approaching alley or simply to pursue her way toward the park.

She glanced quickly at the brougham. Two men rode within, both of them staring out at her. One was lost in shadow, the other clearly visible. He seemed to have half a face. There was something in their staring that convinced her, suddenly and completely, that they weren't casually passing in the night, that they were watching her. She stepped into the narrow alley, tall buildings tilting away above and blocking the driven rain, which ran down the wall to her left, glazing the dirty bricks and flowing into a muddy stream along the center of the alley. She lifted her skirts and ran. There was nothing to do but splash through the ankle-deep rill. She would double back when she found the end of the alley—run all the way to Jermyn Street if need be. The hour didn't matter. Better to betray herself to friends at the Trismegistus Club than to summon a constable. But better anything than to fall into the hands of whoever it was rode in the brougham. And she had a fair idea who it was.

She never reached the end of the alley. It seemed to hover there beyond a haze of rain some hundred yards distant, yellow in the glow of a gaslamp. Into the feeble light stepped a tall figure in a cloak, bent as if with age. Nell slowed, then stopped. She was suddenly certain that whoever it was stood in the mouth of the alley, it wasn't Ignacio Narbondo. She'd been wrong, but the realization didn't console her. She slowed to a walk, shrinking against the comparatively dry right wall, brushing the moist bricks with the back of her hand. She turned. Lightning cracked the sky above her, turning the two slouched figures that approached her into dense shadows against a suddenly bright backdrop. No windows, no doors presented themselves. The walls were steep and slippery. The night was one tumultuous rush of noise, and her scream was lost in a roar of thunder which threatened to collapse the sheer, crumbling bricks above her.

A hand closed over her mouth, then jerked away when she hit it. She stumbled and kicked blindly at the man in the cloak. He cursed and stepped back in a little bent hop, as if he were infirm with age. She blinked rainwater out of her eyes, unwilling to believe what she saw. But it was so. A moment of weakness years earlier had come round to betray her.

A ruined face, the face of a corpse, loomed in front of her, and the ghoul who possessed it slammed her back into the wall, dragging a flour sack over her head. She spun around, tumbled onto her knees in the water, and was jerked upright and pushed forward.

The stumbling, blind walk back down the alley to the waiting brougham seemed endless, yet didn't afford her time for thought. Her second scream was silenced by a jerk at the sack that had been twisted round her neck. She saw two rapid lightning flashes, and automatically, out of sheer numbness, counted the six seconds that followed. The thunder still boomed in the low skies when a hand was laid against the small of her back and she was precipitated into the brougham. She remained on her knees on the floor. She heard the click of the door latch and listened as the coach careered away into the rainy night to the sound of the wheezing, rattling breath of her two strange captors. She grappled with her memory in an effort to find an explanation of her fate. There was none. What she knew, Shiloh knew. She had been, those long years past, a briefly willing convert, who had confessed thoroughly and truthfully. But the knowledge she had revealed, of her guilt and of the whereabouts of the thing in the box, hadn't altered. She could be of no further use to him. Unless it was something else they were after. Would they attempt to use her against the Captain? Was it Jack's emerald they sought? She searched her mind. Had she revealed the existence of the emerald? She almost wished she had, for if they sought to meddle with Captain Powers through her, then they made a mistake—and she heartily wished, as the brougham jerked to a stop minutes later, that it was just such a mistake they'd made.

—*∿∿*—

DR. NARBONDO CARRIED the mutilated carp up the narrow stairs toward his laboratory above Pratlow Street, Willis Pule slouching along behind. The gland he excised was a pitiful thing, itself half ruined by Pule's clumsy foolery. He'd have to mug up some sort of show to satisfy the damned missionary—have Pule hook Joanna Southcote up to the ceiling and dance her like a marionette. The old man would be loathe to part with his money—worthless as it was—if he got no satisfaction at all. In fact, there was no telling what tricks the crazy old man mightn't be up to if his precious mother didn't rise from the slab.

Narbondo, his hands full of fish viscera, kicked the door open and stepped into his cabinet. The lamp above his empty aquarium was alight. Below it, his face half in shadow, stood Shiloh himself, gaunt, haggard, and dripping water onto the floor beside the slab. Dr. Narbondo could see that the old man was far from satisfied. Joanna Southcote wasn't an inspiring sight. She lay in a comfortable heap on the slab, partly disassembled, a rickety, fleshless, collapsed framework of dirt and dust and bones. Tangled wisps of hair were clotted with leaves. Her winding sheet lay in an ignominious heap beside the slab.

A dissecting board onto which was pinned an enormous, flayed toad had been swept from the slab onto the floor along with a sheaf of notes, an ink bottle, and a quill pen. The hunchback dropped the fish onto the slab and pulled off his dripping greatcoat in silence. Shiloh, stupefied with anger, threw out his arm and shoved the fish onto the floor atop the toad. The violence of the effort jarred the slab, and the bones of his mother danced briefly, her jaws clacking shut as if she were admonishing her clumsy son.

"She speaks!" cried the evangelist, lurching forward and grasping her forearm as if to entreat her to continue. Her hand fell off onto the slab. Shiloh stepped back in horror, covering his eyes. Narbondo grunted in disgust, turned to hang his coat on a hook. He stopped, a smile spreading across his face.

"Nell Owlesby," he said. "And after so many long years. What has it been? Fifteen years now since you shot your poor brother, hasn't it?" He paused momentarily and licked his lips. "A very pretty shot, that one. Straight into his heart. Knicked a rib going in and lodged in the left ventricle. Quite a mess. I worked on him for three hours after chasing you half across London, but I couldn't save him. I animated him, though, for a week, but he wasn't worth keeping. Lost his sense. Wept the day out. I cut him to bits, finally—used a piece of him here, a piece of him there."

Nell sat tight-lipped in her corner, staring at the rainwater that beat against the window. "That's a lie," she said finally. "I saw him buried at Christchurch myself. His bones are still there. My mistake was to not shoot you instead of him. I know that now. I knew it an hour after. But the deed was done."

"You're right, of course." Narbondo stooped to pick up his toad. He lay it on a table, repinning one rubbery leg that had fallen loose. He pointed then at the ruined carp. "Your mother's soul," he said, turning to Shiloh, "resides in this carp. It's been beaten. It's a pity, really, but it couldn't be helped. My assistant here pulverized it against a window sill. But it's worlds away healthier than this, eh?" He nodded at the skeleton before frowning just a bit as if not entirely satisfied with it. He stepped slowly across to the window, flung it open, and sailed the carp out into the night.

The old missionary leaped toward him, his cloak flying behind. Narbondo flourished his right hand in front of his face, as if he were a magician uncovering a palmed coin. Between his thumb and forefinger was the little kidney-shaped gland, glistening pink. He winked at the old man, who stopped abruptly. "This is worth two hundred fifty pounds." Narbondo squinted at it, holding it to the light.

"I'll trade you the woman for it," said Shiloh, smiling for the first time that evening.

Narbondo shrugged. "What do I want with her? She's a murderess. I haven't any interest in a murderess, have I?"

"You've been asking after her around the city for a month. You've offered, in fact, nearly twice that sum for news of her. I'm prepared to let her go at a bargain."

The hunchback shrugged. He turned to Nell, who sat as before, staring into the night. She had a faint idea of what brought the two villains together—what information Narbondo craved even after fifteen years.

"Where is the box?" the doctor asked abruptly.

"Ask the old man," Nell said. "He knows."

Narbondo spun round and faced the evangelist, who stood now with a look of satisfaction on his face. He shrugged. "This is," he said slowly, as if contemplating each word, "a matter of mutual gain, is it not?"

Narbondo started to speak, apparently thought better of it, and fell silent. Then, after a pause, said: "Where is the box? I want it. Now."

The old man shook his head. "I'll pay for services rendered. I've seen no services yet." Then, suddenly coming to himself, he gestured at the slab behind him. "Tonight," he said. "Immediately."

Pule groaned, slumping into a chair. Narbondo nodded, as if the request were simple enough, and plucked an apron from a hook, hissing at Pule to prepare for surgery.

"How…?" began Pule, but the hunchback cut him off with a curse. Shiloh backed toward a chair that sat opposite the fire, his face a mixture of reverence, satisfaction, and trepidation.

—◦◦◦—

THEOPHILUS GODALL HURRIED along through the rainy streets, listening to the receding footfalls of Langdon St. Ives, and pondering the strange state of Captain Powers, who had evidently suffered a loss of articles unknown to the rest of them. This business was difficult enough when the bits and pieces were apparent. When they were hidden, it grew frustrating indeed—interesting certainly, but frustrating.

He'd become accustomed to staying up nights. He hadn't any business to speak of, so he could afford to nod off in pursuit of a couple of hours of sleep in the morning. It was close upon two o'clock. The night and the weather would cover his lack of disguise. He puffed thoughtfully on his pipe, tapped his stick decisively on the cobbles, and set a course toward Pratlow Street, rounding the corner as a lit window midway down the block was thrown open and a cylindrical bundle sailed out, smashing to the pavement below, followed by a shout clipped off by the shutting of the window. Godall hurried along and bent over the thing in the street. It was a dead fish of indeterminate sort—its head and most of its body having been reduced to muck by its sudden collision with the roadway. Godall turned and strode away up the stairs into his bare, rented room, arranging the curtains so as to have his usual view of the cabinet of Ignacio Narbondo.

He could see, from his curtain, three men in the room, all of whom were familiar. Shiloh, the self-proclaimed messiah, exhorted the hunchback and his assistant. He seemed to be railing at them, and now and then Godall could make out bits of shouting over the wind and rain. The hunchback squirted yellow mist at a corpse on the slab—a skeleton on the slab—from a hand-held device fed by a coiled tube. A fire roared behind him in the grate. Encased within a heavy, glass, liquid-filled jar was a tiny object of some sort—too small to identify. Herbs burned in a stone chalice. The evangelist

collapsed to his knees in the semblance of prayer, and Narbondo, apparently treading on the old man's hand, stumbled and sprayed his yellow mist onto Pule, who staggered away retching. The hunchback paused to shout at the old man, who arose and stepped back a pace, out of the way of the window.

A fresh flurry of rain dimmed Godall's vision for a moment, but he squinted through it, focusing on the thing that lay on the slab. Surely, thought the tobacconist—surely the hunchback wasn't attempting to animate such a thing. But he was wrong. The machine generated mist that hovered in the air above the corpse. The chalice smoked. Narbondo fished out the business in the jar and, nodding to Pule, shoved it into something that resembled a garlic press and squeezed it into the gaping mouth of the corpse.

The old man fell hack, his hands covering his face. Narbondo pumped at the machine. The thing on the slab lurched once, a scattering of debris falling from its tangle of hair, and seemed to rise as if by levitation. The shouts of Narbondo were audible but were reduced by the windy rain to gibberish.

The body jerked twice, stiffened, and very slowly began to pull itself up onto the elbow of its handless arm, as if it would slide from its slab and walk, It turned its leathery head back and forth, blind, barely animate, an unholy, rusted machine. Its other arm rose and followed the swiveling head as it rotated on its axis toward the window. For one gut-clutching moment Godall was certain the thing was looking at *him,* but the head rotated farther, settling its vacant gaze on the trembling evangelical, its pointing hand hovering in the air, as if in accusation or, just as easily, supplication. The old man clutched his robes, his hands opening and shutting in a gesture of fear and wonder. Then, like a card house tumbling, the corpse dropped straightaway to the table, and the pointing hand clacked to the floor. The old man gasped and reeled forward. Narbondo clouded the room with his vaporizer, casting it down, finally, and plucking up a fallen hand. He fought off the old man's efforts to wrestle it away, then stopped, shrugged, and tossed it onto the slab beside the heaped bones.

The mist still clouded the room. Through it, striding toward the courtyard window, came a woman who appeared to Godall to be about forty. Supposing, perhaps, that she would attempt to meddle with the corpse, the old man rushed at her, protesting. She slammed him in the side of the head with her clenched fist, burst past him, and flung open the casement, leaning out, either for a breath of air or to throw herself from the window. Godall squashed the instinctive urge to drop the curtain and duck back into his darkened room. Instead, he looked straight at her, and, as if he were passing her on the sidewalk at midday, he tipped his hat to her, then slid round so that he could just barely see beyond the casing.

All three of the men in the room opposite dragged her back from the window, mortally fearful, it seemed to Godall, that she would indeed tumble out and fall the three stories to the dark stones of the courtyard below. Godall carefully slid the latch on his own window and shoved it open a crack. He was met by a rush of wet air and a cacophony of voices, accusing and shouting oaths. The men tugged on the woman as if she were a money-filled purse in the hands of thieves, until, with a lurch that threw the hunchback against his aquarium, she yanked herself free. Pule reached for her, and she kicked him in the leg.

The short, uneasy truce that followed was interrupted by the old man, who seemed to suffer a sudden fit of remorse over the state of his fallen mother. "You've ruined her!" he cried, waving at the corpse and turning suddenly on Narbondo. "You'll... you'll...*pay!*"

The hunchback shrugged, suddenly seeming calm. "No," he said, straightening his coat and winking at the woman. *"You'll* pay." And with that he jerked open the door and nodded toward the black hallway without. "I'm not done with your mother. This is something of a success. If our carp hadn't been so thoroughly dealt with, she'd be dancing us a minuet at the moment." And with that he brought his hand down onto the keys of the open piano by the door, dragging his hand along them in a rush of heightening notes.

Shiloh looked from Narbondo to Pule and from Pule to Narbondo, not moving when the hunchback jerked his head toward the door. In the hallway stood two men, one in a turban, the other with a mutilated face. The woman shrank back toward the window once again but was grasped by a frightened Pule. The man in the turban bowed to the old man and produced a pistol from his waistcoat, pointing it at the hunchback.

"Come, my dear," said the evangelist, waving a hand at the woman. Godall could barely hear his suddenly softened voice. The turbaned man leveled the gun across his upraised forearm, directly into the gaping Pule, who shoved the woman into the waiting arms of the old man. "My offer still stands. Each of us wants a particular woman alive. We haven't long, have we?" And not waiting for an answer, Shiloh, the woman, and the toughs stepped through the door and were swallowed by darkness.

Godall took the stairs two at a time and was on the street before them. St. Ives' story of the two men in the house of prostitution left little doubt in his mind of the identity and nature of Shiloh's accomplices. He hoped they were as feeble as St. Ives supposed. On the strength of the brougham parked around the corner on Old Compton, Godall crouched in the dark alcove of the doorway, supposing the party would pass him going out.

A door slammed, footfalls clattered on the steps of the house next door, and a moment later four dim figures hurried past, the woman dragged along unceremoniously by the old evangelical, who made a sort of unidentifiable mewling sound—something between a titter and a groan. Godall stepped silently to the walk behind them, his own footsteps lost in theirs. With no attempt at stealth, he grasped the coat of the turbaned man, jerked it back, and in the instant the man turned toward him in surprise, Godall plucked the revolver from a belt about the man's waist.

It seemed likely that threatening two walking dead men with a revolver would avail him little, so he leaped past both of them, clutched Shiloh by the front of his cloak, and shoved the revolver against the side of his head, holding his stick under his arm.

"I'll thank you to release the woman," said Godall.

The old man let her go without hesitation, waggling both hands over his head as if to demonstrate that he had no intention of arguing.

Godall released the old man's cloak and handed Nell his stick. "Theophilus Godall," he said, bowing, "at your service."

She hesitated for a moment, then said, "Nell Owlesby, sir," and watched Godall's face, which made an incomplete effort to disguise its surprise.

Turning again to the old man, who stared nervously at the gun, Godall said: "You'll accompany us for a ways. Your friends will remain here."

"Of course they will. That's just what they'll do. They'll stay very well put. Won't you, my sons?"

The two were silent. Godall edged backward along the sidewalk, fearing suddenly that the man with the ruined face might also be armed. But he made no movement at all. They stepped from the curb and hurried along toward the end of the street. The east was gray with dawn light, and the city was awakening. Clouds overhead were breaking up, and the moon blinked through, pale as a ghost. The morning was lightening the neighborhood dangerously. If they could slip round the corner and down a block or two, they'd leave the old man to shift for himself and would make away toward Jermyn Street.

The evangelist began to utter monosyllabic spiritual doggerel about damnation and pain, and, still walking backward, he smashed his eyes shut, as if praying or as if clamping out the sight of a world too coarse and evil to he tolerated. He stumbled, nearly precipitating the three of them into the gutter. Godall, hesitating out of general chivalry to cuff an old man, said simply, "Walk, will you!" They rounded the corner and approached the parked brougham.

A horse whinnied. Godall spun toward it, surprised at the sudden noise. A curse rang out from directly over his head, and before he had time to sort the curse from the whinny, someone had dropped like an ape onto his back from the roof of the brougham.

The driver. There had been a driver, thought Godall wildly and ineffectually as he was borne down onto the wet street. His gun clattered away along the cobbles. He grappled with his attacker, striking at the man whose arms encircled his neck. But the backhand blows were worth nothing, and the man slid his forearm in beneath Godall's shoulder and around the back of his neck. Godall's head pressed against his own chest. His right foot kicked back and found the curb. He pushed, rising to his knees. His assailant was curiously light, but light or not, the pressure he exerted on Godall's neck sharpened. His hat had been shoved down half over his eyes and somehow clung there as tenaciously as the man on his back, unwilling to let go. Below the brim he could see the two thugs rounding the corner, loping toward them, and the old evangelist stooping to pick up the fallen pistol.

Godall stamped once in that direction, but accomplished nothing. He stood up, the man clinging like a bug, and ran backwards into the side of the brougham. The wagon lurched on its springs; the horse bolted forward. There was a guttural shriek in Godall's ear as the man on his back twisted away, jerking Godall after him and off balance. As he fell he saw Shiloh recoiling from a blow. It was Nell with Godall's stick. She held it by the tip, and, when Shiloh made another feeble attempt to grasp the fallen pistol, she cracked him in the ear with the ivory moon handle, then turned to thrust the tip into the throat of the turbaned man, who sailed in to aid his fallen comrades.

Godall leaped on the pistol, rolled heavily onto his side, and waved it menacingly. The turbaned man kneeled in a huddle, gagging. The evangelist sat dripping blood along the line of his scalp, shaking his head slowly, casting Nell a dark look of pain and rage. The driver of the brougham lay entangled in the spokes of the rear wheel, which had caught his foot when the horse leaped forward, and had spun him from his perch on Godall's back.

The battle, clearly, was over. Godall hesitated. Should he take the old man with him? But Nell was already hurrying away, carrying his stick. The sky was clear and gray. An approaching wagon jangled in the silent morning. Godall gave the pistol a final wave, turned, and jogged after Nell Owlesby. When he passed Lexington two blocks down he looked back to see the ghouls bent over their hunched saviour. —◦

NINE

Poor Bill Kraken

WILLIS PULE LEANED against the embankment railing, looking out over the tumult of Billingsgate market. The sun was up, but not far, and it cast an orange, rippling slash along the placid waters of the Thames through parted clouds. The streets were clean and wet. Under other circumstances it would have been a pleasant enough morning, what with masts and ropes of sailing vessels rising above tiers of fishing boats against the lavender sky and hundreds of men landing fish along the docks. But Pule hadn't slept that night. Narbondo would have another carp, and he'd have it now. His were dead of swim-bladder disease. The oceanarium couldn't be attempted twice in a single day. There was the chance that breeders from fisheries in Chingford would have carp for sale at Billingsgate. And if they were fresh—if they hadn't begun to dry out—there was the chance they could restore Joanna Southcote after all.

The hunchback had been tearing his hair since the old man had left with Nell Owlesby. Narbondo was mad to suppose they could do anything with the corpse on the slab—even madder to trust Shiloh to keep his end of the bargain. The evangelist would sell them out. And his power was accumulating. Pule could see a half-dozen of his converts passing out tracts in the market, most of which were immediately put to use wrapping fish. None of the supplicants appeared to be Narbondo's animated dead men. Even the farthest-fetched, vilest sort of religious cult could develop a sort of fallacious legitimacy through numbers.

Pule wondered whether his prospects wouldn't be better if he were to throw in with Shiloh, if he were to become a convert. He could do it surreptitiously—keep a hand in with Narbondo—play the one against the other. He stared into his coffee, deaf to the whistles, cries, and shouts of the basket-laden throng around him.

The loss of sleep would play hell with his complexion. He fingered a lump on his cheek. With all the powers of ages of alchemical study at hand, he couldn't seem to prevent these damned boils and pimples. Camphor baths had nearly suffocated him.

Hot towels soaked in rum, vinegar, and—he shuddered to recall it—urine, had merely activated the boils, and it had taken two solid months before he could go abroad without supposing that everyone on the street was whispering and gesturing at his expense. And they probably were, the scum. He rubbed idly at his nose, sniffing at his coffee, the acrid fumes of which just barely disguised the seaweed odors of whelk and oysters and gutted fish—odors that lay like an omnipresent shroud over the market. The smell of fish, of dead, out-of-water fish, sickened him.

Someone tapped him on the shoulder. He looked up darkly into the face of an earnest youth in a cap and neckerchief. A tract fluttered in his hand. "Excuse me," said the youth, smiling vacantly. "A wonderful morning, this." And he looked about him as if he were surrounded by evidence of it. Pule regarded his face with loathing. "I'm here to offer you salvation," said the youth. "It's easy to come by, isn't it?"

"I wouldn't know," responded Pule truthfully.

"It is, though. It's in the sunrise, in the river, in the bounty of the sea." And he waved his hand theatrically at a heap of squid laid out on a sledge below. He smiled all the while at the disheveled Pule, who absentmindedly rubbed a rising blemish on the tip of his nose. The youth, apparently satisfied with the squid illustration, rubbed his own nose, although there was no profit in it. "I'm a member of the New Church," said he, thrusting forth his tracts. "The New Church that won't have a chance to get old."

Pule blinked at him.

"Do you know why?"

"No," said Pule, rubbing at his nose once more.

As if powered by magnetism, the young man was after his own nose again, thinking, perhaps, that something clung to the side of it, a speck that eluded his previous rubbing. Pule noted his behavior and felt his face grow hot. Was the fool having him on? Pule clenched his teeth. "What the hell do you want with me?" he cried.

The violence of Pule's epithet seemed almost to catapult the youth backward. He recovered, pulled the slack out of himself, and smiled all the more widely. "The end is near," he announced, grinning. The idea of Armageddon seemed to appeal to him. "You've days to save your immortal soul. The New Church, I tell you, is the way. He, Shiloh, the New Messiah, is the way! He raiseth people from the grave! He redeemeth the dead! He…"

But Pule interrupted. "So you're saying I should become a convert to save myself? Conversion by extortion is it?"

The youth gazed at him, his smile broader, if anything. "I say," said he, having another innocent go at his nose, "that he who was born of no man can lift you out of misery, can…" and with this, the youth put his hand on Pule's forehead, as if to heal his soul there and then, in the midst of tramping men carrying baskets of shark heads and eels. The touch of a human hand on the ravaged forehead electrified Pule, but in a way other than had been intended.

Pule screamed an oath, dropped his cup and with both hands tore the tracts from the youth and flung them in a heap to the stones of the embankment. "Filthy… blathering…scum!" shrieked Pule, dancing on the tracts, scuffling and tearing at them with the soles of his shoes. He bent, grabbed a handful, and flung them over the railing, the wind sailing them merrily away like penny whirligigs. Pule cut another half-dozen capers, his eyes like saucers, his mouth twisted in rage. The youth, his smile gone with his vanishing tracts, edged backward a step at a time, until, certain that Pule was too far away to leap on him, he cut and ran toward the embankment stairs, cries of "Scum-sucking pig!" and "Damnable filth!" lending him wings. Pule grasped at the railing, oblivious to the stares of passersby, who gave him a wide berth, anxious not to set him off. He had called attention to himself, to his livid face. They would speak to each other, nudge each other, twigging him. He stared into his retrieved cup, chest heaving, until he saw, beneath his feet, a last tattered tract, smeared with gravel and rainwater footprints. He picked the thing up. On it, sketched rudely by someone whose under-standing of perspective was nonsense, was an elongated dirigible, sailing among the clouds. And above it, streaming across a progressively darkening sky, a flaming comet, strangely phallic, arched in toward the flat earth. "The time is at hand!" shouted the caption below the illustration. But what time it was that was at hand wasn't at all clear, lost as it was in the unfortunate footprint. Pule folded the tract and shoved it into the pocket of his coat, then stepped away down the stairs into the interior of the market, the wooden rambling barn packed with shouting vendors and so thick with fish that it seemed impossible that the oceans hadn't been stripped clean.

A woman strung with codfish pushed past, smearing Pule with bloody slime. Directly after came a fat man leering up out of Oyster Street with a basket full of gray shells, shouting so vociferously in Pule's face that for a moment the world seemed to him nothing but a great nose, an open mouth, and a shower of spittle. Pule shrank back in disgust. Fish vendors pushed in on him from all sides. Octopi the size of bumboats seemed to be hovering over him, grasping at him with warty tentacles. Baskets of eels appeared, pushed along on a cart, wriggling out over the sides of their prison only to be ignominiously shoved back in and buried beneath a ballast of cabbage leaves.

Pule gagged. It was close as a tanyard. He'd faint if he didn't have air. "Carp! Carp! Carp!" came a sudden cry. "Who'll have these ha-a-an-some carp! All alive! Alive O! Prime carp! Carp o' the gods!" Pule steered toward the voice, groping for his purse. He wouldn't haggle. This was no time for haggling. He'd have his carp and away. He stumbled, slipped on the carcass of a fish trod to slime by a hundred shoes. In front of him was a plank piled with enormous reddish shrimp, like impossible bugs, their eyes staring on stalks from out of brittle carapaces, huge feelers waving like antennae. Pule rocked against a wagon of squid, nearly upsetting it. "'Ere now!" came a cry, and he was shoved along. There were the carp—seven of them, submerged in a trough of water.

"Fresh as any daisy!" cried the vendor, noting Pule's evident interest.

"How much?"

"Two pounds buys the lot."

Pule produced the money and waved it blindly at the man, who snatched it away and winked at a seller of dried herring beside him. "Want them all, then?"

"I gave you enough, didn't I?"

"No," said the vendor, "you were a pound shy. What're you up to? Precious sort of fellow, aren't you, trying to cheat a poor carp man like me."

Pule looked up at him, astonished, far too tired and frightened to argue. The man dangled a single pound note from his fingers. Pule gave him a look and got another look in return. "How many for a pound?" he whispered.

"What's that?"

"For a pound? What do I get for a pound?"

"One bleeding fish, is what. We had an agreement. Me mate here heard it from your very face, and an unnatural sort of pocky face it is, if I says so myself." And with that he leered across at the herring dealer, who nodded widely and finally.

Pule dug out another pound. "I want the trough too," he said weakly.

"That'll cost you another, carbuncle," said the carp vendor. Pule nodded, his fear and embarrassment metamorphosing into anger. "Here, you!" he cried, gesturing to a costerlad who sat in an empty barrow. "Five shillings to transport this tub of carp out to Soho."

The boy leaped up and grappled with the heavy trough, spilling water. Pule cuffed him on the side of the head.

"Here's a brave one!" shouted the carp man, pocketing the most recent pound note. "Look at moony beat this here lad!" And he burst into laughter, reached across the trough, and jerked Pule's cap off, dipping it full of squid from a passing basket. He shoved the cap back onto the head of the fleeing and humiliated Pule, who, with the barrow at his heels, burst out into the chilly morning sunlight and pitched the cap, squids and all, into the Thames.

"Say!" cried the lad with the barrow. For a moment he looked as if he were going to leap in after them. "That were a good hat, weren't it?" he asked innocently, marveling, perhaps, at the apparent wealth of a man who would throw such a hat into the river. "And they was prime squid too." He shook his head and sloshed along in Pule's wake.

Some hundred yards down the embankment, the cries and odors of Billingsgate market having receded behind him, Pule noticed a sleeping figure, hunched out of the wind beneath a little stony outcropping that had been, before it crumbled, a decorative granite buttress on an ancient bit of river wall. It wasn't the reclining figure that caught his eye so much as the half-exposed object that protruded from a pillowcase which the sleeper cradled in his arms.

Pule slowed and squinted at it. He looked at the man's face. It appeared to be Bill Kraken. And the box? It was a Keeble box. He'd seen Narbondo's sketches. There wasn't any question about it: the grinning face of the clothed hippo that peered out from the folds of the pillowcase, the dancing apes carved into the exposed lid. What rare piece of serendipity *was* this, he asked himself. Could this be heavenly repayment for his recent ill-use?

He studied the sleeping Kraken. He was unacquainted with the man, literally speaking, but perhaps knew enough about him to turn the happenstance of their meeting to profit. He addressed the costerlad: "Run along down the way," he said, "and buy me a bottle of brandy, heated, will you? And two glasses." He gave the boy three shillings. "There's another for you if you come back." He realized as he watched the boy run off that he hadn't had to offer him a bribe to return. He'd have come back after his barrow sure enough. Perhaps he could cheat him of it somehow. Pule turned his attention to Kraken, who snored volubly and held onto his prize.

The sun peeked over the treetops below London Bridge, casting its rays full into Kraken's face. He recoiled in the glare of it, blinking and squinting, then seemed to realize what it was he clutched to his chest, and clutched it all the more tightly, as if it were a beast of some sort that might leap from his arms and run. In an instant he pushed it away, hoping, it seemed, that it would run, then yanked it to him again. He stopped his odd tug of war, however, when he noted Pule, bent over the barrow of carp.

"Good morning to you," said Pule pleasantly, one eye cocked for the approach of the lad with his brandy. Kraken sat in silence. "Cold enough this morning."

"That it is," said Kraken suspiciously.

"Bit of hot brandy would be the ticket."

Kraken swallowed hard. He ran a dry tongue over his lips and regarded Pule. "Have a bit of fish there, have you?"

"That's it. Fish. Carp, actually."

"Carp is it? They say carp is…What do they say? Immortal. That's it."

"Do they?" asked Pule, feigning deep interest.

"Science does. They've studied 'em. In China mainly. Live forever and grow as big as the pool they're kept in. That's a fact. Read up your Bible—it's all there. Loads of talk about the leviathan—the devil's own fish. Shows up as a serpent here, a crocodile there—they can't keep him straight. But he's a carp, sure enough, with his tail in his own mouth. And soon—weeks they say—he's going to let loose and come up out of the sea like one of them monsoons. I'm a man of science and the spirit both, but I don't trust to neither one entirely. There's no affidavit you can sign. That's my thinking."

Pule was momentarily awash. He nodded vehement agreement. "Spirit, is it?" he asked, seeing that the brandy bottle approached at a run from up the embankment. The brandy was delivered, Pule was relieved of another shilling, and the boy pushed the barrow twenty yards farther along and waited.

"Glass of Old Pope?" asked Pule, pouring half a tumbler full for Kraken before he had an answer.

"I am dry, thank you. And I haven't had breakfast yet. What did you say you were?" Kraken sipped at the brandy. Then, as if in rushing relief, he drained half of it, gasping and coughing.

"I'm a naturalist."

"Are you?"

"That's right. I'm an associate of the noted Professor Langdon St. Ives."

Kraken gasped again, without the help of the brandy, then his face dropped into a melancholy scowl of self-pity. Pule poured another dollop into his glass. Kraken drank. The brandy seemed to run the morning chill away. Kraken suddenly thought of the box, which lay on his lap like a coiled serpent. Why had he taken it? What use had he for it? He didn't at all want it. He'd sunk very low. That was certainly the truth. Another glass wouldn't sink him any lower. He wiped a tear from his eye and let go a heaving sigh.

"Interested in the scientific arts, you say?" said Pule.

Kraken nodded morosely, gazing into his empty glass. Pule filled it.

"Of what branch of the sciences are you an aficionado?"

Kraken shook his head, unable to utter a response. Pule loomed in at him, proffering the bottle, stretching his countenance into an expression both pitying and interested. "You seem," said Pule, "if you'll excuse my meddling in your affairs, to be a student of the turnings of the human heart, which, if I'm correct, is as often broken as it is whole." And Pule heaved a sigh, as if he too saw the sad end of things.

Kraken nodded a rubbery head. The brandy rallied him a bit. "You're a philosopher, sir," he said. "Have you read Ashbless?"

"I read little else," Pule lied, "unless, of course, it's scientific arcana. One is forever learning from reading the philosophers. It's nothing more nor less than a study of the human soul. And we're living, I fear, in a world too negligent of that part of man's anatomy."

"There's truth in that," cried Kraken, rising unsteadily to his feet. "Some of us have souls the rag man wouldn't touch. Not with a toasting fork." And with that, Kraken began to cry aloud.

Pule placed a comforting hand on his shoulder. He hadn't any idea where the conversation was leading, but was reasonably certain that he couldn't just relieve Kraken of the box and walk away. He'd have to trust to the fates, who if not positively smiling upon him, were at least grinning in his direction. He poured Kraken another two inches of brandy, wondering if he hadn't ought to have bought two bottles when he had the chance. The effects of the warm liquor, however, seemed to have been somehow cumulative, for Kraken suddenly slumped heavily against the stones of the low wall that fronted the embankment, and it occurred to Pule that it might he possible simply to wait until Kraken was blind drunk and then walk away with his box. "Do you…" asked Kraken, "do you suppose there's a bit of hope?"

"Surely," said Pule, to be safe. Kraken appeared to be satisfied. "You've a great burden."

"That's a fact," muttered Kraken

"I can help you. Trust me. This talk about toasting forks is unhealthy, doubly so: I won't believe it of you on the one hand, and it denies the very root of salvation on the other. There is no better time than this to round the bend, to draw a course for home."

"Do you think so, guv'nor? Would they have me?" Kraken drained his glass.

"What have you done that's so awful? Stolen your master's goods? Checked the missus?"

Kraken heaved another sigh and looked inadvertently at the box.

"What can that be," Pule asked, "but a toy for a child? Stride back in and lay it at the feet of your employer. Brass it out. Admit your guilt."

"Oh no," lamented Kraken. "It's a bit more than a toy. It's the gallows, is what it is for Bill Kraken. It's the gibbet. This here ain't no toy."

"Come, come. What can it be that's so valuable as that? The world loves a man who confesses his sins."

"Then they hang him." Kraken lapsed into silence.

Pule, unspeakably irritated but grinning broadly, filled his glass and cast the empty bottle end over end into the river. "Come now," he said, "tell us what it is you've gotten off with there and I'll see if I can't make it right."

"Can you, guv'nor?" asked the befuddled Kraken, suddenly animated.

"I'm the nephew of the Lord Mayor."

"Ah," said Kraken, considering this. "The Lord Mayor. The Lord Mayor hisself. It's a precious great emerald, is what it is. Poor Jacky's inheritance in a lump. And I've gone and pinched it. It's drink that did it, and that's the truth. Drink and this bonk on the conk." And with that he fingered the freshly healed cut along his forehead.

Pule's mind wrenched and clanked like a broken engine. The emerald. If Narbondo got hold of it, Pule could whistle for a share. Damn the homunculus. Damn the rotten Joanna Southcote and her doddering son. The emerald was worth more than all the hunchback's scientific maundering. And it would be worth twice as much to see Owlesby deprived of it. Dorothy Keeble would regret snubbing him. He'd lure Kraken into an alley and bash him to pieces. But the lad with the barrow. There he stood, waiting stupidly. He would send the lad ahead with the carp. Narbondo had paid for them, after all. Give him his due.

"I think I see away out of this entanglement," said Pule.

"Eh?"

"I say, come along with me and I'll put this right. Straightaway. You'll be back in tune in no time. And for the love of God, don't let go the box there. There's villains in this city would murder you over it soon as tip their hat to you. Look sharp now."

"There's truth in that," said Kraken half to himself, stumbling along behind Pule, who advanced toward the boy with the barrow.

"Look here, lad," said Pule. "Haul these carp to two-sixty-six Pratlow Street, off Old Compton, and be quick as you can about it without sloshing the things onto the road. There'll be a half crown for you there from Mr. Narbondo if the fish are breathing when you get there. Tell him Mr. Pule says he can eat these, with Mr. Pule's regards for salt. Now go along with you." And away the lad went innocently about his task. Pule shook with anticipation, following along the embankment toward Blackfriars. He'd have to act before Kraken sobered up. He played in his mind scenes of Kraken's demise, of the telling blow, the glinting knife, the gasp of drunken surprise.

"What the devil do you here!" came a startling cry from behind him. Pule leaped. A wagon rattled up, and in it sat Ignacio Narbondo in a fury. Pule's stomach felt suddenly empty. "It's coming on ten o'clock! Does it take you half a morning to buy a stinking carp? That damned skeleton is dropping to dust before us and you're out taking the sun. Shiloh the bloody messiah has us by the nub!" He paused in his tirade and looked Pule up and down. "Where's my carp?"

"I sent them ahead with a boy. You'll get your stinking carp."

"And they *will* be stinking at this rate. What's this?" He squinted at Kraken. "It's Bill Kraken, by God! Old Bill Kraken. Diggin' up any corpses, Bill?"

Kraken looked from Pule to Narbondo, then back at Pule, suspicions revolving in his sodden mind.

"By God!" said Narbondo under his breath, noting the box for the first time. He turned on Pule. "So that's your game, is it? Going to slip it to an old rummy like Bill and make away with the box. Leave the poor doctor to fend for himself." He shook his head as if out of sympathy with the idea. "And after all I've taught you."

"That's a lie," said Pule hotly. "I was leading him back to Pratlow Street. The woman on the slab would profit from...*reorganizing*." Pule winked hugely at Narbondo, inwardly fuming, berating himself for taking so monumentally long about the business.

Narbondo frowned at Pule's punning, but his humor seemed instantly to improve. "I can see that he's a man of parts," he said, then burst into momentary laughter, cut off as suddenly as it began. "What's in the Keeble box? Does he know?"

"The emerald," said Pule. There was no reason to dissemble here. He'd either have the emerald or he wouldn't. No, that wasn't so. He'd *have* the emerald, period. Even if he had to feed Narbondo to the carp. He'd wait it out. This simply hadn't been the right moment. One can't get greedy with the fates. One has simply to wait.

Kraken looked sick, whether over his mounting suspicions or over the excess of warm brandy it was impossible to say, but it could be seen at a glance that he was no longer the docile, repentant Kraken who moments before had been following Pule like an obedient dog. A look of resolve flickered across his face. He stepped back a pace and started to speak. But the sight of a suddenly appearing revolver in the hand of the hunchback silenced him. The look of resolve collapsed.

"Into the wagon with you, Bill," said the doctor, gesturing with the pistol. Kraken attempted to climb in and stumbled against the side. "Help the sod, numbskull!" roared Narbondo at Pule. "Heave him in and let's be gone. We've got a day's work ahead. In you go, Bill!" And Pule, hauling on Kraken's legs, tumbled him into the wagon as Kraken clutched the box, doubly certain now of his own damnation. Pule climbed in beside him and took the pistol from Narbondo. The wagon rattled away up the road, passing some half mile down the costerlad wheeling his barrow.

"There's the carp!" cried Pule, pointing.

But Narbondo drove past without slackening his pace. "They'll come along right enough," he said over his shoulder. "We'll just get poor Bill home safe while we're at it. No detours now. Not with the box riding along beside us!" And with that he whipped up the horses, careening around onto the Victoria Embankment and away. —☞

TEN

Trouble at Harrogate

LANGDON ST. IVES marveled at the sunny skies over Harrogate. The clouds that shaded London were invisible beyond the horizon, and the pall that overhung Leeds could only dimly be seen, blown away west and south by chill winds off green Scottish hillsides. The weather was brisk—sunny and brisk—and it fitted St. Ives to a tee.

He'd collected the oxygenator from Keeble at King's Cross Station, the toymaker fearful that he'd been followed, perhaps by his nemesis in the chimney pipe hat—the man Kraken had referred to as Billy Deener. But no such villain showed himself. Nothing at all suspicious occurred until the train was an hour north of London. And that little business, thought St. Ives with a certain amount of satisfaction, he'd dealt with handily enough.

He poured another cup of tea and sank his teeth into a scone. A hammering at a closet door behind him and the muffled grunts of someone apparently locked inside gave him no pause. Hasbro walked in just then, nodding to St. Ives. "Shall I just clear these away, sir?"

"By all means."

"He's still thumping, sir."

"And the other one?"

"Quiet, sir, these last two hours."

St. Ives nodded, satisfied, but saddened in spite of himself. "Dead, do you suppose?"

"From his countenance—as well as I can perceive it through the peephole—I would answer in the affirmative. Dead as a herring, I'd say, sir, to quote the populace."

St. Ives arose, walked into his laboratory, and peered in through a door fixed with a porthole window. On the floor of a tiny room beyond lay a man who appeared to have been dead for a week. On a plate beside him was a quantity of fruit. A pitcher of water stood on a window sill behind. His mouldery clothes fit loosely, as if he'd worn the same suit for a month or two of a starvation diet, and his face was the face of a ghoul. The long, open scar of a bullet wound mutilated his cheek, and through it showed three yellowed teeth.

"Didn't touch the food?"

"Not a bite, sir."

"And dead in a day's time. Very interesting. We'll bury him on the grounds, poor sod. This is a sad business, Hasbro, a sad business. But he was a dead man before we starved him. I could see that when they sat down behind me on the express. They had the odor of death and dust on them. What they were up to I can't say, or even whether they belong to Narbondo or to the old man. Filthy pity, really. Let's have a look at the other."

Back into the library they went, where Hasbro stacked a cup and plate onto a tea tray, dusting with a little horsehair brush the table crumbs onto a tray. St. Ives peered in at the second prisoner. The blood pudding they'd left in the closet was gone, the plate, apparently, licked clean. The prisoner thumped morosely at the door, as if the pounding were something he were doing out of necessity but had no real interest in.

"What does a zombie care about lodgings?" asked St. Ives over his shoulder. "A closet or a hillside, it must be immaterial."

"I rather suppose, sir," said Hasbro, "that the animated dead man might fancy a closet more than a hillside. A closet, if you follow me, is something more like home to him."

"Perhaps he's thumping for another pan of pudding," said St. Ives. "I'm half inclined to give it to him. Reminds me of Mr. Dick—do you recall?—up at Bingley. He built that clever device for trapping roaches and then hadn't the heart to do them in. Fed a small family of them for a week until the cat ate them and destroyed the device. Do you remember that?"

"Very well, sir."

"Damned curious cat, if you ask me. But we won't feed this roach. Not a drop of blood, not a slice of pudding. We'll give him back to the infinite."

The next morning, when St. Ives peered in at the window once again, the second ghoul was dead. Shards of the crockery bowl that had contained the pudding protruded from his mouth like teeth.

St. Ives spent the day testing the aerating device and readying his ship, a spherical iron shell crosshatched with lines of rivets, atop what would appear to the untutored eye to be an enormous Chinese rocket, pointed toward the domed roof of the silo in which it sat. A series of pulleys and chains allowed for the drawing-back of the dome and, St. Ives prayed, for the issuance of the craft. Along either side of the vehicle were arched wings, batlike and close to the hull. And from the base of the wings protruded exhaust and motivator tubes. Windows, heavy with glass, encircled the craft beneath the conical locking mechanism of the hatch. The sight of the ship satisfied St. Ives entirely. He climbed the wooden stairway that spiraled up and around to the hatch, rapping the iron skin of the ship, peering in at the little cluster of potted orchids and begonias that would aid Keeble's box in supplying oxygen. He puffed a lungful of air onto the sensing device that would record prevailing levels of gasses in the cabin. It was a frightful risk, sending the craft into the heavens unmanned. He might quite easily lose it in the sea, or watch horror-struck as it smashed down into the suburbs. But it was preferable, all in all, to being *aboard* an untested craft that suffered such a fate. The needle on the gas detection gauge swung briefly beneath its crystal.

The Keeble box was anchored firmly, the ridiculous hippos and apes carved into the rosewood top grinning out at St. Ives, absolute Keeble trademarks. He pushed the tester button with his finger and a little spray of green chlorophyll dust shot out, carried on a mixture of helium and oxygen. The gauge once again gave a brief leap, then settled as the oxygen dissipated in the general atmosphere of the cabin. St. Ives nodded.

As he clumped back down the stairs, he noted with satisfaction that there wasn't a single compelling reason to return to London. No word had come regarding the endeavors of the Trismegistus Club. Certainly they could carry on without him for a week. It was entirely likely that the wayward Kraken had been found, that Kelso Drake had heeded the Captain's warning and scuttled like a beetle into his dark satanic mills. Godall was a marvel—inscrutable, capable. Captain Powers was a rock. The two alone could defend London against a siege of zombies and millionaires. What were they all fooling about with, anyway? What dreary machinations were worth St. Ives' abandoning the spacecraft, which would, early next morning, angle out through the heavens above West Yorkshire, above the astonished populace of Wetherby and Leeds, to describe its flaming halo in the thin air of the twilit sky and plummet homeward that same evening, already the stuff of legend, to its berth on the moor beyond Robb's Head?

London could wait for him. They'd have him soon enough. But for the moment they'd play second fiddle. It was the consequence of the scientific fates, and—he thought to himself while regarding from the open doorway of the silo the finny sweep of the wings and the brass and silver of the polished hull—of the scientific muses. He set out across the lawn. It was three in the afternoon by his pocketwatch. Late enough by any reckoning for a glass of Double Diamond. Two, perhaps.

But he wasn't halfway to the house when, from the direction on the River Nidd, two shots rang out, echoing against the afternoon stillness. St. Ives began to run, redoubling his pace at the sight of Hasbro, a rifle smoking in his hands, standing among the willows. Hasbro threw the rifle to his shoulder, and settled his cheek against the stock. He jerked just a bit with the recoil, then crouched and peered away east into the foliage along the river.

"What the devil!" cried St. Ives, racing up. He could see nothing among the willows and shrubs.

"A prowler, sir," replied Hasbro, ready, it seemed, to let fly another round if given the least opportunity. "I caught him in the study, and he was out the open window before I could have a go at him. My fetching the rifle, I fear, gave him time to make away along the riverbank. He'd been at your papers, sir—strewed them across the floor, emptied drawers in the press. He was still at it when I happened in— and a lucky circumstance that was—so I'm in hopes he hadn't found what it was he was after."

St. Ives was loping across the lawn when these last words were uttered, leaving Hasbro to poke among the riverside shrubs for the prowler. He burst in through the open front door, past the disheveled study and into the library. He hauled out his copy of *Squires' Complications* and thrust his hand into the broad hiatus left by the stout volume. Behind was the familiar bulk of Owlesby's manuscript, undiscovered.

He sighed with relief, wondering at the same time who it was had been after it. For it had to be Owlesby's manuscript the prowler sought. Like it or not, he thought despairingly, London would have him. Mohammed had refused to go the mountain, so here was the mountain, dragging round to Harrogate to kick apart his personal effects. He couldn't shake the machinations after all. He returned *Squires'* to its niche and walked into the study where Hasbro, having lost his man on the riverbank, was just then stepping in through an open French window.

The study, as Hasbro had promised, was ransacked. What had been heaps of paper were no longer heaped, but were scattered across the plank floor. Books lay higgledy- piggledy. Drawers were yanked from chests, their contents flung and kicked. A plaster bust of Kepler lay split in two, clubbed, apparently, with a heavy Waterford decanter, shards of which glistened in the afternoon sunlight that poured through the windows. Half the destruction was clearly a matter of a wild and hasty search for the manuscript; half of it was pure, irrational villainy.

St. Ives rolled Kepler's broken head with his toe. "Did you get a good look at this man?"

"Tolerably, sir, but he was clothed so strangely that his features were effectively hidden."

"Disguise was it?"

Hasbro shrugged, then shook his head. "Bandages, it seemed to me, swaddling his head. He peered at me through eyeslits, for all the world like one of the Pharaohs at the museum in Cairo. And he reeked of some chemical—carbon tetrachloride, if I'm not mistaken, and something that very much resembled anchovy paste."

"Was it, do you suppose, one of our ghouls?"

"I'd hesitate to say so, sir. He was far too energetic—in the act of beating poor Kepler so altogether viciously that I took him at once for a madman. The rifle, I could see straightaway, was the ticket."

St. Ives nodded. It certainly seemed so, given the mess. Damned foolish way to go about thievery—smashing things up for sport in the middle of the afternoon. St. Ives stiffened, the sudden picture of the man with the chimney pipe hat flickering unbidden into his mind. "Did he wear a hat?"

"No, sir."

"Fairly short, was he? Lank, oily hair? Yellow shirt, perhaps, and a leather coat with the sleeves out at the elbows?"

Hasbro shook his head. "On the stout side, sir, running to fat. Blondish hair in curls."

St. Ives was relieved. He didn't at all *want* it to have been Keeble's garret thief. And what on earth would the man have been after? *Keeble* had the plans to the engine, after all. Blond, curly hair—the description was maddeningly familiar somehow. A face swaddled in chemical-soaked bandages. St. Ives snapped his fingers, then slammed his hand into his open fist. Narbondo's assistant! What was his name? Pigby…Peebles… Publes. St. Ives routed through his mind. Pule! That was it. Willis Pule. Of course it was he. Narbondo had set him to it. But how in the world, he wondered, did the doctor know that St. Ives possessed the papers? "Let's have a look along the river, shall we? Lock the house up and tell Mrs. Langley to shriek like a banshee from the kitchen window if she hears so much as a floorboard creak."

And in moments the two men, each carrying a rifle loaded with birdshot, thrashed among shore grasses and willows, following Pule's evident footprints northwest along the Nidd until, some mile down, they disappeared into the waters of the river itself their quarry having, apparently, swum for it. A man named Binger ferried the two across in a little rowboat, promising, on the strength of a half crown's reward, to return to the manor and keep Mrs. Langley company in the kitchen, and to retrieve the two of them from the opposite shore when they'd worked their way back down.

But across the Nidd there were no footprints at all, and their chances of success declined with the settling dusk. Pule, apparently, had sloshed along in the shallows, perhaps doubled back upriver to confuse them. There were endless boats swirling past and here and there one anchored along shore. He might easily have clambered into one and rowed away downriver to Kirk Hammerton. And who was to say he had no accomplices? Narbondo himself might have been waiting beyond the hill in a wagon. Narbondo! The thought of him sobered St. Ives, who had been caught up in the idea of pursuing Pule, of running him down and delivering the scoundrel to the magistrate.

He'd taken a bit for granted, leaving his cook alone in the manor and merely sending an old man along to her when none of them had any idea what sort of foe it was they hunted. He'd been rash. Pule, after all, hadn't gotten away with a thing. The threat of future danger certainly outweighed the necessity of pursuit.

Stars had flickered on in the evening sky. The lights of Harrogate shown in the west. St. Ives shouldered his rifle, and the two men set out apace for the manor, St. Ives breaking into a jog at the idea of poor Mrs. Langley confronting the hunchbacked doctor or a band of his blood-eating zombies. He and Hasbro were scouring along the last quarter-mile of riverside when the sky beyond the willows changed without warning from deep twilight purple to bright yellow, and a thunderous explosion rocked the meadows.

—◦◦◦—

THE MAN IN the chimney pipe hat sat in the branches of a willow, squinting in wondering assessment at the fleeing figure whose head was a mess of loose rags. Through an open window stepped a tall, balding man in a dark suit, a rifle over his shoulder. Billy Deener hadn't any liking for guns if they were in someone else's hands and here was one in the hands of a man who quite apparently knew what he was about. He threw the weapon to his shoulder and emptied both barrels at the retreating figure, who stumbled, rolled back to his feet, and ran all the faster, weaving back and forth through knee-high grass, white filaments of loosening bandages trailing behind him as if he were an unraveling mummy.

Deener wondered who this interloper was—a common thief? Not at all likely, not with a head wrapped in rags. Countryside thieves wouldn't go abroad dressed so. It was easier by far simply to wear a mask. Whoever the man was, he hadn't been carrying the box, more's the pity. It would have been an easy thing to strangle him with his own loose bandages.

Deener climbed out of his willow and sprinted toward the silo recently vacated by St. Ives. In a moment he was in at the door, out of sight of the two on the riverbank. Luck was with him. They'd be caught up in the pursuit of the bandaged man. It was a perfect diversion. He couldn't have planned a better one.

Before him sat the rocket, the space vehicle perched atop it, almost lost in the shadows of the windowless upper reaches of the silo. Deener climbed the stairway toward the domed ceiling. A rare smile flickered along the set line of his lips. Here was something worth meddling with. Worth smashing up. Worth destroying. He'd have the box for Drake and some fun besides, at the expense of the tweed-coated phony with the idiot false mustache. He was tired of the man and his showy friends. He'd fix the filthy lot of them if he could, starting now. He fiddled with the hatch, twisting at the cone with both hands until, with a sigh of escaping air, it clicked counter clockwise half a turn and the circular hatch popped open like the lid of a jack-in-the-box, narrowly missing his outthrust chin. All was dark inside. He fumbled in his coat pocket for a match, struck it against his shoe, and thrust it into the interior. The light illuminated the cabin briefly, and when it flickered out, Deener lowered himself in, struck a second match, and lit a pair of little gaslamps, one on either side of the cabin.

The interior of the craft was a gothic wonder of potted plants and machinery. Deener scratched his head at it, not knowing where to begin. Best to start at the start, he thought wisely. That had always been his way. It was the box he was after first, or at least it was the box that Drake was after. And there it was, affixed to the wall next to his left ear.

He patted his pantleg, feeling beneath the fabric the flat surface of a prybar and the round bulk of a ballpeen hammer. In a moment he had them out and tapped the prybar under the edge of the box with the hammer. A grinning hippo watched him from the front of the box. He raised the hammer in a sudden rage; he'd beat the thing from the wall. Smash the offending hippo. Reduce the thing beside it to splinters. What the hell was it anyway? A sea monster? An octopod? He'd beat it to bits. He'd… but Drake. What would Drake do to him? He lowered the hammer and breathed heavily for a moment, staring at the loathsome box. Then once again he shoved his bar in under it, gave it a heave, and caught the box as it fell to the floor. He shook it, but nothing rattled inside. He searched for a latch, but there was none. All six sides of the box were identical, aside from the carvings and a cigar-shaped brass pipe issuing from the mouth of a winking basilisk seated on a divan, a tiny book open on a table beside him. A brass crank thrust out from the ear of the basilisk.

Deener shrugged in momentary resignation, shoved through the hatch, and lay the box on the landing outside, then lowered himself back in. Drooping spikes of orchid flowers caught his eye. Flowers offended him almost as much as the hippo foolery of the box. He slashed at a stem, severing it. Then he hacked at another. They were astonishingly brittle. He swept his arm back and slashed at the little forest of stems. Blossoms flew. He stamped at them, danced on them, pummeling the broad leaves of begonias until they sailed like scattered paper in an autumn wind.

The reflection of his face in a porthole window caught his eye, and he lashed out at it, smashing the curved end of the bar against the heavy glass, which thudded with the blow but refused to shatter. That wouldn't do. He smashed at it again and then again, cursing it, wheezing for breath. He threw down the bar and plucked up the hammer. Indestructible, was it? He'd see about that. He grabbed an iron rung on the curved wall of the ship and edged in around a cushioned seat. He couldn't seem to get the right angle. Glancing blows wouldn't do. The damned seat was square in the way. He beat at the chair, the hammerhead ripping into the soft leather. He kicked at it, shrieking, whipping around as if to surprise the window and delivering against it one final blow. The handle of the hammer split as a spider web of cracks sprang into the heavy glass, breaking the reflection of his sweating face into fragments. He threw down the rest of the handle and pulled himself through the hatch, losing his hat in the process. It bounced once on the landing, rolled onto the stairs, and sailed into the diminishing light of the silo, tumbling groundward end over end.

In a rage, he threw his prybar after it, then stooped, grabbed the box, and raised it over his head as if to smash it down too, to reduce it to rubble on the cobbled floor forty feet below. He stood just so, heaving with exertion, animal noises issuing past his teeth, and then slowly lowered the box, visions of Kelso Drake winking into focus across the tangled confusion of his mind. He turned and leaped wildly down the stairs, three at a time, his breath escaping in mewling grunts with each jolt.

He jerked to a stop at the base of the stairs, crouching before a bank of levers on the smooth side of the rocket. He dropped the box and grasped first one and then another of the levers, wrenching them this way and that. One snapped off in his hand and he slammed it against the others, then cast it with such force against the clapboard wall of the silo that it impaled itself, vibrating audibly.

He reached for another lever, but stopped dead. A humming noise, growing louder by the moment, filled the silo. A low rush followed, building toward a roar. Billy Deener leaped back at a quick surge of heat from the base of the rocket. He grinned with sudden anticipation, and in a stooping run, grabbed the box from the stones with one hand, his fallen hat with the other, and was out the door, pounding across the green toward a distant copse that lay like a shadow against the evening sky.

A blast behind threw him onto his face in the grass, and the darkness suddenly evaporated. He crouched, turned his shaded eyes toward the silo, and watched in amazement the domed roof burst outward in a spray of shingles and shards of wood, the debris spinning slowly in the air roundabout the shattered roof. Through the airborne debris rose the rocket, a pinwheel of sparks showering down like bursting fireworks. It seemed hardly to make headway, but angled jerkily, its nose threatening to dip groundward.

Deener was struck with the sudden thought that the entire thing was going nowhere, that it might teeter over and plummet onto the green, onto his head, in fact. He rose slowly to all fours, ready to throw himself flat, then dashed once more for the trees, watching the struggling rocket over his shoulder.

The thing stopped abruptly and hung for a moment in the air. It shuddered, like a dog shaking water from its coat, and the dark little sphere at the top popped off in another wash of sparks, soaring like a champagne cork northward, over the tops of the willows along the River Nidd, whistling as it flew like a rubberized, inflated bat slowly losing air through a tiny hole. The whistling diminished, momentary silence fell, then the remains of the rocket smashed full length onto the meadow, flickering with sparkling little fires before snuffing out into darkness. Deener watched with evident satisfaction from the edge of the wood. He clapped his hat onto his head, tossed his box skyward, caught it, and strode away through the trees toward the village of Kirk Hammerton.

—◆—

"HOLY MOTHER OF God," whispered St. Ives, staring in horror across the tops of the willows. A nebula of sparks whirled from the burst top of the distant silo, lighting a rain of shingles. The suddenly appearing rocket edged skyward, visible above the trees, threatening to soar into the heavens, to shoot away toward the winking stars. But it didn't. It was almost stationary, as if it hung by a sky hook, and just before its nose dipped and the thing fell lifeless to the meadow, the spacecraft, the product of years of work, jumped from the end of the rocket as if shot from a child's pop gun, and arched through the air over their heads, its gaslamps curiously lit within, its hatch flung back on its hinges.

It sailed several hundred yards toward town, stuttering out little jets of smoke and fire through motivator tubes, and making a foolish whistling noise that died out even as the two men watched the craft disappear beyond distant trees. A short, far-off crash sounded. St. Ives lurched. A wave of fear washed through him—fear that some local manor house had been destroyed by his craft, or worse, that people had been hurt, killed perhaps. The fear turned almost at once to anger, and he shouldered his rifle and fired both rounds at the moon, imagining briefly that it was the loathsome, pocked face of Willis Pule, who had, obviously, doubled back on them and launched St. Ives' rocket out of spite.

Well *he'd* see. If it was a fight the bastards wanted, St. Ives would jolly well give it to them. Tomorrow. It was too late to get an evening train; the seven a.m. express would do nicely. London would regret his return. The Trismegistus Club had set out to fight villainy, and here was villainy in spades.

He shouted across the river, but had hardly begun when he noticed that the rowboat was already halfway across, skimming along behind a bow lantern that illuminated the astonished face of old Binger.

"Did you see it!" he cried, slamming up against the grassy bank. St. Ives said nothing, but merely clambered aboard. Hasbro followed, respectfully silent, considering, perhaps, that there was little but cliché to offer when a man's work had gone up, literally, in smoke.

The old man carried on wildly. He'd seen the explosion, the tired flight of the rocket. And it had burst out of a silo too, that anyone would think would be filled with corn. Bang, out the top it came like some kind of bird. It gave a man a start, with all the talk of burglars and such. Did St. Ives suppose it was his man in the river that did it, that set it off? St. Ives did. That beat all, said the old man. He'd seen the little ball pop off and sail away. It was the damnedest thing. He and Mrs. Langley went up to the attic, and there the damned thing went over the trees like a duck and smashed Lord Kelvin's barn to splinters. Right through the roof.

The old man dropped an oar in order to illustrate his story with helpful gestures, sailing his hand in a little arch while he whistled through the gap in his front teeth, then disappearing the hand between his knees, which, St. Ives supposed darkly, represented Lord Kelvin's barn. "Pow!" shouted old Binger, throwing his knees apart to demonstrate the barn's going to bits. He wheezed out a sort of laugh and had another go at his knees. Meanwhile the little rowboat rocked dangerously and slipped downstream.

St. Ives gritted his teeth. It *would* be Lord Kelvin, secretary of the Royal Academy. Pule had reduced his spacecraft and his reputation to rubble in a single, fell yank of a lever. Why the devil hadn't he locked the door to the silo?

St. Ives lurched forward as the rowboat ran up onto the bank, nearly dumping his fowling piece into the river. Off to the north, coming along the highroad, was a scattering of waving lights, flickering against the dark night. They bounced and flared—torches, evidently, carried by any number of people. A murmuring reached them on the breeze. St. Ives was struck suddenly by the ominous implication of the approaching people—a mob, perhaps. What were they about? Did they carry hay forks? Guns?

He'd never seen any profit in advertising his experimentations. Rumors filtered out now and again. He'd been suspected of vivisection and of the building of infernal devices. Men from the metalworks no doubt alerted the populace to his having contracted for the shell of the craft and odd parts. But no one, certainly, besides Hasbro and certain friends—the Trismegistus Club specifically—knew that an hour earlier a launchable space vehicle had been moored in the silo.

He climbed the little rise atop which sat his house, lit, now, like Christmas, Mrs. Langley having apparently decided that an abundance of lights would frighten off villains. Perhaps she was right. The blasted silo sat dark and silent on its meadow, lit only by a little sliver of moon that slipped in a low arc above the horizon. It was impossible at the moment to see that the silo was roofless—a relief, certainly.

The torchbearers approached. St. Ives recognized an old farmer—McNally, it was, and his two pudding-faced sons. And there behind them was Stooton from the post office, and Brinsing, the Scandinavian baker. There were a dozen more, generally speaking, and the lot of them seemed to be in a collective terror; they didn't at all bear accusatory looks. Old Binger, seeing that he had lucked upon a comparatively vast audience, started in on the subject of the sailing bat thing, using hand gestures and grimaces to good effect.

St. Ives was in a sweat to shut him up. It mustn't be known that the imbroglio was sponsored by St. Ives. Hasbro, anticipating as much, silently and unheeded, shoved Binger's rowboat out into the current with his foot, then stepped forward and shouted, "The boat!" in such a commanding and inflammatory tone that Binger stopped in midsentence, his hand having completed only half its customary flight, and bolted through the ferns along the riverbank, shouting at his mutinous boat.

St. Ives nodded appreciatively at Hasbro, and decided to give Binger twice what he owed him when he returned, for the old man would without a doubt be wet through before he found his way home that night to work the space vehicle gestures on his tired wife.

The mob—not one of whom was carrying a hayfork, to St. Ives' immense relief—was full of an undefined fear. The spacecraft, apparently, played second fiddle to a more nefarious threat. An alien had been sighted. It bore, insisted Mr. Stooton, the rag headgear of Islam, and was taken to be a member of that tribe by Mrs. Stooton, who hadn't, as yet, been apprised of the spacecraft that had just pulverized Lord Kelvin's barn and smokehouse.

More sightings had occurred, always the same. A man wound with rags was abroad, a creature, surely, from a distant sun. Wasn't the thing in Lord Kelvin's barn a spacecraft? Could there be any doubt that this wrapped man had driven it? Mightn't he be a very dangerous alien?

No doubt whatsoever, assented St. Ives. He was surely a dangerous villain, this rag man from a far-off galaxy. Beat him into submission first, suggested St. Ives; question him afterward—when he was malleable. The man had been sighted, went the rumor, on the road into Harrogate, fleeing the general area of Lord Kelvin's manor. Two farmers had given chase, one of them managing to hit him in the back of the head with a hastily thrown rock, but the alien made away into the fields and disappeared.

"Toward Harrogate, did you say?" asked St. Ives.

"Right you are, sir," said McNally. "Hoofing it into town like the devil was after him. And he was a bad 'un, too, I can tell you. He beat a dog, he did, on the road. Chased him with a stick long as your arm. A vicious thing, your space man. That was when old Dyke hit him with the rock—slam on the noodle, and away he went. And they'd have had him too, if it weren't for the dog, poor beast. It's thought this alien was going to eat it, raw, right there on the road."

"I wouldn't at all doubt it," said St. Ives grimly, trudging up to the manor with Hasbro beside him and the crowd of men behind. "If I were you," he said, "I'd set out after him with dogs. Run him down. I'm a man of science, you know. What we face here is a threat, and there's no gainsaying it. Dogs are your man for tracking aliens of this sort. They have a distinct smell. Comes from travel through space. And they're prodigious liars. I've studied it out. The first thing he'll do is deny the whole business. But there's his craft, isn't it? And there he is wound up in lord knows what sort of filthy rags. Don't let the creature deny his rotten origins; that's the word from the scientific end. Loosen his tongue for him."

St. Ives' speech worked the mob up thoroughly. Along the road two hundred yards off came another dozen men, and St. Ives could see, in the direction of Kirk Hammerton, a procession of torchlights. By God, he thought, they'd have Pule yet! And if the populace made it warm for the scoundrel, fine. There was, apparently, no end to the man's villainy. Beating a dog on the road! St. Ives fumed. He was suddenly anxious, however, to diminish his role in the night's proceedings. He wondered if there were any identifying marks about the ruinous spacecraft that would give him away before he had a chance to think of something to do. He looked at Hasbro, who stood silently holding both rifles. Hasbro raised his eyebrows and nodded toward the house. This was, he seemed to indicate, no time to be chatting with local vigilantes.

"I'd like to know," St. Ives said to McNally, "if you run this man down. Don't kill him, mind you. Science will need to have a go at him—to study him. This sort of thing doesn't happen every day, you know."

The growing crowd of men agreed that it didn't. They seemed to be waiting for some further word from St. Ives. He could sense that they looked to him for advice, he being the one among them who most understood such strange transpirings. "Keep at it, then!" he said in a stout voice. And he turned on his heel and clumped up the stairs.

"Look there!" cried someone directly behind him. It was a familiar voice—Hasbro's voice. St. Ives spun round, expecting to see some revelation—perhaps Pule being dragged across the meadow by his heels. What he saw was Hasbro pointing in theatrical horror at the blasted silo, clearly visible now in the thin moonlight. A simultaneous murmur of surprise issued from the crowd.

St. Ives flinched. Had Hasbro gone mad? Had he been bought off by Narbondo? He squinted at his otherwise capable gentleman's gentleman with a face which he hoped betrayed nothing to the several dozen onlookers, but which would be an open book to Hasbro.

"The spacecraft, sir, appears to have shorn off the silo roof—blew it to bits, if I'm any judge."

"So it has!" cried McNally.

"The scoundrel!" shouted Brinsing the baker, shaking a fist over his head to illustrate the enormity of the act.

"The filthy dog!" cried St. Ives, echoing the general sentiment and relieved that Hasbro hadn't, after all, gone mad. They'd eventually have seen the silo, after all. It was far safer to explain it away so simply and logically. The ship had destroyed *his* property too—had narrowly missed the house, had strewed all sorts of debris about the meadow. Poor Mrs. Langley! He glanced down and there was old Binger, returned, standing agog, scratching his head. Hasbro's suggestion that the craft had simply ripped the lid from the silo as it passed along overhead ran counter to his memory.

"Binger!" shouted St. Ives suddenly, descending the stairs and collaring the old man. "There's that business of the half pound I owe you. Step along with me now, and I'll pay up. Mrs. Langley has a pie, too, unless I'm mistaken, and we've bottles of ale to wash it down with. Come along, then." And he stepped across the threshold, dragging Binger with him, Hasbro closing in behind.

"Half a pound, sir?" asked the innocent Binger, thoroughly befuddled.

"That's right," said St. Ives. "Step along here now." He turned to the crowd on the meadow, tipping his hat. "Keep at it, lads," he cried, shutting the door behind him and precipitating the old man down the hallway toward the kitchen. "We'll just have a go at that pie now." He smiled and drew a half pound from his pocket. "It'll be in the pantry, I should think. Cool as a cellar in here." The pantry door swung back to reveal two prone corpses on the stone floor—the remains of Narbondo's ghouls. "No pies here," rattled St. Ives, slamming the door shut. "Take care of this, will you?" he whispered to Hasbro.

"Certainly, sir. And I'll just take the wagon along to Lord Kelvin's afterward, don't you think? If I can…collect the spacecraft, sir, we could study it at our leisure."

St. Ives nodded hugely. Hasbro's talk of "studying" the spacecraft was lost on Binger, though, for the man stared open-mouthed at the shut pantry door.

"A five-pound note was it?" asked St. Ives evenly.

"Beg pardon, sir, but…"

"No buts, Mr. Binger," cried St. Ives. "You've rendered us a service, man. And I intend to reward you. Disregard the dead men in the pantry; they're not what you suppose. Sent along by the undertaker, they were. Victims of a wasting disease. Quite conceivably virulent. Here's the note, eh? And here, by heaven, is a bottle of ale. Join me? Of course you will!" He hauled Mr. Binger along toward the parlor. "I was just set to have a go at one of these when that damned alien appeared. Tore the roof right off the silo. You saw that, did you?"

"Aye, sir. What was he doing inside it, sir? I'd swear he come out through the roof."

"Optical illusion, I should think. Difficult scientific matter. These men from the stars aren't like you and me. Not a bit. Liable to do anything, aren't they?"

"But wasn't he down on the river…"

"I don't at all wonder that he was," said St. Ives. "He's been high and low tonight, hasn't he? Smashing my silo, beating dogs up and down the highroad, tearing into Lord Kelvin's barn—you witnessed that, didn't you, Mr. Binger. Quite a sight, I don't doubt. From the attic window, you say, after it beat the devil out of my silo?"

"Yes, sir," said Binger, livening up. He balled his hand into a fist and sailed it along from one side of his chair to the other, burying it between the arm and the cushion.

St. Ives sat transfixed. "Just like that, was it? Remarkable narrative powers you have, Mr. Binger. Really remarkable. Quite an explosion when it struck, was there?" St. Ives opened two more bottles of ale. He needed them every bit as much as he needed to pour them down the confused Binger.

Out of the corner of his eye he could see Hasbro dragging a body down the hallway toward the rear door—the second ghoul, from the look of the checked trousers. Mr. Binger's back was to the hall. St. Ives blinked and grimaced at him, hoping that his evident satisfaction with the man's brief but gesture-ridden tale would encourage him to generate some really colorful, time-consuming detail. The next corpse followed the first out the back door, which slammed after it. And in a moment St. Ives heard the wagon rattle away out of the carriage house. He looked out through the window to see Hasbro driving along toward the river through moonlit dust, the two corpses flung into the wagon behind him.

St. Ives was relieved. It wouldn't do to bury the creatures on the grounds—not with the night's complications. They'd be miles down the Nidd by morning. And if they were discovered, their deaths would be laid to the alien, to Willis Pule. Damn Pule, thought St. Ives. Willis Pule! His very name sounded almost like an obscenity. The spacecraft gone! If Hasbro could retrieve it, he'd put in to have the man declared a saint. He pulled out his pocketwatch. It was coming onto ten o'clock. He'd have to pack. There was no telling when Hasbro would return. They'd be on their way into Harrogate by four in the morning.

"Astonishing business!" cried St. Ives heartily, interrupting the old man's by now oft-told story. "Come round and see us again, my good fellow. That's right. Here's a bottle for the road. Give Mrs. Binger our best. And what of young Binger? Working at the mill is he? Capital, capital." With that Mr. Binger found himself on the front porch, a bottle of ale in each hand, trying to answer all of the professor's questions at once, but finding himself in conversation, all of a sudden, with an oak slab door. He set off down the drive, richer by five pounds, two bottles of ale, and a story that would last him years.

St. Ives tumbled halfway up out of sleep three hours later at the sound of the wagon rolling along the drive. He pulled himself up in bed and peered out into the night. The wagon drove past, the dark bulk of the spacecraft atop the bed. Into the carriage house it went. A door slammed. St. Ives dropped away again and awakened before dawn the next morning to the sound of Hasbro hauling suitcases out the front door.

The two of them drove along toward Harrogate and the London express a half hour later, the sun just peering up over the trees in the east. What strange activities lay before them St. Ives could only guess at, but the set of his mouth and the squint of his eye promised that he was ready for them, that he'd breakfast on them. His error had been that he'd thought himself apart from the villainies of the London underworld. But he saw things more clearly now, much more clearly. —⁕

ELEVEN

Back to London

WILLIS PULE SHIVERED in the undergrowth that choked the empty streambed of a little tributary to the River Nidd. The willow and bracken was thick enough to keep out searching eyes—he'd lie low there until the train was a moment from pulling away toward London. The station was a five minute dash to the south. He'd been a genius to buy his return ticket the day before. His goose would be cooked otherwise. They were scouring the countryside for him. But why, for the love of God? Surely not because of the affair at St. Ives' manor. That would hardly have loosed such a lunatic mob. Perhaps it had something to do with the explosions that had followed his retreat. But for heaven's sake, *he* had had nothing to do with that. Damn these country clowns, he thought to himself, peering above the foliage roundabout him. If he could manage it, he'd exterminate the lot of them. Some sort of infectious disease, perhaps—animated rats that fed on blood and were hopping with plague fleas.

He patted his nose gingerly, arranging the sagging bandages. He'd have torn them off, thrown them into a ditch, but the chemicals they'd been soaked in had lent his face an amber-blue tint that was startling and inexplicable. The bandages were less so. And more than that, they seemed to be having a positive effect. The skin on his face felt drawn and tight, and he'd long ago overcome his compulsion to retch at the smell of the anchovy paste. He tugged at the knots in the end of the bandages, loosened them, and pulled the whole works taut, tying it off once again.

He checked his pocketwatch. It was time to go. He'd simply have to brass it out—there was nothing else to be done, He could hardly sit in the bushes forever, and he'd be caught for sure if he set out down the road. He'd have liked to steal a cart—garrote the owner and make away with the man's goods, but he was in a deep enough mire as it was. The cost of further mayhem might perhaps be greater than the profit.

He peered again over the bushes. Surely the mob had tired itself out long since. No one, apparently, was about, save a thin man in knee breeches who cleaned cod at a trough behind a fish shop. Pule stepped through a gap in the shrubbery and strode away purposefully, not at all, he fancied, like a man fearful of pursuit. The cod man slashed away at his fish, oblivious to him. Pule rounded the corner of the fish shop, saw that the street before him was empty, and bolted for the train station, one hand pressed to his head to keep the bandages from flying apart.

A block from the station he slowed to a walk. He had enough time. It was dangerous to call attention to himself so. There was the open platform, the train chuffing on the track. Some few people climbed aboard. A tired-looking man in a mustache sold scones and coffee through the windows. Pule would kill for a scone—literally, he thought to himself. He was in a regrettable mood, and hunger put an edge on it.

There were the steel steps into the second class car, ten feet ahead of him. No one shouted. No one menaced him. He snatched a newspaper from a boy idling on the platform, sprang into the car, found an empty compartment, and hid behind the newspaper. He'd stay there, he decided, until they were at least halfway to London.

The train edged forward in a hiss of escaping steam, then lurched to a stop. Footsteps rang on the platform. Pule peeked past the edge of his newspaper, horrified to see Langdon St. Ives and his manservant climbing into the train car. Damn! He raised the newspaper. If the door to his compartment opened he'd go out through the window. What else could he do? He hadn't any weapons. Next time he wouldn't be caught weaponless. And there *would* be a next time.

Narbondo would rail at him for having failed to find the papers. It had taken hours to wring Kraken clean of information. Liquor had done it far more neatly than had torture—although Pule rather preferred the latter; since they had no idea whether Kraken had anything to offer them anyway, torture seemed pretty much an end in itself. He'd been a determined old sod, though, and a sorry one, but he'd divulged it all in the end, weeping into his cups. Pule smiled behind his newspaper. He wondered idly whether St. Ives had taken a compartment on his car or had gone along to the next. What did it matter?

Pule was overcome by a sudden idea. He could slip off the train, return to St. Ives' estate, and in the master's absence, ransack it. Torch the place, if it came to it. He'd been hasty—was on the edge of missing his chance. He arose, casting down his paper, when the train lurched forward again, dumping him backward onto the seat. It seemed certain that the train was at last underway. Pule thrust open the compartment door and shoved out his head, only to see some few yards before him the back of St. Ives' servant, who stood in the aisle, speaking to his employer through an open door. Pule slid back in as the train lurched once again to a stop. Was he fated to stay on the damned train? To be robbed of a second chance? He shrugged. What did it matter, after all? It was Narbondo who would profit from his returning to the manor. It was always Narbondo who profited.

"Hot scones!" came a cry from out the window. "Coffee and tea!"

Pule reached out a shilling. The flour-speckled scone seller shrieked and dropped his pastries, tray and all, onto the platform. Coffee flew. The man shrieked again. "The halien!" he cried, falling backward. "The bloody halien!"

A window slid open in the next compartment. "Brinsing!" shouted a voice. A head shoved out into the morning. Pule, casting secrecy onto the scrapheap, peered out at it. Langdon St. Ives stared back, aghast, speechless. The train bolted. Pule jumped for the door. The scone seller continued to shriek. Hasbro rushed at Pule. Pule grabbed the knob of a compartment door and flung it open into the face of his attacker, throwing his shoulder into it in an effort to knock the man down. Behind him in yet another compartment sat a frail old woman, wide-eyed with terror at the sight of the wrapped Pule. Her feet were propped on a steamer trunk, too heavy, no doubt, to be hefted onto the rack.

Pule set his feet against the doorjamb, his back against the door open in the aisle, and dragged the trunk from beneath the woman's feet, cursing it, cursing her, cursing St. Ives. He wedged the trunk against the open door, realizing as he did so that his efforts weren't worth the time he was wasting. Shouting a parting curse, he leaped out the end of the car and into the next, slowing a bit, wondering where on earth a man could hide on a train.

Trees and meadows shot past along the tracks. If it came to it, he thought, he'd leap for it. Perhaps he should jump now, before they disentangled themselves from the door and trunk. They'd never suppose him rash enough to attempt such a thing. But the countryside was flying by wonderfully quickly—dangerously so. Pule strode along through the next car and the next, into a third class car comprising two parallel rows of wooden benches facing the front of the train. The car was empty but for a single man in a chimney pipe hat who dozed in a seat on the aisle.

In his lap was a Keeble box. Pule nearly strangled. He grabbed a seat for support, gripped by vertigo. What did this mean? What weird offspring of fate had come to meet him so peculiarly here? A shouting arose behind him, along with the splintering sound of wood tearing. If he wasn't quick he'd fail. And the fault would be his own. He looked about him, barely breathing. Beneath the seats were metal baggage racks in various states of disrepair. He grasped a section of iron bar that had come unbolted and wrenched at it. He waited for the sound of the door slamming open behind, for the shouting to commence, for the man with the box—quite possibly in league with St. Ives—to awaken and cut off his escape. The bar clanked to the floor. Pule seized it as the sleeper stirred. The man opened one eye as Pule flailed at him, a cry wrenching out of his lungs. The iron bar struck the man's forehead and seemed to settle into it, as if he'd hit a pudding with a wooden spoon. Pule dropped the bar and caught the box as the man fell forward. The door burst in behind him. He was out in a trice, leaping in great hopping strides through a succession of cars, out, finally, into the morning air with no place left to flee. He braced his back against the door, holding it tight. His pursuers clattered hollering up behind. Sheep winked by on a sailing meadow.

The train tipped into a curve, slowing a bit, and Pule, shutting his eyes, catapulted from the moving car, howling and flailing into high grass and rolling down to the edge of a pond to the astonishment of the chewing sheep. He lay for a moment, imagining the damage he'd done to his spleen or his liver. He jiggled his extremities and pronounced himself fit. Inordinately proud of himself, he stood up and strode away across the pasture with the air of a man who'd done a day's work. He fancied, as he limped along the highway, his bandages finally relinquished, what St. Ives' reaction would be if he *did* slip back up to Harrogate and have another go at the house. It would be what an artist would call a finishing touch. But it would also, he could see at a glance, be unwise. He had a good deal to lose by such heroics all of a sudden, and he was determined that no one—not Narbondo, not St. Ives, not revenge—nothing would deny him the prize he'd so handily won. A moment's serendipity had turned the disastrous trip into a victory. He stopped to look at the box. It was the same sort they'd wrested from Kraken the day before. All of Keeble's damned boxes were the same. Was there a second emerald? Was this the fabled homunculus itself?

Pule considered the brass tube and what appeared to be little crank device on the side. Kraken's box hadn't had any such accoutrements—although their presence certainly didn't reveal the contents of the box. They could, quite conceivably, be a breathing mechanism of some sort for a creature housed within. Had Owlesby's manuscript revealed the whereabouts of the creature? Had St. Ives recovered it? Pule's head swan with unanswerable questions. Only one thing seemed certain—that here was a Keeble box that contained a mystery, quite possibly a valuable mystery. Pule possessed it and would continue to possess it. If worse came to worst, if all of Narbondo's plans came to naught, Pule would have the box, a much-needed wild card in a game in which Narbondo held the aces. A wagon clattered toward him along the road, and Pule stepped out to meet it, the morning sun shining down on him in an altogether friendly way.

—◊◊◊—

BILL KRAKEN HAD never before felt so low. He'd done some vile things in his life— robbed graves, pinched carp from the aquarium, been drunk more often than he'd been sober. He'd been a merchant of overripe squid, a failed purl man, a reasonably successful pea pod man, and for a two-month period a year or so after his separation from Owlesby, he'd taken up the pure trade, selling dog waste to the tanyards for enough money to keep himself fed—if cabbage broth and black bread were food. But his worst moments since poor Sebastian had fallen were mere nothings compared to the depths to which he had sunk in the last forty-eight hours. He had betrayed everyone who had befriended him. He'd sold them all. And for what? Nothing. Not a farthing. Not even a handful of beans.

He knuckled his brow and immersed himself in self-loathing. It was drink that did it—strong drink. It made a man mad. There was no way round that truth. But then so did the absence of drink, didn't it? He licked his dry lips. His tongue felt feathered. His hands shook uncontrollably when he held them in front of him. So he sat on them, perched on a stool in a corner of Narbondo's laboratory. He saw things, too, out of the corner of his eye—things he oughtn't to see. It was the horrors, is what it was. And if it wasn't, it would lead to them sure enough, to the gibbering horrors. He hadn't been so dry in a week, a month.

Now, watching out of the edge of his left eye the thing on the slab that lay not fifteen feet distant, he wondered what in the world it would look like to him if he were drunk. Given half a chance, he'd set out to discover the truth of the matter. He patted his coat pocket and there was Ashbless, bullet hole and all. The problem with the philosophers was that they were short on practical advice. They could reveal little to him about his present circumstance. Better the book were hollow and held a pint of gin.

He mashed his eyes closed and held them so. Time passed fearfully slowly. He remembered, fifteen long years past, having wrestled out of open coffins dead men not much prettier than the thing on the slab. Better his eyes had been plucked out. They quite likely would be. They'd beaten him, but he could stand that. He'd been beaten before. And he'd had the horrors before, too. But those he didn't want again. He'd given up squid merchanting when he'd found that the creatures inhabited his dreams, all leggy and cold.

For the hundredth time he looked roundabout him for something to consume—spirits of any sort—but saw nothing but the empty wine glass left with diabolical purpose on a tabletop by the fat boy in curls, along with the carcass of a fowl. The breadth of the glass magnified the depth of the little crimson circle settled in the bottom. In truth there wasn't enough in it to dribble to the edge when the glass was upturned.

Kraken had tried, to be sure. He'd mopped up the dregs with his fingers, but little of substance was accomplished by it. There was even less in the way of food on the plate—nothing but broken bones—just the gristly burnt carcass of a peculiar game bird, a pea hen with the head on, eyeless and charred.

Pule and Narbondo had gone out, locking the doors and windows. They'd abandoned him hours earlier, before night had fallen. The ghostly light of the gaslamps did nothing to enliven the general gloom of the cabinet—simply cast unpleasant shadows on the walls and floor, like the shadow, thought Kraken, barely able to look at it, of the humped, skeletal pea hen across the edge of the piano. They'd left him a pitcher of water. Perhaps if he got desperate enough…

They'd return, he knew, with a body. Pule's trip to Harrogate in search of poor Sebastian's manuscript had ended in a general rage. Curses flew. The doctor had cuffed Pule across the chin, destroyed the pot of carbolic and stewed horsehide that Pule was cooking as a facial treatment. It had smelled awful. Then they'd gone out. The thing on the slab must be vivified, that's what Narbondo had said. Tonight. They would find a donor. If not, hinted the doctor, Kraken would do nicely. Kraken or Pule, either one of them. Pule had smiled through his tirade, like a cat full of milk.

The gaslamps flickered. Shadows danced. The game bird rattled suddenly on its plate as if it were trying to drag itself away. Kraken started in horror. Silence fell once again. Across the room on a small table beside the fishless aquarium sat the Keeble box. What could Kraken do with it? He could smash out the window and pitch it into the street, then dive out after it. But what would it profit him? He was a hunted man. There could be no doubt about that. Newgate was too good for him. It would mean the gibbet if he were caught.

Outside the window swirled a thick fog, most of it river fog off the Thames. Dirty little rivulets dripped down the panes, pooling up along the mullions and dripping off, one by one, onto the sidewalk below. The street outside was silent. It was the silence, dense as the fog, that bothered him. He'd tried singing and whistling, but in the dim, shadow-haunted room the noise had merely been unnatural. It seemed to him, in fact, that the slightest sound would awaken the thing on the slab.

Its head was twisted toward him, dropped crookedly across its chest. Flesh hung beneath its eyesockets like parchment. It seemed as if a breeze through a broken window pane would turn it to dust. Or perhaps the thing would rise in the draft like a kite to twitch and gibber at him, to lurch along toward him, silhouetted against the light that shone dimly through the curtained window of the room across the courtyard. Earlier he'd seen the shadow of a face peer past the curtain—watching him, perhaps; perhaps one of Narbondo's agents.

Kraken shut his eyes, but through the lids he could see the dancing shadows animated by gaslight. He pressed his eyes with his hands, but the horrors that swirled into view against the back of his eyelids were worse than the thing on the table. What had Paracelsus said about such emanations? He couldn't quite recall. Paracelsus was mist in his memory, a product of another age, an age that had ended when he'd stolen the damned emerald from the Captain, the emerald that the smug Narbondo had left so casually beside the aquarium.

On the edge of the slab, as if they had crawled there of their own power, were two skeletal hands, obviously fallen from the hunched corpse behind them. Kraken avoided looking at them. He had been certain an hour earlier that for an instant the things had moved, rattled their fingers atop the table, inched inexorably toward him, and that the ruined pea hen had sighed on its plate, rustling among cold potatoes.

But all had fallen silent. It was the wind through the broken panes, carrying on it the sharp, sooty odor of fog. There lay the hands, almost grasping the edge of the lamplit table, ready, perhaps, to lunge at him. Why in the devil weren't they attached to the corpse? What unholy thing did their separation betoken?

Kraken peered at them, and was certain for one rigid moment that the index finger of the left hand twitched. Beckoning. He glanced away toward the fogbound window and gasped in horror at his own reflection, hovering in the glass, staring in at him. He edged farther into his corner. If the hands crept from the slab would they shatter when they hit the floor? Or would they fall into shadow, pausing for a moment before scuttling out like crabs toward his feet. Kraken was suddenly fearfully cold. Narbondo, perhaps, wouldn't return at all. Perhaps they'd gone out, knowing that Kraken would die in horror during the night, that the thing in the shroud would rush at him like a sheet hauled along a clothesline, would envelop him in dust and rot and clacking bones and suffocate him in horror.

On the wall behind him hung a collection of instruments, but there was nothing with which to defend himself against animated corpses. His eyes settled on a pair of elongated tongs, the jaws of which were wrapped in a rubber casing. He stood up slowly, barely breathing, understanding that the thing on the slab was watching, trying, perhaps, to fathom his fear, his intent.

He very slowly removed the tongs and stepped across toward the slab, wheezing with fear, waiting for the hands to fly at him like papery bugs, like leather-winged bats, to clutch at his throat, to reach into his mouth. At the touch of the tongs, surely they'd leap at him as if spring driven. He knew they would.

But they didn't. He plucked one of the hands up and very gingerly turned, took a step toward the open piano, and shoved the thing onto the silent keys, banging out a wild note with the edge of the tongs and leaping backward, a shriek lodged in his throat. The other hand lay as before. Or did it? Was it turned now? Had it crept about to face him? He clamped the tongs around it, whirled, and dumped it onto the piano keys along with its grisly counterpart, then slammed down the key cover, locking it with a little triangular brass key that lay atop the piano.

Could he bear to do the same with the thing's head—yank it loose and hide it somewhere? Perhaps shove the top of the piano aside and toss it in? He forced himself to look at it, to imagine clamping the tongs against the ivory cheekbones and twisting the head until it snapped. The thought paralyzed him, but he had to do it. He steeled himself. He couldn't be stared at any longer. He stepped toward it, reaching out with the tongs, slowly drawing the jaws apart. He daren't get the tongs in the thing's mouth; it would snap the steel rods like twigs.

The tongs inched closer. Kraken shook so that the loose rivet about which the tongs swiveled rattled like a locust. He gasped for breath. The horrible eye sockets seemed to stare through him—through his forehead beaded with cold sweat, a great salty drop of which rolled into his right eye, nearly blinding him. The tongs settled in against the cheekbones, and, with a thrum of settling bones, the thing on the table gave a quick lurch, as if shaking off the rubber clamp.

Kraken hooted in fear, dropped the tongs onto the top of the slab, and trod backwards toward his corner, slamming into the game bird's table with his right foot. The spindly table leg buckled, and the skeletal bird rolled from the plate in a little cascade of peas and fell to the floor. Kraken watched it in horror, half expecting the thin gray bones of the wings to vibrate and the bird to sail off like a great moth toward the flame of the gaslamp. The tongs banged down on the floor beside it.

This wouldn't do. He couldn't abide the idea of the bird out of sight on the floor behind the table. He must know its movements, if there were any. If it flew out of nowhere at him, he'd simply drop dead. He bent suddenly, summoning his strength. He grasped the tongs, plucked the bird from the floor, and tossed it, tongs and all, into a coal bucket on the hearth next to the piano. The bird whumped into the bucket in a cloud of coal dust; the tongs banged against the wall and dropped onto the hearth tiles. Kraken whirled around at the sound of a sudden scuffling behind him, expecting to find himself confronted by the handless skeleton. But there it sat, unmoving. The scuffling issued from beyond the wall across the room. Something pawed at the wall, trying to get in at him. Kraken slumped backward toward his stool in the corner. —☞

TWELVE

The Animation
of Joanna Southcote

A PANEL IN THE oak wainscot slid abruptly open, and beyond it, tugging weirdly at a pair of shoes, was a bent Willis Pule. He backed into the room, grunting with effort, and Dr. Narbondo appeared behind him, holding up the opposite end of a corpse. Pule dropped it as soon as it was entirely past the wall, as if he were immensely tired. Narbondo kicked the corner of the panel, and it slid shut, cutting off the entrance to what looked to Kraken to be a dark, low hallway. Kraken shrank into his corner, wondering in horror at this new act of villainy, half relieved, however, that it wasn't him that was being dragged down tunnels.

The panel had just slid shut when there came a fearful pounding at the conventional door. Pule swung it open, and there stood Shiloh the messiah with a look on his face that seemed to imply that he would brook no nonsense, that he'd come for his mother and there would be hell to pay, perhaps literally, if he wasn't satisfied. Narbondo scowled back at him. "Where is Nell Owlesby?" he asked suddenly.

"She's safe—safer by far with my flock than with you."

"Half your flock is *my* flock," said Narbondo, "and they'd as soon eat her as give her a tract. Get her.

"Quite impossible, I assure you." Shiloh stepped in and closed the door, frowning at the littered room and at Bill Kraken, who, it seemed, was at least as offensive to him as was the corpse on the floor. "I'll keep my end of the bargain. You don't need the woman for that. *I* know where the box is hidden, and have these ten years. If you do as I say, you'll know too. It's as simple as that. But you needn't worry about the woman. She's worth nothing to you beyond that single bit of knowledge. And *that,* as we both know, is worth an enormous amount, isn't it?"

The old man slouched on a stool, obviously enjoying the advantage he held over Narbondo. He removed a snuffbox from his pocket, pinched out a frightful quantity, and inhaled hugely, surrounding his head in a momentary brown cloud. He sneezed voluminously six times in rapid, deflating succession until he was reduced to a bent, wheezing ruin, his face a mask of mixed pain and satisfaction. Dr. Narbondo shook his head in disgust. Shiloh groped for his pocket, replacing the snuffbox, and wiped his eyes with the hem of his robe. His wrinkled forehead alternately relaxed and contracted like an irritated slug, as if he were experiencing after tremors of his recent snuff-inspired earthquake.

He pulled himself erect and looked straightaway at the Keeble box atop the aquarium; then, before Narbondo could stop him, he stepped across and picked it up. "Very nice article, this."

The hunchback jerked toward him, snatching the box away. The old man put on a theatrically offended face and then looked in mock surprise at his empty hands. Narbondo scowled and set the box gingerly atop the piano.

The heap of bones and winding sheet on the slab seemed to slump just a bit in response to the box having been moved, and the wisp of settling debris struck the grin from Shiloh's face. He seemed to recall suddenly that it was his mother that lay before him. Narbondo wheeled his misting device past on a tea cart, brushing the old man out of the way. Then he hauled out of a cupboard a low gurney. He and Pule tugged the fresh cadaver onto the gurney and cranked it up level with the slab. From a wooden trough beneath the jar of yellow fluid he pulled a dripping, desultory carp, alive but sluggish, and slapped it onto the gurney beside the corpse. He worked quickly and deftly, but with a contracted brow and sweat-beaded forehead, as if he knew precisely what he was about and knew equally well that what he was about was not at all a simple business.

Pule stood silently by, spurred now and then to grudging action when Narbondo snarled out orders, then falling into inactivity, either out of a lack of comprehension or a general unwillingness to be ordered about. The old man twittered near the window like a bird—the approaching experiment having eliminated any veneer of detached coolness. He gasped suddenly and clutched his breast. "Where," he cried, pointing. "Her hands…where are her hands? I swear to heaven, Narbondo, if you've made a hash of this, if you've…"

"Shut up, old man!" cried Narbondo, clipping him off in midsentence. "Where are Lady Southcote's beautiful hands?" he asked Pule. Pule stared at him, then looked around, bending to peer under the slab. Kraken quaked in silence on his stool.

"You foul…!" cried the evangelist, unable to think of a word sufficiently foul to express his indignity. "I'll…"he began again, but this time a wild clattering arose from the direction of the hearth, and a chunk of coal the size of a walnut popped out of the coal bucket onto the floor.

"A rat," whispered Narbondo, reaching for the poker at the far side of the hearth and raising it over his head.

"Damn me!" shouted the old man, enraged that Narbondo had abandoned his mother to chase a rat. Narbondo hunched toward the coal bucket, a finger to his lips. A wild rattling issued from it. Coal dust rose in a cloud. The bucket tipped over with a clang, cascading a little delta of clinkers onto the hearth, atop which rode the blackened remains of the pea hen, its broken wings working furiously, its head swiveling from side to side. And, as if in accompaniment, the piano erupted into discordant play, as if someone were beating randomly on the concealed keys. Kraken crossed himself. Shiloh threw open the window over the courtyard and perched one foot onto the sill, ready to leap. Narbondo swung the poker wildly at the hopping pea hen, slamming it into the piano leg. The bird rose into the air, a thin whistling sound chirping from its stretched throat where ragged, charred skin still clung in patches. The box atop the piano danced in tune to the wild playing, and the pea hen shot off like a stone out of a sling, straight into the wall above the aquarium, smearing coal dust and grease onto the yellowed plaster, then dropping with a splash into the water, sinking slowly to the gravel and staring out at them mournfully before collapsing onto its side.

The piano, meanwhile, banged away. Narbondo, emboldened by the demise of the pea hen and certain that a properly objective attitude would explain away the phenomenon of the mysterious piano, lunged at the instrument and pushed back the lid. He picked up his poker, raised it ceilingward, and peered in to find nothing but flying hammers. Squinting at Pule, who had retreated toward Kraken's end of the room, he pulled gingerly on the key cover. It was locked. Mystified, he found the key, unlocked the cover, threw it back, and shouted in surprise at the weird scene before him the crabbed, skeletal hands of Joanna Southcote, thumping pointlessly on the keys. They flailed across the keyboard in an agitated whirl, hopping onto the floor where they twitched and danced.

"Her hands!" Shiloh shouted, repeating himself, more horrified at their spectacular reappearance than he had been at their absence.

Narbondo lunged for Kraken's fallen tongs, grappling each hand in turn, flopping them onto the slab. The first leaped off immediately, and Narbondo was on it at once, avidly now, slamming it back beside its mate. The two, finally, lay still.

"This is an outrage!" sputtered Shiloh, his mouth working spasmodically.

"This is powerful alchemy!" whispered Narbondo, as much to himself as to anyone else, and he immediately trained his sprayer onto the corpse. She seemed to stretch. Joints crackled. Her neck swiveled and rose a half inch off her chest. "Damn!" cried Narbondo, remembering her hands. He yanked out a roll of thin, braided wire from a box on his desk and affixed her wayward hands to her wrists. Her jaws clacked as if in satisfaction. Kraken was stupefied with terror. He grabbed suddenly for the water pitcher, swallowed a great draught, choked, and collapsed onto the floor, coughing and sputtering. Pule kicked him out of a lack of anything else to do, and Kraken scuttled in behind the stool, holding it in front of him to ward off the detested Pule.

Yellow mist clouded the room, swirling round in the draft as Narbondo excised the carp gland. "Her hands!" cried Shiloh again. "You've got them on backwards!"

"Silence!" shouted the hunchback, beside himself with success. He capered back and forth beside the slab, dancing round the edge of the gurney, spraying mist, affixing coiled tubing into a slit cut in the trachea of the dead man that Pule and he had dragged in through the secret door. He shoved it into his lungs, crying out to Pule to hold the sprayer, to prop up Joanna Southcote, to measure out a beaker of fluids.

"Her thumbs point outward!" whined the evangelist tiresomely, obsessed with Narbondo's mistake.

"She's lucky to have hands at all," responded the doctor, leaping and jigging. "I'll put the hands of an ape on her!"

And as if in response to this last threat, the corpse of Lady Southcote loomed up out of the mist like a marionette in a fever dream, jaws clacking, wavering there atop the slab as if she were adrift on a current of air.

"Mother!" cried Shiloh, collapsing onto his knees. From his robe he produced a stoppered bottle. He twisted it open and shook it liberally at the creature which slouched down the slab toward him. He intoned a nasal prayer, crossing himself, waving and gesturing. Narbondo sprayed on, stamping at a bladder on the ground that pumped something—Lord knew what—from the lungs of the dead man into the shrouded chest cavity of Joanna Southcote. The escaping gasses whistled eerily, like wind through the gap under a door.

"Speak!" implored the evangelist.

"Whee, whee, whee!" hooted the creeping skeleton before dropping off the end of the slab in a clatter of bones.

"Christ!" shouted Narbondo, genuinely dismayed at this new turn. A loose foot slid past him, out of sight under the piano, and a leg, severed from its pelvis, wobbled storklike in the settling mist before collapsing slowly forward, bouncing just a bit when it hit the ground, then clattering into silence. Only the skull, its toothy mouth working, remained animate, chattering round and round in a tight little circle on the slab.

"Command me, Mother!" cried the evangelist, grabbing for it, then stopping suddenly in mid-grab, as if he were reconsidering his actions. "She's a ruin!" he wept, hitting tiredly at Narbondo, who stood nearby, breathing heavily.

Shiloh looked around suddenly, wildly. "She'll come with me!" he cried.

"Gladly," said the doctor, pulling down one of the cast glass cubes. "This is spade work." He turned, humped across to a closet, flung it open, grabbed a dirty spade from among a half-dozen of the things, and turned to see Kraken, eyes whirling with fear, reaching for the box atop the piano.

Narbondo swung the spade at Kraken, who fended it off with his arm, howling in pain and hopping away from the piano. The hunchback spun around, recovered, and set himself to bash Kraken once again, but his quarry had abandoned the box and bolted toward the stairs. Narbondo leaped after him, paused at the top of the dark landing, listening to Kraken pound in wild steps toward the street. He turned once again into the room, where Pule crawled on his hands and knees, scuttling into the path of the skull, which jabbered along toward the street wall. The evangelist leaped back and forth, shouting orders.

"Get out of the way!" shouted Narbondo, storming past both of them and shoveling the head into the glass jar. In a moment Joanna Southcote was captive, the gibbering evangelist snatching a broad volume from a bookshelf and slamming it atop the square mouth of the jar, fearful, perhaps, that the skull, giddy with animation, would clamber out to resume its skittering journey across the oak plank of the floor.

The old man sat wheezing, cradling the prize in his lap. He stared mournfully at the heap of disconnected bone that had, for some few moments, shown such promise. With her he could have astonished the populace of London. Converts would have flocked in. The eyes of kings and dukes would have shot open. The doors of treasuries would have swung to. And here it was, a ruin.

Then again…He peered in at the head, considering. Its mouth worked silently. Without the aid of the air-filled bladder it could say nothing. But what would it take, he wondered, to provide it with a voice, from offstage, perhaps. It seemed like a blasphemy, to trump up a voice for the holy article, but the work mustn't languish. It must go on at any cost. She would have been the first to agree. It looked to him as if she were nodding agreement from within her box, voicing her approval.

He stood up and moved toward the door. Narbondo and Pule stood talking in low tones near the courtyard window, but on perceiving Shiloh's intent, they stepped along after him.

"It's useless," said Narbondo, reaching the door ahead of the tired evangelist. "I've done what I could. No man alive could have done more. If I had the box, there's no telling what sort of restoration we could accomplish. Where is it?"

The old man glared at him. "You can hardly be serious. You've purposely made a mess of this. Out of spite. Out of evil and nothing else. I owe you nothing at all, nothing."

"Then you're a dead man," replied the doctor, drawing his pistol. "Take the head," he snapped at Pule.

"Wait!" cried Shiloh. "This is no time for haste, my son. Perhaps we can reach an agreement—twenty-five converts, shall we say, in recompense for the damage you've done tonight."

"I'll graft her head onto a carp—or better yet, a pig—and show her in carnivals. Take the head!" He waved with the pistol at Pule.

Shiloh glared at the hunchback. "You leave me no choice," he said.

Narbondo nodded, rolling his eyes. "That's correct. No choice at all. Not a bit. There's nothing I'd like more than to shoot you and turn the both of you into some sort of instructive sideshow attraction. Where is the box?"

"Aboard the blimp of Doctor Birdlip. Nell Owlesby gave it to him the night of her brother's death. There's your accursed information—fat lot of good it will do you. When the blimp…"

But Narbondo turned his back and walked toward the courtyard window, stroking his chin. "Of course it is," he muttered.

"Let me say," began the evangelist, catching sight of Willis Pule as if for the first time. He stopped, gazing with sudden astonishment at the sight of Pule's ravaged and discolored face. "My son," he began again, "your countenance is as an open book, the pages recounting a life of degradation. It is not too late. It is…" But what it was, finally, was left unsaid, for Pule lashed out at the proselytizing evangelist with his open palm, swatting him on the forehead and sending him sprawling through the doorway waving the bottled head. The door slammed shut between them. —๑

THIRTEEN

The Royal Academy

I 'VE JUST WITNESSED the most amazing spectacle." said Theophilus Godall with uncharacteristic enthusiasm. Captain Powers hunched forward in his chair to encourage his friend. But he held up his right hand as if to signal for a brief pause and picked up a decanter of port, offering it to Nell Owlesby, who shook her head and smiled at him.

Godall related the story of the animation of the thing on the slab: how he'd watched through the window the sad antics of Bill Kraken; how he'd seen Narbondo enliven a skeleton, dance it about the laboratory; how the thing had gone to bits and Shiloh the evangelist had sunk from view, he and Willis Pule banging about the floor while Narbondo flailed at Kraken with a shovel. Atop the piano had sat the Captain's box, or one very much like it, and Godall had been in a quandary about how to retrieve it. But his well-laid plan had gone awry when Kraken, obviously a prisoner, had fled, and Godall had gone after him, chasing him half across London only to lose him in Limehouse and come away empty-handed.

The Captain nodded over his pipe, clenching and unclenching his fists so that corded muscles danced along his forearms "We'll go in after it, then," he said finally, squinting across at Godall.

His friend nodded. It seemed, certainly, the only clear course—an emerald, after all, big as a fist. It was Jack and Dorothy's livelihood—Jack's inheritance.

Contacting the police would avail them little. Nell would be exposed. And where, they would ask, did this emerald come from? If it was Jack Owlesby's inheritance, why didn't he have it? Why all the secrecy, the convolutions? How, in fact, did Dr. Narbondo come to possess it? Were they accusing *him* of stealing it? No, they weren't. He took it from the man who stole it. And where was this fellow, this Kraken? No one knew. Somewhere in London, maybe. The police would scratch their chins and give each other looks, and in the end, not only would suspicion fall upon

185

the innocent, but no end of skeletons would be dragged, perhaps literally, from dusty old closets.

No, said the Captain, shaking his head with determination, in for a penny, in for a pound. They'd act tomorrow. Godall produced a pen and paper, poured himself a brandy and water, and began to sketch out a plan of Narbondo's cabinet, the building it occupied on Pratwell, his own room opposite, and the courtyard between. Nell filled in elements of the laboratory itself that Godall could only speculate on, much of the room being invisible from his curtain slit.

If Narbondo were out, they'd force the door, walk in, and take the box—reduce the room to rubble, if need be, to find it. Narbondo would have to be watched. He might, after all, remove the box to another location. But why should he? Then, if the doctor was in, Godall could resort to disguise to gain entrance—an official from social welfare, a seller of scientific apparatus—that would do nicely. They'd hold him up like burglars. What would he do? Call the authorities? Shout through the windows? It was hardly likely. He'd know, then, what sort of men he'd fallen out with, said the Captain. He'd find that he'd made a mistake.

There was a slamming of a street door opposite, and the Captain broke off his speculating to look out, in hopes that it was William Keeble coming across to chat. It was high time, he realized now, that the Keebles knew of the presence of Nell Owlesby. They would all have to fall together in this thing. There could be no more secrets, no disconnected pieces of the puzzle. No more boxes hidden under floors. It would quite likely take the vigilance of the lot of them and to spare if they weren't to be borne down by the collective forces of evil.

But it wasn't William Keeble; it was Jack and Dorothy, setting out hand in hand through the murky morning, the fog swirling round the streetlamps, their shoes clumping on the pavement. Jack held a box beneath his free arm. Nell watched over the Captain's shoulder. "I'd give anything to call out to them," she said in a low voice. "Or to run ahead and step out of a doorway and utter his name." She stopped, watching the pair turn up Spade Street and disappear, and she stood silently for a moment, as if lost in thought. "He'd hate me, I suppose, she said finally, "for what happened to his father."

"I think you'd be surprised," the Captain said, squeezing her hand. "He knows what happened to his father. His death wasn't the worst of it, not by a sea mile, and he wouldn't be the lad I know he is if he was blind to what you did, for the reason of it."

Nell remained silent, watching the door of the Keeble house. Godall pretended to be fiddling intently with his pipe, oblivious to the conversation going on three or four feet away. The Captain slapped his ivory leg and said, "First things first, that's my way. We'll pay a visit to this hunchback sawbones first. Get the fun out of the way. There's time enough for work afterwards." And he turned back to the map and to Godall, gesturing at the open courtyard and reaching for his cold pipe.

—◦◦◦—

St. James Square lay torpid beneath the fog and the chill, as if waiting languidly for the murk to lift. But the fog hovered through the morning, shot through now and again with rays of feeble sunlight that faltered and faded almost as soon as they appeared, rays that thinned the murk momentarily, then abandoned any hope of success and fled. Cabs rattled apace along Pall Mall, pale ghosts with lamps glowing fitfully through the gloom, then winking out, making it seem as if they had been nothing but disembodied rattle and clatter that sprang into and then out of muted clarity.

The man in the chimney pipe hat stood in the darkness of the very alley in which Bill Kraken had caught St. Ives' discarded cigar. His hat perched atop a blood-spotted bandage wrapped around his forehead, and threatened to topple at any moment onto the dirt of the sidewalk. He yawned, deciding that he'd risk stepping across to a tavern in a court opposite for a quick pint. The girl wouldn't be out on such a day anyway. Her schedule, after all, hadn't been unvaried. There was some chance that he'd spend another two hours waiting in vain, perhaps be questioned by a constable and sent on his way.

But if he packed it in and *she* was true to her Thursday morning schedule, what then? Time was short. Drake was in no mood for failure. His returning from Harrogate without the box had almost cost him…he didn't know what. It didn't bear thinking about. Time, somehow, was growing short, and Drake's patience with it. The pint could wait. He'd need it all the more desperately in two hour's time anyway.

A distant bell chimed eleven o'clock. Footfalls sounded out of the murk, which had suddenly swirled into such obscurity that the tree in the center of the square was blotted out. Two shapes approached. Billy Deener squinted into the gloom. It was she. But who was this with her? Her young man. This was unexpected.

What was even less expected was the thing he held under his arm—a box, one that Deener recognized even through the gloom. A vivid picture of a bandage-wrapped figure flailing at him with an iron rod leaped into his mind, a figure that stole the box and fled. And here, apparently, he was, come round to give the box up. Here were two birds, hand in hand. Deener smiled malignly. He hefted the sap in his right hand, stepped out of the shadows behind the loitering, chattering couple, grasped the girl's arm, and slammed the sap against Jack's head, chortling through his nose as his prey fell forward onto his face like a toppled tree.

Dorothy screamed at the sudden clutching hand from the shadows, then screamed again at the solid whump of the cosh and Jack's collapse onto the roadway. But her second scream was cut off instantaneously by a rough hand. She bit at it, kicking backwards and scraping her heel down the shin of the man who twisted her arm around behind her. An almost simultaneous scream broke forth from the lips of a woman who herded a covey of children through the square and who stood open-mouthed, pointing, her children cringing horrorstruck beside her, not so much at the sight of Dorothy being dragged into the alley or of Jack lying senseless on the pavement, as at the sound of their horrified mother's shriek. Sporadic crying and screaming broke out, one shriek igniting another, the collective squealing fueling itself. Deener backed down the alley. The hue and cry would mean the end of him. In a moment he'd have to abandon the struggling girl and flee. He had only to drag her forty feet down the alley to freedom through a door left purposely ajar. But there on the ground, beside the meddling youth, lay the box he'd been cheated of once. He was damned if he'd be cheated again. He raised his hand, allowing the struggling girl to pull her right hand free and bury her nails into his bruised forehead. A thrill of pain shot along his scalp, and he yelped in rage, swinging the cosh hard enough to end the struggle there and then. He shoved his hand into his mouth, blew through two fingers, and scuttled out of the alley, picking up the fallen box. A head popped out of the open door. Deener shouted a curse at it, and a man, the owner of the head, loped along the alley toward him.

"Murder! Murder!" cried the woman with the howling children. The cry was followed close on by the sound of stamping feet and the shrill blast of a police whistle. As Deener and his companion—a beefy, lard-faced man in shirtsleeves dragged the inert girl through the yawning door, the mouth of the alley was filled with a growing crowd of dim spirits, peering in, unwilling to follow two seeming murderers into the dim shadows.

Billy Deener eased the door shut, knowing that the general darkness of the alley obscured almost entirely by the fog would serve to hide their movements, and that a subsequent search would reveal nothing more than a crumbled hole below the street, a hole that led into the filthy darkness of the London sewers.

The cellar wall was a tumbled heap of ancient brick some three feet thick, beyond which ran the upper level of the Kermit Street sewer. Mortar had cracked and fallen for a hundred years from hastily pointed joints, and the continual wet of the sewer had caused the wall to slump and the bricks one by one to fall out, until some final bit of mortar or the corner of an ancient brick had decomposed, precipitating the collapse of a long section of sewer wall in a foul-smelling heap of muck.

The sewer was running at low water, but even so, Deener and his accomplice were hard pressed to make headway. They felt their way along planks slimy and rotten with sewage, kicking into the soft surface of the wood with the hobnails of their hoots. A lit candle flickered in a tin holder wrapped around the head of Deener's companion, and the light danced and shrank, was snuffed out and had to be relit time and time again, both men half expecting the flame to set off an explosion in the dense air. Deener, wary of choke damp, breathed through a kerchief tied over his nose and mouth. They stooped along beneath the low ceiling, watching for the mark that would signal their arrival at the house on Wardour Street.

The Kermit Street sewer was badly in need of leveling, for the general sinking of the ground had created long cesspools, the settling water further decomposing what solid ground remained, so that the foundations of houses above cracked and pitched and loathsome sewer gases drifted up into courtyards. But the cesspools which so hampered leveling and flushing had their own value, were the resting place, in fact, for murdered men, not a few of whom had found their way into the sewers with the help of Billy Deener. Their bodies lay mired in offal and garbage and road sweepings emptied down gulley grates, until the corpses swirled at high water into the Thames where, bloated and faceless, they were declared drowned for lack of any sensible alternative.

But the unconscious girl was a different sort of victim. She should, Deener knew, be the one among them to wear the kerchief over her face, but his service to Kelso Drake only stretched so far. The score of minutes she spent below ground wouldn't hurt her. She wasn't even conscious of their passing.

—*∿*—

WHEN DOROTHY AWOKE, a tearing pain pounding in her head, the cigar-chewing face of the man who had stood in the entry hall of her house arguing with her father smiled down at her, the cigar rolling from side to side as if it were alive. His smile, however, was void of humor or concern for anything but Kelso Drake. She was certain, even in her fuddled state, that it was a smile of loathsome self-satisfaction, empty of anything but falsehood.

It swam out of focus and then back in. She felt awful. There was a horrible stench in the room, the smell of an open sewer, and it seemed to her as Drake materialized before her that it was he who smelled so foul, he or the bent man who stood beside him, squinting at her as if she were some sort of interesting specimen. Then she lost interest in either of the two men, drifting away into herself and the pain in her head. She moved her arm, intent upon touching the hair beside her ear, which, pressed against a pillow, felt clotted with dried blood. She'd been hit on the head. She remembered part of it. Surely, though, this was no hospital. Bits and pieces of memory filtered in, scrabbling around in her mind until they joined like interlocking pieces of a puzzle to form the picture of Jack lying senseless on the pavement of St. James Square, of her struggling with a man in a hat, of a woman screaming over and over, of gaping children, of nothing at all after that.

She tried to push herself up onto her left elbow, to swing her right hand at the face before her. But something got in the way. She couldn't move, was fastened, somehow, secured to the bed by a sheet tied across her shoulders. The cigar face laughed. A hand removed the cigar. The mouth said, "She'll do nicely—pay us twice over," and the face laughed again. "Sedate her," it said, and disappeared from view.

The hunchback loomed over her, a cup full of violet liquid in his hand. The sheet was loosed briefly, and she was yanked onto her elbows by a balding man in a black coat. She hadn't the strength to fight. She drank the thin, bitter draught, and very soon swam away into darkness.

—⁓—

LANGDON ST. IVES sawed away at a grilled cutlet that had the consistency of shoe leather. The gray meat lay like a curled bit of tanned hide between a boiled potato and a collection of thumb-sized peas. A sauce—"*Andalouse aux fines herbes*," as the hastily drawn menu had called it—was dribbled stingily over the cutlet, the chef careful not to be so liberal as to allow the liquid to pollute the boiled potato. This last, cold as the plate it sat on, sorely needed the sauce, and St. Ives tried with limited success to spoon a bit onto it. But most of what he scraped from the surface of the cutlet merely glued itself to the spoon in a scum of tomato and pepper, leading St. Ives to curse both the quality and the quantity of it. Rationally, he supposed, he should count himself lucky to be faced with such a meagre plateful of the wretched stuff, but eating, like anything else, wasn't a particularly rational business.

He pushed the tiresome plate away, listening to the droning voice of an equally tiresome bespectacled gentleman who sat opposite, tearing into his own cutlet indifferently, as if the act of eating were merely a matter of satisfying bodily processes. He might as well consume a plateful of leaves and twigs. The man spoke to St. Ives as he masticated his veal and peas, chomp chomp chomp, over and over like a machine grinding rock into cement.

"The digestion," he said, waggling his jaw, "is a tricky business. Gastric juices and all that. It takes a vast quantity of stomach-produced chemicals to break down a lump of sustenance like this pea." And he held a pea aloft for St. Ives' benefit, as if the thing were a fascinating little world which the two of them could examine.

"Biology has never been my forte," admitted St. Ives, who couldn't abide peas under any circumstances.

The man popped the pea into his mouth and ground it up. "Gallons of bodily fluids," he said, "produced, mind you, at great expense to the system. Now this same pea reduced to pulp can be readied for evacuation by a tenth amount of gastro-intestinal juices..."

St. Ives stared out the window, unable to look at his plate. He couldn't work up much enthusiasm for bodily talk. He had nothing against physiology; some of his best friends were physiologists. But it was hardly supper conversation—was it?—all this business about fluids and evacuation. And what was it leading to here? It constituted the friendly sort of banter that preceded really serious discussion—the reason he was once again being fed at the Bayswater Club owned by the Royal Academy of Sciences. With all their powers of scientific perception, thought St. Ives, they ought to be able to see that the supposed veal they were served was in fact a slab of old dairy cow—or worse, a paring of horseflesh, bled pale and bleached with chemicals by the knacker.

No one, however, seemed to be eating save he and old Parsons, whose fellow Academist Lord Kelvin owned a barn in Harrogate alongside his summer house, a barn that, since the debacle of the alien starship, hadn't any roof. He also, according to Hasbro, owned two dead cows, which had suffered the misfortune of having strayed into the barn minutes before the ship caved in the roof.

And now St. Ives would pay the price. He was in a foul humor—he realized that. First the launching of the craft, then the escape of Willis Pule from the train. The man must have been desperate. It was entirely conceivable that he had leaped to his death in the ditch, an unsatisfying thought altogether. Villains, St. Ives considered, ought to be made to account for themselves. Their demise should be both spectacular and humiliating.

"And the molars of a horse can reduce the most surprising weeds to fortifying pulp in moments," his host intoned, working at a mouthful of his own surprising food-stuffs. "Now, like a human being, a horse has only a single stomach, but his intestine is phenomenally elongated, adapted to the digestion of coarse forages. This is all a fasci-nating subject, this business of eating. I've spent a lifetime studying it. And I've found few things more interesting in the eating line than a workhorse—and of the right sort, mind you. Some sorts of hay are superior due to their effects on the bowel." He waved his fork proudly, as if to illustrate this last statement, and speared up a row of peas.

St. Ives took advantage of the man's pausing to yank out his pocketwatch, widen-ing his eyes in alarm, as if he'd just now become conscious of the prodigious passage of time. But his intended attempt to hurry the end of the engagement disappeared into a lecture on the bacterial manifestations of intestinal debris. The man paused some few minutes later to drain a great tumbler of distilled water before him, the cleansing effects of which would "leach away poisons," not at all unlike the exemplary workings of a well-constructed sewage system. He smacked his lips over the water. "Staff of life," he said.

St. Ives nodded, performing his pocketwatch activity all over again, putting on the same face filled with surprise and haste. His companion, however, wasn't so eas-ily put off. He removed his spectacles, causing his eyes to undergo a remarkable and instantaneous shrinkage, and he wiped his face thoroughly with his napkin. "Close in here, what?"

St. Ives nodded, humoring the man. Such men, he told himself, must be humored. One had to nod continually in agreement until, when an opening presented itself, one could nod to one's feet and nod one's way down the stairs, leaving the zealot with the curious mingling of satisfaction in having been so thoroughly agreed with and wonder at being abandoned. But there was no such opportunity here.

"Dr. Birdlip, then," said Parsons suddenly. "You were a friend of his."

St. Ives steeled himself for the inevitable conversation, the same that had occurred weeks earlier, the afternoon of the night he'd been surprised by Kraken in the rain. The

Royal Academy was vastly interested in Dr. Birdlip's flight and its implications in terms of technologic advance and were prevailing upon St. Ives to help elucidate the nature of the doctor's wonderful flight. Birdlip, of course, was not the real genius behind the perpetually propelled craft. They knew that. He was a sort of mystic—wasn't he?—a man who fancied himself a philosopher. More than that, he was a seeker after mysteries. He'd published, to his credit, a strange paper entitled, "The Myth of the Foggy London Night," followed by a paper speculating on the construction of spectacles through which one could see successive layers of passing time like translucent doors opening and shutting along a corridor. What was that one titled? "Time Considered as a Succession of Semi-closed Doors." Yes, said Parsons, it was all terribly—how should he put it—"theoretical," wasn't it? Poetic, almost. Perhaps he'd missed his true calling. The titles alone betrayed the peculiar bent of his mind. Genius it might he, said Parsons, but genius of a speculative and, mightn't we say, of a non-productive nature. Certainly not the sort of thing that would produce an engine such as the one that drives the dirigible. Parsons smiled up at St. Ives ingratiatingly, prodding a pea across his plate with the end of his fork, driving it into a little pool of dried sauce.

"Are you aware," he asked, squinting at St. Ives, "of the religious cult that has sprung up around the sporadic appearances of this blimp? It's rumored that there is some connection between Dr. Birdlip and this self-styled holy man who calls himself Shiloh. There's nothing more dangerous, mind you, than a religious fanatic. They presume to define morality, and their definitions are made at the expense of everyone but themselves."

"I can assure you," said St. Ives, looking first at Parsons, then glancing out the window at activities transpiring three floors below, "that Dr. Birdlip is unacquainted with the mystic. He…"

But Parsons cut him off, his spectacles dropping of their own accord to the tip of his nose. "Rumor has it, my good fellow, that Dr. Birdlip's craft carries aboard it a talisman of some sort, perhaps a device, that the cultists find sacred—a god, as they have it, that resides in a curious box. Scotland Yard has, of course, infiltrated their organization. They're a dangerous lot, and they've got an eye on the dirigible. It's generally unknown whether they wish to destroy it or make a temple of it, but I can assure you that the Academy intends to allow neither."

On the street, wading out of Kensington Gardens through Lancaster Gate, came a tremendous milling throng of people, shouting something in unison—hosannas, St. Ives decided—pushing up toward Sussex Gardens, choking the street below the club. There could be no doubt about it—at the head of the throng strode the old, robed missionary, the nemesis of the Royal Academy.

Parsons recognized him at the same time, and struck his fist upon the tabletop, the sudden appearance of the evangelist having driven home his point. "What I mean to say," he whispered, gesturing at the street, "is that this is no time for foolish misconceptions about friendships, or whatever you'd call it, to interfere with vital scientific study. You're a scientist yourself, man. The projectile that you launched into Lord Kelvin's barn was a remarkable example of heavier than air flight. Your purposes haven't been fully understood, perhaps, by the Academy, but I assure you that if you could prevail upon this toy-maker on Jermyn Street to cooperate with us...that's right," he said, holding up his hand to silence St. Ives, "I told you we were certain that Birdlip himself could not have built the engine. If you could prevail upon this man Keeble to communicate with us, I think you'd find us inclined to consider this last imbroglio with the spirit of scientific inquiry. Reputations are at stake here—you can see that—and much more besides. Religious lunatics gibber in the streets; rumors of blood sacrifices performed in squalid Limehouse taverns filter up from the underworld. Tales of pseudo-scientific horror, of alchemy and vivisection, are daily on the increase. And sailing into it all, like some long awaited sign, some apocalyptic generator, comes the blimp of Dr. Birdlip.

"Two men in a balloon tracked it over the Sandwich Islands weeks ago. There can be no doubt that it is steadily losing altitude at a rate that will soon put an end to its journey. Our mathematicians have it touching down within Greater London. But what will it do? Will it smash through the suburbs, causing great ruin, exploding in an inferno of igniting gases, ending all efforts to establish an understanding of its motivation? Will it drop into the Atlantic to be reduced by storms to sinking debris?"

Parsons grimaced through his spectacles, giving St. Ives ample opportunity to imagine the wrack and ruin the fated return of the blimp would cause if he—that is to say, if Keeble—would not turn out and share with them his knowledge of the workings of Birdlip's craft. The glory of the sciences, said Parsons, was its cold rationality, the absence of the illogical fervor that drove the crowd in the street at this very instant to inexplicable passions. Why did St. Ives hesitate? The toymaker would listen to him. What was the nature of his hesitation if not the same sort of illogical manifestations that fueled the crowds in the street? It was reason, scientific philosophy, practical reality, that must prevail at times such as these. Surely St. Ives...

But St. Ives couldn't quite see it that way. The entire subject was tedious. Keeble would do as he pleased. Birdlip's blimp would do as it pleased. St. Ives would do the same—that is to say, not the same thing as Birdlip and Keeble—what he would do was find Willis Pule and beat the dust out of him. After that, he'd hunt up the spacecraft of the homunculus. He'd find this last or find evidence that put an end to the legends of its existence. But, he said to Parsons, he would talk to Keeble, mention it all to him, feel him out. If the toymaker balked, there would be an end to it.

Parsons was delighted. Such an attitude was reason personified. And why on earth *had* St. Ives launched the projectile through the roof of Lord Kelvin's barn? The scientific community had been once again mystified.

St. Ives shrugged. It had been set off accidentally, without adjustment, without being properly motivated. Parsons nodded, understanding now, able to take the long view. He held out a limp hand, which St. Ives understood to be a signal that the lunch was at an end. There was no further need of talk, not until Keeble had been broached on the subject of his engine.

They want the engine and nothing more, thought St. Ives as he left the room. If Keeble handed it to them tomorrow they'd abandon any interest in Birdlip, about whom they were absolutely correct. Birdlip was engaged in a mission which couldn't be charted and graphed. His pursuit of truth, such as it was, had taken him on a course that paralleled, figuratively speaking, the wind-blown, haphazard course of his blimp. But by God, it *had* led him home again, hadn't it? Its means were unfathomable, inexplicable, but the ends weren't entirely so, not if you looked at it through the right pair of spectacles—which Parsons, of course, didn't own.

St. Ives trotted down the last half-dozen carpeted steps and out the entry hall into the street, where wind had blown the fog away and where a milling crowd strained to hear something. Scores of them sat in trees; some sat astride the shoulders of others; carriages were parked along the street, and atop the carriages stood what seemed to St. Ives to be a moderate portion of the citizenry of London, all of them listening, their ears cocked, to the wind that blew along the silent afternoon street.

There was a brief chattering, like a woodpecker, perhaps, striking a particularly brittle tree. A roar arose from the crowd. Silence followed, then another clacking and a fresh roar. St. Ives pushed his way toward the front, toward where he could see the head of the evangelist above the horizon of the masses. The old man stood, clearly, atop a crate.

He held something before him with both hands. St. Ives couldn't quite make out what it was—a transparent box of some sort. The sea of onlookers parted in front of him. He was struck with the pervasive religious atmosphere that lay heavily over the street. How many people were there? Enough to constitute a multitude, certainly. And here was the Red Sea, parting before him, a miraculous narrow avenue opening up for some few feet. St. Ives edged down it. A man trod on his toe. Another jabbed him in the ribs with an elbow. The wall of people behind him pressed forward suddenly, shoving him nose first into the greasy hair of a woman in what appeared to be a nightshirt. His apology went unheard. "Beg your pardon," he said, twisting through a gap an inch or so wide. Not far ahead of him stood the evangelist, peering at the sky, muttering indecipherably, perhaps speaking in tongues.

A moment later, the victim of hard looks and a pair of rapid-fire curses, St. Ives stood at the front of the crowd—no one before him but a man so short as to be negligible. The old missionary exhorted a glass cube in which sat, St. Ives was horrified to see, a partially mummified head, dusty and brown from the grave.

The thing's teeth were huge—Parsons would have admired them. What the evangelist intended to do with the head wasn't at all clear. St. Ives looked about him at the expectant faces, which seemed to betray that they, too, weren't sure of the nature of the spectacle they were about to witness.

Catcalls erupted from a gang of toughs slouching in the limbs of a great, drooping oak. "Make 'er sing!" came the shout. "Make 'er eat somethin," came another. "A bug!" shouted someone else, close on. "Ave 'er eat bugs!" After that came a roar of laughter from the tree, followed by the screaming fall of one of the toughs, who had come unseated. More laughter erupted from the tree as well as from the crowd, which seemed to be fast losing its patience with the holy man and his posturing. A handful of people passed out tracts, some of the supplicants horribly mutilated and wasted, as if from loathsome disease. Their very presence seemed to lend an air of authenticity to Shiloh's performance. It was hard to argue with people who were so obviously what they claimed to be.

Just as the laughter fell away, the woodpecker chattering resumed, very rapid, from the direction of the old man. St. Ives started. The head in the glass cube had suddenly become animated. Its jaw clacked as if they were driven by an engine. What was this but a clever bit of parlor magic? The skull hopped and bumped with the force of its clacking, stringy hair flopping in time.

"Speak, Mother!" shouted the old man. "What is it that you hear! That you see! Lift the veil that obscures the future, the scales of filth and degradation that stifle and blind us! Speak, we implore thee!" And with this last falsetto petition a hoarse voice squeaked out, as if it were carried on the breeze that whirled leaves up Bayswater Road, as if it were part of that breeze, of the natural turnings of the universe. The crowd fell instantly silent, leaning forward as one, straining to hear the words of the oracle. Silence followed. Then, shattering the silence, the cry: "Get thee to a nunnery! Go!" rang out amid screams of wild laughter, the product of a particularly educated lad in the oak tree.

Shiloh cast the laughing toughs a look of mixed venom and pity, waiting with theatrical patience for silence to descend. Again the teeth chattered, clearly taking the startled evangelist by surprise.

"Hear me…ee…ee!" came the eerie wavering voice.

"Speak!" commanded Shiloh of the dancing teeth.

"Listen to my words!" ululated the head.

"Kiss my arse!" shouted the oak tree.

The skull fell silent.

"You've mined it!" shouted the lady in the nightshirt, directly into St. Ives' ear, obviously enraged at the crowd in the tree.

"Shut up, will you!" shouted a man at St. Ives' elbow, but it was impossible to tell whether the command was directed at the lady in the nightshirt or the laughing toughs. The head began to chatter again. St. Ives wondered exactly how the thing was supposed to be talking when it lacked flesh on its neck, when it lacked, for that matter, a neck of any sort, fleshed or otherwise. Perhaps the crowd was no more interested in physiology than St. Ives had been when sharing leather cutlets with Parsons a half hour earlier. Maybe it was the wind vibrating the bones in its chin—a sort of Aeolian harp effect.

Just as the voice started up again, the teeth gave out, seeming to take the voice by surprise, for it continued momentarily, uttering something about dread things in the sea before closing off like a faucet. Each effort by the toothy skull seemed more tired than the last. Shiloh peered in at it, shaking it just a bit as if fearing that the thing was running down—which it very apparently was, for away it went one last time, getting off a half-dozen staccato chatters before slowly playing out and, whether of its own accord or because of a misstep of the evangelist, falling over onto its side and giving up the ghost.

The crowd pressed forward to have a closer look, all of them, no doubt, feeling cheated of the show they expected, of the revelations that had a half-dozen times clearly been pending. A shower of acorns launched from the oak tree rained around the evangelist, who, St. Ives could see, was clearly puzzled and chagrined. Whatever it was he'd been attempting to accomplish hadn't entirely been a fake, and it had the unmistakable stamp on it of Ignacio Narbondo.

The old man, seeing that the head had given out, attempted to preach to the crowd from atop his crate. But the masses surged forward, anxious to get a look at the deflated prophet, and the old man's supporters rallied round, linking hands in an effort to keep the mob away from their master and his oracle. Easily two-thirds of the supplicants had eaten blood pudding in the last twenty-four hours, St. Ives determined. Parson's fears of the growing army of cultists weren't as terrifying as they might be—it was an army that could be starved out of existence overnight.

Their linking of arms to hold back the throng was futile; St. Ives could see that at a glance. People pushed past him. Without moving he drifted toward the rear of the crowd. Shiloh, in growing dread, made away up the street, surrounded by his supporters. A brougham careered around the corner from the direction of Leinster Terrace, pulled to a halt half a block up from the charging throng, swallowed the evangelist and three of his allies, and galloped off, bearing away the chattering head, the performance of which, thought St. Ives, would not get favorable reviews. —☙

FOURTEEN

Pule Sets Out

THE NEW MESSIAH rode along into Mayfair with his eyes clamped shut so tightly that little flickers of yellow lightning shot out across the back of his eyelids each time the brougham bounced over a dip in the road. What, he wondered, could have gone wrong? What conceivable force could be responsible for the failing of the spirit of his poor, misused mother? She'd been declining—he could see that—ever since he'd brought her away from the laboratory of the accursed Narbondo. It was as if she had fallen asleep, as if whatever animating force she'd been imbued with had drained away. Was this a sign, an indication that his own vanity had to be curbed? But he was selfless, blameless. He hadn't chosen to be what he was—the son of whom he was the son of. Had he? It had been thrust upon him, and he'd suffered for it, long years of deprivation. And here, when he had the means to sway great masses of people, when success lay within his grasp, the machinery of the spirit failed, ran down, fell mute.

He pressed his temples and looked up at the man next to him—a droopy-eyed, pasty man, one of Narbondo's ghouls. The sight of him was tiresome, uncharitable as this might be. Shiloh couldn't suffer it, wouldn't suffer it. He pushed his head out through the curtain and railed at the driver. "Stop!" he shrieked. "Stop, you bleeding fool!

The brougham lurched to a halt. The evangelist threw open the door on the street side. "Out!" he said tiredly. "All of you." They stared at him stupidly. He picked up a heap of tracts on the floor and pitched them out into the dirt. "Fetch those." The man beside him rose obediently, stepping out through the open door. The others followed, the last sailing face first into the road on the heel of the evangelist's boot. The old man reached out and pulled the door shut. "Drive on!" he cried, and away the brougham raced, the old man alone now, contemplating his failure.

There was simply no accounting for it. Or rather there was, but he simply couldn't see it. Something nagged at him—something about the business at Narbondo's: the hands pounding on the piano, the ill-fated flight of the skeletal bird, his mother's brief revitalization. What explained it? Surely not the capering hunchback with his yellow vapors. Something more had been in evidence. A spirit—that was it. Some presence had charged the room, had launched the bird. The explanation of it all lay just out of sight around a turning of his memory.

The box. Had that been it? Of course it had. Narbondo had set the box atop the piano, and straightaway had set off the playing, had stirred the corpse of the bird. What if, wondered Shiloh, squirming in his seat in the glare of sudden illumination, what if the box in Narbondo's hands were the homunculus?

Had the hunchback left the thing in sight to mock him? Knowing that the creature in the box was, in fact, Shiloh's father? A creature with power over life and death? The stinking swine! He'd known all along, hadn't he? Or had he? Why was he so anxious to get hold of Nell Owlesby? And what *of* Nell Owlesby? Had she lied to him those long years ago in Jamaica? Impossible. She'd been too sincere, too much a product of her momentary passions. She could, of course, have been mistaken. There had, after all, been two boxes.

The evangelist stroked his chin. He'd been played, perhaps, for a fool by any number of people. But he'd have the box. That much Narbondo owed him.

Pratlow Street was silent. No one was about, not even a stray dog or cat. The moon, which had shone for an hour or so between the tilting buildings that lined the street, had long since drifted away. No light burned in Narbondo's cabinet, the hunchback having departed for the night. His relative success with the remains of Joanna Southcote and knowledge of the whereabouts of the homunculus box had improved his mood, which had suffered from Pule's failure to obtain Owlesby's manuscript. Narbondo's house call at Drake's Wardour Street address had given him certain ideas, excited certain passions, and he dallied there into the evening.

—◊◊◊—

THE LIGHTS OF Westminster Bridge were ample to read by; Bill Kraken had read in worse light. And the night sounds—the Thames rushing along beneath the bridge, hurrying toward the sea, the low murmur of conversation from the men who lounged against lampposts—all of it seemed to Kraken to mean something, taken collectively. Especially the river. There was a great deal of talk in Ashbless about rivers. He seemed particularly fond of them, and it was a restful chapter that didn't call on the river to serve as an illustration for an abstraction which, without the tea-dark, swirling waters of the Thames to color it, would have been a lifeless and pale reflection of the world.

Kraken had wandered fitfully along the Thames all that day and most of the preceding night, after he'd failed to retrieve the box from the odious doctor. His life seemed to him to be played out. It was empty of substance—hollow. Most of his teeth were gone. His only possession beyond his clothes was the bullet-ridden copy of Ashbless, whose philosophers, try as they might to pour substance into the cavity of his soul, were pow-erless to help him. He was adrift, and would soon enough float out onto a gray sea.

He had speculated his way through Holborn and the City and Whitechapel, plod-ding along, lost in thought, finding himself late in the afternoon below Limehouse, look-ing out over the London docks. It was unimaginable that such commerce existed, that so many thousands of people labored to some particular end, that the basket of tobacco they hauled out of the hold at midday had to be hauled out just then, because at quarter till midday there had been twenty-five baskets atop it—one leading to another sensibly, each pulled off in turn, by design, according, it seemed, to an unwritten script.

But what pattern was it, he wondered while watching it all, governed the sham-bling life of Bill Kraken, squid man, pea pod man, thief. He'd been beaten senseless by criminals and then had become one himself. It didn't stand to reason.

He'd ambled back upriver, past St. Katherine's Docks and London Bridge and the Old Swan Pier, and everywhere people hurried along about their business, as if their lives were read out of a book, with a second page that followed a first, a twenty-fifth page that followed a twenty-fourth. But the pages of Kraken's life had somewhere been dumped onto the road. The wind had caught them and blown them hither and thither over the rooftops. He'd tramped around, ever on the watch for them, but they were scattered and flown, and here he was, at the end of his tramp, leaning over the parapet in the center of Westminster Bridge and watching the black water of the Thames roil below.

He opened Ashbless at random. "Least of all the sins," he read, "is gluttony." That didn't help him a bit. He closed his eyes and pointed. "The stone that the builder refused," promised the text, quoting the Bible, "shall be the cornerstone." He put the book down and thought about it. What was he, if not that very stone? There were thousands—millions—of people chiseled just so, fit into a vast and sensible order, while he, wandering through London, could find no niche into which he could wedge himself. He hadn't been chiseled so.

But how, he wondered practically, could old Bill Kraken be the cornerstone? What was it that would lend him a ticket to enter Captain Powers' shop by the door when he'd gone out once by the window? The emerald, of course. That was the only route. But recovering it would almost certainly mean destruction, wouldn't it? Kraken shoved Ashb-less into his coat and set out apace. Destruction, perhaps, was less odious than other fates. His journey that day had made him weary, but his sudden resolution, his discerning purpose, no matter how fleeting or mistaken, drove him on with a steady gait, north up Whitehall toward Soho and Pratlow Street where he would settle a score with himself.

THE CRAMPED ROOM in the Bailey Hotel was sufficient to hold an iron bed, but the bed, unfortunately, wasn't sufficient to hold Willis Pule. He was sick and tired of kicking the bedstead all night, of jamming his ankle between iron posts. And the gaslamp at the head was always fizzling and sputtering and smelled so overwhelmingly of leaked gas that he had to keep one window jammed open with a pile of books. He longed for the day when he could unbox his library, arrange the volumes along shelves. That's when his really serious study would begin. He would accomplish something then—exercise his genius.

He peered at himself in a glass tipped against another little heap of books. The bandage wrap hadn't accomplished a thing beyond, perhaps, disguising him a bit. His face appeared even in the wan light of the faltering gaslamp to be enflamed. It seemed stretched, almost oily. He picked up a stained copy of Euglena's *Chemical Cures* and studied a long discourse on the application of facial washes. He could see nothing in it. He had tried Lord knows how many plasters. At best they seemed to dry him up. That was the problem; he was certain of it. His cranial capacity, his abundant mental activity, drew fluids from other parts of his body—hence his perpetually dry and scaly hands. Perhaps a loathsome complexion was the price of genius.

He sighed and flopped back onto the creaking bed, cracking his elbow against the wall and cursing. It was his fate to be contained within a body that betrayed him. He felt at times as if he were attached to an enormous vermin—a corrupt physical bag that contained a pure, sensitive, intelligent soul. It was an attitude that might easily produce envy, but in Pule, of course, it didn't. He saw through the world too clearly. There was little in it to attract him.

Pule had often lamented the problem inherent to genius: genius simply wasn't self-evident. It was evident in works, and yet Pule was certain that works were condescending. One hadn't ought to soil one's hands. And what was there in the productions of time that wasn't transparent? That wasn't pretense? When one possessed—was cursed with—genius, with vision, then one saw too clearly the emptiness of it all. One was aware of the shallowness of it, the false and brittle face of things. Even the stuff of poets was, when one ridded oneself of their romantic foolery, nothing but cleverly painted backdrops hung roundabout to veil a gray and empty world.

Pule heaved a sigh and rubbed at the end of his nose. If only he didn't see things with such insight. And Narbondo! Pule had been tormented by the hunchback on the promise of…of what? Who had waylaid Kraken and gotten the box? Pule had. Who had organized and carried off the recovery of Joanna Southcote? Pule had. Who was it that fetched the carp from the oceanarium? Pule. Narbondo was one of those officious inferior, self-serving braggarts who had attained a position of imagined power. And he would profit by it too. He'd muddle along, appropriating that which belonged to Willis Pule, using him, and would, in the end, stroll away with the emerald, leaving Willis Pule to explain their activities to the judge. Or so thought the hunchback.

Pule bent over and groped under the bed, hauling out the Keeble box he'd retrieved from the man on the train. He shook it for the hundredth time, but the box was silent.

What in the world, wondered Pule, could be in it? There was apparently no lid to the thing. It was possible, even, that the box was designed in such a way as to foil uninstructed attempts to open it. Perhaps it would explode. It had the look about it, with its spout and crank mechanism, of an infernal device. The clothed animals painted over it argued against such a thing; but mightn't that be just a clever sort of ruse?

In the laboratory lay the emerald box, or so Kraken had insisted—drunk, to be sure. Who was to say that *this* wasn't the emerald box? The crank, in fact, might be the means of opening the thing. It might, on the other hand, be a detonator—a timed detonator. No one would build a device which would explode in one's hands. It was no doubt a clock-spring mechanism that could be wound with the crank to a desired tension, then wind down of its own to set off the explosion. Or was it? Who could say? Pule's mind drifted, converting the clock-spring mechanism of the box to an analog of his life—a life which had, it seemed to him, run down. It was a consequence of growing awareness, of intellect. As one's understanding of things grew, the things themselves paled, ceased to exist almost. The world hadn't so much wound down as he had wound up, so to speak, become taut through perception to the point at which he'd shed the world—stood alone, as it were, upon an empty hilltop, the common people scurrying below like bugs, like worms, with little or no consciousness.

The way, suddenly, was clear. He'd come to a sort of crossroad, to a point at which a choice was required—an action. To act would save him. He plucked up the box, held it in front of him, and began slowly to wind the crank. If the result was the springing open of the box, then he'd know, wouldn't he, what lay within? If no such result occurred, then he would assume it was a bomb—dynamite perhaps—and he'd simply haul it along the dark streets to Narbondo's laboratory. Once he got there—if he got there; the thing might easily explode on the street—he'd leave it atop the piano in exchange for Kraken's box. And if the result was that Narbondo's cabinet and all of Narbondo's works were blown to hell, the entire transaction would be eminently satisfactory.

It would require tremendous will, he mused, to stroll across Soho with a live bomb under his arm. Its detonation would likely cost the lives of any number of people, but so what? In the long run of things, what were their lives worth? Hadn't he already established that they were worms? There was no crime in stepping on a few of them. And what was crime to him anyway? It was, perhaps, more to the point to pity them the loss of Willis Pule.

He looked at himself in the mirror one last time, arching his eyebrows to heighten the look of natural intelligence and wit. His mind was set. The effort of will that would crush a lesser being had been summoned in the space of moments, and once it was called into existence, no power on earth could gainsay it.

Pule spun the crank more rapidly. He could feel tension within the box—a mechanism winding tight. It was as he thought. A grim smile stretched his lips. Would the lid fly up like a jack-in-the-box to betray the existence of the emerald? Was Kraken's box merely a clever ploy to throw them off the scent? He listened at the spout that thrust out of the front of the box. He could hear the ratchet turnings of the clockworks. He held the box in front of his face so that the light from the gaslamp illuminated the spout. He closed one eye and squinted, following the thread of illumination up the spout and into the interior of the box. There was a click, a whir; Pule jerked back in sudden tenor. *Was* it a suicide device?

A jet of gas wheezed out, spraying over his face. Spitting and coughing, he cast the box onto the bed. He'd been poisoned. He knew it. The box wheezed again, and a great cloud of green dust blew out of the spout with such force that although he threw himself over backwards onto the floor, the gas enveloped him utterly.

He rolled, smashing into the wall beneath the open window. The tower of books that propped the window cascaded into the street, and the window crashed down, sealing the room. Pule shrieked, a high, frightful, elflike ululation that reinforced his fear that he'd been poisoned. The air had been suddenly dyed a livid green. He would choke on poison gas! He'd been tricked. It had been a plot to eliminate the hunchback, and his betrayal of the monster had brought about his own ruin.

He yanked on the window, batting at the frame. It wouldn't budge. He looked wildly about him and lunged for the door, catching sight of his coat on a nail driven into the jamb. Lunging for it, he tore the coat free and flung it over the still spouting box, smothering the escaping gasses. He picked up the mirror and the books in a single heap and flung the lot of them through the closed window, shoving his head out into the night air, breathing great gulps of it and watching books and glass shards cascade onto the street four stories below.

His chest heaved; his head cleared; his equilibrium and sense of proportion returned. Of course it wasn't a poisoned gas device. There would have been no conceivable way to have calculated the odd events that had led him to board that train in Harrogate. His enemies weren't half that clever. This was something else. It was just possible that he'd been a victim of his own zealous actions. What if, he wondered, the box *had* contained an emerald, and was designed so that uninformed tampering would destroy the gem? Was it emerald dust that filled the room? But why in the devil would a man build such a box, or have it built? Had Owlesby been a lunatic who would rather the emerald be destroyed than profit a thief? Or was there more to it? Had Owlesby been a smuggler?

Of course he had. And here, it seemed certain, was a way by which to utterly destroy and disperse evidence that had fallen into the wrong hands. It was frightfully ingenious if it was so.

Pule bent back into the room. Idle speculation was getting him nowhere. One way or another, the box was worth nothing to him. It might, however, give Narbondo a few trying moments. And Narbondo's box—Pule would have that. He tucked the coat around the still whirring box and stepped out through the door, passing on the stairs his hurrying landlord who began to address him, then fell silent, staring at him in horror.

"Damn you!" cried Pule, pushing the man out of the way and drawing himself up as if to flail at him. Pule stood heaving with wrath, the man cowering against the banister, his countenance frozen. "What are you staring at, idiot!" shrieked Pule. "You soulless halfwit!" Pule choked. He couldn't breathe. The man's face seemed to be inflating like a balloon, the shocked look in his eyes testimony to Pule's condition. Blood rushed in Pule's ears. His heart smashed in his chest. His face burned.

With a snarl of released rage he kicked the man in the ribs, possessed by the desire to beat him senseless, to flail at him with the heavy box, to bash him through the tilted railing and watch him fall down the vortex between the spiraling stairs the thirty-odd feet to the distant floor below.

The man's face loosened. He screamed, and the sound of it propelled Pule down the stairs in great leaping strides, hollering curses over his shoulder. An old man stepped out from a door onto a landing as if to detain Pule. He gasped and fled back inside, slamming the door behind him. A bolt rattled into place. At the ground floor Pule crashed through the street door, surprising two women who were just that moment stepping in. They shrieked in unison, one fainting, one leaping across toward a half-open closet as if to hide.

Pule gritted his teeth. His foes were falling before him. And they'd continue to fall. There'd be no stopping him. On the street he took to his heels, fleeing through the black night, neither running from anything nor toward anything, just running, holding the box beneath his arm, beset, it seemed to him, by no end of devils. He slowed, finally, gasping and sweating, outside a low tavern on Drury Lane. A group of men lounged in the gutter, tossing coins at a target chalked on the street. They paid him little heed. As he walked past, a coin rebounded off his heel.

"Hey, mate!" shouted an exasperated, accusing voice.

Pule turned on him. The man blanched, croaked out a halfmouthed curse, and fled into the open door of the tavern. His companions, themselves looking up, shouted, rose in a body, and followed the first man, the door of the tavern sailing shut with such force that rust from the hinges sprayed out into the lamplit road. The sound of scraping tables and benches could be heard from within, clunking against the door.

Pule turned slowly and resumed his journey, pondering darkly the revenge he'd have on them all—the well-placed anarchist bomb blowing to shreds the likes of such idlers along with the leering carp dealers of the world. He set a course for Pratlow Street.

FIFTEEN

Turmoil on Pratlow Street

S HILOH THE NEW Messiah leaned against the wall in a straight-backed
oak chair, all of the joints of which were loose, the glue having dried to dust years
before. He sat in silent meditation—hadn't moved for half an hour. The curtain had
been pulled back from the little shrine across the room, and in it, sitting beside the miniature portrait of Joanna Southcote, was the head of the lady herself in its aquarium.

The crosses we bear...thought Shiloh. He shook his head over it. The afternoon's meeting in Kensington Gardens had been a disaster. It wouldn't stand thinking about. It would
have to be righted; there was no getting round it. One owed as much to one's mother.

A brief chattering ensued from the glass box—three or four tentative clacks, then
silence. The spark hadn't entirely departed the head. There were elements of it left,
apparently, that awakened at odd intervals like bubbles on the side of a glass, released
suddenly for no apparent reason to sail surfaceward and burst. It would be the greatest
miracle of all, he thought to himself, if during one of her sojourns into consciousness
she would speak—give him a sign of some sort. Utter a telling phrase. Refer, perhaps,
to the drawing nigh of the dirigible. But there was nothing, alas, save the random
click-clacking of dry molars.

In an hour the moon would be down. Darkness would serve him well. The hunchback, he knew, was engaged at the house on Wardour Street, and would be until morning or until his filthy habits burst his pea-sized heart.

There was a chance, of course, that Narbondo had removed the box from his
cabinet—an action that would make its recovery infinitely more complicated. But even
so, there were the bones of his mother to consider—bones that he'd foolishly abandoned
to the hunchback and his base experimentation. Shiloh remembered the confused hands
and shuddered. He'd take the bones and the shroud out in a Gladstone bag. The shroud
could be enshrined in its own glass case, not unlike the shroud of Turin. Enthusiasts
were eager for the sort of circumstantial evidence inherent in such relics.

There had been the case of the woman on the Normandy coast who possessed a felt cap into which was indelibly stained the image of the Bambino of Aracoeli. A shrine had been built for it in the little village of Combray, and fully ten thousand people a year paraded through to view it—or, for two francs, to touch it. A drunken sailor from Toulouse had snatched it from its perch and clapped it onto his head, which promptly burst into flame, reducing the sailor and the cap simultaneously to ash. Not surprisingly, the urn of mixed ashes drew half again as many pilgrims yearly at double the price. The evangelist, laughing to himself, contemplated the fact that thus even the most vile sinners are put to work for the church. They rot in hell, of course, despite their works.

He arose, closed the curtain, and found the street. Outside, pasty and silent, stood an obedient convert, who in a moment trotted away up Buckeridge Street to summon the brougham. Shiloh was impatient. Eternity lay before him, just a few short days away, and he was itching to get at it. And he was itching, at the same time, to hasten Narbondo's decline into the pit. He grinned to think of the cursing and gnashing of teeth that would ensue on the morrow when the hunchback dragged himself home, worn and degraded, wondering at his own sanity, perhaps injured from some ill-advised acrobatics, to find that he'd been relieved of the bones and the box in a single evening, that his smug posing hadn't been worth a penny toot. The brougham swung round the distant corner, stopped before the tavern, and waited, as Shiloh climbed in beside the man in the turban.

"Wipe your disgusting face!" shouted the evangelist, watching in horror as the man smeared at his blood-caked lips. The old man shuddered involuntarily, looked straight ahead, and sank into himself as the brougham clattered along into Soho, bound for Pratlow Street.

—⁓—

"I DON'T INTEND to sue them," said St. Ives heatedly, "I intend to beat them senseless. What would a lawsuit avail us? What, for God's sake, would we claim?"

"It bears contemplation, sir, if you'll pardon my saying so. Breaking into a man's house is ill advised, regardless of its location or the motivation of the burglar. The law, I'm afraid, sir, is adamant on that point. Your own argument is solid. What *would* we claim, sir, if we were apprehended as common thieves?"

St. Ives strode on without speaking. They'd taken a cab to Charing Cross Road— far enough away, thought St. Ives, so that not even the most scrupulous detective would connect them to any ill doings on Pratlow Street—supposing, that is, that the authorities were concerned with what was happening on Pratlow Street, which they almost certainly weren't.

He wished heartily that either Godall or the Captain had been in that evening, but neither had—off on some mutual business, no doubt. Scouring Limehouse, perhaps, for the absconded Bill Kraken. St. Ives would have to act without them. This wasn't their affair anyway, this aerator business. It was his—his and Keeble's, who would be imposed upon to build another if St. Ives failed. He could hardly, though, drag the toymaker into it. It had been St. Ives' own idiotic fault that the silo door had been left unbolted, that Pule had been allowed to escape them twice, first at the manor, then later on the train. They must strike while the proverbial iron was still hot. Peculiar events were fast sliding toward possibly dangerous conclusions. Narbondo and Pule sailed in the current of some sort of hellish, swiftly moving stream, which would carry the villains out of reach if St. Ives weren't brisk.

"Toynbee and Koontz would accomplish little," he said to Hasbro, repealing his disinclination to carry the issue to the authorities.

"There aren't a sharper pair of investigators in the Yard," insisted Hasbro. "Koontz is a legend—feared in the London underworld. It's the peculiar look in his eye, if you ask me, that throws the fear into them. That and the cut of his suit. If he can't come it across this Pule, then no one can. He was involved in the Isadora Persano affair, do you recall—the business with the worm and the inside-out pouch of tobacco. His aunt is a fast friend of my sister. We could look him up tonight, I don't doubt. Lay the case before him."

The dim corner of Old Compton Street loomed ahead of them, the sorry buildings disguised by darkness, the sidewalks in utter shadow. St. Ives slowed his pace and asked himself for the first time exactly what it was he intended to do. And the more he thought on it, the more he recalled the faith he held in the remarkable Hasbro, a faith which his headstrong determination to retrieve the aerating device and deal with Pule had momentarily effaced. Hasbro, in fact, was not altogether wrong. If this man Koontz could be prevailed upon to take the case...

He stopped altogether and stepped back into the darkness of an overhanging gable that shadowed a ruined front stoop. This is decidedly unwise, thought St. Ives. The least he should do was wait for Godall and the Captain. The aerator box was their affair in a roundabout way. What was it Godall had said three nights ago in the rain? "The collective spirit," or some such thing. There was truth in that. No good would come from them each hacking out his own path, only to go blundering into one another in some secret, foliage-obscured crossroad.

"Hasbro," whispered St. Ives, the very atmosphere of the dilapidated neighborhood dampening his voice.

"Sir?"

"You're quite right, of course. This man Koontz—can we find him?"

"He's said to have an almost legendary passion for crustaceans, sir, and might conceivably be engaged even now in a late supper in the environs of Regent Street, at a club with the unlikely appellation of Bistro Shrimp-o-Dandy. He's infamous, I'm afraid, for keeping cooks and waiters up until dawn."

"We'll have a look in, then, at this Shrimp-o-Dandy. I've seen reason, Hasbro."

But at that moment, St. Ives saw something more—the running shadow of a man that slipped in and out of darkness across the street, crossing toward the laboratory of Dr. Ignacio Narbondo.

St. Ives and Hasbro stepped as one into a dim corner, the Shrimp-o-Dandy forgotten, and crept along up the sidewalk toward where the mysterious figure had vanished into a doorway. Neither of them spoke. There was no use pointing out that something was afoot, or that they were duty-bound to follow. They'd gone out that evening on the trail of mystery, and here it was, wearing a placard. There was nothing to do but investigate.

—◦◦◦—

BILL KRAKEN, TREMBLING with fear and animated by determination. found himself alone within the dark confines of the cabinet of Dr. Narbondo. Odd noises assailed him—the languid splashing of lazy carp in the tank on the floor, the sound of his own labored breathing, and the tremendous pounding of his heart which might, it seemed, burst like a piece of ripe fruit before he found what it was he sought. And at random intervals came the brief clatter of what sounded like a handful of ivory dominoes being dropped into a sack.

There was nothing either on the slab or on the table—no corpses to leap up or pea hens to dash at him. And there, atop the piano, lay the Keeble box; he could just see the outline of it in the faint light of the flickering candle he carried. He slipped across toward it, walking on tiptoe. This was no time to dillydally. There was nothing in the accursed laboratory that attracted him. He'd just pluck up the box and nip out the way he'd come. If he heard the doctor or Pule ascending the stairs, he'd simply backtrack to an upper floor and wait for them to enter the laboratory, then bolt for the street.

He squinted into the darkness, fearful that Narbondo would surprise him again by entering through the passage in the wainscot. It wouldn't do to actually confront the doctor or, for that matter, his loathsome accomplice. He hauled a chair from beneath the table of the pea hen and jammed it under the door latch, wiggling it for good measure.

Waving the candle in the direction of the box, he sent shadows leaping and flicker-ing up the walls in the yellow light. Before him, lying in the pile where they'd fallen, were the grisly, skull-less remains of Joanna Southcote. The sight of them petrified Kraken, froze him into a wide-eyed, half-bent statue. For while he watched, the bones seemed to shudder and collect themselves, half rise, and then collapse again into a dis-ordered pile, making the clacking sound of dominoes.

Quaking, Kraken groped inside his coat for a flask of gin, half of which he poured down his open throat in a hot, leafy rush. The bones made another effort, no more

successful than the last, one of the backwards hands skittering around the floor like a crab before the whole loose business went limp.

Kraken vowed not to look at it. That was best. If it managed to stand, he could outrun it, or beat it to pieces with the poker that lay now atop the hearth. He was damned if he would allow a heap of bones to frighten him off. He took a last, healthy gulp of the gin, grimaced, and snatched the box from atop the piano. He turned, took a step toward the door, and discovered in horror that the door latch, very softly and slowly, was turning. He heard a shuffling of feet, and saw the faint orange glow of a hooded lantern cast across the threshold.

Kraken backed slowly toward the far wall. What if it were Willis Pule? What if it were Narbondo himself? It would mean the end of him, sure enough, and of any attempt to restore himself in the eyes of Captain Powers and poor Jack Owlesby. Whoever stood without wrestled with the stubborn handle, giving off any attempt at secrecy and wrenching at the thing. Curses rang out in the peculiar, high voice of Willis Pule. There was the sound of a foot kicking the bottom of the door.

Kraken jabbed desperately at the wainscot with his free hand, searching for the moving panel. He pummeled the panels up and down either side, sobbing for breath, listening to the thudding on the door behind him and the sudden scrape of the chair as it pushed across the floor.

With a startling suddenness the smooth panel lurched inward, paused, then slowly swung to. Kraken threw his shoulder against it in desperation. His candle tipped and drowned in its own melted wax as he tumbled into a cold and dusty passage, the panel closing behind him. He lay on the musty floor, stifling his wheezing breath, watching through the diminishing crack the chair with which he'd wedged the door tumble inward, followed by the headlong rush of Willis Pule. Utter darkness followed, but through the wainscot came a sudden raging voice, then Pule's voice even louder, maniacal. A crashing of chairs, the shouting of curses, and the sudden firing of a pistol gave way to silence. Kraken beat his pockets for a match.

———✺———

At the sound of the pistol shot, Langdon St. Ives and Hasbro froze on the stairs. They had determined to remain in the street. The alley door of the house was nailed shut. Any thieves whoever they might be—in the house above would have to exit through the street door. There was precious little to be gained in yammering up the stairs after them, bursting unarmed into a room full of desperate men. They'd simply wait at the bottom of the stairs and confront anyone who came out with the box. Whatever odd machinations had brought about the appearance of the evangelist were none of their business.

But the pistol shot put an edge on the mystery. It was possible that Godall had been too concerned with the collection of villains; they seemed bent on exterminating each other. A door slammed above. Another shot banged out, followed by a howl of pain. A door crashed open. Wild shouting ensued. St. Ives bolted down the few stairs they'd ascended, leaping along at Hasbro's heels. At the bottom landing, just inside the street door, Hasbro ripped open the door of a tiny room—an oversize closet from the look of it—and the two men tumbled in, closing the door but for a crack through which they had a tolerably good view of the stairs. Down those same stairs tumbled, head over heels, a howling Willis Pule, who whumped down onto the landing and lay still. St. Ives could just see Pule's face. There was something peculiarly wrong with it. In the feeble light that shone through the open street door, Pule's face appeared to be a ghastly shade of pallid green, as if he were the victim, perhaps, of a tropical disease.

"What on earth…" began St. Ives, staring at the ruined face in horror, when behind him, against the paneled wall of the closet, came such a fearful banging and moaning that Hasbro leaped with a shout against St. Ives' back, and the two of them would have catapulted out onto the landing if Pule's body hadn't blocked the door.

St. Ives gripped the shoulder of the frightened Hasbro and found himself shrieking involuntarily into his ear as the oaken panel slid back slowly to reveal the ghastly, inhuman, eyeless face of a tottering corpse, dank, clotted hair thrusting out around it like a hideous aura. A fetid odor of decay blew out, and another face peered over the shoulder of the first ghoul—the mouths of both working and smacking like cattle chewing cud.

A light glowed behind the things, revealing, impossibly, a dancing collection of the grim apparitions, in the middle of which stood a wild-eyed Bill Kraken, looking mightily like a corpse himself, frozen in mid-stride, a piercing, inhuman shriek issuing from his open mouth. The first of the ghouls, heaving breaths rattling from his throat, his hands clutching, utterly blind, lurched forward into Hasbro. St. Ives was propelled against the door, pinned by Pule, who flopped a bit farther out onto the landing. St. Ives pushed, the ghoul howling in his ear. Hasbro reached past St. Ives, pounding with both fists on the door. Pule budged farther; St. Ives shoved again— threw his shoulder into it; and Shiloh the evangelist, flanked by the turbaned man on the one side and the earless man on the other, appeared suddenly on the stairs, the old man carrying a Keeble box in one hand and an open Gladstone bag stuffed with bones in the other. The evangelist paused, squinted with obvious amazement at the trapped St. Ives, who was pressed against the door jamb by a closetful of gibbering ghouls, and shouted at his two companions. The two hurled themselves against the door, forcing it shut in the face of St. Ives' protestations. The whump of Pule being rolled once more against the door followed, and St. Ives turned to see Hasbro fending off a score of shambling ghouls in various states of decomposition, the lot of them jigging and jibbering pointlessly as if they were marionettes dangled by a lunatic puppeteer. St. Ives smashed against the door, fighting for footing, and inch by inch once again shoved an inert Pule across the landing. He squeezed out, tripping over Pule's legs, and stumbled against the far wall. In a nonce, Hasbro was out beside him, wheezing and doubled up.

Two arms shot through the hiatus. A shoulder followed along with a foot, two ghouls trying simultaneously to squeeze out through the door. St. Ives placed his foot beneath the knob and shoved, thinking to trap the struggling creatures within the closet. But he suddenly remembered poor Kraken, and heard, it seemed to him, a smothered, purposeful cry from within. He abandoned his efforts, turning instead to the supine Pule. In a trice, St. Ives hauled him away. St. Ives and Hasbro sprang onto the stairs, and a veritable rush of ghouls hobbled, leaped, and crawled through the open closet door, the lot of them fleeing into the open night. Among them, slit-eyed and gibbering like a ghoul himself, strode Bill Kraken.

"Stop him!" shouted St. Ives, but Hasbro could do no more than his master to intercept the determined student of philosophy, who, shielded by ghouls, raced into the street and away, clutching in his arms a Keeble box. Hasbro and St. Ives followed, caught up in a tangle of animated corpses, some few of which had already begun to wind down and collapse—one on the stoop, one across the curb, another on the sidewalk, his legs splayed out like scissors as if they had tried to walk two directions at once.

Around the corner, kicking up sparks from the pavement and clattering like an express train in the still night, drove the evangelist's brougham, dead away down the center of the street, bowling through a little knot of ghouls that flew like ninepins. One door hung open, and the turbaned ghoul, his cap knocked back off his head but hanging yet by a chin strap, dangled out the door. He bounced along until the brougham canted round the distant corner, where he sailed out onto the roadway and rolled to a stop in the gutter. St. Ives could do nothing but watch the coach race away, carrying within it his aerator box. Lord knew what the old man thought he had.

A shout sounded from behind them, down the street in the direction from which the brougham had just appeared. And there, limping along slowly, were Theophilus Godall and Captain Powers, the Captain clutching a bloody shoulder.

"Shot, by God!" shouted St. Ives to no one, and not stopping to wonder why it was that his two stalwart friends should have suddenly appeared out of the night. He and Hasbro reached them simultaneously, and found, happily, that the Captain's shoulder had merely been creased by a bullet fired haphazardly by the old evangelist when the two had sought to grab the reins and stop the brougham's escape.

It was an hour later. The company slumped in chairs in Captain Powers' shop, before the general furor of the night's doings drained out of them and it was revealed to St. Ives what the second Keeble box had contained. St. Ives, in turn, related how in the tumult Kraken had fled once again into the City, seemingly deranged by his bout with the ghouls.

"So that," muttered St. Ives, "is what the man stole." He shook his head. "Do you suppose he was trapped in the passage with the ghouls ever since? No wonder he was gibbering mad."

Godall shook his head and related to St. Ives some few of the intrigues of the past three days. "I knew," said Godall, "that a good number of bodies had been brought to the house. Narbondo must have used the passage as a sort of storehouse. Fancy them all coming round together like that. This is a strange business."

"Cut and run; that's my motto," said the Captain, poking gingerly at his shoulder.

Hasbro shook his head. "The papers will be full of this," he said. "We've stirred up a curious nest of bugs, and not a single gain was made in the process."

No one in the shop could deny it as they sat tired and hungry and watching the early morning sky pale with the dawn. The entire business had become woefully complicated, and the Pratlow Street failure took some of the pleasure out of St. Ives' meeting, after fifteen long years, Nell Owlesby.

The arrival of Parsons, pounding on the door hours later, did little to enliven St. Ives' mood. He cursed himself for having told the man that he could be contacted through Powers' shop, and it took a half hour of lying before the scientist could be dissuaded from knocking up Keeble himself. Even Parsons' revelation that the blimp had been sighted over Limerick, looping over the Irish west coast in a long half elipse that would aim it, they were certain, toward London—even that merely added to the general confusion and early morning muddle. Somehow, it seemed to them, the arrival of Birdlip would be the natural culmination of the tangle of plots they'd become involved in, that the appearance of the blimp, a dot in the distant sky, would place a period, an end mark, to their confused and fruitless efforts to slay the various dragons.

It was hours after dawn, the streets long since awake, when there came a new and furious pounding on the door, startling St. Ives, who dozed in a stuffed chair. His companions were awake, making and discarding plans. Hasbro threw the door open, and there stood Winnifred Keeble, disheveled and tired. "Jack's coming round," she said, then turned and hurried back across the street, the collected members of the Trismegistus Club hauling on coats and following in her wake. ⟶

SIXTEEN

The Return of Bill Kraken

WILLIS PULE RUSHED up out of unconsciousness all in a moment, becoming aware suddenly of the sound of dripping water and of an almost numbing, clammy cold. He lay, it seemed to him, on a stone slab, or on pavement, and lying there had apparently made him overwhelmingly stiff and sore, for when he moved, his joints and muscles shrieked at him.

He opened his eyes. Far above him was a vaulted, cathedral-like ceiling of gray stone. Gaslamps hissed, each throwing out a diffused yellow radiance in a circle around it, precious little of the light drifting down toward the floor below. The room at first seemed to be enormous—a huge subterranean chamber hewn, possibly, out of rock. Pule craned his neck, wincing at a throbbing headache. The room wasn't, he determined, as big as all that. It was built of cut stone. Vast porcelain sinks lined one wall, and beneath them sat rows of glass and wood cabinets, several of their doors standing ajar to reveal boxes of surgical instruments—bone saws and knives and clamps. I'm in a hospital, thought Pule groggily. But what sort of a hospital is it that freezes its patients and requires them to sleep on granite mattresses?

Another wall was nothing but great drawers like oversize file cabinets, one of which was pulled open. A foot thrust out sporting a broad paper tag tied to its big toe with a string. This was no hospital, Pule realized with sudden certainty. He was in a morgue. He was dead. But he couldn't be dead, could he? He was cold as an oyster boat, something a dead man might be, but wouldn't be conscious of. It occurred to him with a shock of horror that perhaps he'd died and somehow been reanimated by Dr. Narbondo for some despicable purpose.

He could remember the fight with the old evangelist: the pistol shot, grappling at the top of the stairs, being pushed headlong down them. He had no recollection at all of having landed, only of sailing through the air. But he must have landed, mustn't he? Landed and worse. He was lying on a slab in the morgue, in among what appeared to be an army of corpses, most of which were laid out in a long line on the floor.

How desperate, he wondered, was his situation? On what grounds could he be arrested? None. He had, it's true, booted his landlord in the ribs and broken the window in his room. But he had no identifying papers on his person. No one here would confront him with that. He was alive and free—that much was clear. But how in the world had he gotten into the morgue, and what sort of débâcle had occurred to bring about the death of so many people? And why, for God's sake, did his hands seem to be tinted green?

On a nearby slab lay a man who was turned toward Pule. His mouth hung open and his eyes stared, as if in accusation. Pule stared back at him. It seemed as if he knew the man, as if he'd seen the face before, looking at him in much the same way. Of course he had—not two weeks before in Westminster Cemetery. Pule sat up, began to pass out, and lay back down, breathing heavily, one hand on his cold brow. He tried again, swinging his legs over the edge of the slab, slumping forward with his head between his knees until the rushing and pounding settled.

He squinted at the row of corpses, which waited as if in line to file back into the grave. All of them, every one, had come from Narbondo's storeroom. There was the woman pulled drowned from the Thames; there was the child run down in the street by a wagon; there was the freshly hanged forger, his neck broken and twisted, stolen from the gibbet by the navvy who had deserted Pule on the night of the recovery of Joanna Southcote. But how on earth? Had the passageway been discovered? That would put an end to Narbondo's freedom—to his life if they caught him. And what of himself? What of Willis Pule? If Narbondo were jailed, Pule would follow.

The room was empty. Pule slid from his slab and stood erect, swaying, faint. He bent over, resting his head for a moment on the cool slab before turning and shuffling toward the door. If he had to run, his goose was cooked. The line of corpses gaped at him—half of them deprived of the dubious joys of becoming members of the Church of the New Messiah, the other half of going into the unremunerative employ of Kelso Drake. Better, perhaps, to be returned to the ground. It was a far more restful business, anyway, was death.

Pule stopped inside the door, peering through into an ill-lit antechamber beyond, where a lone man sat at a desk, facing away. Pule backed off softly, slipping across to the cabinets and rooting quietly among the debris for a weapon—anything. A bone saw would do. In a moment he was back at the door, which creaked as he pushed it farther open and crept through. The man at the desk turned lazily, expecting, perhaps, a fellow worker back from dinner, but not, certainly, the grimacing corpse that confronted him, green and lurching and waving a bone saw—a corpse fresh from the slab, lately of the London streets, which were rife with rumors of the walking dead. The man arose, a shriek on his lips, and Pule was upon him. He slashed with the saw, the blade snapping almost immediately against the edge of the chair. Pule cast it to the floor, grasping a crystal paperweight from atop a heap of papers, leaping after the bloodied man who was halfway through the door, shrieking down a dark hallway. Pule clubbed at him blindly with the paperweight again and again. The man stumbled and fell. Pule found himself holding half the weight, the thing having cracked neatly in two against the man's crushed skull.

Pule dropped the chunk of glass onto the floor, stepped across the dead man, and found himself afoot in the London night, heading for Wardour Street where Ignacio Narbondo awaited his fate. He had been promised Dorothy Keeble as a prize if his sojourn to Harrogate were successful. Well, success was a relative business at best. He'd been swindled of the emerald, swindled of his dreams. But before the day was out, he'd have what was his.

—◦◦◦—

WILLIAM KEEBLE SAT in the corner of the room, his brandy untouched on a table beside him, his head in his hands. He looks done in, thought St. Ives, condemning himself for having been sporting in Harrogate while Dorothy Keeble was being kidnapped in London. The sun was high in the sky, lightening the shadowy room. Keeble rose to draw the drapes tighter, to dim the room, but Winnifred followed behind, pulling them entirely apart, flooding the room with spring sunlight.

"We've enough gloom," she said simply. "We can study this out as easily in the light of day as we can in darkness."

"There's nothing to study out!" cried poor Keeble, gripped by a despair which was deepened by two sleepless nights. "If I hadn't been so damned pig-headed with the engine, if I'd given it over, she'd be here now, wouldn't she? And Jack's head wouldn't be split like a melon, would it? Drake would have pocketed another fortune—so what? Would I be any the worse off for another man's fortune?"

"We all would..." began Theophilus Godall, rising out of a deep, tobacco-enshrouded study. But Keeble, it was clear, wasn't keen on reason, on thrashing it out. He seemed to spiral down into himself and sat poking at the end of a sort of brass grapefruit, each poke precipitating from out of the opposite end the grinning rubber head of a man with enormous ears. Smoke and spark accompanied each issuance.

The device reminded St. Ives, somehow shamefully, of the strange pornographic debris that had fallen out of the drop-front desk at the house on Wardour Street. He found himself wondering how on earth it could—whether this wasn't evidence of some deformity in his own rusted moral apparatus. He needed sleep. He could blame peculiarities of intellect on the lack of it. Then he remembered. The thing Keeble toyed innocently with was the odd device the old man had scrambled after and which had been snatched away from him by the butler. "What is that business?" he asked idly, pointing at the orb and the idiotic rubber man that shot from it.

"Some piece of rot left last night by that man Drake," said Winnifred Keeble. "Heaven knows what it signifies. I would have thrown it in his face if I knew then what Jack has told us since. But I didn't."

"Kelso Drake?" muttered Godall, standing up. "He left this, did he?"

"He asked if William could build him a hundred of the same, then laughed like a man insane. He's utterly daft, if you want my opinion. I wouldn't wonder, though, if there's not some darker purpose in this that I don't see." With that she left the room, up the stairs to the second floor where Jack lay, ministered by his aunt, Nell Owlesby.

Godall bent over St. Ives. "I don't like the look of this at all." he said.

"Of the device there?" asked St. Ives.

"Yes. It's imported, of course, from France."

"I didn't know that," said St. Ives. "What, exactly, is it used for?"

Godall shook his head darkly, as if the Queen's English hadn't the sorts of syllables necessary to reveal the grim truth of the matter. "We've got to get it away from Keeble. If Captain Powers awakens and sees it…well, he's too good a man, too simple and uncorrupted to stand for it. He'll want to beat the stuffing out of someone, and he'll do it too, shoulder or no shoulder."

"What in the world…" began St. Ives, looking once again at the curious device, which was covered, he could see, with nodules of some sort and a little porthole door that opened on either side to reveal what looked for all the world to be glass eyes, staring out from within the ball. Keeble stabbed at the end of it and out popped the rubber man, a puff of smoke and sparks erupting from extended, elephantine ears. A whistle of air poofed from rubber lips. The thing's eyes whirled crazily, and in an instant he was gone, swallowed by the orb. The portholes clamped shut; the sparking stopped; and the thing sat silent and treacherous.

Godall shook his head again grimly. "It's called a Marseilles Pinkie. You can imagine, I'm sure, what the thing is. Only the excesses of a southern climate could have produced it."

"Ah," said St. Ives, wondering at his own unworldliness.

"Keeble, blessedly, hasn't a notion. It was widely used in the last century, after the abduction of young French and Italian noblewomen into white slavery. It was sent to their homes—an announcement, I fear, that no ransom would suffice to return them. Even the most coldhearted royalty have been known to fly head foremost into lunacy at the receiving of one, and, tragically, to disgrace themselves utterly with the device despite their grief. The gesture is wasted here, of course. It's merely a sign of Drake's monumental wantonness and conceit, probably intended in some roundabout and perverse way to parody poor Keeble's attraction to toys. It's also, perhaps, a mistake. It tells us something, I believe, of Dorothy's whereabouts."

Before the conversation had gone forward another inch, there came a terrible knocking at the door, which, when thrown back by a surprised Theophilus Godall, revealed Bill Kraken tottering on the stoop. "Kraken!" cried St. Ives from his chair, but the man had no opportunity to reply—he pitched forward like a dead man onto the carpet.

St. Ives and Godall sprang to his assistance, and even Captain Powers, who was startled out of sleep by St. Ives' shout, bent in to help. It seemed entirely possible that Kraken's sudden appearance betokened his return to right-mindedness.

"Give him air, mates," said the Captain, loosening the dirty kerchief round Kraken's neck. Then, with Godall supporting Kraken's head, Captain Powers poured a thin stream of brandy into his mouth, which St. Ives contrived to open by pinching Kraken's cheeks. "Damn me," said the Captain in a low voice, and wrinkling his nose. "He's covered with sewer muck, isn't he? Get them shoes off him and pitch 'em out the door."

The effects of the brandy were such, though, that Kraken awoke of his own accord as St. Ives wrestled with his shoes. Braced by a mouthful of the elixir, he managed to wave St. Ives away and remove the shoes himself. The result was a small improvement in his general odor, and he was obliged to remove one by one the rest of his outer garments and to suffer the Captain's pouring a bucket of water over his head as he sat in a galvanized tub. Wrapped finally in shawls, he was recovered enough to be fit company. His clothes were sent out to be burnt.

"And so," he was saying to the collected party—including Winnifred Keeble, who had come downstairs for news of her daughter—"I come around at last. It was them ghouls what set it off, is what I think—a state o' shock is what it's called. If you ain't in one, then such a sight puts you there. If you're already sufferin' some sort of brain fever, then the particular sight of all them dead men has the opposite effect. A cure is what it is then.

"I studied it out myself when I come out of the George and Pigmy up in Soho. I'd been shouting, they tell me, about dead men slouched in the walls, when I was hit from behind by a pint mug that fell off the shelf. It was like I woke up—like I been out o' my mind since bein' beat on the head a week past, kind of in a mist, you know. Liquor didn't help—sober was worse. And then I went and fetched away the Captain's box—don't ask me why. I don't know. I been through hell, gentlemen, but I've come back now. That crack on the noggin in the Pigmy, comin' on top o' the corpses, was like a bracer. 'Let me out,' says I. 'Show me the road!' And off I went, straight as a die, and didn't stop neither, till I drew up at Wardour Street—you know the house, sir."

And with that he nodded at St. Ives, who did, indeed, know the house. They tried to waken Keeble, who snored in his chair, oblivious to Kraken's timely return. He slept so profoundly, however, that their efforts were in vain. Kraken was in a state— much more the old Kraken, thought St. Ives, than the tired, morose Kraken who had drifted in and out of the front room in Captain Power's shop Thursday last. St. Ives listened in astonishment to Kraken's strange tale—how when crouched in the passage off

Narbondo's laboratory he had overheard Pule and Shiloh exchanging words, Pule offering to give up his Keeble box if the old evangelist would see him right in the business of Dorothy Keeble—would use his influence to get Pule an audience with her, so to speak, at Drake's house on Wardour Street. The old man had raged about sin and damnation. Shots had been fired and Shiloh had said that he'd just *take* the box, thank you. Then out Kraken had gone, into the depths of the passage where there was no end of dead men, dirt from the grave in their hair, and the lot of them stirring there in the candlelight and rising up and starting for him until he'd just about gone mad, and...

"And wait just a minute," cried St. Ives, furrowing his brow. "These corpses were just lying about until you came in?"

"That's it, guv'nor. Dead as herrings, then all of them jumped to it like they heard the last trumpet. Damn me if they didn't."

"And this business of the dancing skeleton," asked St. Ives of Godall, "and the piano playing and the chicken bones or whatever sort of bird it was..."

"How'd yer know about that?" asked Kraken, amazed.

St. Ives nodded at Godall by way of explanation, as if to indicate that there was little or nothing that the man didn't know. "Where was this box when all of that business was transpiring?"

"On the piano," put in Kraken. "I tried for it, too, but the humpback nearly killed me with a spade."

"By Christ!" whispered St. Ives, striking the table before him with his fist. "What if...what if...Wake up Keeble! Straightaway."

Waking the toymaker took a full minute, either because he was so enormously fatigued or because the very spark of life within him had begun to fade, but in time he was conscious and listening to St. Ives. Yes, he said, the emerald box and the homunculus box were identical, beyond the eccentricities of carving and painting that went with that sort of handiwork. Might Nell Owlesby, in her agitated state, have crossed them up? Of course she might. Nell was summoned. She admitted that such an error was possible. Birdlip, she said, might indeed have the emerald. She paused, frowning. "I beg of you," she said, looking particularly at Captain Powers, "not to think me mad for asking this. But could the little man speak?"

"Absolutely," said St. Ives immediately. "According to your brother's manuscript, it was rarely silent—kept up a night and day harangue, an utterly tiresome performance, in any of a number of languages, not all of them of earthly origin."

Nell nodded. "I never read his papers," she said simply, assuming that her reasoning would be apparent. "I only ask because I suffered in Jamaica the certainty that the emerald spoke to me—the fear, that is, that I was going mad. I was feverish. I'd hidden the box in a table beside my bed. And in the night I awoke in a sweat, tossing, certain that a voice had issued from the box in the darkness, and had uttered the name of the false prophet that we're daily more familiar with. I sought this man out, revealed that

I'd heard his name in a dream, and, I fear, confessed all, going so far as to tell him that the homunculus—a creature he took an unwarranted interest in—was with Doctor Birdlip. I've told no one of this but Captain Powers. It was part of those shameful and dreadful early years. And I'm afraid, dear," she said, addressing the Captain particularly, "that I omitted any reference to the box having spoken. It seemed those long months later to be a product of fever."

Kraken had sat stony-faced through Nell's speech, but he could sit still no longer. "If it please your honor," he said to St. Ives, "I've heard the blasted thing speak too. I'm damned if I haven't. Last Thursday night, it was. Lord knows what it said, buried in the floor there while you gentlemen carried on in the next room. Yes, sir, I've heard it talk, and I didn't have the horrors neither."

"I rather believe, gentlemen," said St. Ives, "that this plays a new light over the page. We're in a less dangerous fix than we thought, barring, of course, the problem of Dorothy. The box, then, what did you do with it?"

"Well, sir," said Kraken, peering into the bottom of a snifter gone empty. "I made straight off for Wardour Street when I left the George and Pigmy, aiming to do my part. I could see, there at Narbondo's, that you lads didn't have what they call the upper hand."

"Right you are there," interrupted Godall, who poured Kraken a generous dollop of spirit.

"Thankee, sir, I'm sure. So I... Well... The long and short of it is, I ain't got the box. I had it, to be sure, but I ain't got it now."

"Where is it, man!" cried St. Ives.

"Billy Deener with the chimney pot hat's got it. Leastways he *had* it. Murderous villain, too, is what I'm telling you. If I'd have been sharp, I'd have left it with a pal o' mine in Farthing Alley, but I warn't sharp. I was uncommon dull from that bonk on the conk—I could see straight, you understand, but I couldn't hardly see clear.

"Well, chimney pot cleared me right out. I seen him before. And pardon me, yer honors, that I didn't care to see him again. So when he 'costed me with that 'ere pistol of his, why I give him the box and run, assumin', in my haste, you see, that he'd let me slide and make away with the prize. And so he did. I blushes to tell it, too. But we can fetch it back, and the girl with it, if you'll give me a chance to say on."

And with that he inhaled hugely and drained his glass again, trusting to the element of suspense to keep the rest of them listening.

"Fetch it back!" cried the Captain. "How, lad? Oil yourself, for the love of God! Don't dry out on us now."

"Don't mind if I do," agreed Kraken, tilting the handy bottle. St. Ives poured an ounce for himself, noting that it was past noon. It was close to the truth to say that it was smack in the middle of a long damned day, a day that would grow a good sight longer before it was played out.

Kraken set in again: "Sewers, is what I said to myself. I worked for Drake; you know that. What I did I daren't say. It don't make no difference now. After the last year with the poor master, Drake's little jobs looked uncommon genteel. We used the sewers, is what we did, for the delicate operations—and not a few of them there is too, when you're in that line o' business."

With that Kraken appeared to see for the first time the instrument that lay beside Keeble's chair, fallen from the toy-maker's fingers when he'd once again drifted off to sleep. "Holy Mother of God," uttered Kraken, turning pale. "Where did that infernal contraption appear from?"

"Drake," said Godall simply, tossing a shawl over the thing.

Kraken shook his head slowly and took a conscientious sip of brandy, cut, now, with water. "If you've seen what Lord Bingley done to himself with such an article up on Wardour Street…" Kraken paused in his shaking and shut his eyes, trying, perhaps, to crush out the memory of Lord Bingley's demise. He didn't speak for thirty seconds by the clock.

"Lord Bingley?" asked St. Ives, exercising his scientific curiosity.

Godall shook his head at St. Ives and held a finger across pursed lips, as if to say that the Lord Bingley business hadn't ought to be brought to light—that some few of the antics of humankind, when illuminated, were all the darker for the light cast upon them.

Kraken failed to acknowledge St. Ives' question anyway, but resumed his story instead. "I cut down the Stilton Lane Sewer and popped in through the trap, clean as a baby, speakin' figural, of course. You seen what the sewer does to a man's boots. And didn't I see some visions." Kraken paused and looked closely at the sleeping Keeble. "Dorothy Keeble's safe, I can tell you again, though what makes her so ain't what a man might choose. She's got a fever, or such like, and Drake won't let nobody near her, excepting, of course, the doctor." With this last utterance Kraken waggled his eyes at the men around him, to let them know, perhaps, which doctor it was who looked on at Dorothy's bedside.

"The filthy scoundrel!" cried the Captain, heaving to his feet as if he were intending to thrash the hunchback there and then.

Kraken held up his hand. "It ain't like that, gentlemen. Drake won't stand for it, for reasons of his own, if you follow me. He aims to clarify her of fever, or so he lets on. I was in a closet, top o' the second floor landing. Pule come in not a nickel's worth after I slipped in unseen. Raging after the girl, he was. Had himself wound with sticking plaster, too. Another of his 'cures' as he called it that night when him and the hunchback was twisting the business of the master's papers out of me. Anyway, there was Pule smelling to high heaven of chemical and his hands painted green. I never hope to see such a thing again. Well, they pitched him out—the bum's rush. He swore he'd kill Narbondo. Then he swore he'd kill Drake. Then he swore he'd kill the whole blessed city. Then they showed him the road. Narbondo left directly, worried, if you ask me, gentlemen, that Pule would make trouble up on Pratlow. But little enough trouble it would be, alongside o' what's been done last night. The doctor was in for a peeper, I can tell you."

Kraken grinned at that, fancying Narbondo's reaction when he witnessed the carnage at the Pratlow Street laboratory, Scotland Yard, perhaps, awaiting him on the stairs, the Keeble box long gone, Narbondo discovering that while he frolicked at Drake's the slats were being generally kicked out of his best-laid plans.

St. Ives struck his fist onto his open palm and leaped to his feet. "It's through the sewer then!" he cried. "Can you take me there? We may as well get on with it. They've had the advantage of us since this business began. We'll turn it round now."

"Whoa on," said Kraken, grinning just a bit. "There's more."

St. Ives stared at him. "What more?"

"Your vehicle, guv'nor, it's in the hall."

St. Ives was baffled. "My space vehicle is in Harrogate, locked away."

"The one you been looking about town for, is the one."

"The alien craft!"

"Aye, that's the one. Polished like a mirror, it is, lookin' out at the dome o' St. Paul's like the two of them was cousins."

St. Ives was in a state. Here was news indeed. Was it possible that within the house on Wardour Street lay the cumulative ends of their search? That they could wade in, pistols drawn, and in minutes take back weeks worth of defeat? Well, by God they'd try. St. Ives clapped his hand onto the arm of the couch in a show of determination. "The report from Swansea forecast the blimp at mid-afternoon. How long for it to make London?"

Kraken sneezed voluminously, waking Keeble up again. They put the question to him. "A few hours, I suppose," he said. "Not longer. This evening, to be sure."

"Can we assume, then, that the fourth box will be aboard?"

Keeble nodded. They might, of course, be fooled again, but it was odds on that when the ubiquitous Dr. Birdlip appeared in the sky overhead, he'd be carrying with him Jack Owlesby's inheritance.

"We've got to be on hand, of course," said Godall.

St. Ives nodded. There was no denying that. Jack's emerald, after all. Unless they snatched it at the first crack, they'd likely lose it. They'd never wrestle it away from the authorities—that much was certain, not without compromising Nell.

"There's a half-dozen of us," said Godall. "We'll break into parties. There's too much risk otherwise—we've too much ground to cover."

Godall was interrupted by a sound on the stairs. There stood Jack Owlesby, leaning on the banister. "Jack!" cried the Captain, limping over and offering the lad his arm.

"Afternoon," said Jack, grinning and stepping gamely but slowly down into the room. He took the Captain's arm for the trip across the rug to the couch, and he sat down gingerly when he got there, grimacing just a bit. Nell Owlesby and Winnifred Keeble followed. "I'm going with you to Drake's," said Jack.

There was a general silence in the room. It was a heroic offer, under the circumstances, but of course was out of the question. No one, however, wanted to deny Jack his part.

Captain Powers, having just that moment sat down, lay down his pipe with exaggerated care and stood up once again.

"Now see here," he said, looking at each one of them in turn. "I sailed a bit in my day—forty years of it, in truth, and commanded who knows how many lads from the Straits o' Magellan to the China Sea. It seems natural to me then to step lively here. We got too many officers and not enough hands, and that's been the long and short of her these last weeks, me bein' guiltier than the rest of you."

St. Ives' protest to this last statement was cut short. "Hear me out," said the Captain, poking his pipe stem in the scientist's direction. "Don't buck me, lad. I'm an old man, but I know what I'm about. Time's drawin' on. That 'ere blimp's got to be circumvented, as they say. And the hunchback doctor—we'll go for him straightaway. There's going to be half o' London out on Hampstead Heath tonight, blow me if there ain't, and it won't do to have any more scuffle than we can avoid, if you see my point. We square things away with the doctor now, is what I mean. Tie him up fast and lay him out in that there closet o' his. We can fetch him out in a week or so if we recalls it. So here's what I say, mates:

"I'm the blasted Captain here, so I'll point and you'll jump, and we'll all run aground out on the Heath when the sun goes down, for that's when we'll need the lot of us and to spare. For now, Professor, you and Keeble here will slide into Drakes' through the sewer. I'd get hold of a couple pair o' India rubber boots for the job."

St. Ives looked at Keeble. Did he have the stuff for it? It was clear he had to be given the chance. Keeble seemed to make a visible effort to pull himself together, to haul in loose limbs and slap some color into his face. He picked up his glass, thought better of it, and set it down hard on the table.

"I'm going with them," said Jack staunchly.

"You're going with *me*," cried the Captain, puffing like an engine on his pipe.

"I'm…" began Jack.

"Enough! You'll take orders or by heaven you'll stay home and scrub the slime out o' Kraken's boots! You and Nell, as I was saying, will lie low outside o' Wardour Street with a wagon. We'll be ready to fly when the Professor and Keeble steps out wi' the girl. It's action enough you'll see then, my lad. Can you fire a pistol?"

Jack nodded silently.

"One thing," interrupted St. Ives. He considered for a moment, his face brightening, his eyes gleaming. "In the event," he said, "that I don't come out—through the door that is—look sharp for me in the sky. I mean to get the starship out of

Drake's just as soon as we've got Dorothy safe. Be ready, then, to make for Hampstead without me."

The Captain shrugged. That was St. Ives' affair. Certainly there would be no way of going back in after the ship, not after the confrontation that would likely occur that afternoon. "And we'll leave ye too, mate. Don't think we won't. I aim to be on hand when Birdlip heaves to. The em'rald's been in my hands these long years, if you follow me, whether it's been in my sea chest or aboard that 'ere blimp. Yes, sir, starship or no, I'm for Hampstead when I see the black of that girl's hair."

St. Ives nodded.

"And you two," he said, nodding first to Hasbro and then to Kraken. "You swabs will take care of this here doctor, like I said."

Kraken chortled and rubbed his hands. "That we will," he said.

Hasbro was more eloquent. "Since his ruffians," said the starchy gentleman's gentleman, "tore the manor to bits and shattered the visage of poor Kepler, I've wanted nothing more than to have words with the good doctor, strong words, perhaps."

"Aye," cried Kraken, leaping up in a rush and whirling away with his fists at phantoms, then sitting down in a rush when he remembered that he wasn't wearing trousers. "Mighty strong words," he said squinting.

"That's the spirit," said the Captain. "Don't take no."

"Not us, sir," replied Hasbro, nodding obediently. "Am I to understand, then, that Mr. Kraken and myself are to rendezvous with the rest of you on the green at Hampstead?"

The Captain nodded vigorously. "That's it in a nut. And mind you, it's the blimp we want. This ain't no social affair. First one in grabs the box. Don't be shy. Don't wait for slackards. Lord knows which of us will get in first."

"Well it won't be me," said Winnifred Keeble, frowning at the Captain. "Apparently I'm to stay home, am I? Well I'm not, and you, sir, can smoke that if you'd like. I'm going in after Dorothy."

"As you say, ma'am," replied the Captain humbly. "The more hands the better when foul weather blows up."

"And I, gentlemen," said Godall, rising and picking up his stick, "intend to confront our evangelist. He has, if I'm not mistaken, one of the boxes in question. Which might it be again?"

St. Ives looked at Hasbro for help. "That would be the aerator box, sir, if I remember aright, which Pule possessed when he leaped from the train. And there will be two of the boxes at Drake's, sir, if you'll allow a gentle reminder—the little man inhabiting the one and the clockwork alligator in the other—both, I believe, of some value to us."

"Quite," said St. Ives, itching to be off. "What detains us then?"

The Captain knocked his ashes out into a glass ashtray. He blew through his pipe, shoved it into his coat pocket, and stood up. "Not a blessed thing," he said.

SEVENTEEN

The Flight of Narbondo

I T WAS VERY little presence of mind that Willis Pule had left. Outrage after outrage had been heaped upon him. And now this last business at Drake's…He strode along down alleys and byways out of the way of the London populace, grimacing at each jarring step at the pain of the chemical bath that heated his face beneath the sticking plaster. There was a good chance that the mixture would quite simply explode, reducing his head to rubble. Well so be it. He grinned at the thought of him strolling with a will into the presence of his collected enemies and, in the midst of a fine speech, detonating, as if his head were a bomb. It would have been a very nice effect, taken altogether. He laughed outright. He hadn't lost his sense of humor, had he? It was a sign that he would prevail. He was a man who could keep his head, he thought, while everyone else was…no, that wouldn't work. He giggled through his bandages, thinking about it, unable to stop giggling. Finally he was whooping and reeling, as if in a drunken passion, laughing down on the occasional loiterer like a madman, sending people scurrying for open doorways.

A mile of shouting and laughing, however, took it out of him, and he fell into a deepening despair, intermittent giggles turning to sobs until, wretched, homeless, and corroded by active chemicals, he stumbled into the dark public house for which he'd been bound.

Some few morose and shifty-eyed customers drank at long tables, looking as if they were ready to rise and flee at the slightest provocation. Pule was enough provocation to cause three unrelated loungers to drop their cups and start up, but upon seeing that he was obviously bound for the curtained doorway that communicated with a rear room, they slid back down onto their benches and simply regarded him with hostility.

The head of a newsboy, just then, was thrust in through the open street door, shouting incoherently the latest horrors that littered the front page of the *Times* and the *Morning Herald*. "Corpses!" he yelled. "Viversuction in Soho."

Pule slipped beneath the curtain, thinking darkly of corpses and vivisection. If it was corpses the public called for, then by God it was corpses they'd have. He descended a steep, broad stairs into a sub-street shop lit only by sunlight through high transom windows around the perimeter. An enormous man with a beard like that of a Nordic berserker pounded away with a hammer at what looked like an iron sausage casing. Dismantled clocks cluttered the bench around him. He wore on his face such a look of loathing and cynical contempt for the world in general that he was immediately recognizable as a revolutionary of the sort with no fixed philosophy beyond explosions. He built, however, what Pule sought—a dynamite bomb, of the spherical sort, cast of iron and with a short fuse. A "roll 'n' run" as they were called by the purveyors of such things. It took a little less than ten minutes before Pule strode along once again, a box under his arm, he and his device bound for Pratlow Street where, if he was lucky, he'd find Narbondo in among his instruments.

Pule stared at the pavement as he walked, his nostrils flaring, his eyes squinting, counting the bits and pieces of abuse he'd countenanced in the months he'd known Narbondo, raging within at the demise of the well-laid plans he'd carried into London. It wouldn't do, he thought, to be careless. He must have his revenge on all of them—there wasn't a one among them who wouldn't feel his wrath. He would settle Narbondo first, and Drake if he were able. And if he weren't, then he'd be on hand when the precious blimp landed, and he'd have his pickings then, wouldn't he? Somehow the chemical preparation vaporized beneath the bandages, and the rising fumes smarted his eyes, generating a steady stream of tears. He mopped at his face. The bandages were loose, unraveling even as he walked along.

Another newsboy chanted past. Rarely had there been as much news. The headlines were wild with it. "Blimp to land!" shouted the boy, waving a newspaper as if it were a banner. "Man from Mars inside! Alien threat! Harmergideon!"

Here, thought Pule, what's this? In a moment he owned a paper, the front page of which was given over equally to the story of the Pratlow Street corpses and the story of the approaching blimp, this last replete with predictions from the Royal Academy itself that the blimp would touch down in Hampstead. The minister of a popular religious sect insisted that aboard the blimp flew an alien creature who would "usher in Armageddon."

There was some confusion as to whether the two stories—the ghouls and the blimp—weren't somehow connected, the ghouls themselves perhaps amounting to aliens in some particularly opaque way. Or, it was equally likely, the ghouls were the first of millions of what Cicero had called the silent majority to rise bodily from their earthly resting place and shake off their shrouds. So said the man called Shiloh, the self-proclaimed messianic figure so common of recent date on London streets, and connected with the recent gatherings at Hyde Park. Why the newly enraptured crowd had chosen to wander down to Pratlow Street and pitch over into the gutter wasn't made at all clear.

Pule read while he walked, paying less attention to direction, perhaps, than would under the circumstances have been wise. His bandages were in full mutiny, his face half-exposed when he stumbled out into the sunlight of Charing Cross Road. He neglected the safer byways and alleys out of interest in the newspaper. Indeed, half the street seemed to have the same interest, for papers, it was clear, were in short demand. People read over each other's shoulders. A great knot of men and women stood in the center of the road, so engrossed in the communal reading of a paper that they were nearly trampled by a hansom cab, the driver of which grappled with a fluttering paper.

The populace, all in all, wore a fairly horrified look on their collective faces—news of aliens and ghouls being, apparently, the sort of ill wind that blew no one any good. Pule, sobbing out of a green malodorous face, dripping unwound sticking plaster, and slouching into the midst of such an assemblage of fear and suspicion, had a predictable effect. A woman shrieked and pointed. Others joined her. People turned where they stood, gaping at Pule, who was, for a moment, oblivious to the developing turmoil. Looking up, though, he saw at once that he'd been mistaken for something awful. For what, no one could immediately determine, neither Pule nor the horrified populace who fell back shrieking and pointing. Could *this* perhaps be the alien? A ghoul? Both? Who could say? Something unnatural it very clearly was.

"It's running!" squeeked a man in a waistcoat several sizes too small for him. And the cry was taken up by the street, Pule's flight seeming to be clear evidence that he was, somehow, what they thought him to be.

He pounded along, ridding himself of newspapers and bandages. If he could have pitched the bomb among them, silenced most of them and given the rest something substantial to shriek about, he would have done so gladly. But they would have been on him before he could act, and he would have been deprived the pleasure of demonstrating the device to Narbondo. The shouts, finally, were fading; no one on the street had been terribly keen on pursuit. It was enough, perhaps, merely to have been a party to the strange events of the day.

He could see very clearly what he had to do. It was a simple business: slip into the passage through the downstairs closet, climb to the laboratory, slide back the panel, and, without a word, roll the lit bomb into the room. Pule prayed that Narbondo would be there. It would almost be worth extinction to stay, to whisper something to the hunchback just as the bomb detonated, to see the look of futility and fear wash across his face, watch him scramble, perhaps, for the device, only to be blown to evil bits, weeping and shouting for mercy. Pule smiled at the thought. It was almost worth it, except that Narbondo was only one of a half score of people who sorely required comeuppance. And there was, of course, the matter of Dorothy Keeble. He wouldn't be deprived entirely of her company. That wouldn't do at all. He angled along down Pratlow, keeping well in toward the dilapidated façades so that an anxious Narbondo wouldn't catch sight of him through the casement. He slid through the street door

at the base of the stairs, nipped into the closet, and punched the corner of the panel
behind which was hidden the spring latch.

———◈———

IT WAS UNLIKELY that there had ever before been such a crowd in Regent's Park. A continual stream of people trudged along either side of the Parkway and up Seven Sisters'
Road. Between the human rivers rattled no end of dogcarts and cabrioles and hackney
coaches and chaises, clattering and hopping across potholes and ruts, their drivers cursing the masses of people that seemed to flow out into the center of the road on a whim,
clogging traffic. Wagons full of people jerked along, then stopped dead for the space of
a half-dozen minutes, then jerked along again, only to stop almost at once to avoid running down three score of travelers who, because of a mud puddle, perhaps, had drifted
again into the roadway, oblivious to the wagons clamoring to get through. If half of
London *isn't* on the march, thought Theophilus Godall as he handed a tract to a gaunt
man in a pince nez, then I'm a corpse. He certainly did his best to look like one—in a
hastily donned suit bought in Houndsditch for a shilling.

He'd had to do little to authenticate it; it was almost dirty enough to suffice. A bit
of shredding, an energetically executed dance on the heaped garments in the street,
some smearing on of mud—all in all it was an effective costume. A putty scar down
the center of his forehead and running under his right eye made it seem probable that
he'd had a rough and tumble life, which, when paired with the once ostentatious suit,
advertised him, perhaps, as a reformed gambler or other sort of rakehell.

At first he supposed that his fellow ghouls were utterly speechless, but that didn't
seem to be the case. Those who had a comparatively fresh look about them, who,
perhaps, had lain in the grave only a day or two before being liberated, could utter
some few syllables through rusted vocal chords. They hadn't, however, any elasticity
to them, and the croaking of the ghouls was, like the production of any unnatural
sound, difficult for a healthy man to imitate. Godall did his best, remaining mute for
the most part.

The evangelist was inflamed with his usual false spirit, fired by the bellows of approaching apocalypse. Part of him gnashed and cursed the loss of the homunculus
box—if that's what it was. That there was another box of inestimable value aboard the
blimp was certain. And he had Pule's wonderful device—hadn't he?—the use of which
a half hour earlier had brought about a miracle, and a very useful miracle at that. He'd
been imbued with the powers of fertility, with the spirit of the Garden, even to the
extent of his visage having turned a mysterious pale green, as if he were the incarnation, perhaps, of a vegetable deity. He'd become a walking illustration of the paradox
of rebirth—the wrinkles of age giving way to the budding of a new spring, the age of
lead wheezing into extinction as the age of gold clambered up out of the wings. And

he'd spoken in a curious voice, squeaky and birdlike—frightening at first; there was no denying it.

But being a vehicle of such cataclysmic change wasn't, to be sure, an easy business and had never been such. The power that had assumed control of his larynx was quite clearly the spirit of his departed mother, hovering in the London aether like a waiting dove. He could remember the particular timbre of her voice, whispering through the dusty halls of memory. When he'd whirled the crank on the device and been sprayed, as it were, by the curious green dust, he'd been gripped by her spirit; he'd spoken for the space of a long moment in his mother's sweet voice. He'd been overwhelmed, amazed. He'd doubted, even. But doubt was everywhere; he knew that. Flesh was weak, vilely weak. It had, often, to be satiated. Give it some harmless trifle to placate it, and by so doing beat it down so that the spirit could go on about its business. "Let the filthy yet be filthy," he said half aloud.

His mind wandered, from the curious box to the crowds surging behind and around him to a young lady in a muslin dress—one of his particular favorites among the live converts. She reminded him of Dorothy Keeble, a prisoner in Drake's establishment. He squinted a bit, as if diminishing the scene roundabout him in order to call up a more immediately pleasurable picture.

His face writhed into something idiotic, a facsimile of a smile. His hands shook and he was gripped by the immediacy of his unspent passion. His chest heaved as he struggled to catch his breath. He reached surreptitiously into his cloak and groped for a flask of medicine—gin and laudanum—the combined wonders of which had a distinctly calming effect. He shuddered and looked round him wondering if, perhaps, he hadn't ought to crank up the device and treat the captive audience around him to the first of the evening's bountiful collection of miracles. There before him, smiling benignly, stood one of Narbondo's animations, bless his enlivened heart. His comparatively uncorrupted countenance suggested that he wasn't one of the mutes, one of the recovered long-dead.

"I can see from the cut of your suit that you were of genteel breeding," said the evangelist benevolently to the man he supposed to be a corpse.

Godall continued to smile at him with the same vacant, empty-headed smile that resided on the faces of the faithful, both living and dead, who milled through the crowds. He decided to respond, having little to lose, even if he were found out. "I was indeed, master," said Godall thickly.

The evangelist gawked at him, surprised. Here was a lively ghoul indeed. Could such a miracle be possible? Of course it could. The end, after all, was drawing nigh. The sea would give up its dead and all would be given tongues so that they might, like lawyers, argue their cases before a holy tribunal. He was fired with the idea. "My son!" he exclaimed into the face of Theophilus Godall. And with that he began to blubber and wheeze, carried away by the sight of London on the march,

232 *James P. Blaylock*

hurrying toward they knew not what. "Stand beside me, my child! You'll be called upon to testify!"

With that admonition, the old man grasped the Keeble box—St. Ives' aerator—and whirled away at the crank, launching a cloud of green vapors that brought forth, as he had hoped, torrents of exclamation from the pressing crowd. A flat-bed wagon sat abandoned in the road before them, its driver having grown impatient and tramped away toward Hampstead Heath on foot.

"Kneel, my son," commanded Shiloh. Godall kneeled. Shiloh placed a foot on his back and boosted himself onto the wagon, waving the spirit box.

The crowd roundabout fell silent. The press was so thick that the audience, for the moment anyway, was literally captive, and there were no oak trees nearby, thank heaven, to provide shelter for mocking sinners. The evangelist gave the box another crank, bathing his face in the dust of fecundity. "Hear me!" he squeaked in a voice weirdly reminiscent of pipid frogs. He motioned wildly at an attendant who lifted above his head the glass case in which rested the skull of Joanna Southcote. The teeth seemed to hop and chatter just a bit, but the effect was negligible. It was impossible to tell whether the result was a matter of the head's sudden animation or of the attendant's having given it a shake.

Shiloh twisted the crank, shoving the tube into his mouth so as to get the full effect of the emitted holy gases. He staggered under the power of it just as the horse in front of the cart lurched. "The hour," piped the old man, "hath come! We hasten toward the gate. Outside are the dogs and sorcerers and fornicators and murderers and idolators..." and halfway through idolators the effects of the gases diminished and with a frightening burst the piping voice gave way to the old man's creaking shout. He whirled away at the crank with a passion, squirting himself down with vapors, playing the green spray on the multitude who stood in silent wonder. "Come!" he resumed. "Come!" he shrieked.

Godall realized suddenly that the old man was shouting particularly at him. "Me?" mouthed Godall, looking up questioningly.

"Yes, my child! Come hither. Leap aboard this chariot!"

Godall complied. Before them, the road had cleared, part of the crowd having moved along. Those that hadn't clustered round the rear of the wagon, watching the prophet in expectation of further miracle. The attendant lay the skull on the wagon, heaving the Gladstone bone-bag up beside it. Godall waved at the crowd, put his foot against the forehead of the erstwhile attendant, and pushed the man down onto the road.

"Here now!" cried the evangelist turning in surprise upon Godall. But the tobacconist grabbed the flapping cloth of the old man's robe and, giving it a jerk, hauled him over backward. Shouts arose from the baffled masses. Godall whirled, grabbed the reins, and whipped up the anxious horses. The cart leaped ahead. A handful of the faithful raced after it as if to climb aboard, but the effort was wasted. The horses tore away up the road while Shiloh the evangelist, flopping and shrieking on the wagon, held onto his collected props as the jigging skull of Joanna Southcote chattered and clattered accusingly into his ear.

Godall raced up Camden Town Road and angled along a narrow, deserted street into comparatively empty countryside, and for ten minutes he rattled along farther and farther from the environs of Hampstead Heath. He reined in the horses, finally, amid the shadows of a scattering of trees and turned on the scrambling missionary, who quaked in fear at the sight of the pistol in Godall's hand. He squinted into his captor's face, slow recognition appearing in his own. "You!" he cried.

Godall nodded. "I should, I suppose, put a bullet into you, mad dog that you are..."

"On the contrary, sir," began Shiloh, interrupting.

"Silence!" cried Godall. "Now, sir. As I say, I'd just as soon drill a hole in your forehead with this pistol as shake your hand. In fact, I'd gladly do the one and wouldn't consider the other. But it's not my place to judge another man..."

"Judge not!" cried the evangelist, waving both hands about his head as if suffering a fit, "lest ye be judged!"

Godall eyed him coolly. "Don't press me, villain, or you'll find yourself respiring through the top of your head. Hear me out. And save your breath; you have a trek before you, carrying all that gear along. You may, I suppose, be mad—I've no reason to believe otherwise—and a madman, though he might commit vile acts, can hardly be held entirely accountable for them. The extent of your crimes, moreover, can only be measured by an examination of the damage done in the infection of innocent people with your dubious proclamations. Such people, perhaps, would have fallen prey to someone else had you not been handy. The judging of the thing, then, is beyond my powers. It will have to be the unpleasant duty of a higher authority.

"But hear me, sir. I have very powerful acquaintances. Your perversions at the house on Wardour Street haven't gone unnoticed, and the coin you so liberally sprinkle about on your own behalf is transparent, to speak figuratively. If you continue, then, to practice your chicanery publicly, to delude the London innocent, then, sir, you'll be called out, the disparity between our ages notwithstanding."

The evangelist stood rigid as a post, his face purple, his eyes squeezed almost shut. Had he been a jack-in-the-box his lid would have blown off in the next moment. "D-d-do you!" he cried, breathing heavily thereafter and scooping up from the leaves on the ground the foolish head. "Do you know, sir, that you've unalterably called down upon you your own vile damnation!" And this last syllable was uttered with such ferocity that Theophilus Godall was certain for a moment that the old man's tongue would fly out, like the poisonous tongue of a newt. The display, all in all, confirmed Godall's suspicion that the old man was the most deluded of his entire flock, if the shepherd can be said to occupy such a position.

Time was wasting. Light was failing. He was an hour and a half out of Hampstead in the borrowed wagon. And if the roads were clogged yet with sightseers, then it would be odds on that the blimp would descend without him. He'd had enough of the old man, and was tempted to tie him to the tree to prevent the possibility of his following along to the heath. But such a course might well burst the man's head. So without another word, Godall took up the ribands, flicked at the horses with the whip, and set off up the road at a canter followed by the receding figure of Shiloh the New Messiah, who struggled cursing along, toting in one hand the Gladstone coffin and in the other the encased skull, and hoping heartily that some few of his congregation might have followed them out of the city.

—◦◦◦—

THE PARTLY SHADED lantern threw an amazingly bright shaft of light across the floor of the cupboard. Hasbro and Kraken had carried it up the passage from the street, finding themselves, finally, beyond the wall of Narbondo's laboratory. The lantern did nothing, however, to generally illuminate the close quarters, and Kraken, bending across to whisper into his companion's ear, smashed his nose against Hasbro's shoulder in the process. "Ugh' whispered Kraken, putting a hand to his face.

"Ssshh!" said Hasbro, who made an effort to peer through a wire-thin crack that ran along the edge of the moving panel. Lamplight shone from beyond, and every now and then someone—the hunchback surely—passed across in front of the crack.

"Shall we clip it open and throttle him, then?" whispered Kraken.

"Patience, sir."

"He's a bad'n, is the doctor. Not a man o' science, mind you. A different sort. A devil. I'm agoing to pummel him," whispered Kraken, jolting around for a moment, perhaps practicing his pummeling. Hasbro peered through the crack, undisturbed. "Science don't slice up dead men," insisted Kraken in a stage whisper of increasing vehemence. "Science don't..." he began, but a noise on the stairs behind interrupted him.

"Sh!" whispered Hasbro, jiggling the covered lamp so that the cloth fell and nipped off the light altogether. The two held their breath. A tramp, scrape, tramp sounded on the stairs. Someone, something approached, ascended toward them. Hasbro squeezed Kraken's shoulder twice, as if signaling that action was imminent. "As silent as possible," he murmured into Kraken's ear.

"Aye," breathed Kraken.

A sputtering light appeared, preceding low giggling and a muffled cough. The light flickered across the landing at the top of the narrow stairs. Both men half expected the appearance on the landing of a ghoul, of one of the walking dead who would shuffle round to face them up the dark corridor. With a last scrape and thud, a knee and a foot appeared; then a head bent into view—the grinning, open-mouthed head of Willis Pule, lit by the unnaturally white light of a sputtering fuse that curled up out of the bowels of an infernal device. He turned and crept toward them, the circle of light cast by the fuse approaching along the floor.

Hasbro crouched there, waiting, ready to spring the moment they were revealed. Kraken shook beside him, his teeth rattling audibly. Pule stopped, canted his head, squinting through the gloom, suspicious.

"Lord!" howled Kraken. "He'll blow us to finders!" And with that he launched himself at the horrified Pule, who made as if to heave the bomb full into Kraken's face. The two went down in a heap of arms and legs, both shouting, Kraken rolling astride Pule and flailing away at him with both fists. The bomb bounced on the wooden floorboards, Hasbro scooping it up and pinching at the fuse, which, despite his efforts, sputtered continually to life.

"This won't do," he said aloud, and he pitched the bomb along the corridor. It bounced, rolled, caromed off the wall and down the stairs, bump, bump, humping along. The corridor was cast into sudden darkness.

"Ow!" cried Kraken. "Filthy animal!"

Hasbro whipped the cloth from atop the lamp and punched at the oak panel before him. Expecting an explosion that would literally bring the house down, he stepped through into an empty laboratory, the door standing ajar. Kraken sprang in beside him, blood pouring down his arm.

"You've been injured, sir," said Hasbro as he strode toward the gaping door.

"Filthy blighter bit me," heaved Kraken, laboring for breath. "So I kicked him down the well."

"Bravo!" cried Hasbro, leaping up the stairs two at a time toward the upper floors.

"He went up, did he?"

"I haven't the foggiest," shouted Hasbro over his shoulder. "But the house might, if it's going up you want."

"Oh Lord, yes!" hooted Kraken, close at Hasbro's heels. In a trice they found the door to the roof, and without slackening pace, leaped across to the next roof, neither pausing to question the possibility of slowing up, but leaping instead to a third just as the expected explosion boomed up from the street. Both men dropped instinctively; then, realizing that the roof they stood on was yet solid, they crept across and peered between chimney pots. In the center of Pratlow Street was a smoking crater. Half a block down, high-stepping toward Holborn as if pursued by goblins, flew a desperate Willis Pule, foiled once again.

"It must ha' gone out the door," observed Kraken.

"I believe you're correct. A pity, really, that it didn't destroy the laboratory."

"We can have a go at that one ourselves," Kraken shouted, the idea clearly appealing to him. "We can smash it and smash it and smash it!"

Hasbro considered Kraken's suggestion, recalling, perhaps, the broken Kepler. "It's growing a bit late," he began, only to cut himself off and shout, for there, half a dozen rooftops away, springing suddenly out of hiding, leaped Dr. Ignacio Narbondo, a satchel in either hand.

Without a word the two were after him, neither knowing what it was they intended to do with him if they caught him, but remarkably keen on the catching.

It was clear, though, before the chase was six minutes old, that the doctor had taken to those same rooftops more than once in the past, for it seemed that he gained two each time the two pursuers crossed one, sliding along gables, clattering across copper sheathing, skidding on the scree of decomposing chimneys and all the time falling farther behind.

They paused, finally, some two blocks from Old Compton, listening to what sounded for all the world like distant laughter ring over the rooftops. For the slice of a moment the doctor appeared at what seemed to be an impossible distance, standing before the brick front of a steep garret, an orange sun beyond him dropping across the afternoon sky. Then he was gone. —⌀

EIGHTEEN

On Wardour Street

LANGDON ST. IVES and William Keeble crouched in the darkness of an ill-lit hallway on the second floor of the house on Wardour Street. Their short journey through the sewers had been both unpleasant and uneventful. It had been such an easy business gaining access to the house, in fact, that last week's song and dance with the clock crystal seemed an idiotically bad idea. Where they were to go now that they were inside, however, remained to be seen.

The air was almost unnaturally still and quiet. There had to have been any number of people within earshot, but in the heavy, somnolent atmosphere, it seemed as if most were asleep—not at all an unlikely thing, given that most of their business was transacted during the night. There was some stirring and banging downstairs, from the kitchen, possibly. Muted voices could be heard, one of which sounded as if it might be the voice of Winnifred Keeble, who, dressed as a washerwoman, might well have gained entrance through the back door. The thought of her confronting the flour-faced cook was bothersome, but Winnifred had insisted. And cleaver or no cleaver, the cook would find Winnifred Keeble a difficult case.

St. Ives and Keeble tiptoed down the hallway, half wondering which room to peer into. Opening the wrong door would be disastrous. Kraken had supposed that Dorothy was somewhere on the third floor, guarded, no doubt, by Drake's toughs, perhaps by Drake himself. So there was no real need to start peeking into doorways on the second floor, except that the doors presented themselves. Who could say what lay behind them?

They approached the wooden balustrade that fronted the great open hall which St. Ives had been deprived of seeing on his previous visit. There, Kraken had said, lay the starship. Would it be merely an empty hull, stripped and rusted by the centuries? And what purpose did Drake put it to? Was it enough just to possess it, or was there, as rumor had it, some darker, foul purpose? St. Ives thought momentarily of the dreaded

Marseilles Pinkle, wrapped in a shawl, lying in the Captain's wagon on the street. There were, apparently, no limits to the perversions concocted by desperate men. What might such men do with the space vehicle of the homunculus? St. Ives couldn't imagine.

A sudden sobbing erupted from beyond the door to their right, followed by the utterance of a low laugh. Keeble straightened, his eyes wide. "Dorothy," he called, half aloud, reaching for the door handle.

St. Ives' attempt to stop him was in vain. He grabbed the back of Keeble's coat, whispered, "Wait!" and was pulled into the room along with the toymaker. On a narrow, unmade bed sat a pasty-faced woman wearing what appeared to be a fruit bowl for a hat. Crawling on his hands and knees on the floor was a man in kneebreeches and a striped topcoat, this last being hauled up over his head, the tails caught up and tied with a broad strip of dotted ribbon. On his feet were pointed, women's shoes, turned around backward and wedged on awkwardly. It was the man on the floor who sobbed in girlish tones.

At the raging issuance of Keeble and St. Ives, the woman on the bed shrieked, and without a second's hesitation, plucked up a glass vase full of wilted roses and pitched the entire affair at the horrorstruck Keeble. The man on the floor stopped his capering at the sound of the shriek and shouted: "What? Who is it!" He struggled, pinioned helplessly in his coat and shoes and bombarded by the fruit that cascaded from the woman's hat. She shrieked again, even though her first shriek had driven Keeble half-way back out into the hallway.

Looking desperately for concealment, St. Ives hauled the toymaker along. Doors slammed on the floor below. Two half-dressed, bearded men thrust their heads through a suddenly opened door, then fled toward the stairs, perhaps assuming that St. Ives and Keeble, rushing at them along the hallway, were police officers. Another door shot open and out dashed an enormous gentleman in ventilated rubber trousers, a sheet of newspaper in front of his face. He too bowled away down the stairs toward the street.

Within moments, it seemed, the cry had gone round the house, and the air was full of shouts and pounding feet and the slamming of doors. Behind St. Ives raged the man with the coat over his head, shouting curses, threatening through a mouthful of tweed. His ridiculous twisted shoes lay on the carpet behind. A head, shouting a fearful string of venomous oaths, shot through the gathered coat, the dotted ribbon and coattails encircling his neck like a clown's collar, his arms cocked up, trapped and thrashing as if he wore a makeshift straightjacket. It was Kelso Drake.

At the sight of Keeble and St. Ives, Drake blanched. His mouth writhed. He flailed away within the confines of his woolen prison. Keeble stopped, dumbstruck. He hesitated a quarter of a second, pondering Drake's bound state, then slid past St. Ives in a rush and struck the industrialist on the nose. Drake was propelled backward, struggling in his coat, in fear now as well as anger. Keeble struck him again. He grasped a handful of coat front, slapped Drake three or four times on the cheek, then tweaked both his ears. Keeble capered and yodeled before his helpless victim as St. Ives, anxious to conclude their business and be away, hauled at the toymaker's collar.

With a rip of rending material, Drake was suddenly free of the restricting garment, and, with the cry of a madman, he launched himself at Keeble, punching and flailing at the toymaker, who, with a deliberation and sobriety that startled St. Ives, pulled from his coat a leather truncheon, and slammed the industrialist on the side of the head, felling him to the carpet. Keeble replaced the truncheon, apparently satisfied, and turned toward St. Ives a face pale and beaded with sweat. "I don't suppose I should kill him," he said slowly.

"No!" cried St. Ives, hauling Keeble once again along the hallway toward the stairs. Jolting up from the ground floor raged two men, obviously not customers. One, St. Ives realized with a shock of horror, was the man with the chimney pot hat, who held in his hand a carving knife. His companion scrabbled in his coat, perhaps after a gun.

"The bench!" cried St. Ives, grappling with the end of the carved Jacobean trestle bench that sat on the landing. Keeble went for the opposite end. The two men swung it in a quick arch, then let it go, Keeble a second or so ahead of St. Ives. Chimney pot flattened himself against the balustrade as Keeble's end of the heavy bench swung round, grazing his forehead, plowing into the neck and chest of his companion, who had, to his own great misfortune, been peering into his coat. The man screamed and pitched over backwards, he and the bench skidding together down the stairs. Chimney pot was after them, waving the knife.

St. Ives skipped up the stairs, Keeble beside him, both men running headlong into a surprised Winnifred Keeble who supported Dorothy around the shoulders with her left arm. In her right hand she clutched a revolver. "Where on earth..." she began before catching sight of the murderous chimney-pipe. "I have your gun!" she cried, pointing the weapon in his general direction.

He slowed momentarily, cocked his head as if debating the extent of the threat, then rushed heedlessly on. Winnifred pushed Dorothy in William's direction, grasped the revolver with both hands, and fired off three or four shots, one after the other, eyes closed. St. Ives dove onto his chest, rolling against the wall of the stairwell, as he watched Billy Deener sail over backward and tumble to the floor below, then roll six feet toward the center of the room, his hands over his head, before scrambling away toward the kitchen. The back door slammed in his wake. Kelso Drake staggered into the room below, then abruptly disappeared after he looked up to see the smoking pistol in the hands of Winnifred Keeble.

The Keebles ushered a stumbling and bewildered Dorothy along to the now empty room, all of them intent only on reaching the street. Fearful that they wouldn't be quick enough, Keeble bent over and scooped the drugged girl into his arms, tilting dangerously for a moment before tossing her just a bit so that she settled in and balanced. St. Ives crouched halfway up the second floor stairs, watching the toymaker and his wife disappear below. He turned, bolted for the top landing, and burst out onto a deserted corridor, lit dimly by gaslamps in the shape of brass cupids, clinging at intervals along the wall.

Twenty feet along, the corridor opened onto the great hall that St. Ives had been denied a look at ten days earlier. He stepped toward it, wafering himself against the wall to peer out over the high, open room, fearful that he'd be seen from below. No one, however, was in the room save Kelso Drake, who limped along across the floor, his head now swathed in bandages. A low murmur arose, as if he were cursing under his breath. Then he shouted at someone unseen about bringing the brougham around. There sounded an answering shout, then a grunt from Drake, then another shout about Deener having "taken the other box."

"Good!" cried Drake, struggling to open a leather bag, the clasp of which refused to cooperate. The millionaire flung it against the back of a velvet couch with a fury that astonished St. Ives, and set to kicking the bag about the room like a football, dancing atop it until he'd stomped the clasp into submission. Then, yanking open the bag, he tore apart the doors of a broad, mirrored buffet, and yanked out a Keeble box, dropping it into the bag and hurrying out of sight. A moment later the front door banged shut and silence reigned. The house, no doubt, contained any number of people, hidden away from daylight and activity like bats in caves.

St. Ives wasted no time. He had no desire to confront murderers or to hide behind potted plants. He would find a way into the strange ship that sat toadlike in the center of the room below. It was apparently nothing more than a curious ornament, like a china vase or a marble cupid, the peculiar bric-a-brac of a millionaire, polished, no doubt, by a cleaning woman with a rag, who assumed it to be some sort of inexplicable and filthy contrivance for the gratification of the abhorrent appetites of wealthy customers. It was thought to be a sort of giant Pinkle, perhaps, the uses of which were veiled from the sight of the uncorrupted.

St. Ives stared at the machine for a long minute, peering at the little crenelations along its fins, its emerald-tinted ports, the silver sheen of its globular bulk. All in all it wasn't vastly different in character from his own ship—they weren't brothers, to be sure, hut they bore each other an unmistakable family resemblance. Curious, thought St. Ives, how two vehicles that hailed from galaxies so immensely distant from each other should have such an obvious affinity. There was a metaphysic there that bore contemplation, but it seemed a good idea to wait until later to contemplate it. He turned and made off down the stairs, pushing through two doors and under a tremendous arch into the hall.

He grasped the rope that hung behind the drawn curtains and gave it a yank, the curtains swinging back and the room flooding with midafternoon sunlight. The vast, unshuttered window looked out onto Wardour Street, obscured partly from view by a scattering of junipers and boxwoods that grew up close along the walls of the house, entangled in the creeping tendrils of climbing fig. It might easily have been years since the foliage had been trimmed, and easily as long since the drape had been drawn to illuminate the dim and unwholesome room with sunlight.

At the sound of a crashing upstairs and what sounded like the whispering of furtive voices, St. Ives hastily manipulated what seemed to him to be the hatch—a circular panel that popped open like the stone door of Aladdin's cave, emitting a little airy chirp as if startled, perhaps, by the touch of the scientist's hand.

At the sudden sight of the interior of the ship, St. Ives found himself trembling so that he could hardly command his hands and feet. He attempted to scale the side, but his foot slid from a protruding bit of polished metal and his hands could find no purchase on the slippery arched edge of the open hatch. His breath whooshed out by the lungful. He felt suddenly giddy and faint, faced, as he was, by the object of a long and sometimes desperate search and fired by the fear that at any moment he'd hear the click of a pistol hammer drawn back or the rough shout of one of Drake's men. He hauled on the arm of a nearby upholstered chair, drawing it up next to the spacecraft, climbing up onto the seat and nearly sinking at once to the level of the floor in the soft, lack-springed cushion. He stepped up onto an arm, teetered back and forth, and slid head first in at the hatch. After yanking the hatch shut, he settled into a cushioned seat and surveyed the interior of the ship.

Before him were a plethora of dials and gauges. He'd wage a sum on his being able to guess out the nature of half a dozen of them, but others were a mystery. The dials were mounted under clock crystals, filled, it seemed, with violet liquid. Scattered in between and roundabout were buttons that one might push, fabricated of what appeared to be ivory and ebony. St. Ives had the sudden urge to jab away at them, like a man with no musical training might poke at the keys of a piano. But the discordant result might easily mean his doom—probably *would* mean his doom. He calculated, trusting to his earlier conclusions about the peculiar but telling affinity of related objects in the universe. His fingers wandered from one switch to the next. Nothing ventured...he told himself, stopping before an ivory button beside which was a sort of hieroglyphic depiction of a sun. He stabbed at it. The dials glowed suddenly through the violet liquid. Emboldened, he pushed another, this one next to a little picture of an aeolus-faced puff of wind. A humming ensued. St. Ives braced himself, then felt, against the back of his neck, a little rush of air. An oxygenator, he thought, smiling at his pair of successes. He jabbed another button and the hatch opened.

"Damn," he said, half aloud. He stooped up through the hiatus, grasped the hatch in order to haul it back down, and looked straight into the ruined face of a ghoul, who stood precariously on the upholstered chair. St. Ives shrieked at it, dropping into the craft, bounding up again to clutch at the hatch, the ghoul meanwhile endeavoring to hoist itself in. Its gaping face, hair tumbling over its forehead, loomed in above St. Ives, who pressed his right hand against the thing's nose and forehead, shoving with all his strength, his feet braced against the deck of the craft. The ghoul stared out stupidly from beneath St. Ives' fingers, its own hands stubbornly clutching the edges of the circular hatch opening. St. Ives banged at the fingers with the fist of his free hand, then reached past, grasped the hatch, and slammed it down on the back of the thing's head.

It lurched forward, eyes widening, then jerked its head out, throwing the hatch open with it. A third hand joined the pair still clutching the ship—another ghoul endeavoring to clamber in. St. Ives banged the hatch down onto the fingers, mashing at them once, then twice, then a third time, grimacing at each blow, expecting a rain of severed fingers. He shut his eyes and slammed the hatch again, it settled into place. Outside were the two ghouls, examining their hands with looks of wonder on their faces, as if having already forgotten how they'd come to be in such a state. Beyond them was another ghoul. Two more slumped in through the door.

St. Ives gritted his teeth and poked an ebony button. The ship lurched and lay still. He poked another. Nothing at all happened. Two ghouls pushed a sofa toward the craft. Another hauled at an oak secretary. Three more wandered into the room and tugged at a piano, inching it forward, intent upon…what? Scuttling St. Ives' ship by burying it in furniture? The scientist settled to his work. A heavy rope end flicked past the window. They were tying the craft to the leg of the upholstered chair, then winding it around the leg of the piano. He'd been wrong about the cleaning woman again. Apparently it was common knowledge, even among ghouls, that the craft was a ship of some sort—not at all a bad thing, thought St. Ives. It argued that the craft worked, that Drake had given orders to prevent its being hijacked.

At the pressing of a button next to the drawing of a spiralling arrow, the ship spun suddenly on its axis, dragging with it the stuffed chair and tearing the rope from the hands of a bent and ragged zombie that crept about under the piano. St. Ives pressed the same button and the movement stopped. He pressed again and the craft resumed its revolution. When he faced the window straight on, he pushed it once again. Then, throwing caution onto the dust heap, he stabbed away at a succession of buttons.

The ship shuddered, lurched, slid forward a foot. The chair in which he sat tilted back, nearly dumping him onto the floor. A wild hum erupted as the craft lurched again, skittered across the floor, and, in an avalanche of cascading glass and tearing vines, rose in a sudden escalating rush, hauling with it the stuffed chair and a single dangling ghoul whose face, smitten with wonder and confusion, pressed against one of the starboard ports for a quick second or so before sliding away and disappearing.

St. Ives, hands flying over the controls in a wild effort to steady the craft, had no time to be concerned with attached zombies. The ship cartwheeled. St. Ives watched in a whirling rush the topsy turvy dome of St. Paul's spin past, followed by a brief glimpse of the spiraling armchair, lost almost immediately to sight and giving way to what was almost certainly a split-second view of the Kennington Oval. The ship shot away to the south and west, bound, it seemed, for the channel.

He was moving prodigiously fast in an utterly uncontrolled flight, pinned to his seat by the laws of physics on a voyage that, he was suddenly certain, was making him sick at his stomach. It would end in disaster. He knew it. He could picture himself catapulting out of hand into the sea. He couldn't, in fact, picture anything else. It was evident that the slightest manipulation of a pair of curved levers at dead center in front of him would cause the ship to tumble or swerve or skip or in some way run mad. Hesitantly, he prodded one. But he succeeded only in once again cavorting along end over end. There was the sea, the lying chair, what appeared briefly to be a pantleg with a shoeless foot dangling from it, this last entangled in the swinging rope. A prod at the other lever sent him plummeting breathlessly toward the sea, his stomach at once in his throat, the chair rising weirdly past the ports followed by the staring face of the zombie, whose ankle was fouled in the line. The gray swell of the Channel hurtled toward him as he edged the lever back, ever so slowly. The craft swung round in a slow arc, leveling off, then rising once again. It was slow deliberation that was called for—the mere consideration of pressure on a lever was nearly sufficient for a change of course.

His stomach returned to its rightful position, the blood in his veins ceased its racing and settled in apace, and with a keen-minded deliberation, tempered by a vision of the collected, astonished visages of the Royal Academy when he swept in among them at prodigious speeds, and encouraged by the vast canvas of the deepening evening sky, St. Ives eased the lever forward with a subtle pressure from his right hand. He steadied the ship with his left, satisfied with the controlled response. He dipped suddenly, evened her out, and smiled, angling in an increasing rush toward the Dover Strait. The ship slanted upward through thinning atmosphere into the purple heavens. The sky above darkened, brimming suddenly with flickering emerald lamps through the tinted ports, as if he stared into a deep, stellar well, half full of dark water and reflected stars. —◌

NINETEEN

On the Heath

FROM HAMPSTEAD HEATH, the lights of London winked and glittered in the darkness, an earthbound counterpoint to the stars amid which St. Ives raced in his borrowed ship miles and miles above. Theophilus Godall stood with Captain Powers and Hasbro, alternately watching the wash of lights and the heavens, the first for no practical reason save beauty, the latter for the appearance of the dark bulk of Birdlip's blimp.

The village of Hampstead was choked with people, slogging in the mud of the streets, jamming the taverns, perching in trees. Pots of ale and cups of gin and rum were carried around by hustling children, who got no farther than a dozen feet from their doors before their wares were snatched away and consumed and a hundred voices called for more of the same. Half the populace of Greater London seemed to have found itself in the vicinity of Hampstead, although a good part of them got no farther than Hampstead Village or Camden Town before encamping, either having little interest in approaching blimps, or, more likely, having little idea what it was that approached, satisfied to be afoot on a warm evening in the carnival atmosphere.

Godall professed to Captain Powers that he hoped the ale and spirits would hold up. And just when he finished the sentence, a great crash sounded from across the green on which they stood, and a low building collapsed in a heap of flying debris. Screams and moaning erupted from a score of people who had moments before been perched atop it and had been singing a tumultuous hymn. A band of robed faithful, two of whom supported a worn but animated Shiloh between them, hurried toward the wrecked shack, pitching handfuls of tracts to the enthusiastic crowds they passed along the way.

The Royal Academy clustered within the confines of a roped-off rectangle on the green onto which had been arranged lawn chairs. The perimeter of the rectangle was threatened roundabout by the pressing multitude. Parsons, a powdered wig canted across the top of his head, shouted over a sheaf of foolscap at his fellows, but his words were one with the general mêlée, and not a scientist among them had his eyes on anything but the stars.

Godall was faintly surprised to see the evangelist. There seemed to be no end to the perspicacity of a zealot. The old man appeared, however, to be deflated, to have had the wind taken out of his sails. In the glass cube, still clutched under his arm, lay the head of Joanna Southcote, mute now and toppled over onto its side. It was hard to imagine that the evangelist would cause them trouble. It was the blimp he was interested in. When it landed, *then* they'd have to look sharp. But he'd hardly risk attacking them outright, despite the affront of being manhandled by Godall hours earlier.

Kelso Drake, though, was a different proposition. He'd ridden up minutes after the arrival of the Captain's wagon, then had vanished immediately—an ominous thing, all in all. Godall would far sooner keep him in sight. It was impossible to say whose ghouls lurched about the heath, Shiloh's or Drake's—quite conceivably both. Kraken was crouched in the upper limbs of a particularly tall alder fifty meters away, a whistle in his teeth. He was on the watch, especially, for the man in the chimney pipe hat. The Keebles were ensconced in the wagon, neither Jack nor Dorothy being in condition to venture out among the multitude. Dorothy, however, was coming round, the haste of their retreat from Wardour Street having chased off some of the effects of the drugs. William Keeble looked about furtively, his right hand on the pistol in his coat, utterly certain that Drake would attempt to repay him for the pummeling in the hallway. Wrapped in a shawl beneath his feet lay the notorious Marseilles Pinkle.

Once, as the wagon had banged and rattled up the hill from Hampstead, they'd rounded a corner, pressing through a mob of trudging merrymakers, and among them, a broad-brimmed hat yanked across his eyes, Willis Pule had bent along slowly. He had glanced up, as if to join the bulk of the mob in cursing the wagon, and his eyes might as well have been pinwheels. If ever Keeble had seen a madman, Pule was it, and no mistake. His face was awash with a deadly, green pallor, as if his head were a pocked and cratered ball of green cheese gouged from the moon.

At the sight of the wagon pushing past, the spinning rear wheels sluicing mud onto Pule's trousers and Pule himself understanding in a rush who it was that rode in the wagon, his mouth twitched open spasmodically, and his suddenly whirling eyes rolled back up under the brim of his hat. He'd lurched forward to grab the wheel, as if to yank the wagon to a stop. But the crowd, finally, had thinned, and the horses leaped forward onto the clear quarter mile of road appearing ahead. Pule was dragged along in a sudden head-over-heels tumble, onto his back like a roach in the mud and moaning unrepeatable curses.

The episode had mystified Keeble. What on earth, he wondered, had befallen Pule to have brought him to such a pass, and why had the sight of the wagon so enraged him? There was much, clearly, in the world that Keeble didn't understand—much that he didn't care to understand.

Parsons strode back and forth across the green—ten steps this way, ten steps that. He paused in mid-stride coming and going to address comments to his fellows, remarking on the direction of prevailing winds, the possibility of warm valley air rushing in a dangerous updraft and pushing the blimp along to Chingford or Southgate or farther. Winds, after all, were treacherous things. Like teeth, actually. But if one knew their peculiarities, their habits, they would reveal monumental knowledge and could be read and deciphered, much like the interior winds of the human organism could be relied upon to betray gastrointestinal peculiarities. If only Birdlip, Parsons lamented, had been a different breed of scientist—what the man mightn't have learned, adrift on the skytides for close onto fifteen years! Ah, but they could hope for little, expect even less. Wish for the worst, he insisted, and one was rarely disappointed. He strode up and down, hauling out his pocketwatch at intervals, then shoving it back into his vest pocket.

A dozen gray beards wagged behind him, and no end of brass telescopes were trained on the empty heavens—empty, that is, but for a wash of stars and a crescent moon risen to the top of the sky. A cry arose, and a finger or two pointed briefly at the ivory slice of moon, but whatever it was that had prompted the cry had disappeared. Something, apparently, had for a brief moment been silhouetted there, but had sailed at once into darkness. Parsons pronounced the mystery a bat, whose nocturnal eating habits accounted for its astonishingly proficient digestive system. Still there was no sign of the blimp.

Parsons wished heartily that the populace would go home. The shouting and singing and general drunkenness were at best a distraction, and certainly had no place at a function of this magnitude. Their presence was due solely to the idiotic posing of the charlatan evangelist, whose apocalyptic tracts had stirred a million Londoners into unwholesome exodus. The man should be in a madhouse. There he stood, one foot planted squarely on the back of each of two kneeling parishioners. What he shouted into the night air was lost in the general cacophony, and Parsons couldn't fathom a bit of it. The few phrases that blew across the green were tangles of hellfire, final trumpets, avenging angels, and—remarkably—creatures from the stars. This last, under calmer circumstances, would have appealed to Parsons, but it was such utter blather here that to attend to it for ten seconds running was a tiresome business.

The hands of the old evangelist rose slowly over his head, and in them, held for the crowd to appreciate, was a cube of some sort. It was far too dark, despite burning clumps of brush scattered round the green, for Parsons to see clearly what it was—a holy object, no doubt. People pressed in around the evangelist, listening. The starry sky and the distant lights of London winking and glittering on the plain below enlivened the night with a spirit of mysticism.

The evangelist exhorted the crowd. There was an answering shout, a confirmation, it seemed. A scream followed. Hands pointed heavenward. A general shouting arose. Spyglasses were aimed toward where a tiny pinprick of light arced out of the sky, falling toward the Heath and brightening as it fell. The general tumult gave way to an awed silence, broken by the shouting evangelist. "And the name of the star," he cried, "is Wormwood!"

But the utterance of the last syllable was followed by a sudden shriek as the evangelist catapulted forward off the backs of his supplicants. The box he held over his head sailed some few feet above the green until it was snatched out of the air by a running figure in a broad-brimmed hat, who dashed among the multitude, knocking people aside like billiard balls and racing as a man possessed toward where Parsons stood before the assembled scientists.

"What in the devil is *this*?" cried Parsons, an utterance that might easily have applied to either mystery—to the glowing orb that plummeted earthward, or to the gibbering, fright-masked lunatic who capered up, yowling at the thing in his hands and lurched to a stop not ten feet in front of the collected Royal Academy. He regarded the cube as if stupefied, betrayed. Parsons could see now that it was built of glass and contained some rattling object. The madman's mouth worked, gibbering silently. With a sobbing heave, as if the strange cube were perhaps the most inconceivably disheartening thing he'd run across in recent years, he dashed it to the ground, then slumped off unpursued. For the minions of the evangelist, along with the old man himself, watched in growing wonder the thing in the sky—a glowing, spheroid ship, fallen from the stars.

Parsons blinked. He looked at the receding madman. He looked at the approaching starship. He looked at the decayed head, toothy and brown, that rolled to a stop at his feet, peering up at him through empty sockets. Its jaws clacked once, as if in a tired attempt to bite his shoes or to utter some final lamentation. Then it lay still. "What on earth…" murmured Parsons.

———

St. Ives could once again see Greater London spread out below him, but this time it wasn't spinning like a top. It lay below like jeweled pinpoints flung along the winding dark ribbon of the Thames. To the west the sky was tinged red with dying sunlight, which quickly deepened to purple then blue-black as his craft dropped toward Hampstead Heath. Behind him lay the uncharted oceans of deep space—oceans traversed by comets and moons and planets and asteroids, the vast and lonely sailing ships that plied the trade lanes among the stars, and among which, for a few brief minutes, St. Ives had maneuvered his little coracle of a star vessel.

But he was destined now for Hampstead Heath. The wonders of the heavens would wait for him, of that there could be little doubt. But the machinations of earthbound villainy would not. His friends at that moment were embroiled in God knew what sorts of dangers and intrigues. St. Ives smiled as he diminished the speed of the craft sliding in toward the fires that dotted the hillsides like beacons above the lights of Hampstead.

The great oval green was thick with people who swirled and parted and fell back. There, he could see, was a knot of people on chairs in a cordoned area—the Royal Academy, without a doubt. And before them—that had to be Parsons. St. Ives angled in toward him, looking in vain for his own companions. But there were horse carts aplenty, and one looked pretty much like another from such lofty heights. The ground sailed up at him. Upturned faces, mouths agape, swam into clarity. St. Ives fingered the levers, toyed with them, eased them this way and that, settling, finally, onto the green, dead center between two roaring fires, with no more jarring than if he'd sailed in on a feather.

He arose, flipped open the hatch, thrust out his head, and was amazed to see, sitting directly in front of the ship, its back turned toward him, the upholstered chair from the house on Wardour Street, still tethered to the ship, the luckless ghoul bound into it by three turns of hempen rope. The thing's hair stood on end—elevated by the spate of rapid travel through space—and its face was pulpy and bent, as if shoved and pummeled by atmospheric pressures. The ghoul seemed to be staring straightaway toward an open-mouthed Parsons, who held in his right hand, of all things, the severed, diminished head of Joanna Southcote.

St. Ives smiled and nodded at Parsons, who, quite apparently, was going to weep. He'd clearly been affected by the glorious issuance of the craft. St. Ives had underestimated Parsons; that much was certain. What was even more certain was that the members had underestimated St. Ives. Their countenances betrayed them.

"Gentlemen!" cried Langdon St. Ives, having prepared a small speech while cavorting through the upper reaches of the atmosphere. But his speech ended as abruptly as it began, for there arose immediately a furious shouting from the direction of the village of Hampstead, a shouting that climbed the hill like an approaching giant. And there, hovering out of the starry distances, sailed the blimp of Doctor Birdlip, swinging slowly on the breeze, making for Hampstead Heath.

As wonderful as St. Ives' arrival had been, the approach of the wonderful dirigible diminished it. The Royal Academy pushed past the star vessel in a rush, leaving St. Ives to address the back of the head of the thing in the chair. Duty, thought St. Ives, recalling the point of his journey to the Heath. His friends were somewhere nearby, as were his enemies. Birdlip approached, carrying with him the inheritance of Jack Owlesby— independence for Jack and Dorothy, Sebastian Owlesby's only respectable legacy. And there would be no end of villains afoot with an eye toward it.

St. Ives was torn. He dare not leave the craft unattended. Who could say what deviltry might be perpetrated against it? Drake, certainly, would attempt to repossess it, Pule to blow it to bits, Shiloh to claim it as a chariot of some peculiar god or another. Still, what could he do? Sit in it? Let the same crowd overrun the blimp, pluck the jewel from their grasp? He bent through the hatch, overbalancing and sliding out onto the riveted shell of the craft, grabbing at a pair of brass protrusions to haul himself free.

The shouting increased in volume. St. Ives slid head first onto the dewy grass of the heath, then scrambled onto his feet, yanking at his rumpled clothes. A loud crack

sounded behind him along with the snap and zing of something ricocheting off the hull
of the ship. Another crack rang out, and St. Ives was once again in the grass, scuttling
like a lobster around the ship, peering out beneath the lower curve of the thing at a man
in the chimney pipe hat—Billy Deener—crouched beneath the spreading limbs of a
shadowy oak. A pistol smoked in his hands. Beside him was a horse and wagon, empty,
tethered to the tree. Deener took aim with his pistol and stepped forward, as if to stride
toward St. Ives in order to flush him out. There could be no doubt that it was murder
he intended. And there in the tumult on the Heath he'd get away with it too. They'd
find St. Ives stiff as a gaffed fish on the green and half a million Londoners suspect.

St. Ives edged round the far side of the ship. Would it be wise to run, trusting the
increasing distance to confound Deener's aim? He peeked out and a shot banged off the
hull of the ship, the bullet singing past his ear. St. Ives contracted like a startled snail.
He could, perhaps, clamber into the ship, shut the hatch, and sail away, but the man
would he on him like a dog—St. Ives would be found murdered, dangling from the
hatch, exterminated in a sorry effort to flee. It was run or nothing. Zigzag—that was
the ticket. He'd dash away toward a far stand of trees. He'd keep the ship between them
so that Deener would have to fire past it.

St. Ives leaped up and ran for it. "Hey! Hey! Hey!" he shouted, for no purpose other
than to alert the night to the ensuing mayhem. He glanced over his shoulder as soon as
he was underway, unable to stand the idea of not knowing where the assassin stood.

But there was no assassin—not standing, anyway. A man leaned out of the tree
like an ape above Deener, and even as St. Ives watched, he slammed the chimney pipe
hat cockeyed with what appeared to be a cricket bat. The hat sailed off end over end as
Deener collapsed forward onto his knees. The man dropped from the tree, his own hat
tumbling to the ground, and gripping the club with both hands smashed Deener again.
Drake's hireling fell poleaxed onto his face in the weeds.

The man with the bat raised it aloft for another blow. St. Ives set out cautiously toward
the ship. This is thick, he thought. There was, after all, such a thing as common decency,
even toward a would-be murderer. The cricket bat descended, cracking against Deener's
skull, then again and again, as if the man who wielded it was wild with fury. "Here now!"
cried St. Ives, setting off at a run. The man cast the bat haphazardly into the air, turned
toward the approaching St. Ives, and bent to pick something up out of the grass. It was
the pistol. He leveled it at St. Ives, who lurched to a skipping halt, reversed direction, and
weaved away across the green, tempted to run downhill toward the assembled masses below, but fearful that some innocent Londoner might take a bullet intended for him.

St. Ives ducked in once again behind the ship, wondering wildly at the strange
course of events that had led Willis Pule to save him from the murderous Billy Deener,
for it had been Pule, gibbering mad, who had leaned out of the tree with the cricket bat
to pulverize Deener. But why? In order, apparently, to have the pleasure of killing St.
Ives himself. But Pule had given up the idea. He strode across to the tethered horse and

wagon, rummaged among Deener's effects, and hauled something out—a Keeble box. Even from a distance there could be no doubting it.

The gun forgotten, St. Ives leaped from his cover and raced toward Pule. Which of the boxes it was that Pule was even then making away with, St. Ives couldn't say. But visions of the spark-throwing rocket bursting through the silo roof and of Willis Pule smashing about in his study, beating poor Kepler's bust into pieces, leant St. Ives a sudden disregard for danger. Madness, however, had given the student of alchemy wings, for he paid the advancing St. Ives no heed at all, but raced away into the night, gabbling to himself as he ran, half sobbing, his words utterly indecipherable. Billy Deener, St. Ives discovered, was dead.

The blimp swayed in the night sky on winds which seemed to be blowing into the stars. The moon rode at anchor, heaving on a heavenly groundswell, encircled by a radiant halo of stellar light, as if the stars themselves were ship's lamps that illuminated the invisible avenue down which rode Birdlip's craft, its gondola creaking to and fro in practiced rhythms. St. Ives wondered how many people were mesmerized there on the green; how many were perched in the treetops, peered skyward through unshuttered windows, or stood craning their necks along the dark and muddy roads that led up out of smoky London. Hundreds of thousands? And all of them still—not even the peep of a slanting bat or the chirp of a cricket in the nearby wood broke the silence. There was simply the shrub-scented night, heavy, quiet, expectant, and the slow creak, creak, creak of the swaying gondola, lit now by the sliver of moon. There at the helm stood the skeletal Birdlip, the indomitable pilot, his coat a tatter of webby lace, wisping 'round the ivory swerve of his ribcage. The moon showed straight through the coat like lamplight through muslin— seemed magnified, if that were possible, as if the coat were a wonderful bit of glass spun of silk and silver that drew through it the accumulated light of the heavens.

St. Ives couldn't move. What did it mean, this humming dirigible that had, after years of circuitous wanderings in the atmosphere, decided to wend its way homeward at last? What did it signify? Birdlip knew. He'd pursued something—a demon, a will o' the wisp, the reflection of a phantom moon that beckoned on the night wind and receded toward unimagined horizons. Had Birdlip caught it? Had it eluded him? And what, in the name of all that was holy, would poor Parsons make of it? He'd shortly be faced with yet another fleshless visage. What, wondered St. Ives, did it all mean?

The blimp hovered fifty feet above the heath, seeming actually to rise now, following the natural curve of the hill, intent upon landing not just anywhere, but at some predetermined spot, an utterly necessary spot, as if it were indeed piloted yet by the straddle-legged doctor. His French cocked hat was settled low over his forehead, shading his empty eye sockets, the jellied orbs within having long since been burned by a remorseless sun and picked away by seabirds. What strange eyesight did Birdlip retain? How clearly did he see? —◦

TWENTY

Birdlip

BILL KRAKEN, SITTING astride the limb of an oak some five feet above the heads of the crowd below, wondered much the same thing. In none of Kraken's investigations into science was there anything as grand, as majestic, as the homeward bound Birdlip and his astonishing craft. Something, Kraken was certain, was pending. He could feel it in the air—a static charge that shivered through the masses who stood mute with anticipation.

The descending blimp swung low overhead. People leaned out of the uppermost branches of trees, endeavoring to touch it. It seemed to Kraken as if the sky was nothing but blimp. He glanced back over his shoulder, looking proudly at Langdon St. Ives who stood before his own incredible ship. The night, indeed, was full of marvels. And he, Bill Kraken, squid merchant, pea pod man, had a hand in them. The man beside him in the branches, an unshaven pinch-faced man in a stocking cap, hadn't. Kraken smiled at him good-naturedly. It wasn't his fault, after all, that he didn't hobnob with geniuses. The man gave him a dark look, disliking the familiarity. Someone above trod on the top of Kraken's head in an effort to boost himself even higher. Below him on the green, stumbling from shadow to shadow as if working his way surreptitiously toward where the blimp seemed destined to land, lurched a man who appeared to be sick or drunk. Kraken squinted at him, disbelieving. It was Willis Pule.

Kraken dangled one leg down along the trunk, feeling for the crotch of two great limbs that forked up some six feet from the ground. Things, apparently, were hotting up. Pule disappeared into the shadows, then reappeared again beyond a heaped bonfire, the dancing orange light of which seemed to intensify the darkness behind it.

Not twenty paces behind Pule, possessed by a determination that belied his age, Shiloh the New Messiah limped along, accompanied by a straggling covey of converts strung along like quail, half intent on catching up to the disappeared Pule, half intent on Birdlip's craft. The blimp hung now over the green, suspended by the magic, perhaps, of its Keeble engine. The evangelist was lit for a moment by the same firelight which had illuminated Pule and which now betrayed on the old man a face twisted slantwise in a rictus of loathing, the messiah pursuing the worm, the devil who had made away with the head of his mother, and who now carried one of the fabulous boxes, quite conceivably the same box stolen hours ago by the imposter in the wagon.

And there, sliding along down the edge of the crowd, came Theophilus Godall, carrying with *him,* Kraken was horrified to see, a round, metallic object that could be nothing other than the Marseilles Pinkle, glinting in the firelight. He was clearly unseen either by Pule or the old man. But Bill Kraken saw him, and so did St. Ives. The tune had begun to he called, and it was time for Kraken to dance to it. He slid to the ground and set out, running straight on into Kelso Drake, an inch and a half of cigar protruding from Drake's mouth like a blackened tongue.

If he'd had time to think, Kraken would have sailed back into his tree, scaled the slippery trunk like an ape. But he had no such time. He launched himself at the millionaire. "Here's for Ashbless!" he cried, an obtuse reference to the bullet Billy Deener had drilled into his treasured volume. And he struck Drake squarely on the chin, snatching the Keeble box from his hands as Drake fell sputtering, stupefied with surprise, his hat sailing off to reveal a bandaged head.

Kraken turned and ran, holding the box before him as if it were a pitcher of water he daren't spill. Drake pounded along behind, filling the suddenly tumultuous night with curses, drowned out when a hundred thousand voices arose in a sudden monumental cheer. The blimp, its time come round at last, shot forward and settled in onto the green, not twenty-five feet from St. Ives' space vehicle. The bulk of the crowd surged up the hill behind it. The ghoul in the stuffed chair sat placid as a man at tea in front of it. The Royal Academy, directed by the indomitable Parsons, clustered around it, eager to have a look at the skeletal sailor, home at last from the sea.

Kraken angled away into the rushing crowd. There was the Captain, stumping along, and William Keeble at the heels of his stalwart wife, all of them charging toward the blimp, toward the fourth and final box that rode within. "Cap'n!" shouted Kraken, capering along behind them, carried in a rush by the swarming masses, A sea of heads cut off his view. Someone trod on his toe. He stumbled. A dozen people smashed past him. He was pushed from his knees onto his face, nearly trampled, lying atop the Keeble box.

"Filthy piece of dirt!" hissed a voice in his ear, and as he hunched forward in an effort to stand, he was borne down again by the weight of Kelso Drake, his cigar gone, his jaws working as if he were full of speeches too vile to utter.

Kraken plowed his elbow into Drake's nose. A hand closed over his face, tugging his head back. He clamped his scattered teeth onto a finger and chewed away until the teeth closed against bone. A shriek erupted in his ear, and the hand was jerked away, nearly tearing the precious tooth away with it.

Kraken stumbled forward, half rose, and was elbowed sideways into a host of people, slowing now in the press. He was on his feet, though. Indeed, it would be difficult to fall, closed in as he was by the throng. Over his shoulder he could see Kelso Drake, cursing at the people around him—people who were in no mood to be cursed. A fist shot out and clipped Drake in the ear. He lurched aside. Kraken grinned. Drake was obviously possessed by the thought that millionaires ought not to be treated so. He railed at the man who he supposed had hit him—the wrong man, as it turned out, a man who had the general shape of a hogshead and the facial consistency of a bag of stones.

"Here now!" shouted the man, not wasting words, and he slammed Drake on the nose to the general encouragement of the crowd. Kraken pushed toward the erupting mêlée, shouting happily to see the color of Drake's blood. The industrialist flailed like a windmill, utterly ineffectively, so far gone was he in his anger and loathing.

Kraken hoped to get in a blow or two of his own, but his hopes were dashed when, with sudden inspiration, he shouted: "That's the man who murdered the child!" at the top of his lungs, pointing past the circle of Drake's tormenters into the millionaire's face. A cry of disgust and abandonment arose, and before Kraken could have a go at him, Drake disappeared beneath a monsoon of whirling fists. "Get him!" cried Kraken, but the suggestion, he quickly saw, was unnecessary. He pushed along toward the blimp, hugging his box.

Ahead of him, two dozen or so men scrambled to string ropes around the craft, cordoning it off against the possible rush of the masses. But the London populace, apparently, harbored suspicions, fears, and perhaps reverence, for they hovered round the perimeter of an oblong patch of ground on which sat the blimp, the corpse in the chair, and the starship. Parsons directed the roping efforts, arguing all the while with both the Captain and St. Ives. Captain Powers grew more heated by the moment, shouting that Parsons had no "jurisdiction." Parsons attempted to ignore him, but cast meaningful glances at St. Ives, as if to encourage the scientist to calm his bellowing friend.

St. Ives, however, was distracted by a scuffling and shouting off to his right, beyond the bonfire, which blazed now with increased ferocity, fed by a hail of limbs and forest debris tossed by the enthusiastic mob. St. Ives stepped along toward the scuffle when he saw amid it the head and shoulders of Theophilus Godall. Bill Kraken sprang into view just then, hurrying toward St. Ives, carrying his Keeble box like a trophy.

Willis Pule writhed and grunted, heaving in a tangle of grasping fanatics that included Shiloh the New Messiah. Godall circled round, intent on the box that Pule clutched. Jack Owlesby circled gamely beside him, looking for an opportunity. Pule shrieked; the box jumped out of his hands and was snatched by a beefy young man in a soiled robe. Shiloh hauled the box away from the man and lurched toward clear ground, jabbering excitedly, having no earthly idea which of the many strange boxes he possessed, but certain that the lot of them were somehow holy and somehow rightfully his.

Jack Owlesby strode along after him. The several parishioners who made as if to stop Jack found themselves peering at the business end of Godall's pistol. Jack reached past the old man and snatched the box, leaping away toward the blimp. Shiloh turned, an unuttered shriek stretching his mouth. Godall, smiling calmly, thrust the Pinkle into the old man's outstretched hands.

"What!" cried the evangelist, setting in to pitch the thing away. He saw it clearly for the first time even as he threw it. His eyes, yellow in the light of the fire, seemed to expand like balloons. He checked his throw, warbling out a little deflating cry. But it was too late. The Pinkle threw out a spoonful of sparks that whirled around the thrusting rubber head and flew in a wheeling arc into a stand of shadowy bracken and broom that muffled the strange noises and lights emitted by the orb.

The evangelist stiffened, his mouth going suddenly slack. Jack was beyond his reach. The bird he'd had momentarily in hand had flown. But here was another in the bush. He turned, ignoring Godall, who made no move to stop him. In a second he was gone, creeping through the dark shrubs on his hands and knees, as unheeding of the apocalyptic gyrations on the Heath roundabout him as if he'd been one of Narbondo's ghouls.

The evening, in the space of five minutes, had begun to look very satisfactory to St. Ives. Here was Jack Owlesby, toting a recovered Keeble box. Here was Bill Kraken, toting another. There was Theophilus Godall with yet another. St. Ives smiled at Jack and reached out to shake the lad's hand. Evil, it was clear, was fairly literally being pummeled. Jack grinned, the flames roared, the Captain shouted, and Bill Kraken, with in alarming suddenness, pitched forward toward the edge of the fire.

Behind him, his face bleeding, his right eye shut, his left arm dangling uselessly, crouched a lunatic Kelso Drake. Kraken shouted and threw out his hands. The Keeble box set sail as if shot from a catapult. St. Ives leaped for it, knocking it askew in its flight, saving it from the fire but sending it cartwheeling toward where the enigmatic ghoul reclined in his chair. The box struck him on the chin, snapped his head down onto his chest, and landed in his lap.

With an oath, Drake limped forward, grimacing murderously. But there was Godall, smiling in the circle of firelight, his pistol drawn and mimed at Drake's chest. The millionaire lurched to a stop, raising his bands.

A cry arose from the crowd. St. Ives turned toward the blimp, expecting a revelation. But the blimp sat silent and dark on the Heath, surrounded by scientists scribbling in notepads, casting looks at the insistent Captain who held the sputtering Parsons by the collar.

Another cry. Hands pointed. It was the corpse in the chair, stirring. His back straightened; his fists clenched; air gasped through his closed teeth. The Captain released Parsons, who goggled at the corpse as it stood upright, dragging the ropes loose from where they were entangled among the springs of the chair. It held the box aloft, almost with reverence.

"Lord have mercy," muttered Kraken. Jack stood mute. The ghoul shuffled forward, bearing the Keeble box.

"Homunculus!" whispered St. Ives. Godall nodded beside him, his pistol disappeared. In his right hand now was St. Ives' aerator, in his left was a handful of Pule's jacket, the murderous student of alchemy slouching beside him like a man stuffed with rags, his mouth agape. Thousands of pairs of eyes watched the dumb show on the heath.

The ghoul hunched toward Parsons, who stepped back, regretting suddenly that he'd gotten rid of the severed head he'd been given earlier. Would this ghoul demand it? Or would it hand Parsons yet another inexplicable item? What, for God's sake, was in the damned box?

But the ghoul strode past him unhindered, toward the gondola where stood the strident Birdlip. Only Captain Powers had the temerity to follow him. Parsons said nothing. The Captain fell in behind, hearing as he did the incessant demanding voice that jabbered from the Keeble box in the ghoul's hand.

Dr. Birdlip, suddenly, seemed to shake himself. Those on the edge of the crowd gasped. Was it the wind? A trick of moonlight? Birdlip released his hold on the wheel—a grip he'd maintained without pause for a decade. Finger bones picked at the rotted cords that lashed him to the gondola. The cords fell. Birdlip turned, jerking forward toward the little swinging stile door fallen back on its hinge. Firelight danced and leaped. Parsons gaped. St. Ives barely breathed. Godall stood bemused. The Captain nodded politely to the skeleton of Doctor Birdlip, then bent suddenly and picked something up from the floor of the gondola. St. Ives knew what it was. Birdlip seemed to heed nothing—nothing but the proferred box, which the ghoul relinquished, seeming to deflate almost and stagger just a bit, backwards, stepping toward the stuffed chair as if suddenly fatigued to the point of collapse. Parsons began to step along after him, wondering at the nature of the animate corpse that gaped at him, opening and shutting its mouth like a conger eel.

"Speak, man!" cried the biologist.

The corpse dropped dead into the chair.

Birdlip jerked down onto the green in quick little lurching, stiff-jointed steps, holding the Keeble box, his skull canted sideways as if in perplexity. The dead silence was broken by the utterance of an immense sob, as Willis Pule, taking the startled Godall by surprise, twisted out of his coat in a rush. Pule sailed down on Birdlip, ducking under a murderous blow aimed at him by the stalwart Captain. But Pule, apparently, hadn't theft in mind as a motive. All such practical pursuits had been abandoned; it was mayhem and ruin he coveted, gibbering destruction, the mindless, drooling desire to tear the weary world to bits.

In an instant he snatched the box from Birdlip, who tottered there on the green, suddenly enervated. Pule raised the box overhead and smashed it to the green. The

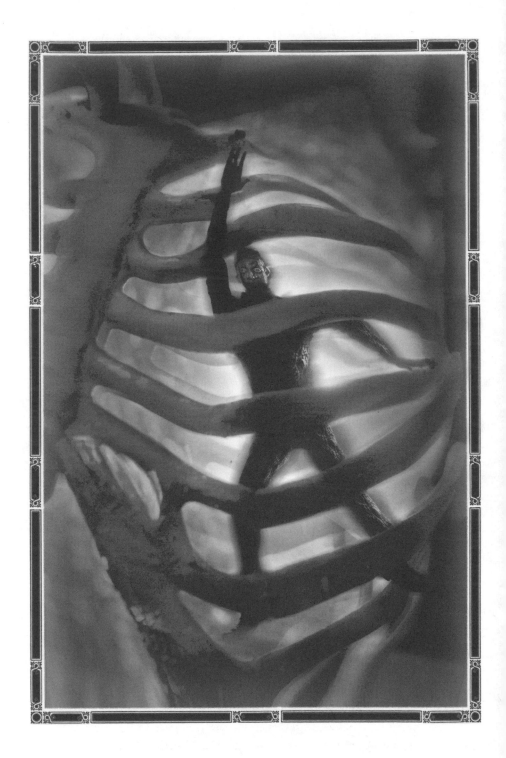

clever joinery of the Keeble box flew asunder as the thing cracked against a stone. The lid wheeled away into the astonished crowd. Ten thousand mouths gaped in wide wonder to see a tiny man tumble forth—the fabled homunculus—and leap to his feet on the green free of his prison at long last. Even though he wore a hat he couldn't have been eight inches tall.

What, wondered the treetop crowds and the staring masses on the heath, what thing was this that ran dead away toward the skeletal Birdlip, past the goggling Parsons, through spring grasses that waved round his ears, step by tiny step? It clearly had a destination in mind. What, conceivably, could it desire?

Willis Pule clutched at his head, his wild loathing played out. He was reduced to a thing as empty as the airy gondola sitting like the bleached bones of a dinosaur on the green behind the teetering Birdlip. Theophilus Godall watched Pule creep away into shadow. He'd allow the spent thing to wander away unpursued, to take up a life, perhaps, of begging or of geeking in some low sideshow. A great wind blew up out of the south, buffeting the dark dirigible, which swayed on its makeshift moorings, threatening to tumble over onto its side like a wounded beast. The crowd gasped and surged away, fearful of being crushed. The homunculus confronted Doctor Birdlip, spoke to him, pointed, it seemed, toward the heavens. It doffed its clever little hat and gestured animatedly with it. Then, with a startling alacrity, it leaped onto the swaying skeleton, grappling its way into the doctor's ribcage, peering out as if through the bars of Newgate Prison. Birdlip took a tentative step forward, animate once again, and, to the degree that a skull can reflect emotion, he seemed smitten with sudden elation, perhaps a flowering of the sense of wanderlust that had motivated his journey through the heavens.

A cheer arose from those close enough to perceive this sudden illumination. Jack Owlesby, perhaps, cheered most loudly of all, but his cheer was cut short when, with a sudden whump, he was struck in the small of the back, and the box that he carried flew from his hands. Kelso Drake, having gone down the same twisted road as Willis Pule, shrieked past Godall into the firelight and endeavored to dance on the box, to smash it up. He was stopped cold, however, by the simultaneous effort of Godall and St. Ives, and by the curious behavior of the fallen box.

It shuddered there in front of the teetering Birdlip, in front of the astonished Parsons, clearly illuminated in the fireglow. Dr. Birdlip jerked round and stood still. Kelso Drake stepped a pace back toward the fire. The top of the box sprang away with a suddenness that brought a cry from any of a number of treetops. And very slowly and majestically there arose from the depths of the box the bird-eating cayman, snatching up one then another and another and another of the little fowl before sinking again into his tomb.

"Hooray!" shouted a hundred voices, a thousand. The cheer was taken up by the multitude, who could have no earthly idea what it was they cheered. And with the salutory cries fueling his departure, Dr. Randal Birdlip, himself piloted now by the little man within him, clacked jerkily over the grass, Parsons at his heels. He stopped at the side of the starship, turned and gazed one last long moment at the jeweled lights of London, bent over and unknotted the rope from round one of the little feet of the starship and clambered woodenly into the open hatch. The hatch slammed shut. Emerald lights burned suddenly within the ship. The ground seemed to shudder momentarily, and in the wink of an eye the ship was nothing but a speck of fire in the vast heavens, the intrepid Dr. Birdlip piloting the craft of the homunculus among the countless stars that hung suspended above the streetcorners of space like gaslamps. —⌀

Epilogue

S T. IVES DIDN'T rue the loss of the ship for a moment. He'd had his voyage. And the future, he was certain, held the promise of more. Here was Dorothy Keeble, recovered, clutching Jack's arm, the two of them smiling at the Captain, who held before them an open Keeble box in which lay a tremendous emerald, big as a fist and seeming to burn green and immense in the firelight.

A moaning filled the night. Branches tossed on the trees. The tall grasses blew in undulating waves. The blimp canted sideways, mooring lines snapped, and people scurried like bugs, running to get out of the way. Slowly and majestically the blimp toppled over, tearing itself to bits, escaping gases whooshing through rents in the fabric of the thing. The ribby gondola, hauled onto its side, broke apart like a wooden ship beaten against rocks by high seas. And first one, then twenty, then a hundred onlookers rushed in to salvage a bit of it as a souvenir. Wood snapped. Fabric ripped. Great sheets of deflated blimp were stripped loose, clutched at by uncounted hands and rent to fragments. Within moments the once rotund blimp was nothing but a flattened bit of wreckage that had disappeared beneath an antlike swarm of Londoners. An hour later, when the crowds, finally, abandoned their pursuit of relics and surged wearily homeward at last, not a fragment, not a scrap of Birdlip's craft remained on the heath.

St. Ives and his companions kicked through the grass, gazing at the place where the blimp had lain. Bill Kraken said that the loss of it was shameful. William Keeble wondered at the fate of its engine, carried happily away in pieces by drunken green-grocers and costermongers and beggars who hadn't the foggiest notion of the magic it had once contained. Jack and Dorothy gazed at each other with an intensity of expression that seemed far removed from any wondering over disappeared blimps, an expression very like the one shared by Captain Powers and Nell Owlesby, who stood hand in hand beside Jack and Dorothy.

Ten paces away sat Parsons, astride the arm of the stuffed chair, the corpse slumped beside him, restful now and refusing to respond to Parson's chatter. "Sheep," the biologist insisted, "aren't like you and me. They produce vast quantities of methane gas. Very inflammatory, I assure you…"

St. Ives strode across and laid a hand on the poor man's shoulder. Parsons grinned at him. "Telling this fellow about the gaseous mysteries of grass feeders."

"Fine," said St. Ives. "But he seems to have fallen asleep."

"His eyes, though…" began Parsons, glancing at the aerator box that St. Ives held in the crook of his arm. He shuddered, as if gripped by a sudden chill. "You don't mean to open that here, do you?"

St. Ives shook his head. "Not at all," he said. "Wouldn't think of it."

Parsons seemed relieved. "Tell me," he said slowly, looking askance at the head of Joanna Southcote, which lay now up to its nonexistent ears in weeds beside the stuffed chair, "does the night seem uncommonly full of dead men and severed heads to you?"

St. Ives nodded, searching for words with which to respond to Parson's very earnest question. His search, though, came to an abrupt end with the sudden issuance of Shiloh the New Messiah, his face haggard, his cloak stained and mired, the ghastly Marseilles Pinkle tooting in his grip, its rubber head shooting in and out, throwing sparks like a pinwheel and smelling of burnt rubber and unidentifiable decay. With a mad cry the old man fell forward onto his face and lay still, his torn and soiled robes splayed out around him. Dead, apparently, he hopped once or twice as the Pinkle, trapped beneath him, continued to sputter and whir before rolling free.

St. Ives shook his head. Parsons arose and very slowly stepped across to where the Pinkle spun itself out on the green, the rubber head tooting out a final, blubbery whistle. Parsons shook his head ponderously and wandered away into the dark, weaving toward Hampstead like a rudderless boat.

St. Ives watched him in silence, wondering whether his own reputation as a scientist had in any way been cemented by the night's odd events, and determining finally that he didn't really care a rap one way or the other. The evening had taken its toll, certainly, on the good as well as the wicked. His companions trudged along toward the wagon, on the seat of which sat a placid Hasbro. St. Ives was suddenly dead tired. The morrow would see him at Harrogate. There was work ahead; that was sure. "Well," he said to Godall, "so ends the earnest endeavors of the Trismegistus Club. And with a modicum of success, too."

"For the moment," said Godall enigmatically. "We haven't, possibly, seen the last of our millionaire. But I rather believe him to be a spent force. I'll call upon him myself in a day or two."

"What ever became of Willis Pule, do you think?" asked St. Ives. "He was utterly mad there at the last."

Godall nodded. "Madness, I'm certain, is the wages of villainy. He met an old friend, in fact."

"What's that?" asked St. Ives, surprised.

"The hunchback."

"Narbondo!"

Godall nodded. "In a dog cart full of carp. Pule lay face down among them, comatose."

"Poor devil," said St. Ives. "I don't suppose Narbondo had come to his rescue."

"Not very bloody likely," said Godall darkly, and the two men hoisted themselves onto the wagon, sitting with their feet dangling over the back so that they faced the sweep of hill on which, two hours earlier, had sat the long-awaited blimp.

Ahead of them, some distance away, trudged half of London, not a man or woman among them with the least understanding of the mysteries that had supplied the evening's entertainment. What understanding have any of us, wondered St. Ives. Not a nickel's worth, not really. Not even Godall, for all the man's intellectual prowess. Intellect wouldn't answer here, wouldn't explain why the cold and measured tread of science had strayed from chartered paths and wandered unsuspecting into the curious moonlight of Hampstead Heath. Poor Parsons. What did he make of the blimp now? Would he awaken at midday having somehow clipped the evening apart and reassembled it into a more tolerable pattern, like a man who whistles his way through a dark and lonely night, then abandons his fears in the light of a noonday sun?

St. Ives gazed with sleepy wonder at empty, receding green as the wagon bumped around a muddy swerve of road into Hampstead, the village dark now and silent. He tried to summon a picture of the blimp riding at anchor, of Doctor Birdlip visible beyond the slats of the wooden gondola, legs wide set to counter the roll of an airy swell. But the Heath lay empty above, the blimp fragmented, disappeared. And it seemed as if the strange craft had never been more than a ghostly will o' the wisp, a bit of sleepy enchantment woven out of nothing, that whirled and faded now across the back of his closed eyes until he seemed to be sailing with it above the clouded landscape of a dream. —

Two Views of a Cave Painting

'M OPPOSED TO giving advice and making weighty statements on general principle; we're wrong as often as not, and look like fools. But it's safe to say this: ruination, utter ruination, might be as close to us now as is the proverbial snake, and but for the grace of the Deity and the cleverness of friends, we might at any moment find that by a slip of memory we've brought about the collapse of worlds.

I wouldn't have thought it so. I've believed that there was room in our lives for casual error, that we could shrug and grin and suffer mild regret and the world would wag along for better or worse. Well, no more; recent events have proven me wrong. The slightest slip of the hand, the forgetting of the most trivial business, the uttering of an unremarkable bit of foolishness might plunge us, as Mr. Poe would have it, into the maelstrom. It fell out like this:

We'd been out on the Salisbury—Plain Professor Langdon St. Ives; his man Hasbro; and myself, Jack Owlesby—digging for relics. I haven't got much taste for relics, but the company was good, and there is an inn that goes by the name of The Quarter Pygmy in Andover where I've eaten Cornish pasty that was alone worth the trip down from London.

St. Ives discovered, quite by accident one hot, desolate, fly-ridden afternoon, a cave beneath an isolated hillside, covered in shrub and lost to the world thousands of years ago. If you've been to Salisbury and ridden across the plain as a tourist in a coach-and-four, then you know how such a thing could be; there's nothing there, for the most part, to attract anyone but an archeologist, and most of them are chasing down Druids. St. Ives was after fossils.

And he found them too; by the bushel-basketful. They littered the cave floor, dusty and dry, the femurs of megatheria, the tusks of wooly mammoths, the jawbones of heaven-knows-what sorts of sauria. St. Ives rather suspected they'd be there. He intended, he said, to make use of them.

The cave had been occupied in a distant age. Neanderthal man had lived there, or at least had come and gone. There was a cave painting, is what I'm trying to say, on the wall.

I know nothing of the art of painting on cave walls, but I can tell you that this one was very nice indeed. It was the painting of a man, bearded and hairy-headed like an unkempt lion and barely decent with a loose covering of pelts. His countenance was bent into a thoughtful frown—a pensive cave man, if such a thing were possible. The painting was a self-portrait, and, said St. Ives, in quality it rivaled the famous bison painting from the cave of Altamira, Spain, or the reindeer drawings from the cavern of Aurignac. The artist had caught his own soul in berry-tinted oil, as well as his beetling brow and shaggy head.

This strikes you, I'm certain, as a weighty discovery. But you'd look in vain in the scientific journals for word of it. Our enterprises there fell out rather ill, as you might have judged from the tone of the first page of this account, and it's only recently that I've been able to take up the pen and reveal the grim truth of it. In the months since our return from that cave on the Salisbury Plain I've invented reasons, any number of them, to cast a shadow over our enterprise. St. Ives and Hasbro, the two men who might have given me away, are gentlemen through and through, and have kept quiet on the score. But you might have read in the *Times* a week past news of an explosion—an "upheaval of the earth," I believe they called it, in their uncomprehending, euphemistic way—which collapsed a section of countryside a bit north and west of Andover on the Salisbury Plain. They heard the explosion, no doubt, at the Pygmy. In fact, I know they did; I was there, and I heard it myself.

"An act of God!" cried the Royal Academy, and so unwittingly they paid the highest compliment, albeit it a trifling exaggeration, that they've paid yet to my mentor and friend, Langdon St. Ives. The business had his mark on it, to be sure, although I'll insist that I myself had no hand in it. With the collapse of the bit of countryside. however, was buried forever the only known evidence of my abominable folly and buried along with it were months of worry and guilt, which St. Ives no doubt grew weary and sorrowful for at long last.

I wish to heaven such were the end of it, but I can't, of course, be entirely sure. I'm taking it on faith here. In matters involving the curiosities of traveling in time, and the complexities of meddling with the very structure of the universe itself, one must expect the odd surprise: the Neanderthal man in a hair piece, the Azilian mummy with a Van Dyke beard. One never knows, does one? It fell out like this:

When the volcano business was over with and St. Ives's great nemesis, Dr. Ignacio Narbondo, had been swallowed by a frozen lake in Scandinavia, the professor had, for the first time in decades, the leisure time to pursue a study he'd gotten on to some ten years earlier. Time travel isn't news anymore. Mr. H. G. Wells has put it to good use in a book which the casual reader would doubtless regard as a fiction. And perhaps it was. I, certainly, haven't seen the wonderful machine, although I have met the so-called Time Traveler, or someone masquerading as the man, broken and teary-eyed at Lady Beech-Smythe's summer house in Tadcaster. He was weeping into his ale glass—a man who had seen more than was good for him.

I have too, which is what I'm writing about here. Though to be more accurate, it wasn't so much what I *saw* that has stayed my pen these past months as what I *did*. This, then, is a confessional as much as anything else, and if it's wrath such a thing provokes, I'm your man to suffer it.

St. Ives, in a word, had cast upon a way to travel through time, quite independent of the methods of Wells's hero. The professor had been studying iridium traces in fossil bone, and had developed theories about the decline of the prehistoric monsters. But it wasn't entirely the scientific data that put him in the way of a method to leap through time, it was something *other* than that. I won't say *more* than that, for there is no room here to drag in questions of a spiritual or mythologic nature.

Let it suffice that there is something *in* a fossil—in the stony little trilobite which, five hundred million years ago, crept along Devonian seabottoms; or, say the femur of a great toothed whale that shared Eocene seas with fish lizards and plesiosaurs. St. Ives possessed, I remember, the complete skeletal remains of a pterodactyl, which reposed in mid-flight twelve feet above the floor of his vast library in Harrogate, as if the books and busts and scattered furniture of the room below were the inhabitants of a Cretaceous jungle clearing, and the thunder of the train rattling past toward Stoke Newington were the ebb and flow of prehistoric tides on a trackless beach.

There is enchantment in a fossil, is what I mean to say. St. Ives saw that straight-away. It might well be enchantment that scientists of the graph-and-caliper variety would wave into nonexistence if they had a chance at it. But Haitian islanders, in their ignorance of modern science, can dissolve a man's nose by splashing chicken blood into the face of a doll. I've seen it done. Hand the chicken blood and the doll—made of sticks and rags—to the president of the Royal Academy, and ask *him* to have a go at it. Your man's nose will be safe as a baby.

There are forces at work, you see, that haven't yet been quantified. They hover roundabout us in the air, like wraiths, and you and I are blind to them. But a man like St. Ives—that man carries with him a pair of spectacles, which, in a fit of sudden inspiration, he claps over his eyes. He frowns and squints. And there, winging it across the misty, cloud-drift sky, is—what? In this case it was a device which would enable him to travel through time. I don't mean to say that the device itself could be seen winging it through the clouds. I was speaking figuratively there. I'm afraid, now that I'm pressed, that my discussion of his device must remain in that vague and nebulous level, for I'm no scientist, and I hadn't a foggy notion on that morning when I stepped into the device and clutched the copper grips, whither the day's adventure might take me. It was enough, entirely enough, that I had St. Ives's word on the matter.

It wasn't electricity, despite the copper, nor was it explosives that hurtled us backward through time. There was a shudder and a gust of faint wind that smelled like the first fall of rain on paving stones. The little collection of fossils that were heaped on a copper plate on the floor between us shook and seemed for the moment to levitate. I had the frightening sensation of falling a great distance, of tumbling head over heels through a black void. At the same time it seemed as if I were watching myself fall, as if somehow I were having one of those out-of-body experiences that the spiritualists rely upon. In short, I was both falling and hovering above my falling self at one and the same time. Then, after an immeasurable passage through the darkness, an orange and murky light began to dawn, and without so much as a sigh, the fossils settled and the falling rush abated. I was whole once more, and together we stepped out into the interior of that cavern on Salisbury Plain.

I'd seen the cavern before, of course, any number of times in a distant age, and so I was understandably surprised that the painting of the cave man was missing. On the wall were sketches of Paleolithic animals, freshly drawn, the oily paint still soft. I remembered them as a sort of background for the more intricately drawn human in the foreground. St. Ives immediately pointed out what I should have understood—that the artist had only begun his work, and that he would doubtless finish it in the days that followed.

If we had arrived an hour earlier or later, we might well have caught him at it. St. Ives was relieved that such a thing hadn't happened. The cave artist mustn't see us, said the Professor. And so adamant was he on the issue that he hinted, to my immense surprise, that if he *had* been there, laboring over the tail of an elephant, turning around in wonder to see us appear out of the mists of time, we mightn't have any choice but to kill the man then and there—and not with the pistol in St. Ives's bag, but we must crush his head with a stone and, God help us, finish his cave painting ourselves. St. Ives produced a sketch of it, accurate to the last hair of the man's unkempt beard.

Traveling in time, it was to turn out, was a vastly more complicated business than I could have guessed. The curious talk of beaning the cave man with a stone was only the beginning of it. St. Ives had unearthed his fossils in that very grotto, and, in the years that followed, he had stumbled across two immeasurably sensible ideas: first, that the use of fossil forces as a means of time travel would impel one not just *anywhere* in prehistory, but to that time in prehistory from whence came the fossil. Second, one had to make very sure, when he disappeared from one age and appeared abruptly in another, that he didn't, say, spring into reexistence in the middle of a tree or a hillside or, heaven help him, in the space occupied by some poor cave painter bent over his work. This last we had had to take our chances on.

St. Ives determined that by launching from the interior of the cave itself, utilizing fossils discovered at that precise spot—perhaps the gnawed bones of a Cro-Magnon feast—we would be guaranteed a landing, so to speak, in the very same cave thirty-five thousand years past, and not in an adjacent tree-thick forest. The reasoning was sound. It would have been much more convenient, of course, to have launched from the laboratory in Harrogate, and so have dispensed with the arduous task of secretly transporting the device and the fossils nearly three hundred kilometers across central

England. But that wouldn't have done at all. St. Ives assures me that a very grand and destructive explosion might have been the result, and the three of us reduced to atoms.

So there we were, three men from 1902, carrying Gladstone bags, scrutinizing a cave painting on which a real live Neanderthal man had been daubing paint a half hour earlier, utterly unaware that hurtling toward him through the depths of time was a machine full of spectacled men from the future. It would almost have been worth it to see his face when we winked into existence behind him. Well, not entirely worth it, I suppose; not if we'd had to beat him with a stone.

The morning was fast declining, and although we had, as I said, Ruhmkorff lamps, and had brought along food in our bags, and so could have passed a comfortable enough night there on the plain, St. Ives was in a hurry to finish his research and be off. The lamps were an emergency precaution, he said. If all went according to plan, we'd while away the afternoon and launch at dusk. We mustn't be seen, he reminded us again. We had accomplished a third of our mission by having arrived at all—the half-completed painting was proof enough that we'd effectively disposed of several hundred centuries. We would accomplish another third when we found ourselves safe at home at last, or at least once again in our own century, where we could spend the night on the plain if we chose to. The final third was simple enough, it seemed to me: we'd observe, is what we'd do. A "field study" St. Ives called it, although it seemed to *him* to be the most ticklish business of the lot. We would lounge about, keeping ourselves hidden behind a tumble of rock a hundred meters above the cave, and every now and again we'd pop up and snap a photograph of a wandering bison or cave bear, and haul the evidence back to London, where the Royal Academy would be toppled onto their collective ear.

I hefted my bag and slung a tripod over my shoulder and made as if to set out. St. Ives nearly throttled himself stopping me. "Your footprints" he said, pointing to the soft silt of the cave floor. And there, sure enough, were the prints of a pair of boots bought in Bond Street, London, either three weeks or thirty-five centuries earlier, I couldn't have said for certain at the time. St. Ives yanked a feather duster out of his bag and went to work on the prints. He was a man possessed. There mustn't be a trace, he said, of our coming and going. It took us the better part of an hour, sneaking and skulking and breaking our backs with the hurry of it, to transport the machine, which, thank heaven, was remarkably light and could be partially dismantled, up to our aerie in the rocks. Then we were at it for another hour in the gloom of evening, dusting away tracks, replacing pebbles kicked aside in haste, grafting the snapped limb of a scrub plant back onto itself—taking frightful care, in other words, that no sentient being could remark our passing, and all the time Hasbro keeping watch above, whistling us into hiding at the approach of so much as a rodent.

We daren't, said St. Ives, meddle with anything. The slightest alteration in the natural state of the landscape might have ungovernable consequences in ages to come.

The universe, it seems, is but a tenuous, delicate composition, rather like the reflected jumble of tinted jewels in a kaleidoscope. If one holds still while gazing into the end of the thing, the jewels sit there perfectly at ease, as if the reflected pattern isn't a clever ruse after all, but is a church window fixed into a wall of cut stone. But the slightest jiggling—the blink of an eye or the tremor of a sudden chill—casts the jewels into disarray, and no earthly amount of twisting and shaking and wishing will fetch them back again in the lost order. And so goes the universe.

What if a bug, said St. Ives, were crushed inadvertently underfoot, and that bug weren't as a result, eaten, say, by the toad which, historically, would have eaten that bug had the bug not been crushed by a bootheel that had no business being there in the first place. That toad might die—mightn't he?—for lack of a bug to eat, or from having eaten another bug out of desperation that he hadn't ought to have eaten. And the wild dog that would have eaten the toad, he'd go hungry, you see, and attempt the conquest of a toad which the universe had earmarked for an utterly different dog, who, everything being built upon everything else, like the crystals, as I said, in a kaleidoscope, would have to turn out and eat a rabbit. And that rabbit, which otherwise would have lived into a satisfying old age and bore six dozen rabbits very much like it, would be dead—wouldn't it?—and no end of prehistoric beasts would be denied the pleasure of dining on those six dozen rabbits.

You see how it goes. When St. Ives laid it out for me I was transfixed. I could tell straightaway that our puny comings and goings through the veil of time were as nothing in the eyes of the universe, compared to the brief few hours we intended to spend among the stones of the hillside. A bug and a toad and six dozen rabbits and pretty soon the entire local crowd is in an uproar. The universe they thought they could depend on has gone to smash. A megatherium looks for roots to nibble one morning and the roots are gone, because a half score wild dogs have moved to the coast where the rabbit population is more dependable, and the rabbits, finding travel a safer thing than it was last week, reproduce tenfold and make up, as they say, for lost time. Their offspring eat the roots that the megatherium thought he could count on and so he eats someone else's roots and so on and so on, magnified over countless centuries.

The crowning result is that the people of London aren't the people of London anymore at all. The Romans never arrived, for reasons that can be traced, if one had the right instruments, to the crushed bug. The Greeks, say, got in before them, and lived in the countryside in huts, spinning philosophies, and made peace with their Celtic neighbors and the middle ages crept past without so much as a mention of feudal states. I can tell you that it boggled my mind, to use the popular phrase, when St. Ives told me about it. That crushed bug, depend on it, would send the jewels tumbling, and where they'd fall, no one on Earth could puzzle out, try as he might and given a notebook and pen to calculate with.

—⁓—

WE WERE DUSTY and hot before we were done that evening. A mammoth had come past, as if looking for something he'd lost, and St. Ives snapped a dozen photographs of the beast before it ambled away. Then a rhinoceros of some vintage appeared, and out came the camera again. I was a frightful mass of dirt and stinging insects and, indelicate as it sounds, perspiration, and was surprised to find a pool of clear water in the rocks, the product of a slowly running spring. I spent a cool half hour scrubbing up, and was happy enough to have brought along the requisite toiletries.

One is tempted—or at least I am—to dispense with the niceties when traveling rough. What purpose is there in trimming one's mustache, you ask, when one is tenting in the Hebrides? We can take a lesson from Robinson Crusoe, who maintained a degree of gentility even when lost forever, he supposed, on a desert island. Which one of us wouldn't have run naked with the savages before the month was gone? Not Crusoe. And so with me. I tread on the temptation to run with the savages, and although in truth I neglected to bring a mustache scissors (we were to be away, at most, for half a day) I carried with me a comb and brush and a bottle of rose oil, and, as I say, I wielded those tools to good effect while St. Ives, caught up in the fever of his picture taking, let me go about my business.

And I was careful. There were tiny fish, in fact, down in that shallow pool, fish that had no need for a dose of rose oil. I skimmed three broken hairs from the placid surface—which surface I had used as a mirror—and I put the hairs in my pocket and carried them back with me.

I had finished up and felt entirely restored when the sun, with a rapidity which never fails to amaze me, sank beyond the primeval horizon. Night descended like a lead curtain, and almost at once there sounded roundabout us such a shrieking and mewling and growling as I hope never to hear again. The night was alive with prowling beasts, and us with neither shelter nor fire. We were at it again, hustling the machine back into the cave. Our cave painter hadn't yet returned. With a cloth thrown over a lamp, once again we scoured out our footprints, watching with wary nervousness the pairs of eyes that shined at us out of the darkness. We launched an hour after sunset, and I heartily believed, along with St. Ives and Hasbro, that we left behind us not a trace of our having been there—nothing which might in the least joggle the delicate mechanism of the temporal and spacial universe.

We arrived in the twentieth century, in the familiar cave on the Salisbury Plain. All of us, since St. Ives' remonstrances, were leery of what we'd find. Stonehenge, we feared, would be whisked away and replaced by a picket fence enclosing a pumpkin patch. The wagon load of tourists bound for Wiltshire would have their hats on backward or would wear spectacles the size and shape of starfish. When one thought about it, it seemed almost a miracle that no such incongruity confronted us when we peered out of the door of that cave. There was the plain, dusty and hot, Marlborough to the north, Andover to the east, London, for aught we could determine, bustling along the shores of the Thames some few miles away, beyond the horizon.

I, for one, breathed a hearty sigh of relief. The last third of our mission had been ticked off the list, and another chapter in the great book of the adventures of Langdon St. Ives had come to a happy close. His camera was full of photographs. His time machine was faultless. There lay our cart and tarpaulin. We had only to load the device and the gear and away. The Royal Academy was a plum for the plucking.

I hefted my bag, grinning. For the moment. Something, however, seemed to be tugging at the corners of my mouth, effacing the grin. What was it? I gave St. Ives a look, and he could see quite clearly, from the puzzlement on my face, that something was amiss. I felt, abruptly, like a caveman smitten across the noggin with a stone.

My toiletries kit—I'd left it by the spring! There wasn't a thing in it, beyond a comb and brush, a bar of soap and a bottle of rose oil for the hair. I tore open my bag, hoping, in spite of my certain knowledge to the contrary, that I was wrong. But such wasn't the case. The kit was gone, lost in the trackless centuries of the past.

Our first thought was to retrieve it. But that wouldn't do. As fine as St. Ives's calculations were, we might as easily arrive a week early or a week late. We might appear, as I've said, while the cave painter was at work, and have to knock him senseless in order to squelch the news of our scissoring at the fabric of time. The universe mustn't get onto us, although, as I pointed out to St. Ives, it already had, due to my incalculable stupidity. St. Ives pondered for a moment. Returning would, quite likely, compound the problem. And there was our wagon, wasn't there? The universe hadn't gone so far afoul as to have eradicated our wagon. Surely the Romans had arrived after all. Surely the megatherium had nosed a sufficient quantity of roots out of the dirt to satisfy itself and the universe both. The toad had eaten his bug and all was well. The panic had been for nothing.

We turned, intending to dismantle the ship, to hoist it onto the wagon preparatory to returning to Harrogate via London. There on the wall before us was the cave painting—the likeness of the artist himself, the scattered beasts beyond. We stood gaping at it, unbelieving. I blinked and stepped forward, running my hand across the time-dried paint. Was this some monstrous hoax? Had some grinning devil had a go at the painting at our expense while we dawdled in pre-history?

The painting was wonderfully detailed—his broad nose, his overhung brow, his squinty little pig eyes. But instead of that troubled frown, his face was arched with a faint half smile that Da Vinci would have paid to study. His hair, in another lifetime shaggy and wild, was parted down the center and combed neatly over his ears. The artist had been clever enough to capture the sheen of rose oil on it, and the passing centuries hadn't diminished it. His beard, still monumental by current standards, was combed out and oiled into a cylinder like the beard of a pharaoh. My comb was thrust into it by way of ornament. He held my brush in one hand; in the other, gripped at the neck and drawn with reverential care, was the bottle of hair oil, tinted pink and orange in the dying sunlight.

———

I FEAR THAT after the shock of it had drained the color from my face, I pitched over onto that same article and had to be hauled away bodily in the cart. The rest you know. The cave on the Salisbury plain is no more, and, happily, the tenuous and brittle fabrication of the universe isn't quite so tenuous and brittle after all. Or so I tell myself. With the cave went the great mass of St. Ives's evidence. His photographs were cried down as frauds—waxwork dummies covered in horsehair. He's planning another journey, though. He's found the foreleg of a dinosaur in a sandpit in the forest near Heidelberg, and he intends to compel it to spirit us back to the Age of Reptiles.

Whether I accompany him or stay in Harrogate to look after the tropical fish is a matter I debate with myself daily. You can understand what an unsettling thing it must be to teeter on the brink of bringing down the universe in a heap, and then to be snatched away at the last moment by the timely hand of Providence. And besides, I'm thinking of writing a monograph on the Crusoe matter—a little business regarding the civilizing influences of a good tortoiseshell comb. Desperate as it was, the incident of the toiletries bag has rather revived my interest in the issue. The truth of it, if I'm any judge, has been borne out quite nicely. - ☙

Lord Kelvin's Machine

Murder in the Seven Dials

R AIN HAD BEEN falling for hours, and the North Road was a muddy ribbon in the darkness. The coach slewed from side to side, bouncing and rocking, and yet Langdon St. Ives was loathe to slow the pace. He held the reins tightly, looking out from under the brim of his hat, which dripped rainwater in a steady stream. They were two miles outside Crick, where they could find fresh horses—if by then it was fresh horses that they needed.

Clouds hid the moon, and the night was fearfully dark. St. Ives strained to see through the darkness, watching for a coach driving along the road ahead. There was the chance that they would overtake it before they got into Crick, and if they did, then fresh horses wouldn't matter; a coffin for a dead man would suffice.

His mind wandered, and he knew he was tired and was fueled now by hatred and fear. He forced himself to concentrate on the road ahead. Taking both the reins in his left hand, he wiped rainwater out of his face and shook his head, trying to clear it. He was foggy, though. He felt drugged. He squeezed his eyes shut and shook his head again, nearly tumbling off the seat when a wave of dizziness hit him. What was this? Was he sick? Briefly, he considered reining up and letting Hasbro, his gentleman's gentleman, drive the coach. Maybe he ought to give it up for the rest of the night, get inside and try to sleep.

His hands suddenly were without strength. The reins seemed to slip straight through them, tumbling down across his knees, and the horses, given their head, galloped along, jerking the coach behind them as it rocked on its springs. Something was terribly wrong with him—more than mere sickness—and he tried to shout to his friends, but as if in a dream his voice was airy and weak. He tried to pluck one of the reins up, but it was no use. He was made of rubber, of mist…

Someone—a man in a hat—loomed up ahead of the coach, running out of an open field, up the bank toward the road. The man was waving his hands, shouting something into the night. He might as well have been talking to the wind. Hazily, it occurred to St. Ives that the man might be trouble. What if this were some sort of ambush? He flopped helplessly on the seat, trying to hold on, his muscles gone to pudding. If that's what it was, then it was too damned bad, because there was nothing on earth that St. Ives could do to save them.

The coach drove straight down at the man, who held up a scrap of paper—a note, perhaps. Rainwater whipped into St. Ives's face as he slumped sideways, rallying his last few remnants of strength, shoving out his hand to pluck up the note. And in that moment, just before all consciousness left him, he looked straight into the stranger's face and saw that it wasn't a stranger at all. It was himself who stood at the roadside, clutching the note. And with the image of his own frightened face in his mind, St. Ives fell away into darkness and knew no more.

—◆◆◆—

THEY HAD TRAVELED almost sixteen miles since four that afternoon, but now it was beginning to seem that continuing would be futile. The black night was cold, and the rain still beat down, thumping onto the top of the coach and flooding the street six inches deep in a river that flowed down High Holborn into the Seven Dials. The pair of horses stood with their heads bowed, streaming rainwater and standing nearly to their fetlocks in the flood. The streets and storefronts were empty and dark, and as Langdon St. Ives let the drumming of raindrops fill his head with noise, he dreamed that he was a tiny man helplessly buried in a coal scuttle and that a fresh load of coal was tumbling pell-mell down the chute...

He jerked awake. It was two in the morning, and his clothes were muddy and cold. On his lap lay a loaded revolver, which he meant to use before the night was through. The coach overturning outside Crick had cost them precious hours. What that had meant—seeing the ghost of himself on the road—St. Ives couldn't say. Most likely it meant that he was falling apart. Desperation took a heavy toll. He might have been sick, of course, or tired to the point of hallucination, except that the fit had come over him so quickly, and then passed away entirely, and he had awakened to find himself lying in the mud of a ditch along the roadway, wondering how on earth he had gotten here. It was curious, but even more than curious, it was unsettling.

Long hours had gone by since, and during those hours Ignacio Narbondo might easily have spirited Alice away. He might have . . . He stared out into the darkness, shutting the thought out of his mind. The chase had led them to the Seven Dials, and now the faithful Bill Kraken, whose arm had been broken when the carriage overturned, was searching through a lodging house. Narbondo *would* be there, and Alice with him. St. Ives told himself that, and heedlessly rubbed the cold metal of the pistol, his mind filled with thoughts even darker than the night outside.

Generally, he was the last man on earth to be thinking about "meting out justice," but there in the rainy Seven Dials street he felt very much like that proverbial last man, even though Hasbro, his gentleman's gentleman, sat opposite him on the seat, sleeping heavily, wrapped in a greatcoat and carrying a revolver of his own.

And it wasn't so much a desire for justice that St. Ives felt; it was cold, dark murder. He hadn't spoken in three hours. There was nothing left to say, and it was too late at night, and St. Ives was too full of his black thoughts to make conversation; he was empty by now of anything save the contradictory thoughts of murder and of Alice, and he could find words for neither of those. If only they knew for certain where she was, where he had taken her...The Seven Dials was a mystery to him, though—such a tangle of streets and alleys and cramped houses that there was no sorting it out even in daylight, let alone on a night like this. They were close to him, though. Kraken would root him out. St. Ives fancied that he could feel Narbondo's presence in the darkness around him.

He watched the street past the wet curtain. Behind them a mist-shrouded lamp shone in a second-story window. There would be more lamps lit as the night drew on into morning, and for the first time the thought sprang into St. Ives's head that he had no desire to see that morning. Morning was insupportable without Alice. To hell with Narbondo's death. The gun on St. Ives's lap was a pitiful thing. Killing Narbondo would yield the satisfaction of killing an insect—almost none at all. It was life that mattered, Alice's life. The life of the London streets on an April morning was a phantasm. Her life alone had color and substance.

He wondered if he was bound, ultimately, for a madhouse, following in the sad footsteps of his father. Alice was his sanity. He knew that now. A year ago such a thought would have puzzled him. Life had largely been a thing of beakers and calipers and numbers. Things change, though, and one became resigned to that.

There was a whistle. St. Ives sat up, closed his fingers over the revolver handle, and listened through the rain. He shoved half out through the door, the coach rocking gently on its springs and the sodden horses shaking themselves in anticipation, as if finally they would be moving—somewhere, anywhere, out of the flood. A sudden shout rang out from ahead, followed by the sound of running footsteps. Another shout, and Bill Kraken, looking nearly drowned, materialized through the curtain of water, running hard and pointing wildly back over his shoulder.

"There!" he shouted. "There! It's him!"

St. Ives leaped into the street and slogged after Kraken, running heavily, the rain nearly blinding him.

"The coach!" Kraken yelled, out of breath. He turned abruptly and grabbed for St. Ives's arm. There was the rattling sound of another coach in the street and the clop of horse's hooves. Out of the darkness plunged a teetering old cabriolet drawn by its single horse, the driver exposed to the weather and the passenger half hidden by the curtain fixed across the narrow coffin-shaped side chamber. The cab slewed around into the flood, the horse throwing streamers of water from its hooves, and the driver—Ignacio Narbondo—whipping the reins furiously, his feet jammed against the apron to keep himself from flying out.

St. Ives leaped into the street, lunging for the horse's neck and shouting futilely into the rain. The fingers of his right hand closed over a tangle of streaming mane, and he held on as he was yanked off his feet, waving the pistol in his left hand, his heels dragging on the wet road as the horse and cab brushed past him and tore away, slamming him backward into the water. He fired the already-cocked pistol straight into the air, rolled onto his side as he cocked it again, and fired once more at the hurtling shadow of the cab.

A hand clutched his arm. "The coach!" Kraken yelled again, and St. Ives hauled himself heavily out of the water-filled gutter and lunged after him.

Hasbro tossed at the reins even as St. Ives and Kraken clambered in, and the pair of horses lurched off down the narrow street, following the diminishing cab, which swayed and pitched and flung its way toward Holborn. As soon as St. Ives was in and had caught his balance, he threw the coach door open again and leaned out, squinting through the ribbons of water that flew up from the wheels and from the horses' hooves. The coach clattered along, tossing him from side to side, and he aimed his pistol in a thousand directions, never fixing it on his target long enough for him to be able to squeeze the trigger.

They had Narbondo, though. The man was desperate. Too desperate, maybe. Their haste was forcing him into recklessness. And yet if they didn't pursue him closely they would lose him again. An awful sense of destiny swarmed over St. Ives. He held on and gritted his teeth as the dark houses flew past. Soon, he thought. Soon it'll be over, come what will. And no sooner had he thought this than the cabriolet, charging along a hundred yards ahead now, banged down into a water-filled hole in the street.

Its horse stumbled and fell forward, its knees buckling. The tiny cab spun like a slowly revolving top as Narbondo threw up the reins and held on to the apron, sliding half out, his legs kicking the air. The cab tore itself nearly in two, and the sodden curtain across the passenger chamber flew out as if in a heavy wind. A woman—Alice—tumbled helplessly into the street, her hands bound, and the cabriolet crashed down atop her, pinning her underneath. Narbondo was up almost at once, scrambling for a footing in the mire and staggering toward where Alice lay unmoving.

St. Ives screamed into the night, weighed down by the heavy dreamlike horror of what he saw, of Alice coming to herself, suddenly struggling, trapped beneath the overturned cabriolet. Hasbro reined in the horses, but for St. Ives, even a moment's waiting was too much waiting, and he threw himself through the open door of the moving coach and into the road, rolling up onto his feet and pushing himself forward into the onslaught of rain. Twenty yards in front of him, Narbondo crawled across the wreckage of the cab as the fallen horse twitched in the street, trying and failing to stand up, its leg twisted back at a nearly impossible angle.

St. Ives pointed the pistol and fired at Narbondo, but the bullet flew wide, and it was the horse that whinnied and bucked. Desperately, St. Ives smeared rainwater out of his face with his coat sleeve, staggering forward, shooting wildly again when he saw suddenly that Narbondo also had a pistol in his hand and that he now crouched over the trapped woman. He supported Alice's shoulders with his left arm, the pistol aimed at her temple.

Horrified, St. Ives fired instantly, but he heard the crack of the other man's pistol before he was deafened by his own, and through the haze of rain he saw its awful result just as Narbondo was flung around sideways with the force of St. Ives's bullet slamming into his shoulder. Narbondo managed to stagger to his feet, laughing a hoarse seal's laugh, before he collapsed across the ruined cab that still trapped Alice's body.

St. Ives dropped the pistol into the flood and fell to his knees. Finishing Narbondo meant nothing to him anymore. —⌒

PART 1

In The Days Of The Comet

The Peruvian Andes,
One Year later

LANGDON ST. IVES, scientist and explorer, clutched a heavy alpaca blanket about his shoulders and stared out over countless miles of rocky plateaus and jagged volcanic peaks. The tight weave of ivory-colored wool clipped off a dry, chill wind that blew across the fifty miles of Antarctic-spawned Peruvian Current, up from the Gulf of Guayaquil and across the Pacific slope of the Peruvian Andes. A wide and sluggish river, gray-green beneath the lowering sky, crept through broad grasslands behind and below him. Moored like an alien vessel amid the bunch grasses and tola bush was a tiny dirigible, silver in the afternoon sun and flying the Union Jack from a jury-rigged mast.

At St. Ives's feet the scree-strewn rim of a volcanic cone, Mount Cotopaxi, fell two thousand feet toward steamy open fissures, the crater glowing like the bowl of an enormous pipe. St. Ives waved ponderously to his companion Hasbro, who crouched some hundred yards down the slope on the interior of the cone, working the compression mechanism of a Rawls-Hibbing Mechanical Bladder. Coils of India-rubber hose snaked away from the pulsating device, disappearing into cracks in the igneous skin of the mountainside.

A cloud of fierce sulphur-laced steam whirled suddenly up and out of the crater in a wild sighing rush, and the red glow of the twisted fissures dwindled and winked, here and there dying away into cold and misty darkness. St. Ives nodded and consulted a pocket watch. His left shoulder, recently grazed by a bullet, throbbed tiredly. It was late afternoon. The shadows cast by distant peaks obscured the hillsides around him. On the heels of the shadows would come nightfall.

The man below ceased his furious manipulations of the contrivance and signaled to St. Ives, whereupon the scientist turned and repeated the signal—a broad windmill gesture, visible to the several thousand Indians massed on the plain below. "Sharp's the word, Jacky," muttered St. Ives under his breath. And straightaway, thin and sailing on the knife-edged wind, came a half-dozen faint syllables, first in English, then repeated in Quechua, then giving way to the resonant cadence of almost five thousand people marching in step. He could feel the rhythmic reverberations beneath his feet. He turned, bent over, and, mouthing a quick silent prayer, depressed the plunger of a tubular detonator.

He threw himself flat and pressed an ear to the cold ground. The rumble of marching feet rolled through the hillsides like the rushing cataract of a subterranean river. Then, abruptly, a deep and vast explosion, muffled by the crust of the earth itself, heaved at the ground in a tumultuous wave, and it appeared to St. Ives from his aerie atop the volcano as if the grassland below were a giant carpet and that the gods were shaking the dust from it. The marching horde pitched higgledy-piggledy into one another, strewn over the ground like dominoes. The stars in the eastern sky seemed to dance briefly, as if the earth had been jiggled from her course. Then, slowly, the ground ceased to shake.

St. Ives smiled for the first time in nearly a week, although it was the bitter smile of a man who had won a war, perhaps, but had lost far too many battles. It was over for the moment, though, and he could rest. He very nearly thought of Alice, who had been gone these twelve months now, but he screamed any such thoughts out of his mind before he became lost among them and couldn't find his way back. He couldn't let that happen to him again, ever—not if he valued his sanity.

Hasbro labored up the hillside toward him carrying the Rawls-Hibbing apparatus, and together they watched the sky deepen from blue to purple, cut by the pale radiance of the Milky Way. On the horizon glowed a misty semicircle of light, like a lantern hooded with muslin—the first faint glimmer of an ascending comet. —⌒

Dover, Long Weeks Earlier

THE TUMBLED ROCKS of Castle Jetty loomed black and wet in the fog. Below, where the gray tide of the North Sea fell inch by inch away, green tufts of waterweed danced and then collapsed across barnacled stone, where brown penny-crabs scuttled through dark crevices as if their sidewise scramble would render them invisible to the men who stood above. Langdon St. Ives, wrapped in a greatcoat and shod in hip boots, cocked a spyglass to his eye and squinted north toward the Eastern Docks.

Heavy mist swirled and flew in the wind off the ocean, nearly obscuring the sea and sky like a gray muslin curtain. Just visible through the murk some hundred-fifty yards distant, the steamer H.M.S. *Ramsgate* heaved on the ground swell, its handful of paying passengers having hours since wended their way shoreward toward one of the inns along Castle Hill Road—all the passengers, that is, but one. St. Ives felt as if he'd stood atop the rocks for a lifetime, watching nothing at all but an empty ship.

He lowered the glass and gazed into the sea. It took an act of will to believe that beyond the Strait lay Belgium and that behind him, a bowshot distant, lay the city of Dover. He was overcome suddenly with the uncanny certainty that the jetty was moving, that he stood on the bow of a sailing vessel plying the waters of a phantom sea. The rushing tide below him bent and swirled around the edges of thrusting rocks, and for a perilous second he felt himself falling forward.

A firm hand grasped his shoulder. He caught himself, straightened, and wiped beaded moisture from his forehead with the sleeve of his coat. "Thank you." He shook his head to clear it. "I'm tired out."

"Certainly, sir. Steady on, sir."

"I've reached the limits of my patience, Hasbro," said St. Ives to the man beside him. "I'm convinced we're watching an empty ship. Our man has given us the slip, and I'd sooner have a look at the inside of a glass of ale than another look at that damned steamer."

"Patience is its own reward, sir," replied St. Ives's manservant.

St. Ives gave him a look. "My patience must be thinner than yours." He pulled a pouch from the pocket of his greatcoat, extracting a bent bulldog pipe and a quantity of tobacco. "Do you suppose Kraken has given up?" He pressed curly black tobacco into the pipe bowl with his thumb and struck a match, the flame hissing and sputtering in the misty evening air.

"Not Kraken, sir, if I'm any judge. If our man went ashore along the docks, then Kraken followed him. A disguise wouldn't answer, not with that hump. And it's an even bet that Narbondo wouldn't be away to London, not this late in the evening. For my money he's in a public house and Kraken's in the street outside. If he made away north, then Jack's got him, and the outcome is the same. The best…"

"Hark!"

Silence fell, interrupted only by the sighing of wavelets splashing against the stones of the jetty and by the hushed clatter of distant activity along the docks. The two men stood barely breathing, smoke from St. Ives's pipe rising invisibly into the fog. "There!" whispered St. Ives, holding up his left hand.

Softly, too rhythmically to be mistaken for the natural cadence of the ocean, came the muted dipping of oars and the creak of shafts in oarlocks. St. Ives stepped gingerly across to an adjacent rock and clambered down into a little crab-infested grotto. He could just discern, through a sort of triangular window, the thin gray line where the sky met the sea. And there, pulling into view, was a long rowboat in which sat two men, one plying the oars and the other crouched on a thwart and wrapped in a dark blanket. A frazzle of black hair drooped in moist curls around his shoulders.

"It's him," whispered Hasbro into St. Ives's ear.

"That it is. And up to no good at all. He's bound for Hargreaves's, or I'm a fool. We were right about this one. That eruption in Narvik was no eruption at all. It was a detonation. And now the task is unspeakably complicated. I'm half inclined to let the monster have a go at it, Hasbro. I'm altogether weary of this world. Why not let him blow it to smithereens?"

St. Ives stood up tiredly, the rowboat having disappeared into the fog. He found that he was shocked by what he had said—not only because Narbondo was very nearly capable of doing just that, but also because St. Ives had meant it. He didn't care. He put one foot in front of the other these days out of what?—duty? revenge?

"There's the matter of the ale glass," said Hasbro wisely, grasping St. Ives by the elbow. "That and a kidney pie, unless I'm mistaken, would answer most questions on the subject of futility. We'll fetch in Bill Kraken and Jack on the way. We've time enough to stroll round to Hargreaves's after supper."

St. Ives squinted at Hasbro. "Of course we do," he said. "I might send you lads out tonight alone, though. I need about ten hours' sleep to bring me around. These damned dreams…In the morning I'll wrestle with these demons again."

"There's the ticket, sir," said the stalwart Hasbro, and through the gathering gloom the two men picked their way from rock to rock toward the warm lights of Dover.

—◦◦◦—

"I CAN'T IMAGINE I've ever been this hungry before," said Jack Owlesby, spearing up a pair of rashers from a passing platter. His features were set in a hearty smile, as if he were making a strong effort to efface having revealed himself too thoroughly the night before. "Any more eggs?"

"Heaps," said Bill Kraken through a mouthful of cold toast, and he reached for another platter at his elbow. "Full of the right sorts of humors, sir, is eggs. It's the unctuous secretions of the yolk that fetches the home stake, if you follow me. Loaded up with all manners of fluids."

Owlesby paused, a forkful of egg halfway to his mouth. He gave Kraken a look that seemed to suggest he was unhappy with talk of fluids and secretions.

"Sorry, lad. There's no stopping me when I'm swept off by the scientific. I've forgot that you ain't partial to the talk of fluids over breakfast. Not that it matters a bit about fluids or any of the rest of it, what with that comet sailing in to smash us to flinders..."

St. Ives coughed, seeming to choke, his fit drowning the last few words of Kraken's observation. "Lower your voice, man!"

"Sorry, Professor. I don't think sometimes. You know me. This coffee tastes like rat poison, don't it? And not high-toned rat poison either, but something mixed up by your man with the hump."

"I haven't tasted it," said St. Ives, raising his cup. He peered into the depths of the dark stuff and was reminded instantly of the murky water in the night-shrouded tide pool he'd slipped into on his way back from the tip of the jetty last night. He didn't need to taste the coffee; the thin mineral-spirits smell of it was enough. "Any of the tablets?" he asked Hasbro.

"I brought several of each, sir. It doesn't pay to go abroad without them. One would think that the art of brewing coffee would have traveled the few miles from the Normandy coast to the British Isles, sir, but we all know it hasn't." He reached into the pocket of his coat and pulled out a little vial of jellybean-like pills. "Mocha Java, sir?"

"If you would," said St. Ives. "'All ye men drink java,' as the saying goes."

Hasbro dropped one into the upheld cup, and in an instant the room was filled with the astonishing heavy aroma of real coffee, the chemical smell of the pallid facsimile in the rest of their cups retreating before it. St. Ives seemed to reel with the smell of it, as if for the moment he was revitalized.

"By God!" whispered Kraken. "What else have you got there?"

"A tolerable Wiener Melange, sir, and a Brazilian brew that I can vouch for. There's an espresso too, but it's untried as yet."

"Then I'm your man to test it!" cried the enthusiastic Kraken, and he held out his hand for the little pill. "There's money in these," he said, plopping it into his full cup and watching the result as if mystified. "Millions of pounds."

"Art for art's sake," said St. Ives, dipping the end of a white kerchief into his cup and studying the stained corner of it in the sunlight shining through the casement. He nodded, satisfied, then tasted the coffee, nodding again. Over the previous year, since the episode in the Seven Dials, he had worked on nothing but these tiny white pills, all of his scientific instincts and skills given over to the business of coffee. It was a frivolous expenditure of energy and intellect, but until last week he could see nothing in the wide world that was any more compelling.

He bent over his plate and addressed Bill Kraken, although his words, clearly, were intended for the assembled company. "We mustn't, Bill, give in to fears about this... this...heavenly visitation, to lapse into metaphysical language. I woke up fresh this morning. A new man. And the solution, I discovered, was in front of my face. I had been given it by the very villain we pursue. Our only real enemy now is time, gentlemen, time and the excesses of our own fears."

St. Ives paused to have another go at the coffee, then stared into his cup for a moment before resuming his speech. "The single greatest catastrophe now would be for the news to leak to the general public. The man in the street would dissolve into chaos if he knew what confronted him. He couldn't face the idea of the earth smashed to atoms. It would be too much for him. We can't afford to underestimate his susceptibility to panic, his capacity for running amok and tearing his hair whenever it would pay him in dividends not to."

St. Ives stroked his chin, staring at the debris on his plate. He bent forward, and in a low voice he said, "I'm certain that science will save us this time, gentlemen, if it doesn't kill us first. The thing will be close, though, and if the public gets wind of the threat from this comet, great damage will come of it." He smiled into the befuddled faces of his three companions. Kraken wiped a dribble of egg from the edge of his mouth. Jack pursed his lips.

"I'll need to know about Hargreaves," continued St. Ives, "and you'll want to know what I'm blathering about. But this isn't the place. Let's adjourn to the street, shall we?" And with that the men arose, Kraken tossing off the last of his coffee. Then, seeing that Jack was leaving half a cup, he drank Jack's off too and mumbled something about waste and starvation as he followed the rest of them toward the hotel door.

—◦◦◦—

Dr. Ignacio Narbondo grinned over his tea. He watched the back of Hargreaves's head as it nodded above a great sheet of paper covered with lines, numbers, and notations. Why oxygen allowed itself to flow in and out of Hargreaves's lungs Narbondo couldn't at all say; the man seemed to be animated by a living hatred, an indiscriminate loathing for the most innocent things. He gladly built bombs for idiotic anarchist deviltry, not out of any particular regard for causes, but simply to create mayhem, to blow things to bits. If he could have built a device sufficiently large to obliterate the Dover cliffs and the sun rising beyond them, there would have been no satisfying him until it was done. He loathed tea. He loathed eggs. He loathed brandy. He loathed the daylight, and he loathed the nighttime. He loathed the very art of constructing infernal devices.

Narbondo looked round him at the barren room, the lumpy pallet on the ground where Hargreaves allowed himself a few hours' miserable sleep, as often as not to lurch awake at night, a shriek half uttered in his throat, as if he had peered into a mirror and seen the face of a beetle staring back. Narbondo whistled merrily all of a sudden, watching Hargreaves stiffen, loathing the melody that had broken in upon the discordant mumblings of his brain.

Hargreaves turned, his bearded face set in a rictus of twisted rage, his dark eyes blank as eclipsed moons. He breathed heavily. Narbondo waited with raised eyebrows, as if surprised at the man's reaction. "Damn a man that whistles," said Hargreaves slowly, running the back of his hand across his mouth. He looked at his hand, expecting to find heaven knew what, and turned slowly back to his bench top. Narbondo grinned and poured himself another cup of tea. All in all it was a glorious day. Hargreaves had agreed to help him destroy the earth without so much as a second thought. He had agreed with uncharacteristic relish, as if it was the first really useful task he had undertaken in years. Why he didn't just slit his own throat and be done with life for good and all was one of the great mysteries.

He wouldn't have been half so agreeable if he knew that Narbondo had no intention of destroying anything, that his motivation was greed—greed and revenge. His threat to cast the earth forcibly into the path of the approaching comet wouldn't be taken lightly. There were those in the Royal Academy who knew he could do it, who supposed, no doubt, that he might quite likely do it. They were as shortsighted as Hargreaves and every bit as useful. Narbondo had worked devilishly hard over the years at making himself feared, loathed, and, ultimately, respected.

The surprising internal eruption of Mount Hjarstaad would throw the fear into them. They'd be quaking over their breakfasts at that very moment, the lot of them wondering and gaping. Beards would be wagging. Dark suspicions would be mouthed. Where was Narbondo? Had he been seen in London? Not for months. He had threatened this very thing, hadn't he?—an eruption above the Arctic Circle, just to demonstrate the seriousness of his intent, the degree to which he held the fate of the world in his hands.

Very soon—within days—the comet would pass close enough to the earth to provide a spectacular display for the masses—foolish creatures. The iron core of the thing might easily be pulled so solidly by the earth's magnetic field that the comet would hurtle groundward, slamming the poor old earth into atoms and all the gaping multitudes with it. What if, Narbondo had suggested, what if a man were to give the earth a push, to propel it even closer to the approaching star and so turn a long shot into a dead cert, as a blade of the turf might put it? And with that, the art of extortion had been elevated to a new plane.

Well, Dr. Ignacio Narbondo was that man. Could he do it? Narbondo grinned. His advertisement of two weeks past had drawn a sneer from the Royal Academy, but Mount Hjarstaad would wipe the sneers from their faces. They would wax grave. Their grins would set like plaster of Paris. What had the poet said about that sort of thing? "Gravity was a mysterious carriage of the body to cover the defects of the mind." That was it. Gravity would answer for a day or two, but when it faded into futility they would pay, and pay well. Narbondo set in to whistle again, this time out of the innocence of good cheer, but the effect on Hargreaves was so immediately consumptive and maddening that Narbondo gave it off abruptly. There was no use baiting the man into ruination before the job was done.

He thought suddenly of Langdon St. Ives. St. Ives was nearly unavoidable. For the fiftieth time Narbondo regretted killing the woman on that rainy London morning one year past. He hadn't meant to. He had meant to bargain with her life. It was desperation had made him sloppy and wild. It seemed to him that he could count his mistakes on the fingers of one hand. When he made them, though, they weren't subtle mistakes. The best he could hope for was that St. Ives had sensed the desperation in him, that St. Ives lived day-to-day with the knowledge that if he had only eased up, if he hadn't pushed Narbondo so closely, hadn't forced his hand, the woman might be alive today, and the two of them, St. Ives and her, living blissfully together, pottering in the turnip garden. Narbondo watched the back of Hargreaves's head. If it was a just world, then St. Ives would blame himself. He was precisely the man for such a job as that—a martyr of the suffering type.

The very thought of St. Ives made him scowl, though. Narbondo had been careful, but somehow the Dover air seemed to whisper "St. Ives" to him at every turning. He pushed his suspicions out of his mind, reached for his coat, and stepped silently from the room, carrying his teacup with him. On the morning street outside he smiled grimly at the orange sun that burned through the evaporating fog, then he threw the dregs of his tea, cup and all, over a vine-draped stone wall and strode away east up Archcliffe Road, composing in his mind a letter to the Royal Academy.

—⁕—

"DAMN ME!" MUMBLED Bill Kraken through the fingers mashed against his mouth. He wiped away furiously at the tea leaves and tea that ran down his neck and collar. The cup that had hit him on the ear had fallen and broken on the stones of the garden. He peered up over the wall at Narbondo's diminishing figure and added this last unintended insult to the list of villainies he had suffered over the years at Narbondo's hands.

He would have his turn yet. Why St. Ives hadn't given him leave merely to beat the stuffing out of this devil Hargreaves Kraken couldn't at all fathom. The man was a monster; there was no gainsaying it. They could easily set off one of his own devices—hoist him on his own filthy petard, so to speak. His remains would be found amid the wreckage of infernal machines, built with his own hands. The world would have owed Bill Kraken a debt.

But Narbondo, St. Ives had insisted, would have found another willing accomplice. Hargreaves was only a pawn, and pawns could be dealt with easily enough when the time came. St. Ives couldn't afford to tip his hand, nor would he settle for anything less than fair play and lawful justice. That was the crux of it. St. Ives had developed a passion for keeping the blinders on his motivations. He would be driven by law and reason and not fuddle things up with the odd emotion. Sometimes the man was scarcely human.

Kraken crouched out from behind the wall and slipped away in Narbondo's wake, keeping to the other side of the road when the hunchback entered a stationer's, then circling round to the back when Narbondo went in at the post office door. Kraken stepped through a dark, arched rear entry, a ready lie on his lips in case he was confronted. He found himself in a small deserted room, where he slid behind a convenient heap of crates, peeping through slats at an enormously fat, stooped man who lumbered in and tossed Narbondo's letter into a wooden bin before lumbering back out. Kraken snatched up the letter, tucked it into his coat, and in a moment was back in the sunlight, prying at the sealing wax with his index finger. Ten minutes later he was at the front door of the post office, grinning into the wide face of the postman and mailing Narbondo's missive for the second time that morning.

—⁂—

"Surely it's a bluff," said Jack Owlesby, scowling at Langdon St. Ives. The four of them sat on lawn chairs in the Gardens, listening with half an ear to the lackluster tootings of a tired orchestra. "What would it profit him to alert the *Times*? There'd be mayhem. If it's extortion he's up to, this won't further his aim by an inch."

"The threat of it might," replied St. Ives. "If his promise to pitch the earth into the path of the comet weren't taken seriously, the mere suggestion that the public be apprised of the magnetic affinity of the comet and the earth might be. Extortion on top of extortion. The one is pale alongside the other one. I grant you that. But there could be a panic if an ably stated message were to reach the right sort of journalist—or the wrong sort, rather." St. Ives paused and shook his head, as if such panic wasn't to be contemplated. "What was the name of that scoundrel who leaked the news of the threatened epidemic four years ago?"

"Beezer, sir," said Hasbro. "He's still in the employ of the *Times*, and, we must suppose, no less likely to be in communication with the doctor today than he was then. He would be your man, sir, if you wanted to wave the bloody shirt."

"I rather believe," said St. Ives, grimacing at the raucous climax of an unidentifiable bit of orchestration, "that we should pay this man Beezer a visit. We can't do a thing sitting around Dover. Narbondo has agreed to wait four days for a reply from the Academy. There's no reason to believe that he won't keep his word—he's got nothing to gain by haste. The comet, after all, is ten days off. We've got to suppose that he means just what he claims. Evil begets idiocy, gentlemen, and there is no earthly way to tell how far down the path into degeneration our doctor has trod. The next train to London, Hasbro?"

"Two-forty-five, sir."

"We'll be aboard her." —෴

London and Harrogate

THE BAYSWATER CLUB, OWNED by the Royal Academy of Sciences, sat across from Kensington Gardens, commanding a view of trimmed lawns and roses and cleverly pruned trees. St. Ives peered out the window on the second floor of the club, satisfied with what he saw. The sun loomed like an immense orange just below the zenith, and the radiant heat glancing through the geminate windows of the club felt almost alive. The April weather was so altogether pleasant that it came near to making up for the fearful lunch that would at any moment arrive to stare at St. Ives from a china plate. He had attempted a bit of cheerful banter with the stony-faced waiter, ordering dirt cutlets and beer as a joke, but the man hadn't seen the humor in it. What he *had* seen had been evident on his face.

St. Ives sighed and wished heartily that he was taking the sun along with the multitudes in the park, but the thought that a week hence there mightn't be any park at all—or any multitudes, either—sobered him, and he drained the bottom half of a glass of claret. He regarded the man seated across from him. Parsons, the ancient secretary of the Royal Academy, spooned up broth with an enthusiasm that left St. Ives tired. Floating on the surface of the broth were what appeared to be twisted little bugs, but must have been some sort of Oriental mushroom, sprinkled on by a chef with a sense of humor. Parsons chased them with his spoon.

"So you've nothing at all to fear," said Parsons, dabbing at his chin with a napkin. He grimaced at St. Ives in a satisfied way, like a proud doggy who had fetched in the slippers without tearing holes in them. "The greatest minds in the scientific world are at work on the problem. The comet will sail past us with no commotion whatsoever. It's a matter of electromagnetic forces, really. The comet might easily be drawn to the earth, as you say, with disastrous consequences. Unless, let's imagine, if we can push ourselves so far, the earth's magnetic field were to be forcibly suspended."

"Suspended?"

"Shut off. Current interruptus." Parsons winked.

"Shut off? Lunacy," St. Ives said. "Sheer lunacy."

"It's not unknown to have happened. Common knowledge has it that the magnetic poles have reversed themselves any number of times, and that during the interim between the establishing of new poles, the earth was blessedly free of any electromagnetic field whatsoever. I'm surprised that a physicist such as yourself has to be informed of such a thing." Parsons peered at St. Ives over the top of his pince-nez, then fished up out of his broth a tendril of vegetable. St. Ives gaped at it. "Kelp," said the secretary, slathering the dripping weed into his mouth.

St. Ives nodded, a shiver running up along his spine. The pink chicken breast that lay beneath wilted lettuce on his plate began, suddenly, to fill him with a curious sort of dread. His lunches with Parsons at the Bayswater Club invariably went so. The secretary was always one up on him, simply because of the food. "So what, exactly, do you intend? To *hope* such an event into existence?"

"Not at all," said Parsons smugly. "We're building a device."

"A *device?*"

"To reverse the polarity of the earth, thereby negating any natural affinity the earth might have for the comet and vice versa."

"Impossible," said St. Ives, a kernel of doubt and fear beginning to sprout within him.

"Hardly." Parsons waved his fork with an air of gaiety, then scratched the end of his nose with it. "No less a personage than Lord Kelvin himself is at work on it, although the theoretical basis of the thing was entirely a product of James Clerk Maxwell. Maxwell's sixteen equations in tensor calculus demonstrated a good bit beyond the idea that gravity is merely a form of electromagnetism. But his conclusions, taken altogether, had such terrible and far-reaching side implications hat they were never published. Lord Kelvin, of course, has access to them. And I think that we have little to fear that in such benevolent hands, Maxwell's discoveries will lead to nothing but scientific advancement. To more, actually—to the temporary reversal of the poles, as I said, and the switching off, as it were, of any currents that would attract our comet. Trust us, sir. This threat, as you call it, is a threat no more. You're entirely free to apply your manifold talents to more pressing matters."

St. Ives sat silently for a moment, wondering if any objections would penetrate Parsons's head past the crunching of vegetation. Quite likely not, but St. Ives hadn't any choice but try. Two days earlier, when he had assured his friends in Dover that they would easily thwart Ignacio Narbondo, he hadn't bargained on this. Was it possible that the clever contrivances of Lord Kelvin and the Royal Academy would constitute a graver threat than that posed by the doctor? It wasn't to be thought of. Yet here was Parsons, full of talk about reversing the polarity of the earth. St. Ives was duty-bound to speak. He seemed to find himself continually at odds with his peers.

"This…device," St. Ives said. "This is something that's been cobbled together in the past few weeks, is it?"

Parsons looked stupefied. "It's not something that's been *cobbled* together at all. But since you ask, no. I think I can safely tell you that it is the culmination of Lord Kelvin's lifelong work. All the rest of his forays into electricity are elementary, pranks, gewgaws. It's this engine, sir, on which his genius has been expended."

"So he's had the lifelong ambition of reversing the polarity of the earth? To what end? Or are you telling me that he's *anticipated* the comet for the past forty years?"

"I'm not telling you either of those, am I? If I chose to tell you the truth about the matter, which I clearly don't choose to do, you wouldn't believe it anyway. It would confound you. Suffice it to say that the man is willing to sacrifice ambition for the good of humanity."

St. Ives nodded, giving his chicken a desultory poke with the end of his finger. It might easily have been some sort of pale tide-pool creature shifting in a saline broth on the plate. Ambition…He had his own share of ambition. He had long suspected the nature of the device that Lord Kelvin tinkered with in his barn in Harrogate. Parsons was telling him the truth, or at least part of it. And what the truth meant was that St. Ives, somehow, must possess himself of this fabulous machine.

Except that the idea of doing so was contemptible. There were winds in this world that blew a man into uncharted seas. But while they changed the course of his action, they ought not to change the course of his soul. Take a lesson from Robinson Crusoe, he told himself. He thought about Alice then, and of the brief time they had spent together. Suddenly he determined to hack the weeds out of her vegetable garden, and the thought buoyed him up. Then, just as suddenly, he was depressed beyond words, and he found himself staring at the mess on his plate. Parsons was looking contentedly out the window, picking at his teeth with a fingernail.

First things first, St. Ives said to himself. Reverse the polarity of the earth! "Have you read the works of young Rutherford?" he asked Parsons.

"Phiiwinnie Rutherford of Edinburgh?"

"Ernest Rutherford. Of New Zealand. I ran across him in Canada. He's done some interesting work in the area of light rays, if you can call them that." St. Ives wiggled loose a thread of chicken, carried the morsel halfway to his mouth, looked at and changed his mind. "There's some indication that alpha and beta rays from the sun slide away along the earth's magnetic field, arriving harmlessly at the poles. It seems likely, at a hasty glance, that without the field they'd sail in straightaway—we'd be bathed in radioactivity. The most frightful mutations might occur. It has been my pet theory, in fact, that the dinosaurs were laid low in precisely that same fashion—that their demise was a consequence of the reversal of the poles and the inherent cessation of the magnetic field."

Parsons shrugged. "All of this *is* theory, of course. But the comet is eight days away, and *that's* not at all theory. It's not a brontosaurus, my dear fellow, it's an enormous chunk of iron that threatens to smash us into jelly. From your chair across the able it's easy enough to fly in the face of the science of mechanics, but I'm afraid, sir, that Lord Kelvin will get along very well without you—he has in the past."

"There's a better way," said St. Ives simply. It was useless to lose his temper over Parsons's practiced stubbornness.

"Oh?" said the secretary.

"Ignacio Narbondo, I believe, has showed it to us."

Parsons dropped his spoon onto his lap and launched into a choking fit. St. Ives held up a constraining hand. "I'm very much aware of his threats, I assure you. And they're not idle threats, either. Do you propose to pay him?"

"I'm constrained from discussing it."

"He'll do what he claims. He's taken the first steps already."

"I realize, my dear fellow, that you and the doctor are sworn enemies. He ought to have danced his last jig on the gallows a long time ago. If it were in my power to bring him to justice, I would, but I have no earthly idea where he is, quite frankly, and I'll warn you, with no beating about the bush, that this business of the comet must not become a personal matter with you. I believe you take my meaning. Lord Kelvin sets us all an example."

St. Ives counted to ten very slowly. Somewhere between seven and eight, he discovered that Parsons was very nearly right. What he said was beside the point, though. "Let me repeat," St. Ives said evenly, "that I believe there's a better way."

"And what does a lunatic like Narbondo have to do with this 'better way'?"

"He intends, if I read him aright, to effect the stoppage of certain very active volcanoes in arctic Scandinavia via the introduction of petrifactive catalysts into open fissures and dykes. The subsequent detonation of an explosive charge would lead to the eruption of a chain of volcanic mountains that rise above the jungles of Amazonian Peru. The entrapped energy expended by such an upheaval would, he hopes, cast us like a Chinese rocket into the course of the comet."

"Given the structure of the interior of the earth," said Parsons, grinning into his mineral water, "it seems a dubious undertaking at best. Perhaps…"

"Are you familiar with hollow-earth theory?"

Parsons blinked at St. Ives. The corners of his mouth twitched.

"Specifically with that of McClung-Jones of the Quebec Geological Mechanics Institute? The 'thin-crust phenomenon'?"

Parsons shook his head tiredly.

"It's possible," said St. Ives, "that Narbondo's detonation will effect a series of eruptions in volcanoes residing in the hollow core of the earth. The stupendous inner-earth pressures would themselves trigger an eruption at Jones's thin-crust point."

"Thin-crust point?" asked Parsons in a plonking tone.

"The very Peruvian mountains toward which our man Narbondo has cast the glad eye!"

"That's an interesting notion," muttered Parsons, coughing into his napkin. "Turn the earth into a Chinese rocket." He stared out the window, blinking his eyes ponderously, as if satisfied that St. Ives had concluded his speech.

"What I propose," said St. Ives, pressing on, "is to thwart Narbondo, and then effect the same thing, only in reverse—to propel the earth temporarily out of her orbit in a long arc that would put the comet beyond her grasp. If the calculations were fined down sufficiently—and I can assure you that they have been—we'd simply slide back into orbit some few thousand miles farther along our ellipse, a pittance in the eyes of the incalculable distances of our journeying through the void."

St. Ives sat back and fished in his coat for a cigar. Here was the Royal Academy, unutterably fearful of the machinations of Ignacio Narbondo—certain, that is, that the doctor was not merely talking through his hat. If they could trust to Narbondo to destroy the earth through volcanic manipulation, then they could quite clearly trust St. Ives to save it by the same means. What was good for the goose, after all. St. Ives took a breath and continued. "There's been some study of the disastrous effects of in-step marching on bridges and platforms—military study mostly. My own theory, which abets Narbondo's, would make use of such study, of the resonant energy expended by a troop of synchronized marchers…"

Parsons grimaced and shook his head slowly. He wasn't prepared to admit anything about the doings of the nefarious doctor. And St. Ives's theories, although fascinating, were of little use to them here. What St. Ives wanted, perhaps, was to speak to the minister of parades…

Then there was this man Jones. Hadn't McClung-Jones been involved in certain ghastly lizard experiments in the forests of New Hampshire? "Very ugly incident, that one," Parsons muttered sadly. "One of your hollow-earth men, wasn't he? Had a lot of Mesozoic reptiles dummied up at a waxworks in Boston, as I recall, and insisted he'd found them sporting in some bottomless cavern or another." Parsons squinted shrewdly at St. Ives. It was *real* science that they would order up here. Humanity cried out for it, didn't they? Wasn't Lord Kelvin at that very moment riveting together the carcass of the device that Parsons had described? Hadn't St. Ives been listening? Parsons shrugged. Discussions with St. Ives were always—how should one put it?—revealing. But St. Ives had gotten in out of his depth this time, and Parsons's advice was to strike out at once for shore—a hearty breaststroke so as not to tire himself unduly. He patted St. Ives on the sleeve, waving the wine decanter at him.

St. Ives nodded and watched the secretary fill his glass nearly to the top. There was no arguing with the man. And it wasn't argument that was wanted now, anyway. It was action, and that was a commodity, apparently, that he would have to take with his own hands.

———

ST. IVES'S MANOR house and laboratory sat some three quarters of a mile from the summerhouse of William Thomson, Lord Kelvin. The River Nidd ran placid and slow between, slicing neatly in two the broad meadow that separated the grounds of the manor from the grounds of the summerhouse. The willows that lined the banks of the Nidd effected a rolling green cloudbank that almost obscured each house from the view of the other, but from St. Ives's attic window, Lord Kelvin's broad low barn was just visible atop a grassy knoll. Into and out of that barn trooped a platoon of white-coated scientists and grimed machinists. Covered wagons scoured along the High Road from Kirk Hammerton, bearing enigmatic mechanical apparatus, and were met at the gates by an ever-suspicious man in a military uniform.

St. Ives watched their comings and goings through his spyglass. He turned a grim eye on Hasbro, who stood silently behind him. "I've come to a difficult decision, Hasbro."

"Yes, sir."

"I've decided that we must play the role of saboteur, and nothing less. I shrink from such deviltry, but far more is at stake here than honor. We must ruin, somehow, Lord Kelvin's machine."

"Very good, sir."

"The mystifying thing is that I thought it was something else that he was constructing in that barn. But Parsons couldn't have lied so utterly well. He isn't capable of it. We've got to suppose that Lord Kelvin will do just what he says he will do."

"No one will deny it, sir."

"Our sabotaging his machine, of course, necessitates not only carrying out the plan to manipulate the volcanoes, but implies utter faith in that plan. Here we are setting in to thwart the effort of one of the greatest living practical scientists and to substitute our own feeble designs in its stead—an act of monumental egotism."

"As you say, sir."

"But the stakes are high, Hasbro. We *must* have our hand in. It's nothing more nor less than the salvation of the earth, secularly speaking, that we engage in."

"Shall we want lunch first, sir?"

"Kippers and gherkins, thank you. And bring up two bottles of Double Diamond to go along with it—and a bottle or two for yourself, of course."

"Thank you, sir," Hasbro said. "You're most generous, sir."

"Very well," mumbled St. Ives, striding back and forth beneath the exposed roof rafters. He paused and squinted out into the sunlight, watching another wagon rattle along into the open door of Lord Kelvin's barn. Disguise would avail them nothing. It would be an easy thing to fill a wagon with unidentifiable scientific trash—heaven knew he had any amount of it lying about—and to dress up in threadbare pants and coat and merely drive the stuff in at the gate. The guard would have no inkling of who he was. But Lord Kelvin, of course, would. A putty nose and false chin whiskers would be dangerous things. If any members of the Academy saw through them they'd clap him in irons, accuse him very rightly of intended sabotage.

He could argue his case well enough in the courts, to be sure. He could depend on Rutherford, at least, to support him. But in the meantime the earth would have been beat to pieces. That wouldn't answer. And if Lord Kelvin's machine was put into operation and was successful, then he'd quite possibly face a jury of mutants—two-headed men and a judge with a third eye. They'd be sympathetic, under the circumstances, but still…

⁓

THE VAST INTERIOR of Lord Kelvin's barn was awash with activity—a sort of carnival of strange debris, of coiled copper and tubs of bubbling fluids and rubber-wrapped cable thick as a man's wrist hanging from overhead joists like jungle creepers. At the heart of it all lay a plain brass box, studded with rivets and with a halo of wires running out of the top. This, then, was the machine itself, the culmination of Lord Kelvin's life's work, the boon that he was giving over to the salvation of mankind.

The machine was compact, to be sure—small enough to motivate a dogcart, if a man wanted to use it for such a frivolous end. St. Ives turned the notion over in his mind, wondering where a man might travel in such a dogcart and thinking that he would gladly give up his entire fortune to be left alone with the machine for an hour and a half. First things first, he reminded himself, just as three men began to piece together over the top of it a copper pyramid the size of a large doghouse. Lord Kelvin himself, talking through his beard and clad in a white smock and Leibnitz cap, pointed and shouted and squinted with a calculating eye at the device that piece by piece took shape in the lamplight. Parsons stood beside him, leaning on a brass-shod cane.

At the sight of Langdon St. Ives standing outside the open door, Parsons's chin dropped. St. Ives glanced at Jack Owlesby and Hasbro. Bill Kraken had disappeared. Parsons raised an exhorting finger, widening his eyes with the curious effect of making the bulk of his forehead disappear into his thin gray hair.

"Dr. Parsons!" cried St. Ives, getting in before him. "Your man at the gate is a disgrace. We sauntered in past him mumbling nonsense about the Atlantic cable and showed him a worthless letter signed by the Prince of Wales. He tried to shake our hands. You've *got* to do better than that, Parsons. We might have been anyone, mightn't we?—any class of villain. And here we are, trooping in like so many ants. It's the great good fortune of the Commonwealth that we're friendly ants. In a word, we've come to offer our skills, such as they are."

St. Ives paused for breath when he saw that Parsons had begun to sputter like the burning fuse of a fizz bomb, and for one dangerous moment St. Ives was fearful that the old man would explode, would pitch over from apoplexy and that the sum of their efforts would turn out to be merely the murder of poor Parsons. But the fit passed. The secretary snatched his quivering face back into shape and gave the three of them

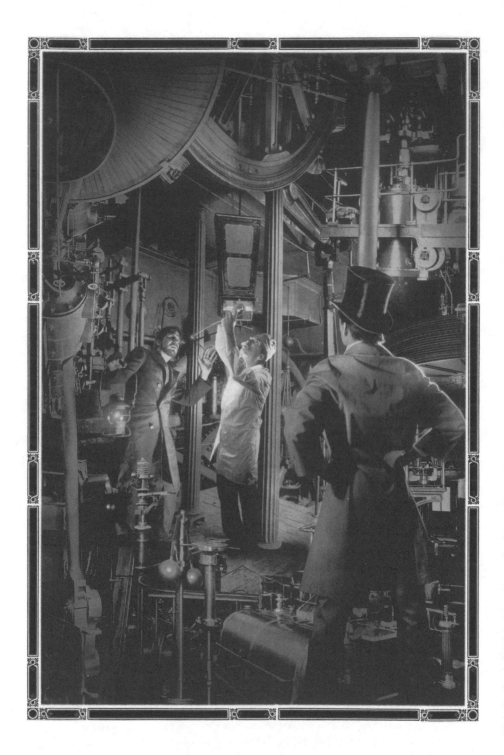

an appraising look, stepping across so as to stand between St. Ives and the machine, as if his gaunt frame, pinched by years of a weedy vegetarian diet, would somehow hide the thing from view.

"*Persona non grata,* is it?" asked St. Ives, giving Parsons a look in return, then instantly regretting the action. There was nothing to be gained by being antagonistic.

"I haven't any idea how you swindled the officer at the gate," said Parsons evenly, holding his ground, "but this operation has been commissioned by Her Majesty the Queen and is undertaken by the collected members of the Royal Academy of Sciences, an organization, if I remember aright, which does not count you among its members. In short, we thank you for your kind offer of assistance and very humbly ask you to leave, along with your ruffians."

He turned to solicit Lord Kelvin's agreement, but the great man was sighting down the length of a brass tube, tugging on it in order, apparently, to align it with an identical tube that hung suspended from the ceiling fifteen feet away. "My lord," said Parsons, clearing his throat meaningfully, but he got no response at all, and gave off his efforts when St. Ives seemed intent on strolling around to the opposite side of the machine.

"*Must* we make an issue of this?" Parsons demanded of St. Ives, stepping across in an effort to cut him off and casting worried looks at Hasbro and Jack Owlesby, as if fearful that the two of them might produce some heinous device of their own with which to blow up the barn and exterminate the lot of them.

St. Ives stopped and shrugged when he saw Bill Kraken, grimed with oil and wearing the clothes of a workman, step out from behind a heap of broken crates and straw stuffing. Without so much as a sideways glance at his employer, Kraken hurried to where Lord Kelvin fiddled with the brass tube. Kraken grasped the opposite end of it and in a moment was wrestling with the thing, hauling it this way and that to the apparent approval of his lordship, and managing to tip St. Ives a broad wink in the process.

"Well, well," said St. Ives in a defeated tone, "I'm saddened by this, Parsons. Saddened. I'd hoped to lend a hand."

Parsons seemed mightily relieved all of a sudden. He cast St. Ives a wide smile. "We thank you, sir," he said, limping toward the scientist, his hand outstretched. "If this project were in the developmental stages, I assure you we'd welcome your expertise. But it's really a matter of nuts and bolts now, isn't it? And your genius, I'm afraid, would be wasted." He ushered the three of them out into the sunlight, smiling hospitably now and watching until he was certain the threat had passed and the three were beyond the gate. Then he called round to have the gate guard relieved. He couldn't, he supposed, have the man flogged, but he could see to it that he spent an enterprising year patrolling the thoroughfares of Dublin. —◦

London and Harrogate Again

I T WAS LATE evening along Fleet Street, and the London night was clear and unseasonably warm, as if the moon that swam in the purple sky beyond the dome of St. Paul's were radiating a thin white heat. The very luminosity of the moon paled the surrounding stars, but as the night deepened farther away into space, the stars were bright and thick enough to remind St. Ives that the universe wasn't an empty place after all. And out there among the planets, hurtling toward earth, was the vast comet, its curved tail comprising a hundred million miles of showering ice, blown by solar wind along the uncharted byways of the void. Tomorrow or the next day the man in the street, peering skyward to admire the stars, would see it there. Would it be a thing of startling beauty, a wash of fire across the canvas of heaven? Or would it send a thrill of fear through a populace still veined with the superstitious dread of the medieval church?

The shuffle of footsteps behind him brought St. Ives to himself. He wrinkled his face up, feeling the gluey pull of the horsehair eyebrows and beard, which, along with a putty nose and monk's wig, made up a very suitable disguise. Coming along toward him was Beezer the journalist, talking animatedly to a man in shirtsleeves. Beezer chewed the end of a tiny cigar and waved his arms to illustrate a story that he told with particular venom. He seemed unnaturally excited, although St. Ives had to remind himself that he was almost entirely unfamiliar with the man—perhaps he always gestured and railed so.

St. Ives fell in behind the two, making no effort to conceal himself. Hasbro and Jack Owlesby stood in the shadows two blocks farther along, in an alley past Whitefriars. There was precious little time to waste. Occasional strollers passed; the abduction would have to be quick and subtle. "Excuse me," St. Ives said at the man's back. "Mr. Beezer is it, the journalist?"

The two men stopped, looking back at St. Ives. Beezer's hands fell to his side. "At's right, Pappy," came the reply. Beezer squinted at him, as if ready to doubt the existence of such a wild figure on the evening street.

"My name, actually, is Penrod," said St. Ives. "Jules Penrod. You've apparently mistaken me for someone else. I have one of the twelve common faces."

Beezer's companion burst into abrupt laughter at the idea. Beezer, however, seemed impatient at the interruption. "Face like yours is a pity," he said, nudging his companion in the abdomen with his elbow. "Suits a beggar, though. I haven't got a thing for you, Pappy. Go scrub yourself with a sponge." And with that the two of them turned and made away, the second man laughing again and Beezer gesturing.

"One moment, sir!" cried St. Ives, pursuing the pair. "We've got a mutual friend."

Beezer turned and scowled, chewing his cigar slowly and thoughtfully now. He stared carefully at St. Ives's unlikely visage and shook his head. "No, we don't," he said, "unless it's the devil. Any other friend of yours would've hung himself by now out of regret. Why don't you disappear into the night, Pappy, before I show you the shine on my boot?"

"You're right, as far as it goes," said St. Ives, grinning inwardly.

"I'm a friend of Dr. Ignacio Narbondo, in fact. He's sent me round with another communication."

Beezer squinted at him. The word *another* hadn't jarred him.

"Is that right?" he said.

St. Ives bowed, clapping a hand hastily onto the top of his head to hold his wig on.

"Bugger off, will you, Clyde?" Beezer said to his friend.

"That drink…" came the reply.

"Stow your drink. I'll see you tomorrow. We'll drink two. Now get along."

The man turned away regretfully, despondent over the lost drink perhaps, and St. Ives waited to speak until he had crossed Whitefriars and his footsteps faded. Then he nodded to the still-scowling Beezer and set out on the sidewalk again, looking up and down the street as if to discern anything suspicious or threatening. Beezer fell in beside him. "It's about the money," said St. Ives.

"The money?"

"Narbondo fears that he promised you too much of it."

"He's a filthy cheat!" cried Beezer, eliminating any doubts that St. Ives might have had about Beezer's having received Narbondo's message, mailed days past from Dover.

"He's discovered," continued St. Ives, "that there are any of a number of journalists who will sell out the people of London for half the sum. Peabody at the *Herald*, for instance, has agreed to cooperate."

"The filthy scum-sucking cheat!" Beezer shouted, waving a fist at St. Ives's nose. "Peabody!"

"Tut, tut," admonished St. Ives, noting with a surge of anxious anticipation the darkened mouth of the alley some thirty feet distant. "We haven't contracted with Peabody yet. It was merely a matter of feeling out the temperature of the water, so to speak. You understand. You're a businessman yourself in a way." St. Ives gestured broadly with his left hand as if to signify that a man like Beezer could be expected to take the long view. With his right he reached across and snatched the lapels of Beezer's coat, yanking him sideways. Simultaneously he whipped his left hand around and slammed the startled journalist square in the back, catapulting him into the ill-lit alley.

"Hey!" shouted Beezer, tripping forward into the waiting arms of Jack Owlesby, who leaped in to pinion the man's wrists. Hasbro, waving an enormous burlap bag, appeared from the shadows and flung the bag like a gill net over Beezer's head, St. Ives yanking it down across the man's back and pushing him forward off his feet. Hasbro snatched at the drawrope, grasped Beezer's shoulders, and hissed through the canvas, "Cry out and you're a dead man!"

The struggling Beezer collapsed like a sprung balloon, having an antipathy, apparently, to being a dead man. Jack clambered up onto the bed of a wagon, hauled open the lid of a steamer trunk, and, along with St. Ives and Hasbro, yanked and shoved and grappled the feebly struggling journalist into the wood and leather prison. He banged ineffectively a half-dozen times at the sides of the trunk, mewling miserably, then fell silent as the wagon rattled and bounced along the alley, exiting on Salisbury Court and making away south toward the Thames.

A half hour later the wagon had doubled back through Soho, St. Ives having set such a course toward Chingford that Beezer couldn't begin to guess it out from within his trunk. Hasbro, always prepared, had uncorked a bottle of whiskey, and each of the three men held a glass, lost in his own thoughts about the warm April night and the dangers of their mission. "Sorry to bring you in on this, Jack," said St. Ives. "There might quite likely be the devil to pay before we're through. No telling what sort of a row our man Beezer might set up."

"I'm not complaining," Jack said.

"It was Dorothy I was thinking about, actually. We're only weeks finished with the pig incident, and I've hauled you away again. There she sits in Kensington wondering what sort of nonsense I've drummed up now. She's a stout woman, if you don't mistake my meaning."

Jack nodded, glancing sideways at St. Ives, whose voice had gotten heavy with the sound of regret. St. Ives seemed always to be on the edge of a precipice, standing with his back to it and pretending he couldn't see that it was there, waiting for him to take an innocent step backward. Work furiously—that had become the byword for St. Ives, and it was a better thing, perhaps, than to go to pieces, except that there was something overwound about St. Ives sometimes that made Jack wonder if it wouldn't be better for him to try to see into the depths of that pit that stretched out behind him, to let his eyes adjust to the darkness so that he might make out the shadows down there.

But then Jack was settled in Kensington with Dorothy, living out what must look to St. Ives like a sort of storybook existence. The professor couldn't help but see that Dorothy and Alice had been a lot alike, and Jack's happiness must have magnified St. Ives's sorrow. If Dorothy knew, in fact, what sort of business they pursued this time, she probably would have insisted on coming along. Jack thought of her fondly. "Do you know…," he began, reminiscing, but the sound of Beezer pummeling the sides of the trunk cut him off.

"Tell the hunchback!" shrieked a muffled voice, "that I'll have him horsewhipped! He'll be sulking in Newgate Prison again by the end of the week, by God! There's nothing about him I don't know!"

St. Ives shrugged at Hasbro. Here, perhaps, was a stroke of luck. If Beezer could be convinced that they actually *were* agents of Narbondo, it would go no little way toward throwing the man off their scent when the affair was over, especially if he went to the authorities with his tale. Beezer hadn't, after all, committed any crime, nor did he contemplate one—no crime, that is, beyond the crime against humanity, against human decency. "Narbondo has authorized us to eliminate you if we see fit," said St. Ives, hunching over the trunk. "If you play along here you'll be well paid; if you struggle, you'll find yourself counting fishes in the rocks off Southend Pier." The journalist fell silent.

Early in the predawn morning the wagon rattled into Chingford and made for the hills beyond, where lay the cottage of Sam Langley, son of St. Ives's longtime cook. The cottage was dark, but a lamp burned through the slats in the locked shutters of a low window in an unused silo fifty yards off. St. Ives reined in the horses, clambering out of the wagon at once, and with the help of his two companions, hauled the steamer trunk off the tailgate and into the unfastened door of the silo. Jack Owlesby and Hasbro hastened back out into the night, and for a moment through the briefly open door, St. Ives could see Sam Langley stepping off his kitchen porch, pulling on a coat. The door shut, and St. Ives was alone in the feebly lit room with the trunk and scattered pieces of furniture.

"I'm going to unlock the trunk…," St. Ives began.

"You sons of…," Beezer started to shout, but St. Ives rapped against the lid with his knuckles to silence him.

"I'm either going to unlock the trunk or set it afire," said St. Ives with great deliberation. "The choice is yours." The trunk was silent. "Once the trunk is unlocked, you can quite easily extricate yourself. The bag isn't knotted. You've probably already discovered that. My advice to you is to stay absolutely still for ten minutes. Then you can thrash and shriek and stamp about until you collapse. No one will hear you. You'll be happy to know that a sum of money will be advanced to your account, and that you'll have a far easier time spending it if you're not shot full of holes. Don't, then, get impatient. You've ridden out the night in the trunk; you can stand ten minutes more." Beezer, it seemed, had seen reason, for as St. Ives crouched out into the night, shook hands hastily with Langley, leaped into the wagon, and took up the reins, nothing but silence emanated from the stones of the silo.

—◦◦◦—

Two evenings earlier, on the night that St. Ives had waylaid Beezer the journalist, the comet had appeared in the eastern sky, ghostly and round like the moon reflected on a frosty window—just a circular patch of faint luminous cloud. But now it seemed fearfully close, as if it would drop out of the heavens toward the earth like a plumb bob toward a melon. St. Ives's telescope, with its mirror of speculum metal, had been a gift from Lord Rosse himself, and he peered into the eyepiece now, tracking the flight of the comet for no other reason, really, than to while away the dawn hours. He slept only fitfully these days, and his dreams weren't pleasant.

There was nothing to calculate; work of that nature had been accomplished weeks past by astronomers whose knowledge of astral mathematics was sufficient to satisfy both the Royal Academy and Dr. Ignacio Narbondo. St. Ives wouldn't dispute their figures. That the comet would spin dangerously close to the earth was the single point that all of them agreed upon. His desire in watching the icy planetoid, beyond a simple fascination with the mystery and wonder of the thing, was to have a look at the face of what might easily be his last great nemesis, a vast leviathan swimming toward them through a dark sea. He wondered if it was oblivion that was revealed by the turning earth.

Hasbro packed their bags in the manor. Their train left Kirk Hammerton Station at six. Dr. Narbondo, St. Ives had to assume, would discover that same morning that he had been foiled, that Beezer, somehow, had failed him. The morning *Times* would rattle in on the Dover train, ignorant of pending doom. The doctor would try to contact the nefarious Beezer, but Beezer wouldn't be found. He's taken ill, they would say on Fleet Street, repeating the substance of the letter St. Ives had sent off to Beezer's employers. Beezer, they'd assure Narbondo, had been ordered south on holiday—to the coast of Spain. Narbondo's forehead would wrinkle with suspicion, and the wrinkling would engender horrible curses and the gnashing of teeth. St. Ives almost smiled. The doctor would know who had thwarted him.

But the result would be, quite likely, the immediate removal of Narbondo and Hargreaves to the environs of northwestern Scandinavia. The chase, thought St. Ives tiredly, would be on. The comet loomed only a few days away, barely enough time for them to accomplish their task.

A door slammed in the manor. St. Ives slipped from his stool and looked out through the west-facing window of his observatory, waving to Hasbro who, in the roseate light of an early dawn, dangled a pocket watch from a chain and nodded to his employer. In a half hour they were away, scouring along the highroad toward the station in Kirk Hammerton, where St. Ives, Hasbro, and Jack Owlesby would leave for Ramsgate and the dirigible that would transport them to the ice and tundra of arctic Norway. If the labors of Bill Kraken were unsuccessful, if he couldn't sabotage

Lord Kelvin's frightful machine, they would all know about it, along with the rest of suffering humanity, two days hence.

—◦◦◦—

BILL KRAKEN CROUCHED in the willows along the River Nidd, watching through the lacey tendrils the dark bulk of Lord Kelvin's barn. The device had been finished two days earlier, the ironic result, to a degree, of his own labor—labor he wouldn't be paid for. But money wasn't of particular consequence anymore, not like it had been in the days of his squid merchanting or when he'd been rescued from the life of a lowly peapod man by the charitable Langdon St. Ives.

Kraken sighed. Poor St. Ives. There was suffering and there was suffering. Kraken had never found a wife, had never fathered children. He had been cracked on the head more often than he could remember, but so what? That kind of damage could be borne. The sort of blow that had struck St. Ives, though—that was a different thing, and Kraken feared sometimes that it would take a heavy toll on the great man before they all won through. Kraken wanted for nothing now, not really, beyond seeing St. Ives put right again.

In a cloth bag beside him wriggled a dozen snakes, collected from the high grass beyond the manor house. In a wire-screen cage beneath the snakes was a score of mice, hungry, as were the snakes, from days of neglect. A leather bellows dangled from his belt, and a hooded lantern from his right hand. No one else was on the meadow.

The Royal Academy had been glad to be quit of Ignacio Narbondo, who had taken ship for Oslo to effect his preposterous machinations. That was the rumor around Lord Kelvin's barn. The Academy would reduce his threats to drivel now that the machine was built. Why Narbondo hadn't followed through with his plan to alert the press no one could say, but it seemed to Secretary Parsons to be evidence that his threats were mere bluff. And that crackpot St. Ives had given up, too, thank God. All this had lightened the atmosphere considerably. A sort of holiday air had sprung up around what had been a business fraught with suspicion and doubt. Now the Academy was free to act without impediment

Kraken bent out from under the willows and set out across the meadow carrying his bundles. It would do no good to run. He was too old to be cutting capers on a meadow in the dead of night, and if he tripped and dropped his mice or knocked his lantern against a stone, his plan would be foiled utterly. In an hour both the moon and the comet would have appeared on the horizon and the meadow would be bathed in light. If he was sensible, he'd be asleep in his bed by then.

The dark bulk of the barn loomed before him, the pale stones of its foundation contrasting with the weathered oak battens above. Kraken ducked along the wall toward a tiny mullioned window beneath which extended the last six inches of the final section of brass pipe—the very pipe that Kraken himself had wrestled through a hole augered into the barn wall on that first day he'd helped Lord Kelvin align the things.

What, exactly, the pipe was intended to accomplish, Kraken couldn't say, but somehow it was the focal point of the workings of the device. Beyond, some twenty feet from the barn and elevated on a stone slab, sat a black monolith, smooth as polished marble. Kraken had been amazed when, late the previous afternoon, Lord Kelvin had flung a ball peen hammer end over end at the monolith, and the collected workmen and scientists had gasped in wonder when the hammer had been soundlessly reflected with such force that it had sailed out of sight in the general direction of York. That the hammer had fallen to earth again, not a man of them could say. The reversal of the poles was to be accomplished, then, by emanating toward this monolith the collected magnetic rays developed in Lord Kelvin's machine, thus both exciting and deflecting them in a circuitous pattern, and sending them off, as it were, astride a penny whirligig. It was too much for Kraken to fathom, but Lord Kelvin and his peers were the giants of electricity and mechanics. A job like this had been child's play to them. Their heads weren't like the heads of other men.

Kraken squinted through the darkness at the monolith, doubly black against the purple of the starry night sky, and wondered at the remarkable perspicacity of great scientists. Here sat the impossible machine, primed for acceleration on the morrow. Could Kraken, a man of admittedly low intellect, scuttle the marvelous device? Kraken shook his head, suddenly full of doubt. He had been entrusted with little else than the material salvation of humanity…Well, Kraken was just a small man with a small way of doing things. He had seen low times in his life, had mucked through sewers with murderers, and so he would have to trust to low means here. That was the best he could do.

He quit breathing and cocked an ear. Nothing but silence and the distant hooting of an owl greeted him on the night air. He untied the bellows from his belt and shook them by his ear. Grain and broken biscuits rattled within. He shoved the mouth of the bellows into the end of the brass tube and pumped furiously, listening to the debris clatter away, down the tilted pipe. Long after the last of the grain had been blown clear of the bellows, Kraken continued to manipulate his instrument, desperate to send the bulk of it deep into the bowels of the apparatus. Haste would avail him nothing here.

Finally satisfied, he tied the bellows once again to his belt and picked up the mouse cage. The beasts were tumultuous with excitement, stimulated, perhaps, by the evening constitutional, or sensing somehow that they were on the brink of an adventure of powerful magnitude. Kraken pressed the cage front against the end of the tube and pulled open its little door. The mice scurried around in apparent amazement, casting wild glances here and there, curious about a heap of shredded newspaper or the pink ear of a neighbor. Then, one by one, they filed away down the tube like cattle down a hill, sniffing the air, intent suddenly on biscuits and grain.

The snakes were a comparatively easy case. A round dozen of the beasts slithered away down the tube in the wake of the mice, anxious to be quit of their sack. Kraken wondered if he hadn't ought to wad the sack up and shove it into the tube, too, in order to make absolutely sure that the beasts remained trapped inside. But the dangers of doing that were manifold. Lord Kelvin or some particularly watchful guard might easily discover the stopper before Kraken had a chance to remove it. They mustn't, said St. Ives, discover that the sabotage had been the work of men—thus the mice and snakes. It might easily seem that the natural residents of the barn had merely taken up lodgings there, and thus the hand of Langdon St. Ives would go undetected.

It was very nearly within the hour that Bill Kraken climbed into bed. But his dreams were filled that night with visions of mice and snakes dribbling from the end of the tube and racing away into the darkness, having consumed the grain and leaving nothing behind sufficient to foul the workings of the dread machine. What could he do, though, save trust to providence? The shame of his failure—if failure it should be—would likely be as nothing next to the horrors that would beset them after Lord Kelvin's success. God bless the man, thought Kraken philosophically. He pictured the aging lord, laboring night and day to complete his engine, certain that he was contributing his greatest gift yet to humankind. His disappointment would be monumental. It seemed almost worth the promised trouble to let the poor man have a try at it. But that, sadly, wouldn't do. The world was certainly a sorrowful and contradictory place. —◦

Norway

THE BRIGHT APRIL weather had turned stormy and dark by the time St. Ives and Hasbro had chuffed into Dover, and the North Sea was a tumult of wind-tossed waves and driving rain. St. Ives huddled now aboard the Ostende ferry, out of the rain beneath an overhanging deck ledge and wrapped in an oilcloth, legs spread to counter the heaving swell. His pipe burned like a chimney, and as he peered out at the roiling black of the heavens, equally cloudy thoughts drew his eyes into a squint and made him oblivious to the cold and wet. Had this sudden turn of arctic weather anything to do with the experimentation of the Royal Academy? Had they effected the reversal of the poles prematurely and driven the weather suddenly mad? Had Kraken failed? He watched a gray swell loom overhead, threatening to slam the ferry apart, only to sink suddenly into nothing as if having changed its mind, and then tower up once again overhead, sheets of flying foam torn from its crest and rendered into spindrift by the wind.

His plans seemed to be fast going wrong. The dirigible he had counted upon for transport had been "inoperable." The fate of the earth itself hung in the balance, and the filthy dirigible was "inoperable." They would all be inoperable by the end of the week. Jack Owlesby had stayed on in Ramsgate where a crew of nitwits fiddled with the craft, and so yet another variable, as the mathematician would say, had been cast into the muddled stew. Could the dirigible be made operable in time? Would Jack, along with the flea-brained pilot, find them in the cold wastes of arctic Norway? It didn't bear thinking about. One thing at a time, St. Ives reminded himself. They had left Jack with a handshake and a compass and had raced south intending to follow Narbondo overland, trusting to Jack to take care of himself.

But where was Ignacio Narbondo? He must have set sail from Dover with Hargreaves hours earlier, apparently under a false name—except that the ticket agent could find no record of his having boarded the Ostende ferry. St. Ives had described him vividly: the hump, the tangle of oily hair, the cloak. No one could remember having seen him board. He might have got on unseen in the early morning, of course.

It was conceivable, just barely, that St. Ives had made a monumental error, or that Narbondo had tricked the lot of them, had been one up on them all along. He might at that moment be bound, say, for Reykjavik, intent on working his deviltry on the volcanic wastes of the interior of Iceland. He might be sitting in a comfortable chair in London, laughing into his hat. What would St. Ives do then? Keep going, like a windup tin soldier on the march. He could imagine himself simply ambling away into Scandinavian forests, circling aimlessly through the trees like a dying reindeer.

But then in Ostende the rain let up and the wind fell off, and the solid ground beneath his feet once again lent him a steadiness of purpose. In the cold station, a woman stirred a caldron of mussels, dumping in handfuls of shallots and lumps of butter. Aromatic steam swirled out of the iron pot in such a way as to make St. Ives lightheaded. "Mussels and beer," he said to Hasbro, "would revive a body."

"That they would, sir. And a loaf of bread, I might add, to provide bulk."

"A sound suggestion," said St. Ives, striding toward the woman and removing his hat. He liked the look of her immediately. She was stooped and heavy and wore a dress like a tent, and it seemed as if all the comets in the starry heavens couldn't knock her off her pins. She dumped mussels, black and dripping, into a cleverly folded newspaper basket, heaping up the shells until they threatened to cascade to the floor. She winked at St. Ives, fished an enormous mussel from the pot, slid her thumbs into the hiatus of its open shell, and in a single swift movement pulled the mollusk open, shoved one of her thumbs under the orange flesh, and flipped the morsel into her open mouth. "Some don't chew them," she said, speaking English, "but I do. What's the use of eating at all if you don't chew them? Might as well swallow a toad."

"Indubitably," said St. Ives, happy enough to make small talk. "It's the same way with oysters. I never could stand simply to allow the creatures to slide down my throat. I fly in the face of custom there."

"Aye," she said. "Can you imagine a man's stomach, full of beasts such as these, whole, mind you, and sloshin' like smelts in a bucket?" She dipped again into the caldron, picked out another mussel, and ate it with relish, then grimaced and rooted in her mouth with a finger. "Mussel pearl," she said, holding up between thumb and forefinger a tiny opalescent sphere twice the size of a pinhead. She slid open a little drawer in the cart on which sat the caldron of mussels, and dropped the pearl in among what must have been thousands of the tiny orbs. "Can't stand debris," she said, grimacing.

The entire display rather took the edge off St. Ives's appetite, and the heap of mussels in his basket, reclining beneath a coating of congealing butter and bits of garlic and shallot, began to remind him of certain unfortunate suppers he'd consumed at the Bayswater Club. He grinned weakly at the woman and looked around at the hurrying crowds, wondering if he and Hasbro hadn't ought to join them.

"Man in here this afternoon ate one shell and all," she said, shaking her head. "Imagine the debris involved. Must have given his throat bones some trouble, I daresay."

"Shell and all?" asked St. Ives.

"That's the exact case. Crunched away at the thing like it was a marzipan crust, didn't he? Then he took another, chewed it up about halfway, saw what he was about, and spit the filthy thing against the wall there. You can see bits of it still, can't you, despite the birds swarming round. There's the smear of it against the stones. Do you see it there?—bit of brown paste is all it amounts to now."

St. Ives stared at the woman. "Big man?"

"Who?"

"This fellow who ate the shells. Big, was he, and with a beard? Seemed ready to fly into a rage?"

"That's your man, gents. Cursed vilely, he did, but not at the shells. It was at the poor birds, wasn't it, when they come round to eat up what your man spit onto the wall there. You can see it there, can't you? I never..."

"Was he in the company of a hunchback?"

"Aye," said the woman, giving her pot a perfunctory stirring. "Greasy little man with a grin. Seemed to think the world is a lark. But it ain't no lark, gentlemen. Here you've been, wasting my time this quarter hour, and not another living soul has bought a shell. You've frightened the lot of them off, is what I think, and you haven't paid me a penny." She glowered at St. Ives, then glowered at Hasbro.

"What time this afternoon?" asked St. Ives.

"Three hours past, say, or four. Might have been five. Or less."

"Thank you." St. Ives reached into his pocket for a coin. He dumped a half crown into her outstretched hand and left her blinking, he and Hasbro racing through the terminal toward the distant exit, each of them clutching a bag in one hand and a paper satchel of mussels in the other. The streets were wet outside, but the clouds were broken overhead and taking flight in the gray dusk, and the wind had simmered down to a billowy breeze. A bent man shambled past in trousers meant for a behemoth, clutching at a buttonless coat. St. Ives thrust his mussels at the man, meaning to do him a good turn, but his gesture was mistaken. The man cast him a look of mingled surprise and loathing, fetching the basket a swipe with his hand that sent the entire affair into the gutter. St. Ives hurried on without a word, marveling at misunderstood humanity and at how little space existed between apparent madness and the best of intentions.

In a half hour they were aboard a train once again, in a sleeping car bound for Amsterdam, Hamburg, and finally, to Hjørring, where on the Denmark ferry they'd once again set sail across the North Sea, up the Oslofjord into Norway.

St. Ives was determined to remain awake, to have a look at the comet when it sailed in over the horizon sometime after midnight. But the sleepless nights he had spent in the observatory and the long hours of travel since had worn him thin, and after a tolerable meal in the dining car, and what might likely turn out to be, on the morrow, a regrettable lot of brandy, he dropped away at once into a deep sleep, and the comet rose in the sky and fell again without him, slanting past the captive earth.

In Oslo Hargreaves had beaten a man half senseless with the man's own cane. In Trondheim, two hours before the arrival of St. Ives and Hasbro on the express, he had run mad and threatened to explode a greengrocer's cart, kicking the spokes out of one of the wheels before Narbondo had hauled him away and explained to the authorities that his companion was a lunatic bound for a sanitorium in Narvik.

St. Ives itched to be after them, but here he sat, becalmed in a small brick railway station. He stared impatiently out the window at the nearly empty station. A delay of a minute seemed an eternity, and each sighing release of steam from the waiting train carried upon it the suggestion of the final, fateful explosion. Hasbro, St. Ives could see, was equally uneasy at their motionless state, for he sat hunched forward on his seat as if trying to compel the train into flight. Finally, amid tooting and whooshing and three false starts, they were away again, St. Ives praying that the engineer had understood his translated request that they make an unscheduled stop on the deserted tundra adjacent to Mount Hjarstaad. Surely he would; he had accepted the little bag of assorted coffee tablets readily enough. What could he have understood them to be but payment?

Darkness had long since fallen, and with it had fled the last of the scattered rain showers. Ragged clouds pursued by arctic wind capered across the sky, and the stars shone thick and bright between. The train developed steam after puffing along lazily up a steepening grade, and within a score of minutes was hurtling through the mountainous countryside.

St. Ives was gripped once more with the excitement and peril of the chase. He removed his pocket watch at intervals, putting it back without so much as glancing at it, then loosening his already-loosened collar, peering out across the rocky landscape at the distant swerve of track ahead when the train lurched into a curve, as if the engine they pursued must surely be visible a half mile farther on.

The slow labored climb of steep hills was almost instantly maddening and filled him again with the fear that their efforts would prove futile, that from the vantage point of the next peak they would witness the detonation of half of Scandinavia: crumbling mountainsides, hurtling rocks. But then they would creep, finally, to another summit void of trees, where the track was wafered onto ledges along unimaginable precipices. And the train would plunge away again in a startling rush of steam and clatter.

They thundered through shrieking tunnels, the starry sky going momentarily black and then reappearing in an instant only to be dashed again into darkness. And when the train burst each time into the cold Norwegian night, both St. Ives and Hasbro were pressed against the window, peering skyward, relieved to see the last scattered clouds fleeing before the wind. Then all at once, as if waved into existence by a magic wand, the lights of the aurora borealis swept across the sky in lacey showers of green and red and blue, like a semitransparent Christmas tapestry hung across the wash of stars.

"Yes!" cried St. Ives, leaping to his feet and nearly pitching into the aisle as they rushed howling into another tunnel. "He's done it! Kraken has done it!"

"Indeed, sir?"

"Absolutely," said St. Ives, his voice animated. "Without the shadow of a doubt. The northern lights, my good fellow, are a consequence of the earth's electromagnetic field. It's a simple matter—no field, no lights. Had Lord Kelvin's machine done its work, the display you see before us would have been postponed for heaven knows how many woeful years. But here it is, isn't it? Good old Bill!" And on this last cheerful note, they emerged once again into the aurora-lit night, hurtling along beside a broad cataract that tumbled down through a boulder-strewn gorge.

Another hour's worth of tunnels, however, began to make it seem finally as if there were no end to their journey, as if, perhaps, their train labored around and around a clever circular track, that they had been monumentally hoaxed one last fateful time by Dr. Ignacio Narbondo. Then, in an effort of steam, the train crested yet another treeless summit, and away to the west, far below them, moonlight shimmered on the rippled surface of a fjord, stretching out to the distant Norwegian Sea. Tumbling down out of the rocky precipices to their right rushed the wild river they had followed for what seemed an age, the torrent wrapping round the edge of Mount Hjarstaad and disappearing into shadow where it cascaded, finally, into the vast emptiness of an abyss. A trestle spanned the cataract and gave out onto a tundra-covered plain, scattered with the angular moon shadows of tilted stones.

Ahead of them, some ten yards from the track and clearly visible in the moonlight, lay a strange and alien object—an empty steamer trunk, its lid thrown back and its contents removed. Beyond that, a hundred yards farther along, lay another, also empty and yanked over onto its side. The train raced past both before howling to a steam-shrieking stop that made St. Ives wince. So much for subtlety, he thought, as Hasbro pitched their bags onto the icy plain and the two leaped out after them, the train almost immediately setting forth again, north, toward Hammerfest, leaving the world and the two marooned men to their collective fate.

St. Ives hurried across the plain toward the slope of Mount Hjarstaad. A footpath wound upward along the edge of the precipice through which the river thundered and roiled. The air was full of cold mist and the booming of water. "I'm afraid we've announced our arrival through a megaphone," St. Ives shouted over his shoulder.

"Perhaps the roar of the falls...," said Hasbro at St. Ives's back. But the rest of his words was lost in the watery tumult as the two men hurried up the steepening hill, keeping to the edge of the trail and the deep shadows of the steep rocky cliffs.

St. Ives patted his coat, feeling beneath it the hard foreign outline of his revolver. He realized that he was cold, almost numbed, but that the cold wasn't only a result of the wet arctic air. He was struck with the overwhelming feeling that he was replaying his most common and fearful nightmare, and the misty water of the falls seemed to him suddenly to be the rain out of a London sky. He could hear in the echoing crash the sound of horse's hooves on paving stones and the crack of pistols fired in deadly haste.

The revolver in his waistband suddenly was almost repulsive to him, as if it were a poisonous reptile and not a thing built of brass and steel. The notion of shooting it at any living human being seemed both an utter impossibility and an utter necessity. His faith in the rational and the logical had been replaced by a mass of writhing contradictions and half-understood notions of revenge and salvation that were as confused as the unfathomable roar of the maelstrom in the chasm.

There was a shout behind him. A crack like a pistol shot followed, and St. Ives was pushed from behind. He rolled against a carriage-sized boulder, throwing his hands over his head as a hail of stones showered down around him, and an enormous rock, big as a cartwheel, bounded over his head, soaring away into the misty depths of the abyss.

·   He pushed himself to his knees, feeling Hasbro's grip on his elbow, and he peered up into the shadowy gloom above. There, leaping from perch to rocky perch, was a man with wild hair and beard—Hargreaves, there could be little doubt. Hasbro drew his revolver, steadied his forearm along the top of a rock, and fired twice at the retreating figure. His bullets pinged off rocks twenty feet short of their mark, but the effect on the anarchist was startling—as if he had been turned suddenly into a mountain sheep. He disappeared on the instant, hidden by boulders.

St. Ives forced himself to his feet, pressing himself against the stony wall of the path. Hasbro tapped his shoulder and gestured first at himself and then at the mountainside. St. Ives nodded as his friend angled away up a rocky defile, climbing slowly and solidly upward. He watched Hasbro disappear among the granite boulders, and for a moment he felt the urge to sit down right there in the dirt and wait for him.

He couldn't do that, though. There was too much at stake. And there was Alice to think of. Always there was Alice to think of. If revenge was the compelling motive for him now, so what? He had to call upon something to move him up the path; it might as well be raw hatred.

He sidled along carefully, grimly imagining himself following the course of the rock that had plummeted over his head moments ago. Icy dirt crunched underfoot, and the hillside opened up briefly on his right to reveal a wide, steep depression in the rock—a sort of conical hole at the bottom of which lay a black, silent tarn. The water of the tarn brimmed with reflected stars that were washed with the blue-red light of the aurora. It was a scene of unearthly beauty, and it reminded him of the alluring darkness of pure sleep.

Abruptly he jerked himself away and climbed farther up the trail, rounding a sharp bend. He could see high above him the mouth of the smoking crater. Perched on the rim and hauling on the coils of a mechanical bladder was the venomous Dr. Narbondo, the steamy reek of boiling mud swirling about his head and shoulders. Hargreaves capered like a lunatic beside him, dancing from one foot to the other like a man treading on hot pavement.

They were too distant to shoot at, but St. Ives compelled himself to take the pistol out of his waistband anyway. Calmly and with a will, he began to sing "God Save the Queen" in a low voice. It didn't matter what song—what he needed was a melody and a set of verses with which to sweep his mind clear of rubble. Narbondo worked furiously, looking back over his shoulder, scanning the rocky mountainside. There was nothing for St. Ives to do but step out into the open and rush up the path toward the two of them. It might be futile, exposing himself like that…He sang louder, but the thought that Hargreaves would simply kill him caused him to scramble the words, and for a moment he considered going back down to where Hasbro had cut off into the rocks, maybe following his friend's trail. But that would be a retreat, and he couldn't allow that.

He cocked his pistol and stepped forward in a crouch. Hargreaves grappled now with a carpetbag, pulling out unidentifiable bits and pieces of mechanical debris, which he fumbled with, trying to assemble them. His curses reached St. Ives on the wind. Narbondo raged beside him, turning once again to survey the rocks behind and below him. He looked straight down into St. Ives's face. Despite the distance, his expression was clear in the moonlight; hatred and fear and passion played across his features, and for a moment he stood stock-still, as if he had seen his fate standing there below him.

A pistol shot rang out, echoing away somewhere among the rocks, and Narbondo spun half around, grabbing his shoulder and shouting a curse. He worked his arm up and down as if testing it, and then pushed Hargreaves aside, tearing at the contents of the bag himself and shouting orders. Hargreaves immediately disappeared behind a tumble of rocks, and St. Ives scrambled for cover as the anarchist popped up almost at once to shoot wildly down at him. Another shot followed close on, and for an instant St. Ives saw Hasbro leaping across a granite slope, only to disappear again when Hargreaves spun around and fired at him.

St. Ives stood and darted up the path, breathing heavily in the thin air. There was the sound of another gunshot just as a spatter of granite chips sprayed into his face, nearly blinding him. He blinked and spit, creeping along until he could see Hargreaves above him, looking down. Hargreaves dropped like a stone, then stood up at once and fired again twice, the bullets pinging off the rocks beside St. Ives's head.

St. Ives yanked himself down, the smell of powdered granite in his nose. He smiled grimly, wiping at his watering eyes, the sudden danger surging over him like a sea wave, washing away his muddled doubts. He stood up to draw Hargreaves's fire, ducking immediately and hearing two shots, one after another, from Hargreaves and Hasbro both. He stood again, resting his forearm across the cold stone and setting up to fire carefully now. Hargreaves set out at a run, down and across the rocks. But he was too far away and moving too fast, and St. Ives was no kind of marksman. He waited too long, and his man again disappeared.

St. Ives stepped at once out onto the path, half expecting a bullet and half expecting Hasbro to provide covering fire. There sounded two more shots, from roughly the same direction, but St. Ives forced himself to ignore them, intent now on Narbondo, who worked madly, casting futile glances down at him and bellowing for Hargreaves, the roar of the falls drowning his words before they reached St. Ives, who ran straight up the path, leveling his pistol. He hadn't bothered to reload after the last couple of shots, but somehow it didn't matter to him. What he wanted now was to put his hands on Narbondo's throat. He had failed once before; he wouldn't fail again.

There was a warning shout, though—Hasbro's voice—and St. Ives turned to see Hargreaves scrambling toward him, ignoring Hasbro, who stood like a statue, his pistol raised and pointed at Hargreaves's back. Narbondo was oblivious to them all, as if he would cheerfully die rather than give up his loathsome dream. He peered suddenly skyward, though, his forearm thrown across his brow as if to shade his eyes from moonlight. St. Ives followed Narbondo's gaze, and there, below the moon, dropping past the pale blue wash of the aurora, drifted the dark ovoid silhouette of a descending dirigible.

St. Ives bolted forward, as if the sight of it had brought the world to him once again, had reminded him that he wasn't a solitary man facing a solitary villain, but that there was such a thing as duty and honor…He heard the crack of Hargreaves's pistol almost at the same time that the bullet struck him in the shoulder. He cried out and dropped to his knees, his revolver spinning away into the void on the opposite side of the path as he scuttled like a crab down again into the shelter of the rocks.

A shriek followed, and St. Ives looked up to see Hargreaves dancing next to Narbondo now, the two of them shouting and cursing. Hasbro stepped determinedly toward them as Narbondo furiously worked a mechanical detonator. It was too late for him, though, and he knew it. He hadn't had enough time. St. Ives was full of something like happiness, although it was cold and cheerless, and he stepped out onto the path again, gripping his bleeding shoulder.

Hargreaves raised his hand to shoot at Hasbro. But there was no sound at all, even though the man continued to pull the trigger. He pitched the gun away from him in disgust, picking up the carpetbag as if he would fling it into Hasbro's face. He turned with it, though, and slammed Narbondo in the back, roaring nonsense at him. Hasbro stood still twenty feet below them, his arm upraised, and shot Hargreaves carefully and steadily.

The anarchist lurched round, teetered for a moment on the edge of the crater, and then toppled off, disappearing into the mouth of the volcano as Narbondo made one last futile grab at the bag clutched in Hargreaves's flailing hand.

There was an instant when no one moved, all of them waiting, and then a thunderous explosion that rocked the mountainside—the volatile contents of the bag having been detonated by the fires of Mount Hjarstaad. The three men pitched to the ground as the explosion echoed away, replaced by the low roar of rocks tumbling toward the plain below. Hasbro was up at once, stepping toward the crater's edge, leveling his pistol at Narbondo, who stood still now, hangdog, his head bowed like that of a man defeated at the very moment of success. He raised his hands in resignation.

Then, without so much as a backward glance, he bolted down the footpath toward St. Ives, gathering momentum, running headlong at the surprised scientist. Hasbro spun around and tracked him with the pistol.

"Shoot!" St. Ives shouted, but a shot was out of the question unless he himself backed away, out of the line of fire. He scrambled back down the path toward the bend in the trail as Narbondo leaped along in great springing strides behind him, wild to escape, his face contorted now with fear and wonderment as he hurtled uncontrollably toward St. Ives. The scientist stopped to face him, but saw at once that Narbondo would run him down like an express train.

St. Ives turned and hurried downward, hearing Narbondo's footsteps slamming along and knowing he would be overtaken in seconds. The path widened just then, but turned sharply at the edge of the cliff, and St. Ives saw below him the waters of the starlit tarn, deadly still in the moonlight. In an instant he took it all in—Narbondo was moving too quickly. He would plummet off the edge of the path where it turned, hurtling into the abyss below. There was no hope for him.

And good riddance, St. Ives thought. But then, almost instinctively, he braced himself against two rocks, and as Narbondo raged past, St. Ives reached out to pull him down. He bulled past like a runaway express, though, and St. Ives, meaning to grab him by the arm, was slammed sideways instead, back into the rocks, managing only to knock Narbondo off-balance. His feet stuttered as he tried to stop himself, and then with a shriek he catapulted forward, away from the abyss, head over heels, caroming against a rock and then somersaulting like a circus acrobat across the steep scree-slippery slope until he plunged into the black waters of the tarn. The reflection of the moon and stars on the surface of the water disintegrated, the bits and pieces dancing wildly. But by the time Hasbro had made his way down to where St. Ives stood staring into the depths of the pool, the surface was lapping itself placid once again.

"He's gone," said St. Ives simply.

"Will he float surfaceward, sir?"

"Not necessarily," replied the scientist. "The fall must have knocked the wind from him. It might have killed him outright. He'll stay down until he bloats with gasses—until he begins to rot. And the water, I fear, is cold enough to slow the process substantially, perhaps indefinitely. We could wait a bit, just to be certain, but I very much fear that I've done too much waiting in my life."

Hasbro was silent.

"I might have saved him, there at the last," St. Ives said.

"Very doubtful, sir. I would cheerfully have shot him. And there'd be no use in saving him for the gallows. He wouldn't escape Newgate Prison a second time."

"What I wanted was to grab his arm, pull him down. But it seems I gave him a shove instead."

"And a very propitious shove, to my mind."

St. Ives looked at him tiredly. "I'm not sure I understand any of it," he said. "But it's over now. This part is." And with that St. Ives nodded at the horizon where glowed a great arc of white fire. As the two men watched, the flaming orb of the comet crept skyward, enormous now, as if it were soaring in to swallow the puny earth at a gulp.

Hasbro nodded quietly. "Shall we fetch their equipment, sir?"

"We'll want the lot of it," said St. Ives. "And to all appearances, we'll want it quickly. We've a long and wearisome journey ahead of us before we see the mountains of Peru." He sighed deeply. His shoulder began suddenly to ache. He turned one last time toward the tarn in which Narbondo had found an icy grave. His confrontation with Narbondo had rushed upon him, the work of a confused second, and had found him utterly unprepared, his actions futile. It almost seemed choreographed by some chaotic higher authority who meant to show him a thing or two about confusion and regret and what most often happened to man's best-laid plans.

Hasbro stood in silence, waiting, perhaps, for St. Ives to come once again to life. Finally he set off up the path toward the summit, to fetch Narbondo's apparatus and leaving St. Ives to welcome Jack Owlesby, whose hurried footfalls scuffed up the trail behind them. —◌

London

B ILL KRAKEN LEANED against the parapet on Waterloo Bridge and grinned into the Thames. Four pints of Bass Ale had banked and stoked the fires of good cheer within him. Tomorrow would see the return of his companions; tonight would see the ascent of the diminishing comet. It was nearing midnight as he finished reading the last half paragraph in his ruined copy of Ashbless's *Account of London Scientists,* happy to note that although the Royal Academy had never publicly recognized the genius of his benefactor, Ashbless had devoted the better half of his book to accounts of St. Ives's successes and adventures.

Kraken closed and pocketed the book. The adventure of Lord Kelvin's machine had ended nicely, if strangely, three afternoons past. The mice and snakes that had rained on Leeds like a Biblical plague had mystified the populace, from the unbelieving Lord Kelvin to the man in the street, taking flight in wondering speculation. The newspapers had been full of it. Every reporter with, perhaps, the exception of Beezer had set out to investigate the incident, but the Royal Academy had put the cap on it—had hushed it up, had hauled away the clogged machine in the night to dismantle it in secret.

Poor Lord Kelvin, thought Kraken, shaking his head. The odd sight of the rocketing beasts had rather unnerved him—perhaps more so even than the ruination of his device. And the muck clogging the tube just before the explosion...Kraken giggled. But his success wasn't entirely a cause for celebration. There were questions of a philosophic nature to be asked, for sure—questions concerning his lordship's manufactured failure and the sleepless nights of vain speculation that failure would engender, questions of the expendability of dumb animals for the sake of saving mankind. Kraken wasn't sure he liked either notion, but he liked the idea of a mutant future even less.

These scientists, thought Kraken, there was no telling what sorts of tricks they'd get up to, scampering like so many grinning devils astride an engine, laboring to turn the old earth inside out like a pair of trousers, one of them yanking at a pant leg with a calipers while another filled the pockets with numbers and gunpowder. And here on the horizon, slipping as if by magic into the sky, rose the comet, the stars paling round-about like lanterns enfeebled by sudden daylight.

Kraken tipped his hat at the sky and set out. He trudged past Westminster Pier and the Houses of Parliament and climbed into a waiting dogcart, pausing just a moment to look once again over his shoulder at the ascending comet. He took up the reins and shrugged, then reached out to pat the flank of his horse. Success, he thought to himself as he set out at a leisurely canter toward Chingford, is a relative business at best. —☙

PART II

The Downed Ships:
Jack Owlesby's Account

The Hansom Cab Lunatic

I WAS COMING ALONG down Holborn Hill in December, beneath a lowering sky and carrying a tin of biscuits and a pound of Brazilian coffee, when a warehouse exploded behind Perkins inn. Smoke and lumber and a twisted sheet of iron, torn nearly in half from the blast, blew out of the mouth of the alley between Kingsway and Newton Street and scattered the half-dozen pedestrians like autumn leaves.

I was clear of it, thank God, but even so the concussion threw me into the gutter, and I dropped the biscuits and coffee and found myself on the seat of my pants, watching a man stagger away from the explosion, out of the mouth of the alley to collapse bloody on the pavement.

I jumped up and ran for the man on the ground, thinking to help but really not thinking at all, when a second blast ripped through and slammed me against a bakery storefront. Glass shattered where my elbow went through the window, and then the rest of me followed, snapping the mullions and tumbling through in an avalanche of buns.

Directly there was another roar—not an explosion this time, but a roof caving in, and then a billow of black smoke pouring out of the alley and a fire that reminded you of the Gordon Riots. I could walk, if you call it that, and between the two of us, the baker and I, we pulled the bloody man across to where my coffee lay spilled out in the gutter. We needn't have bothered; he was dead, and we could both see it straight off, but you don't leave even a dead man to burn, not if you can help it.

I couldn't see worth anything all at once, because of the reek. It was a paper company gone up—a common enough tragedy, except that there was an element or two that made it markedly less common: Mr. Theophilus Godall was there, for one. Maybe you don't know what that means yet; maybe you do. And the paper company wasn't just any paper company; it was next door but one to an empty sort of machine works overseen by the Royal Academy, specifically as a sort of closed-to-the-public museum used to house the contrivances built by the great Lord Kelvin and the other inventive geniuses of the Academy.

—⁓—

MY NAME IS Jack Owlesby, and I'm a friend of Professor Langdon St. Ives, who is perhaps the greatest, mostly unsung, scientist and explorer in the Western Hemisphere. Mr. Oscar Wilde said something recently along the following lines: "Show me a hero," he said, "and I will write you a tragedy." He might have taken St. Ives as a case in point. I'm rather more inclined to enlarge upon the heroism, which is easier, and of which you have a remarkable surplus when you tackle a subject like Langdon St. Ives. You yourself might have read about some few of his exploits; and if you have, then I'll go as far as to tell you that this business of the exploding paper company won't turn out in the end to be altogether foreign to you.

As for Theophilus Godall, he owns the Bohemian Cigar Divan in Rupert Street, Soho; but there's more to the man than that.

—⁓—

LUCKILY THERE WAS a sharp wind blowing down Kingsway toward the Thames, which scoured the smoke skyward almost as soon as it flooded out of the alley, so that the street was clear enough in between billows. The blast brought a crowd, and they didn't stand and gawk, as crowds have got a reputation for. Two men even tried to get up the alley toward the fire, thinking that there might have been people trapped there or insensible, but the baker stopped them—and a good thing, too, as you'll see—pointing out quick that this being a Sunday the paper company was closed, as was everything else in that direction except Perkins Inn, which was safe enough for the moment. He had been out for a look, the baker had, not a minute before the explosion, and could tell us that aside from the dead man there hadn't been a soul dawdling in the alley except a tall gentleman of upright carriage in a greatcoat and top hat.

All of us looked as one down that grim black alley, all of us thinking the same thing—that the man in the coat, if he had in fact been dawdling there, was dead as a nailhead. The two men who had a minute earlier been making a rush in that direction were happy enough that they had held up, for the flames licked across at the brick façade opposite the paper company, and a wide section of wall crumbled outward in a roar of collapsing rubble.

The baker, as if coming to, clapped a hand onto the top of his baldhead and sprinted for his own shop—thinking to get some few of his things clear before it went up too. The heat drove him back, though, and I can picture him clearly in my mind today, wringing his hands and scuffing his feet in the spilled coffee next to the dead man, and waiting for his shop to burn.

It didn't, though; thank heaven. It began to rain, is what it did, with such a crashing of thunder that, with the first bolt, we thought another roof had caved in. The drops fell thick and steady, as if someone were pouring it out of a bucket, and the baker fell to his knees right there in the street and clasped his hands together with the rainwater streaming down his face. I hope he said a word for the dead man behind him—although if he did, it was a brief one, for he stood up just as quick as he had knelt, and pointed across at a man in a greatcoat and hat, walking away in the direction of the river.

He carried a stick, and his profile betrayed an aquiline nose and a noble sort of demeanor—you could see it in his walk—that made him out to be something more than a gentleman: royalty, you'd think, except that his hat and coat had seen some wear, and his trousers were splashed with mud from the street.

The baker shouted. Of course it was the man he'd seen loitering in the alley directly before the blast. And two constables had the man pinned and labeled before he had a chance to run for it. He wouldn't have run for it anyway, of course, for it was Godall, as you've no doubt deduced by now.

I was possessed by the notion that I ought to go to his defense, tell the constables that they'd collared the wrong man. I didn't, though, having learned a lesson from that earlier unthinking dash of mine into what the newspapers, in their silly way, sometimes call "the devouring elephant," meaning the fire, and still limping from it, too. They would arrest me along with Godall, is what they would do, as an accomplice. My word is nothing to the constabulary. And I was certain that they wouldn't keep him two minutes anyway, once they knew who he was.

The rain fell harder, if that were possible, and the flames died away almost as fast as they'd risen, and the fire brigade, when it clanged up, had nothing at all to do but wait. The smoke boiled away, too, on the instant. Just like that. You would have thought there'd be a fresh billow, what with the sudden rain and all, but there wasn't; it was simply gone, leaving some whitish smoke tumbling up out of the embers of the dwindling fire.

It struck me as funny at the time, the fire and blast so quick and fierce, and then the smoke just dying like that. It's a consequence of hanging about with men like St. Ives and Godall, I guess, that you jump to conclusions about things; you want everything to be a mystery. No, that's not quite it: you *suspect* everything of being a mystery; what you *want* is a different story, which is to say, no story at all. There was a story in this, though. It took about thirty seconds of thought to conclude that it had been an incendiary bomb and a lot of chemical smoke, which had fairly quickly used itself up. The explosion had to have been manufactured.

My biscuits, it turned out—the tin I'd dropped in the road—had been trampled, and I left for Jermyn Street empty-handed. It's a good walk in the rain—by that I mean a long one—but it gave me time to think about two things: whether the tragedy that afternoon had anything to do with Lord Kelvin's machine (the presence of Godall rather argued that it had) and what I would tell Dorothy about it all. Dorothy, if you don't already know, is my wife, and at the moment she was a wife who wouldn't be keen on my getting caught up in another of St. Ives's adventures when the last one hadn't quite got cold yet. I had the unsettling notion that "caught up" was just the right verb, even if a little on the passive side; this had all the earmarks of that sort of thing.

St. Ives wasn't in Harrogate, at his laboratory. He was in London paying a visit to my father-in-law—Mr. William Keeble of Jermyn Street, the toy maker and inventor—consulting him on the building of an apparatus that doesn't concern us here, and is too wild and unlikely for me to mention without throwing a cloud of suspicion and doubt over the whole story. But it was fortuitous, St. Ives's being in London, because if he hadn't been I would have had to send a message up to Harrogate, and he would have come quick enough, maybe to find nothing at all and have wasted a trip.

As it was, I ran him down that night in an oyster bar near Leicester Square. The rain had given off, but the clouds hadn't, and it felt like snow. St. Ives sat reading a *Standard* that wasn't long off the presses. News of the explosion, however, didn't appear on the front page, which was fairly bursting with an extravagant story of another sort altogether. And here my own story digresses for a bit.

I wish I could quote it to you, this second story, but I haven't got it anymore; so I'll tell it to you straight out, although I warn you that I can't do it justice, and that you wouldn't half believe me if I could. Any good library, though, can afford you a copy of a London newspaper from the day in question, if you're the sort of Thomas in the popular phrase.

And note that I haven't tried to sandbag you with the notion that I'd *seen* this second tragedy as well as the explosion up in Holborn: what I'm telling you now is neither art nor journalism, but a sort of lager and lime mix-up of both, and maybe nearer the truth for that.

—∿∿∿—

IT WAS WHAT the *Standard* referred to as an "imbroglio," although that, I'm afraid, is a small word, and this was no small matter. A lorry had very nearly overturned on White-friars Street. It had been running along south, heavily laden, toward the Embankment, its load covered in canvas, several layers, and lashed down against the wind and possible rain. Some few witnesses claimed that there was a man beneath the canvas, too, peering out at the day, although no one saw him so clearly as to identify him beyond their generally agreeing that he ran to tall and thin, and was hatless and nearly bald.

The lorry, angling round across Tudor Street and onto Carmelite, caught a bit of stone curb with its wheel. There was a shifting of cargo and a horrible shout from the half-hidden man on board, and the wagon, as if it were a great fish on the end of a played-out line, shuddered almost to a stop, the horses stumbling and their shoes throwing sparks on the pavement. A terrible mechanical howling set in, as if an engine had just that minute been started up.

The driver—an enormous man with a beard—cursed and slammed at the reins and whipped the poor beasts nearest him as if to take the hide off their flanks. They tried to drive on, too—desperately, to hear the witnesses tell of it—but the lorry, or rather the cargo, seemed to compel the horses back, and for the space of a long minute it looked as if time had stopped dead, except for the suddenly falling rain and the cursing and the flailing of the driver. Then there was the snap of a stay chain coming loose and the lorry lurched forward, the chain swinging round into the spokes, and there was such a groaning and screeching and banging that it seemed sure the wagon would go to pieces on the road and the horses plummet down Carmelite and into the river.

It wasn't the lorry, though, that was tearing itself apart. The air suddenly was full of flying debris, shooting out of the buildings along the street: nails and screws pried themselves out of door casings and clapboards; an iron pot flew from an open window as if it had been thrown; door knockers clanked and clattered and hammered in the hands of a dozen anxious ghosts and then tore away from their doorfronts with a screech of overstrained steel. Even the two iron hitching posts in front of the Temple Inn lurched out of the ground in a shower of dirt and stone fragments, and all of it shot away in the direction of that impossible lorry, a sort of horizontal hailstorm of hardware clanging and banging against the mysterious cargo and clamping tight to it as if glued there.

A man on the street, the paper said, was struck down by one of the posts, and wasn't expected to recover his senses, and two or three others had to be attended to by the surgeon, who removed "shrapnel and all manner of iron debris." Shopwindows were shattered by stuff inside flying out through them, and the wagon itself, as if possessed, rocked up and down on its hounds like a spring pole.

During the mêlée there sounded an awful screaming and scrabbling from under the canvas, where the unfortunate passenger (fortunate, actually, that he was padded by several folds of heavy canvas) fought to clamber farther around behind the cargo. His cries attested to his partial failure to accomplish this feat, and if the strange business had gone on a moment longer he would have been beaten dead, and half a dozen houses along Tudor and Carmelite dismantled nail by nail and left in a heap.

The howling noise stopped, though, just like that. The horses jerked forward and away, hauling the lorry with its broken stay chain and spokes, and disappearing around onto the Embankment as the rush of iron debris fell straight to the roadway in a shower, clanking along in the wake of the wagon until it all tired out and lay still.

The street lay deathly silent after that, although the whole business took only about a minute and a half. Rain began to pour down (I've already described it; it was the same rain that saved the baker's shop up in Holborn), and the lorry got away clean, no one suspecting that the whole odd mess involved any definable crime until it was discovered later in the afternoon that a building owned by the Royal Academy—a machine works—had been broken into and a complicated piece of machinery stolen and the paper company next door ignited…It was thought at first (by anyone who wasn't certifiable) that this business of the flying iron might be connected to the theft of the machine.

The peculiar thing, then, was that a spokesman from the Royal Academy—the secretary, Mr. Parsons—denied it flat out and quick enough so that his denials were printed in the *Standard* by nightfall. There wasn't any connection, he said. Couldn't be. And he was extremely doubtful about any nonsense concerning flying door knockers. Science, Mr. Parsons seemed to say, didn't hold with flying door knockers.

Tell that to the man laid out by the iron post, I remember thinking, but it was St. Ives and Godall who between them made the whole thing plain. I forgot to tell you, in fact, that Godall was at the oyster bar, too—he and Hasbro, St. Ives's gentleman's gentleman.

But this is where art leans in and covers the page with her hand—she being leery of making things plain when the story would be better left obscure while the reader draws a breath. "All in good time" has ever been the way of art.

—⁓⁓—

AND ANYWAY IT wasn't until the first of the ships went down in the Dover Strait that any of us was certain—absolutely certain; or at least Godall was, from the deductive end of things, and St. Ives from the scientific. I wasn't certain of anything yet.

I was sitting on one of Godall's sofas, I remember, waiting for the arrival of St. Ives and thinking that I ought to take up a pipe and thinking too that I had enough vices already—indolence being one of them—when a man came in with a parcel. Godall reacted as if the Queen had walked in, and introduced the man to me as Isaac Laquedem, but aside from the odd name and his great age and frailty, there seemed to be nothing notable about him. He was a peddler, actually, and I forgot about him almost at once, their business having nothing to do with me—or with this story except in a peripheral way.

My father-in-law, William Keeble, had been teaching me the trade of toy-making, and I sat there meddling with an India-rubber elephant with enormous ears that I had finished assembling that very morning. Its trunk would rotate when you pushed its belly, and the ears would flap, and out of its mouth would come the magnified noise of ratcheting gears, which sounded, if you had an imagination, like trumpeting—or at least like the trumpeting of a rubber elephant with mechanical nonsense inside. It was funny to look at, though.

I remember wondering what it would have been like if Keeble himself had built it, and thinking that I at least ought to have given it a hat, maybe with a bird in it, and I

listened idly to Godall and the old fellow talk about numismatics and about a clock-work match that the man was peddling. Then he left, very cheerfully, entirely forgetting his parcel of matches and going away up Rupert Street toward Brewer.

A minute passed, neither of us noticing the parcel. Then Godall spotted it and shouted damnation, or something, and I was up and out the door with it under my arm and with my elephant in my other hand. I ran up the street, dodging past people until I reached the corner, where I found the old man in a tearoom trying to sell little cheesecloth bags of green tea that could be dropped into a cup of boiling water and then retrieved again—not for the purpose of being reused, mind you, but so that the leaves wouldn't muck up the brew. The proprietor *read* tea leaves, though, as well as palms and scone crumbs, and wasn't at all interested in the invention, although I thought it was fairly clever and said so when I returned his automatic matches. He said that he admired my elephant, too, and I believe he did. We chatted over a cup of tea for ten minutes and then I strolled back down, thinking correctly that St. Ives would have shown up by then.

There at the side of the street, half a block up from the cigar divan, was a hansom cab, rather broken-down and with a curtain of shabby velvet drawn across the window. As I was passing it, the curtain pushed aside and a face popped out. I thought at first it was a woman, but it wasn't; it was a man with curled hair to his shoulders. His complexion was awful, and he had a sort of greasy look about him and a high effeminate collar cut out of a flowery chintz. It was his eyes, though, that did the trick. They were filled with a mad unfocused passion, as if everything around him—the cab, the buildings along Rupert Street, me—signified something to him. His glance shot back and forth in a cockeyed vigilance, and he said, almost whispering, "What is that?"

He was looking up the street at the time, so I looked up the street too, but saw nothing remarkable. "Beg your pardon," I said.

"That there."

He peered down the street now, so I did too.

"There."

Now it was up into the air, toward a bank of casements on the second floor. There was a man staring out of one, smoking a cigar.

"Him?" I asked.

He gave me such a look that I thought I'd landed upon it at last, but then I saw that I was wrong.

"That. In your hand."

The elephant. He blinked rapidly, as if he had something in his eye. "I like that," he said, and he squinted at me as if he knew me. There was something in his face, too, that I almost recognized. But he was clearly mad, and the madness, somehow, had given him a foreign cast, as if he were a citizen from nowhere on earth and had scrambled his features into an almost impenetrable disguise.

I felt sorry for him, to tell you the truth, and when he reached for the rubber elephant, I gave it to him, thinking, I'll admit, that he'd give it back after having a look. Instead he disappeared back into the cab, taking the elephant with him. The curtain closed, and I heard from him no more. I knocked once on the door. "Go away," he said.

So I did. He wanted the creature more than I wanted it. What did I want to build toys for, anyway, if not for the likes of him? And besides, it pretty clearly needed a hat. That's the sort of thing I told myself. It was half cowardice, though, my just walking away. I didn't want to make a scene by going into the cab after him and be found brawling with a madman over a rubber elephant. I argued it out in my head as I stepped into Godall's shop, ready to relate the incident to my credit, and there, standing just inside the threshold, impossibly, was the lunatic himself.

I must have looked staggered, for Hasbro leaped up in alarm at the sight of my face, and the person in the doorway turned on her heel with a startled look. She wasn't the fellow in the truck; she was a woman with an appallingly similar countenance and hair, equally greasy, and with a blouse of the same material. This one wore a shawl, though, and was older by a good many years, although her face belied her age. It was almost unlined due to some sort of unnatural puffiness—as if she were a goblin that had come up to Soho wearing a cleverly altered melon for a head. This was the mother, clearly, of the creature in the cab.

She smiled theatrically at me. Then, as if she had just that instant recognized me, her smile froze into a look of snooty reproach, and she ignored me utterly from then on. I had the distinct feeling that I'd been cut, although you'd suppose that being cut by a madwoman doesn't count for much—any more than having one's rubber elephant stolen by a madman counts for anything.

"A man like that ought to be brought to justice," she said to St. Ives, who gestured toward the sofa and raised his eyebrows at me.

"This is Mr. Owlesby," he said to the woman. "You can speak freely in front of him."

She paid me no attention at all, as if to say that she would speak freely, or would not, before whomever she chose, and no one would stop her. I sat down.

"Brought to justice," she said.

"Justice," said St. Ives, "was brought to him, or he to it, sometime back. He died in Scandinavia. He fell into a lake where he without a doubt was frozen to death even before he drowned. I...I saw him tumble into the lake myself. He didn't crawl out."

"He did crawl out."

"Impossible," said St. Ives—and it *was* impossible, too. Except that when it came to the machinations of Dr. Narbondo you were stretching a point using the word *impossible,* and St. Ives knew it. Doubt flickered in his eyes, along with other emotions, too complex to fathom. I could see that he was animated, though. Since his dealings with the comet and the death of Ignacio Narbondo, St. Ives had been enervated, drifting from one scientific project to another, finishing almost nothing, lying on the divan in his study through the long hours of the afternoon, drifting in and out of sleep. For the space of a few days he had undertaken to restore Alice's vegetable garden, but the effort had cost him too much, and he had abandoned it to the moles and the weeds. I could turn this last into a metaphor of the great man's life over the last couple of years, but I won't. I promised to leave tragedy alone.

"Look here," the woman said, handing across what appeared to be a letter. It had been folded up somewhere for years, in someone's pocket from the look of it, and the cheap paper was yellowed and torn. It was addressed to someone named Kenyon, but the name was new to me and the contents of the letter were nothing of interest. The handwriting was the point as was the signature: Dr. Ignacio Narbondo. St. Ives handed it across to Godall, who was measuring out tobacco on a balance scale in the most disinterested way imaginable.

She handed over a second letter, this one fresh from last week's post. It was in an envelope that appeared to have been dropped in the street and trod upon by horses, and part of the letter inside, including the salutation, was an unreadable ruin. The first two paragraphs were written in a plain hand, clearly by a man who cared little for stray blots and smudges. And then, strangely, the final several sentences were inscribed by the man who had written the first missive. It didn't take an expert to see that. There was a flourish in the *T*'s, and the uppercase *A*, of which there were two, was several times the size of any other letter, and was printed rather than enscripted, and then crossed pointlessly at the top, giving it an Oriental air. In a word, the handwriting at the end of this second letter was utterly distinct, and utterly identical to that of the first. The signature, however, was different. "H. Frost," it read, with a scattering of initials afterward that I don't recall.

The text of this second letter was interesting. It mentioned certain papers that this H. Frost was anxious to find, and would pay for. He was a professor, apparently, at Edinburgh University, a chemist, and had heard rumors that papers belonging to our madwoman's father were lost in the vicinity of the North Downs some forty years ago. He seemed to think that the papers were important to medical science, and that her father deserved a certain notoriety that he'd never gotten in his tragic life. It went on so, in flattering and promising tones, and then was signed, as I said, "H. Frost."

St. Ives handed this second letter to Godall and pursed his lips. I had the uncanny feeling that he hesitated because of his suspicions about the woman, about her reasons for having come round with the letters at all. "The doctor is dead, madam," was what he said finally.

She shook her head. "Those letters were written with the same hand; anyone can see that."

"In fact," said St. Ives, "the more elaborate the handwriting, the easier it is to forge. The reproduction of eccentricities in handwriting is cheap and easy; it's the subtleties that are difficult. Why someone would want to forge the doctor's hand, I don't know.

It's an interesting puzzle, but one that doesn't concern me. My suggestion is to ignore it utterly. Don't respond. Do nothing at all."

"He ought to be brought to justice is what I'm saying."

"He's dead," said St. Ives finally. And then, after a moment of silence, he said, "And if this mystery were worth anything to me at all, then I'd have to know a great deal more about the particulars, wouldn't I? What papers, for example? Who was your father? Do you have any reason to think that his lost papers are valuable to science or were lost in the North Downs forty years ago?"

Now it was her turn to hesitate. There was a good deal that she wasn't saying. Bringing people to justice wasn't her only concern; that much was apparent. She fiddled with her shawl for a moment, pretending to adjust it around her shoulders but actually casting about her mind for a way to reveal what it was she was after without really revealing anything at all. "My father's name was John Kenyon. He was…misguided when he was young," she said. "And then he was misused when he was older. He associated with the grandfather of the man you think is dead, and he developed a certain serum, a longevity serum, out of the glands of a fish, I misremember which one. When the elder Narbondo was threatened with transportation for experiments in vivisection, my grandfather went into hiding. He went over to Rome…"

"Moved to the Continent?" asked St. Ives.

"No, he became a papist. He repented of all his dealings in alchemy and vivisection, and would have had me go into a nunnery to save me from the world, except that I wouldn't have it. His manuscripts disappeared. He claimed to have destroyed them, but I'm certain he didn't, because once, when I was about fifteen, my mother found what must have been them, in a trunk. They were bound into a notebook, which she took and tried to destroy, but he stopped her. They fought over the thing, she calling him a hypocrite and he out of his mind with not knowing *what* he intended to do.

"But my father was a weak man, a worm. He saved the notebook right enough and beat my mother and went away to London and was gone a week. He came home drunk, I remember, and penitent, and I married and moved away within the year and didn't see him again until he was an old man and dying. My mother was dead by then for fifteen years, and he thought it had been himself that killed her—and it no doubt was. He started in to babble about the notebook, again, there on his deathbed. It had been eating at him all those years. What he said, as he lay dying, was that it had been stolen from him by the Royal Academy. A man named Piper, who had a chair at Oxford, wanted the formulae for himself, and had got the notebook away from him with strong drink and the promise of money. But there had never been any money. I ought to find the notebook and destroy it, my father said, so that he might rest in peace.

"Well, the last thing I cared about, I'll say it right out, was him resting in peace. The less peace he got, the better, and amen. So I didn't do anything. I had a son, by then, and a drunk for a husband who was as pitiful as my father was and who I hadn't seen in a fortnight and hoped never to see again. But I was never a lucky one. That part don't matter, though. What matters is that there *are* these papers that he mentions, this notebook. And I know that it's him—the one you claim is dead up in Scandinavia—that wants the papers now. No one else knows about them, you see, except him and a couple of old hypocrites from the Royal Academy, and they wouldn't need to ask *me* about them, would they, having stolen the damned things themselves. He's got his methods, the doctor has, and this letter doesn't come as any surprise to me, no surprise at all. If you know him half as well as you claim to, gentlemen, then it won't come as any surprise to you either, no matter how many times you think you saw him die."

And so ended her speech. It just rushed out of her, as if none of it were calculated, and yet I was fairly certain that every word had been considered and that half the story, as they say, hadn't been told. She had edited and euphemized the thing until there was nothing left but the surface, with the emotional nonsense put in to cover the detail that was left out.

She had got to St. Ives, too. And Godall, it seemed to me, was weighing out the same bag of tobacco for the tenth time. Both of them were studying the issue hard. If she had come in through the door intending to address their weightiest fear, she could hardly have been more on the money than she was. Something monumental was brewing, and had been since the day of the explosion and the business down by the Embankment. No run-of-the-mill criminal was behind it; that weeks had gone by in the meantime was evidence only that it was brewing slowly, that it wouldn't be rushed, and was ominous as a result.

"May we keep the letters?" asked St. Ives.

"No," she replied, snatching both of them off the counter where Godall had laid them. She turned smiling and stepped out onto the sidewalk, climbing into the waiting cab and driving away, just like that, without another word. She had got us, and that was the truth. St. Ives asking for the letters had told her as much.

Her sudden departure left us just a little stunned, and was Godall who brought us back around by saying to St. Ives, "I fancy that there is no Professor Frost at Edinburgh in any capacity at all."

"Not a chemist, certainly. Not in any of the sciences. That much is a ruse."

"And it's his handwriting, too, there at the end."

"Of course it is." St. Ives shuddered. Here was an old wound opening up—Alice, Narbondo's death in Scandinavia, St. Ives once again grappling with weighty moral questions that had proven impossible to settle. All he could make out of it all was guilt—his own. And finally he had contrived, by setting himself adrift, simply to wipe it out of his mind. Now this—Narbondo returning like the ghost at the feast...

"It's just the tiniest bit shaky, though," Godall said, "as if he were palsied or weak but was making a great effort to disguise it, so as to make the handwriting of this new letter as like old as possible. I'd warrant that he wasn't well enough to write the whole thing, but could only manage a couple of sentences; the rest was written for him."

"A particularly clever forger, perhaps...," began St. Ives. But Godall pointed out the puzzle:

"Why forge another man's handwriting but not use his name? That's the key, isn't it? There's no point in such a forgery unless these are deeper waters than they appear to be."

"Perhaps someone wanted the letter to get round to us, to make us believe Narbondo is alive..."

"Then it's a puzzling song and dance," said Godall, "and far more a dangerous one. We're marked men if she's right. It's Narbondo's way of calling us out. I rather believe, though, that this is his way of serving her a warning, of filling her with fear; he's come back, he means to say, and he wants that notebook."

"I believe," said St. Ives, "that if I were her I'd tell him, if she knows where it is."

"That's what frightens me about the woman," said Godall, sweeping tobacco off the counter. "She seems to see this as an opportunity of some sort, doesn't she? She means to tackle the monster herself. My suggestion is that we find out the whereabouts of this man Piper. He must be getting on in age, probably retired from Oxford long ago."

Just then a lad came in through the door with the *Standard*, and news that the first of the ships had gone down off Dover. It was another piece to the puzzle, anyone could see that, or rather could sense it, even though there was no way to know how it fit.

—⁓—

THE SHIP HAD been empty, its captain, crew, and few paying passengers having put out into wooden boats for the most curious reason. The captain had found a message in the ship's log—scrawled into it, he thought, by someone on board, either a passenger or someone who had come over the side. It hadn't been there when they'd left the dock at Gravesend; the captain was certain of it. They had got a false start, having to put in at Sterne Bay, and they lost a night there waiting for the cargo that didn't arrive.

Someone, of course, had sneaked on board and meddled with the log; there had never been any cargo.

What the message said was that every man on board must get out into the boats when the ship was off Ramsgate on the way to Calais. They must watch for a sailing craft with crimson sails. This boat would give them a sign, and then every last one of them would take to the lifeboat and row for all he was worth until they'd put a quarter mile between themselves and the ship. Either that or they would die—all of them.

It was a simple mystery, really, baffling, but with nothing grotesque about it. Until you thought about it—about what would have happened if the captain hadn't opened the logbook and those men hadn't got into the boat. The message was in earnest. The ship sank, pretty literally like a stone, and although the crew was safe, their safety was a matter of dumb luck. Whoever had engineered the disaster thought himself to be Destiny, and had played fast and high with the lives of the people on board. That had been the real message, and you can bank on it.

The captain lost his post as well as his ship. Why hadn't he turned about and gone back to Dover? Because the note in the log didn't hint that the ship would be destroyed, did it? It was more than likely a hoax, a prank—one that would kill a couple of hours while they tossed in the lifeboat and then rowed back over to her and took possession again. He had never even expected to see the doubtful sailcraft. And they were already a day late because of the stopover at Sterne Bay. It was all just too damned unlikely to take seriously, except the part about getting into the boat. The captain wouldn't risk any lives, he said.

But there it was: the ship had gone down. It hadn't been the least bit unlikely in the end. There were only two things about it that *were* unlikely, it seemed to us: one was that the crew, every man jack of them, had remained in Dover, and shipped out again at once. The word of the captain was all that the authorities had; and he, apparently, was a Yank, recently come over from San Francisco. The second unlikelihood was that this business with the ship was unrelated to the two London incidents. —೧

The Practicing Detective
at Sterne Bay

W E HAD NO choice but to set out for the coast by way of Sterne Bay. It wasn't just the business of the downed ship; it was that St. Ives discovered that Dr. Piper, of the Academy, had retired years past to a cottage down the Thames, at Sterne Bay. Godall stayed behind. His business didn't allow for that sort of jaunt, and there was no reason to suppose that London would be devoid of mysteries just because this most recent one had developed a few miles to the east.

St. Ives had put in at the Naval Office, too, in order to see if he couldn't discover something about this Captain Bowker, but the captain was what they call a shadowy figure, an American whose credentials weren't at all clear, but who had captained small merchant ships down to Calais for a year or so. There was no evidence that he was the sort to be bought off—no recorded trouble. That was the problem; nothing was known about the man, and so you couldn't help jumping to the conclusion that he was just the sort to be bought off. It seemed to stand to reason.

We rattled out of Victoria Station in the early morning and arrived in time to breakfast at the Crown and Apple in Sterne Bay before setting about our business. Nothing seemed to be particularly pressing. We took over an hour at it, shoving down rashers and eggs, and St. Ives all the while in a rare good humor, chatting with the landlady about this and that—all of it entirely innocent—and then stumbling onto the subject of the ship going down and of Captain Bowker. Of course it was in all the papers, being the mystery that it was, and there was nothing at all to suggest that we had anything but a gossip's interest in it.

Oh, she knew Captain Bowker right enough. He was a Yank, wasn't he, and the jolliest and maybe biggest man you'd meet in the bay. He hadn't an enemy, which is what made the business such a disaster, poor man, losing his ship like that, and now out of a situation. Well, not entirely; he had taken a position at the icehouse, tending the machinery—a good enough job in a fishing town like Sterne Bay. He was generally at it from dawn till bedtime, and sometimes took dinner at the Crown and Apple, since he didn't have a family. He slept at the icehouse too, now that his ship was gone and he hadn't got a new one. He was giving up the sea, he said, after the disaster, and was happy only that he hadn't lost any men. The ship be damned, he liked to say—it was his men that he cared about; that was ever the way of Captain Bowker.

St. Ives said that it was a good way, too, and that it sounded to him as if the world ought to have a dozen more Captain Bowkers in it, but I could see that he was being subtle. His saying that had the effect of making her think we were the right sort, not busybody tourists down from London. That was St. Ives's method, and there was nothing of the hypocrite in it. He meant every bit of it, but if being friendly served some end too, before we were done, then so much the better.

Now it happened that Hasbro had an aunt living in the town, his jolly old Aunt Edie. She had been a sort of lady-in-waiting to St. Ives's mother—almost a nanny to him—and now, as unlikely as it sounds, she had taken to the sea, to fish, on a trawler owned by her dead husband's brother, Uncle Botley. So after breakfast St. Ives and Hasbro went off to pay her a visit, leaving me to myself for an hour. I wanted to sightsee, although to tell you the truth, I felt a little guilty about it because Dorothy wasn't along. I've gotten used to her being there, I guess, over the years, and I'm glad of it. It's one of the few things that I've got right.

It was a damp and foggy morning, getting along toward late—the sort of morning when every sound is muffled, and even though there are people out, there's a sort of curtain between you and them and you walk along the damp cobbles in a gray study, lost in thought. I strolled down the waterfront, thinking that Sterne Bay was just the sort of place to spend a few leisurely days, maybe bring along a fishing rod. Dorothy would love it. I would propose it to her as soon as we got back. The thought of proposing it to her, of course, was calculated to rid me of some of the guilt that I was feeling, out on holiday, really while Dorothy was stuck up in London, trapped in the old routine.

Then I thought of poor St. Ives, and of Alice, whom he had loved for two short years before that awful night in the Seven Dials. Thank God I wasn't there. It's a selfish thing to say, perhaps, but I can't help that. The man had lived alone before Alice, and has lived alone since. And although he'll fool most people, he doesn't fool me—he wasn't born to the solitary life. He's been worn thin by it. Every emotional shilling was tied up in Alice. He had put the lot of it in the savings bank until he had the chance to invest it in her, and it had paid off with interest. All that was gone now, and the very idea of a romantic holiday on the water was impossible for him to bear. He's been disallowed from entertaining notions that other people find utterly pleasant and common...

And just then, as I was strolling along full of idle and sorrowful thoughts, I looked up and there was a three-story inn, like something off a picture postcard.

It was painted white with green gingerbread trim and was hung with ivy vines. From what I could see, a broad veranda ran around three sides of it. On the veranda sat pieces of furniture, and on the willow furniture sat a scattering of people who looked just about as contented as they had any right to look—a couple of them qualifying as "old salts," and very picturesque. There was a wooden sign over the stairs that read THE HOISTED PINT, which struck me as calculated, but very friendly and with the right general attitude.

I stepped up onto the veranda, nodding a hello in both directions, and into the foyer, thinking to inquire about rates and availability. Spring was on the horizon, and there would be a chance of good weather—although the town was admirably suited to dismal weather too—and there was no reason that I shouldn't simply cement the business of a holiday straightaway, so as to make Dorothy happy.

She would love the place; any doubts I might have had from the street were vanished. There were wooden floors inlaid with the most amazing marquetry depicting a whale and whaling ship—the sort of work you don't see anymore—and there were potted plants and a great stone fireplace with a log fire burning and not a piece of coal to be seen. A small woman worked behind the long oak counter, meddling with papers, and we talked for a moment about rooms and rates. Although I didn't like her very much, or entirely trust her, I set out finally for the door very well satisfied with the inn and with myself both.

That's when I thought I saw my rubber elephant lying atop a table, half hidden by a potted palm. I was out the door and onto the veranda before I knew what it was that I'd seen—just the bottom of him, his round feet and red-painted jumbo trousers. It was the impossibility of it that made it slow to register, and even by the time it did, by the time I was sure of it, I had taken another step or two, half down the stairs, before turning on my heel and walking back in.

The woman looked up from where she dusted at furniture now with a clutch of feathers. She widened her eyes, wondering, perhaps, if I hadn't forgotten something, and I smiled back, feeling like a fool, and asking weakly whether I didn't need some sort of receipt, a confirmation—implying by it, I suppose, that her bookwork there behind the counter wasn't sufficient. She frowned and said that she supposed she could work something up, although…And I said quite right, of course but that as a surprise to my wife I thought that a little something to put into an envelope on her breakfast plate…That made her happy again. She liked to see that in a man, and said that she was anxious to meet the young lady. When I glanced across the room there wasn't any elephant, of course, or anything like it.

I don't doubt that you're going to ask me why I didn't just *inquire* about the woman and her son, who carried a rubber elephant with enormous ears. There would have been a hundred friendly ways to phrase it. Well, I didn't. I still felt like half a fool for having blundered back in like that and going through the song and dance about the breakfast plate, and I was almost certain by then that I hadn't seen anything at all, that I had invented it out of the curve of a leaf and the edge of a pot. It was a little farfetched, wasn't it? Just as it had seemed improbable to the captain of the downed ship that the nonsense in his log ought to be taken seriously.

I had imagined it, and I told myself so as I set out toward the pier again, where, just like that, I nearly ran over old Parsons, the secretary of the Royal Academy of Sciences, coming along with a bamboo pole and creel in his hand, got up in a woolen sort of fishing uniform and looking as if even though he mightn't catch a single fish, at least he had got the outfit right, and that qualified him, as the scriptures put it, to walk with the proud.

I was surprised to see him. He was thoroughly disappointed to see me. It was the company I kept. He assumed straight off that St. Ives was lurking somewhere about, and that meant, of course, that the business of the Royal Academy was being meddled in again. And he was right. *His* being there said as much. It was an altogether unlikely coincidence. If I had looked at it from the angle of a practicing detective, then I'd have had suspicions about his angling outfit, and I'd have concluded that he was trying too hard to play a part. He was up to something, to be sure.

"What are *you* doing here?" he asked.

I gave him a jolly look, and said, "Down on holiday, actually. And you, going fishing?"

Foolish question, I guess, given what he looked like, but that didn't call for him to get cheeky. "I'm *prospecting*," he said, and held up his bamboo pole. "This is an alchemical divining rod, used to locate fishes with coins in their bellies."

But just then, when I was going to say something clever, up came a gentleman in side whiskers and interrupted in order to wring Parsons's hand. "Dreadfully sorry, old man," he said to Parsons. "But he was tired, and he'd lived a long life. Very profitable. I'm happy you could come down for the funeral."

Parsons took him by the arm and led him away down the pier pretty briskly, as if to get him away from me before he said anything more. He had already said enough, though, hadn't he? This man Piper was dead, and Parsons had come down to see him buried.

It was a full morning, taken all the way around. There was a half hour yet before I was to meet St. Ives and Hasbro back at the Apple. I was feeling very much *like* a detective by then, although I couldn't put my finger on exactly what it was I had detected, besides this last bit. I decided that wasn't enough, and went across toward the ramshackle icehouse, a wooden sort of warehouse in a weedy lot not far off the ocean.

I went in at a side door without knocking. The place was cold, not surprisingly, and I could hear the hiss of steam from the compressors. The air was tinged with the smell of ammonia and wet straw. The jolly captain wasn't hard to find; he confronted me as soon as I came in through the door. He seemed to be the only one around, and he was big, and he talked with an accent, stretching out his vowels as if they were made of putty. I won't try to copy it, since I'm no good at tricking up accents, but he was full of words like *tarnation* and *fleabit* and *hound dog* and *ain't* and talked altogether in a sort of apostrophic "Out West" way that struck me as out of character in a sea captain. I expected something salty and maritime. I made a mental note of it.

That was after I had shaken his hand and introduced my self. "I'm Abner Benbow," I said, thinking this up on the spot and almost saying "Admiral Benbow," but stopping myself just in time. "I'm in the ice trade, up in Harrogate. They call me 'Cool Abner Benbow,'" I said, "but they don't call me a cold fish." I inclined my head just a little, thinking that maybe this last touch was taking it too far. But he liked it, saying he had a "monicker" too.

"Call me Bob," he said, "Country Bob Bowker. Call me anythin' you please, but don't call me too late for dinner." And with that admonition he slammed me on the back with his open hand and nearly knocked me through the wall. He was convulsed with laughter, wheezing and looking apoplectic, as if he had just that moment made up the gag and was listening to himself recite it for the first time. I laughed too, very heartily, I thought, wiping pretended tears from my eyes.

"You're a Yank," I said. And that was clever, of course, because it rather implied that I didn't already know who he was, despite his recent fame.

"That's a fact. Wyoming man, born and bred. Took to the sea late and come over here two years ago just to see how the rest of the world got on. I was always a curious man. And I was all alone over there, runnin' ferries out of Frisco over to Sarsleeto, and figured I wouldn't be no more alone over here."

No more than any common criminal, I thought, assuming straight off, and maybe unfairly, that there was more to Captain Bowker's leaving America than he let on. I nodded, though, as if I thought all his nonsense very sage indeed.

"Been here long?" I asked, nonchalant.

He gave me a look. "Didn't I just say two year?"

"I mean here, at the icehouse."

"Ah!" he said, suddenly jolly again. "No. *Just* got on. If you'd of come day before yesterday you wouldn't have found me. Old man who ran the place up and died, though. Pitched over like he was poisoned, right there where you're a-standing now, up and pitched over, and there I was an hour later, looking in at the door with my hat in my hands. I knew a little about it, being mechanical and having lived by the sea, so I was a natural. They took me right on. What's all that to you?"

"Nothing. Nothing at all," I said, realizing right off that I shouldn't have said it twice; there was no room here to sound jumpy. But he had caught me by surprise with the question, and all I could think to say next, rather stupidly, was, "*Up* and died?" thinking that the phrase was a curious one, as if he had done it on purpose, maybe got up out of a chair to do it.

You can see that I had got muddled up. This wasn't going well. Somehow I had excited his suspicions by saying the most arbitrary and commonplace things. Captain Bowker was another lunatic, I remember thinking—the sort who, if you passed him on the street and said good-morning, would squint at you and ask what you *meant* by saying such a thing.

"Dropped right over dead on his face," said Captain Bowker, looking at me just as seriously as a stone head.

Then he grinned and broke into laughter, slapping me on the back again. "Cigar?" he asked.

I waved it away. "Don't smoke. You have one. I like the smell of tobacco, actually. Very comfortable."

He nodded and said, "Drives off the 'monia fumes," and then he gnawed off the end of a fat cigar, spitting out the debris with about twice the required force.

"So," I said. "Mind if I look around?"

"Yep," he said.

I started forward, but he stepped in front of me. "Yep," he said again, talking past his cigar. "I *do* mind if you look around." Then he burst into laughter again so that there was no way on earth that I could tell what he minded and what he didn't mind.

He plucked the unlit cigar out of his mouth and said, "Maybe tomorrow, Jim. Little too much going on today. Too busy for it. I'm new and all, and can't be showing in every Dick and Harry." He managed, somehow, to get me turned around and propelled toward the door. "*You* understand. You're a *businessman*. Tomorrow afternoon, maybe, or the next day. That's soon enough, ain't it? You ain't going nowhere. Come on back around, and you can have the run of the place. Bring a spyglass and a measure stick."

And with that I was out in the fog again, wondering exactly how things had gone so bad. In the space of ten minutes I'd been Abner and Jim and Dick and Harry, but none of us had seen a thing. At least I hadn't given myself away, though. Captain Bowker couldn't have guessed who I really was. I could relate the incident to St. Ives and Hasbro without any shame, There was enough in the captain's manner to underscore any suspicions that we might already have had of the man, and there was the business of his not wanting me to see the workings of the icehouse, innocent as such workings ought to be.

I lounged along toward the Apple—it wasn't the weather for hurrying—and had got down past the market, maybe a hundred yards beyond The Hoisted Pint, when I heard the crack of what sounded like a firecracker from somewhere above and behind me. Immediately an old beggar with his shoes wound in rags, standing just in front of me, stiffened up straight, as if he'd been poked in the small of the back, and a wash of red blood spread out across his shirtfront where you could see it through his open coat.

Before I could twitch, he sat down in the weeds and then slumped over backward and stared at the sky, his mouth working as if he were trying to pray, but had forgot the words. He had been shot, of course—in the heart—by someone with a dead-on aim.

A woman screamed. There was the sound of a whistle. And without half knowing what I was about, I had the man's wrist in my hand and was feeling for a pulse. It was worthless. Where the *hell* do you find a man's pulse? I can't even find my own half the time. I slammed my hand over the hole in his chest and leaned into it, trying to shut off the rush of blood and feeling absolutely futile and stupid until a doctor strode up carrying his black bag. He crouched beside me, squinted at the corpse, and shook his head softly to tell me that I was wasting my time.

Reeling just a little from the smell of already-drying blood, I stood up and stumbled over to sit on a bench, where I hunched forward and pretended for a bit to be searching for a lucky clover until my head cleared. I sat up straight, and there was a constable looming over me with the look in his eye of a man with a few pressing questions to ask. If I was a rotten actor in front of Captain Bowker, I had improved a bit in the score of minutes since, and it was a simple thing to convince the constable that I knew nothing of the dead man.

I avoided one issue, though: I seemed to be *collecting* dead men all of a sudden. First there was the tragedy up in Holborn, now a man drops dead at my feet, shot through the heart. Most of us go through our lives avoiding that sort of thing. Now I was getting more than my share of it. It was evidence of something, but not the sort of evidence that would do the constable any good, not yet anyway.

It wasn't quite noon when I got back to the Crown and Apple and cleaned myself up, and when St. Ives and Hasbro found me I was putting away my second pint and not feeling any better at all. This last adventure had taken the sand out of me, and I couldn't think in a straight enough line to put the pieces of the morning together in such a way that they would signify.

"You're looking rotten," said St. Ives with his customary honesty. He ordered a pint of bitter, and so did Hasbro, although St. Ives had lately been under a new regime and had taken to drinking nothing but cider during the day. They were following my lead in order to make it seem perfectly natural that I was swilling beer before lunch. St. Ives winked at Hasbro. "It's the clean sea air. You're missing the London fogs. Your lungs can't stand the change. Send for Dorothy." He said this last to Hasbro, who pretended to get up, but then sat back down when the two fresh pints hove into view.

They were joking, of course—being jolly after their morning visit. And I was happy for it, not for myself, but for St. Ives. I hated to tell them the truth, but I told them anyway. "There's been a man shot," I said.

St. Ives scowled. "The news is up and down the bay by now. We heard a lad shouting it outside the window of Aunt Edie's cottage. Sterne Bay doesn't get many shootings."

"I saw the whole thing. Witnessed it."

St. Ives looked up from his pint glass and raised his eyebrows.

"He wasn't a half step in front of me. A tramp from the look of him, just about to touch me for a shilling, I suppose, and then, crack! just like that, and he's on his back like a bug, dead. Shattered his heart."

"He was a *half step* in front of you? That's hyperbole, of course. What you meant to say is that he was nearby."

"As close to me as I am to you," I said, thinking what he was thinking.

St. Ives was silent for a moment, studying things. It had taken me a while to see it too, what with all the complications of the morning. Clearly the bullet hadn't been meant for the beggar. There's no profit in shooting a beggar, unless you're a madman. And I had been running into too many madmen lately. The odds against there being another one lurking about were too high. Picture it: there's the beggar turning toward me. From back toward The Hoisted Pint, I must have half hidden him. The bullet that struck him had missed me by a fraction.

So who had taken a shot at me from The Hoisted Pint, from a second-story window, maybe? Or from the roof of the icehouse; that would have served equally well. I thought about the disappeared elephant and about the captain and his "Out West" mannerisms. But why on earth...?

I ordered a third pint, swearing to myself to drink it slowly and then go up to take a nap. I'd done my work for the day; I could leave the rest to Hasbro and St. Ives.

"I saw Parsons on the pier," I said. "And I talked to Captain Bowker. And I think your woman with the letters is skulking around, probably staying at The Hoisted Pint, down toward the pier." That started it. I told them the whole story, just as it happened—the toy on the table, Parsons in his fishing regalia, the captain jollying me around—and they sat silent throughout, thinking, perhaps, that I'd made a very pretty morning of it while they were off drinking tea and listening to rumors through the window.

"He thought you were an agent," said St. Ives, referring to Captain Bowker. "Insurance detective. What's he hiding, though, that he wouldn't let you look around the icehouse? This log of his, maybe? Not likely. And why would he try to shoot you? That's not an act calculated to cement the idea of his being innocent. And Parsons here too..." St. Ives fell into a study, then thumped his fist on the table, standing up and motioning to Hasbro, who stood up too, and the both of them went out leaving their glasses two-thirds full on the table. Mine was empty again, and I was tempted to pour theirs into mine in order to secure a more profound nap and to avoid waste. But there was the landlady, grinning toward me and the clock just then striking noon.

She whisked the glasses away with what struck me as a sense of purpose, looking across her spectacles at me. I lurched up the stairs and collapsed into bed, making up for our early rising with a nap that stretched into the late afternoon.

—⁓—

I WAS UP and pulling on my shoes when there was a knock on the door. It's St. Ives, I thought, while I was stepping across to throw it open. It might as easily have been the man with the gun—something that occurred to me when the door was halfway open. And for a moment I was tempted to slam it shut, cursing myself for a fool and thinking at the same time that half opening the door and then slamming it in the visitor's face would paint a fairly silly picture of me, unless, of course, it *was* the man with the gun...

It wasn't. It was a man I had never seen before. He was tall, gaunt, and stooped, almost cadaverous. He wore a hat, but it was apparent that he was bald on top and didn't much bother to cut the tufts of hair above his ears. He would have made a pretty scarecrow. There were deep furrows around his lips, the result of a lifetime of pursing them, I suppose, which is just what he was doing now, glaring down his hooked nose at me as if he didn't quite approve of the look on my face.

Afternoon naps always put me in a wretched mood, and the sight of him doubled it. "You've apparently got the wrong room," I said, and started to shut the door. He put his foot in the way.

"I'm an insurance agent," he said, glancing back down the hallway. "Lloyd's. There's a question or two..."

"Of course," I said. So that was it. Captain Bowker *was* under investigation. I swung the door open and in he came, looking around the room with a slightly appalled face, as if the place was littered with dead pigs, say, and they were starting to stink. I didn't like him at all, insurance agent or not.

He started in on me, grilling me, as they say. "You were seen talking to Captain Bowker today."

I nodded.

"About what?"

"Ice," I said. "My name is Adam Benbow, from up in Harrogate. I'm a fish importer down on holiday."

He nodded. He was easier to fool than the captain had been. I was bothered, though, by the vague suspicion that I had gotten my name wrong. I had, of course. This morning it had been Abner. I could hardly correct it, though, not now. And how would he know anyway? What difference did my name make to him?

"We're investigating the incident of the downed ship. Did you talk to him about that?"

"Which ship?"

"The *Landed Catch,* sunk off Dover days ago. What do you know about that ship?"

"Not a thing. I read about it in the papers, of course. Who hasn't?"

"Are you acquainted with a man named Langdon St. Ives?" he asked abruptly. He half spun around when he said this, as if to take me by surprise.

It worked, too. I sputtered there for a moment, blinking at him. And when I said, "Langdon who?" the attempt was entirely worthless. I was as transparent as window glass.

He acted as if I had admitted everything. "We believe that Mr. St. Ives is also investigating the business of the *Landed Catch,* and we're wondering why."

"I'm sure I don't know. Who was it again? Saint what?" It was worthless pretending, and I knew it. I had to dummy up, though. I wasn't about to answer the man's questions. St. Ives could do that for himself. On the other hand, I suppose it was pointless to insist that I didn't know St. Ives. The man was onto my game, what with the false names and the Harrogate business.

"What did you *see,* exactly, at the icehouse?"

"*See?* Nothing. The man wouldn't allow me in. He seemed anxious, to tell you the truth. Like he didn't want me snooping around. He has something to hide there; you can take that much from me."

"Something to hide, you think?"

"Bank on it."

The man nodded, suddenly jolly, grinning at me. "I think you're right," he said. "He's hiding something horrible, is what I think. These are dangerous waters. Very rocky and shallow. He's a subtle man, Captain Bowker is. My advice is to steer clear of him. Leave him to us. He'll be in Newgate Prison waiting to swing, if only for this morning's shooting."

I must have jerked my eyes open when he said this last, for he grinned at the look on my face and nodded, pursing his lips so that his mouth almost disappeared. "You were a lucky man," he said. "But you're safe now. We're onto him, watching him from every angle. You don't have to hide in your room like this."

"I wasn't hiding, actually. I…"

"Of course, you weren't," he said, turning toward the door. "Quite a welcome you've had. Don't blame you. Look me up. Binker Street."

He was out the door then, striding away down the hail. I shut the door and sat on the edge of the bed, studying things out. I understood nothing—less than before. I was vaguely happy, though, that someone was watching the captain. Of course it must have been him who had fired the shot—him and his cowboy upbringing and all. Much more likely than my hansom cab lunatic. I could see that now.

There was another knocking on the door. It's the agent, I thought, back again. But it wasn't. It was the landlady with a basket of fruit. What a pleasant surprise, I remember thinking, taking the basket from her. "Grape?" I asked, but she shook her head.

"There's a note in it," she said, nodding at the basket.

From Dorothy, I thought, suddenly glad that I'd made the reservation at The Hoisted Pint. Absence was making hearts grow fonder. And quickly, too. I'd only left that morning. There was the corner of an envelope, sticking up through the purple grapes and wedged in between a couple of tired-looking apples. The whole lot of fruit lay atop a bed of coconut fiber in a too-heavy and too-deep basket.

It was the muffled ticking that did the trick, though—the ticking of an infernal machine, hidden in the basket of fruit.

My breath caught, and I nearly dropped the basket and leaped out the door. But I couldn't do that. It would bring down the hotel, probably with me still in it. I hopped across to the window, looking down on what must have been a half-dozen people, including St. Ives and Hasbro, who were right then heading up the steps. I couldn't just pitch it out onto everybody's heads.

So I sprinted for the door, yanking it open and leaping out into the hallway. My heart slammed away, flailing like an engine, and without bothering to knock I threw open the door to the room kitty-corner to my own, and surprised an old man who sat in a chair next to a fortuitously open casement, reading a book.

It was Parsons, not wearing his fishing garb anymore. —⌒

Aloft in a Balloon

ARSONS LEAPED UP, wild with surprise to see me rushing at him like that, carrying my basket. "It's a bomb!" I shouted. "Step aside!" and I helped him do it, too, with my elbow. He sprawled toward the bed, and I swung the basket straight through the open casement and into the bay in a long, low arc. If there had been boats roundabout, I believe I would have let it go anyway. It wasn't an act of heroics by that time; it was an act of desperation, of getting the ticking basket out of my hand and as far away from me as possible.

It exploded. Wham! Just like that, a foot above the water, which geysered up around the sailing fragments of basket and fruit. Everything rained down, and then there was the splashing back and forth of little colliding waves. Parsons stood behind me, taking in the whole business, half scowling, half surprised. I took a couple of calming breaths, but they did precious little good. My hand— the one that had held the basket—was shaking treacherously, and I sat down hard in Parsons's chair.

"Sorry," I said to him. "Didn't mean to barge in."

But he waved it away as if he saw the necessity of it. It was obvious that the device had been destined to go out through the window and into the sea. There had been no two ways about it. I could hardly have tucked it under my coat and forgotten about it. He stared for a moment out the window and then said, "Down on holiday," in a flat voice, repeating what I'd said to him on the pier that morning and demonstrating that, like everyone else, he had seen through me all along. I cleared my throat, thinking in a muddle, and just then, as if to save me, St. Ives and Hasbro rushed in, out of breath because of having sprinted up the stairs when they'd heard the explosion.

The sight of Parsons standing there struck St. Ives dumb, I believe. The professor knew that Parsons was lurking roundabout, because I'd told him, but here, at the Apple? And what had Parsons to do with the explosion, and what had I to do with Parsons?

There was no use this time in Parsons's simply muttering, "Good day," and seeing us all out the door. It was time for talking turkey, as Captain Bowker would have put it. Once again, I was the man with the information. I told them straight off about the insurance agent.

"And he knew my name?" said St. Ives, cocking his head.

"That's right. He seemed to know…" I stopped and glanced at Parsons, who was listening closely.

St. Ives continued for me. "He made sure who you were, and he found out that you had suspicions about what was going on at the icehouse, and then he left. And a moment later the basket arrived."

I nodded and started to tell the story my way, to put the right edge on it, but St. Ives turned to Parsons and, without giving me half a chance, said, "See here. We're not playing games anymore. I'm going to tell you, flat out and without my beating about the bush, that we know about Lord Kelvin's machine being stolen. A baby could piece that business together, what with the debacle down on the Embankment, the flying iron and all. What could that have been but an electromagnet of astonishing strength? There's no use your being coy about it any longer. I've got a sneaking hunch what they've done with it, too. Let's put everything straight. I'll tell you what I know, and you tell me what you know, and together maybe we'll see to the bottom of this murky well."

Parsons held his hands out in a theatrical gesture of helplessness. "I'm down here to catch a fish," he said. "It's you who are throwing bombs through the window. You seem to attract those sorts of things—bombs and bullets."

St. Ives gave Parsons a weary glance. Then he said to me,

"This agent, Jack, what did he look like?"

"Tall and thin, and with a hooknose. He was bald under his hat, and his hair stuck out over his ears like a chimney sweep's brush."

Parsons looked as though he'd been electrocuted. He started to say something, hesitated, started up again, and then, pretending that it didn't much matter to him anyway, said, "Stooped, was he?"

I nodded.

"Tiny mouth, like a bird?"

"That's right."

Parsons sagged. It was a gesture of resignation. We waited him out. "That wasn't any insurance agent."

The news didn't surprise anyone. Of course it hadn't been an insurance agent. St. Ives had seen that at once. The man's mind is honed like a knife. Insurance agents don't send bombs around disguised as fruit baskets. We waited for Parsons to tell us who the man was, finally, to quit his tiresome charade, but he stood there chewing it over in his mind, calculating how much he could say.

Parsons is a good man. I'll say that in the interests of fair play. He and St. Ives have had their differences, but they've both of them been after the same ends, just from different directions. Parsons couldn't abide the notion of people being shot at, even people who tired him as much as I did. So in the end, he told us:

"It was a man named Higgins."

"Leopold Higgins!" cried St. Ives. "The ichthyologist. Of course." St. Ives somehow always seemed to know at least half of everything—which is a lot, when you add it up.

Parsons nodded wearily. "Oxford man. Renegade academician. They're a dangerous breed when they go feral, academics are. Higgins was a chemist, too. Came back from the Orient with insane notions about carp. Insisted that they could be frozen and thawed out, months later, years. You could keep them in a deep freeze, he said. Some sort of glandular excretion, as I understand it, that drained water out of the cells, kept them from bursting when they froze. He was either an expert in cryogenics or a lunatic. It's your choice. He was clearly off his head, though. I think it was opium that did it. He claimed to dream these things.

"Anyway, it was a glandular business with carp. That was his theory. All of it, mind you, was wrapped up in the notion that it was these secretions that were the secret of the astonishing longevity of a carp. He hadn't been back from China a year when he disappeared. I saw him, in fact, just two days earlier, in London, at the club. He burst in full of wild enthusiasm, asking after old—after people I'd never heard of, saying that he was on the verge of something monumental. And then he was gone—out the door and never seen again."

"Until now," said St. Ives.

"Apparently so."

St. Ives turned to Hasbro and myself and said, "Our worst fears have come to pass," and then he bowed to Parsons, thanked him very much, and strode out with us following, down the hallway and straightaway to the train station.

———∽∽∽———

WE SPENT THE night on the Ostende ferry. I couldn't sleep, thinking about the *Landed Catch* sinking like a brick just to the south of the very waters we were plowing, and I was ready at the nod of a head to climb into a lifeboat and row away. The next day found us on a train to Amsterdam, and from there on into Germany and Denmark, across the Skaggerak and into Norway. It was an appalling trip, rushing it like that, catching little bits of hurried sleep, and the only thing to recommend it was that there was at least no one trying to kill me anymore, not as long as I was holed up in that train.

St. Ives was in a funk. A year ago he had made this same weary journey, and had left Narbondo for dead in a freezing tarn near Mount Hjarstaad, which rises out of the Norwegian Sea. Now what was there but evidence that the doctor was alive and up to mischief? It didn't stand to reason, not until Parsons's chatter about cryogenics. Two things were bothering St. Ives, wearing him thinner by the day. One was that somehow he had failed once again. Thwarting Narbondo and diverting the earth from the course of that ghastly comet had stood as his single greatest triumph; now it wasn't a triumph anymore. Now it was largely a failure, in his mind, anyway. Just like that. White had become black. He had lived for months full of contradictions of conscience. Had he brought about the doctor's death, or had he tried to prevent it? And never mind that— had he tried to prevent it, or had he attempted to fool himself into thinking he had? He couldn't abide the notion of working to fool himself. That was the avenue to madness. So here, in an instant, all was effaced. The doctor was apparently alive after all and embarked on some sort of murderous rampage. St. Ives hadn't been thorough enough. What Narbondo wanted was a good long hanging.

And on top of that was the confounding realization that there wasn't an easier way to learn what we had to learn. St. Ives knew no one in the wilds of Norway. He couldn't just post a letter asking whether a frozen hunchback had been pulled from a lake and revived. He had to find out for himself. I think he wondered, though, whether he hadn't ought simply to have sent Hasbro about the business, or me, and stayed behind in Sterne Bay.

We were in Trondheim, still hurtling northward, when the news arrived about the sinking of the other two ships, just below where the first had disappeared. Iron-hulled vessels, they'd gone down lickety-split, exactly the same way. The crew had abandoned the first one, but not the second. Ten men were lost in all. It had been Godall who sent the cable to Norway. He had prevailed upon the prime minister to take action. St. Ives was furious with himself for having done nothing to prevent the debacle.

What could he have done, though? That's what I asked him. It was useless to think that he could have stopped it. Part of his fury was directed at the government. They had been warned, even before Godall had tackled them. Someone—Higgins, probably— had sent them a monumental ransom note. They had laughed it away, thinking it a hoax, even though it had been scrawled in the same hand as had Captain Bowker's note, and warned them that more ships would be sunk. The Royal Academy should have urged them to take it seriously, but they had mud on their faces by now, and had hesitated. All of them had been fools,

Shipping now was suspended in the area, from the mouth of the Thames to Folkestone, at an inconceivable expense to the Crown and to private enterprise. Half of London trade had slammed to a halt, according to Godall. It was a city under siege, and no one seemed to know who the enemy was or where he lay…St. Ives was deadly silent, frustrated with our slow travel northward, with the interminable rocky landscape, the fjords, the pine forests.

What could he do but carry on? That's what I asked him. He could turn around, that's what. He made up his mind just like that. We were north of Trondheim and just a few hours from our destination, St. Ives would take Hasbro with him. I would go on alone, and see what I could see. He and Hasbro would rush back to Dover where St.

Ives would assemble scientific apparatus. He had been a fool, he said, a moron, a nitwit, It was he and he alone who was responsible for the death of those ten men. He could have stopped it if he hadn't been too muddleheaded to see. That was ever St. Ives's way, blaming himself for all the deviltry in the world, because he hadn't been able to stop it. The sheer impossibility of his stopping all of it never occurred to him,

Hasbro gave me a look as they hefted their luggage out onto the platform. St. Ives was deflated, shrunken almost, and there shone in his eyes a distant gleam, as if he were focused on a single wavering point on the horizon—the leering face of Ignacio Narbondo—and he would keep his eyes fixed on that face until he stared the man into oblivion.

Hasbro took me aside for a moment to tell me that he would take care of the professor, that I wasn't to worry, that we would all win through in the end. All I had to do was learn the truth about Narbondo. St. Ives must be desperately certain of the facts now; he had become as methodical as a clockwork man. But like that same man, he seemed to both of us to be running slowly down. And for one brief moment there on the platform, I half hoped that St. Ives would never find Narbondo, because, horrible as it sounds, it was Narbondo alone that gave purpose to the great man's life.

Narbondo had had a long and curious criminal history: vivisection, counterfeiting, murder—a dozen close escapes capped by his fleeing from Newgate Prison very nearly on the eve of his intended execution. There was nothing vile that he hadn't put his hand to. He dabbled in alchemy and amphibian physiology, and there was some evidence that, working with the long-forgotten formulae of Paracelsus, he had developed specifics that would revive the dead. His grandfather, the elder Narbondo, had elaborated the early successes of those revivification experiments in journals that had been lost long ago. And those, of course, were the papers alluded to by the woman in Godall's shop.

It was a mystery, this business of the lost journals—a far deeper mystery than it would seem on the surface, and one that seemed to have threads connecting it to the dawn of history and to the farthest corners of the earth. And it was a mystery that we wouldn't solve. We would tackle only the current manifestation of it, this business of Higgins the academician and Captain Bowker and the revived Narbondo and the ships sinking in the Dover Strait. There was enough in that to confound even a man like St. Ives.

It was St. Ives's plan to resort again to the dirigible. I would proceed to Mount Hjarstaad by train and make what discoveries I could, while waiting for the arrival of the dirigible, which would put out of Dover upon St. Ives's return to that city. Ferries were still docking there, but only if they had come in from the north: Flanders and Normandy ferries had stopped running altogether. So St. Ives would send the dirigible for me, in an effort to fetch me back to England in time to be of service.

We should have hired the dirigible in the first place, lamented St. Ives, standing on the platform in the cold arctic wind. We should have this, we should have that.

I muttered and nodded, never having seen him in such despair. There was no arguing with him there in that rocky landscape, which did its part to freeze one's hope. I would have to go on with as stout a heart as I could fabricate.

And so away they went south, and I north, and I didn't learn another thing about their adventures until I met up with them again, days later, back in Sterne Bay, the dirigible rescue having come off without a hitch and skived at least a couple of days off my wanderings about Norway, but having sailed me into Dover too late to join my comrades in their dangerous scientific quest. I'm getting ahead of myself, though. It's what I found out in Hjarmold, near the mountain, that signifies.

Narbondo *had* been fished out of his watery grave, all right—by a tall thin man with a baldhead. It had to have been Leopold Higgins, although he had registered at the hostel under the name Wiggins, which was evidence either of a man gone barmy or of a man remarkably sure of himself. I got all this from the stableboy, whose room lay at the back of the stables, and who had seen a good deal of what transpired there. No real effort had been made for secrecy. Higgins and an accomplice—Captain Bowker, from the description of him—had ridden in late one afternoon with Narbondo lying in the back of the wagon, stiff as a day-old fish. They claimed that he had just that morning fallen into the lake, that they had been on a climbing expedition. There was nothing in their story to excite suspicions. Higgins had professed to be a doctor and had stopped them from sending up to Bodø for the local medicine man.

Curiously, he hadn't taken Narbondo inside the hostel to thaw him out; he had set up camp in the stables instead, insisting that Narbondo's recovery must be a slow business indeed, and for the first two nights Narbondo slept on his table without so much as a blanket for covering. Higgins fed him nothing but what he said was cod-liver oil, but which he referred to as "elixir." And once, when Narbondo began to moan and shudder, Higgins said that he was "coming round too soon," and he hauled Narbondo out into the freezing night and let him stiffen up some.

The stableboy who told me all of this was a bright lad, who had smelled something rotten, as it were, and it wasn't the fish oil, either. He had a sharp enough eye to recognize frauds like Higgins and Bowker, and he watched them, he said, through a knothole when they thought he was asleep. It was on the fourth night that Narbondo awakened fully, if only for a few seconds. Higgins had set up some sort of apparatus—hoses, bladders, bowls of yellow liquid. Throughout the night he had sprayed the doctor with mists while Captain Bowker snored in the hay. An hour before dawn, Narbondo's eyes blinked open in the lamplight, and after a moment of looking around himself, puzzled at what he saw, he smiled a sort of half-grin and said the single word, "Good," and then lapsed again into unconsciousness.

I knew by then what it was I had come for, and I had learned it in about half an hour. St. Ives had been right to turn around; it didn't take three men to talk to a stableboy. After that I was forced to lounge about the village, eating vile food, wondering what it was that my companions were up to and when my dirigible would arrive, and worrying finally about one last bit of detail: the frozen man, according to my stableboy, had had milky-white hair and pale skin, like a man carved out of snow or dusted with frost; and yet Narbondo had had lanky black hair, just going to gray, when he had catapulted into that tarn.

The phrase "dusted with frost" wasn't my own; it was the artful creation of my stableboy, who had lived for ten years in York and might have been a writer, I think, if he had put his mind to it. Here he was mucking out stables. It made me wonder about the nature of justice, but only for a moment. Almost at once it brought to mind the letter we had read in Godall's shop, the one signed H. Frost, of Edinburgh University.

—◦◦◦—

MEANWHILE, LANGDON ST. Ives and Hasbro arrived back in Dover without incident— no bombs, no gunfire, no threats to the ship. I believe that our sudden disappearance from Sterne Bay had confounded our enemies. Perhaps they thought that the fruit-basket bomb had frightened us away, although Narbondo—or Frost—knowing St. Ives as well as he did, shouldn't have made that mistake. Anyway, in Dover, St. Ives arranged for the dirigible to fetch me out of Norway, and then set about hiring a balloon for himself and Hasbro. They didn't wait for me—they couldn't—and I'm narrating their exploits as accurately as I can, having got the story secondhand, but straight from the horse's mouth, of course.

St. Ives set about constructing a bismuth spiral, which, for the reader unfamiliar with the mysteries of magnetism, is a simple snail-shell spiral of bismuth connected to a meter that reads changes of resistance in the spiral to determine intensities of magnetic fields. It's a child's toy, comparatively speaking, but foolproof. The very simplicity of St. Ives's notion infuriated him even further. It was something that ought to have been accomplished a week earlier, in time to save those ten men.

He affixed the spiral to a pole that they could slip down through a small hiatus in the basket of the balloon, so as to suspend the spiral just above the waves, making the whole business of taking a reading absolutely dangerous—almost deadly, as it turned out—because it required their navigating the balloon perilously close to the sea itself. Why didn't they use a length of rope, instead—play out the line while staying safely aloft? That was my question too; and the answer, in short, is that the science of electricity and magnetism wouldn't allow for it: the length of wire connecting the bismuth to the meter must be as short as possible for the reading to be accurate—that was how St. Ives understood it, although his understanding was nearly the death of him.

He meant to discover where Lord Kelvin's machine—the enormously powerful electromagnet stolen from the machine works in Holborn—lay beneath the sea, some-where in the Dover Strait. He assumed that it rested on a submerged platform or on

a shallow sandy shoal. Maybe it was anchored, but then again maybe it was slowly drifting at the whim of deepwater currents. He suspected the existence of a float or buoy of some sort, both to locate it and, perhaps, to effect its switching on and off.

The two of them were aloft within a day. It was doubtful that the ban on local shipping would last out the week; the economy wouldn't stand it. The government would pay the ransom or get used to the notion of losing ships. The Royal Academy still denied everything, right down to the ground, while at the same time working furiously to solve the mystery themselves.

St. Ives and Hasbro scoured the surface of the sea, from Ramsgate to Dungeness. Hasbro, an accomplished balloonist—the blue-ribbon winner, in fact, of the Trans-European balloon races of 1883—grappled with the problem of buoyancy, of keeping the basket above the licking waves in order not to drown St. Ives's apparatus. The wind blew down out of the North Sea in gusts, buffeting them southward toward the coast of France, and it took all of Hasbro's skill to steady their course at all. St. Ives had fashioned a sort of ballasted sea anchor that they dragged along and so avoided being blown across the coast of Normandy before discovering anything.

Even so, it finally began to seem as if their efforts were in vain—the Strait being almost inconceivably vast from the perspective of two men in a balloon. It was sometime late in the afternoon, when they were just on the edge of giving up, that they saw a sloop flying the ensign of the Royal Academy. St. Ives could see Parsons on the deck, and he waved to the man, who, after seeming to ascertain who it was that hailed him, replied with a perfunctory little nod and went immediately belowdecks. There was the chance, of course, that the Academy had already discovered the spot where the device had been sunk. And there was the chance that they were still searching. What would St. Ives do? What *could* he do?

They swept across her bow and passed her, St. Ives lowering the bismuth spiral one last time to take another reading. It registered some little bit of deviation, the needle swinging around fairly sharply as they drove along south and west, away from Parsons's sloop.

They were two hundred yards off his port bow when the balloon lurched, throwing both the professor and Hasbro into the basket wall in a tangle of arms and legs. The basket tilted ominously, nearly pouring them into the sea. Hasbro hacked furiously at the rope holding the sea anchor, thinking that it had caught itself in something, while St. Ives held on to his pole and meter, which burst suddenly in his hands. That is to say the meter did—exploded—its needle whirling around and around like a compass gone mad, until it twisted itself into ruin,

St. Ives let go of the apparatus, which shot straight down into the water as the balloon strained at her lines, trying to tug the basket skyward, but having no luck. The basket, torn in the opposite direction by an unseen force, spun and dipped crazily, fighting as if it had been grappled by a phantom ship.

The crew of the sloop, including Parsons, lined the deck, watching the wild balloon and the two men clinging helplessly to her. It must have appeared as if she were being torn asunder by warring spirits—which she was, in a sense, for it was the powerful forces of hot air and magnetism that tugged her asunder. The ruined meter told the tale. St. Ives had found the sunken device right enough; the iron-reinforced base of the balloon basket was caught in its electromagnetic grip.

With a tearing of canvas and snapping of line, the basket lurched downward, almost into the ocean. A ground swell washed across them, and in an instant they were foundering. St. Ives and Hasbro had to swim for it, both of them striking out through the cold water toward the distant sloop, the nails in their bootheels prising themselves out. St. Ives fished out his clasp knife and offered it up to the machine in order that his trousers pocket might be saved. Finally, when they were well away from the snapping line and rollicking bag, they stopped swimming to watch.

For a moment their basket still tossed on the surface of the water. Then it was tugged down into the depths, where it hung suspended just below the surface. The still-moored balloon flattened itself against the sea, humping across the rolling swell, the gasses inside snapping the seams apart with Gatling-gun bursts of popping, the hot air inside whooshing into the atmosphere as if a giant were treading the thing flat.

Within minutes the deflated canvas followed the basket down like a fleeing squid and was gone, and St. Ives and Hasbro trod water, dubious about their obvious success. If it weren't for the sloop sending a boat out after them, they would have drowned, and no doubt about it. Parsons, seeing that clearly, welcomed them aboard with a hearty lot of guffawing through his beard.

"Quite a display," he said to St. Ives as the professor slogged toward a forward cabin. "That was as profitable an example of scientific method as I can remember. I trust you took careful notes. There was a look on your face, man—I could see it even at such a distance as that—a look of pure scientific enlightenment. If I were an artist I'd sketch it out for you…" He went on this way, Parsons did, laughing through his beard and twigging St. Ives all the way back to Dover, after leaving the area encircled with red-painted buoys.

———

AT THE VERY moment that they were aloft over the Strait, I was aloft in the dirigible, watching the gray seas slip past far below, and captain of nothing for the moment but my own fate. I was bound for Sterne Bay. The business of the icehouse had become clear to me while I lounged in Norway. Days had passed, though, since my confrontation with Captain Bowker, and in that time just about anything could have happened. I might rush back to find them all gone, having no more need of ice. On the other hand, I might easily find a way to do my part.

At the Crown and Apple I discovered that St. Ives and Hasbro hadn't yet returned from their balloon adventure. Parsons was gone too. I was alone, and that saddened me. Parsons's company would have been better than nothing. I sat on the edge of the bed contemplating a pint or two and a nap, wanting to escape my duty by going to sleep—drink and sleep being a substitute, albeit a poor one, for company. Sitting there reminded me of that last fateful knock on the door, though—reminded me that while I slept, no end of frightful business might be transpiring. Who could say that the door mightn't swing open silently and an infernal machine, fuse sputtering, mightn't roll like a melon into the center of the floor...

A nap was out of the question. But what would I do instead? I would go to the icehouse. There was no percentage in my pretending to be Abner Benbow any longer. Might I disguise myself? A putty nose and a wig might accomplish something. I dismissed the idea. That was the sort of thing they would expect. My only trump card was that they would have no notion of my having returned to Sterne Bay.

Still, I wouldn't take any unnecessary risks. I was ready for them now. I went out through the second-story door at the back of the inn, and down rickety steps that led out past a weedy bit of garden and through a gate, right to the edge of the bay. A half score of rowboats were serried along a dock of rotting wooden planks that ran out into the water fifty good yards or so before becoming a mere thicket of broken pilings. There was no one about.

The tide was out, leaving a little stretch of shingle running along beside a low stone seawall. I clambered down and picked my way along the shingle, thinking to emerge into the village some distance from the Apple, so that if they *were* onto me, and someone was watching the inn, I'd confound them.

Some hundred yards down, I slipped back over the seawall and followed a narrow boardwalk between two vine-covered cottages, squeezing out from between them only a little ways down from where my beggar man was shot before he could borrow any money from me. I hiked along pretty briskly toward the icehouse, but the open door of The Hoisted Pint brought me up short.

I had never discovered whether my rubber elephant inhabited a room there, largely because I had been coy, playing the detective, and was overcome by the woman behind the counter, who, I was pretty sure, had taken me for a natural fool. The truth of it is that I'm too easily put off by an embarrassment. This time I wouldn't be. I angled toward the door, up the steps, and into the foyer. She stood as ever, meddling with receipts, and seemed not to recognize me at all. My hearty, "Hello again," merely caused her to squint.

She pushed her spectacles down her nose and looked at me over them. "Yes?" she said.

Somehow the notion of her having forgotten me, after all the rigamarole just a few days earlier, put an edge on my tone. I was through being pleasant. I can't stand cheeky superiority in people, especially in clerks and waiters, who have nothing to recommend them but the fact of their being employed. What was this woman but a high-toned clerk? Perhaps she owned the inn; perhaps she didn't. There was nothing in any of it that justified her putting on airs.

"See here," I said, leaning on the counter. "I'm looking for a woman and her son. I believe they're staying here or at any rate were staying here last week. They look remarkably alike, frighteningly so, if you take my meaning. The son, who might be as old as thirty, carries with him an India-rubber elephant that makes a noise."

"A *noise*?" she said, apparently having digested nothing of the rest of my little speech. The notion of an elephant making a noise, of my having gone anatomical on her, had shattered her ability to understand the clearest sort of English, had obliterated reason and logic.

"Never mind the noise," I said, losing my temper. "Disregard it." I caught myself, remembering St. Ives's dealings with the landlady at the Crown and Apple. Tread softly, I reminded myself, and I forced a smile. "That's right. It's the woman and her son that I wanted to ask you about. She's my mother's cousin, you see. I got a letter in the post, saying that she and her son—that would be, what? my cousin twice removed, little Billy, we used to call him, although that wasn't his name, not actually—anyway, that she's here on holiday, and I'm anxious to determine where she's staying."

The woman still looked down her nose at me, waiting for me to go on, as if what I had said so far hadn't made half enough sense, couldn't have begun to express what it was I wanted.

I winked at her and brassed right along. "I asked myself, 'Where in all of Sterne Bay is my mother's favorite cousin likely to stay? Why, in the prettiest inn that the town has to offer. That's the ticket.' And straightaway I came here, and I'm standing before you now to discover whether she is indeed lodged at this inn."

That ought to have made it clear to the woman, and apparently it did, for the next thing she said was, "What is the lady's name?" in a sort of schoolteacher's voice, a tone that never fails to freeze my blood—doubly so this time because I hadn't any earthly idea what the woman's name was.

"She has several," I said weakly, my brain stuttering. "In the Spanish tradition. She might be registered under Larson, with an *o*."

I waited, drumming my fingers on the oak counter as she perused the register. Why had I picked Larson? I can't tell you. It was the first name that came to mind, like Abner Benbow.

"I'm sorry," she said, looking up at me.

"Perhaps...," I said, gesturing toward the book. She hesitated, but apparently couldn't think of any good reason to keep it away from me; there was nothing in what I asked to make her suspicious, and she wouldn't, I suppose, want to insult the favored cousin several times removed of one of her registered guests. So she pushed her glasses back up her nose, sniffed at me, and turned the book around on the counter.

Fat lot of good it would do me. I didn't know what the woman's name was. What sort of charade was I playing? The rubber elephant had been my only clue, and that hadn't fetched any information out of her. If I brought it back into the conversation now, she'd call the constable and I'd find myself strapped to a bed in Colney Hatch. I was entirely at sea, groping for anything at all to keep me afloat.

I gave the list a perfunctory glance, ready to thank her and leave. One of the names nearly flew out at me: Pule, Leona Pule.

Suddenly I knew the identity of the madman in the coach. I knew who the mother was. I seemed to know a thousand things, and from that knowledge sprang two thousand fresh mysteries. It had been Willis Pule that had stolen my elephant. I should have seen it, but it had been years since he had contrived a wormlike desire for my wife Dorothy, my fiancée then. You wouldn't call it love; not if you knew him. He went mad when he couldn't possess her, and very nearly murdered any number of people. He was an apprentice of Dr. Narbondo at the time, but they fell out, and Pule was last seen insane, comatose in the back of Narbondo's wagon, being driven away toward an uncertain fate.

I noted the room number. They hadn't left. They might be upstairs at the moment. The nonsense in the coach—his taking the elephant—was that a charade? Was that his way of toying with me? Was it Willis Pule that had shot my beggar man? I thanked the woman at the counter and stepped away up the shadowy stairs, half thinking to discover whether from room 312 a man might have a clear rifle shot down toward the green.

I'll admit it: right then I was foolishly proud of myself for being "on the case," and was half wondering about the connection between Pule's grandfather and the elder Narbondo, which mirrored, if I saw things aright, the relationship between Pule and the doctor. How did Higgins fit, though? Had he discovered references to the lost alchemical papers that had ruined Mrs. Pule's family? Had he thought to revive Narbondo in order to enlist his aid in finding them? And now they were all skulking about in Sterne Bay, perhaps, carrying out their deadly plans for the machine, waiting for the ransom, thawing Narbondo out slowly at the icehouse.

I felt awfully alone at the moment, and wished heartily that St. Ives and Hasbro weren't off doing whatever they were doing. The stairs creaked. The evening sunlight filtering through the landing windows was insufficient, and the deepening shadows above me seemed to be a waiting ambush as I stepped cautiously out onto the dim third-floor landing.

An empty hallway stretched away in either direction. Room 312 was either up or down; it didn't matter to me, for it was clear at once that the landing window would suffice if what you wanted to do was shoot a man. The iron hinges of the double casement were rusted. I got onto my hands and knees and peered at the floor in the failing light. It was swept clean, except for right along the floor moldings, where flakes of rust dusted the very corner. The window wasn't opened very often; but it had been recently. The varnished wood of the sill was etched with a scraped indentation where someone had forced open the jammed casement, the wood beneath the scratch still fresh and clean, barely even dusty.

I slipped the latch and pulled, but the old window, swollen by sea air and the wet spring weather, was jammed shut. I wiggled it open just far enough to wedge my fingers in behind it, and then it was easy enough to work the window open, scraping it again across the sill. I leaned out then, peering through the gloom toward the green where the beggar had died.

The sounds of the village settling into evening struck me as being very pleasant, and the rush of sea wind in my face awakened me from the morbid reverie of dread that I'd slipped into while climbing the darkened stairs. I could even see the lights of the Crown and Apple, and they reminded me of supper and a pint. But then I looked down three long stories to the paving stones of the courtyard below, and with a dreadful shudder I was reminded of danger in all its manifold guises, and I bent back into the safety of the hallway, imagining sudden hands pushing against the small of my back, and me tumbling out and falling headlong....Being handed a bomb in a basket has that effect on me.

I knew what I had to know. Confrontations would accomplish nothing, especially when I had no idea on earth what it was, exactly, I would discover upon knocking on the door of the Pules' room. Better to think about it over supper.

I forced the window shut, then stood up and turned around, thinking to steal back down the stairs and away. But I found myself staring into the face of the ghastly Mrs. Pule, the woman in Godall's shop. —᠀

My Adventure at
The Hoisted Pint

I GASPED OUT A sort of hoarse yip while she grinned out of that melon face of hers—a hollow grin, empty of any real amusement. She pointed a revolver at me.

Down the hail we went. I would be visiting their room after all, and I'll admit that I didn't like the notion a bit. What would St. Ives do? Whirl around and disarm her? Talk her out of whatever grisly notion she had in mind? Prevail upon her better judgment? I didn't know how to do any of that. St. Ives wouldn't have gotten himself into this mess in the first place.

She knocked twice on the door of the room, then paused, then knocked once. It swung open, but nobody stood there; whoever had opened the door was hidden behind it, not wanting to be seen. Who would it be? Captain Bowker, perhaps, waiting to lambaste me with a truncheon. I couldn't have that. Ignoring the revolver, I ducked away to the left into the room and spun around to face whoever it was that would emerge when the door swung shut.

It was the lunatic son—Willis Pule. He pecked out coyly, just his head, and his mother had to snatch the door shut because he didn't want to let go of it. She reached across and pinched him on the ear, and his coy smile evaporated, replaced by a look of theatrical shock, which disappeared in turn when he got a really good glimpse at the fright that must have been plain on my face. Then, suddenly happy, he affected the wide-eyed and round-mouthed demeanor of the fat man in the comical drawing, the one who has just that moment noted the approach of someone bearing an enormous plate of cream tarts. Pule pulled his right hand from behind his back and waved my elephant at me.

There was a buzzing just then, and the woman strode across to where the outlet of a speaking tube protruded from the wall. She slid open its little hatch-cover, jammed her ear against it, listened, and then, speaking into the tube, she said, "Yes, we've got him." She listened again and said, "No, in the hallway." And after another moment of listening she snickered out, "Him? Not hardly," and closed the hatch-cover and shut off the tube.

She had obviously just spoken to the landlady. The place was a rat's nest. Everything was clear to me as I slumped uninvited into a stuffed chair. All my detective work was laughable; I'd been toyed with all along. Even the elephant under the potted plant—that had been the work of the landlady too. She had snatched it away, of course, when I'd gone out through the door. She was the only one who was close enough to have got to it and away again before I had come back in. And all the rigamarole about my mother's cousin with the improbable names

She must have taken me for a child after that, watching me stroll away up the stairs to my probable doom. "Him, not hardly…" I grimaced. I thought I knew what that meant, and I couldn't argue with it. Well, maybe it would serve me some good in the end; maybe I could turn it to advantage. I would play the witless milksop, and then I would strike. I tried to convince myself of that.

Willis Pule tiptoed across to a pine table with a wooden chair alongside it. His tiptoeing was exaggerated, this time like a comic actor being effusively quiet, taking great silent knee-high steps. What was a madman but an actor who didn't know he was acting, in a play that nobody else had the script for? He sat in the chair, nodding at me and working his mouth slowly, as if he were chewing the end of a cigar. What did it all mean, all his mincing and posing and winking? Nothing. Not a damned thing. All the alterations in the weather of his face were nonsense.

He laid the elephant on the table and removed its red jumbo pants with a sort of infantile glee. Then he patted his coat pocket, slipped out a straight razor, and very swiftly and neatly sawed the elephant's ears off. A look of intense pity and sadness shifted his eyes and mouth, and then was gone.

I forgot to breathe for a moment, watching him. It wasn't the ruining of the toy that got to me. I had built the thing, after all, and I've found that a man rarely regrets the loss of something he's built himself; he's always too aware of the flaws in it, of the fact that it wants a hat, but it's too late to give it one. It was the beastly cool way that he pared the thing up—that's what got to me: the way he watched me out of the corner of his eye, and looked up once to wink at me and nod at the neat bit of work he was accomplishing, almost as if to imply that it was merely practice, sawing up the elephant was. And, horribly, he was dressed just like his mother, too, still got up in the same florid chintz.

His mother walked past him, ignoring him utterly. I hoped that she might take the razor away from him. A razor in the hands of an obvious lunatic, after all…But she didn't care about the razor. She rather approved of it, I think,

"Willis likes to operate on things," she said matter-of-factly, the word *operate* effecting a sort of ghastly resonance in my inner ear. I nodded a little, trying to smile, as if pleased to listen to the chatter of a mother so obviously proud of her son. "He cut a bird apart once, and affixed its head to the body of a mouse."

"Ah," I said,

She cocked her head and favored me with a horrid grimace of sentimental wistfulness, "It lived for a week. He had to feed it out of a tiny bottle, poor thing. It was a night-and-day job, ministering to that helpless little creature. A night-and-day job. It nearly wore him out. And then when it died I thought his poor heart would break, like an egg. He enshrined it under the floorboards along with the others. Held a service and all."

I shook my head, wondering at the notion of a heart breaking like an egg. They were both barmy, and no doubt about it. And given Pule's years in apprenticeship with Narbondo, all this stuff about vivisection very likely wasn't just talk. I glanced over at the table. Pule had managed to stuff a piece of candle through the holes where the beast's ears had been. He lit it with a match at both ends, so that the twin flames shot out on either side of its head, melting the wax all over the tabletop and filling the room with the reek of burning rubber.

"Willis!" shrieked the mother, wrinkling up her nose at the stink. In a fit of determination she leaped up and raced toward the sleeping room. She was immediately out again, brandishing a broad wooden paddle, and her son, suddenly contrite, began to howl and beg and cry. Then, abruptly, he gave off his pleading and started to yell, "Fire! Fire!" half giggling, half sobbing, as he slammed away at the burning elephant with his cap, capering around and around the table and chair as his mother angled in to swat him with the paddle.

It was an appalling sight— one I hope never again to witness as long as I live. I was up in a shot, and leaping for the door, getting out while the getting was good. The getting wasn't any good, though; the door was locked tight, and both the mother and son turned on me together, he plucking up the razor and she waving the paddle.

I apologized profusely. "Terribly sorry," I said. "Terribly, terribly sorry." I couldn't think of anything else. But all the while I looked around the room, searching out a weapon, and there was nothing at all close to hand except a chair cushion. I believe that if I could have got at something with a little weight to it I would have pounded them both into jelly right then and there, and answered for the crime afterward. There wasn't a court in all of England that would have condemned me, not after taking a look at that mad pair and another look beneath the floorboards of their house in London.

They advanced a step, so I shouted, "I know the truth!" and skipped away against the far wall. It was a nonsensical thing to shout, since I didn't any more know the truth than I knew the names of my fictitious cousins, but it stopped them cold. Or at least it stopped her. He, on the other hand, had fallen entirely into the role of being a menace, and he stalked back and forth eyeing me like a pirate, and she eyeing him, until, seeing her chance, she walloped him on the posterior with the paddle, grinning savagely, and very nearly throwing him straight razor and all into the chair I'd been sitting in.

He crept back to his table tearfully, like a broken man, whimpering nonsense at her, apologizing. He slumped over the ravaged elephant, hacking off its feet with the razor and then slicing its legs to ribbons, the corners of his mouth turned down in a parody of grief and rage.

"Where are they?" she asked.

What are they; that was the question. I ought to have had the answer, but didn't. It could be she meant people—St. Ives, maybe, and Hasbro. She thought, perhaps, that they were lurking roundabout, waiting for me. It didn't sound like that's what she meant, though. I scrambled through my mind, recalling her conversation at Godall's shop.

"I can lead you to them." I was clutching at straws, hoping wasn't as utterly obvious as it seemed to be.

She nodded. The son peered at me slyly.

"But I want some assurances," I said.

"An affidavit?" she asked, cackling with sudden laughter. "*I'll* give you assurances, Mr. High-and-mighty."

"And I'll give you *this*!" cried the son, leaping up as if spring-driven and waving his straight razor in the air like an Afghani assassin. In a sudden fit he flailed away with it at the remains of the elephant, chopping it like an onion, carving great gashes in the tabletop and banging the razor against the little gear mechanism inside the ruined toy, the several gears wobbling away to fall off the table and onto the floor. Then he cast down the razor, and, snarling and drooling, he plucked up the little jumbo trousers and tore them in half, throwing them to the carpet, alternately trodding on them and spitting at them in a furious spastic dance, and meaning to say, I guess, that the torn pants would be my head if I didn't look sharp.

His mother turned around and slammed him with the paddle again, shouting "Behavior!" very loud, her face red as a zinnia. He yipped across the room and sank into the chair, sitting on his hands and glowering at me.

"Where?" asked the woman. "And no games."

"At the Crown and Apple," I said. "In my room."

"*Your* room." She squinted at me.

"That's correct. I can lead you there now. Quickly."

"You won't lead us anywhere," she said. "We'll lead ourselves. You'll stay here. There's not another living soul on this floor, Mr. Who-bloody-is-it, and everyone on the floor below has been told there's a madman spending the night, given to fits. Keep your lip shut, and if we come back with the notebooks, we'll go easy on you."

Willis Pule nodded happily. "Mummy says I can cut out your tripes," he assured me enthusiastically, "and feed them to the bats."

"The bats," I said, wondering why in the world he had chosen the definite article, and watching him pocket the razor. So it was the notebooks…Both of them donned webby-looking shawls and toddled out the door like the Bedlam Twins, she covering me all the time with the revolver. The door shut and the key clanked in the lock.

I was up and searching the place for a window, for another key, for a vent of some sort—for anything. The room was on the inside of the hallway, though, and without a window. And although both of them were lunatics, they were far too canny to leave spare keys roundabout. I sat down and thought. The Crown and Apple wasn't five minutes' walk. They'd get into my room right enough, search it in another five minutes, and then hurry back to cut my tripes out. Revolver or no revolver, they'd get a surprise when they pushed in through the door. She would make him come through first, of course, to take the blow...I studied out a plan.

What the room lacked was weapons. She had even taken the wooden paddle with her. There were a couple of chairs that would do in a pinch, but I wanted something better. I had worked myself into a bloodthirsty sort of state, and I was thinking in terms of clubbing people insensible. Chairs were too spindly and cumbersome for that.

I went to town on the bedstead—a loose-jointed wooden affair that wanted glue. Yanking the headboard loose from the side rails, I listened with satisfaction as the mattress and rails bumped to the floor, loud enough to alert anyone below that visiting lunatic was doing his work. Then I leaned on one of the posts of the headboard itself, smashing the headboard sideways, the posts straining to tear away from the cross-members. Dowels snapped, wood groaned, and after a little bit of playing ram-it-against-the-floorboards the whole thing went to smash, leaving the turned post free in my hands. I hefted it; I would have liked it shorter, but it would do the trick.

The doorknob rattled just then. They were back, and quick, too. Either that or else maybe the landlady, noticing that the lunatic had been doing his job too well, had come round to investigate. I slid across to stand by the door, thinking that I wouldn't smash the landlady with my club, but would simply push past her instead, and away down the stairs. If it was a man, though...

Whoever it was was having a terrible time with the lock. It seemed like an eternity of metallic clicking before the door swung to. I tensed, the club over my shoulder. A man's face poked in from the dark hallway, the rest of the head following, I closed my eyes, stepped away from the wall, and pounded him one, slamming the club down against the back of his head, and knowing straight out that it wasn't Willis Pule at all, but someone perhaps even more deadly: it was Higgins, the academician-gone-to-seed, still gripping a skeleton key in his right hand.

The blow left him half senseless, knocking him onto his face on the floor. He lay writhing. I stepped across, thinking to give him another one, a sort of cricket swing to the cranium, but he was already down and I couldn't bring myself to do it—something I'm happy about today, but which took all my civilized instincts at the time.

The door lay open before me, and I was out of it quick, bolting for the stairs, throwing the post onto the floor of the hallway, and wondering about Higgins sneaking around like that. He wasn't expected; that was certain. He had seen them both go out, perhaps, and had crept in, no doubt searching for the very notebooks that they were off ransacking my room for. They weren't in league, then, but were probably deadly enemies. The Pules would take good care of him if they found him on the floor of their room.

I peered cautiously down the dark and empty stairwell, and then leaped down the stairs three at a time toward the second-floor landing, thinking to charge into the foyer at a run, knocking down anyone between me and the door and maybe shouting something clever at the landlady to regain some lost dignity. I fairly spun around the baluster and onto the bottom flight of stairs, straight into the faces of the two Pules, who puffed along like engines, coming up, she holding the revolver under her shawl and he going along before, both of them with a deadly resolve.

"Here now!" piped the son, clutching my arm in the devil's own grip.

"Hold him!" she cried. "*We'll* make him sing! Up the stairs, Bucko!"

I kicked him on the shin as hard as I could, my momentum lending it some mustard. He howled and slammed backward against the railing, nearly knocking his mother down. He didn't let go of my arm, though, but pulled me over with him, both of us flailing and rolling and me jerking free and scrabbling back up toward the landing like an anxious crab, expecting to be shot. I was on my feet and jumping up the stairs three at a time toward the third floor, listening to the curses and slaps and yips behind me as Mrs. Pule rallied her son.

There was no shot, despite the way being clear for it and the range close, but I ducked and danced down the third-floor hall anyway, trying to convince myself that she was loathe to fire the gun in public and bring about the collapse of her plans. I should have thought of that an hour ago, when she collared me at the window, but I didn't, and wasn't convinced of it now.

I blasted past the room again, its door still open and Higgins on his hands and knees on the floor, ruminating. The sight of him brought the Pules up short as they came racing along behind me, and for the moment they let me go in order to attend to him. I headed straight toward a French window, grappled with the latch, pulled it open, and looked out, not onto three stories of empty air, thank heaven, but onto a little dormer balcony. There was a hooting from the open door of the room, and a grunt, and then an outright shriek, as the Pules visited the sins of Jack Owlesby onto the head of poor Higgins.

I closed the window behind me, although I couldn't latch it. In a moment they'd be through it and upon me. Without a bit of hesitation I hoisted myself over the railing, swinging myself down and in, landing on my feet on an identical balcony below and immediately crumpling up, my ankles ringing with the impact. I was up again, though, climbing across this railing too, and clutching two handfuls of ivy tendrils with the nitwit idea of clambering down through it to safety like an ape in a rain forest. I scrabbled in the vines with my feet as the ivy tore loose in a rush, and I slid along through it shouting, landing in a viney heap in a flower bed.

The window banged open upstairs, and I was on my feet and running, trailing vines, wincing at the pain in my ankles, but damned if I'd let any of it slow me down.

I expected a shot, but none came—just a litany of curses cried into the night and then cut off abruptly when a voice from a window in a nearby house shouted, "Wot the hell!" and the strollers down along the street to the pier began to point. Mrs. Pule, blessedly, wasn't keen on calling attention to herself just then.

I ran straight toward the gap between the two houses that would lead me to the seawall, not slowing down until I was there, clambering over the now-damp stone and jumping to the shingle below, where I found myself slogging through ankle-deep water, the tide having come up to lap against the wall. I nearly slipped on the slick stones, and forced myself to slow down. There was no sound of pursuit, nothing at all, and the wild sense of abandon that had fueled my acrobatic leap from the top balcony drained away, leaving me cold and shaking, my shoes filled with seawater.

I climbed back over the wall and tramped along to the Crown and Apple, up the backstairs to find the door unlocked. I slipped into my room, dead tired and even more deadly thirsty. In fifteen minutes I strolled into the dining room in *dry* shoes, feeling tolerably proud of myself, and there sat St. Ives and Hasbro, stabbing at cutlets and with a bottle of Burgundy uncorked on the table. It did my heart good, as they say.

—⁓⁓—

"NOT WITH A revolver, she didn't," said St. Ives. "You were too far away for anyone to have brought off so close a shot. My guess is that it was a Winchester, and that it was your man Bowker who fired it. Clearly they and the Pules are working at cross-purposes, although both of them chase the same ends—which have little to do, I'm convinced, with drawing ships to their doom. That's a peripheral business—quick cash to finance more elaborate operations."

St. Ives emptied the bottle into Hasbro's glass and waved at the waiter, ordering a second bottle of wine and another pint for me. I'm a beer man generally; red wine rips me up in the night. St. Ives studied his plate for a moment and then said, "It's very largely a distraction, too, the ship business, and a good one. Godall seems to think that the Crown is on the verge of paying them what they ask, in return for their solemn assurance that they'll abandon the machine where she lies. Imagine that. Those were Parsons's words, 'Their solemn assurance.' The man's gone round the bend. Now that we've found the machine, though, they'll wait on the ransom. We've accomplished that much. The Academy has the area cordoned off with ships and are going to try to haul it up out of there."

St. Ives drained his glass, then scowled into the lees, swirling them in the bottom. "If I had half a chance…," he said, not bothering to finish the sentence. I thought I knew what he meant, though; he had harbored a grim distrust of the machine ever since Lord Kelvin had set out to reverse the polarity of the earth with it. What were they keeping it for, if not to effect some other grand and improbable disaster in the name of science? I half believed St. Ives knew what it was, too—that there was far more to the machine than he was letting on and that only the principal players in the game fully understood. I was a pawn, of course, and resolved to keeping to my station. I'm certain, though, that St. Ives had contemplated on more than one occasion going into that machine works up in Holborn and taking it out of there himself. But he hadn't, and look what had come of his hesitating. That's the way *he* saw it—managing to blame himself from a fresh angle.

I tried to steer the subject away from the business of the machine. "So what *do* they want?" I asked.

"The notebooks, for the moment. The damnable notebooks. They think that they're an ace away from immortality. Narbondo very nearly had it ten years ago, back when he was stealing carp out of the aquarium and working with Willis Pule. He was close— close enough so that in Norway Higgins could revive him with the elixir and the apparatus. For my money Narbondo was pumped up with carp elixir when he went into the pond; that's what kept him alive, kept his entire cellular structure from crystallizing. Higgins's idea, as I see it, is that he would revive the doctor, and the two of them would search out the notebooks and then hammer out the fine points; together they would bottle the Fountain of Youth. How much they know about the machine I can't say.

"Higgins had been tracking them—the notebooks—and he wrote to Mrs. Pule, who he suspected might know something of their whereabouts, but his writing to her just set her off. She came around to Godall's very cleverly, knowing that to reveal to us that the notebooks existed and that Narbondo was alive would put us on the trail. She and the son merely followed us down from London."

It made sense to me. Leave it to St. Ives to put the pieces in order. "Why," I asked, "are they so keen on killing *me*, that's what I want to know. I'm the lowly worm in the whole business."

"You were available," said St. Ives. "And you were persistent, snooping around their hotel like that. These are remarkably bloodthirsty criminals. And the Pules, I'm afraid, are amateurs alongside the doctor. Higgins didn't have any idea on earth what it was he was reviving, not an inkling."

St. Ives pushed his plate away and ordered a bit of custard. It was getting along toward ten o'clock, and the evening had wound itself down. The beer was having its way with me, and I yawned and said that I would turn in, and St. Ives nodded thoughtfully and said that he'd just stroll along over to the icehouse in a bit and see what was up. I slumped. I wasn't built for it, not right then, and yet it was me who had found out about the business up in Norway. I was pretty sure that I understood the icehouse, and it didn't seem fair that I be left out. "It's early for that, isn't it?" I asked.

St. Ives shrugged. "Perhaps."

"I suggest a nap. Just a couple of hours to rest up. Let's tackle them in the middle of the night, while they sleep."

St. Ives considered, looked at his pocket watch, and said, "Fair enough. Stroke of midnight. We'll be across the hail, just in case anyone comes sneaking around."

"Knock me up with fifteen minutes to spare," I said, getting up. And with that I toddled off to my room and fell asleep in my clothes.

———≈≈≈———

THE NIGHT WAS howling cold and the sky clear and starry. There was a moon, but just enough to hang a coat on. We had slipped out the back and taken my route along the seawall, none of us speaking and with the plan already laid out. Hasbro carried a revolver and was the one among us most capable of using it.

Absolutely no one was about. Lamps flickered here and there along the streets, and a single light glowed in one of the windows of The Hoisted Pint—Willis Pule turning Higgins into an amphibian, probably. The shadowy pier stretched into the moonlit ocean, and the icehouse loomed dark and was empty in the weeds—very ominous, it seemed to me.

We wafered ourselves against the wall and waited, listening, wondering what lay within. After a moment I realized that Hasbro was gone. He had been behind me and now he wasn't; just like that. I tugged on St. Ives's coat, and he turned around and winked at me, putting a finger to his lips and then motioning me forward with a wave of his hand.

We crept along, listening to the silence and ducking beneath a bank of dirty windows, hunching a few steps farther to where St. Ives stopped outside a door. He put a finger to his lips and a hand on the latch, easing the latch down gently. There sounded the hint of a click, the door swung open slowly, and we were through, creeping along across the floor of a small room with a broken-down desk in it.

Some little bit of moonlight filtered in through the window—enough to see by now that our eyes had adjusted. Carefully, St. Ives pushed open another heavy door, just a crack, and peered through, standing as if frozen until he could make out what lay before him. He turned his head slowly and gave me a look—just a widening of the eyes—and then pushed the door open some more.

I caught the sound of snoring just then, low and labored like that of a hibernating bear, and when I followed St. Ives into the room, both of us creeping along, I looked for Captain Bowker, and sure enough there he was, asleep on a cot, his head turned to the wall. We slipped past him, through his little chamber and out into the open room beyond.

It was fearfully cold, and no wonder. Great blocks of ice lay stacked in the darkness like silvery coffins beneath the high ceiling. They were half covered with piled straw, and there was more straw littering the floor and a pair of dumpcarts and a barrow and a lot of shadowy odds and ends of tongs and tools and ice saws along the wall—none of it particularly curious, considering where we were.

St. Ives didn't hesitate. He knew what he was looking for, out and I thought I did too. I was wrong, though. What St. Ives was after lay beyond the ice, through a weighted door that was pulled partly open. We stepped up to it, dropping to our hands and knees to peer beneath it. Beyond, in a square slope-ceilinged room with a double door set in the far wall, was a metal sphere, glowing dully in the moonlight and sitting on four squat legs.

It's Lord Kelvin's machine!—I said to myself, but then saw that it wasn't. It was a diving bell, a submarine explorer, built out of brass and copper and ringed with port-holes. Mechanical armatures thrust out, with hinged elbows so that the device looked very jaunty, as if it might at any moment shuffle away on its piggy little legs. We rolled under the door, not wanting to push it open farther for fear of making a noise. And then all of a sudden, as we got up to dust ourselves off, there was noise to spare—the rattling and creaking of a wagon drawing up beyond the doors, out in the night.

A horse snorted and shook its head, and there was the sound of a brake clacking down against a wheel. I dropped to the ground, thinking to scramble under and into the ice room again before whoever it was in the wagon unlocked the outside doors and con-fronted us there. St. Ives grabbed my coat, though, and shook his head, and in a moment there was a fiddling with a lock and I stood up slowly, ready to acquit myself like a man.

The doors drew back, and between them, pulling them open, stood the remark-able Hasbro. St. Ives didn't stop to chat. He put his shoulder against one of the doors, pushing it fully open while Hasbro saw to the other one, and then as St. Ives latched on to the harness and backed the horses and dray around and through the doors, Has-bro clambered up onto the bed, yanked loose the wheel brake, and began to unlatch a clutch of chain and line from the post of a jib crane bolted to the bed.

I stood and gaped until I saw what it was we were up to, and then I hitched up my trousers and set to. Lickety-split, passing the line back and forth, looping and yanking, we tied the diving bell in a sort of basket weave. Hasbro hoisted it off the ground with the jib crane, which made the devil's own creaking and groaning, and St. Ives and I guided it by the feet as it swung around and onto the bed of the dray, clunking down solidly. Hasbro dropped down onto the plank seat, plucked up the ribands, clicked his tongue, and was gone in a whirl of moonlit dust, cantering away into the night.

It was a neat bit of work, although I had no real notion of its purpose. If the ma-chine in the Strait was guarded by Her Majesty's navy, then our villains had no real use for the diving bell anyway; that part of their adventure, it seemed to me, had already drawn to an unsuccessful close. But who was I to question St. Ives? He was damned glad to get the bell out of there; I could see that in his face.

But we weren't done yet; I could see that too. Why hadn't we ridden out of there with Hasbro? Because St. Ives was in a sweat to see what else lay in that icehouse. Narbondo himself was in there somewhere, and St. Ives meant to find him. We bellied straightaway under the weighted door, back into the ice room, St. Ives first and me following, and stood up to peer into the grinning face of the jolly Captain Bowker, who stood two yards distant, staring at us down the sights of his rifle. —⌐

Villainy at Midnight

H E WOULDN'T MISS this time. I was determined to play the part of the cooperative man, the man who doesn't want to be shot. The door slammed up and open behind us, and there stood Higgins, dressed in a lab coat, his head bandaged and him winded and puffing. Tufts of hair poked through the bandage. He smelled awful, like a dead fish in a sack.

"Leopold Higgins, I presume," said St. Ives, bowing. "I am Langdon St. Ives."

"I know who you bloody well are," he said, and then he looked at me for a cold moment, smiled, and said, "How did you like the fruit?"

Clearly he didn't know it was me who had beaned him at The Hoisted Pint when he was sneaking into the Pules' room. That was good; he wouldn't have been making jokes otherwise. Despite the gloom of the icehouse I could see that his face was bruised pretty badly. That must have been the work of the wonderful Pules.

"Catch it?" asked the captain, still training the rifle on us.

"Got away right enough," said Higgins. "What sort of watch was that you were keeping? Napping is what I call it. Sleeping like a baby while these two…"

The captain swiveled the rifle around and—blam!—fired a round past Higgins's ear. I leaped straight off my feet, but not nearly so far off them as Higgins did. He threw himself facedown into the straw on the floor, mewling like a wet cat. Captain Bowker chuckled until his eyes watered as Higgins, pale and shaken, struggled back up, fear and fury playing in his eyes.

"Who cares?" said the captain.

Higgins worked his mouth, priming his throat. "But the diving bell…"

"Who cares about the filthy bell? It ain't worth a nickel to me. *You* ain't worth a nickel to me. I'd just as leave kill the three of you and have done with it. You'll get your diving bell back when the tall one finds out we've got his friends."

This last added an optimistic flavor to the discussion. "The tall one" was clearly Hasbro, who, of course, would happily trade a dozen diving bells for the lives of dear old Jack and the professor. I didn't at all mind being held for ransom; it was being dead that bothered me.

"Or *one* of his friends, anyway." The captain shifted his gaze from one to the other of us, as if coming to a decision. There went the optimism. I was surely the most expendable of the two of us, since I knew the least. Captain Bowker sniffed the air and wrinkled up his face. "Gimme the 'lixir," he said to Higgins.

"*He* needs it," said Higgins, shaking his head. It was a brave act, considering, for the captain trained the rifle on Higgins again, dead between the eyes now, and started straight in to chuckle. Without an instant's hesitation, Higgins's hand went into the pocket of his lab coat and hauled out a corked bottle, which he reached across toward the captain.

The captain grabbed for it, and St. Ives jumped—just when the rifle was midway between Higgins and us. It was the little pleasure in baiting Higgins that tripped the captain up.

"Run, Jack!" shouted St. Ives when he threw himself at the captain. In a storm of arms and legs he was flying forward, into the air, sideways into Captain Bowker's expansive stomach. The captain smashed over backward, his head banging against the floorboards and the bottle of elixir sailing away toward the stacked ice with Higgins diving after it. I was out both doors and into the night, running again toward the two houses before St. Ives's admonition had faded in my ears. He had commanded me to run, and I ran, like a spooked sheep. Live to fight another day, I told myself.

And while I ran I waited for the sound of a shot. What would I do if I heard it? Turn around? Turning around wasn't on my mind. I pounded down the little boardwalk and angled toward the seawall, leaping along like an idiot instead of slowing down to think things out. No one was after me, and I was out of sight of the icehouse, so there was no longer any chance of being shot. It was cold fear that drove me on. And it was regret at having run in the first place, at having left St. Ives alone, that finally slowed me down.

I was walking when I got to the water, breathing like an engine. Fog was blowing past in billows, and the moon was lost beyond it. In moments I couldn't see at all, except for the seawall, which I followed along up toward the Apple, moving slowly now and listening to the dripping of water off eaves and to what sounded like the slow dip of oars out on the bay. Suddenly it was the heavy silence that terrified me, an empty counterpoint, maybe, to the now-faded sound of gunfire and the moment of shouting chaos that had followed it.

Where was I bound? Back to the Apple to hide? To lie up until I learned that my friends were dead and the villains gone away? Or to confront the Pules, maybe, who were awaiting me in my room, honing their instruments? It was time for thinking all of a sudden, not for running. St. Ives had got me out of the icehouse. I couldn't believe that his heroics were meant simply to save my miserable life—they *were*, without a doubt, but I couldn't admit to it—and so what I needed was a plan, any plan, to justify my being out of danger.

I just then noticed that a lantern glowed out to sea, coming along through the fog, maybe twenty yards offshore; you couldn't really tell. The light bobbed like a will-o'-the-wisp, hanging from a pole affixed to the bow of a rowboat sculling through the mist. I stopped to finish catching my breath and to wait out my hammering heart, and I watched the foggy lantern float toward me. A sudden gust of salty wind blew the mists to tatters, and the dark ocean and its rowboat appeared on the instant, the boat driving toward shore when the man at the oars out got a clear view of the seawall. The hull scrunched up onto the shingle, the stern slewing around and the oarsman clambering into shallow water. It was Hasbro. His pant legs were rolled and his shoes tied around his neck.

He looped the painter through a rusted iron ring in the wall and shook my hand as if he hadn't seen me in a month. Without a second's hesitation I told him about St. Ives held prisoner in the icehouse, about how I was just then formulating a plan to go back after him, working out the fine points so that I didn't just wade in and muck things up. Captain Bowker was a dangerous man, I said. Like old explosives, any little quiver might detonate him.

"Very good, Mr. Owlesby," Hasbro said in that stony butler's voice of his. Wild coincidence didn't perturb him. Nothing perturbed him. He listened and nodded as he sat there on the wet seawall and put on his shoes. His lean face was stoic, and he might just as well have been studying the racing form or laying out a shirt and trousers for his master to wear in the morning. Suddenly there appeared in my mind a picture of a strangely complicated and efficient clockwork mechanism—meant to be his brain, I suppose—and my spirits rose a sizable fraction. As dangerous as Captain Bowker was, I told myself, here was a man more dangerous yet. I had seen evidence of it countless times, but I had forgot it nearly as often because of the damned cool air that Hasbro has about him, the quiet efficiency.

Here he was, after all, out on the ocean rowing a boat. A half hour ago he was tearing away in a wagon, hauling a diving bell to heaven knows what destination. *That* was it—the difference between us. He was a man with destinations; it was that which confounded me. I rarely had one, unless it was some trivial momentary destination— the pub, say. Did Dorothy know that about me? Was it clear to the world as it was to me? Why on earth did she humor me day to day? Maybe because I reminded her of her father. But this was no time for getting morose and enumerating regrets. Where had Hasbro been? He didn't tell me; it was later that I found out.

At the moment, though, both of us slipped along through the fog, and suddenly I was a conspirator again. A destination had been provided for me. I wished that Dorothy could see me, bound on this dangerous mission, slouching through the shadowy fog to save St. Ives from the most desperate criminals imaginable. I tripped over a curb and sprawled on my face in the grass of the square, but was up immediately, giving the treacherous curb a hard look and glancing around like a fool to see if anyone

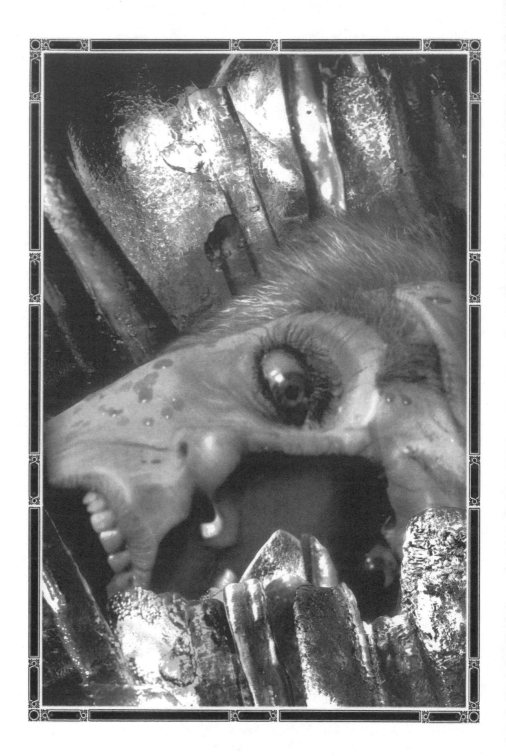

had been a witness to my ignominious tumble. Hasbro disappeared ahead, oblivious to it—or so he would make it seem in order not to embarrass me.

But there, away toward the boardwalk and the pier, across the lawn…It was too damnably foggy now to tell, but some one had been there, watching. Heart flailing again, I leaped along to catch up with Hasbro. "We're followed," I hissed after him.

He nodded, and whispered into my ear. "Too much fog to say who it is. Maybe the mother and son."

I didn't think so. Whoever it was was shorter than Willis Pule. Narbondo, maybe. He was somewhere about. It wasn't certain that he was on ice; that was mere conjecture. Narbondo skulking in the fog—the idea of it gave me the willies. But we were in view of the icehouse again, and the sight of it replaced the willies with a more substantial fear. The glow of lamplight filtered through a dirty window, and Hasbro and I edged along toward it, just as St. Ives and I had done an hour earlier.

I kept one eye over my shoulder, squinting into the mists, my senses sharp. I wouldn't be taken unawares; that was certain. What we saw through the window, though, took my mind off the night, and along with Hasbro I gaped at the three men within—none of whom was St. Ives.

What we were looking at wasn't a proper room, but was a little niche cut off from the ice room with a canvas drape. It was well lit, and we had a first-rate view of the entire interior, what with the utter darkness outside. The floor was clean of litter, and the whole of the room had a swabbed-out look to it, like a jury-rigged hospital room. On a wheeled table in the middle of it, lying atop a cushion and wearing what appeared to be a rubber all-together suit, was Dr. Narbondo himself, pale as a corpse with snow white hair that had been cropped short. Frost was a more appropriate name, certainly. Narbondo *had* met his fate in that tarn; what had risen from it was something else entirely.

He lay there on his cushion, with fist-sized chunks of ice packed around him, like a jolly great fish on a buffet table. Captain Bowker sat in a chair, looking grizzled, tired, and enormous. His rifle stood tilted against the back corner of the room, always at hand. Higgins hovered over the supine body of the doctor. He meddled with chemical apparatus—a pan of yellow cataplasm or something, and a rubber bladder attached by a coiled tube to a misting nozzle. On a table along the wall sat the bottle of elixir that Higgins had apparently saved from its flying doom an hour past.

He showered the doctor with the mist, pulling open either eyelid and spraying the stuff directly in. The interior of the room was yellow with it, like a London fog. Narbondo trembled, as if from a spine-wrenching chill, and shouted something— I couldn't make out what—and then half sat up, lurching onto his elbows and staring round about him with wide, wild eyes. In seconds the passion had winked out of them, replaced by a placid know-it-all look, and he took up the bottle of elixir, uncorked it with a trembling hand, and drank off half the contents. He glanced at our window, and

I nearly tumbled over backward, but he couldn't have seen us out there in the darkness and the fog.

What to do; that was the problem. Where was St. Ives? Dead? Trussed up somewhere within? More than likely. There were too many issues at stake for them to waste such a hostage as that. I nudged Hasbro with my elbow and nodded off down the dark clapboard wall of the icehouse, as if I were suggesting we head down that way—which I was. I saw no reason not to get St. Ives out of there. Hasbro was intent on the window, though, and he shook his head.

It was the doctor that he watched, Dr. Frost, or Narbondo, whichever you please. He had sat up now and was turning his head very slowly, as if his joints wanted oil; you could almost hear the creak. A startled expression, one of dread and confusion, passed across his face in waves. He was obviously troubled by something, and was making a determined effort to win through it. He slid off onto the floor and stood reeling, turning around with his back to us and with his hands on the table. I saw him pluck up a piece of ice and hold it to his chest, an artistic gesture, it seemed to me, even at the time.

Higgins hovered around like a mother hen. He put a hand on the doctor's arm, but Narbondo shook it off, nearly falling over and then grabbing the table again to steady himself. He turned slowly, letting go, and then, one step at a time, tramped toward the canvas curtain like a man built of stone, taking three short steps before pitching straight over onto his face and lying there on the floor, unmoving. Captain Bowker stood up tiredly, as a man might who didn't care a rap for fallen doctors, and he trudged over to where Higgins leaped around in a fit, shouting orders but doing nothing except getting in the way. The captain pushed him against the wall and said, "Back off!" Then he picked the doctor up and laid him back onto his bed while Higgins hovered about, gathering up the ice chunks knocked onto the floor.

"It's not working!" Higgins moaned, rubbing his forehead. "I've *got* to have the notebooks. I'm so *close!*"

"Looks like a bust to me," said the captain. "I'm for making them pay out for the machine. I'm for Paris, is what I'm saying. Your friend here can rot. Say, gimme some more of that 'lixir now. He won't be needing no more tonight."

It was then, while the captain's back was turned and Higgins was furiously snatching up the bottle of elixir to keep it away from him, that the canvas curtain lifted and into the little room slipped Willis Pule and his ghastly mother, she holding her revolver and he grinning round about him like a giddy child and carrying a black and ominous surgeon's bag.

Captain Bowker was quick; I'll give him that. He must have seen them out of the corner of his eye, for he half turned, slamming Willis on the ear with his elbow and knocking him silly, if such a thing were possible. Then he lunged for his rifle; and it's here that he moved too slowly. He would have got to it right enough if he hadn't taken the time to hit Willis first. But he had taken the time, and now Mrs. Pule lunged forward with a look of insane glee on her face, shoving the muzzle of the revolver into the captain's fleshy midsection so that the barrel entirely disappeared and the explosion was muffled when she fired. He managed to knock her away too, even as the bullet kicked him over backward in a sort of lumbering spin. He clutched at his vitals, his mouth working, and he knocked his rifle down as he caved in and sank almost like a ballerina to the floor, where he lay in a heap.

It was the most cold-blooded thing I've ever seen, and I've seen a few cold-blooded things in my day. Mrs. Pule turned her gun on Higgins, who couldn't stand it, apparently, and leaped at the canvas curtain. But Pule, who still sat on the floor, snaked out his arm and clutched Higgins's leg, and Higgins went over headforemost as if he *had* been shot. Pule climbed up onto his back and sat there astride him, giggling hysterically and shouting "Horsey! Horsey!" and poking Higgins in the small of the back with his finger, trying to tickle him, as impossible as that sounds, and then cuffing him on the back of the head with his open hand. "Take that! Take that! Take that!" he shrieked, as if the words were hiccups and he couldn't stop them.

Mrs. Pule saw her chance, and leaned in to slap Willis a good one, shouting, "Behavior!" again, except that this time the word had no effect on her son, and she was forced to box his ears, and so it went for what must have been twenty seconds or so: Willis slapping the back of Higgins's jerking head and yanking his ears and pulling his hair, and Mrs. Pule cuffing Willis on the noggin, and both of the Pules shouting so that neither of them could make themselves heard. Finally the woman grabbed a handful of her son's hair and gave it a yank, jerking him over backward with a howl, and Higgins flew to his knees and scrambled for the canvas, his bandages falling loose around his shoulders and fresh blood seeping through them.

They had him by the feet, though, just as quick as you please, and hauled him back in. They jerked him upright and slammed him into the late Captain Bowker's chair, trussing him up with the captain's own gaiters.

It was then that I saw someone right at the edge of my vision, down at the far end of the icehouse. I was certain of it. Someone was prowling around and had come out into the open, I suppose, at the sound of the gunfire and the scuffle, and then had seen us still standing by the window, doing nothing, and had darted away again, assuming, maybe, that there wasn't any immediate alarm.

By the time I nudged Hasbro there was no one there, and there was precious little reason to go snooping off in that direction, especially since whoever it was, it wasn't one of our villains; they were all present and accounted for. It's someone waiting, I thought at the time—waiting to see how things fell out before making his move, waiting for the dirty work to be done for him.

And all the while Dr. Narbondo lay there on ice, seemingly frozen. Willis seemed to see him for the first time. He crept across to peer into the doctor's face, then blanched with horror at what he saw there. Even in that deep and impossible sleep, Narbondo terrified poor Willis. And then, as if on cue, the doctor flinched in his cold slumber and mumbled something, and Pule fell back horrified. He cringed against the far wall, crossing his arms against his chest and drawing one leg up in a sort of flamingo gesture, doing as much as he could do to roll up into a ball and still stay on his feet—so that he could run, maybe, if it came to that.

———

HIS MOTHER HUNCHED across, goo-gooing at him, and rubbed his poor forehead, fluttering her eyelids and talking the most loathsome sort of baby talk to comfort him while still holding on to the revolver and stepping over the captain's splayed legs, straight into the blood that had pooled up on the floor. She nearly slipped, and she caught on to her son's jacket for support, giving off the baby talk in order to curse, and then wiping the bottom of her shoe very deliberately on the captain's shirt. Maybe Hasbro couldn't see this last bit from where he stood, but I could, and I can tell you it gave me the horrors, and doubly so when she went straightaway for her son again, calling him a poor lost thing and a wee birdy and all manner of pet names. I couldn't get my eyes off that horrifying bloody shoe-smear on the captain's already gruesome shirtfront. I was sick all of a sudden, and turned away to glance at Hasbro's face. He had taken the whole business in. His stoic visage was evaporated, replaced by a look of pure puzzlement and repulsion; he was human, after all.

"Let's find the professor," I whispered to him. I had no desire to watch what would surely follow; they wouldn't leave the doctor alive, and his death wouldn't be pretty. These two were living horrors—but even then, bloodthirsty and hypocritical as it sounds, somehow I didn't begrudge them their chance to even the score with Narbondo; I just didn't want to see them do it.

We stepped along through the weeds, around to the door that opened onto what had been Captain Bowker's sleeping quarters. The door was secured now, the hasp fitted with a bolt that had been slipped through it—enough merely to stop anyone's getting out. We got in, though, quick as you please, and there was St. Ives, tied up hands and feet and gagged, lying atop the bed. We got the gag out and him untied, and we indicated by gestures and whispers what sort of monkey business was going on in the room beyond. He was up and moving toward the door to the ice room, determined to stop it. It didn't matter who it was that was threatened. St. Ives wouldn't brook it; even Narbondo would have his day before the magistrate.

He tugged open the door, and you can guess who stood there—Mrs. Pule, grinning like a gibbon ape and holding the gun. I whirled around to the outside door, which still stood open, ready to leap out into the night, and thinking, of course, that one of us ought to get out in order to find the constable, to summon aid. Could I help it if it was always me who was destined for such missions? But there stood Willis, right outside, looking haggard and wearing the mask of tragedy—and training the captain's rifle on me with ominously shaking hands. I stopped where I stood and waited while Mrs. Pule took Hasbro's revolver away from him. So much for that.

They marched us back through the ice room, the floor of which was wet and mucky with meltwater and sopping hay, and smelled like an ammoniated swamp. I was desperately cold all of a sudden, and thought about how unpleasant it was to have to face death when you were shaking with cold and dead tired and it was past three in the morning. The night had been one long round of wild escapes, followed by my striding back into various lion's dens and tipping my hat. There was no chance of another go at it now, though, with one of them in front and one behind.

St. Ives started right in, as soon as he saw Narbondo lying there on the table. He felt for a pulse, nodded, and raised one of the doctor's eyelids. Next he examined the bladder apparatus and sniffed the elixir, and then, as if it was the most natural and unpretentious thing in the world, he slipped the bottle of elixir into his coat pocket.

"Out with it!" hissed the woman, tipping the revolver against my head. My eyes shot open in order to better watch St. Ives remove the bottle.

"Wake him up," she said, removing the revolver from my temple and gesturing toward the sleeping doctor.

St. Ives shook his head. "I'd love to," he said. "But I don't know how. It would be the happiest day of my life if I could animate him in order that he be brought to justice."

She laughed out loud. "Them's my words," she said, referring to that day in Godall's shop. "Justice! We'll bring him justice, won't we, Willis?"

Willis nodded, wild with happiness now—partly, I thought, because of St. Ives's insisting that the doctor couldn't be awakened. Pule didn't want him awake. He picked up his bag of instruments and set it on the table. When he opened it, I could smell burnt rubber, and sure enough, he pulled out the hacked and charred fragments of the toy elephant and the little collection of gears, put back together now. "This is what I did to his elephant," he said, nodding at me, but looking at Higgins.

"Elephant?" Higgins said, casting me a terrified and wondering glance. This obscure reference to the elephant must have struck him as significant in some unfathomable way, largely because what Pule held in his hand no longer had anything to do with elephants. It was simply a limp bit of flayed rubber and paint.

I shrugged at Higgins and started to speak to the poor man, but Willis cut me off, shouting, "Shut up!" in a lunatic falsetto and blinking very fast and hard. He wasn't interested in hearing from me. He was caught up in his own twisted story, and he happily set about laying out an array of operating instruments—scalpels and clamps and something that looked a little like a bolt cutters and a little like a pruning shears and was meant, I guess, for clipping bone.

He made a bow in our direction, and, gesturing at Narbondo, he said, as if he were addressing a half score of students in a surgery, "I intend to affix this man's head to the fat man's body, and then to wake him up and make him look at himself in a mirror and see how ugly he is. Then I'm going to install this mechanism"—and here he plucked up the reassembled gears from the elephant—"in his heart, so that I can control him with a lever. And this man," Pule said, pointing at poor terrified and befuddled Higgins, "I'm going to cut apart and put together backward, so that he has to reach behind himself to button his shirt, and then I'm going to sell him to Mr. Happy's Circus."

Pule was madder than I thought him. What on earth did he mean by nonsense like "put him together backward"? It was clear that he could actually accomplish none of this. What real evidence was there that he had any skills in vivisection at all? None, and never had been—only his association with Narbondo, which proved nothing, of course, except that he was capable of committing vile acts. He was simply going to hack three men up—two of them alive at the moment—for the same utterly insane reasons that he had hacked up my elephant or that he chopped apart birds and hid them under the floorboards of his house. And he would do it all with relish—I was certain of it.

Poor Higgins was even more certain, it seemed, for just as soon as Pule mentioned this business about selling him to Mr. Happy's Circus, he began to utter a sort of low keening noise, a strange and mournful weeping. His eyes rolled back up into his head just as he slumped forward, tugging at the gaiters that held him to the chair, his voice rising another octave.

Mrs. Pule handed Willis the revolver, and he shifted the rifle to his left hand, not wanting to put it down. She picked up the dish of yellow chemical and advised Higgins to pipe down. But he couldn't, and so she splashed the stuff into Higgins's face, at which Higgins lurched upright, spitting and coughing, and she slapped him one, catching him mostly on the nose because of his twitching around. "Did you *hear* him?" she hissed.

"What! What! What!" cried Higgins, out of his mind now.

"You can save yourself," she said. "Or else…" She hunched over and whispered the rest of the sentence in his ear.

"Merciful Jesus! I'm what?" he shouted. "You're going to *what*? Mr. Happy!" His voice cracked. He began to gibber and moan.

They had gone too far. She had wanted to bargain with him, but she had made the mistake of driving him mad first, and now he was beyond bargaining. So she hit him again, twice—slap, slap—and he sat up straight and listened harder.

"The notebooks," she said. "Where are they?"

St. Ives cleared his throat, and very cheerfully, as if he were talking to a neighbor over the garden wall, he said, "I don't believe that the man knows…"

"Shut up!" she cried, turning on the three of us.

"Shut up!" cried her son, rapidly opening and closing his eyes and training the revolver on me, of all people; *I* hadn't said anything. I shrugged, very willing to shut up.

St. Ives was a different kettle of fish. "I mean to say, madam," he said, calmly and deliberately, "that Professor Higgins is utterly ignorant of the whereabouts of the notebooks. It was he who posted that letter to you, after he had revived the doctor. And since then he hasn't found them, although he's made a very pretty effort. Your torturing him now won't accomplish a thing, unless, as I suspect, you're torturing him for sport."

"You filthy…," she said, leaving it unfinished, and in a wild rage she snatched the revolver away from her son and pointed it at the professor. "You scum-sucking pig! You know *nothing*. I'll *start* with you, Mr. Hooknose, and then Willis will make a scarecrow of you."

She croaked out a laugh just as I lunged at her; don't ask me why I did it—making up for lost opportunities, maybe. I threw myself onto the revolver and grabbed it by the barrel, hitting her just as hard as I could on the jaw, which was plenty hard enough to knock her over backward.

Willis grappled with the rifle, but hadn't gotten it halfway up before Hasbro clipped him neatly on the side of the head, and he sank to his knees and slumped forward.

It was over, just like that. I'd had to hit a woman to accomplish it, but by heaven I would hit her once more, harder, if I had it to do again.

"Go for the constable, Jack," cried St. Ives, taking the revolver from me. "Bring him round, quick. I won't leave Narbondo's side, not until he's in a cell, sleeping or awake, I don't care."

I turned and started out, but didn't take more than a step, for the canvas pulled back, and there stood the constable himself, the one that had questioned me on the green, and Parsons stood with him, along with two sleepy-looking men who had obviously been routed out as deputies. For it had been Parsons who was lurking about, waiting for his chance. When it had got rough, and he had realized what a spot we had got ourselves into, he had himself run for the constable, and here they were, come round to save us now that we didn't want saving.

"I'll just take those weapons," said the constable, very officiously.

"Certainly," said St. Ives, handing over the revolver as if it were a snake.

Then there was a lot of talk about Narbondo, on the table, him and a fetching of more ice, and a cataloging of the bits and pieces of scientific apparatus, and finally St. Ives couldn't stand it any longer and he asked Parsons, "The notebooks. You've got them, haven't you?"

Parsons shrugged.

"It was Piper, wasn't it? The oculist. He had got them from the old man, and had them all along. And when he died you came down and fetched them."

"Accurate to the last detail," said Parsons, smiling to think that at last he'd put one across St. Ives, that at last he had been in ahead of us. "What you *don't* know, my good fellow, is that I've destroyed them. They were a horror, a misapplication of scientific method, an abomination. I burned them in Dr. Piper's incinerator without bothering to read more than a snatch of them."

"Then it's my view," said St. Ives, "that Narbondo is dead, or as good as dead. How long he can last in this suspended state, I don't know, but it's clear that Higgins couldn't entirely revive him. Neither can I, and without the notebooks, thank God, neither can you."

Parsons shrugged again. "Keep him on ice," he said to the constable. "The Academy will want him. He'll make an interesting study."

The use of the word *study* had a Willis Pule ring to it that I didn't like, and I was reminded of what it was about Parsons that set the men of the Academy apart from a man like St. Ives. I was almost sorry that Narbondo at last had fallen into their hands.

St. Ives, however, didn't seem in the least sorry. "I suggest we retire to the Crown and Apple, then," he said. "I have a few bottles of ale in my room. I suggest that we sample it—toast Professor Parsons's success."

"Here, here," said Parsons, a little vainly, I thought, as we trooped out into the night, leaving the icehouse behind. In fact, though, a couple of bottles of ale and a few hours of sleep would settle me right out. Our adventure was over, and tomorrow, I supposed, it was back to London on the express. I patted my coat pocket, where I still had the proof of my reserving a room for me and Dorothy at The Hoisted Pint. You'd think that I would have had my fill of the place, but in fact I was determined to stay there as I'd planned, under happier circumstances, especially since whoever it was that we would find tending to the guests, it wouldn't be the woman who had hoodwinked me. The constable had already sent someone around to collect her.

—◦◦◦—

So THERE WE were, sitting in St. Ives's room, and him passing around opened bottles of ale, until he got to Parsons and said, "You're strictly a water man, aren't you?"

"You've got an admirable memory, sir. Water is the staff of life, the staff of life."

"And I've got a bottle of well water right here," said St. Ives, uncorking just such an object. Parsons was delighted. He took the glass that St. Ives gave him and swirled the water around in it, as if it were Scotch or Burgundy or some other drinkable substance. Then he threw it down heartily and smacked his lips like a connoisseur, immediately wrinkling up his face.

"Bitter," he said. "Must be French. Lucky I'm thirsty after tonight's little tussle." He held out his glass.

"Mineral water," said St. Ives, filling it up.

I was tempted to say something about "tonight's little tussle" myself, but I put a lid on it. Hasbro had fallen asleep in his chair.

Parsons winked at the professor. He was as full of himself as I've ever seen him. "About revivifying Narbondo," he said. "I've got a notion involving Lord Kelvin's machine. You've read of Sir Joseph John Thomson's work at the Cavendish Laboratory."

St. Ives's face betrayed what he was thinking, as if he had known that it would come to this, and here it was at last. "Yes," he said, "I have. Very interesting, but I don't quite see how it applies."

This made Parsons happy. To hear St. Ives admit such a thing was worth a lifetime of waiting and plotting. He had the face of a man holding four aces and looking at a table mounded with coin. "Electrons," he said, as if such a word explained everything.

"Go on," said the professor.

"Well, it's rather simple, isn't it? They spin sphere-wise around their atom. An intense electromagnetic field yanks them into a sort of oval, rather like the shifting of tides on the earth, and in animate creatures causes immediate and unrestrained cellular activity. What if Narbondo were subjected to such a force—a tremendous dose of electromagnetism? It might—how shall I put it?—'start him up,' let's say, like turning over an Otto's four-stroke engine."

"It might," said St. Ives darkly. "It might do a good deal more. I'll get directly to the point here; this isn't a matter for dalliance. The Academy undertook to start that damnable machine once, and to be straight with you, I had my man sabotage it. Do you remember?"

Of course Parsons remembered. It had been the incident of Lord Kelvin's machine that had caused the deepening of the chasm between the two men. Parsons looked almost sneery for a moment and said, "He loaded the contrivance with field mice, if I remember aright. Very effective, if a little bit—what?—primitive, maybe."

"Well," continued St. Ives, going right on, "some few of those field mice lived to tell the tale, as my friend Jack might put it. I carried on a study of them for almost two years in the fields round about the manor, until I was certain, finally, that the last of those poor creatures was dead, and what I discovered was a remarkably horrendous syndrome of mutations and cancers. It's my theory quite simply that this 'unrestrained cellular activity,' as you put it, is more likely ungovernable cellular growth. Your engine analogy may or may not apply. It doesn't matter. You simply cannot start the machine for any purpose, especially for something as frivolous as this. Leave Narbondo's fate in the hands of the Almighty, for heaven's sake."

"Frivolous!" shouted Parsons. "I don't give a rap for Narbondo's fate. Imagine, though, what this will mean. Here's poor Higgins, who has devoted a lifetime to the study of cryogenics. Here's Narbondo and a lifetime's study of chemistry. He was a monster, certainly, but so what? You must be a pitifully shortsighted scientist if you can't see the effect the sum total of their work will have on the future of the human race. And it's Lord Kelvin's machine that will usher in that future. To put it simply, my ship is putting in and I mean to board her." Parsons struck the arm of his chair with his fist to punctuate his speech. Then his eyes half closed and his head nodded forward. He shook himself awake and mumbled something about being suddenly sleepy, and then his head fell against his chest and straightaway he began to snore through his beard, having said, apparently, all he had to say.

The sight of him sleeping so profoundly put me in mind of my own bed, and I was just yawning and starting to say that I would turn in too, when St. Ives leaped to his feet, dropped an already-prepared letter into Parsons's lap and cried out, "It's time!" Then he roused Hasbro, who himself leaped up and headed straight for the door.

"Coming or not, Jacky?" asked the professor.

"Why, coming, I suppose. Where? Now?"

"To the Dover Strait. You can sleep on board."

With that he rushed into Parsons's room, coming back out with a bundle of the man's clothes, and I found myself following them through the night—out the backdoor of the inn, down along the seawall, and clambering into the tethered rowboat. Hasbro unshipped the oars and we were away, through the patchy fog, dipping along until the shadowy hull of a small steam trawler rose out of the mists ahead of us. We thunked into the side of her and clambered aboard, then winched up the rowboat after us. Up came the anchor, and I found myself saying hello to Hasbro's stalwart Aunt Edie and to the grizzled Uncle Botley, pilot of the trawler. Roped onto a little barge behind us rested the diving bell that we had stolen earlier that very night from the icehouse.

St. Ives had drugged poor Parsons. The water bottle had been doctored, and Parsons, in the joy of his victory, had swallowed enough of it to make him sleep for half a day. We would get into the Strait before him, towing the bell, and when we did... —⌒

Parsons Bids Us Adieu

W E FOUND THE WATERS around the submerged machine alive with a half-dozen ships, all of them at anchor a good distance away. They had attached a buoy directly to it, to track it so as to avoid either losing it or coming too near it. We showed no hesitation at all, but steamed right up to the line. That was where I played my part, and played it tolerably well, I think.

Up onto the deck I came, wearing an enormous white beard and wig and dressed in Parsons's clothes, which St. Ives had stolen from his room at the Apple. St. Ives stayed hidden; his face would excite suspicion in any of a number of people. He coached me, though, from inside a cabin, and together we bluffed our way through that line of ships with a lot of what sounded to me like convincing talk about having learned how to "disarm" the machine and having brought along a diving bell for the purpose.

Anyway, certain that I was Parsons, they let us through right enough, and we navigated as close to the buoy as we dared, then set out in the rowboat, towing the barge with the bell standing on whittle-legged atop the deck, the jib crane attached to the barge now with brass carriage bolts, its chain pulled off and replaced entirely with heavy line. We would have to be quick, though. Uncle Botley had removed as much iron from the rowboat and barge as he could manage, but there was still the chance that if we didn't look sharp, the machine would start to tug our nails and would scuttle us.

Hasbro and I manned the oars—work that I was admirably suited to from my days of punting on the Thames. They must have been surprised, though, to see old Parsons hauling away like that, given that he was upward of eighty-five years old. The idea of it amused me, and I pulled all the harder, watching over my shoulder as we drew slowly nearer to the buoy.

St. Ives was in the bell itself, making ready. His was the dangerous work. He was going down without air, because a compressor would have been pulled to pieces. But it was a shallow dive, and it wouldn't take him long. That was his claim, anyway. "Give me eight minutes by the pocket watch," he had told us, "and then pull me out of there. I can go down again if need be. And," he said darkly, "if the rowboat starts to go to pieces, or if there's trouble down below, cut the line and get away as quick as you can."

Hasbro insisted at once on going with him, as did I, neither one of us keen on getting away. But that wasn't St. Ives's method and never had been. He was still in a funk because of the time he thought we had wasted and because of the two ships that had gone down needlessly. And there was the fact of his—as he saw it— having allowed the machine to exist all these years, sitting placidly in that machine works, only to be stolen and misused. He was the responsible party, and he would brook no nonsense to the contrary. There was a certain psychological profit, then, in his going down and facing the danger alone; his face seemed to imply that if something went wrong and we had to leave him, well, so be it; it was no more than he deserved.

Then there was the business of Alice, wasn't there? It hovered over the man's head like a rain cloud, and I believe that I can say, without taking anything away from his natural courage, that St. Ives didn't care two figs whether he lived or died.

And although in truth I had no idea how much air one working man would breathe at a depth of eight fathoms, I accepted his assurances that two men would breathe twice as much and increase the dangers accordingly. The controls were meant for a single man, too, and St. Ives had been studying and manipulating them all the way out from Sterne Bay. Hasbro and I would have been nothing but dangerous baggage, trying to demonstrate our loyalty by our willingness to die along with him, if it came to that. He didn't need any such demonstrations.

Down he went, into the dark ocean. One of the handlike armatures of the bell held on to a bundle of explosives wrapped in sheet rubber and sealed with asphaltum varnish. There was a timing device affixed to it. St. Ives had never meant to "disarm" the machine at all. He had meant all along to blow it to kingdom come, and he had stolen Higgins's bell for just that purpose.

The Strait was blessedly placid—just a trace of wind and a slightly rolling ground swell. Line played slowly out through the oaken blocks, and we watched the bell hover deeper, down toward the vast black shadow below. I hadn't expected quite what I saw— a sort of acreage of shadow down there, but then I realized that what I saw wasn't merely the machine, but was a heap of derelict iron ships clustered together, the whole heap lying, I supposed, on a sandy shoal.

And that was why St. Ives hadn't done the obvious—merely wrapped a hunk of iron into that package of explosives and tossed it over the side. It might easily have affixed itself to the hull of a downed ship and blown it up, leaving the machine alone. What the professor had to do was drop onto the machine itself, or grapple his way to it by the use of the bell's armatures, and plant the explosives just so; otherwise they were wasted. Eight minutes didn't seem like such a long time after all.

But then the line went suddenly slack and began to coil onto the top of the water. St. Ives had hooked on to something—the machine, a ship. All of us studied our pocket watches.

You'd think that the minutes would have flown by, but they didn't; they crept. The breeze blew, clouds slipped across the sky, the loose circle of ships rolled on the calm waters, no one aboard them suspecting who I really was in my beard and wig. Hasbro counted the minutes aloud, and Uncle Botley stood at the winch. At the count of eight the three of us put our backs into it. The line went quivering-taut, spraying droplets. The blocks groaned and creaked. The bell very slowly swam into view, and in a rush of ocean water it burst out into the air, St. Ives visible within, the explosive package gone. He had either succeeded or failed utterly; it didn't matter which, not at the moment.

Thunk went the bell onto the deck, and while Uncle Botley lashed it down, Hasbro and I bent to the oars and had that barge fairly skimming, if I do say so myself. There's nothing like a spot of work when you know what the devil you're doing and, of course, when there's an explosion pending.

A cheer went up from the ships waiting in a circle around us, and I took my hat off and waved it in the air, my wig nearly blowing away in the sea wind. I clapped the hat back down and gave up the histrionics, hauling us through the chop, bang up against the hull of our trawler. We clambered aboard, taking the barge in tow and setting out at once.

We didn't leave St. Ives in the bell, of course. He climbed out at the last possible minute, taking the risk now of being seen. "Let's go," he said simply, and into the cabin he went as I took up the speaking trumpet and started to shout at the nearest ship, on which a half-dozen men stood at attention along the rail, and a captain or some such thing awaited orders. In my best Parsons voice, helpfully disguised by the speaking tube, I gave him all the orders he needed—that we had set into motion the disarming of the machine, but that its excess electromagnetic energies would reach capacity just before she shut down. Move away, is what I told him, for safety's sake, or risk going to the bottom!

That drew their attention. I think they would have run for it even if my beard had been plucked off right then by a sea gull. Flags were run up; whistles blew; men scrambled across the decks of the several ships, which began to make away another quarter of a mile, just as I told them, where they would await orders. We kept right on going—steaming back toward Sterne Bay. That must have confounded them, our racing off like that. For my money, though, it didn't confound them half as much as did the explosion that followed our departure. We were well away by then, on the horizon, but we saw the plume of water, and then heard the distant whump of the concussion.

—⁂—

So LORD KELVIN's machine was nothing but sinking fragments, an instant neighborhood for the denizens of the sea. Dr. Narbondo would continue his cold sleep until whatever it was that animated him had played itself out. Parsons, poor man, wouldn't be at the helm of whatever grand ship he had imagined himself piloting into the harbor of scientific fame. His schemes were a ruin—blown to pieces. Even his victory over St. Ives had been a short-lived one—toasted to with drugged water.

St. Ives wasn't happy with that part. He felt guilty about Parsons, and he felt even worse that Narbondo would sleep through what ought to have been his public trial and execution. Ah well, I was happy enough. I wasn't fond of Parsons in the first place, and had rather enjoyed parading around in the beard and wig. I wish there had been some way to let him know about that, just to make him mad, but I guess there wasn't. He would hear most of it, likely enough, but he probably wouldn't guess it had been me, and that was too bad.

We landed in Sterne Bay, our business done. And we parted company with Hasbro's aunt and with Uncle Botley. At the Crown and Apple we found a note under St. Ives's door—the same note, in fact, that St. Ives had left on Parsons's lap. The old man had scrawled on it the words, "I'm on the afternoon train to London; you might have the kindness to see me off." Just that. You would have expected more—some little bit of anger or regret—given what St. Ives had revealed to him. But there was no anger, just the words of a sad man asking for company.

We hurried down to the station to do his bidding. It was the least we could do. His just giving in like that made the business doubly sorrowful, and although I was tempted for a moment to wear them, I left the beard and wig at the Apple.

The train was chuffing there on the track, the passengers already boarded. We ran along the platform. St. Ives was certain that there was some good reason for Parsons's having summoned him, and that it was his duty, our duty, after exploding Parsons's dreams, to see what it was that the old man wanted, what last tearful throwing-in-the-towel statement he would utter. Let him complain to our faces, I thought, taking the long view. He had been riding high just yesterday, astride his charger, but now, as they say, the mighty had fallen. The race was not always to the swift. Parsons could have his say; I wouldn't begrudge him.

But where was he? The cars were moving along. We trotted beside them, keeping up, out toward the empty tracks ahead, the train chugging forward and away. Then, as the last car but one rolled past, a window slid down, and there was Parsons's face grinning out at us like a winking devil. "Haw! Haw! Haw!" he shouted, apparently having run mad, the poor bastard.

Then he dangled out the window a bound notebook, tattered and old-looking. Streaked across it in faded ink was the name "John Kenyon," written in fancy-looking heavy script—the name, of course, of Mrs. Pule's derelict father. Despite what was utterly obvious, and thinking to put on a show of being interested in the old man's apparent glee, I was witless enough to yell, "What is it?" as we watched the train pick up speed and move away from us toward London.

And he had the satisfaction of leaning out even farther in order to make a rude gesture at us, shouting in a sort of satisfied whinny, "What the hell do you think it is, idiot?" Then the damned old fool drew the notebook in and slammed the window shut, clipping off the sound of his own howling laughter.

The train bore Parsons away to London, along with—if the half-frozen doctor had only been aware of his victory, of this renewed promise of resurrection—the gloating still-animate body of Ignacio Narbondo. —◦

PART III

The Time Traveler

In the North Sea

AIR HISSED THROUGH rubber tubing like the wheezing of a mechanical man. There was the odor of machine oil and metal in the air, mixed with the damp aquarium smell of seawater seeping slowly past riveted joints and rubber seals. The ocean lay silent and cold and murky beyond porthole windows, and St. Ives fought off the creeping notion that he had been encased in a metal tomb.

One of the bathyscaphe's jointed arms clanked against the brass hull with a dull echo, a sound from a distant world. St. Ives felt it in his teeth. He smeared cold sweat from his forehead and focused his mind on his task—recovering Lord Kelvin's machine from the debris-covered sandbar forty feet beneath the Dover Strait. The hulks of three ships lay roundabout, one of them blown apart by the dynamite bomb that St. Ives had dropped into its hold six months past.

He pulled a lever in the floor, feeling and hearing the metallic ratchet of the pair of retractable feet that thrust out from the base of the bathyscaphe. Laboriously, inch by inch, the spherical device hopped across the ocean floor. Fine sand swirled up, obscuring the portholes, and for the space of a minute St. Ives could see nothing at all. He shut his eyes and pressed his hands to his temples, aware again of the swish of air through tubing and of the sound of blood pounding in his head. He felt a great pressure, all imaginary, but nonetheless real for that, and he began to breathe rapidly and shallowly, fighting down a surge of panic. The portholes cleared, and a school of John Dory lazied past, gaping in at him, studying him as if he were a textbook case on the extravagances of human folly…

"Stop it!" he said out loud. His voice rang off the brass walls, and he peered forward, trying to work the looped end of line around the far side of the machine.

"Pardon me, sir?" The stalwart voice of Hasbro sounded through the speaking tube.

"Nothing. It's close down here."

"Perhaps if I had a go at it, sir?"

"No. It's nothing. I'm at the end of it."

"Very well," the voice said doubtfully.

He let go of the line, and it slowly sank across the copper shell of the machine, drifting off the far edge and settling uselessly on the ocean floor. Failure—he would have to try again. He closed his eyes and sat for a moment, thinking that he could easily fall asleep. Then the idea of sleep frightened him, and he looked around himself, taking particular note of the dials and levers and gauges. He needed something solid to use as ballast for his mind—something outside, something comfortable and homely.

Abruptly he thought of food, of cottage pie and a bottle of beer. With effort, he began to think through the recipe for cottage pie, reciting it to himself. It wouldn't do to talk out loud. Hasbro would haul him straight out of the water. He pictured the pie in his head—the mashed potatoes whipped with cream and butter, the farmer's cheese melted across the top. He poured a mental beer into a glass, watching it foam up over the top and spill down the sides. Keeping the image fresh, he pulled in the line again, working diligently until he gripped the noose once more. Then, slowly, he carried it back out with the mechanical hand. He dropped it carefully, and this time it floated down to encircle a solid piece of outthrust metal.

"Cottage pie," he muttered.

"I'm sorry, sir?"

"Got its . . . eye," he said weakly, realizing that this sounded even more lunatic than what he *had* said. It didn't matter, though. He was almost through. Already the feeling of desperation and confinement was starting to lift. Carefully, he clamped on to the line again, pulling it tight inch by inch, working steadily to close the loop. If he could attend to his work he would be on the surface in ten minutes. Five minutes.

"Up we go," he said, loud this time, like a sea captain, and in a matter of seconds there was a jolt, and the bathyscaphe tilted just a little, lifting off the ocean floor. It rose surfaceward in little jerks, and the school of John Dory followed it up, nosing against the portholes. St. Ives was struck suddenly by how friendly the fish were, nosing against the glass like that. God bless a fish, he thought, keeping a man company. The water brightened around him, and the feeling of entombment began to dissipate. He breathed deeply, watching bubbles rush past now and the fish turn in a school and dart away. Suddenly the wave-lapped surface of the gray ocean tossed across the porthole, and then the sea gave way to swirling fog, illuminated by a morning sun and enlivened by the muffled sound of water streaming off the sides of the bathyscaphe. Then there was the solid clunk of metal feet settling on a wooden deck.

St. Ives opened the hatch and climbed out, and immediately he and Hasbro swung the dripping bathyscaphe across the deck so as to make room for Lord Kelvin's machine. They unfastened it from the jib crane and lashed it down solidly, hiding it beneath oiled canvas, working frenziedly while the sun threatened to burn off the fog and to reveal their efforts to the light of day. Hurrying, they fixed the line that grappled Lord Kelvin's machine to the jib crane and set about hauling it out of the water, too, afterward hiding it beneath more tied down canvas.

In another twenty minutes the steam trawler, piloted by the man that St. Ives knew as Uncle Botley, made off northward. St. Ives remained on deck for a time, watching through the mist. Soon they would be far enough from the site that they could almost pretend to be innocent—to have been out after fish.

It had been six months since anyone from the Royal Academy had been lurking in the area. So they ought to have been safe; the issue of the machine was officially closed. Yet St. Ives was possessed with the notion that he would be discovered anyway, that there was something he had missed, that his plans to save Alice would fail if he wasn't vigilant night and day. Fears kept revealing themselves to him, like cards turned up in a deck. He kept watch for another hour while the fog dissipated on the sea wind. The horizon, when he could see it, was empty of ships in every direction.

Exhausted, he went below deck and fell into a bunk as the trawler steamed toward Grimsby, bound, finally, up the Humber to Goole. In three days he would be home again, such as it was, in Harrogate. Then the real work would start. Secrecy now was worth—what? His life, pretty literally. Alice's life. They would transport the machine overland from Goole, after disguising it as a piece of farm machinery. Even so, they would keep it hidden beneath canvas. No one could be trusted. Even the most innocent bumpkin could be a spy for the Royal Academy.

When they reached the environs of Harrogate they would wait for nightfall, sending Kraken ahead to scout out the road. That's when the danger would be greatest, when they got to within hailing distance of the manor. If the Academy was laying for St. Ives, that's where they would hide, waiting to claim what was theirs. How desperate would they be? More to the point, how far would St. Ives go to circumvent them?

He knew that there were no steps that Parsons wouldn't take in order to retrieve the machine. If Parsons knew, that is, that the machine was retrievable. For the fiftieth time St. Ives calculated the possibility of that, ending up, as usual, awash with doubts. Parsons was a doddering cipher. He had out-tricked St. Ives badly in Sterne Bay, and the only high card left to St. Ives now was the machine itself. Parsons hadn't expected St. Ives to destroy it, and he certainly couldn't have expected St. Ives to *pretend* to destroy it. Perhaps he should pretend to destroy it again, and so confuse the issue utterly. He could spend the remainder of his life pretending to have destroyed and recovered the machine. They could scuttle Uncle Botley's trawler after transferring the machine to some other vessel, making Parsons believe that it was still on board. Of course, Parsons didn't know it was on board in the first place; they would have to find a way to reveal that. Then they could pretend to pretend to scuttle the ship, maybe not move the machine off at all, but only pretend to...

He tossed in his bunk, his mind aswirl with nonsense. Finally the sea rocked him to sleep, settling his mind. Water swished and slapped against the hull, and the ship creaked as it rose and fell on the ground swell. The noises became part of a dream—the sounds of a coach being driven hard along a black and muddy street.

He was alone on a rainy night in the Seven Dials, three years past. At first he thought his friends were with him, but around him now lay nothing but darkness and the sound of rain. There was something—he squinted into the night. A shop-window. He could see his own reflection, frightened and helpless, and behind him the street, rain pelting down. The rainy curtain drew back as if across a darkened theater stage, and a picture formed in the dusty window glass: a cabriolet overturned in the mud, one spoked wheel spinning round and round past the upturned face of a dead woman…

He jerked up out of his bunk, fighting for breath. "Cottage pie," he said out loud. Damn anyone who might hear him. What did they know? He was a man alone. In the end, that was what had proved to be true. It wasn't anybody's fault; it was the way of the world. He lay down again, feeling the ship rise on the swell. He thought hard about the pie, about the smell of thyme and rosemary and sage simmering in a beef broth, about the herb garden that Alice had started and that was now up in weeds. He hadn't given much of a damn about food before he knew Alice, but she had got him used to it. He had kept the herb garden flourishing for a month or so, in her memory. But keeping the memory was somehow worse than fleeing from it. Moles were living in the garden now—a whole village of them.

He drifted off to sleep again, dreaming that he watched the moles through the parlor window. One of them had the face and spectacles of old Parsons. It pretended to be busy with mole activities, but it regarded him furtively over the top of its spectacles. Away across the grounds lay the River Nidd, fringed with willows. Through them, his beard wagging, stepped Lord Kelvin himself, striding along toward the manor with the broad ever-approaching gait of a man in a dream. He wasn't in a jolly mood, clearly not coming round to chat about the theory of elasticity or the constitution of matter. He carried a stick, which he beat against the palm of his hand.

Willing to take his medicine, St. Ives stepped out into the garden to meet him, nearly treading on the mole that looked like Parsons. Weeds crackled underfoot and the day was dreary and dim, almost as if the whole world were dilapidated. This wasn't going to be pretty. Lord Kelvin wasn't a big man, and he was getting on in years, but there was a fierce look in his eyes that seemed to say, in a Glasgow brogue, "You've blown my machine to pieces. Now I'm going to beat the dust out of you."

What he said was, "I spent twenty-odd years on that engine, lad. I'm too old to start again." His face was saddened, full of loss.

St. Ives nodded. One day, maybe, he would give it back to the man. But he couldn't tell him that now.

"I'm truly sorry…," he began.

"Ye can't imagine what it was, man." He gestured with the stick, which had turned into a length of braided copper wire.

On the contrary, St. Ives had imagined what it was on the day that he walked into

Lord Kelvin's barn, looking to ruin it. He took the braided wire from the old man, but it fell apart in his hands, dropping in strands across his shoes.

"We might have gone anywhere in it," the old man said wistfully. "The two of us. Traveled across time…" He could be open and honest now that he thought the machine was blasted to pieces. There was nothing to hide anymore. St. Ives let him talk. It was making them both feel better, filling St. Ives with remorse and happiness at the same time: the two of them, traveling together, side by side, back to the Age of Reptiles, forward to a day when men would sail among the stars. St. Ives had worked too long in obscurity, shunned by the Academy and so pretending to despise it—but all the time pounding on the door, crying to be let in. That was the sad truth, wasn't it? Here was its foremost member, Lord Kelvin himself, talking like an old and trusted colleague.

Lord Kelvin nodded his head, which turned into a quadrant electrometer. In his hand he held a mariner's compass of his own invention. The needle pointed east with awful, mystifying significance.

"I knew what it…what it was," St. Ives said remorsefully. "But I wanted the machine for myself, to work my own ends, not yours. I've given up science for personal gain." He couldn't help being truthful.

"You'll never be raised to the peerage with that attitude, lad."

St. Ives noticed suddenly that the mole with Parsons's face was studying him out of its squinty little eyes. Hurriedly, it turned around and scampered away across the meadow, carrying a suitcase. Lord Kelvin looked at his pocket watch, which swung on the end of a length of transatlantic cable. "If he hurries he can catch the 2:30 train to London. He'll arrive in time."

He showed the pocket watch to St. Ives. The crystal was enormous, nearly as big as the sky, filling the landscape, distorting the images behind it like a fishbowl. St. Ives squinted to make things out. The hands of the watch jerked around their course, ticking loudly. Behind them, on the watch face, a figure moved through the darkness of a rainy night. It was St. Ives himself, wading through ankle-deep water. It was fearsomely slow going. Like quicksand, the water clutched his ankles. Going round and round in his head was a hailstorm of regrets—if only the ships hadn't gone down, if he hadn't missed his train, if he hadn't come to ruin on the North Road, if he could tear himself loose now from the grip of this damnable river…He wiped rainwater out of his eyes. Crouched before him in the street was Ignacio Narbondo, a smoking pistol in his hand and a look of insane triumph on his face.

St. Ives jackknifed awake again. The air of the cabin was cold and wet, and for a moment he imagined he was once more in the bathyscaphe, on the bottom of the sea. But then he heard Uncle Botley shout and then laugh, and the voice, especially the laughter, seemed to St. Ives to be a wonderful fragment of the living world—something he could get a grip on, like a cottage pie.

St. Ives studied his face in the mirror on the wall. He was thin and sallow. He felt a quick surge of terror without an object, and he realized abruptly that he had gotten old. He seemed to have the face of his father. "Time and chance happeneth to them all," he muttered, and he went out on deck in the gathering night, where the lights of Grimsby slipped past off the starboard bow, and the waters of the Humber lost themselves in the North Sea. —◦

The Saving of Binger's Dog

S T. IVES SAT in the chair in his study. It was a dim and wintry day outside, with rain pending and the sky a uniform gray. He had been at work on the machine for nearly six months, and success loomed on the horizon now like a slowly approaching ship. There had been too little sleep and too many missed or hastily eaten meals. His friends had rallied around him, full of concern, and he had gone on in the midst of all that concern, implacably, like a rickety millwheel. Jack and Dorothy were on the Continent now, though, and Bill Kraken was off to the north, paying a visit to his old mother. There was a fair chance that he wouldn't see any of them again. The thought didn't distress him. He was resigned to it.

A fly circled lazily over the clutter on the desk, and St. Ives whacked at it suddenly with a book, knocking it to the floor. The fly staggered around as if drunk. In a fit of re-morse, St. Ives scooped it up on a sheet of paper, walked across and opened the French window, and then dumped the fly out into the bushes. "Go," he said hopefully to the fly, which buzzed around aimlessly, somewhere down in the bushes.

St. Ives stood breathing the wet air and staring out onto the meadow at the brick silo that rose there crumbling and lonely, full to the top with scientific aspirations and pretensions. It looked to him like a sorry replica of the Tower of Babel. Inside it lay Lord Kelvin's machine, along with Higgins's bathyscaphe. St. Ives had removed and discarded most of the shell of the machine, hauling the useless telltale debris away by night. What was left was nearly ready; he had only to wheedle what might be called fine points out of the gracious Lord Kelvin who would abandon Harrogate for Glasgow tomorrow morning.

St. Ives hadn't slept in two days. Dreaming had very nearly cured him of sleep. There would be time enough for sleep, though. Either that, or there wouldn't be. On impulse, he left the window open, thinking to show other flies that he harbored no ill will toward them, and then he slumped back across to the chair and sat down heavily, sinking so that he rested on his tailbone. A shock of hair fell across his eyes, obscuring his vision. He harrowed it backward with his fingers, then nibbled at a grown-out nail, tearing it off short and taking a fragment of skin with it. "Ouch," he said, shaking his hand, but then losing interest in it almost at once. For a long time he sat there, thinking about nothing.

Coming to himself, finally, he surveyed the desktop. It was a clutter of stuff—tiny coils and braids of wire, miniature gauges, pages torn out of books, many of which torn pages now marked places in other books. There was an army of tiny clockwork toys littering the desktop, built out of tin by William Keeble. Half of them were a rusted ruin, the victims of an experiment he had performed three weeks past. St. Ives looked at them suspiciously, trying to remember what he had meant to prove by spraying them with brine and then leaving them on the roof.

He had waked up in the middle of the night with a notion involving the alteration of matter, and had spent an hour meddling with the toys, leaving them, finally, on the roof before going back to bed, exhausted. In the morning, somehow, he had forgotten about them. And then, days later, he had seen them from out on the meadow, still lying on the roof, and although he remembered having put them there, and having been possessed with the certainty that putting them there was good and right and useful, he couldn't for the life of him recall why.

That sort of thing was bothersome—periods of awful lucidity followed by short bursts of rage or by wild enthusiasm for some theoretical notion having to do with utter nonsense. Moodily, he poked at the windup duck, which whirred momentarily to life, and then fell over onto its side. There were ceramic figures, too, sitting among comical Toby mugs and glass gewgaws, some few of which had belonged to Alice. Balls of crumpled paper lay everywhere, along with broken pens and graphite crumbs and fragments of India-rubber erasers. A lake of spilled ink had long ago dried beneath it all, staining the brown oak of the desktop a rich purple.

Filled with a sudden sense of purpose, he reached out and swept half the desk clear, the books and papers and tin toys tumbling off onto the floor. Carefully, he straightened the glass and ceramic figurines, setting a little blue-faced doggy alongside a Humpty Dumpty with a ruff collar. He stood a tiptoeing ballerina behind them, and then, in the foreground, he lay a tiny glass shoe full of sugar crystals. He sat back and looked at the collection, studying it. There was something in it that wasn't quite satisfying, that wasn't—what? Proportionate, maybe. He turned the toe of the glass shoe just a bit. Almost…He rotated the Humpty Dumpty so that it seemed to be regarding the ballerina, then slid the dog forward so that its head rested on the toe of the shoe.

That was it. On the instant, meaning had evolved out of simple structure. Something in the little collection reminded him of something else. What? Domestic tranquillity. Order. He smiled and shook his head nostalgically, yearning for something he couldn't recall. The comfortable feeling evaporated into the air. The nostalgia, poignant as it had been for that one moment, wasn't connected to anything at all, and was just so much vapor, an abstraction with no concrete object. It was gone now, and he couldn't retrieve it. Maybe later he would see it again, when he wasn't trying so hard.

Frowning, he returned to the window where he worked his fingers through his hair again. There was a broken limb on the bush where he had dropped the fly, as if someone had stepped into it clumsily. For a moment he was puzzled. There hadn't been any broken limb a half hour ago.

A surge of worried excitement welled up in him, and he stepped out through the window, looking up and down along the wall of the house. Here he is again! he said to himself. No one was visible, though.

He sprinted to the corner, bursting quickly past it to catch anyone who might still be lurking. He looked about himself wildly for a moment and then ran straight toward the carriage house and circled entirely around it. The door was locked, so he didn't bother going in, but headed out onto the meadow instead straightaway toward the silo. He realized that he should have fetched Hasbro along with him, or at any rate brought a weapon.

He had left the silo doors double-locked, though. They were visible from the house, too—both from the study and from St. Ives's bedroom upstairs. Hasbro's quarters also looked out onto the meadow, and Mrs. Langley could see the silo from the kitchen window. St. Ives had been too vigilant for anyone to have...And no one had. The doors were still locked, the locks untouched. Carefully, he inspected the ground finding stray shoeprints here and there. He stepped into them, realizing only then that he was in his stocking feet. Still, there was one set of prints that were smaller even than his unshod foot. They wouldn't belong to Hasbro, then. Possibly they were Bill Kraken's, except that Kraken was up in Edinburgh and these prints were fresh. Parsons! It had to be Parsons, snooping around again. Who else could it be? No one.

Finally he jogged off toward his study window, pounding his fist over and over into his hand in a fit of nervous energy. His mind was a turmoil of conflict. He *had* to sort things out...The ground outside the French windows was soft, kept wet by water falling off the overhanging eaves. A line of shoeprints paralleled the wall, as if someone had come sneaking along it, stepping onto the bush in order to sandwich himself in toward the window without being seen. In his excitement St. Ives hadn't seen the prints, but he stooped to examine them now. The toes were pressed deeply into the dirt, so whoever it was had been hunched over forward, keeping low, moving slowly and heavily. Small shoeprints again, though. Certainly not his own.

St. Ives hurried back into the study. He opened a desk drawer and rooted through it, pulling out papers and books until he found a cloth-wrapped parcel. He pulled the cloth away, revealing four white plaster-of-Paris shoeprint casts. He turned them over, and, on the bottom, printed neatly in ink, were dates and place-names. The first set was dated six months past, taken in Sterne Bay from the dirt outside the icehouse.

The second pair were taken a week past, down along the River Nidd. They were from different pairs of shoes of the same size.

He put the first pair back into the drawer and carried the second outside, laying them into appropriate prints. They settled in perfectly. On his hands and knees he squinted closely at one of the heel prints in the dirt. The back outside corner of the heel was gone, worn away, so that the heel print looked like someone's family crest, but with a quarter of the shield lopped away. An image leaped into his mind of Parsons walking along in his usual bandy-legged gait, scuffing the leather off the corners of his heels. The heels on the plaster casts were worn out absolutely identically. There couldn't be any doubt, or almost none. Parsons had come snooping around. He couldn't have been entirely positive that the man he had seen skulking along the river had been Parsons. It had been late evening, and drizzling. Whoever it had been, though, it was the same man who, within the last half hour or so, had sneaked along the wall of the house, stepped into the bush and broke off the limb, and then, no doubt, peered in at the window.

He climbed back into the room, rewrapping the plaster casts and closing them up in the drawer. Then, pulling on his coat, he strode out across the meadow once again like a man with a will, noticing only when he was halfway to the River Nidd that he still wasn't wearing any shoes.

—⁓—

HE RETURNED LATE that afternoon in an improved mood, although he felt agitated and anxious. He had spent three hours with Lord Kelvin. The great scientist had come to understand that tragedy had turned St. Ives into a natural fool. He had even patted St. Ives on the head once, which had been humiliating, but to some little extent St. Ives had been grateful for it—a sign, he realized, of how dangerously low his spirits had fallen. But things were looking up now. His efforts weren't doomed after all, although he was certain that he was running a footrace with Parsons and the Royal Academy. When they were sure of themselves, they would merely break down the silo door—come out with a dozen soldiers and checkmate him. The game would be at an end.

The idea of it once again darkened his thoughts. His elation at having swindled Lord Kelvin out of certain tidbits of information suddenly lapsed, and he slumped into his chair feeling fatigued and beaten. He seemed to swing between two extremes—doom and utter confidence. Middle ground had become the rarest sort of real estate. What he needed, desperately, was to be levelheaded, and here he was atilt again, staggering off course.

Tomorrow, though, or the next day, he would set out. Right now he would rest. Lord Kelvin had taken pity on him this afternoon. That was the long and the short of it. One look at St. Ives's face, at his disheveled clothes, and Lord Kelvin had been ready to discuss anything at all, as if he were talking to the village idiot. The man had a heart like a hay wagon, to be sure. St. Ives's wandering over without any shoes on had probably done the trick. Kelvin had finally warmed to the subject of time travel, and St. Ives had led him through a discussion of the workings of the machine itself as if he were a trained ape.

That was clever, he told himself, going out shoeless was. He half believed it for a moment. Then he knew that it hadn't been clever at all; he had gone out shoeless without meaning to, and in late autumn, yet. He would have to watch that sort of thing. They'd have him tied down in Colney Hatch if he wasn't careful. He was too close to success. He couldn't chance a strait-waistcoat. Seeing things clearly for the moment, he looked at himself in the cheval glass on the desk. A haircut wouldn't be a bad idea, either. Perhaps if a man affected sanity carefully enough…

Almost happy again, he stepped into his slippers and lit a pipe, sitting back and puffing on it. Failure—that's what had squirreled him up. Too much failure made a hash of a man's mind…He thought for a moment about his manifold failures, and suddenly and inexplicably he was awash with fear, with common homegrown panic. He found that he could barely keep his hands still.

Immediately, he tried to recite the cottage-pie recipe, finding that he couldn't remember it. He pulled a scrap of paper from his shirt pocket and studied the writing on it. There it was—sage and sweet basil. Not sweetbread. He could feel his heart flutter like a bird's wings, and he felt faint and light-headed. Desperately, he breathed for a moment into a sack until the light-headedness began to abate. Sweetbread? Why had he thought of sweetbread? That was some kind of gland, wasn't it? Something the French ate, probably out of buckets and without the benefit of forks.

With an unpleasant shock, he noticed just then that someone had cleaned up his desk. The debris on the floor was separated into tidy piles against the wall. The papers were shuffled, and the books stacked. The glass and ceramic figurines were dusted and lined up together. The neatened desk baffled him for a moment. Then, slowly, a dark rage began to rise in him, and the whole business of an orderly desk became an affront.

He bent down and tossed together the stuff on the floor, mixing it into a sort of salad. Then he kicked through it, sending it flying, winding himself up. He turned to the desk itself, methodically picking up books and shaking out the loose leaves so that they fluttered down higgledy-piggledy. He picked up a heavy iron elephant paperweight and one by one smashed his quill pens, accidentally catching the squared-off edge of the crystal ink bottle and smashing it too, so that ink spewed out across his shirtfront. The shock of smashing the glass made him bite down hard on the stem of his pipe. He heard and felt the stem crack, and quickly let up on it. The pipe fell neatly into two pieces, though, so that the stem stayed in his mouth and the bowl fell down onto the desktop, wobbling around in the ink and broken glass like a drunkard. Furious, he picked up the elephant again and smashed the pipe, over and over and over, until he noticed with a deep rush of demoralizing embarrassment that Mrs. Langley stood in the open door of the room, her eyes wide open with horror and disbelief.

Coldly he put the elephant down and turned to her, realizing without knowing why that she had become an obstruction to him. Somehow, his rage had been transferred en masse to the housekeeper, to Mrs. Langley. He had no need for a housekeeper He saw that clearly. What he had a need for was to be left alone. His desk, his books, his things, wanted to be left alone. Soon he would be gone altogether, perhaps never to return. A page in his life was folding back, a chapter coming to a close. The world was rife with change.

And this wasn't the first time that she had cut this sort of caper. He had spoken to her about it before. Well, the woman had been warned, hadn't she? There wouldn't be any need to speak to her about it again. "As of this moment, Mrs. Langley," he said to her flatly, "you are relieved of your duties. You'll have three months' severance pay."

She put her hand to her mouth, and he realized that his eye was twitching badly and that every muscle in his body was stiff with tension, his hands opening and closing spasmodically. He gestured toward the window, the open road. "*Must* you stare so?" he demanded of her.

"He's gone stark," she muttered through her fingers.

He clenched his teeth. "I have *not* gone stark," he said. "Understand that! I have *not* gone stark!" Even as he said it, there flickered across his mind a vague understanding of what it meant—that he *had* gone mad, utterly. He wasn't quite sane enough to admit it, though, to hold on to the notion. He was too far around the bend to see it anymore, but could merely glimpse its shadow. He knew only that he couldn't have Mrs. Langley meddling with his things, chasing after him with a dust mop as if he wanted a keeper. He watched her leave, very proudly, with her head up. She wasn't the sort to forgive easily. She would be gone, up to her sisters. Well…For a moment he nearly called her back, but was having difficulty breathing again. He put his head into the sack.

After a moment he sat back down in his chair and contrived to rearrange the four objects amid the clutter on the desktop. His hand shook violently, though, and he accidentally uncorked the glass shoe, spilling out half the sugar crystals. Then he knocked the Humpty Dumpty over twice. He concentrated, making himself breathe evenly, placing the objects just so. Surely, if he could get them right, he would regain that moment of indefinable satisfaction that he had felt a few hours past. It would settle him down, restore a sense of proportion. It wouldn't work, though. He couldn't manage it.

He forced himself to concentrate on the desktop again. There was something in the arrangement that was subtlely wrong. The figurines stood there as ever, the dog with his head on the shoe, the Humpty Dumpty gazing longingly at the ballerina. But there was no pattern any longer, no art to it. It was as if the earth had turned farther along its axis and the shadows were different.

He found his shoes, putting them on this time before going out. Work was the only mainstay. He would let Mrs. Langley stew for a while and then would commute her sentence. She must learn not to treat him like a child. Meanwhile he would concentrate on something that would yield a concrete result. With effort, with self-control, he would have what he wanted within twenty-four hours. Where the machine would take him was an utter mystery. Probably he would be blown to fragments. Or worse yet, the machine would turn out to be so much junk, sitting there in the silo with him at the controls, making noises out of his throat like a child driving a locomotive built out of packing crates. He stood by the window, focusing his mind. There wasn't time to regret this business with Mrs. Langley. There wasn't time to regret anything at all. There was only time for action, for movement.

His hands had stopped shaking. As an exercise, he coldly and evenly forced himself to recite the metals in the order of their specific gravities. The cottage-pie recipe was well and good when a man needed a simple mental bracer. But what he wanted now was honing. He needed his edges sharpened. With that in mind, he worked through the metals again, listing them in the order of their fusibility this time, then again backward through both lists, practicing a kind of dutiful self-mesmerization.

Halfway through, he realized that something was wrong with him. He was light-headed, woozy. He held on to the edge of the desk, thinking to wait it out. He watched his hand curiously. It seemed to be growing transparent, as if he had the flesh of a jellyfish. It was happening to him again—the business on the North Road, the ghostly visitation. His vision was clouded, as if he were under water. He slid to the floor and began to crawl toward the window. Maybe fresh air would revive him. Each foot, though, was a journey, and all at once his arms and legs gave way beneath him and he slumped to the floor, giving up and lying there unhappily in front of the open window, thinking black thoughts until suddenly and without warning he thought no more at all.

And then he awakened. His head reeled, but he was solid again. He stood up and studied his hand. Rock steady. Opaque. How long had he been away? He couldn't say. He was confused for a moment, trying to make sense of something that didn't want sense to be made of it. Either that or it already made sense, and he was looking for something that was now plain to him.

Suddenly full of purpose, he straightened his collar and went out into the deepening twilight, having already forgotten about Mrs. Langley but this time wearing his shoes.

—∿—

His COD HAD got cold, and the restaurant, the Crow's Nest in Harrogate, had emptied out. Lunch was over, and only a couple of people lingered at their tables. St. Ives sat in the rear corner, his back to the window, doodling on a pad of paper, making calculations.

He felt suddenly woozy, light-headed. Lack of sleep, he told himself, and bad eating habits. He decided to ignore it, but it was suddenly worse, and he had to shove his feet out in order to brace himself. Damn, he thought. Here it was again—another seizure. This time he would fight it.

He heard muffled laughter from across the room and looked up to see someone staring back at him, someone he didn't recognize. The man looked away, but his companion sneaked a glance in St. Ives's direction, his eyes full of furtive curiosity. Nettled, St. Ives nodded at the man and was suddenly aware of his own slept-in clothes, of his frightful unshaven face. His fork, along with a piece of cod, fell from his hand, dropping onto his trousers, and he stared at it helplessly, knowing without trying that his hand would refuse to pick it back up.

In a moment he would pass out. Better to simply climb down onto the floor and be done with it. He didn't want to, though, not in public, not in the condition he was in. He pressed his eyes shut. Slowly and methodically he began to recite the cottage-pie recipe, forcing himself to consider each ingredient, to picture it, to smell it in his mind. He felt himself recover momentarily, as if he were grounding himself somehow, holding on to things anchored in the world.

Hearing a noise, he slumped around in his chair, looking behind himself at the window. Weirdly, a man's face stared back in at him, past the corner of the building. He was struck at first with the thought that he was looking at his own reflection—the disheveled hair, the slept-in clothes. But it wasn't that. It was himself again, just like on the North Road, his coat streaked with muck, as if he had crawled through every muddy gutter between Harrogate and London. The ghost of himself waved once and was gone, and simultaneously St. Ives fell to the floor of the restaurant and knew no more until he awoke, lying in a tangle among the table legs.

The two men who had been staring were endeavoring to yank on him, to pull him free of the table. "Here now," one of them said. "That's it. You'll be fine now."

St. Ives sat up, mumbling his thanks. It was all right, he said. He wasn't sick. His head was clear again, and he wanted nothing more than to be on his way. The two men nodded at him and moved off, back to their table, one of them advising him to go home and both of them looking at him strangely. "I tell you he bloody well disappeared," one man said to the other, staring once more at St. Ives. His companion waved the comment away.

"Disappeared behind the table, you mean." They went back to their fish, talking between themselves in low voices.

St. Ives was suddenly desperate to reach the sidewalk. These spells were happening too often, and he believed that he understood what they meant, finally. What could he have seen but his future-time self, coming and going, hard at work? He had seen the dominoes falling, catching glimpses of them far down the line. The machine would be a success. That must be the truth. He was filled with optimism, and was itching to be away, to topple that first domino, to set the future into motion.

He left three shillings on the table and nodded his thanks at the two men as he strode toward the door. They looked at him skeptically. He burst out into the sunlight, nearly knocking straight into Parsons, who retreated two steps away, a wild and startled look on his face, as if he had been caught out. Parsons yanked himself together, though, and reached out a hand toward St. Ives. For a moment St. Ives was damned if he would shake it. But then he saw that such a course was unwise. Better to keep up the charade.

"Parsons!" he said, forcing animation into his voice.

"Professor St. Ives. *What* an unbelievable surprise."

"Not terribly surprising," St. Ives said. "I live right up the road. What about you, up on holiday?" He realized that his voice was pitched too high and that he sounded fearful and edgy. Parsons by now was the picture of cheerful serenity.

"Fishing holiday, actually. Lot of trout in the Nidd this time of year. Fly-fishing. Come into town to buy supplies, have you? Going somewhere yourself?" He squinted at St. Ives, taking in the down-at-heels look of him. Parsons couldn't keep an element of discomfort out of his face, as if he regretted encountering a man who was so obviously out humiliating himself. "You look…tired," he said. "Keeping late hours?"

"No," St. Ives said, answering all of Parsons's questions at once. Actually, he *had* been keeping late hours. Where he was going, though, he couldn't rightly say. He knew just where he wanted to go. He had the coordinates fined down to a hair. His mind clouded over just then, and he again felt momentarily dizzy, just as he had the other three times. Some sort of residual effect, perhaps. He couldn't attend to what Parsons was saying, but was compelled suddenly to concentrate merely on staying on his feet. Basil, potatoes, cheese…he said to himself. It was happening again—the abysmal and confusing light-headedness, as if he would at any moment float straight up into the sky.

Parsons stared at him, and St. Ives shook his head, trying to clear it, realizing that the man was waiting for him to say something more. Then, abruptly, as if a trapdoor had opened under him, St. Ives sat down hard on the sidewalk.

He was deathly cold and faint. There could be no doubt now. Here he was again—his future-time self—the damned nitwit. He had better have a damned good excuse. His brain seemed to be a puddle of soft gelatin. He pictured the pie in his head, straight out of the oven, the cheese melting. Sometimes he made it with butter rather than cheese. Never mind that. Better to concentrate on one thing at a time.

There was a terrible barking noise. Some great beast…He looked around vaguely, still sitting on the sidewalk, holding on to his mind with a flimsy grasp. A dog ran past him just then, a droopy-eyed dog, white and brown and black, its tongue lolling out of its mouth. Even in his fuddled state he recognized the dog, and for one strange moment he was filled with joy at seeing it. It was Furry, old Binger's dog, the kind of devoted animal that would come round to see you, anxious to be petted, to be spoken to. A friend in all kinds of weather…Another dog burst past, nearly knocking

Parsons over backward. This one was some sort of mastiff, growling and snarling and snapping and chasing Binger's dog. Weakly, St. Ives tried to throw himself at the mastiff, nearly getting hold of its collar, but the dog ran straight on, as if St. Ives's fingers were as insubstantial as smoke.

Through half-focused eyes, St. Ives saw Binger's poor dog running straight down the middle of the road, into the path of a loaded dray. The air was full of noise, of clattering hooves and the grinding of steel-shod wheels. And just then a man came running from the alley behind the Crow's Nest. He waved curtly to Parsons as he leaped off the curb, hurtling forward into the street, his arms outstretched. St. Ives screwed his eyes half-shut, trying to focus them, the truth dawning on him in a rush. He recognized the tattered muddy coat, the uncombed hair. It was the same man whose reflection he had seen in the glass. It was himself, his future-time self. Parsons saw it too. St. Ives raised a hand to his face, covering his eyes, and yet he could see the street through his hand as if through a fog.

The running man threw himself on the sheepdog. The driver of the dray hauled back on the reins, pulling at the wheel brake. A woman screamed. The horses lunged. The dog and its savior leaped clear, and then the street and everything in it disappeared from view, winking out of existence like a departing hallucination.

———◆◇◆———

SUDDENLY HE COULD see again. And the first thing he noticed was Parsons, hurrying away up the sidewalk in the direction taken by the St. Ives that had saved the dog. There's your mistake, St. Ives said to himself as he struggled to his hands and knees. You're already too late. He felt shaky, almost hung over. He staggered off toward the corner, in the opposite direction as that taken by Parsons. The man would discover nothing. The time machine had gone, and his future-time self with it. St. Ives laughed out loud, abruptly cutting off the laughter when he heard the sound of his own voice.

Mr. Binger's dog loped up behind him, wagging its tail, and St. Ives scratched its head as the two of them trotted along. At the corner, coming up fast, was old Binger himself. "Furry!" he shouted at the dog, half mad and half happy to see it. "Why, Professor," he said, and looked skeptically at St. Ives.

"Have you got your cart?" St. Ives asked him hastily.

"Aye," said Binger. "I was just coming along into town, when old Furry here jumped off the back. Saw some kind of damned mastiff and thought he'd play with it, didn't he?" Binger shook his head. "Trusts anybody. Last week…"

"Drive me up to the manor," St. Ives said, interrupting him. "Quick as you can. There's trouble."

Binger's face dropped. He didn't like the idea of trouble. In that way he resembled his dog. "I don't take any stock in trouble," he had told St. Ives once, and now the look on his face seemed to echo that phrase.

"Cow in calf," St. Ives lied, defining things more carefully. He patted his coat, as if somehow there was something vital in his pocket, something a cow would want. "Terrible rush," he said, "but we might save it yet."

Mr. Binger hurried toward his cart, and the dog Furry jumped on behind. Here was trouble of a sort that Mr. Binger understood, and in moments they were rollicking away up the road, St. Ives calculating how long it would take for Parsons to discover that the man he was chasing was long gone, off into the aether aboard the machine. He was filled with a deep sense of success, transmitted backward to him from the saving of old Furry. It was partly the sight of himself dashing out there, sweeping up the dog. But more than that, it was the certainty that he was moments away from becoming a time traveler, that he could hurry or not hurry, just as he chose. It didn't matter, did it?

The truth was that he was safe from Parsons. The saving of the dog meant exactly that, and nothing less. He was destined to succeed that far, at least. He laughed out loud, but then noticed Mr. Binger giving him a look, and so he pretended to be coughing rather than laughing, and he nodded seriously at the man, patting his coat again.

The manor hove into view as Mr. Binger drove steadily up the road, smoking his pipe like a chimney. There, on the meadow, grazed a half-dozen jersey cows. A calf, easily two months old, stood alongside its mother, who ruminated like a philosopher. "Well, I'll be damned," St. Ives said, jerking his thumb in the direction of the calf. "Looks like everything's fine after all." He smiled broadly at Mr. Binger, in order to demonstrate his deep delight and relief.

"That ain't…," Mr. Binger started to say.

St. Ives interrupted him. "Pull up, will you? I'll just get off here and walk the rest of the way. Thanks awfully." Mr. Binger slowed and stopped the horses, and St. Ives gave him a pound note. "Don't know what I'd do without you, Mr. Binger. I'm in your debt."

Mr. Binger blinked at the money and scratched his head, staring out at the two-month-old calf on the field. He was only mystified for a moment, though. The look on his face seemed to suggest that he was used to this kind of thing, that there was no telling what sorts of shenanigans the professor might not be up to when you saw him next. He shrugged, tipped his hat, turned the wagon around, and drove off.

St. Ives started out toward the manor, whistling merrily. It was too damned bad that Mrs. Langley had gone off to her sister's yesterday without having waited for morning. St. Ives hadn't had time to put things right with her. What had he been thinking of, talking to her in that tone? The thought of his having run mad like that depressed him. He would fetch her back. He had tackled the business of Binger's dog; he could see to Mrs. Langley, too. With the machine he would make everything all right.

Then he began to wonder how on earth he had known about Binger's dog. In some other historical manifestation he must have witnessed the whole incident, and it must have fallen out badly—Binger's dog dead, perhaps, smashed on the street. Via the machine, then, St. Ives must have come back around, stepping in out of time and snatching the dog from the jaws of certain death. Now he couldn't remember any of that other manifestation of time. The first version of things had ceased to exist for him, perhaps now had never existed at all. There was no other explanation for it, though. He, himself, must have purposefully and effectively altered history, *even after history had already been established,* and in so doing had obliterated another incarnation of himself along with it. Nothing is set in stone, he realized, and the thought of it was dizzying—troubling too. What else might he have changed? Who and what else might he have obliterated?

He would have to go easy with this time-traveling business. The risks were clearly enormous. The whole thing might mean salvation, and it might as easily mean utter ruin. Well, one way or another he was going to find out. He no longer had any choice, had he? There he had been, after all, peeking in at the window, saving the dog in the road. There was no gainsaying it now. What would happen, would happen—unless, of course, St. Ives himself came back and made it happen in some other way altogether.

His head reeled, and it occurred to him that there would be nothing wrong, at the moment, with opening a bottle of port—a vintage, something laid down for years. Best taste it now, he thought, the future wasn't half as secure as he had supposed it to be even twenty minutes past. He set out for the manor in a more determined way, thinking happily that if a man were to hop ten years into the future, that same bottle of port would have that many more years on it, and could be fetched back and…

Something made him turn his head and look behind him, though, before he had taken another half-dozen steps. There, coming up the road, was a carriage, banging along wildly, careering back and forth as if it meant to overtake him or know the reason why. Mrs. Langley? he wondered stupidly, and then he knew it wasn't.

Fumbling in his pocket for the padlock key, he set out across the meadow at a dead run, angling toward the silo now. For better or worse, the past beckoned to him. The bottle of port would have to wait. —◆

The Time Traveler

EVEN AS HE was climbing into the machine he could hear them outside, through the brick wall of the silo: the carriage rattling up, the shouted orders, then a terrible banging on the barred wooden doors. He shut the hatch, and the sounds of banging and bashing were muffled. In moments they would knock the doors off their hinges and be inside—Parsons and his ruffians, swarming over the machine. They would have to work on getting in, though, since it was unlikely that they'd brought any sort of battering ram. St. Ives prayed silently that Hasbro wouldn't try to stop them. He could only be brought to grief by tangling with them. They meant business this time, doubly so, since Parsons knew, or at least feared, that he was already too late, and that fear would drive him to desperation. And St. Ives's salvation lay in the machine now, not in his stalwart friend Hasbro, as it had so many times in the past.

He settled himself into the leather seat of what had once been Leopold Higgins's bathyscaphe. It made a crude and ungainly time machine, and most of the interior space had been consumed by Lord Kelvin's magnetic engine, stripped of all the nonsense that had been affixed to it as modification during the days of the comet. There was barely room for St. Ives to maneuver, what with the seat moved forward until his nose was very nearly pressed against a porthole. An elaborate system of mirrors allowed him to see around the device behind him, out through the other porthole windows.

He glanced into the mirrors once, making out the dim floor of the silo: the tumbled machinery and scrap metal, the black forge with its enormous bellows, the long workbench that was chaos of debris and tools. What a pathetic mess. The sight of it reminded St. Ives of how far he had sunk in the last couple of years—the last few months, really. His mental energy had been spent entirely, to its last farthing, on building the machine; he hadn't enough left over to hang up a hammer. He remembered a dim past day when he had been the king of regimentation and order. Now he was the pawn of desperation.

It was then that he saw the message, scrawled in chalk on the silo wall. "Hurry," it read. "Try to put things right on the North Road. If at first you fail..." The message ended there, unfinished, as if someone—he himself—had abandoned the effort and fled. And just as well. It was a useless note, anyway. He would remember that in the future. Time was short; there was none left over for wasted words and ready-made phrases.

He concentrated on the dials in front of him, listening with half an ear to the muffled bashing of the doors straining against the bar. He knew just exactly where he wanted to go, but harmonizing the instrumentation wanted minutes, not seconds. Measure twice, cut once, as the carpenter said. Well, the carpenter would have to trust to his eye, here; there was no time to fiddle with tape measures. Hastily, he made a final calculation and delicately turned the longitudinal dial, tracking a route along the Great North Road, into London. He set the minutes and the seconds and then went after the latitudinal dial.

There was a sound of wood splintering, and the murky light of the silo brightened. They were in. St. Ives reeled through the time setting, hearing the delicate insect hum of the spinning flywheel. The machine shook just then, with the weight of someone climbing up the side. Parsons's face appeared in front of the porthole. He was red and sweating, and his beard wagged with the effort of his shouting. St. Ives winked at him, and glanced into the mirrors again. The silo door was swung wide open, framing a picture of Hasbro, carrying a rifle, running across the meadow. Mrs. Langley followed him, a rolling pin in her hand.

Mrs. Langley! God bless her. She had gone away miffed, but had come back, loyal woman that she was. And now she was ready to hammer his foes with a rolling pin. St. Ives very nearly gave it up then and there. She would sacrifice herself for him, even after his shabby treatment of her. He couldn't let her do that, or Hasbro either.

For a moment he hesitated. Then, stoically and calmly, he set his mind again to his instruments. By God, he *wouldn't* let them do it. He was a time traveler now. He would save them all before he was through, whatever it took. If he stayed, if he abandoned the machine to Parsons, he would be a gibbering wreck for ever and ever. If he lived that long. He'd be of no use to anyone at all.

He heard the sound of someone fiddling with the hatch. The moment had come. "Hurry," the message on the wall had said. He threw the lever that activated the electro-magnetic properties of Lord Kelvin's machine. The ground seemed suddenly to shake beneath him, and there was a high-pitched whine that rose within a second to the point of disappearing. Parsons pitched over backward as the bathyscaphe bucked on its splayed legs. Simultaneously, there was a shouting from overhead, and a pair of legs and feet swung down across the porthole. Parsons scrambled upright, latching on to the dangling man and pulling him free.

And then, abruptly, absolute darkness prevailed, and St. Ives felt himself falling, spinning round and round as he fell, as if down a dark and very deep well. His first impulse was to clutch at something, but there was nothing to clutch, and he seemed to have no hands. He was simply a mind, spiraling downward through itself, seeming already to have traveled vast distances along endless centuries and yet struck with the notion that he had merely blinked his eyes.

Then he stopped falling, and sat as ever in the bathyscaphe. He realized now that his hands shook treacherously. They had been calm and cooperative when the danger was greatest, but now they were letting themselves go. He was still in darkness. But where? Suspended somewhere in the void, neither here nor there?

He saw then that the darkness outside was of a different quality than it had been. It was merely nighttime, and it was raining. He was in the country somewhere. Slowly, his eyes accustomed themselves to the darkness. A muddy road stretched away in front of him. He was in an open field, beside the North Road.

From out of the darkness, cantering along at a good pace, came a carriage. St. Ives—his past-time self—was driving it. The horses steamed in the rain, and muddy water flew from the wheels. Bill Kraken and Hasbro sat inside. Somewhere ahead of them, Ignacio Narbondo fled in terror, carrying Alice with him. They were nearly upon him…

Shrugging with fatalistic abandon, the St. Ives in the machine scribbled a note to himself. He knew that it was possible that he could deliver the note, if he hurried. He knew equally well what attempting to deliver it might mean. He had experienced this fiasco once before, seeing it through the eyes of the man who drove the wagon. He was filled suddenly with feelings of self-betrayal.

Still, he reminded himself, he *could* change the past: witness the saving of Binger's dog. And in any event, what would he sacrifice by being timid here? His failing to act would *necessarily* alter the past, and with what consequences? It wouldn't serve to be stupid and timid both; one mistake was enough.

He read hastily through the finished note. "N. will shoot Alice on the street in the Seven Dials," the note read, "unless you shoot him first. Act. Don't hesitate." As a lark he nearly wrote, "Yrs. sincerely," and signed it. But he didn't. There was no time for that. Already the man driving the horses would be losing his grip on the reins. St. Ives had waited long enough, maybe too long. He tripped the lever on the hatch and thrust himself through, into the rainy night, sliding down the side of the bathyscaphe onto his knees in ditch water. Rain beat into his face, the fierce roar of it mixing with the creaking and banging of the carriage.

He cursed, slogging to his feet and up the muddy bank, reeling out onto the road. The carriage hurtled toward him, driven now by a man who was nearly a ghost. There was a look of pure astonishment in its eyes. He had recognized himself, but it was too late. His past-time self was already becoming incorporeal. St. Ives reached the note up, hoping to hand it to himself, hoping that there was some little bit of substance left to his hands. His past-time self spoke, but no sounds issued from his mouth. He bent down and flailed at the note, but hadn't the means to grasp it.

St. Ives let go of it then, although he knew it was too late. "Take it!" he screamed, but already the carriage was driverless. His past-time self had simply disappeared from the carriage seat, reduced to atoms floating now in the aether. The note blew away into the rainy darkness like a kite battered by a hurricane, and for one desperate moment St. Ives started to follow it, as if he would chase it forever across the countryside. He let it go and turned momentarily back to the road, watching the reins flop across the horses' backs as they hauled the carriage away, bashing across deep ruts, smashing along toward certain ruin.

St. Ives couldn't stand to watch. They'll survive, he told himself. They'll struggle on into Crick where a doctor will attend to Kraken's shoulder, and then they'll be off again for London, with Narbondo almost hopelessly far ahead. Kraken would search him out in Limehouse, surprising him in the middle of one of his abominable meals, and they would pursue him to the Seven Dials, losing him again until early morning when…

There it was, laid out before him, the grim future, or, rather, the grim past, depending on one's perspective. The time machine was a grand success, and his bid to alter the past a grand failure. It was spilled milk, though. What he had to do now was get out fast. Just as the note had said. Hurry, always hurry. Still he didn't move, but stood in the rain, buffeted by wind. He couldn't see far enough up the dark road to make anything out.

"Where to?" he said out loud. Back to the silo, possibly to confront Parsons? Surely not. Back to the silo day before yesterday, perhaps? He could avoid insulting Mrs. Langley that way. But what then? He would be taking the chance of making a hash of everything, wouldn't he? There was no profit in reliving random periods in his life. Only one event was worth reliving. Only one thing had to be obliterated utterly. Suddenly, he was struck dumb with fear at the very idea of it.

Like a bolt of lightning it struck him: who was to say that his time traveling wouldn't merely change things for the worse? What if he had managed to give himself that note, and had gotten away in the machine in time? Quite likely they would have overtaken Narbondo within the hour. There would have been no wreck on the North Road, no lost day in Crick, no confrontation in the Seven Dials. The note would then have meant nothing. It would have been turned into senseless gibberish. And the ghastly irony of the business, he shuddered to realize, was that his time traveling, his desperate effort to avert Alice's death, had been the very instrument that set into motion the sequence of events that would bring about her death. He had killed her, hadn't he?

Suddenly he began to laugh out loud. The rain pounded down, washing across his face and down his coat collar as he hooted and shrieked in the mud, beating his fists against the brass wall of the time-traveling bathyscaphe until he was breathless, his energy spent. The night was black and awful, and his shoes were sodden lumps of muck and mud from the ditch. His chest heaved and his head spun. Slowly, implacably, he forced himself to crawl back up the rungs to the hatch, shuddering with little spurts of uncontrollable laughter. "Cottage pie," he said, fumbling with the latch. "Basil, sage, potatoes..." The list meant nothing to him, but he recited it anyway, until, weary and shivering, he sat once again looking out through the porthole at the night, his laughter finally spent. "Cheese," he said.

He set the dials and at once activated the machine. There was the familiar bucking and shuddering and the abruptly silenced whine, and then once again he was adrift in the well. It wasn't night when he materialized, though. There was sunlight filtering through murky water. He was on the bottom of Lake Windermere. He had got the location right. The time ought to have been fifty years past, before he had been born. So there would be no hapless past-time St. Ives in the process of disappearing. He could take his time now, safe from Parsons, safe from himself, invisible to anybody but fish. What he wanted was practice—less hurry, not more of it.

He cast about in his mind, looking for an adequate test. He had the entirety of history to peek in at—almost too much choice. He studied the lake bed outside the porthole. There was nothing but mud and waterweeds. Carefully he manipulated the dials, then threw the lever. There was an instant of black night, then water-filtered sunlight again. He was still on the lake bottom, but in shallow water now, only partly submerged. A slice of sky shone at the top of the porthole.

Cautiously, he pushed up the hatch and peered out, satisfied with where he had found himself. Across twenty yards of reeds lay a grassy bank. Sheep grazed placidly on it, with not a human being in sight. He shut the hatch, fiddled with the controls, and jumped again, into full sunlight this time. The machine sat on the meadow now, among the startled sheep, which fled away on every side. He raised the hatch cover once more and looked around him. He could see now that there was a house some little way distant, farther along the edge of the lake. Two women stood in the garden, picking flowers. One turned suddenly and pointed, shading her eyes. She had seen him. The other one looked, then threw her hand to her mouth. Both of them turned to run, back toward the house, and St. Ives in a sudden panic retreated through the hatch, slamming it behind him, and then once again set the dials, leaping back down into the bottom of the lake, five years hence, safe from the eyes of humankind.

Nimbly, he bounced forward once more, and then back another sixty years, up onto the meadow again. The house was gone, the fields empty of sheep. He crept forward, a year at a time. Sheep came and went. There was the house, half-built. A gang of men labored at lifting a great long roof beam into place. St. Ives crept forward another hour. The beam was supported now by vertical timbers. The sound of pounding hammers filled the otherwise silent morning.

He was ready at last. He was bound for the future, for Harrogate and an encounter with Mr. Binger's dog. That would be the test. Or would it? He thought for a moment. Perhaps a better test would consist of his *not* saving Mr. Binger's dog. That might answer his questions more adequately. But what then? Then the dog would die. The answer to that particular question was evident. Old Furry would run under the wheels of that carriage. St. Ives had no choice.

He alighted in a yard off Bow Street, around the corner from the Crow's Nest. This time there was no hesitation. He climbed out through the hatch and sprinted down the sidewalk, slowing as he approached the corner. He could picture himself bursting out, snatching up the dog, thumbing his nose at Parsons.

Something was wrong, though. He knew that. There was no barking. And no dray, either. He was early. Seeing his mistake he stopped abruptly, swung around, and started back, running toward the machine. How early was he? He thought he knew, but he couldn't take any chances. He must know for certain. Abruptly, he angled into the weedy back lot behind the Crow's Nest, slowing down and sneaking along the wall. Carefully he peered around the corner, looking in the rear window of the almost-empty restaurant. There he sat, his past-time self, just then dropping his fork onto his trousers. Slowly the St. Ives inside the restaurant turned around to face the window, and for a split second he looked himself straight in the eye, holding his own gaze long enough for both of him to understand how haggard and drawn and cockeyed he appeared.

Then with that lesson in mind, he was off and running again, leaving his past-time self to grapple with the mystery. He climbed in at the hatch, bumped the time dial forward, and skipped ahead five minutes. When he opened the hatch it was to the sound of barking dogs. He climbed hastily down the side, looking up toward the street corner where he could see the dray already coming along. Christ! Was he too late? He slid to the ground and started out at a run, but the barking abruptly turned to a single cut-off yelp, then silence. The driver shouted, and one of the horses bucked.

Already St. Ives was clambering back into the machine, sweating now, panicked. He backed the dial off slightly, giving himself twenty seconds. Again he leaped backward, rematerializing in an instant and leaping without hesitation at the hatch. He was down and running wildly toward the corner. He could hear the dray again, but this time he couldn't yet see it. The barking of old Furry, though, seemed to fill the air along with the snarling of the mastiff.

He leaped straight down off the curb, looking back at where a stupefied Parsons stared at him in wide-eyed alarm. Reaching down, he snatched up the dog, nearly slamming into the horses himself. He threw himself backward, turning, holding the struggling dog, and staggered toward the curb, where he let the creature go. Then he took one last precious second to shout like a lunatic at the snarling mastiff, which turned and fled, howling away down the street to disappear behind a milliner's shop.

"Run," St. Ives said, half out loud. And he was away up Bow Street again, pursued by Parsons, who huffed along with his hand on his hat. Full of wild energy, St. Ives easily outdistanced the old man, climbing into the machine and closing the hatch. He knew where he was going, where he *had* to go. He had done all the necessary calculations at the bottom of Lake Windermere.

As he adjusted the dials, he half expected Parsons to clamber up onto the bathy-scaphe or to peer into the porthole and shake his fist. But Parsons didn't appear.

Of course he won't, St. Ives thought suddenly. Parsons was too shrewd for that. He was right then searching out a constable, commandeering a carriage in order to race up to the manor and beat the silo door in. St. Ives tripped the lever to activate Lord Kelvin's machine, and once again he felt himself falling, downward and down-ward through the creeping years, until he came to rest once again, in London now, in Limehouse, sometime in 1835. —⌐

Limehouse

A COLD AUTUMN FOG was settling over Limehouse, and St. Ives counted this as a piece of luck, a sign, perhaps, that his fortunes were turning. The mist would hide his movements on the rooftop, anyway, although it would also make it tolerably hard to see. There was a moon, which helped, but which also would expose his skulking around if he didn't keep low and out of sight. For the moment, though, he was fascinated with the scene round about him. He looked down onto Pennyfields and away up West India Dock Road and watched the flickering of lights in windows and the movements of people below him—the streets were crowded despite the hour—sailors mostly, got up in strange costumes. There were Lascars and Africans and Dutchmen and heaven knew what-all sorts of foreigners, mingling with coal-backers and ballast-heavers and lumpers and costermongers and the thousands of destitute rag-bedraggled poor who slept in the streets in fair weather and under the bridges in foul.

The roof beams beneath his feet sagged under the weight of the bathyscaphe, but the machine was safe enough for the moment, and St. Ives intended to stay no longer than he had to. Had to—he wondered what that meant. He had been compelled, somehow, to travel to Limehouse, but he found that he couldn't say why that was, not in so many words. Beneath his feet, in a garret room over a general shop, lay Ignacio Narbondo, probably asleep. What was he?—three or four years old? St. Ives couldn't be certain. Nor could he be certain what emotions had carried him here. He could, without any difficulty at all, murder Narbondo while he slept, ridding the world of one of its most foul and dangerous criminal minds…But the idea of that was immediately repellent, and he half despised himself for admitting it into his mind. Then he thought of Alice, and he despised himself less. Still, murder wasn't in him. What he wanted was to study his nemesis close at hand, to discover what forces in the broad universe had conspired to turn him into what he had become.

The rest of Limehouse didn't sleep. The tide was rising and the harbors navigable, so ships were loading and unloading, with no regard for the sun or for the lateness of the hour. Directly below him, from the open door of the shop, light shone out into the foggy street, illuminating a debris of broken iron, soiled overcoats, dirty bottles and crockery and linens and every other sort of household refuse that might conceivably find a use for itself, although it was an effort for St. Ives to imagine how destitute a man might be before he saw such trash as useful. He was filled, suddenly, with horror and melancholy and hopelessness, and he realized that his head ached awfully, and that he couldn't remember entirely when he'd last slept. He had always had a penchant for confused philosophy when he was tired. He recognized it as one of the sure signs of mental fatigue.

"Hurry," he muttered, as if speaking to the woman who sat below, guarding the detritus that spilled out of the shop as if it were a treasure. He looked down onto the tattered bonnet on her head and into the bowl of the short pipe that she smoked, and tried to fathom what it would be like to have one's life circumscribed and defined by a couple of filthy streets and a glass of bad gin.

Giving it up as a dead loss, he backed away from the edge of the roof, turning toward a tall garret window that stood behind him, its glass streaked and dirty and cracked and looking out on the fog and chimney pots like an occluded eye. He crept toward it across the slates, hoping that it wasn't latched, but prepared to open it by force if it was. He had a pocket full of silver, and he wondered what they would make of a strangely clothed gentleman creeping in at the window in the middle of the night for no other purpose, apparently, than to give them money—which is exactly what he intended to do if they caught him coming in at the window. He liked the idea: tiptoeing around the rooftops of Pennyfields, bestowing shillings on mystified paupers. The notion became abruptly despicable, though, a matter more of vanity than virtue. More likely he would have to use the silver to buy his freedom before the night was through.

There was no latch on the window at all, which was jammed shut with a folded-up bunch of paper torn out of a book. Without hesitation he wiggled it open and bent quietly down into the dark interior, wishing he had brought along a lantern and nearly recoiling from the fetid smell of sickness in the close air of the room. He held on to the window frame and felt around for the floor with his foot, kicking something soft, which shifted and let out a faint moan. Abruptly he pulled his foot back, perching on the sill like an animal ready to bolt. Slowly his eyes adjusted to the darkness, which, despite the thickening fog, was still lit by pale moonlight.

The room was almost empty of furniture. There was an old bed against one wall, a couple of wooden chairs, and a palsied table. Against another wall was a broken-down sideboard, almost empty of plates and glasses, as if it had no more day-today reason to exist than did the two sleeping humans who inhabited the room. A book lay open on the table, and more books were scattered and piled on the floor, looking altogether like superfluous wealth, an exotic treasure heaped up in a dark and musty pirates' cavern. The rags beneath his feet moved again and groaned, and then shook as the child covered by them was convulsed with coughing. On the bed someone lay sleeping heavily, unperturbed by the coughing.

Carefully now, St. Ives reached his foot past the sleeping form on the floor and pushed himself into the room, swinging the window shut behind him. He stepped across to the table to examine one of the books, which was moderately new. He was only half surprised to find that it was a volume of the *Illustrated Experiments with Gilled Beasts,* compiled by Ignacio Narbondo senior. St. Ives shook his head, calculating how long ago it must have been that Narbondo senior had been transported for the crime of vivisection. Not long—a matter of a couple of years. This collection of books seemed to be the only thing he had left to his abandoned family, except for his taste for corrupt knowledge. And now the son, young as he was, already followed in the father's bloody footsteps.

The little boy sleeping on the floor began to breathe loudly—the labored, hoarse wet breathing of someone with congested lungs. St. Ives bent over the convulsed form, gently pulling back the dirty blanket that covered it. He lay stiffly on his side, neck straight, as if he were endeavoring to keep his throat open. His arms were sticklike, and his pallid cheeks sagging. St. Ives ran his hand lightly down the child's spine, looking for the bow that would develop one day into a pronounced hump.

Strangely, there was no bow; the back was ramrod stiff, the flesh feverish. Through the thin blanket he could feel the air gurgling in and out of the child's lungs. St. Ives stood up, looking around the room again, and then immediately stepped across and fetched a glass tumbler from the sideboard. He stooped again and pressed the open end to the child's back, then listened hard to the closed end. The lungs sounded like a troubled cesspool.

The boy was taken with another coughing fit, hacking up bloodstained froth as St. Ives jerked away and stood up again. Clearly, he was far gone in pneumonia. There could be no doubt about it. He had been nauseated, too. In his weakened condition the child would die. The sudden knowledge of that washed over St. Ives like a dam breaking. Murder wasn't in the cards at all. Even if such a thing had appealed to St. Ives, it would be a redundant task. Nature and circumstance and the poverty of a filthy and overcrowded city would kill Narbondo just as surely as a bullet to the brain. St. Ives had only to crouch back out through the window and lose himself in the future.

And yet the idea of it ran counter to what he knew to be the truth. How could Narbondo die without St. Ives's helping him to do it? A man might alter the future, but how could the future alter itself? He examined the child's face, thinking things through. He needed light. Hurrying to the sideboard again, he carefully opened cupboard doors until he found candles and sulphur matches. The woman on the bed wouldn't awaken. She was lost in gin, snoring loudly now, her head covered with blankets. He struck a match and lit the candle, bending over the child and studying his face, looking for a telltale rash. There was nothing, only the sweating pale skin of an undernourished sick child.

Surely it hadn't a chance of survival. The boy would be dead tomorrow. Two days, maybe. Pneumococcal meningitis—that was his guess. It was a hasty candlelight-and-glass-tumbler diagnosis, but the pneumonia was certain, and alone was enough to kill him. He stood for a moment thinking. Meningitis could explain the hump. If Narbondo lived, the spinal damage might easily pull him into a stoop that would become permanent over the years.

It really didn't matter how accurately he understood the child's condition. The boy was doomed; of that St. Ives was certain. He pulled the blanket back up, taking off his coat and laying that too over the sleeping child, who exhaled now like a panting dog, desperately short of breath. St. Ives couldn't bring himself to equate the suffering little human with the monster he had shot in the Seven Dials. They simply were not the same creature. "Time and chance…," he thought, then remembered that he'd said the same thing not six months back—about himself and what he had become, and the feelings of melancholy and futility washed over him again.

He had a vision of all of humanity struggling like small and frightened animals in a vast black morass. It was easy to forget that there had ever been a time when he was happy. Surely this dying child couldn't remember any such happiness. St. Ives sighed, rubbing his forehead to drive out the fatigue and doom. That sort of thinking accomplished nothing. It was better to leave it to the philosophers, who generally had the advantage of having a bottle of brandy nearby. Right now all abstractions were meaningless alongside the fact of the dying child. Abruptly, he made up his mind.

He left his three silver coins on the table and stepped out through the window, pulling it shut, leaving his coat behind. If he failed to return, they could have the coat and the silver both; if he did return, they could have it anyway. He shivered on the rooftop, hurrying across toward the bathyscaphe, no longer interested in the early morning bustle below.

—⁓—

As HE STEPPED into the study through the open French window—all still very much as he remembered it—he half expected to see himself as an old man, disappearing into the atmosphere. But by now he would already have vanished. It had taken that long to get out through the window of the silo and sneak across to the manor. He might be long ago dead, of course. It was 1927, a date he had struck upon randomly. The manor might have a new owner, perhaps a man with a rifle loaded with bird shot. The interior of the silo, however, argued otherwise. It was full of faintly mystifying apparatus now, but it was the sort of apparatus that only a scientist like St. Ives would possess, and it wasn't rusty and scattered, either; instead it was orderly, not the ghastly mess that he had let it decline to back…when? For a moment he was disoriented, unable to recall the date.

The study was neatened up, too—no books scattered around, no jumbled papers. He thought guiltily of Mrs. Langley, and then quickly pushed the thought from his mind. Muddling himself up wouldn't serve. Mrs. Langley would wait. There were interesting and suggestive changes in the room around him. From the study ceiling hung the wired-together skeleton of a winged saurian, and leaning against one wall, braced by a couple of wooden pegs, was the femur of a monstrous reptile, something the size of a brontosaurus. So he had followed his whims, had he? He had taken up paleontology. How so? Had he utilized the time machine? Traveled back to the Age of Reptiles? A thrill of anticipation surged through him along with the knowledge, once again, that things, ultimately, must have fallen out for the best. Here was evidence of it—the well-apportioned room of a man in possession of his faculties.

Then it struck him like a blow. He wasn't any such man yet. There was no use being smug. He had to go back, to return to the past, to drop like a chunk of iron into the machinery of time, maybe fouling it utterly. This was one manifestation of time, no more solid than a soap bubble. He caught sight of himself in the mirror just then, recoiling in surprise. A haunted, gaunt, unshaven face stared out at him, and involuntarily he touched his cheek, forgetting his newfound optimism.

A note lay on the cleaned-off desk. He picked it up, noticing only then that a bottle of port and a glass stood at the back corner. He smiled despite himself, remembering suddenly all his blathering foolishness about fetching back bottles of port from the future. To hell with fetching anything back; he would have a taste of it now. "Cheers," he said out loud.

He settled himself into a chair in order to read the note. "I cleared out the silo," it read. "You would have materialized in the center of a motorcar if I hadn't, and caused who-knows-what kind of explosion. Quit being so proud of yourself. You look like hell. Talk to Professor Fleming at Oxford. He can be a bumbling idiot, but he possesses what you need. We're friends, after a fashion, Fleming and I. Go straightaway, and then get the hell out and don't come back. You're avoiding what you know you have to do. You're purposefully searching out obstacles. Look at you, for God's sake. You should make yourself sick."

Frowning, St. Ives laid the note onto the desk, drinking off the last of his glass of port. He was in a foul mood now. The note had done that. How dare he take that tone? Didn't he know whom he was talking to? He had half a mind to…what? He looked around, sensing that the atoms of his incorporeal self were hovering roundabout somewhere, grinning at him. Maybe they inhabited the bones of the pterodactyl hanging overhead. The thing regarded him from out of ridiculously small, empty eye sockets, reminding him suddenly of a beak-nosed schoolteacher from his childhood.

He searched in the drawer for a pen, thinking to write himself a note in return. What should he say? Something insulting? Something incredibly knowledgeable? Something weary and timeworn? But what did his present-time self know that his future-time self didn't know? In fact, wouldn't his future-time self know even the contents of the insulting note? He would simply rematerialize, see the note, and laugh at it without having to read it. St. Ives put down the pen dejectedly, nearly despising himself for his helplessness.

The door opened and Hasbro stepped in. "Good morning, sir," he said, in no way surprised to see St. Ives and laying out a suit of clothes on the divan.

"Hasbro!" St. Ives shouted, leaping up to embrace the man. He was considerably older. Of course he would be. He still wasn't in any way feeble, though. Seeing him so trim and fit despite his white hair caused St. Ives to lament his own fallen state. "I'm not who you think I am," he said.

"Of course you're not, sir. None of us are. This should fit, though."

"It's good to see you," St. Ives said. "You can't imagine…"

"Very good, sir. I've been instructed to trim your hair." He looked St. Ives up and down, squinting just a little, as if what he saw amounted to something less than he'd anticipated. He went out again, saying nothing more, but leaving St. Ives open-mouthed. In a moment he returned, carrying a pitcher of water and a bowl. "The ablutions will have to be hasty and primitive," he said. "I'm afraid you're not to visit any other room in the house for any reason whatever. I've been given very precise instructions. We're to go straightaway to Oxford, returning as soon as possible and keeping conversation to a minimum. I have a pair of train tickets. We board at the station in fifty-four minutes precisely."

"Yes," said St. Ives. "You would know, wouldn't you?" He hastily removed his shirt, scrubbing his face in the bowl, dunking the top of his head into the water and soaping his hair. Within moments he sat again in the chair, Hasbro shaving his over-grown beard. "Tell me, then," St. Ives said. "What happens? Alice, is she all right? Is she alive? Did I succeed? I must have. I can see it written all over this room. Tell me what fell out."

"I'm instructed to tell you nothing, sir. Tilt your head back."

Soapy water ran down into St. Ives's shirtfront. "Surely a little hint…," he said.

"Not a word, I'm afraid. The professor has informed me that the entire fabric of time is a delicate material, like old silk, and that the very sound of my voice might rip it to shreds. Very poetic of him, I think."

"He talks like a fool, if I'm any judge," St. Ives said angrily. "And you can tell him that from me. Poetic…!"

"Of course, sir. Just as you say. We'll need to powder your hair."

"Powder my hair? Why on earth…?"

"Professor Fleming, sir, up at Oxford. He knows you as a considerably older man. Due to your fatigued and malnourished state, of course, you appear to *be* an older man. But we mustn't assume anything at all, mustn't take any unnecessary risks. You can appreciate that."

"Older?" said St. Ives, looking skeptically at himself in the mirror again. It was true. He seemed to have aged ten years in the last two or three. His face was a depressing sight.

"You'll be young again, sir," Hasbro said reassuringly, and suddenly St. Ives wanted to weep. It seemed to him that he was caught up in an interminable web of comings and goings in which every action necessitated some previous action and would promote some future action and so on infinitely. And what's more, no outcome could be certain. Like old silk, even the past was a delicate thing…

"What does this Fleming have, exactly?" asked St. Ives, pulling himself together.

"I really must insist that we forego any discussion at all, sir. I've been instructed that you are to be left entirely to your own devices."

St. Ives sat back in the chair, regarding himself in the mirror once more. The stubble beard was gone, and his hair was clipped and combed. He felt worlds better, although the clothes that Hasbro fitted him with were utterly idiotic. Who was he to complain, though? If Hasbro had been instructed that it was absolutely necessary to hose him down with pig swill, he would have to stand for it. His future-self held all the cards and could make him dance any sort of inconceivable jig.

Together they went back out through the window, Hasbro insisting that St. Ives not see anything of the rest of the house. A long sleek motorcar sat on the drive. St. Ives had seen motorized carriages, had even toyed with the idea of building one, but this was something beyond his dreams, something—something from the future. He climbed into it happily. "Fueled by what?" he asked as they roared away toward Harrogate. "Alcohol? Steam? Let me guess." He listened closely. "Advanced Giffard injector and a simple Pelton wheel?"

"I'm terribly sorry, sir."

"Of course it's not. I was testing you. Tell me, though, how fast will she go on the open road?"

"I'm afraid I'm constrained from discussing it."

"Is the queen dead?"

"Lamentably so, sir. In 1901. God bless her. Royalty hasn't amounted to as much since, I'm afraid. A trifle too frivolous these days, if you'll pardon my saying so."

St. Ives discovered that he didn't have any real interest in what royalty was up to these days. He admitted to himself that there was a good deal that he didn't want to know. The last thing on earth that appealed to him was to return to the past with a head full of grim futuristic knowledge that he could do damn-all about. It was enough, perhaps, that Hasbro was hale and hearty and that he himself—if the interior of the silo was any indication—was still hard at it. Suddenly he wanted very badly just to be back in his own day, his business finished. And although it grated on him to have to admit it, his future-time self was absolutely correct. Silence was the safest route back to his destination. Still, that didn't make up for the hard tone of the man's note.

OXFORD, THANK HEAVEN, was still Oxford. St. Ives let Hasbro lead him along beneath the leafless trees, toward the pathology laboratory, feeling just a little like a tattooed savage hauled into civilization for the first time. His clothes still felt ridiculous to him, despite his harmonizing nicely with the rest of the populace. Their clothes looked ridiculous too. There wasn't so much shame in looking like a fool if everyone looked like a fool. His face itched under the powder that Hasbro had touched him up with in a careful effort to make him appear to be an old man.

Professor Fleming blinked at him when they peeked in at the door of the laboratory. They found him hovering over a beaker set on a long littered tabletop. His hair hung in a thatch over his forehead, and he gazed at them through thick glasses, as if he didn't quite recognize St. Ives at all for a moment. Then he smiled, stepping across to slap St. Ives on the back. "Well, well, well," he said, his brogue making him sound a little like Lord Kelvin. "You're looking…somehow…" He gave that line up abruptly, as if he couldn't say anything more without being insulting. He grinned suddenly and cocked his head. "No hard feelings, then?"

"None at all," St. Ives said, wondering what on earth the man was talking about. Hard feelings? Of all the confounded things…

"My information was honest. No tip. Nothing. You've got to admit you lost fair and square."

"I'm certain of it," St. Ives said, looking at Hasbro.

"That's two pounds six, then, that you owe me." He stood silently, regarding St. Ives with a self-satisfied smile. Then he turned away to adjust the flame coming out of a burner.

"For God's sake!" St. Ives whispered to Hasbro, appealing to him for an explanation.

Past the back of his hand, Hasbro whispered, "You've taken to betting on cricket matches. You most often lose. I'd keep that in mind for future reference." He shook his head darkly, as if waging sums was a habit he couldn't countenance.

St. Ives was dumbstruck. Fleming wanted his money right now. But two and six? He rummaged in his pocket, counting out what he had. He could cover it, but he would be utterly wiped out. He would go home penniless after paying off the stupid gambling debt run up by his apparently frivolous future-self.

"This is an outrage," he whispered to Hasbro while he counted out the money in his hand.

"I beg your pardon," Fleming said.

"I say that I'm outraged that these men can't play a better game of cricket." He was suddenly certain that the cricket bet had been waged merely as a lark—to tweak the nose of his past-time self. The very idea of it infuriated him. What kind of monster had he become, playing about at a time like this? Perhaps there was some sort of revenge he could take before fleeing back into the past.

Fleming shrugged, taking the money happily and putting it away in his pocket without looking at it. "Care to wager anything further?"

St. Ives blinked at him, hesitating. "Give me just a moment. Let me consult." He moved off toward the door, motioning at Hasbro to follow him. "Who is it that I lost money on?" he whispered.

"The Harrogate Harriers, sir. I really can't recommend placing another wager on them."

"Dead loss, are they?"

"Pitiful, sir."

St. Ives smiled broadly at Fleming and wiped his hands together enthusiastically. "I'm a patriot, Professor," he said, striding across to where Fleming filled a pipette with amber liquid. "I'll wager the same sum on the Harriers. Next game."

"Saturday night, then, against the Wolverines? You can't be serious."

"To show you how serious I am, I'll give you five to one odds."

"I couldn't begin to…"

"Ten to one, then. I'm filled with optimism."

Fleming narrowed his eyes, as if he thought that something was fishy, perhaps St. Ives had got a tip of some sort. Then he shrugged in theatrical resignation. Clearly he felt he was being subtle. "I normally wouldn't make a wager of that magnitude," he said. "But this smells very much like money in the savings bank. Ten to one it is, then." They shook hands, and St. Ives nearly did a jig in the center of the floor.

"Well," Fleming said, "down to work, eh?"

St. Ives nodded as Professor Fleming held out to him a big two-liter Mason jar full of clear brown liquid.

"A beef broth infusion of penicillium mold," he was saying.

"Ah," St. Ives said. "Of course." Mold? What the hell did the man mean by that? He looked at Hasbro again, hoping to learn something from him.

"I've been constrained…," Hasbro started to say, but St. Ives ignored him. He didn't want to hear the rest.

"I'm not certain of the result of an oral dosage," Fleming said. "I'm a conservative man, and I hesitate to recommend this even to a scientist such as yourself. It needs time yet—months of study…"

"I appreciate that," St. Ives said. "It's a case of life and death, though. Literally—the life of a child who, for the sake of history, mustn't be allowed to die." He realized suddenly that this must sound like the statement of a lunatic, but Professor Fleming didn't seem confused by it. What had his future-time self told the man? Did Fleming know? He couldn't know; otherwise Hasbro wouldn't have gone through the rigamarole with the powder. "Can you give me a rough dosage, then?"

"Pint a day, taken in two doses until it's used up. Keep it cold, mind you."

"Cold," said St. Ives, suddenly worried. He would have to have a word with the mother. They could keep the stuff outside, on the roof. The London autumn would keep it cold. He hoped that the woman wasn't too far gone in gin to comprehend. But how *could* she comprehend? Here he was, a gentleman with a jar of beef broth, stepping in out of the future. He could claim to be the Angel of Mercy, perhaps show her the bathyscaphe in order to prove it. Better yet, he would show her a purse full of money, promising to come back with more if she carried out his instructions. Damn it, though; he didn't have any money. He would have to go back after some. Suddenly he was fiercely hungry, and he realized that he hadn't eaten in—how long? About eighty-odd years as the crow flies.

He took the jar from Fleming. He had what he came for, but this was too good an opportunity. Here he was in 1927, in the pathology lab of a man who was apparently one of the great minds in the field. Now that he looked about him, St. Ives could see that the laboratory was filled with unidentifiable odds and ends. He must at least know more about this beef broth elixir. "I'm still confused on a couple of issues," he said to Fleming. "Tell me how it was that you came across this penicillium."

Fleming clasped his hands together, stretching his fingers back as if he were loosening up, warming to the idea of telling the tale thoroughly. "Well," he began, "it was almost entirely by accident..." At which point Hasbro pulled out a pocket watch, contorting his face with a look of dismay.

"Our train," Hasbro said, interrupting.

"Oh, damn our train, man." St. Ives cast him a look of thinly veiled disgust.

"I'm afraid I must insist, sir." He put a hand into his coat, as if he had something in there to enforce his insistence.

St. Ives was filled with black thoughts. Here was an opportunity gone straight to hell. They had him on a leash, and they weren't going to reel out any slack line. Hasbro was deadly serious; that was the only thing that kept St. Ives in check. He knew too well that one didn't argue with Hasbro when the man was serious. Hasbro would prevail. You could chisel that legend in stone without any risk. And when Hasbro was in a prevailing mood, he generally had reason to be. It wouldn't do to argue.

The two of them left, proceeding directly to the station, and then, after no more than five minutes' wait, back to Harrogate where they drove once again out to the manor, St. Ives holding on to the jar of beef broth all the way home.

At last they stood awkwardly on the meadow, near the silo door. Hasbro held the keys in his hand. It was clear that they weren't going back into the manor. St. Ives would have liked another small glass of port before toddling off to the past again, but there he wasn't about to ask for it. Like as not, Hasbro would have complied, but there was still such a thing as dignity. Best to do what the note had instructed, leave straightaway. He had what he came for. "I'll be setting out now," he said.

"Best of luck, sir."

"I'll see you, then, when this is through."

"That you will, sir. I'd like to buy you a drink when the time comes."

"You can buy me two," St. Ives said, striding away through the weeds toward the silo. "And then I'll buy you two," he shouted, turning to wave one last time. Hasbro stood on the lonely meadow, watching him depart, the picture of an old and trusted friend saddened at this dangerous but necessary leave-taking. Either that or he was hanging about to make damn well certain that St. Ives wouldn't cut any last-moment capers.

Seated in the bathyscaphe at last, he wrapped the jar in his new coat and secured it beneath the seat, then turned his attention to the instruments. He had the wide world to travel through, but ultimately he left the spatial coordinates alone, returning simply to his own time, some two hours after his first departure so that he wouldn't run into an astonished Parsons still snooping around the silo.

He was filled with relief at being back in his own time at last, and he sat back with a sigh, regarding his surroundings. Grinning, he thought all of a sudden of the bet he'd made with Fleming. All the hindsight in the world hadn't been worth a farthing to his future-self, had it? He still couldn't believe that he had taken to betting on cricket matches. He simply wouldn't. He was warned now. Who the hell had that been? The Harrogate Haberdashers? He laughed out loud. What a lark! His future-self would be hearing the news from Hasbro about now: "I what...!"

He climbed out of the machine, weary as a coal miner but still smiling. There was no sign of Parsons, nothing but silence round about him. The silo was dim, but even in the gray twilight he could see clearly enough to know that something had changed—something subtle. Terror coursed through him. This wasn't good. This was what he had feared. It was exactly what his future-time self had been desperate to avoid.

He couldn't at first determine what it was, though. His tools lay scattered as ever... Then he saw it suddenly—the chalk marks on the wall. The message was different now. In clean block letters a new message was written out: "Harriers 6, Wolverines 2."

Mrs. Langley's Advice

THERE WAS TOO much danger in staying. St. Ives would have liked to sleep, to eat, to sit in his study and look at the wall. The beef broth, though, wouldn't allow for it. Time—that commodity that he ought to have had plenty of—wouldn't allow for it. It would insist on going on without him, piling up complications, altering everything. Never had he been so aware of the ticking of the clock.

He sneaked into the manor by way of the study window, remaining long enough to fetch out a purse containing twenty pounds in silver, and then, without so much as a parting glance, he loped back out to the silo, climbed into the machine, and sailed away in the direction of midcentury Limehouse.

He arrived a week earlier than he had on his previous visit. The child wouldn't be so far gone this time around. It was just after midnight, and to St. Ives, looking down over Pennyfields, it seemed as if nothing had changed. There was no fog, and the moon was high in the sky. But the old woman sat as ever, smoking her pipe amid the scattered junk slopping out of the door of the general shop. Sailors came and went from public houses. The seething Limehouse night was oblivious to the tiny tragedy unfolding in the attic room above.

He pulled the garret window open and stepped in carefully, setting the jar beneath the sill. The child slept on the floor, although not under the window now. He breathed heavily, obviously already congested, lying on his back with the ragged blanket pulled to his chin. But for the sleeping child, the room was empty.

"Damn it to hell," St. Ives muttered. He *must* talk to the mother. He couldn't be popping back in twice a day to feed the child the beef broth. He could think of nothing to do except leave, climb back into the bathyscaphe and reset the coordinates, maybe arrive three hours from now, or maybe yesterday. What a tiresome thing. He would make the child drink the broth now, though, just to get it started up. Trusting to the future was a dangerous thing. A bird in the hand…he told himself.

There was a noise outside the door just then, a woman's high-pitched laughter followed by a man's voice muttering something low, then the sound of laughter again.

A key scraped in the lock, and St. Ives hurried across toward the window, thinking to get out onto the roof before he was discovered. The door swung open, though, and he stopped abruptly, turning around with a look of official dissatisfaction on his face. He would have to brass it out, pretend to be—what? Merely looking grave might do the trick. Thank heaven he had shaved and cut his hair.

In the open doorway stood the woman who must have been the child's mother. She was young, and would have been almost pretty but for the hardness of her face and her general air of shabbiness. She was half drunk, too, and she stood there swaying like a sapling in a breeze, looking confusedly at St. Ives. Sobering suddenly, she peered around the room, as if to ascertain that she hadn't opened the wrong door by mistake. Then, as her countenance changed from confusion to anger, she said, "What are you doing here?"

The man behind her gaped stupidly at St. Ives. He was drunk, too—drunker than she was. A look of skepticism came into his eyes, and he took a step backward.

"Who's this?" asked St. Ives, nodding at the man. He pitched it just as hard and mean as he could, as if it meant something, and the man turned around abruptly, caromed off the hallway wall, and scuttled for the stairs. There was the sound of pounding feet and a door slamming, then silence.

"There goes half a crown," she said steadily. "I'm not any kind of bunter, so if you've been sent round by the landlord, tell him I pay my rent on time, and that there wouldn't be half so many bunters if they didn't gouge your eyes out for the price of a room."

"Not at all, my good woman," St. Ives said, surprised at first that she was moderately well-spoken. Then he realized that it wasn't particularly surprising at all. She had been the wife of a famous, or at least notorious, scientist. The notion saddened him. She had fallen a long way. She was still youthful, and there was something in her face of the onetime country girl who had fallen in love with a man she admired. Now she was a prostitute in a lodging house.

She stood yet in the doorway, waiting for him to explain himself, and St. Ives realized almost shamefully that she held out some little bit of hope—of what? That she wouldn't have lost her half crown after all? St. Ives, her eyes seemed to say, was the sort of man she would expect to find in the West End, not your common sailor rutting his way through Pennyfields before his ship set sail.

"I'm a doctor, ma'am."

"Really," she said, stepping into the room now and closing the door. "You wouldn't have brought a drain of gin, would you? A *doctor*, is it? Brandy more like it." She gave him what was no doubt meant to be a coy look, but it disfigured her face awfully, as if it weren't built for that sort of theatrics, and it struck him that a great deal had been taken away from her. He could hear the emptiness in her voice and see it in her face. The country girl who had fallen in love with the scientist was very nearly gone from her eyes, and there would come a day when gin and life on the Limehouse streets would sweep it clean away.

"I'm afraid I haven't any brandy. Or gin, either. I've brought this jar of beef broth, though." He pointed at the jar where it sat beneath the window.

"What is it?" She looked at him doubtfully, as if she couldn't have heard what she thought she heard.

"Beef broth. It's an elixir, actually, for the child." He nodded at the sleeping boy, who had turned over now and had his face against the floor molding. "Your son is very sick."

Vaguely, she looked in the child's direction. "Not so sick as all that."

"Far sicker than you realize. In two weeks he'll be dead unless we do something for him."

"Who the devil *are* you?" she asked, finally closing the door and lighting a lantern on the sideboard. The room was suddenly illuminated with a yellow glow, and a curl of dirty smoke rose toward a black smudge on the ceiling. "Dead?"

"I'm a friend of your husband's," he lied, the notion coming to him out of the blue. "I promised him I'd come round now and then to check on the boy. Three times I've been here, and each time there was no one to answer my knock, so this time I let myself in by the window. I'm a doctor, ma'am, and I tell you the boy will die."

At the mention of her husband, the woman slumped into a chair at the table, burying her face in her hands. She remained so for a moment, then steeled herself and looked up at him, some of the old anger rekindled in her eyes. "What is it that you want?" she asked. "Have your say and get out."

"This elixir," he said, setting to work on the child, "is our only hope of curing him." The boy awoke just then, recoiling in surprise when he saw St. Ives huddled over him.

"It's all right, lamby," his mother said, kneeling beside him and petting his lank hair. "This man is a doctor and a friend of your father's."

At the mention of this, the child cast St. Ives such a glance of loathing and repugnance that St. Ives nearly toppled over backward from the force of it. The complications of human misery were more than he could fathom. "Do you have a cup?" he asked the mother, who fetched down the tumbler from the sideboard—the same tumbler that St. Ives, a week from now, would use to…

What? He reeled momentarily from a vertigo that was the result of sudden mental confusion.

"Careful" the woman said to him, taking the half-filled tumbler away.

"Yes," he said. "Have him drink it down. All of it."

"What about the rest of it?" she asked. "A horse couldn't drink the whole jar."

"Two of these glasses full a day until the entire lot's drunk off. It *must* be done this way if you want the boy to live."

She looked at him curiously, hesitating for a moment, as if to say that life wasn't worth so much, perhaps, as St. Ives thought it was. "Right you are," she said finally, returning the glass to the sideboard. "Go back to sleep now, lamby," she said to the boy, who pulled the blanket over his head and faced the wall again. She patted her hair, as

if waiting now for St. Ives to suggest something further, as if she still held out hope that he might be worth something more to her than the half crown she had lost along with the sailor.

"Well," he said awkwardly, stepping toward the window. "I'll just…" He looked down at the jar again. In his haste to leave he had nearly forgotten it. Now he was relieved to see it, if only to have something to say. "This has to be kept cold. My advice is to leave it on the roof, outside the window."

In truth, the room itself was nearly cold enough to have done the trick. It was a good excuse to swing the window open and step through it, though. Hurrying, he nearly fell out onto the slates. He stood up, brushing at his knees, and leaned in at the window.

"Leaving by way of the roof?" she asked, making it sound as if she had been insulted. It was clear to her now that this was just what St. Ives was doing. He wasn't interested in what she had to sell. He had chased off the sailor, and to what end? Now she would have to go down into the street again…"Stairs aren't good enough for you?" she asked, raising her voice. "Don't want to be seen coming down from the room of a *whore?* Precious bloody doctor…"

He nodded weakly, then checked himself and shook his head instead. "My…carriage."

"On the roof, is it?"

"Yes. I mean to say…" He hesitated, stammering. "What I meant to say was that there was the matter of the money."

"To hell with your filthy money. I wouldn't take it if I were dying. Lord it over someone else. If the boy gets well, I'll thank you for it. But you can bloody damn well leave and take your money with you."

"It's not *my* money, madam, I assure you. Your husband and I wagered a small sum four years back. I've owed him this, with interest." St. Ives pulled out the purse he'd taken from his study in Harrogate, full of money that would no doubt mystify her. She would make use of it, though. Here goes another twenty, he thought, handing it in to her. She paused just a moment before snatching it out of his hand. It would buy a lot of gin, anyway…Ah well, he would win it back from Fleming someday in the hazy future. Time and chance, after all…

He tipped his hat and walked away across the roof, having nothing further to say. He would trust to fate. He climbed in through the hatch and calibrated the instruments, his head nearly empty of thought. Then he realized that during the entire exchange in the room he had never once associated the sick child with Dr. Ignacio Narbondo. There seemed to be no earthly connection between the two. Even the look on the child's face at the mention of his father—a shadow so deep and dark that it belied the child's age. Well…it didn't bear thinking about, did it?

As he switched on Lord Kelvin's machine, he glanced out one last time through the porthole. There was the woman, holding the purse, staring out through the open window with a look of absolute and utter amazement on her face. Then, along with the rest of the world, she vanished, and he found himself hurtling up the dark well of time, her face merely an afterimage on the back of his eyelids.

———*⁄∿⁄*———

THERE WAS ONE more task ahead of him before the end. He would pay a visit to Mrs. Langley. Into his head came the vision of her stumping across the grass toward the silo, ready, on his behalf, to beat men into puddings with her rolling pin. He wondered suddenly how it was that virtues seemed to come so easily to chosen people, while other people had to work like dogs just to hold on to the few little scraps they had.

He reappeared directly outside his study this time, on the lawn, and he sat for a moment in the time machine, giving himself a rest. The silo, right now, contained its own past-time version of the bathyscaphe, which would right at that moment be in the process of itself becoming incorporeal. As his future-self had pointed out in the nastily written note, it wouldn't do to drop straight into the middle of it.

He sat for a moment orienting himself in time. Soon, within the next couple of hours, his past-time self would wander shoeless over to Lord Kelvin's summerhouse and would hit upon the final bit of information he would need to make the machine work. But right now, his past-time self was disintegrating into atoms, crawling unhappily toward the window. Well, it couldn't be helped. If his past-time self was irritated at this little visit, then he was a numbskull. It was his own damned fault, treating Mrs. Langley as if she were a serf.

After another few moments, he climbed out onto the ground, nervously keeping an eye open for Parsons even though he knew from experience that he would easily accomplish his task and be gone before Parsons came snooping around. He checked his pocket watch, calculating the minutes he had to spare, then climbed in through the window. He couldn't bring himself to look at the desk. It was a mess of broken stuff from when he'd hammered everything with the elephant.

Suddenly he staggered and nearly fell. A wave of vertigo passed over him, and he braced himself against the back of a chair, waiting for it to subside. For a moment he was certain what it meant—that one of his future-time selves was paying him a visit, that in a moment there would be *two* invisible St. Iveses lying about the room. The time machine would sit on the lawn unguarded, except that it, too, would disappear. The whole idea of it enraged him. Of all the stupid…

But that wasn't it. The vertigo passed. His skin remained opaque. He didn't disappear at all. This was something else. Something was wrong with his mind, as if bits of it were being effaced. It struck him suddenly that his memory was faulty. Expanses of it were dissipating like steam. Vaguely, he remembered having gone to Limehouse twice, but he couldn't remember why. The events of the last few hours—the trip to Oxford, then back to Limehouse to dose the child—those were clear to him. But what did he even mean by thinking, *"back* to Limehouse"? *Had* he been there twice?

Now for an instant it seemed as if he had, except that one of his visits had the confused quality of a half-forgotten dream that was fading even as he tried desperately to hold on to it. Fragments of it came to him—the smell of the sick child's room, the sensation of treading on the sleeping form, the cold tumbler pressed against his ear.

All this, though, was swept away again by an ocean of memories that were at once new to him and yet seemed always to have been part of him. These new memories were roiled up and stormy, half-hidden by the spindrift of competing, but fading, recollections that floated and bobbed on this ocean like pieces of disconnected flotsam going out with the tide: the tumbler, the candle, his stepping across to open a heavy volume lying on a decrepit table. Beyond, bobbing on the horizon, were a million more odds and ends of memory, already too distant to recognize. For a moment he was neither here nor there, neither past nor present, and the storm tossed in his head. Then the sea began to calm and authentic memory took shape, shuffling itself into order, solid and real and full.

Those bits of old flotsam still floated atop it, though, half submerged; he could still make a few of them out, and he knew that soon they would sink forever. Frantically, he searched the desk for a pen and ink. Then, finding them, he began to write. He forced himself to recall the hard, cold base of the tumbler against his ear. And with that, the memory of his first past-time trip to Limehouse ghosted up once again like a feebly collapsing wave, a confused smattering of images and half-dismantled thoughts. The pen scratched across the paper. He barely breathed.

Then, abruptly, it was gone again, whirled away. The very idea of the tumbler against his ear vanished from his head. Weirdly, he could recall that the image of a tumbler had meant something to him only seconds ago; he even knew what tumbler it was that his mind still grappled with. He could picture it clearly. But now it was half full of beef broth, and the mother was feeding it to her sick child, calling him pet names.

Hurriedly, he read over the notes he had scrawled onto the paper—fragments of memory written out in half sentences. "Woman in bed, snoring. Stepping on child. Child nauseated, feverish. Pneumococcal meningitis diagnosed. Child near death. Inflamed meninges cause spinal deformity; hence Narbondo the hunchback? Left coat, money on table. Watch for Parsons snooping along the window…" There was more of the same, then the writing died out. What did it all mean? He no longer knew. It was all fiction to him. It had no reality at all. What coat? He was wearing his coat—or what would *become* his coat, anyway. Hunchback? Narbondo a hunchback? He cast around in his mind, trying to make sense of it all. Narbondo was not a hunchback. And why would Parsons come snooping along the window? Parsons was no stranger at the manor, not since Lord Kelvin had discovered that St. Ives possessed the machine. Parsons was petitioning him daily to give it up.

Just then he saw something out of the corner of his eye, near the window, but when he turned his head, it was gone. It had looked for all the world like a body, lying crumpled on the floor. His heart raced, and he half stood up, wondering, squinting his eyes. There was nothing, though, only the meadow with the machine sitting among wildflowers like an overgrown child's toy. St. Ives looked away, but when he did, he saw the thing again, peripherally. He held his gaze steady, focusing on nothing. The thing lay by the window; he must have stepped on it when he came in. It was his past-time self, lying where he had fallen by the window—or rather it was the ghost of his past-time self, unshaven and with wild hair—waiting for his future-time self to leave.

Ghosts—it all had to do with ghosts, with the fading of one world and the solidifying of the next. Just as concrete objects—he, the machine, any damned thing at all—began to fade when a copy of that object appeared from another point in time, so did memory. Two conflicting memories could not coexist. One would supplant the other. Whatever Narbondo had been, or would have become if St. Ives had left him alone, he wasn't that anymore. St. Ives had dosed him with Fleming's potion, and he had got well. And the result was that he hadn't become a hunchback at all, which is what he must have become in that other history that St. Ives had managed to efface. Which meant, if St. Ives read this right, that the sickly child *would not have died at all,* but must ultimately have recovered, although deformed by the disease.

Fear swarmed over him again. He had gone and done it this time. He was a victim of his own compassion. He had meddled with the past, and the result was that he had come back to a different world than he had left. How much it was different, he couldn't say. He had forgotten. And it didn't matter now, anyway; there was no recalling that lost fragment of history. All of that had simply ceased to exist.

What a fool he had been, jaunting around through time as if he were out for a Sunday ramble. Why in heaven's name hadn't his future-time self warned him against this? The damned old fool. Perhaps he could go back and unchange what he had changed. Except, of course, that he had made the change over fifty years ago. He would have to return to Limehouse and convince himself not to leave Fleming's elixir with the mother, but to dump it off the roof instead. Let the child suffer…Well…

Going back would make a bad matter worse. He could see that. He sighed, getting a grip, finally. What else might all this mean? Anything might have changed, maybe for the better. Mightn't Alice be alive? Why not? He was filled with a surge of hope, which died out almost at once. Of course she wasn't alive. That much hadn't changed. His mind worked furiously, trying to make sense of it. Here was his littered desk and his ghostly unshaven self lying in a heap by the window. What was all that but a bit of obscure proof that this world must be in most ways similar to the one he had buggered up?

And more than that, he *remembered* it, didn't he?—the business of his going out barefoot, of his finally putting the machine right, of his saving Binger's dog, of Alice murdered in the Seven Dials.

Where was Mrs. Langley? He *must* talk to her. At once. Speak to her and get out. He was only a day away from his own rightful time. Minimize the damage, he told himself, and then go home.

He went out into the kitchen. There she was, the good woman, putting a few things into a carpetbag, packing her belongings. She was going to her sister's house. Her face was full of determination, but her eyes were red. This hadn't been easy for her. St. Ives hated himself all of a sudden. He would have fallen to his knees to beg her forgiveness, except that she disliked that sort of indignity almost as much as he did.

"Mrs. Langley," he said.

She turned to look at him, affecting a huff, her mouth set in a thin line. She wasn't about to give in. By damn, she was bound for her sister's house, and soon, too. This had gone on entirely long enough, and she wouldn't tolerate that sort of tone, not any longer. Never in all her born years, her face seemed to say.

Still, St. Ives thought happily, ultimately she *wouldn't* go, would she? She would be there to take on Parsons with a rolling pin. St. Ives would succeed, at least in this one little thing. She was regarding him strangely, though, as if he were wearing an inconceivable hat. "I've come to my senses," he said.

She nodded. Her eyes contradicted him, though. She looked at him as if he had lost his senses entirely this time, down a well. Inadvertently he brushed at his face, fearing that something...Wait. Of course. He wasn't the man that he had been a half hour ago. He was clean-shaven now, his hair cut. He wore a suit of clothes with idiotic lapels, woven out of the wool of sheep that didn't yet exist. He was a man altered by the future, although there would be nothing but trouble in telling her that.

"What I mean to say is that I'm sorry for that stupid display of temper. You were absolutely right, Mrs. Langley. I *was* stark raving mad when I confronted you on the issue of cleaning my desk. I know it wasn't the first time, either. I...I regret all of it. I've been...It's been hard for me, what with Alice and all. I'm trying to put that right, but I've made a botch of it so far, and..."

He found himself stammering and was unable to continue. Dignity abandoned him altogether, and he began to cry shamelessly, covering his face with his forearm. He felt her hand on his shoulder, giving him a sympathetic squeeze. Finally he managed to stop, and he stood there sniffling and hiccuping, feeling like a fool.

She brought him a glass of water, which he drank happily. "It's not every man," she said to him, "who can eat crow without the feathers sticking to his chin." She nodded heavily and slowly. "Nothing wrong with a good cry now and then. It's like rain—washes things clean."

"God bless you, Mrs. Langley," he said. "You're a saint."

"Not by a considerable sight, I'm not. You come closer, to my mind. But I'm going to be bold enough to tell you that you're not cut out for saint work. You've got the instinct, but you haven't got the constitution for it. And if I was you I'd find a new situation just as quick as I might. Go back to science, Professor, where you belong."

"Thank you," he said, in control of his emotions once more. "That's just where I intend to go, just as you advise. There's one little bit of business to attend to first, though, and by heaven, if there were one person on earth I could bring along to help me see it through, you would be that person, Mrs. Langley."

"I'm good with a ball of dough, sir, but not much else."

"You're a philosopher, my good woman, whether you know it or not. And from now on your salary is doubled."

She started to protest, but he cut her off with a gesture. "I've got to hurry," he said. "Carry on here."

With that he left her, returning to the study and going out through the window, stepping carefully over that bit of floor where his ghost lay invisible. He clambered straight into the bathyscaphe and left. His past-time self would materialize again and set to work on the machine, never knowing that the Mrs. Langley problem had been solved. It occurred to him too late that he might have written himself a note, explaining that he had come back around to patch things up with her. But to hell with that. His past-time self was a fool—more of a fool, maybe, than his future-time self was—and would probably contrive to muck things up in some new lunatic way, threatening everything. Better to let him go about his business in ignorance.

In the time machine, he returned to the now-empty silo, some couple of hours past the time when he had fled from Parsons and the constable. It occurred to him, unhappily, that there had been no Langdon St. Ives existing in the world during the last two hours, and that the world didn't give a rotten damn. The world had teetered along without him, utterly indifferent to his absence. It was a chilling thought, and was somehow related to what Mrs. Langley had been telling him. For the moment, though, he put it out of his mind.

There were more immediate things to occupy him. It mightn't be safe to leave the machine in the silo yet, but he couldn't just plunk down on the meadow every time he reappeared. Parsons had petitioned him, as one scientist to another, to give it up. It belongs to the Crown, he had said. Parsons hadn't known until that very afternoon in Harrogate, though, that the time machine was workable, that St. Ives had got the bugs out of it at long last. Well, he knew now. There wouldn't be any more petitions. And next time Parsons wouldn't just bring the local constable along to help.

St. Ives climbed out wearily, looking around him at the sad mess of tools and debris. He had half a mind to set in on it now—neaten it up, stow it away as if it was himself he was putting right. He couldn't afford the time, though.

Then he saw the chalk markings—changed again. Lord help us, he thought, feeling again a surge of distaste for his future-self. This was no lark, though. It was a warning: "Parsons looming," the message read. "Obliterate this and take the machine out to Binger's." —◦

The Return of Dr. Narbondo

S MOKING VERY SLOWLY on his pipe, Mr. Binger stood staring at St. Ives, who smiled cheerfully at him from halfway out of the bathyscaphe hatch. St. Ives had just arrived from out of the aether, surprising Mr. Binger in the pasture. "Good afternoon, Mr. Binger," St. Ives said.

Furry hopped around, happy to see St. Ives and not caring a rap that he had appeared out of nowhere. Binger looked up and down the road, as if expecting to see a dust cloud. There was nothing, though, which seemed to perplex him. Finally, he removed his pipe and said, nodding at the bathyscaphe, "No wheels, then?"

"Spacecraft," St. Ives said, and he pointed at the sky. "You remember that problem with the space alien some few years back?"

"Ah!" Binger said, nodding shrewdly. That would explain it. Perhaps it would suffice to explain everything—St. Ives's sudden arrival, his strange clothes, his being clean-shaven and his hair trimmed. Just a little over two hours ago St. Ives had been in town, disheveled, hunted, looking like the Wild Man of Borneo. He had been babbling about cows and seemed to be in a terrible hurry. Now the mysteries were solved. It was space men again.

St. Ives climbed down onto the ground and petted Furry on the back of the head. "Can you help me, Mr. Binger?" he asked.

"Aye," the man said. "They say it was you that saved old Furry up to town today."

"Do they?"

"They do. They say you come near to killing yourself over the dog, nearly struck by a wagon. Chased off that bloody mastiff, too. That's what they say."

"Well." St. Ives was at a momentary loss. "They exaggerate. Old Furry's a good pup. Anyone would have done the same."

"Anyone didn't do it, lad. You did, and I thank you for it."

Anyone didn't *know* to do it, St. Ives thought, feeling like a fraud. He hadn't so much chosen to save the dog as he had been *destined* to save the dog. Well, that wasn't quite true, either. The past few hours had made a hash of the destiny notion—unless there were infinite destinies waiting in the wings, all of them in different costumes. One destiny at a time, he told himself, and with the help of Binger and his sons, St. Ives hauled the time machine to the barn, in among the cows, and then Mr. Binger drove him most of the way back to the manor. He walked the last half mile, thinking that if Parsons was lurking about, it would be better not to reveal that Binger was an accomplice.

It was dark when he bent through the French window again and lay down on the divan, telling himself that he ought not to risk waiting, that he ought to be off at once and finish what he had meant to finish. But he was dog-tired, and what he meant to do wouldn't allow for that. Surely an hour's sleep…

The street in the Seven Dials came unbidden into his mind—the rain, the mud, the darkness, the shadowy rooftops and entryways and alleys—but this time he let himself go, and he wandered into his dream with a growing sense of purpose rather than horror.

—◦◦◦—

HASBRO SHOOK HIM awake in the morning. The sun was high and the wind blowing, animating the ponderous branches of the oaks out on the meadow. "Kippers, sir?" Hasbro asked.

"Yes," said St. Ives, sitting up and rubbing his face blearily.

"Secretary Parsons called again, sir, early this morning. And Dr. Frost, too, some little time later."

"Yes," said St. Ives. "Did you tell them to return?"

"At noon, sir. An hour from now."

"Right. I'll…" He stood up slowly, wondering what it was he would do. Eat first. Mrs. Langley came in just then, carrying the plate of kippers and toast and a pot of tea. She handed him a newspaper along with it, just come up from London. The front page was full of Dr. Frost, lately risen from his long and icy sleep. He had got the ear of the Archbishop of Canterbury, it said, who had taken a fancy to Frost's ideas regarding the rumored time-travel device sought after by the Royal Academy.

The journalist went on to describe the fanciful device in sarcastic terms, implying that the whole thing was quite likely a hoax perpetrated for the sake of publicity by Mr. H. G. Wells, the fabulist. Frost already had a large following, though, and considered himself a sort of lay clergyman. He had taken to wearing white robes, and his followers had no difficulty believing that his rising from an icy sleep held some great mystical import. Accordingly, there was widespread popular support for Frost's own claim to the alleged time-travel device. What Frost had proposed that had won the heart of the Archbishop yesterday afternoon was that a journey be undertaken to the very dawn of human time, to the Garden itself, where Frost would pluck that treacherous apple out of Eve's hand by main force and beat the serpent with a stick…

The article carried on in suchlike terms, the journalist sneering openly at the whole notion and lecturing his readers on the perils of gullibility. St. Ives didn't sneer, though. Frost's, or Narbondo's, capacity for generating mayhem and human misery didn't allow for sneering. The journalist was right, but really he knew nothing at all. Frost would take the machine if he could; but he jolly well wouldn't travel back to eat lunch with Adam and Eve.

St. Ives scraped up the last of the kippers and watched the meadow grasses blow in the wind. Parsons, too. He intended to make careful scientific journeys, he and his cronies. They knew St. Ives had the machine. The evidence was all circumstantial, but it was sufficient. Two days ago they had finished their search of the sea bottom off Dover. There was no trace of the machine, no wreckage beyond that of the sunken ships. And Parsons had made it very clear to St. Ives that Lord Kelvin, just yesterday afternoon, had recorded strange electromagnetic activity in the immediate area of Harrogate.

Parsons had been diplomatic. St. Ives, he had said, was always the most formidable scientist of them all—far deeper than they had supposed. His interest in the machine, his pursuit of it, could not have culminated in his destroying it. Parsons admired this, and because he admired it, he had come to appeal to St. Ives to give the thing up peaceably. There was no profit in coming to blows over it. The law was all on the side of the Academy.

Well, today it would come to blows. His future-time self knew that, and had returned to warn him with the chalk markings in the silo. And Parsons was right. The device *did* belong to the Academy, or at least to Lord Kelvin. When had Kelvin deduced that St. Ives had it? It was conceivable that he suspected it all along, and that he had let St. Ives fiddle away on it, thinking to confiscate it later, after the dog's work was done.

Hasbro appeared just then. "Secretary Parsons," he announced.

"Tell him to give me five minutes. Pour him a cup of tea."

"Very good, sir."

St. Ives stood up, straightened his clothes, ran his hands through his hair, and went out again at the window, heading at a dead run for the little stable behind the carriage house. Sitting in the parlor, Parsons wouldn't see him, and given a five-minute head start, St. Ives didn't care a damn what Parsons saw. Across the meadow the silo stood as ever, but now with the door ajar. They had broken into it, thinking simply to take the machine, but finding it gone. So much for being peaceable. He laughed out loud.

Hurriedly, he threw a saddle onto the back of old Ben, the coach horse, and old Ben immediately inflated his chest so that St. Ives couldn't cinch the girth tight. "None of your tricks, Ben," St. Ives warned, but the horse just looked at him, pretending not to understand. There was no time to argue. St. Ives had to get across the river before he was seen. He swung himself into the saddle and walked the horse out through the open stall gate, heading for the river. The saddle was sloppy, and immediately slid to the side, and St. Ives wasted a few precious moments by swinging down and tugging on the girth, trying to cinch it tighter. Old Ben reinflated, though, and St. Ives gave up. There was no time to match wits with a horse, and so he remounted, hunkering over to the left and trotting out toward the willows along the river.

They crossed the bridge and cantered along the river path, emerging through the shrubbery on the opposite bank. Now the manor was completely hidden from view, and so St. Ives kicked old Ben into the semblance of a run. They skirted the back of Lord Kelvin's garden and angled toward the highroad, St. Ives yanking at the saddle to keep it on top of the horse. On the road he headed east at a gallop, leaning hard to the left to compensate and keeping his head down along Ben's neck, like a jockey. Old Ben seemed to recall younger and more romantic days, and he galloped away without any encouragement at all, his mane blowing back in St. Ives's face.

St. Ives smiled suddenly with the exhilaration of it, thinking of Parsons unwittingly drinking tea back at the manor, wondering aloud of Hasbro whether St. Ives wasn't ready to see him yet. Suspicions would be blooming like flowers. The man was a simpleton, a bumpkin.

The saddle inched downward again, and St. Ives stood up in the stirrups and yanked it hard, but, all the yanking in the world seemed to be useless. Gravity was against him. The right stirrup was nearly dragging on the ground now. There was nothing for it but to rein up and cinch the saddle tight. He pulled back on the reins, shouting, "Whoa! Whoa!" but it wasn't until old Ben had stopped and begun munching grasses along the road, that St. Ives, still sitting awkwardly in the saddle, heard the commotion behind him. He turned to look, and there was a coach and four, kicking up God's own dust cloud, rounding a bend two hundred yards back.

"Go!" he shouted, whipping at the reins now. "Get!"

The horse looked up at him as if determined to go on with its meal of roadside grass, but St. Ives booted it in the flanks, throwing himself forward in the teetering saddle, and old Ben leaped ahead like a charger, nearly catapulting St. Ives to the road. They were off again, pursued now by the approaching coach. The saddle slipped farther, and St. Ives held on to the pommel, pulling himself farther up onto the horse's neck. His hat flew off, and his coat billowed out around him like a sail.

He turned to look, and with a vast relief he saw that they would outdistance the coach, except that just then the saddle slewed downward and St. Ives with it, and for a long moment he grappled himself to the horse's flank, yanking himself back up finally with a handful of mane. He snatched wildly at the girth, trying to unfasten the buckle as old Ben galloped up a little rise. St. Ives cursed himself for having bothered with the saddle in the first place, of all the damned treacherous things. Somehow the girth was as tight as it could be now, wedged around sideways like it was. And it was behind his thigh, too, where he couldn't see it, and old Ben didn't seem to care a damn about any of it, but galloped straight on up the middle of the road.

They crested the rise, and there before them, coming along peaceably, was another coach, very elegant and driven by a man in bright red livery. The driver shouted at St. Ives, drawing hard on the reins and driving the coach very nearly into the ditch.

A white-haired head appeared through the coach window just then—Dr. Frost himself, his eyes flying open in surprise when he saw who it was that galloped past him on a horse that was saddled sideways. Frost shouted, but what he said was lost on the wind. St. Ives tugged hard on the girth, feeling it give at last, and then with a sliding rush, the saddle fell straight down onto the road, and old Ben tripped right over it, stumbling and nearly going down. St. Ives clutched the horse's neck, his eyes shut. And then the horse was up again, and flying toward Binger's like a thoroughbred.

When St. Ives looked back, Frost's coach had blocked the road. It was turning around, coming after him. Parsons's coach was reining up behind it. Good, let them get into each other's way. He could imagine that Parsons was apoplectic over the delay, and once again he laughed out loud as he thundered along, hugging old Ben's neck, straight through Binger's gate and up the drive toward the barn.

"They're after me, Mr. Binger!" St. Ives yelled, leaping down off the horse.

"Would it be men from the stars again?" Binger asked, smoking his pipe with the air of a farmer inquiring about sheep.

"No, Mr. Binger. This time it's scientists, I'm afraid."

Binger nodded, scowling. "I don't much hold with science," he said, taking his pipe out of his mouth. "Begging your honor's pardon. You're not like these others, though. The way I see it, Professor, there's this kind of scientist, and then there's that other kind." He shook his head darkly.

"This is that other kind, Mr. Binger." And right then St. Ives was interrupted by a clattering out on the road—both the coaches drawing up and turning in at the gate. St. Ives strode straight into the barn, followed by Binger, who still smoked his pipe placidly. One of his sons was mucking out a pen, and old Binger called him over. "Bring the hayfork," he said. The dog Furry wandered out of the pen along with him, happy to see St. Ives again.

At the mention of the hayfork, St. Ives paused. "We mustn't cause these men any trouble, Mr. Binger," he said. "They're very powerful…" But now there was a commotion outside—Parsons and Frost arguing between themselves. St. Ives would have liked to stop and listen, but there wasn't time. He climbed aboard the bathyscaphe, pulling the hatch shut behind him. Settling himself in the seat, he began to fiddle with the dials, his heart pounding, distracted by what he saw through the porthole.

Seeing the hatch close down, Frost and Parsons gave off their bickering and hurried along, followed by the driver in livery and two other men who had accompanied Parsons. Binger pointed and must have said something to Furry, because as Parsons and one of the other men made a rush forward, the dog bounded in among them, catching hold of Parsons's trousers and ripping off a long swatch of material. Parsons stumbled, and the other man leaped aside, swiping at the dog with his hand.

Binger's son shoved the end of the hayfork into the dirt directly in front of the man's shoe, and he ran into the handle chin-first, recoiling in surprise and then pushing past it toward the machine as Furry raced in, nipping at his shoe, finally getting hold of his cuff and worrying it back and forth.

Parsons was up and moving again and Frost along with him. Together they rushed at the machine, pushing and shoving at each other, both of them understanding that they had come too late. Furry let loose of his man's cuff and followed the two of them, growling and snapping so that they were forced to do a sort of jug dance there in front of the porthole while they implored St. Ives with wild gestures to leave off and see reason.

But what St. Ives saw just then was darkness, and he heard the by-then-familiar buzzing and felt himself falling down and down and down, leaving that far-flung island of history behind him, maybe never to return. And good riddance—Narbondo, somehow, wasn't born to be a man of the cloth. He looked cramped and uncomfortable in his new clothing. And Parsons—well, Parsons was Parsons. You could take a brickbat to history six-dozen times, and somehow Parsons would stride into every altered picture wearing the same overgrown beard.

Just then there was darkness of a different caliber again, nighttime darkness and rain falling. St. Ives came to himself. He patted his coat pocket, feeling the cold bulk of the revolver. He had come too far now to be squeamish about anything, but it occurred to him that there was something ironic about setting out to kill the man whose life you had recently worked so hard to save. But kill him he would, if it took that.

He climbed out into the wind-whipped rain, looking around him, and realized with a surge of horror that he was on the wrong street. He could see it straight off. He had dreamed that line of storefronts and lodging houses too many times to make any mistake now. What he saw before him was utterly unfamiliar. He had been rushed by the imbroglio in Binger's barn and had miscalibrated the instruments. But how? Panicked, he ran straight up the street, slogging through the flood, listening hard to the sounds of the night.

Lancing suddenly through his head came the confused thought that it might be worse than a mere miscalculation. It was conceivable that anything and everything might have changed by now. He had wanted the same street, but what did the notion of sameness mean to him anymore? He slowed to a stop, rain falling on him in torrents.

Then he heard it—the clatter of a coach. Gunfire!

He ran toward the sound, wiping the water out of his eyes, breathing hard. Another gunshot rang out and then a shriek and, through the sound of the rain, the tearing and banging of the cabriolet going over in the street. He could picture it in his mind—his past-time self running forward, hesitating to shoot until it was too late, and...

He rounded the corner now, his pistol drawn, and nearly ran Narbondo down as he crouched over Alice, whose leg was pinned under the overturned cabriolet. Narbondo pointed his pistol at her head, staring at the rainy street where Langdon St. Ives ought to have been, but wasn't. Hasbro and Kraken stared at the street, too, but there was nothing at all there save the empty coach, and although St. Ives alone knew why that was, he didn't give it a moment's thought, but lashed out with the gun butt and hammered Narbondo across the back of the head.

St. Ives's hand was in the way, though, and he managed only to hit Narbondo heavily with his fist. Narbondo's head jerked down, and his hands flew outward as he tumbled away from Alice. He rolled forward, still holding his pistol, struggling to one knee and looking back wild-eyed at St. Ives, then immediately aiming the pistol and shooting it wildly, without an instant's hesitation.

Already St. Ives was lunging toward him, though, and the shot went wide. Three years of pent-up energy and fear and loathing drove St. Ives forward, unthinking. Narbondo staggered backward, sprawling through the water, starting to run even before he was fully on his feet. St. Ives ran him down in three steps. Too wild to shoot him, St. Ives grabbed the back of Narbondo's coat and clubbed him again with the pistol butt, behind the ear this time, and Narbondo's head jerked sideways as he brought his pistol up, firing it pointlessly in the air. St. Ives hammered him again, still clutching his jacket as Narbondo slumped to his knees, his pistol falling into the street. A hand seized St. Ives's wrist as he raised his gun yet again, and St. Ives turned savagely, ready to strike. It was Hasbro, though, and the look on his face made St. Ives drop his own pistol into the water.

"He shot her," St. Ives mumbled. "I mean..." But he didn't right then know what he meant. He was vastly tired and confused, and he remembered the child drinking medicinal beef broth in Limehouse. He looked back down the street. Alice wasn't shot—of course she wasn't shot. Kraken bent over her, lifting off the top end of the cabriolet and then stooping to untie her. St. Ives walked toward them, as old suppressed memories freshened and grew young again in his mind. Mercifully, the rain let off just then, and the moon shone through the clouds, lightening the street.

"That were a neat trick, sir," Kraken said to him enthusiastically, standing up and making way for him. "I could have sworn you was in the coach. Why, I even seen you stepping out through the open door. Then you was gone, and then here your honor was again, smashing your man in back of the head." He looked at St. Ives with evident pride, and St. Ives kneeled in the flooded street, feeling for a pulse, fearing suddenly that it was too late after all. The crash alone might have...Then Alice opened her eyes, rubbed the back of her head with her hand, winced, and smiled at St. Ives. She struggled to sit up.

"I'm all right," she said.

Kraken let out a whoop, and Hasbro, who had dragged Narbondo to the roadside, helped both St. Ives and Alice to their feet, pulling them into a doorway out of the rain.

"Tie Narbondo up with something," St. Ives said to Kraken.

Kraken looked disappointed. "Begging your honor's pardon," he said, taking St. Ives aside, "but hadn't we ought to kill him? I should think that would be recommended, seeing as who he is. You know he would have shot her. A life don't mean nothing to the likes of him. Give me the word, sir, and I'll make it quick and quiet."

St. Ives hesitated, then shook his head tiredly. "No, he's got too much to do yet. All of us do. Heaven alone knows what will come of the world if we don't all play our parts—heroes, villains, spectators, and fools. Perhaps it's already too late," he said, half to himself. "Perhaps this changes the script utterly. So tie him up, if you will. He'll spend some time in Newgate before he escapes."

Kraken nodded, although he looked confused, like a man who understood nothing. St. Ives left him to it and faced Alice again. He sighed deeply. She was safe. Thank God for that. "I'll have to go," he said to her.

"What?" Alice looked at him in disbelief. "Why? Aren't I going with you? We'll all go, the sooner the better."

St. Ives was swept with a wave of passion and love. He kissed her on the mouth, and although she was surprised by the suddenness of it, she kissed him back with equal passion.

Hasbro cleared his throat and went off abruptly toward where Kraken was tying up Narbondo with the reins from the wrecked cabriolet.

I *will* stay, St. Ives thought suddenly. Why not? His past-time self—now nothing but a ghost—wouldn't be any the wiser. He was already gone, flitted away, into the mists of abandoned time. Why not start anew, right now? They would take a room in the West End, make it a sort of holiday—nothing but eating and the theater and lounging about all day long. He suddenly felt like Atlas, having at last shrugged off the world, ending what had turned out to be merely a lengthy nightmare.

Alice was regarding him strangely, though. "You look awful," she said, squinting at him as if she realized something was wrong but had no notion how to explain it. He knew what she had meant to say. She had meant to say that he looked old, worn-out, thin, but she had caught herself and had said something more temporary so as to preserve his feelings. "What's wrong?" she asked suddenly, and his heart sank.

He looked out into the street, where his past-time self lay invisible in the water and muck of the road. You fool, he said in his mind. I *earned* this, but I've got to give it to you, when all you would have done is botch it utterly. But even as he thought this, he knew the truth—that he wasn't the man now that he had been then. The ghost in the road was in many ways the better of the two of them. Alice didn't deserve the declined copy; what she wanted was the genuine article.

And maybe he could become that article—but not by staying here. He had to go home again, to the future, in order to catch up with himself once more.

"I won't be gone but a moment," he said, glancing back toward where he had left the machine. "And when I appear again, I might be confused for a time. It'll pass, though. When you see me next, tell me that I'm a mortal idiot, and I'll feel better about it all."

"What on *earth* are you talking about?" she asked, looking at him fearfully, as if he had lost his mind.

He almost started to explain, but it was too much for him. Now that he had made up his mind to leave, the future was calling to him, and the shortest route back to it sat in the middle of the street a block away. "Trust me," he said. "I won't be gone a moment." He kissed her again, and then stepped out of the doorway, turned, and loped off, not looking back, his heart full of gladness and regret. —◦

Epilogue

HE LANDED ON the meadow, half expecting heaven knew what. There was no telling what was what anymore. Maybe Parsons would leap out of the bushes and claim the machine. Maybe Narbondo, or Frost, or whatever he called himself now, would menace him with a revolver. Maybe anything at all—he didn't care. They could have the machine. He didn't want it anymore. His work was done, and he was ready to confront the results, whatever they were, and then to give up his chasing around through time. At least for the moment.

What he couldn't do, though, was face himself. There were two present-time copies of him now, and he was determined to let the other one depart gracefully and, he hoped, privately. What sort of man had he become? A happy man, perhaps, who wouldn't relish the idea of this copycat St. Ives popping in at the window to replace him? Or, just as easily, a miserable man, who might gladly hand over the reins and disappear forever.

Fragments of his memory were even now starting to wink out like candle flames in a breeze. His nightmares about the Seven Dials, the very fact of his returning there, his whole tiresome rigamarole life during the past three years—all of it would become vapor.

And good riddance, too. He would welcome new memories, whatever they were. He realized that this was bluff, though. He thought one last time of the child Narbondo, huddled in dirty rags in Limehouse, and of his mother and the sailor in the doorway. There were memories worse than his own. That's partly why he was still sitting there in the machine, wasn't it? He had no idea what he would find inside the manor—who he would discover himself to be.

He climbed through the hatch into the wind. It was sunny and fine with just the hint of a smoky autumn chill in the air. He pulled his coat straight and fiddled with his tie, realizing that he was a wet and dirty mess. But he felt fit, somehow, as if a great weight had fallen away from him, and then, in a confused shudder of memory, it occurred to him that he couldn't bear eating eggplant again. Not once more.

His head reeled, and he nearly fell over. Eggplant? It was starting. His memories would depart like rats from a ship. Disconcerted, he hurried through the window, into the study, and there stood Hasbro, staring at him strangely.

"We'll have to move the time machine into the silo," St. Ives said to him. "I wasn't sure whether it was empty or not."

"I beg your pardon, sir?"

"The machine on the meadow," St. Ives said. "We'll want to get it into the silo, out of the weather."

"I'm sorry, sir. I wasn't aware that Dr. Frost had returned it. This comes as a surprise. I was under the impression that he had stolen it from Secretary Parsons. He's brought it here, has he?"

"Stolen it?" St. Ives was gripped by vertigo just then. His memory shifted. He fought to hold on to it, afraid to let pieces of it go completely. "Of course," he said. "It's a mystery to me, too, but there it sits." He gestured out the window, where the machine glinted in the sunlight.

Narbondo had taken it! That was funny, hilarious. Now St. Ives had reappeared with it, and that meant that Narbondo's copy was in the process of disappearing, out from under his nose, and stranding him, St. Ives hoped, in some distant land. Either that or the villain was gone somewhere in time, and would someday perhaps return, and then St. Ives's machine would disappear. Time and chance, he reminded himself.

And then new memories, like wraiths, drifted into his mind, shifting old memories aside. "Alice!" he cried. "Is she here then?"

"She's still in the parlor, sir," Hasbro said, looking skeptical again. "Where you left her moments ago. I really must advise you against that suit, by the way. The tailor is certifiable. Perhaps if I laid something else out…"

"Yes," St. Ives said, hurrying through the door. "Lay something out."

He was dizzy, foggy with memories, drunk on them. And as if he were literally drunk, he felt free of the depressing guilt and worry that had plagued him…for how long? And why? He couldn't entirely remember. It seemed so long ago. His mind was a confusion of images now, stolen from the man whose ghost was where? Blowing away on the wind, across the meadow? Would he remain to haunt the manor, exercising a ghostly grudge against his other-time self for having returned to supplant him?

Mrs. Langley loomed out of the kitchen, her hands white with baking flour.

"I've taken your advice, Mrs. Langley," he said.

"Beg pardon, sir? What advice?"

"I…" What advice, indeed? He didn't know. He pulled at the collar of his shirt, which was too tight for him. "Nothing," he said. "Never mind. I was thinking out loud." She nodded, baffled, and he forced himself along, walking toward the parlor. Steady on, he told himself. Keep your mouth closed. There's too much you don't know yet, and too much of what you do know is nonsense.

And then there sat Alice, reading a book. He was astonished by the sight of her. She hasn't aged a day, he thought joyfully, and then he wondered why on earth he thought any such thing, and a garden of memories, like someone else's anecdotes, sprung fully bloomed in his mind. His head swam, and he sat down hard on a chair. Maybe he ought to have waited, to have grappled with the business of memory before wading in like this. But he hadn't, and now that he got a good look at Alice, with her dark hair done up in a ribbon, he was happy that he hadn't wasted another moment.

"I'm sorry about the eggplant," she said to him, just then glancing up from her book. She squinted at the sight of him, looking unhappily surprised, and he grinned back at her like a drunken man. "That awful suit of clothes," she said. "You look rather like a dirty sausage in them, don't you? I've seen those before…

"I'm just getting set to burn them," St. Ives said hurriedly. "They're a relic, from the future. A sort of…costume."

"Well," she said. "The trousers might look better if you hadn't waded across the river in them. But I *am* sorry about the eggplant. I don't mean to make you eat it every night, but Janet's cook, Pierre, is apparently fixing it for us this evening. Will you be ready to leave in a half hour? You looked wonderful just moments ago."

"Eggplant? Janet?" His mind fumbled with the words. Then through the parlor window he saw Alice's garden, laid out in neat rows. Purple-green eggplants hung like lunar eggs from a half-dozen plants.

"Oh, *Janet*," he said, nodding broadly. "From the Harrogate Women's Literary League!"

"What on earth is wrong with you? Of course that Janet, unless you've got another one hidden somewhere. And don't go on about the eggplant this time, will you?"

Suddenly he could taste the horrible sour stuff. He had eaten it last night mixed up with ground lamb. And the night before, too, stewed up with Middle Eastern spices. He had been on a sort of eggplant diet, a slave to the vegetable garden.

"You could use a bath, too, couldn't you? At least a wash up. And your hair looks as if you've been out in the wind for three days. What *have* you been up to?"

"I…old Ben," he began. "Mud. Up to his blinkers."

But then he was interrupted by a sort of banshee wail from somewhere off in the house. It rose to a crescendo and then turned into a series of squalling hoots.

He stood up, looking down at Alice in alarm. "What…"

"It's not all that bad," she said, nearly laughing. "Look at you! Anyone would think you hadn't ever changed his nappies before. They can't be a tremendous lot dirtier than your trouser cuffs, can they?"

The baby's crying had very nearly inundated him with fresh memories. Little Eddie, his son. He smiled broadly. *It was his turn to change the nappies.* They had agreed against a nanny, were bringing up the child themselves, spoon-feeding it with stuff

mashed up out of the garden. Eddie wouldn't eat eggplant either, wouldn't touch it on a bet. "Good old Eddie!" he said out loud.

"That's the right attitude," Alice said.

And now in the shuffle of the old being washed out by the new, he saw it all clearly for one last long moment. His fears for the future had come to nothing. Alice was safe. They had a son. The garden was growing again. They were happy now. *He* was happy, nearly delirious. He found that he couldn't think in terms of future-time selves and past-time selves any longer. None of his other selves mattered to him at all.

There was only he and Alice and Eddie and…rows and rows of eggplant. He nearly started to whistle, but then the baby squalled again and Alice widened her eyes, inviting him to do something about it.

"I've changed my mind," he said, heading for the stairs. "I love eggplant." And he very nearly meant it, too. —☙

Parenthetically Speaking

by James P. Blaylock

TITLES HAVE NEVER been easy for me, but they were a special problem twenty or thirty years ago when I was writing my Steampunk stories. Chekhov once stated that he could write a story about anything—that if a person asked him to write a story about a bottle, he'd do it, and he'd call it "The Bottle." I, on the other hand, would set out to write a story about a bottle, and before it was done it would also be about apes and severed heads and doughnut-eating skeletons, and the simple title wouldn't work. One day a couple of lifetimes ago I was sitting around at Fullerton College, where I was teaching at the time, and I happened to be holding a copy of *Homunculus*, which had just recently been published—a novel that had come dangerously close to being titled (on Tim Powers's recommendation) *And Your Winged Crocodiles*, a phrase that Tim had found in a poem by Byron. A woman sitting nearby tried unsuccessfully to puzzle out the pronunciation. "What's it mean"? she asked. "It means 'little man,'" I told her. "In Latin." She nodded and asked if I'd written any other books, and I told her that my previous book had been titled *The Digging Leviathan*. "And what does that mean," she asked (unimpressed), "*big* man?" "Pretty much," I said, and it came into my mind that if I combined the two into a third novel I could call it *Little Big Digging Man*, except that it might be confused with the Thomas Berger novel unless it was rendered into Latin. Maybe a novel about a time-traveling beatnik: *Little Man Digging Big*...

It was about then that Susan Allison, my editor at Ace, began to have serious second thoughts about allowing me to title my own books. Probably she was right. Almost certainly she was. I was awash, however, with wild ideas for titles, including my favorite—one that I had borrowed from Tim: "Uncle Hinky Beards Fat Billy Winger in his Den." My idea was to write a 20-page chapter under this title and mail it off to Susan as a sort of joke, assuring her that I was hard at work on further chapters. The nifty thing was that throughout those 20 pages Uncle Hinky would be asleep in his armchair. Proust, after all, had taken 60 pages to have his man turn over in bed. I saw no reason at all for my character to wake up—ever. There was something stunningly postmodern in the idea. I killed two days writing the 20 pages, and then called Tim, laughing like an idiot, to tell him my "plan." Tim convinced me not to mail the 20 pages to Ace, for which I almost certainly owe him my career.

None of that actually has much to do with Steampunk, but neither did I, really—not at the time, at least. *Homunculus* was simply a variety of historical novel that I had written largely because I was crazy for *The Strange Case of Dr. Jekyll and Mr. Hyde* and because I had grown up reading Jules Verne and H.G. Wells, and my idea of science fiction had always had to do with backyard scientists and fabulous submarines and spacecraft that housed onboard greenhouses. And of course no one had heard the word "Steampunk" (or Cyberpunk, either) back when Tim, K.W. Jeter, and I were first writing our Victoriana. The term hadn't been coined yet, and wouldn't be for years. And certainly we had no idea that we were inventing a sub-genre of science fiction. We were merely writing stories that amused us, and we often had an equally amusing time recounting to each other aspects of the amusing stories that we intended to write.

I remember a fairly typical afternoon involving popcorn and beer at O'Hara's Pub in Orange sometime in 1977. (I've written about this particular afternoon before, and I wonder now whether it's *particular* at all, but is instead a sort of archetypal afternoon that lingers in my mind, a couple of dozen afternoons run together.) I was working back then as a finish carpenter for a room addition contractor and had recently begun teaching composition classes in the evening. Tim was employed at a Tinderbox tobacco store and had sold his first novels to Laser Books, as had K.W., who, if I remember correctly, was working nights at the local Juvenile Hall. I had already written 'The Ape-box Affair" (which I'm going to insist was the first published Steampunk story. If there's evidence to the contrary, let me know.) I had it in my mind that Langdon St. Ives would be a series character, although I hadn't given much thought to his further adventures, because I was spending most of my literary time rewriting a novel that I had been working on for a couple of years by then, currently titled *Sanctity of Moontide* (which title, according to Phil Dick, was the worst ever conceived). Previously I had called it *The Chinese Circus* (which ranks pretty high on the worst title list). The unfinished (and unfinishable) novel was to be a modern *Tristram Shandy*, narrated by a man who might or might not be a lunatic and who had certain knowledge of a pending cataclysm that would be triggered when a mechanical mole burrowed through the earth's crust. I had recently finished reading all of Proust, winding up with his letters and his early novel, *Jean Santieul*, and my head was full of Proustian language as well as characters who slept too much. Why not, I wondered with a thrill of artistic anticipation, revise the novel so that it was a hybrid of Proust and Laurence Sterne, but was set in Glendale and Eagle Rock and involved Bulgarian acrobats, the mechanical mole, and a dairy that was manufacturing faux milk out of plaster of Paris? (I've read that deranged people are sometimes fundamentally happy, because they're utterly certain that they're correct in all aspects of their thinking, whereas the rest of us are unhappily certain that we're very often wrong. In that sense the inspired lunacy of early artistic insight is a lot like madness, because a writer in the grip of the muses is often certain that he or she is engaged in an endeavor of great genius.)

So there we were at O'Hara's Pub, talking about something vital, with a fresh bowl of popcorn, a pitcher of beer, and an empty afternoon before us…. (And just as none of us knew that we were about to write the first "Steampunk" stories and spawn a literary movement, none of us knew that we were rapidly using up our cardboard carton full of empty afternoons. These thirty years later I can see the looming shadow of empty afternoons in my future again, but of a decidedly different sort.) K.W. rolled his eyes at something I'd said (something involving "science") and suggested that given my curious notions of that subject I'd be likely to write a story in which someone plugged a black hole with a Fitzall Sizes cork. After a momentary silence I asked him whether, with all due respect, he was willing to let me have that idea or whether he wanted it for himself. He said I was welcome to it, and I went home and wrote "The Hole in Space" and sent it off to *Starwind* magazine, which closed its doors a week after accepting the story and mailing me the forty dollar check. I never sent the story back out, and it languished in the drawer for over 25 years before it saw daylight again. But it was writing that second St. Ives story that somehow made it inevitable that I write more. A conversation at Roy Squires's house in Glendale (as well as a bottle of Laphroaig scotch) inspired "The Idol's Eye," and an article in the Los Angeles *Times* about a local comet chaser gave rise to a lengthy, unpublished, plotless story that turned out to be notes for *Homunculus*. "The Ape-box Affair" was also the result of my love of Robert Louis Stevenson's work (something that still hasn't worn off) and you can find its beginnings and the beginnings of *Homunculus* in Stevenson's *The Wrong Box* and in the stories that make up *New Arabian Nights*. Langdon St. Ives's last name came from the Stevenson's *St. Ives*, although it was perhaps the only Stevenson novel that I hadn't read and still haven't. (I don't know whether the "St. Ives" of the novel is a person or is the place that the man in the rhyme was going to. One of these days I'll read the book and find out.) Langdon St. Ives, by the way, is a distant forebear of Edward St. Ives, who would make his appearance years later in *The Digging Leviathan*, which was the novel that *Sanctity of Moontide* turned into once I got rid of Proust and Sterne and figured out how to write it.

Meanwhile, K.W. and Tim Powers contracted with Roger Elwood to write books in a series that would involve the reincarnation of King Arthur throughout history. The series was scrapped before their novels were published. (I submitted a proposal for a novel involving a plot against George III involving poisoned snuff and William Blake, not knowing that Ray Nelson was already writing *Blake's Progress*, the first book in the series. Elwood sent me a rejection letter complaining that I was apparently making a mockery of his project. I wasn't, actually, and I remember wondering whether it was a good thing or a bad thing that my writing seemed so effortlessly to make mockeries of things. It wouldn't, alas, be the last time the problem surfaced.) At about that time K.W. met Elwood in Los Angeles to discuss the project, and when the waiter took their drink order, Elwood asked for a "Vanilla 500." K.W. said he'd have the same. The drink turned out to be milk on the rocks, which, K.W. told us at O'Hara's later that same afternoon, contained neither vanilla nor 500. K.W.'s Arthurian novel, *Morlock Night*, was published by Daw, and Tim's novel, *The Drawing of the Dark*, was published by Del Rey. *The Drawing of the Dark* wasn't Steampunk in its setting, but it was Steampunk in spirit, and of course it would be followed up with *The Anubis Gates*, which is arguably the best novel of the genre.

Late in the 1990's I received a letter from the University of Bologna inviting me to speak at a conference that was to be put on by the Department of Utopian and Dystopian Studies. The subject of the conference was Steampunk, and there was to be a day (out of three) dedicated to my work with me as keynote speaker. My Italian publisher, Mondadori, would host a party. I'd be the talk of the town. I was pleasantly bowled over. I imagined Umberto Eco reading *Homunculus* with his eyes bulging out— perhaps the scene in which Dr. Narbondo (a name I had borrowed from Borges) tries to animate the skeleton of Joanna Southcote with a bladder full of chemical gas. Eco, of course, would see immediately that the episode was not only a subtle nod to Borges, but to Flaubert, also—to Madame Bovary's lengthy and fairly hilarious death scene. With tears in his eyes he'd wave me onto the stage: thunderous applause, chants from the audience of "Steampunk! Steampunk!" (rendered into Italian).

Unfortunately the University could only offer me several million lire to pay for the trip, which turned out to be about thirty dollars, give or take fifty cents. I couldn't afford to go, which was just as well, because my memory of Umberto Eco goggling over my books, by then fixed in my mind, has remained unsullied all these years since. Certainly that was the best conference I never attended. It was also my first inkling that Steampunk was "big in Europe" and apparently still is.

Lord Kelvin's Machine is my most recent effort (although ideally not my final effort) to write out another episode in the life of Langdon St. Ives. It's hard to believe that I wrote that book fifteen years ago, a time of great change in my own life. As ever, I didn't foresee the change or perceive it occurring (although I can see its shadow in the novel, now that I reread it). Coming to understand change is always a matter of looking back, which is just what I've been doing in this afterword, with no other motive, really, aside from nostalgia. —✲

Jim Blaylock
Orange, California
December 10, 2007